More Praise for William R. Trotter's *Sands of Pride*

"William R. Trotter has crafted a magnificent Civil War novel, epic in proportion and sweeping in its treatment of the first three years of that bloody conflict."
—*BookPage*

"A swashbuckling, bodice-ripping (at least bodice untying) historical novel." —*Star-News* (Wilmington, North Carolina)

"Vividly rendered and swiftly paced." —*The Providence Journal*

"An epic, colorful narrative that makes for happy hours of reading."
—*The News & Record* (Greensboro, North Carolina)

"This masterful epic will appeal to the countless fans of *Cold Mountain.*" —*Publishers Weekly* (starred review)

"Definitely a page-turner . . . an abundance of adventure, romance, [and] tragedy."
—*Booklist*

"Monumental, bombs-bursting-in-air epic." —*Kirkus Reviews*

William R. Trotter, an authority on the Civil War, is the author of thirteen books, including the novel *Winter Fire* and the nonfiction trilogy *The Civil War in North Carolina.* He lives in Greensboro, North Carolina.

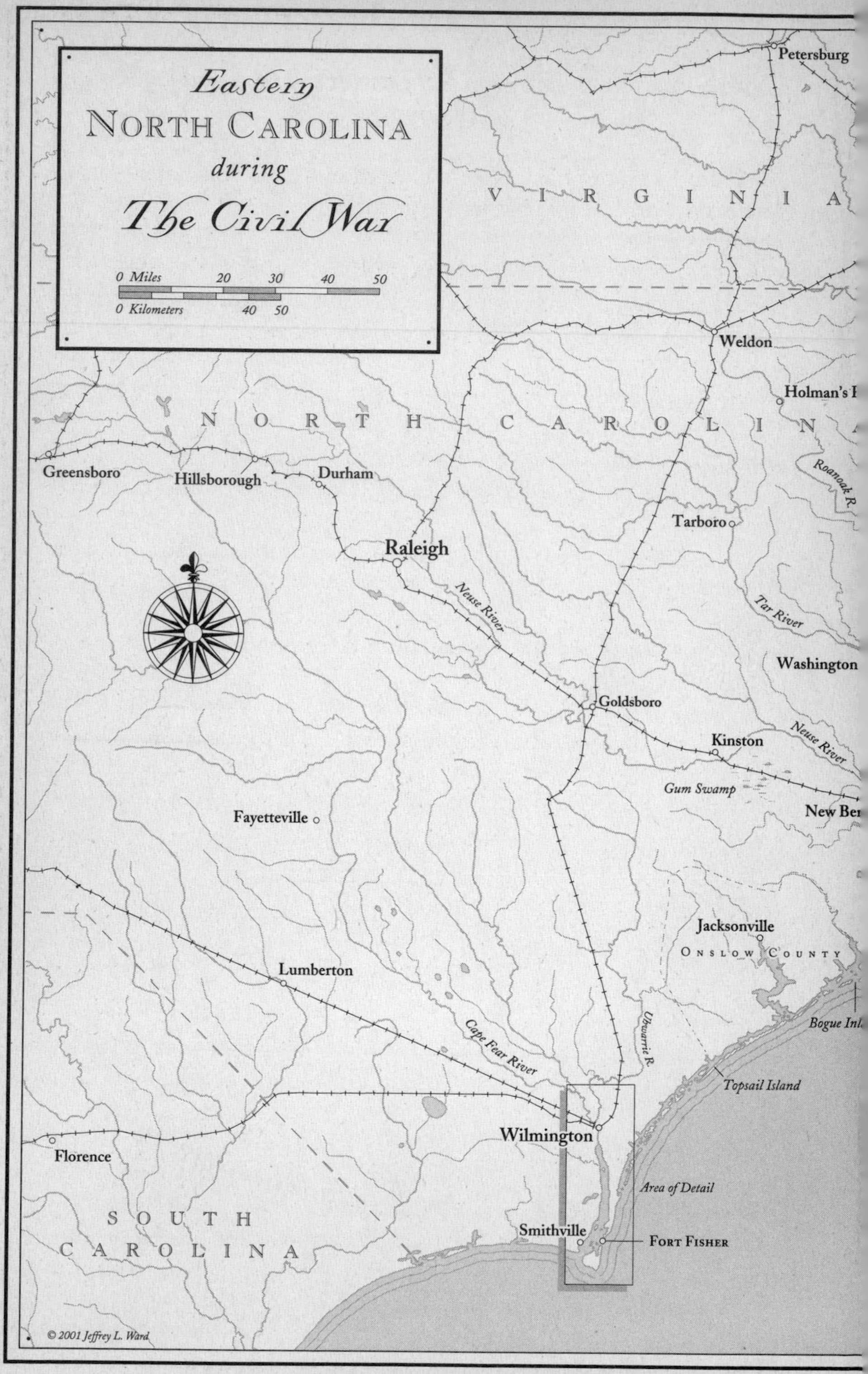
Eastern
NORTH CAROLINA
during
The Civil War
0 Miles 20 30 40 50
0 Kilometers 40 50
VIRGINIA
NORTH CAROLINA
SOUTH CAROLINA
Petersburg
Weldon
Greensboro
Hillsborough
Durham
Raleigh
Tarboro
Roanoak R.
Neuse River
Tar River
Washington
Goldsboro
Kinston
Neuse River
Gum Swamp
Fayetteville
Jacksonville
ONSLOW COUNTY
Lumberton
Cape Fear River
Ubwarrie R.
Topsail Island
Wilmington
Florence
Area of Detail
Smithville
FORT FISHER
© 2001 Jeffrey L. Ward

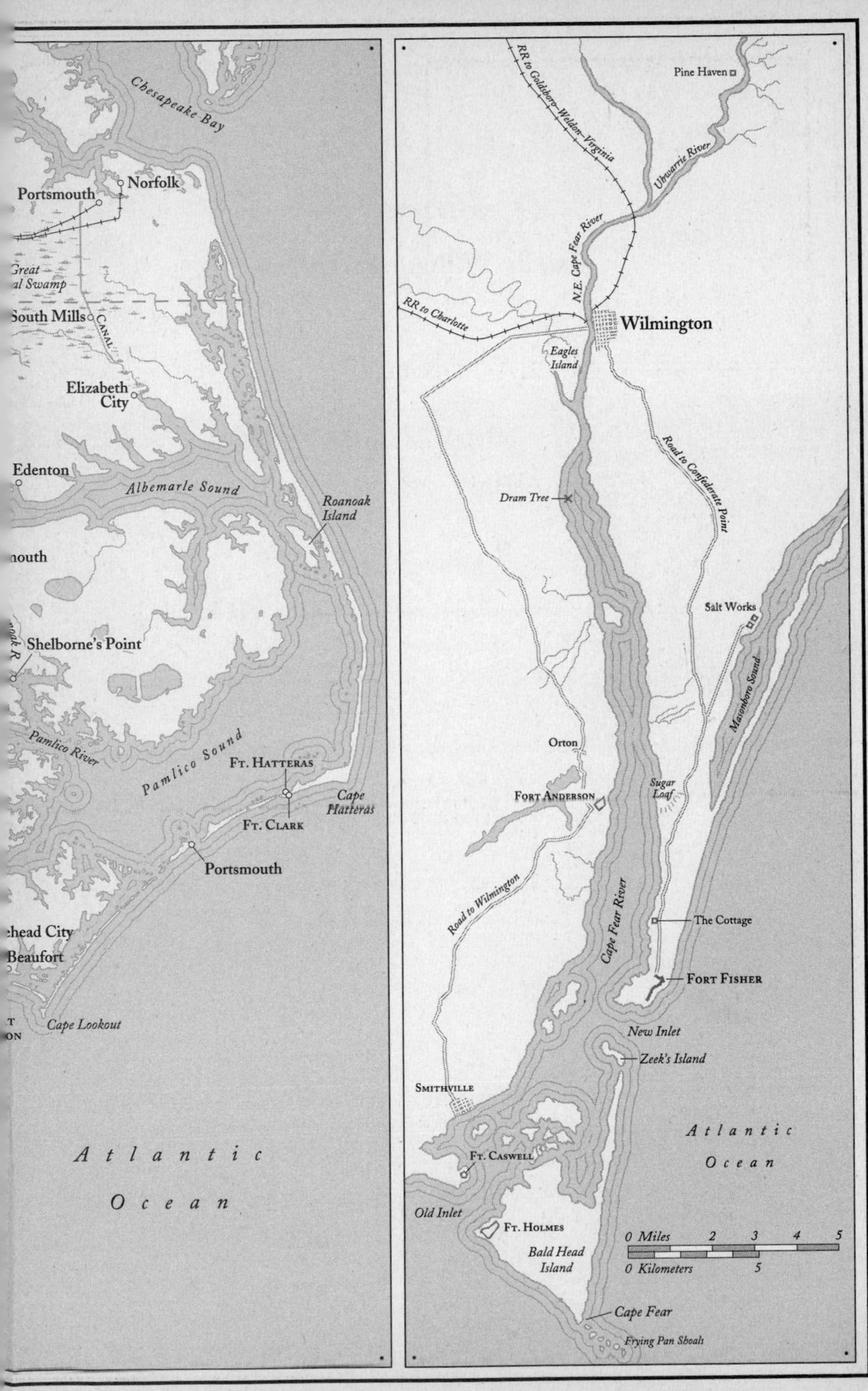

Chesapeake Bay
Norfolk
Portsmouth
Great
al Swamp
South Mills
CANAL
Elizabeth City
Edenton
Albemarle Sound
Roanoak Island
nouth
Shelborne's Point
Pamlico River
Pamlico Sound
FT. HATTERAS
Cape Hatteras
FT. CLARK
Portsmouth
ehead City
Beaufort
Cape Lookout
Atlantic
Ocean
RR to Goldsboro–Weldon–Virginia
Pine Haven
Ubwarrie River
N.E. Cape Fear River
RR to Charlotte
Wilmington
Eagles Island
Road to Confederate Point
Dram Tree
Salt Works
Masonboro Sound
Orton
Sugar Loaf
FORT ANDERSON
Road to Wilmington
Cape Fear River
The Cottage
FORT FISHER
New Inlet
Zeek's Island
SMITHVILLE
Atlantic
Ocean
FT. CASWELL
Old Inlet
FT. HOLMES
Bald Head Island
0 Miles 2 3 4 5
0 Kilometers 5
Cape Fear
Frying Pan Shoals

Also by William R. Trotter

Fiction

Winter Fire
Honeysuckle

Nonfiction

Life Begins at Forte: Stokowski as Musical Hobo (1942–1960)
Deadly Kin: A True Story of Mass Family Murder
Silk Flags and Cold Steel, The Civil War in North Carolina, volume 1
Bushwhackers!, The Civil War in North Carolina, volume 2
Ironclads and Columbiads, The Civil War in North Carolina, volume 3
A Frozen Hell: The Russo-Finnish War of 1939–1940
(Awarded the Finlandia Foundation Arts and Letters Prize)
Priest of Music: The Life of Dimitri Mitropoulos
Close Combat: Normandy Campaign
Close Combat: A Bridge Too Far

The SANDS *of* PRIDE

A Novel of the Civil War

WILLIAM R. TROTTER

A PLUME BOOK

To Elizabeth, who once told me that the apple would fall when it was ripe.

PLUME
Published by the Penguin Group
Penguin Group (USA) Inc., 375 Hudson Street, New York, New York 10014, U.S.A.
Penguin Books Ltd, 80 Strand, London WC2R 0RL, England
Penguin Books Australia Ltd, 250 Camberwell Road,
Camberwell, Victoria 3124, Australia
Penguin Books Canada Ltd, 10 Alcorn Avenue, Toronto, Ontario, Canada M4V 3B2
Penguin Books (N.Z.) Ltd, Cnr Rosedale and Airborne Roads,
Albany, Auckland 1310, New Zealand

Penguin Books Ltd, Registered Offices: 80 Strand, London WC2R 0RL, England

Published by Plume, a member of Penguin Group (USA) Inc. This is an authorized reprint of a hardcover edition published by Carroll & Graf Publishers. For information address Carroll & Graf Publishers, 161 William Street, 16th Floor, New York, New York 10038.

First Plume Printing, June 2003
10 9 8 7 6 5 4 3 2 1

CIP data is available.
ISBN 0-7867-1013-6 (hc.)
ISBN 0-452-28442-2 (pbk.)

Printed in the United States of America
Original hardcover design and flag illustration by Michael Walters

PUBLISHER'S NOTE
This is a work of fiction. Names, characters, places, and incidents either are the product of the author's imagination or are used fictitiously, and any resemblance to actual persons, living or dead, business establishments, events, or locales is entirely coincidental.

Methinks her patient sons before me stand,
Where the broad ocean leans against the land,
Pride in their port, defiance in their eye,
I see the lords of humankind pass by.

—Oliver Goldsmith, "The Traveler"

And the Lord answered and said unto His people:
"Behold, I will send you corn, and wine, and oil,
And ye shall be satisfied therewith;
And I will no more make you a reproach among the nations;
But I will remove far off from you the Northern One,
And will drive him into a land barren and desolate,
With his face toward the eastern sea,
And his hinter part toward the western sea ..."

—The Book of Joel 2:19

Contents

The Sands of Pride

Major and Supporting Characters

Historical figures are marked with an asterisk below and described in past tense, while fictional characters are described in present tense.

The Confederacy

Battle, Richard (*): The trusted and tireless secretary of North Carolina governor Zebulon Vance.

Benjamin, Judah P. (*): The most prominent southern Jew, he served first as Confederate Attorney General, then as secretary of war, and finally as secretary of state.

Bragg, Braxton, General (*): A fine administrator but a bafflingly inert field commander, he won just a single victory, at Chickamauga.

Branch, William, Naval Commander, later Flag Officer. In the war's early months, he leads the Mosquito Fleet with great audacity, but ennui and frustration, as well as a deepening addiction to opium, render him an ineffectual leader of Wilmington's naval forces.

Bright, Fitz-John: Overseer of Pine Haven Plantation who becomes navigator/pilot of the blockade-runner Banshee.

Burgwyn, Harry, Major-General (*): Zebulon Vance's executive officer in the Twenty-sixth North Carolina regiment, then its commander after Vance was elected governor.

Cantwell, John, Colonel (*): Hotheaded leader of Wilmington's militia during the months before secession.

Clark, Henry T. (*): Speaker of the North Carolina House, then governor, briefly, after John Ellis died of a heart attack. He was succeeded by Zebulon Vance.

Conver, Ezekial Jeremiah Prosper-For-Me de Vonell (*): Probably the smallest man in the Rebel army (just over four feet tall), Conver performed with outstanding heroism during the Battle of Fort Fisher.

Davis, Jefferson (*): President of the Confederate States of America.

Ellis, John William (*): Governor of North Carolina in 1861, Ellis reluctantly led his state out of the Union and ably organized its resources for war, until felled by a heart attack.

Fulton, John (*): A bombastic, cheerfully bigoted, and a zealous Confederate, Fulton edited The Wilmington Journal throughout the war; many of his editorials are included as chapter openers in this novel.

Harper, Stepney: Father of Mary Harper Sloane, owns Limerick Plantation, near Charleston.

Huger, Benjamin, General (*): Fat, indolent, and a terrible strategist, his staggering incompetence during the Peninsula campaign caused Robert E. Lee to sack him in disgrace.

Johnston, Joseph E., General (*): First commander of the Army of Northern Virginia and a consummate professional soldier, he often crossed swords with President Davis.

Lamb, Daisy (*): Wife of Colonel William Lamb.

Lamb, William, Colonel (*): A lawyer and journalist by training, and an innate genius as a military engineer, his brilliant design made Fort Fisher the strongest earthen fortress ever built in America.
Landau, Jacob: Bavarian Jew and a prominent Wilmington merchant, his mission in life is to found the city's first synagogue. An ardent Confederate patriot, he is part owner, with Matthew Sloane and Augustus Hobart-Hampden, of the blockade-runner Banshee.
Landau, Largo:. A free-spirited young woman, Jacob's daughter becomes the lover of the mysterious Hobart-Hampden, and champion of the downtrodden denizens of Paddy's Hollow, Wilmington's red light district.
Loyall, Benjamin P., Lieutenant (*): The reassuringly named naval officer served in numerous engagements along the North Carolina coast and was admired by all who served with him.
O'Neal, Belle: A daring Rebel spy, her affairs with prominent Federal officers allow her to pass vital intelligence to the Confederacy.
Parker, Samuel, Naval Commander: After valiant early service in the Mosquito Fleet, he masterminds the construction of the ironclad Hatteras.
Reilly, Frederick, Sergeant, then Major (*): An expert gunner and inventor, Reilly commanded most of Fort Fisher's artillery.
Satchwell, Dr. Baccus: Prominent Wilmington physician and friend of the Landaus.
Sloane, Mary Harper: Wife of Matthew Sloane, mistress of Pine Haven Plantation.
Sloane, Matthew: Owner of Pine Haven Plantation and later a highly successful blockade-runner with the Banshee, until he falls under Belle O'Neal's amorous charms.
Smith, Peter (*): Mechanical genius and owner of the Holman's Ferry shipyard where Parker and his men built the Hatteras.
Vance, Zebulon Baird (*): A fiery orator from the mountains around Asheville, North CarCarolina, Vance was one of the Confederacy's greatest political figures, and among President Davis's fiercest critics.
Whiting, Chase, General (*): Vigorous commander of North Carolina's coastal defenses, he was fully supportive of Lamb's imaginative strategy.

The Union

Baker, Lafayette (*): Second-in-command of the new U.S. Secret Service, Baker was feared, powerful, and utterly ruthless.
Bone, Cyrus: Confederate deserter, and vicious bushwhacker, Bone organizes and leads the renegade Buffaloes, displaying remarkable gang-leader charisma.
Burnside, Ambrose, General (*): His amphibious campaign in North Carolina was brilliant, though his subsequent Civil War record was quite mixed,
Butler, Benjamin, General (*): Notoriously ugly and a vicious political infighter, Butler held various commands, including military governor of New Orleans, where he looted so many valuables from the local Rebels that he was nicknamed "Spoons" Butler.
Cushing, William Barker, Master's Mate, later Naval Commander (*): The

most decorated naval hero of the war, for either side, his exploits are many and colorful; he often led his men on operations that might reasonably have been described as "suicidal," such as the attempted capture of General Chase Whiting, depicted in this novel.

Fairless, Jack: A gangly hillbilly, Jack enlists in the Rebel army mainly to earn a cash bounty to help his kinfolk through a hard winter. At the urging of Cyrus Bone, he deserts and follows him into Union service as second-in-command of the Buffaloes.

Flusser, Charles, Commander (*): Flusser commanded all the Union gunboat flotillas in the North Carolina sounds and rivers, and was a patron to his hot-headed younger colleague, Will Cushing.

Foster, John G., General (*): He replaced Burnside as overall Union commander in North Carolina.

Hawkins, Rush, Colonel, later General (*): His early exploits with Burnside are factual; so is his chumminess with Ben Butler. His involvement in this novel with the "Butler Cabal," is fictional—though quite plausible.

Lee, Samuel Phillips, Admiral (*): A distant cousin to Robert E. Lee, he completely reorganized the Union blockade effort in late 1862 and improved its effectiveness throughout the war.

Reubens, Bonaparte: An "octaroon" free black from the French Indies, he is arrogant and perhaps mad. He winds up commanding the Negro company in the "Buffaloes."

Rowan, Stephen, Commodore, USN (*): Commander of Union shallow-draft naval forces during the war's first year.

Stringham, Silas, Commodore, USN (*): Crusty naval commander of the expedition against the Hatteras forts, he was later promoted to command the blockade squadron, but he was soon retired in favor of Admiral Lee.

Welles, Gideon (*): Lincoln's secretary of the navy, known as "Old Neptune" because of his gruff manners and trademark biblical whiskers.

The British

Armstrong, Sir George (*): Fabulously rich industrialist who donates a gigantic cannon to the defense of Fort Fisher, by which he hopes to gain lucrative contracts from the Confederacy.

Blayley, Charles John (*): Wartime governor of Nassau, the Bahamas.

Hobart-Hampden, Augustus (*): Known as H-H, and by the alias "Captain Roberts," he was one of the most colorful blockade-runners. He had once served as captain of Queen Victoria's yacht, before seeking extended leave, so he could make a fortune in the Confederacy while spying for the Crown. His recreational use of hashish is speculative, but the practice was not uncommon among officers posted to the wilder reaches of the empire. For all his prominence, H-H remained quite mysterious—here is the only major character whose musings I have never explicitly set forth in print. He acted virtually as a law unto himself, and others interacted with him, even attribute motives to him, but I have not written a single sentence with the phrase, "He thought . . . "

1861

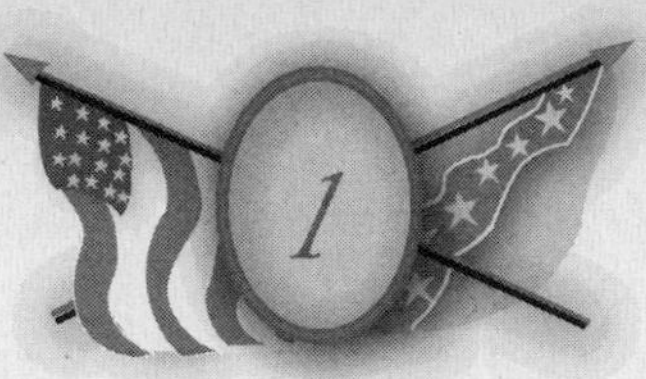

"For God's Sake, Don't Waste the Powder!"

$10 REWARD—"Run-away" from subscriber, about three months hence, a negro woman named "Bridgett." She walks lame but quick, of dark complexion, low built, between about 35 or 40 years. She is supposed to be lurking on the Sound near Wrightsville. The above reward will be paid upon her confinement in the Wilmington jail, by the Subscriber: Jere. J. King.

—The Wilmington Daily Journal, March 21 1861

On the last day of the year 1860, John William Ellis sat alone at his desk in the governor's mansion in Raleigh, North Carolina. Beyond his window the sky was a curdled mass of charcoal-colored clouds, and a slow, cold, miserable rain nibbled at the leaves of the noble old elm trees that shaded the mansion's front lawn. From the tall flagpole in front of the porte cochere the flag of the United States hung like a soggy dishrag, flattened against its staff as though in shame and in fear of the elements. Ellis wryly observed that the North Carolina flag had been lowered conscientiously and taken in by someone on his staff. A small but significant sign of the times, he thought.

Rising slowly, his joints protesting against the chill, Ellis walked to the fireplace and threw another scuttle of coal on the ebbing flames. Then, impatient for the fire to grow, he poured a glass of sherry into a goblet embossed with the Great Seal of North Carolina and its motto, "*Esse quam vederi*"—"To be, not to seem."

Warmed by the wine, he returned to his desk and began methodically to read through the document that he had only had time to scan this morning. Fresh from the printers, still fragrant of ink, this volume too bore the Great Seal and motto. Ranked upon its pages were the vital signs of North Carolina, the final tabulations of the census of 1860. With a scholar's eye, Ellis extracted the more salient data and stored it in his mind, trying to extrapolate what the numbers would really mean if the growing political crisis could not be resolved peacefully.

He presided, it seemed, over a population of almost 1 million souls, a fact that made North Carolina the twelfth most populous state in the Union. The economy was still primarily rural and agrarian—barely one quarter of the population lived in towns and cities, and of that number, only one percent was engaged in manufacturing.

There was a good railroad network serving the central and coastal regions, but not a foot of track west of Salisbury, the gateway to the Appalachians. Inhabitants of the mountain counties were almost as isolated from the rest of their state as they had been a century earlier. Where primitive roads existed, the unforgiving grain of the mountain ranges made it easier for them to trade with their neighbors across the borders of Tennessee, Virginia, and northwest Georgia than with the more prosperous regions of their own state.

While North Carolina's coastline was vast and the state's major rivers wormed deeply into the central Piedmont, most of the ports were small and dedicated mainly to modest intracoastal commerce. Only the bustling city of Wilmington, tucked snuggly beyond reach of the often-furious storms that battered Cape Fear, enjoyed regular commerce with the outside world. Elsewhere, poor roads retarded agricultural development, and the South's most valuable commodity, cotton, did not thrive in the state's red-clay soil. Corn, on the other hand, did just fine, as did long-leaf tobacco, rye, sweet potatoes, and barley, so that even the poor enjoyed a healthy if monotonous diet.

And what will happen to that fragile way of life if war comes and the farmers are off bearing arms instead of tending their crops?

Ellis sighed. The state was fertile but defenseless, and the treasury barely took in enough taxes to maintain the essentials of administration. Four-fifths of the voting males owned no slaves and never expected to. While the average citizen voiced anger at the trouble-making activities of the abolitionists, the passionate and biblically buttressed defenses of slavery that rang so shrilly in the state assemblies and editorials of the Deep South states were, in most of North Carolina, muted and morally ambiguous. Only in the coastal counties, where Negro labor was essential in maintaining the big rice plantations and turpentine groves, did such stridency prevail.

In the two generations since North Carolina's delegates had

scratched their pens on the Constitution, the Union had been good to and for the state. Until the galvanizing bolt of Lincoln's election in November, politics, like horse racing, had been a gentleman's hobby. But in the seven weeks since that event, passion and polarization had increased beyond reason. When South Carolina declared secession, five days before Christmas, the hotheaded secessionists of Wilmington had wheeled forth some dusty cannons from a militia warehouse and fired a salute of one hundred shots. Ellis's first reaction to that piece of news had been to exclaim: "For God's sake, don't waste the powder!"

Ellis knew the electorate of his state; he had worked the stump hard in his last campaign, and at that time the general populace had seemed industrious, hardworking, God-fearing, and quite preoccupied with minding its own business. Such was no longer the case. Now, at one polarity, there were growing numbers of secessionists—most of them motivated more by fear and envy regarding the North's economic and industrial power than by any heartfelt love of slavery as an institution; on the other extreme, particularly in the mountain counties, there were increasing numbers of pro-Union zealots. The only thing that kept the lid on, for the moment anyway, was the preponderant majority in between those poles—people who only sought, with diminishing success, to remain neutral, to go on about their customary activities with only an occasional glance at the storm clouds gathering overhead.

As governor, however, Ellis could not afford to turn away from the very real possibility of civil war. Setting aside the census report, he contemplated the legislative agenda he would present to the General Assembly when it reconvened in early January. His highest priority was the appropriation of $300,000 for modernizing the militia and fortifying the coast; next came the extension of rail service westward to Asheville; thirdly . . . Ellis glanced up at the diffident knock that sounded on his office door. "Yes, come in." There stood his dour but efficient secretary, Theophilus Hart, gripping the doorknob as though it was a living creature struggling to escape his fist.

"Excuse me, Your Excellency, but a delegation has just arrived from Wilmington, and they insist on seeing you. Shall I tell them to make a proper appointment and come back tomorrow?"

"What difference will tomorrow make? Show them in, please, and be gracious about it."

Ellis was not totally surprised. The day after Christmas, he had received a rather breathless telegram from one Colonel John Cantwell, recently elected commander of a group calling itself the Cape Fear

Minute Men. Until that moment, Ellis had never heard of such a unit, but that, too, was no surprise; volunteer "regiments" (usually not much larger than a company) were springing up all over the state, many of them adopting bellicose or historically reverberant names: the Goldsboro Grizzlies, the Lexington Wildcats, the Rockingham Invincibles. So many of these reports had crossed Ellis's desk since Lincoln's election that he could no longer keep track of them all.

"Colonel" Cantwell's telegram had requested the governor's permission to seize two lightly manned Federal posts in the Wilmington vicinity. The proposition made military sense—if war seemed imminent, Washington would certainly dispatch reinforcements to those posts as quickly as they could be loaded onto transports. Why not forestall these reinforcements by preemptive seizure? Ellis was, for a moment, tempted to give authorization, but after some reflection he wired back a negative reply. For the moment, North Carolina was part of the United States and the action proposed by Cantwell would be illegal as well as rashly provocative.

Brushing rudely past Mr. Hart, four men crowded into the governor's office. Each man had apparently selected his "uniform" from whatever he could lay hands upon: ostentatious caps, cartridge pouches stitched together from stable leather, tunics of various colors, home-sewn insignia of rank; and each man dragged behind him a clanking sword of varying length and vintage. If the expressions on their faces had not been so grim, the delegation would have looked like the chorus from a comic opera.

During a half-minute of awkward silence, the men from Wilmington and the governor regarded each other warily. Then a tall, clean-shaven man with bristling eyebrows stepped forward and saluted.

"Colonel John Cantwell, Your Exellency, representing the Southern patriots of Wilmington."

Ellis rose and shook hands with Cantwell, then with the other three men.

"Welcome to Raleigh, gentlemen. I assume you are here to press the case outlined in your recent telegram."

"Indeed we are, sir!" Now that Ellis was physically close to the men, he could feel their frustration, their coiled-spring energy. Whatever might happen, they were ready for war—hungry for it as so many hot-blooded young men were who had not seen its face. Cantwell removed his cavalier's hat, a broad-brimmed accessory garishly trimmed with peacock feathers, and held it respectfully in front of his waist, twisting the brim in red-knuckled fingers. How earnest he is, thought Ellis, and how faintly absurd.

"Governor Ellis, we are here to plead with you in person. We have received intelligence from several sea captains, recently arrived from various Northern ports, that a Federal cutter is being loaded with troops, guns, and provisions. The vessel's destination is well known: in a few days, a week at the most, it will bring reinforcements to Fort Caswell and Fort Johnston. If we act before those reinforcements arrive, we can occupy both positions without bloodshed and set about strengthening them for the conflict to come."

Ellis thought that might take considerable doing. "Fort" Johnston, located in the small fishing port of Smithville, thirty miles south of Wilmington, was an empty barracks, not really a fort at all; and Fort Caswell, guarding the western shore of the older of the two Cape Fear River inlets, was a crumbling pile of obsolete masonry. Both places held a "garrison" of just one man, a fort keeper who was supposed to keep things tidy in case the Federal government suddenly decided to occupy the positions in strength.

"Colonel Cantwell, I too have heard this rumor, but so far it is only that. Rest assured that if a Federal warship had set sail on such a mission, I would have learned about it within the hour. For the moment, sir, North Carolina remains part of the Union, and I am bound by my oath of office to discourage any acts which may be construed as illegal, not to say inflammatory. I am not insensitive to your argument, nor without sympathy. Only yesterday, I telegraphed President Buchanan and asked him bluntly what were his intentions with regard to those two locations. His reply, which arrived this morning, plainly states that Washington has *no* plans to garrison either post."

"Buchanan will not be president much longer," responded Cantwell. "And Mister Lincoln will not be so timid, once he is installed in office. He will surely act on this matter."

"And if it comes to that, sir, if Lincoln masses troops against us, then everything will be changed, and our state must take its stand alongside the states which have already seceded. I pray to God that does not happen, that reason and diplomacy might still prevail—North Carolina has invested eighty years in the Union, and played a vital role in its creation. Such a relationship cannot be swept away overnight by suspicion and petulance."

Cantwell bristled at those words. "By God, Mister Ellis, 'reason and diplomacy' have availed us nothing! War is coming, sir, war!"

Ellis stared coldly at the red-faced Rebel leader. "You forget yourself, sir. The first duty of a soldier, even an *amateur* soldier, is to obey the orders of his superior. As governor, I am entitled to your respect and obedience. If you and your men act rashly, I shall call you to heel. Is that clear, *Mister* Cantwell?"

Suddenly deflated, Cantwell pulled himself to attention and bowed. "Forgive me, Your Excellency. I spoke from passion."

Ellis nodded. "And in all likelihood, the South will soon have need of such passion, Colonel. But for the time being, we must not provoke the Federal government. Buchanan has but a short time to remain in office and is most unlikely to take aggressive steps. Mister Lincoln, on the other hand, is already under tremendous political pressure to take stern measures against the secessionists as soon as he takes the oath. If that happens, my orders to you will be more to your liking, for the actions you propose are strategically sensible." Ellis opened his arms to include the whole delegation. "Be patient, gentlemen—events are moving in your direction, though I wish with all my heart that they were not."

Chastened and somewhat mollified, Cantwell saluted. "As loyal sons of North Carolina, we will of course comply with Your Excellency's orders."

"I thank you for that loyalty, gentlemen. Now that our business is concluded, let me invite you to stay the night as my guests. My secretary will show you to comfortable quarters, and you may rest from your journey until dinnertime. We dine promptly at six o'clock, and the kitchen staff sets a good table. Until then . . . "

Cantwell took the hint and bustled his men out of the office.

When he was alone again, Ellis took a deep breath, surprised at the tension knotting his shoulders. He poured another glass of sherry and observed, with a curious intellectual detachment, that his hands were trembling.

Outside, the storm had grown stronger. Rain came down in sheets and gusts of wind moaned against the window. As he drank, Ellis stared morosely at the downpour. Manhandled by a powerful wind, the rain-soaked Union flag stirred fitfully and slapped against the flagstaff, in a rhythm suggestive of marching men.

William Lamb woke just before dawn, to face another February day in the coldest winter Norfolk had seen in many years. He could see his breath, despite the darkness. On the street outside, a wagon rolled past, and he could hear ice cracking under its wheels. He was in no hurry to rise from his cocoon of quilts, for he had fallen asleep spooned against the heated silken back of his wife, Daisy, the two of them murmuring sleepy endearments, the fireplace still blazing, the air still vibrant with the no-longer-mysterious but always wonderful scent of their lovemaking.

Ritualistically, Lamb prepared his body for the first shock of cold air. Two deep breaths, a determined knotting of muscles, and his customary phrase of self-admonition: *Prepare thyself, Young Soldier of the Lord!*

Soldier or not, the first contact between his bare feet and the icy wooden floor brought a shudder. Shaking it off, he scurried across to the fireplace, poked some life into its coals, threw in some kindling and pine knots. A series of huffs and puffs rewarded him with spurting flames and the cheerful sputter of pine resin. Hunkering down on his haunches, Lamb toasted his face and hands by the burgeoning fire, then stood, still naked below the hem of his nightshirt, and turned his buttocks toward the heat.

Now that the room was bright again, William Lamb could see his wife as she lay sleeping. Black and glossy as a raven's wing, Daisy's hair spilled down her pillow like a dark river. Her cheeks seemed to glow as if they welcomed the firelight and its warmth, and her lips—so proper and delicate in everyday conversation, so avid when they made love—were slightly parted.

Her full name was Sarah Anne Chaffee, and she was a Yankee, born and bred in Providence. Lamb's family had moved there in 1855 to escape a yellow fever outbreak in Norfolk, and William had lingered after the danger was past, paying court to the petite, sparkling brunette who had caught his eye at a dinner party.

Both the Lambs and the Chaffees occupied similar positions within their respective communities. William's father was a prominent lawyer, thrice elected Mayor of Norfolk. From the year of his birth, 1835, William Lamb had been groomed to be a Southern gentleman; starting with his tenth birthday, he received rigorous instruction in riding, fencing, boxing, shooting, and dancing. With his father's encouragement, he read and devoured biographies of Napoleon, Alexander, Caesar, and George Washington. This martial aspect of his education was balanced by heavy doses of theology. William absorbed all of these subjects readily, with a determined, at times ebullient, optimism borne of material comfort and complemented by an almost

Roman sense of noblesse oblige. By the age of twelve, he was writing out daily prayers to the Almighty in the style of military dispatches, signing himself Young Soldier of the Lord.

At age fourteen, he enrolled as a cadet in the Rappahanock Military Academy, where he learned the basics of drill, maneuvers, and leadership. He particularly excelled in the subjects of engineering and artillery science, developing an almost fetishistic attachment to the cannon.

Obedient to his father's wishes, William then pursued a law degree at the College of William and Mary. He graduated, Phi Beta Kappa, at the age of nineteen—too young to practice his profession. He therefore returned to Norfolk in a state of energized frustration. He was not idle for long, however. His father had bought controlling interest in a newspaper, the *Southern Argus*, and at the age of twenty, William became its editor, and an ardent early proponent of secession. The motto of his editorial page was "Government without Oppression—Liberty without Anarchy." Day after day, the *Southern Argus* denounced the growing power of the Federal establishment and railed against the emerging "Republican host," which Lamb characterized as the "real and true foe of Democracy."

When the yellow fever broke out in 1855, William took an enforced vacation from politics and in so doing found the love of his life. Daisy Chaffee was as well educated as any young woman of her class could be. She shared William's passion for books and, to his surprise and wonderment, his political convictions as well. Daisy viewed the South as a land of romance and chivalry, and her new suitor as a gallant paladin embodying its highest values. As for the moral issues of slavery, they were convinced that the South could solve that problem in its own way and in its own good time, if only it were left alone by what Daisy referred to as "the meddlesome fanatics of the North."

As the courtship deepened, William and Daisy realized that, beneath their intellectual compatibility, their mutual idealization of the Southern way of life, and their rampant Victorian sentimentality, was a mutual physical attraction that was almost frightening in its intensity. Both recognized this for what it was and both yearned for the sanctification of marriage to legitimize their desire.

When the yellow fever outbreak subsided, William and his bride moved back to Virginia. Daisy adapted quickly to Norfolk society, becoming so passionate a convert to the Southern point of view that people soon stopped regarding her as a curiosity and accepted her as one of their own.

In the autumn of 1858, William Lamb found a practical outlet for his military training; he helped organize a company of Norfolk militia, the Woodis Rifles, and was elected their captain in 1859. Not long after, the unit was ordered to peacekeeping duties at the hanging of John Brown. That grimly sensational event made a profound impression on William, crystallizing his attitude toward secession. "Sooner or later," he editorialized in the *Argus* not long after, "the ties, which now link together the North and the South, must be sundered." That prediction seemed to be realized when Lincoln was elected. While many of his peers still viewed secession as a desperate last resort, Lamb embraced it as a creed.

Now, in the final days of February 1861, the sundering of the Union was a fact and William Lamb was certain that war was inevitable. This morning, after a brief visit to his newspaper office, he would march straight to the field where his company spent two days a week drilling and practicing the manual of arms. Now that the bedroom was warm again, and the first pale hint of dawn crept over the distant sea, he opened the doors of a mahogany wardrobe and began to don his uniform, first pausing to wash himself from a basin of bracingly cold water.

Through a haze of contentment, Daisy watched her husband dress. He looked so splendid in his uniform! She admired him in all of his parts, especially his mutable blue eyes, which could flash with ardor or soften to the dreaminess of a poet. She loved his slim yet well-muscled body, his thick brown hair, even the sparse ginger-colored goatee he was trying assiduously to cultivate. Her William was the Southern beau ideal made flesh, and in him lived resolve, honor, and tempered audacity. He was born to wear a sword. The North, in her experience, produced few such men. His idealism was both a bulwark and a comfort. She stretched languorously beneath the quilts, surprised to feel a reverberation of last night's desire still chiming softly in her loins.

"Oh, William," she murmured.

Lamb turned, pleasantly surprised to hear her voice. He buttoned the collar of his gray tunic, leaned his sword belt against the wardrobe, and returned to the edge of the bed. Wordlessly, he stroked Daisy's hair and cheeks, lingering for a sleepy and sensual kiss.

"I tried not to wake you," he said.

"It's so early, my darling. Surely your soldiers are still abed."

"Surely they are, but their commander is fully awake, as he should be."

"Give me another kiss and I'll fix some breakfast."

"I will gladly give you a kiss, but there is no need for you to leave the warmth of our bed. I have to finish an editorial before the *Argus* goes to press, then I'll breakfast at the café near the drill field."

He leaned into her welcoming arms and nuzzled the silky down at the base of her neck. Daisy whispered in his ear: "I always dreamed of a husband who would also be a great lover. How fortunate we are!"

"God has blessed us, my dearest. And I would gladly die to protect you."

"Protect me if the need arises," she chided, "but do not even speak of dying."

She held him until she could sense his need to be up and about his duties, a surge of disciplined energy that ran through him like a galvanic current. She slowly disengaged from their embrace and sat up against the headboard. William rose and buckled on his sword. As he opened the bedroom door, he gazed back at her longingly.

"May I have the honor of escorting you to lunch, Mrs. Lamb?"

She batted her eyes teasingly. "Indeed, sir, you are most forward. I will consider your invitation."

"If you turn it down, there are many ladies eager to accept."

Laughing, she threw a pillow at him. "Go to your soldiers, you scoundrel!"

He gave a mock salute and took an overcoat from the wardrobe. As he was struggling into the garment, Daisy called out once more, in a small and earnest voice.

"William, will there really be a war?"

Slowly he nodded. "I can feel it coming in the very pressure of the air, like the vanguard winds of a hurricane."

Suddenly, there was nothing more to say. Lamb took his leave.

Outside, Norfolk stirred. Already there was considerable wagon traffic in the streets. Shrouded in scarves and top hats, passing citizens nodded to one another, ejecting clouds of steam that made each man appear to be puffing on a cigar. Ruts and watering troughs, skimmed with rime ice, glowed with the cold lavender of sunrise. Lamb heard the clank of pails, the crystalline jingle of harness tackle, the disgruntled snorts of mules, the distant hoot of a harbor steam whistle. He inhaled the clean frigid air with spartan relish, feeling the last vestiges of sleep wash from his blood. Carefully stepping around several fresh piles of steaming dung, he strode briskly to the offices of the *Southern Argus.*

Inside the building, Lamb found the apprentice typesetter industriously scanning yesterday's newspapers from Washington. The boy had already put a pot of coffee on top of the cast-iron stove, and the scent of its brewing was like a breath from Heaven.

"Good morning, Tom," said Lamb, hanging his overcoat on a hook near his desk.

"Morning, Captain Lamb. Coffee's about ready—shall I pour you a cup?"

"That would be splendid. Anything exciting in the latest papers?"

"The usual rhetorical flatulence from the Republicans; otherwise there is nothing out of the ordinary."

"Good. Then I can finish my editorial and you can set the type while I'm at drill with my men."

Sipping strong and scalding coffee from a tin mug, Lamb sat down at his desk and poised his pen above the last sentence he had written yesterday. He marshaled his thoughts efficiently, then began to write:

> The forbearance with which the South has borne these indignities and wrongs, has utterly failed to secure a corresponding forbearance upon the part of our aggressors. The spirit of fanaticism by which they are influenced, has at last so far united the Northern masses as to enable them to seize upon the general Government with all its power of purse and sword. A clearer case of foreign domination towards us could not well be presented. It can but be manifest that a blow aimed at one of the Southern States would involve the whole country in civil war, the destructive consequences of which, to us, could only be controlled by our ability to resist those engaged in waging it.
>
> The civilization of the age, surely, ought to be a sufficient guarantee for the prevention of so great a calamity as intestine war. But should the incoming administration be guilty of the folly and wickedness of drawing the sword against any Southern State, whose people may choose to seek that protection out of the Federal Union which is denied to them within it, then we of Virginia would owe it to ourselves—and to the liberties we have inherited from our fathers—to the peace of our homes and families, dearer to us than all Governments, to resist it to the last extremity.

When Lamb rested his pen, an hour had passed. He wiped some ink from his fingers, proofread his copy, then handed it to the young printer. Glancing at his watch, he saw that he still had time for a leisurely breakfast before the commencement of drill.

Norfolk's militia traditionally held muster on an open sward of parkland just high enough to provide occasional views of the sea. By the time Lamb arrived, twenty minutes before the scheduled starting time of ten o'clock, a dozen of his men had already assembled. They stood around a fire at one end of the field, warming their hands against the morning chill, exchanging rumors and boasts. When they caught sight of Lamb, they hurriedly extinguished pipes and cigars and braced themselves at attention.

Lamb returned their salute, greeted several men by name, and strode off to the east. How different the men's attitude had become since Lincoln's election, he thought. As late as last summer, the Woodis Rifles, at that time numbering about fifty men, had mustered on a monthly basis. The men had been more concerned with cutting a sharp figure before the female onlookers than with the niceties of drill. Usually, after an hour of marching, the formation dissolved and the event turned into a social affair complete with picnic lunches, punch bowls, and flirtations.

Things were much different now. Lamb's company was full strength, 112 men, handsomely dressed in uniforms designed by a committee of Norfolk's more prominent wives: short gray jackets with dark blue piping, dark gray trousers with red stripes, and kepi hats with gay red horsehair cockades. Drills had increased from one a month to two per week, and the mood was no longer social but businesslike. Lamb had instituted regular target practice, but so far the results were as mixed as the weaponry shouldered: heirloom flintlocks converted to accept percussion caps, shotguns, and an assortment of small-caliber varmint rifles. Neither the company's firepower nor its accuracy yet amounted to much, but Lamb's father had prevailed upon the city government to order one hundred .58-caliber Harper's Ferry rifles from the Springfield ordnance works—with luck, those weapons should arrive soon.

Lamb glanced at his watch: five minutes to ten. Behind him, he could hear more and more men arriving and greeting their comrades. Beneath their bantering tone was a discernible tension borne of the realization that they were no longer playing soldier, but girding for real warfare.

The wind picked up, bringing to Lamb's nostrils the scents of the harbor: tar and fish, salt and oak. From his vantage point, he could see a patch of water framed by the roofs of two warehouses. Centered there was the dazzling glare of a winter sun, with a darker shape blurred against the rippling gold. Lamb focused intently, shading his eyes with one hand, until the abstraction became concrete. No doubt about it now: that was a Federal warship, one of the new steam frigates, riding smugly at anchor a half-mile offshore. It had not been there the last time Lamb had savored this view. What was it here for now? he wondered. Surely matters had not deteriorated to the point of a blockade. More likely, the vessel was on its way to a Northern port and had stopped at Norfolk for coal or victuals. Of course, while it was anchored off Virginia's busiest seaport, its captain could survey the land in detail and report back to his superiors regarding the state of any new fortifications that might be under construction.

In sudden anger, Lamb slapped his leather gloves against his side. That warship was a tempting target, and easily ranged from even this modest elevation. What was it Lord Nelson had said? *A ship's a fool to fight a fort.* Indeed, thought William Lamb, that was almost always the case. Baring his teeth in a most ungentlemanly growl, the Young Soldier of the Lord shook his fist at the Yankee ship, hoping her captain might be looking at him through his telescope.

Oh God, for a pair of big rifled guns!

"Mind the fruit punch, Aurelia! The sugar water has boiled quite long enough, I think." Mary Harper Sloane had not anticipated the thirst of her guests; two bowls of fruit punch usually sufficed for the number of people she and Matthew had invited to their spring fete, Pine Haven Plantation's traditional way of marking the start of the rice-planting season. Since the March evening was mild and the extended parlor well ventilated, simple heat did not explain the unusual consumption. Perhaps the constant talk of politics and war had dried every throat.

"It only been bile-ing for six minutes, ma'am. I'se watching the timer glass real close."

Mary Harper checked her impatience—Aurelia was an attentive, hardworking slave, and she had tended to the party preparations as if her own pride were involved. To a certain extent, that was probably true; Aurelia ruled the kitchen with the same firmness and eye for detail that Mary Harper's husband exercised in running the rest of the plantation's daily business.

"I don't mean to snap at you," she said over her shoulder. "I'm just trying to guess how much more whiskey punch the men are going to want."

Aurelia laughed knowingly. "What they be wantin' tonight is all you can serve them, Mizzuz Sloane! Talkin 'bout politics always works up a powerful thirst in men."

Indeed, thought Mary Harper. Pine Haven served its whiskey without stint, to those guests who favored it, and tonight it seemed as though even the ordinarily moderate drinkers were emptying their cups as rapidly as the table-tending servants could refill them.

Leaving Aurelia to finish preparing the nonalcoholic punch, Mary Harper concentrated on mixing a fresh bowl of the more potent beverage, plucking the ingredients from the linen-covered jars arrayed beside a mammoth cut-glass serving bowl: a quart of strawberries, two handfuls of sliced peaches, three-quarters of a pound of powdered sugar, two brimming cups of dark rum, two cups of lemon juice, and two bottles of whiskey. For a proper blend, the mixture should be allowed to stand for two hours, but she doubted if any of the men would object to a certain rawness—not at this stage of the evening.

When both punch bowls were filled—the fortified one and the sugary one for the teetotaling guests—Aurelia stepped outside to get some boys to carry them into the parlor. Like most plantations, Pine Haven maintained its kitchen facilities in a building detached from the main house; this arrangement minimized the danger of fire and also prevented the cooking fires' heat from spreading through the Sloanes' living quarters. Mary Harper's kitchen was spacious and divided into three parts: two rooms for preparation and cooking and a third for storage. When both of the big iron stoves were going full-blast, the temperature was close to infernal, even during the winter months.

Mary Harper took advantage of her brief privacy to fan herself with a scallop-shaped palmetto frond and to check her appearance in a small hand mirror; it was permissible for the guests to perspire—indeed, that was a sign of revelry and high spirits—but distasteful for the hostess. "Horses sweat, men perspire, and ladies *glow*," her mother often said, as though three distinct types of moisture were involved. Mary Harper saw that her forehead did indeed "glow," and she carefully dabbed a bit of flour on two fingers and rubbed it in until her skin was once more smooth and dry-looking.

A woman with a ruddier complexion would have used a more

refined cosmetic, but Mary Harper's skin was outstandingly fair, the unblemished hue of good vellum. She burned easily under the sometimes brutal sunlight of the coast, and she was compelled to wear a hat and long-sleeved clothing even when she ventured out during the hottest days. Although she was but one year shy of thirty, she looked very much as she had when she married Matthew Sloane ten years ago. Her face was a clear ivory oval, framed by dark chestnut hair teased by curling irons into long symmetrical columns that brushed her shoulders. High dark brows, angled upward toward her temples, accented her hazel eyes, and her wide cheeks set off a full mouth whose lips tended, without the help of any cosmetics, to a strawberry red. Matthew had always found her stirringly attractive—or so he said, and so his actions once had demonstrated, even though their moments of physical intimacy were now comparatively rare and . . . she searched for a word. In their society, the vocabulary pertaining to sexual relations was meager and oblique. "Incomplete" might be the right term.

It had not been so in previous years. Mary Harper, of course, had been a virgin when she married Matthew; Matthew might or might not have been the same—it would have been unthinkable for her to inquire—but he was patient and tender, and he had (instinctively, she hoped, rather than from coarse practice) shown some degree of expertise, and their wedding night had not been the grim but needful ritual her mother had warned her about. She had borne two children—Henrietta, six, and Francis Marion, eight—and the pleasure of *begetting* had compensated for the misery of carrying a child to term in such a climate. But her third pregnancy had not gone well; in the final weeks she had contracted a malarial fever and the child, another son, had been stillborn. The doctor from Wilmington had told Matthew that another childbirth might kill her, and since then Matthew had treated her as though she were made of Limoges china. When he did approach her bed, he did so almost apologetically, and touched her with an unwelcome diffidence. His crisis came quickly, and instead of reveling in it, as he once had, he always withdrew from her and spent upon the sheet, groaning more from frustration than from pleasure, and leaving her, always, raw and unsatisfied. Mary Harper assumed, given the accumulated wisdom of the centuries, that there were . . . *methods* . . . by which two loving people might satisfy their desires without risking a pregnancy, but such knowledge was certainly not found in any book she knew about and on the few occasions when she had delicately tried to kindle a frank discussion,

Matthew had become so embarrassed, so flustered, that she felt guilty for even broaching the subject.

Aurelia returned now, and in her wake was Agrippa, her brother, and two teenage cousins, all dressed in formal black coats. The youths picked up the fruit punch, and Agrippa, long-armed and powerful in the hands, took up the whiskey. Leaving Aurelia to replenish the supply of smoked-ham biscuits, Mary Harper led the punch procession back into the main house.

Pine Haven took its name both from the forested acres that bounded the inland flank of its rice fields and from the lustrous yellow heart-pine planks used to construct its frame and floors. Matthew's father, Ezra Sloane, had built the Greek Revival structure in 1840 and it was handsome and comfortable rather than ostentatiously grand in the manner of Limerick, the estate of Mary Harper's parents—three thousand acres that sprawled along a fertile plain in St. James County, near Charleston. Pine Haven was two stories high, faced with plain white weatherboards, and all but surrounded by a single-story porch supported by dignified Doric columns. Its low, hipped roof was surmounted by two pairs of corbeled interior chimneys that carried out the smoke of a dozen fireplaces. On the eastern side of the house, where a flagstoned path led from the kitchen to the main rear entrance, the porch columns concealed wooden downspouts that fed rainwater into a brick cistern constructed at basement level; this supplied their needs for bathing and laundry, while a dependable well adjacent to the smokehouse provided drinking water. The house was faced with many windows, the better to catch any breeze that might appear, and each of the twelve-foot-high ceilings contained a rotating ventilation duct that helped move cool air in and hot air out. Except for the really torrid months of July and August, the house was usually comfortable.

Mary Harper followed the punch bowls up the graceful stairs and onto the porch. Now she could hear the music of a quadrille and the sounds of well-lubricated conversation. Ordinarily, Agrippa or one of the two boys would have hurried forward to open the door for her, but there was no way they could do it without losing their grip on the punch, so Mary Harper swept to the head of the line and opened it for them. Each of the three Negroes bowed solemnly to her as they filed inside and headed for the back parlor with their burdens.

Ordinarily, the front and back parlors were separated by folding pocket doors. The front parlor, by far the more formal in appearance and furnishings, was reserved for company and the children were not allowed to play there except at Christmas. The back parlor was a multipurpose space in which the whole family gathered. In addition to a brick fireplace, it also contained a small iron stove and in the winter it was the warmest, snuggest room in the house. It doubled therefore as a sickroom and, on rarer occasions, a birthing room. Mary Harper had delivered her two living children there, attended by a midwife from Wilmington, Aurelia and two other house slaves, and a semicircle of hot kettles and clean linen. For tonight's party, the two parlors had been joined into one big room, the nonessential furniture had been moved out, the rugs rolled up into a corner, and the dancing area sprinkled with cornmeal to provide a proper surface. In the southeast corner, a trio of musicians—black freedmen from Wilmington who earned their living by playing all over the Cape Fear region—gave rhythm and vitality to the occasion with banjo, fiddle, and spoons.

As soon as Agrippa deposited the whiskey bowl on its assigned table, thirsty men gathered round and filled their cups. The Sloane children were off in one corner, listening to an elderly planter recount his—notoriously exaggerated—seafaring exploits during the War of 1812. The old fellow was waving an imaginary cutlass and the flush on his cheeks indicated which punch bowl he was frequenting. Couples were dancing, suitors were courting or at least flirting, and the air was pungent with cigar smoke.

She stood in the doorway for a moment, as though negotiating a profound change in air pressure—from the cool, quiet outdoors to the bright, loud whirl of the dance floor—then squared her shoulders, summoned her best smile, and moved into the light. Cousins, neighbors, and Matthew's business associates all nodded to her as she entered. In this part of the state, anyone who lived within a twenty-mile radius was considered a neighbor, even if you only saw him two or three times a year.

Matthew Sloane noticed her return and waved to her from behind the whiskey bowl, where he had moved Agrippa aside and was generously plying the ladle to every empty cup extended in his direction. Clustered around him were Mary Harper's mother and father, Stepney and Rosalee Harper, and a vaguely familiar young man in a spanking new militia uniform. When Mary Harper joined them, her husband automatically extended a cup of whiskey punch in her direction and, just as automatically, she accepted it, pretending not to notice the sudden disapproving arch of her mother's brows. Old Stepney, who was obviously rather deep in his own cups, affected not to notice—his daughter was a grown woman with two children and her own estate to run, and if she wanted a drink, by God, she could have one. He said all this with a single don't-you-dare scowl at his wife, a plump, still-handsome woman whose wide imperious head bobbed atop a vast hooped pyramid of black bombazine twill. Mary Harper drained half the cup in one long swallow and shivered with pleasure as the whiskey blossomed in her stomach. Returning the ladle to Agrippa, Matthew introduced the man in uniform as Colonel John Cantwell, newly elected commander of the Cape Fear Minute Men. Cantwell bowed gallantly and kissed her gloved hand.

"My dear, this punch is even better than the first batch!"

"It is certainly stronger, Matthew, which amounts to the same thing by this stage of the party."

Cantwell laughed appreciatively. "Matthew and I were just discussing the economic possibilities of the coming war. He is well situated, I think, to enjoy great prosperity."

"Indeed? I did not know that prosperity was a casus belli for the South. From my reading of history, it seems that wars usually bring just the opposite."

Cantwell looked at her curiously, as though suddenly unsure of her intellectual measure.

"I defer to your knowledge of history, madam. Wars do, of course, bring their quotient of misery and suffering. But armies must be fed and soldiers cannot eat cotton. If conflict breaks out, the value of your rice crop will multiply, especially since your husband has his own ship."

"Come now, John," said Matthew, "the *Banshee* is only fit for coastal trading now. She cannot compete with steamers on the open sea."

Stepney Harper raised his cup to make a point. "She could, Matthew, if you trimmed her masts and mounted a steam engine amidships. She could take rice to Wilmington, sell it for a good profit, then you could reload her with cotton and make a quick run to Bermuda, where the English factors will pay in gold for every bale they can get. She's got plenty of room belowdecks."

"Yes, Stepney, I know." All slave ships had "plenty of room belowdecks," and during the busiest decades of the African trade, the *Banshee* had carried a multitude. Rice cultivation was dependent, even more than cotton, on plentiful labor, and the Negro, whether he came from Angola or Barbados, was considered more fit for such steamy, oppressive work than even the poorest white. Stepney Harper had made a few slaving voyages himself, during his youth, but when he inherited Limerick from his father, he had left that task to hired men, men more hardened to the necessary brutalities. Stepney seldom spoke of the business, but it was clear when he did that he had had no taste for the stink and cruelty of it.

At the time Matthew Sloane assumed de facto ownership of the *Banshee*, as the major portion of Mary Harper's dowry, the ship was at sea in the Indies, and when it returned, Matthew traveled to Wilmington to oversee the sale of its human cargo. He was no abolitionist, and indeed his father-in-law would have spurned him if he had been, but when the auction was over, he pocketed the profits, dismissed the crew, and laid the *Banshee* up in James Cassidey's shipyard, where the benches and chains and other accoutrements of her former trade were removed and the spacious holds made suitable for conventional cargo. When the ship was ready, Matthew hired a skeleton crew and sailed the *Banshee* upriver to Pine Haven. Since that time, she had carried rice to Wilmington after the harvest and returned with a winter's worth of supplies along with farm implements or furniture too bulky to be transported by wagon.

Whatever Stepney Harper's private feelings might have been, he tacitly gave his blessing to this new arrangement. Unspoken by either man was the notion that it was one thing to profit from Negro labor—the South's whole economy rested on bent, sweating, ebony shoulders—but another and lesser thing to personally traffic in human flesh. A Northern zealot might see this distinction as hypocritical and clouded with sophistry, but to men like Harper and Sloane, it was as natural as the turn of seasons.

"Your father-in-law has a point," said Cantwell, breaking into Matthew's reverie. "If war does come, the South will have to trade its agricultural products for European manufactured goods. My advice to you is to order a steam engine now, from a reputable Northern company, before the break comes and such commerce is no longer possible. When the machinery arrives in Wilmington, you can sail downriver and oversee its installation. Even if war can somehow be averted, it would be a worthy investment. A *modernization.*" Cantwell rolled the word as though its syllables were savory—steam and iron were the paths of the future for all ships, civilian or military.

Mary Harper observed how Matthew digested the idea and immediately began gnawing on it like a dog with a new bone. Matthew subscribed to agricultural and scientific journals; he thought of himself as a progressive man, a trait he had inherited from his father. Pine Haven had been one of the first rice plantations to install a threshing mill, back in 1835, and one of the first houses in the region to sprout lightning rods. Whenever Matthew stepped behind the helm of the *Banshee*, he beamed with almost childish pride. Clearly, the idea of *modernizing* her held great appeal. Was that not what he had done when he converted her from a slaver to a freighter?

When Matthew seized upon a new idea, his very features transformed. The sharp crescent ends of his goatee seemed to embrace the corners of his downturned lips; he would chew on them, she suspected, if he could reach them. His close-set blue eyes brightened and his brows knitted toward the fan of wrinkles spreading from the top of his nose to the center of his forehead. He was not, she supposed, a conventionally handsome man—the chin whiskers seemed almost an afterthought, since the rest of his face was smooth-shaven, and the quick parade of his emotions gave him a quizzical, somehow unresolved expression. From their first encounter, Mary Harper had been attracted to his energy and quickness of mind. Other, better-looking suitors had courted her, but Matthew had always seemed more interesting and therefore a better investment. At the time of their marriage, she had been more "fond" of him than "in love" with him, and she had been delightfully surprised when their marital relations proved to be mutually rewarding. Now that those relations had perforce become sporadic and incomplete, she had fallen back upon her reserves of affection. To see him become thus animated, even if the mood was partially a by-product of the whiskey punch, made her feel close to him again.

"Gentlemen, it is all well and good to talk of rice and cotton, but we should not overlook yet a third possibility."

"Indeed, Mrs. Sloane?" Cantwell leaned forward with what seemed like genuine interest. "And what might that be?"

"Well, sirs, if there is to be a war, then there will have to be a navy as well as an army. If only to protect this expanded trade you speak of. And that means a vigorous market for naval goods."

"I believe the term is 'naval stores,' daughter," said Stepney Harper in his most patronizing tone.

"Please, Father, what difference does it make? I mean tar, and pitch, and turpentine. The more ships that ply these waters, the greater the need. And here at Pine Haven, we have three thousand acres of splendid heart-pine forest standing idle."

"My dear Mrs. Sloane," said Cantwell, "have you any idea of the toil required to turn pine sap into naval stores?"

"We are not afraid of hard work, Colonel, not on this plantation. We should at least study the possibility."

"Darling," said Matthew, "we have enough on our hands without venturing into new territory."

Mary Harper glared sternly across the punch bowl. "Only a moment ago, Matthew, you were contemplating, with some excitement, an even riskier venture into 'new territory.' "

"She has you there, old fellow!" chuckled Cantwell. Rosalee Harper wagged a plump finger at her daughter. "Mary, you are being just a touch impertinent!"

"I rather thought, Mother, that I was being shrewd. If Matthew wants to put a steam engine on the *Banshee*, then I can at least make a study of the likely demand for these naval stores and determine if Pine Haven can support a new activity."

Mary Harper's spirits were now roused to defiance, and the punch-bowl banter might have turned into an argument, but at that moment her son, Francis Marion, tugged on her dress.

"Mommy, Mommy! Aurelia says we have to go to bed now! Please let us stay up longer!"

Mary Harper glanced at the clock on the mantelpiece. "Aurelia is right, darling. It is almost eleven, and well past your bedtime. Say good night to your grandparents and go upstairs. I'll tuck you in after a while."

The children did as they were told and Aurelia, with practiced efficiency, swept them from the room and up the stairs.

Mary Harper had finished her cup by now, and wanted another. It would not be proper, however, for her to ladle out a second helping so soon after the first, so she excused herself, on the pretext of checking on the hors d'oeuvres, and went back to the kitchen. Finding herself alone, she poured a generous dollop of straight whiskey and went outside to savor it in privacy.

All around her, the night held its breath, poised between seasons. Today was March the fourteenth; the crisp and frosty days of winter were all but gone, and the gardens had not yet started to bloom—in another three weeks, the air would be ripe with scents and the arduous planting season would be in full vigor. She stood at the convergence of several gravel paths that meandered through groves of poplar and live oaks and waxy magnolias, embraced well-tended ranks of azaleas, camellias, pansies, hydrangea, and crepe myrtle, and eventually led to the ring of outbuildings that surrounded the big house—the kitchen, the barn, the blacksmith's shed, the smokehouse, and finally the long rows of slave cabins on the boundary between the pine forest and the first embankment of the rice fields.

Seduced by the quietude, the late-winter absence of nocturnal insects, and the rare, near-perfect temperature, Mary Harper followed one of the paths until it reached the edge of the rice fields. A waxing half-moon had risen above the tree line, and the shallow irrigation trenches glowed like veins of silver. So peaceful and orderly was the scene that she could scarcely imagine the contrast it would present on Monday morning, when a hundred Negroes would fill the landscape, each one toiling with a hoe, digging shallow grooves, ten inches apart, laying rice seed at carefully spaced intervals, then shielding them with a light covering of earth. The planting would take from mid-March to early June, and if there were no floods, each acre should yield twenty-five to thirty bushels of rice. After subtracting Pine Haven's own supply and the amount required for next season's planting, the bulk of the harvest would be disposed by factors in New Bern and Wilmington. Matthew would deliver the goods himself, sailing the *Banshee* on a course dictated by the highest profits.

Mary Harper passed through the fields like a ghost, following moonbeams toward the distant glint of the Uwharrie River—named by the early English settlers, with unintended irony, in honor of a small, friendly Indian tribe that had been wiped out by smallpox not long after the river was so designated. Ideally, rice should be cultivated in low and marshy ground situated near water that was close enough to the sea to rise and fall with the tides, yet not so close as to be brackish. Pine Haven was well situated. The Uwharrie was a large tributary of the Cape Fear River; from the point where it joined the big river, it twisted north some thirty miles before melting into a vast region of swamps and black-water creeks and losing its identity. Along that distance, a number of smaller rivers, most of them nameless and unused, connected with the ocean. A few miles north of the Pine Haven wharf, the Uwharrie suddenly became shallow, but from the plantation all the way to the Cape Fear inlets, it was navigable even for ships as large as the *Banshee*. Yet for all its distance from the open sea, the Uwharrie still responded sluggishly to the push and pull of the tide, and thus could easily be diverted to irrigate the fields, with only a modicum of mechanical help.

So many factors converged here, thought Mary Harper Sloane, that the place seemed unnaturally blessed by its circumstances. As it had prospered in decades of peace, so it seemed destined to prosper in war.

She continued east, walking now along the rutted wagon trail that led to and from the wharf. She passed the sluice gates that controlled the flow into the irrigation system, their iron frameworks gleaming in the moonlight like prehistoric monuments, and paused to catch her breath (for the whiskey had suddenly made itself felt in a brief wave of dizziness) beside the tin-roofed sheds that clustered hard against the riverbank.

Before her rose the gangplank that led to the *Banshee*'s foredeck. The ship loomed high above her, dwarfing the little steam launch that was Pine Haven's primary link to the rest of the world. Like many slavers, the *Banshee* had been built for speed and evasion, and she drew less water than most vessels her size, so that she could skulk undetected in the shallows off West Africa or the jungly coves of the Indies. One hundred and fifteen feet long and disproportionately wide, she boasted rakish lines and triple masts that carried a lot of sail. Now, of course, even fully rigged and with a stout wind at her back, a modestly powered steamship could overtake her.

Mary Harper finished her whiskey and carefully walked up the gangplank. Bathed in moonlight, scrubbed, and well maintained, the *Banshee* seemed peaceful yet filled with potential energy. Put a good steam engine on her, Mary Harper thought, and she would positively fly. She strode across the deck and leaned against the starboard railing, contentedly watching the moon-slick river, now flowing gently south, echoing the distant ebbing tide of the great Atlantic. In response to either the tide or the moonlight, frogs had started to croak in the nearby marshes. *Unk—Ungh—Rung-it!* Perhaps if she stood here long enough, she could learn to interpret their speech.

"Noisy ta-night, ain't they, ma'am?"

Startled, Mary Harper turned. Instantly, she recognized the gawky, almost impossibly skinny figure of Master Fitz-John Bright, Pine Haven's overseer.

"Whom do you mean, Mister Bright?"

"Why, them TOW-ahds, ma'am. Must be getting an early start on their mating NUP-shals, eh?"

As usual, it took Mary Harper a moment to adjust to Bright's peculiar patterns of speech. There were those who thought him soft in the head, because he blithely persisted in pronouncing words according to some private understanding of English. Matthew had long since stopped attempting to correct Bright's eccentric speech habits, but Mary Harper still found them unsettling.

"Oh. You mean the *toads.*"

"Yessum. Lots of TOW-ahds abroad tonight."

Bright sucked on a corncob pipe and the glow of it momentarily illuminated his skull-like features. His eyes were a watchful, watery blue, constantly rolling from one side of his head to the other, and his ears stuck out like the handles of a jug. He had worked for Pine Haven since Matthew was a child, and eventually became a permanent fixture of the place. A native of Morehead City, he knew the coastal waters of North Carolina intimately and served as Matthew's pilot whenever the *Banshee* sailed. Bright was somewhere between forty and fifty years old. Firm but humane with the slaves, plodding but conscientious in his bookkeeping, he was competent in all his duties, but his conversation could be disconcerting in large doses. When he mispronounced common words, Mary Harper had to repress the urge to shake him violently. He did it so often, and with such impenetrable innocence, that had she actually given in to that impulse, she would have had little time left for more productive communication. It was as though the man's ears were uniquely formed so that everything he heard registered on his brain and reproduced on his tongue according to the rules of a foreign language, although what language that might be was anybody's guess.

Bright gestured toward the river. "Saw a big al-i-GAH-tor a while ago, big as a loco-mo-TIF, he was!"

"Indeed? If he returns, Mister Bright, lecture him and scare him off."

Bright slapped his rump and guffawed—"Hro-hro-hro!"—sprinkling himself with glowing pipe ashes.

"Do you have the time, Mister Bright?"

"Yessum, Ah do." He retrieved a watch from his waistcoat and bent to read it. "The NOCK-turn-ul hour is breasting toward midnight, ma'am."

Mary Harper processed that information. At times, Bright could be as amusing as he was infuriating. But his unexpected appearance had broken her mood and reminded her of her duties back at the big house.

"Well, in that case, I should return and set the clocks back an hour. It wouldn't be proper to keep dancing into the Sabbath, would it?"

"Nor should the re-VELS end just yet, eh? Hro-hro-hro!"

"Not when everyone is having a good time. Won't you join the party, Mister Bright? The whiskey punch is especially good tonight."

"Yessum, yessum. Ah'll come along directly, just as soon as that al-li-GAH-tor swims by again."

"Um, Mister Bright, exactly *why* are you waiting for the alligator?"

"Well, ma'am, Ah reckon me and MIS-ter Sloane will be takin' the old ship out a lot, now, what with see-CESSHUN comin' into a FACT. One THING Ah learned as a chile, is that al-li-GAT-ors be very old and very wise. Could be this GAT-or will im-PART some wisdom as to CUR-rents, or tides, or sand BARS, and such like."

"Am I to understand that you communicate with this reptile?"

"Only in a MAN-ner of speakin'. Mostly, Ah just lis-TEN to the way he moves through the WAD-der."

"Oh. Well, good night, Mister Bright. Do come join us when you and the 'gator have finished your colloquy."

Mary Harper puzzled over this exchange as she returned along the wagon road. If Bright were a little bit mad, what difference did it make? Perhaps alligators *did* speak to him. In wartime, a touch of madness might prove useful.

Only then did it cross her mind that war signified more than a business opportunity. If Matthew sailed for the South, he might die for the South.

By the time she reached the big house, Mary Harper Sloane was shivering.

The Sailor and the Mountaineer

AN EDITORIAL REFLECTION ON THE NORTHERN AND SOUTHERN ARMIES—In no respect does the difference between the feeling which animates the North and South appear more strikingly than in the material which composes the two sections under arms.

Besotted Irishmen, illiterate Germans, rapacious Israelites, street loafers, penniless adventurers, and vagrants fill up the ranks of the Yankee regiments. The "solid citizens" of the North, and their sons and relations, prudently keep out of the range of danger, while they send the floating scum of the working class out to do the work of vandals and marauders.

In the South, the volunteers who spring to arms with so much alacrity are men of substance and position, wealthy farmers and planters, with their sons; professional men, merchants and clerks; intelligent and industrious mechanics; sturdy yeomen eager to defend their modest estates; and indeed, from every art, trade, and profession, the backbones of our society have rallied for the defense of liberty, their homes, and the assertion of their constitutional rights.

—The Wilmington Journal, August 30 1861

If there was salt water in the veins of William Barker Cushing, it probably came from his grandfather, Zattu, who was born near the sea in Plymouth, Massachusetts, in 1770, and worked as an apprentice to a master shipwright until 1789, when the post–Revolutionary War depression drove him and many other young New England lads to seek their fortunes in "the West." During a stopover in Albany, however, Zattu met and married a handsome young woman named Rachael Buckingham. After the birth of their first son, Milton, the Cushings decided to put down roots not in crowded Albany but in the newly incorporated frontier village of Fredonia, where greater opportunities existed for a man of Zattu's talents.

An upright and honorable man, Zattu Cushing was elected Chief Justice of Chatauqua County in 1811. He was an enthusiastic backer of the Erie Canal project, and when the canal opened for business in 1825, Zattu was majority stockholder in the first successful canal boat, the *Fredonia Enterprise.* He prospered greatly and enjoyed watching his five children grow up; he died peacefully in 1839.

His oldest child, Milton, had by then taken a medical degree, set up practice in Columbus, Ohio, and fathered four children with his first wife, who died in 1833. But Milton proved to be "too highly strung" for a physician—family rumors hinted of too much fondness for laudanum—and he would pass along this tendency toward excitability to several of his sons. Temporarily abandoning his medical practice, he went into the mercantile trade and achieved more success as a dry-goods salesman than he ever had as a physician.

Three years after his first wife's death, Milton married again, this time to a well-connected Bostonian named Mary Barker Smith, whom he met while she was visiting relatives in Columbus. Mary had, it was said, more cousins than anyone else in Ohio, and among them were members of the Madison, Hancock, Phillips, and Adams families. President John Adams was a remote cousin, as was Commodore Joseph Smith. The family tree was heavy with patriots, lawyers, politicians, and congressmen. Milton Cushing and Mary Barker Smith Cushing must have been potently attracted, for in rapid order they produced seven children, two of whom did not survive infancy. William Barker Cushing was the fifth son, born on November 11, 1842.

Milton's "nervous condition," whatever it might have been, suddenly vanished. Invigorated and confident, he resumed the practice of medicine, and this time he prospered. His prospects seemed so much improved that he decided, in 1844, to move to Chicago, where he settled on the lakeshore and established a thriving practice in the front rooms of a large and comfortable house.

And it was from that waterfront home, at the age of three, that Will Cushing made his first attempt to walk on water. No one had told him he could not, and he had become fascinated by the small boats that plied back and forth in front of his house. One afternoon when Mary was busy with the washing, he simply put on his father's black stovepipe hat—so large that he had to keep pushing it up from his eyes with both tiny fists—and waddled down to the nearest dock. Upon seeing a fishing boat pass by, Will ran toward it and leaped off the end of the pier, astonished, more than frightened, when he sank. A nearby fisherman dove in and rescued him. For Will, the worst part of his punishment was the fact that he was sternly forbidden ever to wear his father's hat again, until such time as his head grew to fit it.

One year later, after his father had purchased an unbroken colt and stabled him in the barn behind the house, Will Cushing made his second attempt to see the world. This time, he would venture forth on horseback. But when he sneaked into the stable, he discovered that the new horse had not been shod, and hence could not be expected to carry him very far. This was not a major problem for Will: he had watched enough blacksmiths to have a clear idea of how they did their work. From his father's workbench he fetched a hammer, a quartet of iron horseshoes, and a handful of nails. Then he boldly approached the colt, cooing to it with four-year-old assurance. The animal tolerated having its left rear hoof lifted, but balked at the first fumbling hammer-stroke. He reared, snorting with indignation, and kicked out with all the temper in his blood. Hearing the commotion, Mary rushed from the house and found the lad unconscious and missing four of his front teeth. He did not seem to mind the pain, but the loss of so many baby teeth caused him to wail: "Now Willie can't eat no 'tatoes 'n' turkey!"

Dr. Cushing caught pneumonia and died in the autumn of 1846. Mary and the children accompanied his body back to Fredonia. She found the place more appealing than she remembered, and Zattu's numerous descendants furnished moral support. She had enough resources to lease a modest house and establish a private school, a place where the rising middle class could send their children for a bit of polish. The children and stepchildren helped as best they could. Will and Alonzo, ages five and six respectively, became inseparable companions. But while Alonzo was sober and dutiful, Will was increasingly self-assured, believing himself to be a favored child of Providence and destined for great deeds. They complemented each other perfectly, and when one brother got into a school-yard fight, the other immediately pitched in to help. Together or separately, "Allie" and Will Cushing whipped every neighborhood bully who challenged them.

These fights were often started by taunts about the Cushings' genteel poverty. Even though her academy was well regarded, Mary Barker Cushing faced a constant struggle to keep her own children well fed and decently clothed. Her wardrobe, as the years went by, became more patched and worn. Will, who thought his mother to be still the radiant beauty she had been ten years ago, wanted more than anything to see her dressed accordingly. He tried to comfort her with dreams of a future in which he might come to her rescue. "Mother," he would sometimes say, "when I grow up and become famous, I will buy you a beautiful new dress, made of satin, or a velvet robe. Which shall it be?"

And Mary would reply, "I think satin is more suitable for me."

"Well then, satin it shall be!"

Not until the autumn of 1854 did Will Cushing have a glimmer of how it might be possible to realize his dreams. An uncle by marriage, Mr. Francis Smith Edwards, who was happily wed to one of Mary Cushing's sisters, ran for Congress on the Know-Nothing ticket. He was handily elected to represent the Thirty-fourth District of New York State, and in March 1855, just before he departed for Washington, he called on Mary and told her that he would do whatever he could to help Will and Allie better their prospects. After a private discussion, both adults summoned Will to the parlor. Impressed with the seriousness of the moment, the normally agitated boy stood quite still while Mr. Edwards extended an invitation for him to work as a congressional page. For Alonzo, who was almost old enough, he would attempt to procure an appointment to West Point.

"Your duties will not start until next summer, William. Between now and then, you must study very hard—especially your Latin, which your mother tells me is your weakest subject. These are exciting times in our nation's capital, and you will see the making of much history."

When Will Cushing, just turned fourteen, shook hands with Congressman Edwards, he felt an electric current run through his flesh. A new road had opened before him, and he was resolved to stride down it manfully.

All through his last year at Fredonia Academy, William followed the news from Washington. The Kansas-Nebraska Bill was hotly debated, the newly formed Republican Party seemed to go from strength to strength, and for the first time the ordinary citizens of Fredonia began asking one another: "Will it—could it possibly—come to war?"

In the fall of 1856, Washington was rough, hustling, unfinished, and malodorous. Scaffolding alone seemed to hold up the unfinished wings of the Senate and House, the White House stood in solitary splendor in front of a dust-and-mud desert named Pennsylvania Avenue, and most of the city's garbage, including the collected riches of its countless outhouses, rotted on the Potomac Flats, only ten blocks distant from the president's living quarters. As a capital, the city was no more formed and polished than the sprawling and divided nation it represented. But to a fourteen-year-old boy from the shores of Lake Erie, it was as magical as any gilded citadel of the Moguls.

Until he grew acclimated, Will Cushing stayed with his cousins, the Edwardses. When space became available for him in the official pages' residence, just before Christmas, he moved in there. His duties were not onerous—mostly he sat silently behind the Speaker's platform and waited for someone to give him an errand. He used his spare time to assiduously cultivate friendships with a multitude of cousins, and on those occasions, he presented himself as a sober and dedicated young man. One such cousin was Commodore Joseph Smith, chief of the Bureau of Navy Yards and Docks. Smith had gotten a taste of action during the Mexican War and he found young Cushing an attentive and passionate listener. When he orated about the manly glories of seafaring life, his colorful but mostly exaggerated yarns fell on receptive ears. The old officer and the teenager shared two heroes—Admiral Horatio Nelson and John Paul Jones—and Smith was surprised at how capably Will Cushing applied his mind to questions of tactics and strategy. After their friendship had ripened for several months, Smith procured for his nephew a midshipman's appointment to Annapolis, and Will Cushing took the oath on September 25, 1857.

From the first hour, he seemed easily to absorb all the routines and traditions of the academy. When, on his second day as a "middie," he was cornered after breakfast by an upperclassman, he responded promptly to the challenge.

"You! Midshipman! What is your name?"

"William Barker Cushing, sir!"

"Can you tell me, Mister Cushing, what is the proper order of a midshipman's loyalties?"

"Yes, sir! A messmate before a shipmate, a shipmate before a stranger, a stranger before a dog, and a dog before a soldier!"

There were reasons for this attitude. West Point had been in existence since 1802, and its graduates had brought glory to the institution by their remarkable performance in the war with Mexico. The Naval Academy, by contrast, had not been founded until forty years later and had always been treated by Congress as the poor stepchild of military institutions. When Cushing entered the ranks, it had graduated fewer than 250 officers, not one of whom had yet fired a broadside in anger. The buildings, inherited from a small army post called Fort Severn, were old and decrepit, with bowed walls, leaking ceilings, doors aslant, and windows that could neither be fully closed in winter nor fully opened in summer.

Always pinched for funds, the administration devoted most of its attention to finding halfway competent instructors who would work for tradesman's wages and had little time or resources to spare on maintaining order. Upperclassmen were expected to keep their underlings in check and under some modicum of discipline, but they, too, had no routine supervision and it was not unusual to find mixed groups of middies carousing in the streets of Annapolis at all hours, or firing impromptu salvos from the campus's two batteries of big guns. For a time after the academy opened, they also fired off the brass Napoleons—captured from the British in the War of 1812—that decorated the grounds of the Maryland State House, until the irate legislators had the guns spiked in 1850.

Demerits were of course given out for infractions and misdeeds, even as they were at West Point, but no midshipman could be kicked out unless he accumulated 200 of them during a single year. Cushing managed to garner 99 during his first nine months; the next year, he did considerably better, reaching a total of 188.

None of his offenses was dire, but he could not resist participating in any prank that came along. By midway through his second year, he was acknowledged as the prime instigator of several pranks that quickly passed into Annapolis lore.

His academic record was consequently very uneven. He applied himself diligently to such courses as gunnery, seamanship, and navigation, less so to ethics, algebra, and drawing. Each year, as his accumulated demerits rose toward the dreaded two hundred, he restrained his energies and became, for a few weeks at least, a model midshipman. And always, he *looked* the part, as though the uniform had been individually tailored for him alone: double-breasted navy-blue jacket with a rolling collar bearing a gold anchor on both wings, a fluffy cap with a silver anchor (flattened down on one side and rolled up jauntily on the other), a snow-white shirt with a black silk scarf for a tie, and slim-cut dark blue trousers. He was thin, although possessed of considerable wiry strength; he wore his hair to his shoulders, in a pageboy cut, and he had the sunken cheeks and sensual mouth of a poet. A proud aquiline nose dominated his smooth-shaven face and shadowed his haunted eyes, eyes of the deepest, brightest blue, which seemed lit from within by some smoldering spiritual fire.

Through it all, he chaffed to be at sea. In May 1860, a few weeks before he was scheduled to have his first extended cruise on the sloop *Plymouth*, he wrote to his brother Alonzo, who was by then finishing his last year at West Point: *"I want to see every nook and corner of this old world! I want to live on the sea and die on the sea, and when once I have set foot on a good ship as her commander, I never want to leave her till I leave her a corpse. A ship at sea is a complete system unto itself. The Captain is king, and as absolute a monarch as any who ever lived. The officers are his House of Lords, and the crew his subjects. If a seaman be ordered to do an act, it must be done. One looks with as much pride and affection upon one's ship as on one's wife. A man cannot, it seems to me, be happier than when he is bowling along at fourteen knots under a good breeze. I do believe and declare that I would rather be an officer on a man-of-war than President of the United States."*

He sailed in early June, bound for the Azores. At the first kiss of moderate waves, many of his classmates scurried white-faced for the railings and paid their time-honored tribute to Neptune. Cushing simply adjusted to the motions and felt at home with them; this was what he had expected, was it not? He strode briskly behind the wretched men hung over the rails, slapping their backs and cheerily admonishing: "Grin and bear it, lads! It's all in getting used to it, that's all!"

Although the weather was benign and the seas moderate for the first four days of their voyage, Cushing secretly prayed for a storm. He had never experienced anything more frightening than a rainsquall in Chesapeake Bay, but he had listened in awe as older men recounted the power and majesty of the storms they had survived. It seemed to him that no spectacle on Earth could possibly rival the sight of the sea in full bellowing cry. He often speculated on how he would respond to this challenge. Would he become paralyzed with fear? Would he learn suddenly and to his eternal chagrin that he was not, after all, cut out for a sailor's life? Or would the sheer thrill of peril energize his will and flesh as nothing else could, like some powerful intoxicant? He had never shrunk from any challenge before, whether it was a school-yard bully to be fought or an unbroken horse to be shod, but neither had he measured himself against anything so vast and implacable as the sea.

On the fifth day of the voyage, he got his wish. As was now his daily custom, he climbed the rigging after supper and roped himself to a yardarm to watch the sun go down, trying to gauge, from the state of the clouds and the colors, what the weather would be on the morrow. This exercise helped his stomach come to terms with the rancid boiled ham, pasteboard-flavored beans, and wormy biscuits that were the ship's staple fare.

The sky on this day was dominated by a great curling promontory of cloud to the southeast, salmon-pink and seemingly as substantial as curd. It rose in near-solitary grandeur above a sea stained orange by the sun's final crescent, dominating a sky so delicately blue as to seem translucent. If he stared hard enough, Cushing thought, he could see the stars beyond. A clean wind rinsed from him the grime and perspiration of the day's work, combing his long fine hair into a light brown coxcomb. At such a moment he forgot the dreadful food and the numbing tedium of soapstoning the decks beneath a brassy sun, and he was filled with a contentment that had no name, or rather had too many. His place was here, his purpose fixed, his destiny as bright as the rising diamond of Venus.

Then he felt a curious vibration, piquant and subtle, communicated to the keel of the ship, up through the timbers of her hull, drawn like some finespun thread through the piercing height of the masts and thence into his flesh. He listened hard, as though the sea were communicating something urgent, but to all appearances the steady rhythm of the swells did not change, nor did the wind freshen and grow fitful. But he saw, spreading starboard and port as far as he could discern, a subtle change in the horizon. From the base of that solitary pillar of sun-washed cloud spread a crenellated line as purple as a bruise. Something huge and dark was gathering below the horizon in front of the vessel. He could sense its force and the malevolence that was its nature. He was certain that if he rode the lines to the deck and consulted the barometer, he would have seen it starting to drop. The storm he had envisioned, half-longingly and half-fearfully, was lurking below the rim of his world, like a great beast gathering its strength. And like an elusive beast, it masked itself in thickening shadows, showing only a hint of its mass, and when night came down fully, it would rush forth and fall upon the ship in all its pent-up fury. Cushing felt no fear, only a tingling of heightened awareness. Let it come. He would embrace it, fight it, win through or be destroyed. As though in confirmation, a sudden cold nocturnal wind slapped at the *Plymouth*'s sails and made them crack like bullwhips. He peered down and saw the upturned faces of his startled mates. A low and solemn moan issued from the rigging, and Cushing felt as though his face were being cupped in two cold but strangely intimate hands, and into that wind he spoke: *"And they that go down to the sea in ships shall see the wonders of the Lord!"*

Wrapped in utter contentment, he climbed back down and went to his bunk. He would need his strength, and while a few hours of peace remained, he would sleep for a time and thus wake fresh to meet whatever the sea might deploy against him.

"All hands aloft to shorten sail!"

Cushing sprang to his feet, already fully dressed, and knew at once, from the sustained roar that enveloped the ship, that the storm whose vanguard he had detected at sunset had not only reached them, but had grown immeasurably in power. He ran past several sleep-stunned messmates, struggling into their gutta-percha foul-weather capes, and flung himself upstairs, his senses galvanic, his pulse racing.

When he emerged on deck, he entered chaos. Men were running about, yelling and cursing, but the sounds they made were inaudible in the fury that surrounded them, that raked their cheeks and hissed on their bared teeth and stabbed its tiny bladepoints of driven rain against their eyelids. Wind shrieked through every rope and cleat and stanchion, a high, blind, tooth-aching scream. Cushing pushed forward through a curtain of spray and focused on the sea. At first he could see nothing but tumultuous eruptions of spray. Then, when a rocket's tail of horizontal lightning exploded, he beheld mountain ranges of ebonite marching against one another, hard and sleek as muscle fibers. Foam boiled in demented whorls and geysers, as though vast whips were scourging the water. The sea undulated, erupted in black seething lava, then melted in upon itself, only to rise again in higher crests, a murderous phosphorescent broth, parabolas of streaked and gleaming jet. Now came a massive and ponderous swell that cut across his sight like a blade, and the ship shot forward to the edge of a trough and hung there on the storm's rhythm, like a lover verging on a climax whose intensity will carry some hint of extinction, then plunged down helplessly into a lightless canyon. Cushing turned his head forward and saw the bow as it dipped, and then all illumination died as the lightning faded and he had the sensation of being trapped on a mountain that was tipping over the edge of the world. The vessel seemed to slide down forever, its angle inching toward the perpendicular, its bowsprit pointing toward the bottom of the

Atlantic. Surely, Cushing thought, enraptured by the wonder of it all and—some calculating part of his brain was pleased to discover—not in the least afraid, surely the ship could not plunge deeper, nor angle more steeply, or they would never come out of this trough but would just keep going, arrow-straight, all the way to the cold black mud of the bottom. Then the ship bit darkness with her prow and the sea exploded as though smote with a great axe. Darts of foam cut the air like clammy shrapnel and the ship regained its fragile purchase.

An officer was yelling at Cushing now, his face pale as ivory under the lash of lightning, gesturing upward. Although Cushing could not hear anything the man said, his meaning was clear. There was still canvas to be furled aloft, sails whose weight was increasing with every gust of rain, whose surfaces opposed the wind and made the *Plymouth* increasingly sluggish. Cushing stuck a marlinespike and a knife in his belt and immediately began shinnying up the mainmast, into the gale's very jaws.

Those who watched him later swore that they saw a pale transfiguring light shining from within him, as though he were inhabited by the soul of Saint Elmo's Fire. Fearlessly, and at first single-handedly, Cushing wrestled with the rigging, hauling with the strength of ten men (or so it was claimed), waging some kind of berserk personal war against the tempest. His example shamed other men into action, and soon a half-dozen sodden sailors were aloft with him, following his orders, reefing and hauling, gradually gaining on the storm, shortening the sails. At one point, a vicious stroke of lightning lashed at the ship, so close that the air in its wake smelled raw and bloody, and one of the men nearest Cushing flailed out, stunned by the bolt. Knocked unconscious, the man dangled precariously in a web of rope and would surely have fallen to his death had Cushing not come to his aid. First, though, he finished tying off the last ragged flap of sail on the yardarm, coolly calculating that there was nothing more to be done to secure the mainmast; only then did he climb down, like a furious bedraggled spider, wrap the dangling man in one skinny arm, and somehow summon the strength to carry him to the comparative safety of the deck.

But during that last moment of hesitation, when he appeared to be methodically surveying the rigging to make sure his duties aloft were thoroughly done, Cushing had actually been frozen by one more sublime vision. From his high vantage, he was staring down at a vast mountain of moving darkness, the storm's climactic statement, which moved majestically upward like the shoulder of some great animal. A sustained burst of lightning vouchsafed to him a glimpse of the wave's anatomy, obscenely intimate: gleaming tendons and taut planes of muscle, arteries of foam, gaping mouths of darkness, cavities and organs and torrents of slick black blood. Then the wave moved on, sparing him, as though the sea had only wanted a closer look at him before rewarding his courage with a rare gesture of mercy, and the wallowing *Plymouth* steadied, more responsive now to the helm, turning into the wind, no longer in danger of broaching to.

In his report on the storm, the *Plymouth*'s captain cited Midshipman Cushing for leadership and bravery, adding: *"Although his record of deportment is not the best in his class, Mr. Cushing acted on this occasion as a man born to the sea. His example stirred a frightened crew and contributed materially to saving his ship."*

But as the autumn term of 1860 began, seamanship yielded to politics. If war came, Annapolis would become a strategic target for both sides, both by virtue of its commanding location and its inventory of ordnance. No one knew how Maryland would go; the state seethed with debate and in the streets of Baltimore, pro- and antisecessionists often came to blows. A new superintendent, a crusty disciplinarian named Blake, was appointed by Congress to bring a strongly pro-Union influence to the campus.

Half of Will Cushing's classmates were Southern, and he listened to their arguments studiously. The South had a case, he thought, and if the Union would not even acknowledge that much, it would be cowardly of the Southern states to remain a part of it. Nevertheless, his loyalties were steadfastly Northern. Emotions ran high during the autumn, and when Alabama left the Union, on January 11, 1861, one of Cushing's closest friends, an honors-man named Sampson, dutifully tendered his resignation—the first of many. On Sampson's last day, a Sunday, his entire class marched with him one last time, arm in arm, across the parade ground, singing a slow and quiet song. As they wheeled past the superintendent's house, Commodore Blake opened his front door and hailed them sternly.

"What is the meaning of this demonstration on the Sabbath?" he demanded.

"No demonstration, sir!" responded Cushing. "We are only bidding our classmate farewell."

Blake snarled, "A traitor deserves no farewell. You will all disperse and return to barracks immediately!"

From that moment on, the mood at Annapolis changed. Blake's words were perceived as a slap to the collective honor of the midshipmen, causing shame to the Northerners and rage in the hearts of the Southerners, whose numbers diminished by one or two every week as more states went out and attitudes hardened. Instead of becoming more disciplined, the remaining midshipmen became more openly rebellious. Will Cushing, who felt personally affronted by his confrontation with Blake, naturally became the ringleader. When Blake tightened security, deploying more and more armed sentries around the walls of the academy, Cushing devised more elaborate stratagems for outwitting them. The rash of insubordinate pranks, nocturnal cannon-firing, and whiskey-fueled barracks' parties usually found Northern men and Southern men joined together in an emotional, almost desperate attempt to cement their present comradeship, whatever the future might bring.

Blake responded by cracking down harder. He implemented a new regimen, emphasizing close-order drill and field artillery practice, and he made the insulting mistake, finally, of importing a West Point man to oversee this infantrylike training. This drillmaster, a colonel named Lockwood, was a pompous, red-faced martinet who made no effort to hide his professional contempt for the "sailors" under his command. No more egregious insult to the midshipmen could have been delivered. From Lockwood's first bombastic speech, a state of guerrilla war existed between himself and the midshipmen, especially those of the graduating class, who took umbrage at having to set aside their hard-earned nautical expertise in favor of basic infantry drills that went on for hours. One morning, Lockwood strode out of his room for breakfast only to trip a bucket of water carefully planted above his door. A few days later, when Lockwood was off campus on official business, his room was mysteriously filled with horse manure. Lockwood had been warned by Blake to be wary of Midshipman Cushing, and so blame for these outrages naturally focused on Cushing, justly or not.

So vexed did Lockwood become, by mid-March, that he began to stutter when bellowing commands. Naturally, this only inspired tittering in the ranks, not pity. Although the midshipmen knew exactly what Lockwood meant when he turned "Right face!" into "R-r-r-r-r-right face!," they did not respond until the angry man finally managed to spit out the final syllable, but continued to march affably on.

Matters reached a climax on March 22. Cushing's class was marching quick-time in the general direction of the Severn River and as they neared the steep embankment, Lockwood naturally called out "Halt!" Only on this occasion, he got stuck on the first consonant and all that emerged from his sputtering lips was: "H-h-h-h-h-h-h-h." As the marchers reached the end of the drill field, they turned to Cushing for guidance. With a quick nod of his head, he indicated that they should keep marching until poor Lockwood managed to reach that distant and elusive "t." Down the slope they went, all order lost now, and with implacably set faces they marched into the river. Lockwood jumped up and down in a fury, waving his sword, but still unable to shout anything but "H-h-h-h-huh!" With Cushing in the lead, the entire Class of '61 marched on, knee-deep, thigh-deep, hip-deep into the cold water. By the time Lockwood finally managed to scream, "Halt, God damn your eyes!" several of the shorter cadets were so far under that only their caps bobbed on the surface.

To no one's surprise, a summons arrived the following morning from the superintendent's office: Midshipman Cushing was to present himself, in dress uniform, at once.

His meeting with Superintendent Blake did not last long. He remained standing after salutes were exchanged, and Blake did not offer him a seat. Instead, he pulled open the ribbons fastening Cushing's official records and read from those documents in a funereal tone: " 'Midshipman William Barker Cushing, Class of Eighteen Sixty-One. Deficient in Spanish and French. Aptitude for study: good. Habits of study: irregular. General conduct: deplorable. Suitability for naval command: very low. Accumulated demerits as of March twenty-second: One hundred and ten. Accumulated demerits as of this date: two hundred, ninety having been applied as a consequence of gross insubordination bordering on outright mutiny.'

"Only two courses are open to you, sir: expulsion or resignation. If you sign this resignation, you are still eligible for naval service if you choose to reenlist after the passage of ninety days. If you compel me to expel you, you forfeit even that privilege."

Without a word, Cushing signed the document of resignation. Then he snapped a salute, turned briskly on his heel, and strode back to the barracks. There, his classmates greeted him with emotion and anger. Some of them wept as they watched him pack. Among the most demonstrative were several of his Southern comrades. Stoically, Cushing shook hands all around. Before taking his final walk across the parade ground, he admonished them all: "Do not let my fate become yours, gentlemen. This may not be the last time you must serve under petty tyrants, but you have only to put up with this batch for a few more weeks. When you have gained your commissions, remember how unfairly I have been sacrificed and be resolved to treat your own men with honor and fairness. I am sure I will see some of you again, on one side of the cannon or the other."

Will Cushing telegraphed his mother that he would be coming home unexpectedly, nothing more. Then, before taking a train to Philadelphia on the first leg of his journey, he went to the finest millinery in Annapolis and spent the last of his wages on the most beautiful silk dress in stock. When he got off the train in Fredonia and embraced Mary Cushing, he thrust into her hands the fancy box he had been carrying for two days, and said to her in a choked and halting voice: "Mother, I will buy you a satin dress or a velvet robe. Which shall it be?"

"I think satin will be most suitable for me," responded Mary, remembering.

"Then satin it shall be."

Not until Mary Cushing actually tried on the dress and saw that it was the most beautiful dress she had ever owned, did she weep for her son. But by the time she left her room to show it off to him, she was dry-eyed once again.

To Zebulon Baird Vance, nothing quickened a man's spirits more than the coming of spring to the Appalachian Mountains. There was a cool sweetness in the breezes, spiced by the keen minty smell of rhododendron, and the emerald-green fragrance of balsam, fir, and mountain laurel. The myriad creeks, swollen by the last melting snow, made a lively music as they tumbled through their beds of gleaming black stone. During his years at the state university in Chapel Hill, Vance had studied natural history, and even the names of the mountains' minerals were, to his sensibilities, agleam with Shakespearean music: beryl, corundum, and garnet—olivine, opal, and quartz—tourmaline, turquoise, and zircon.

He had paused, just east of the Asheville city limits, to contemplate a favorite view: an unbounded field of azaleas, riotous with color, and beyond them a vast blue-shadowed gorge flanked by serried peaks until the whole landscape vanished in a pearlescent mist. In the great gulf of sky, two hawks circled gracefully. Vance drank in the beauty of his homeland, sure and certain that his beloved mountains were one of God's happier inspirations as a landscape architect.

His reverie was short—he was due to make a speech in Asheville in one hour. Gently, he urged his horse into motion and guided it from the meadow, where it had been grazing with a contentment that matched its owner's, back to the twisting dirt track that led westward.

Vance would just as soon have foregone today's speechifying. He had seen and heard his fill of the increasingly bitter debate about the Union's future; indeed, he had participated until his voice was permanently hoarse. Day after day, ever since South Carolina and six other Southern states had seceded, the oratory had become more fractious, more belligerent, until it seemed to him that the entire House of Representatives was drowning in a tidal wave of rodomontade, but as one of the youngest congressmen in North Carolina's history, Vance took his responsibilities very seriously, and he had striven to articulate the hopes, fears, and often ambiguous aspirations of the mountain people who comprised his electorate.

He knew them well because he was one of them. Zebulon Baird Vance was descended from distinguished forebears on both sides of the Mason-Dixon line. His grandfather, David Vance, had come to western North Carolina in 1749, as part of the first great wave of Scotch-Irish immigrants. David could have settled, in relative comfort, in the town of Salisbury or Winston-Salem, where there was, even then, a modicum of civilized amenities, but instead he had paused in Salisbury only long enough to purchase powder and shot, salt, seed, and a few basic farm implements; then he pushed on to the west, leaving behind all certainties.

Zebulon Vance understood the motives of his ancestor. Over him the mountains had woven their spell, compelling him to follow the beckoning blue undulations on the horizon. It had been more than simple pioneer restlessness, of course, although that had been a part of it. Mountain land was cheap and plentiful, and the early settlers could claim as much of it as they liked, using their own sweat as legal tender. Hundreds of families came into the region in the latter half of the eighteenth century, looking for that elusive place of perfect beauty that might lie down the next cove, around the next bend, over the next ridge. Sooner or later, they would find it and take root. Mountain people did not live *at* a certain place, they were a *part* of that place, as much as the rocks and streams and meadows.

David Vance put down roots in Rowan County and married a local girl in 1755. Two decades later, when he was in his forties, he served with distinction in the Continental army, seeing action at

Brandywine, Germantown, and King's Mountain, and enduring the brutal winter at Valley Forge. At the end of his service, David Vance returned to his family and resettled on Reems Creek, twelve miles north of Asheville. There he constructed a two-story house of hewn yellow pine, and thirty-five years later, his grandson Zebulon was born in an upstairs bedroom.

Captain Vance, like his grandson, believed in public service. He served four terms in the North Carolina General Assembly and was a member of the commission that finally settled the boundary line between North Carolina and Tennessee. When Buncombe County was formed out of parts of Rutherford and Burke, he was appointed clerk of court for the new district, a post he filled honorably until his death in 1813.

As a boy, Zeb heard many stories about his grandfather and no one was surprised when he chose to follow a career in politics. The prerequisite for such a career was a law degree, so at twenty-one he enrolled at the University of North Carolina at Chapel Hill, and in 1852 he was admitted to the bar. The qualities that had made him popular at Chapel Hill—his charm, his good nature, his quick wit, and his facility with words—also made him a successful lawyer almost from the day he hung out his shingle in Asheville.

Zeb married in 1853 and one year later ran for the state's General Assembly on the Whig ticket. He served three years with middling distinction, and was defeated in the state senatorial campaign of 1856. He returned to private practice for the next two years. His second call to political service came in 1858, when the congressman from North Carolina's Eighth District, Thomas L. Clingman, resigned in order to become a U.S. senator. Vance promptly began campaigning to fill the remainder of Clingman's unexpired term; he won by a sizable majority and took his seat in Congress on December 7, 1858. His first year was fairly routine. He kept his eyes and ears open, learned the system, and applied himself diligently to committee work. After filling out Clingman's term, he stood for reelection and won handily.

Vance's second term in Congress was anything but routine. When he took his seat for the convening of the Thirty-sixth Congress, the nation was still reeling from the shock of John Brown's rebellion. Events plunged recklessly toward disunion, acquiring a sinister momentum of their own. By the time Vance braved the cold winds on the reviewing stand at Lincoln's inauguration on March 4, 1861, seven Southern states had seceded. North Carolina, however, was not one of them and Vance had considerable doubt that she ever would be. The spirit that had moved his grandfather to take up arms to rout the Tories at King's Mountain remained strong in the grandson's heart. The Union was no petty ephemeral construct, and Vance believed that the men who were urging the South to open conflict were unrealistic hot-heads. In this matter, his thinking reflected—at least for the present—the majority of his mountaineer constituency, most of whom had more in common with the farmers of New England than with the "slave-ocracy" of the Deep South.

Only one thing would change that, Vance thought as he caught sight of Asheville's modest skyline: armed invasion by the North. One week ago, Vance had been in Washington, where the general feeling was that such a provocation was a "last resort" whose time had not yet come. What worried Zeb Vance was the fact that many of his mountain friends also spoke of a "last resort"—what would happen if the two last resorts collided? Well, he would cross that bridge if he came to it, and in the meantime, he would continue passionately to debate the cause of the Union.

Vance reigned in his horse at a small rough-hewn bridge just outside of town. A rider approached, his horse flinging clods of red spring mud behind him.

"Hey, Zeb! Zeb Vance, you ol' rascal!"

Now Vance recognized his friend and neighbor Edward Swain, Asheville's only doctor and one of Buncombe County's staunchest Union men. Swain halted when the two horses were practically nose to nose. Both horse and rider looked somewhat blown—Swain's face was choleric beneath his bristly, unkempt beard, and his eyes were ablaze.

"Well met, Edward! I trust I'm not too late for the start of the debate?"

"Right on time, I'd say, as usual."

The two men fell in side by side and rode together into town. Having become used to the Romanesque scale of the nation's capitol, Vance was both amused and touched by the raw isolation of Asheville. It was still nothing more than a rustic frontier village, its few streets narrow and ungraded. It lacked sidewalks, sewers, railroad, telegraph, and public lighting. But today, its main street was clogged with people, wagons, and mules.

"Half of Buncombe County must be here," he said.

"Probably more. They all come out to hear the best stump speaker in the state. Hell, the best stump speaker that ever was! The meetin' hall's overflowing. Why, they's even folks hangin' from the windowsills."

Indeed, as Vance rode slowly through the crowd, he was greeted effusively. The mood of the crowd reminded him of a simmering kettle. He felt a subtle excitement in the air.

"They seem a mite anxious, Edward."

"Well, Zeb, I reckon most folks figure you will give 'em the truth about what's going on in Washington. The Unionists hope you will solidify their feelings, and the secessionists hope to persuade you to see things their way. It is a hot crowd, considerin' this is neither an election speech nor a good public hangin'."

Vance scanned the crowd—every other male, it seemed, was toting an earthenware jug. "It would seem that a fair amount of liquor has been drunk, even though it's mighty early in the day for that sort of thing."

"Well, by God, that reminds me!" Swain groped in his saddlebag and produced a cork-stoppered bottle of whiskey. He yanked the cork with his teeth and handed the bottle to Vance. Vance held the container up to the light and admired the clarity of its contents. A few swallows of prime local moonshine would cut the dust of his journey and lubricate his speechifying. He drank boldly, shuddered as the raw corn-liquor smote his belly, then handed the bottle back to his friend.

Swain had not exaggerated: the town's largest church, which doubled as the municipal meeting place, was packed, and the overflow crowd jammed the open windows. After hitching his horse, Vance followed Swain through the press. Blindly, he shook all the hands that were extended and winced at the force of the callused palms that whapped him on the back. When he and Swain finally made it into the room, he felt as though he had entered a gigantic beehive, so restive and numerous were the onlookers.

The crowd stirred mightily when Zeb Vance made his way to the podium. He was a big man, but most of his 230 pounds was carried in his shoulders and torso—as a youth, he had been well acquainted with the axe and the firewood wedge. He had a powerful-looking head centered on a muscular neck, a spacious forehead, strong dark brows, and a determined mouth framed by a modest and dapper moustache. He wore his hair long and brushed straight back, without a part, tucked fastidiously behind the arch of his rather prominent ears. His clear, frank, blue-eyed gaze flashed with an abundance of manly vitality. There was nothing ordinary about his demeanor or his speech, yet there was nothing high-flown or immodest either. His gestures were forceful and eloquent, as a great politician's ought to be, yet never did they seem studied, overrehearsed.

Many politicians felt exposed and uncomfortable "on the stump." Not Zeb Vance. The more grueling the campaign, the more contentious the face-to-face arguments, the more Vance seemed to thrive. He knew that compared to the sleek machinery behind big-city elections, the political process in rural America was rough and approximate, but by the Lord, it gave the voters a chance to measure the candidates in the flesh, to pepper them with needling questions, to gauge their ability to think on their feet and under pressure, to witness firsthand the quickness of their verbal parries, and to evaluate the depth and genuineness of their wit. The electorate thus had a fair chance to determine, at the very least, whether or not a man was a nincompoop.

Vance's opponent for this debate, a fierce secessionist named Alvan Dugger, had recently been elected county sheriff by the slimmest of margins. His supporters comprised the region's wealthiest land and slave owners, and according to persistent rumors, more than a few of his votes had been purchased with greenbacks or whiskey. Dugger was scheduled to speak first. When he rose, scowling, to offer Zeb Vance the obligatory handshake, he wafted a potent fragrance of alcohol, but then, so did Vance. As they sniffed each other like wary dogs, each man caught the other's scent and just a flicker of mutual respect passed through their grips—two mountain men who enjoyed their tipple without shame or pretense.

Dugger proved to be as bombastic as he was inflammatory. He railed against the usurpation of state's rights, although he was somewhat vague as to the particulars of the Constitution that obtained on the matter, denounced the greed and arrogance of Yankee businessmen, the moral turpitude of Lincoln and his coterie of "nigger-lovers," the usual litany of secessionist bluster and cant. The man is preaching to the choir, thought Vance, and his rhetoric was not likely to influence anyone who did not already hold to the same opinions. Only once did Dugger rouse the entire audience to noisy demonstration, and that was when he spoke of the dire consequences that would attend any military action by the North. On that matter, at least, nearly everyone seemed to feel mighty Southern. For that matter, Vance too joined in the applause at that point in Dugger's tirade.

When Dugger finally finished, the hall was seething with raw emotion. Vance rose into its buffeting currents and stood, tall and patient and severe, until quiet returned. If Dugger had fed the crowd raw meat, Vance was determined to serve them a cool drink of water.

"My friends, I have come to you—perhaps I should say 'I have come home'—directly from Washington, where I have heard many a Southern politician play the same medley of tunes that our friend Sheriff Dugger has here performed with so much passion. And as he sought to appeal to your passions, so I seek to address your faculties of reason.

"I have seen with my own eyes the actual and potential strength of the North, and I tell you that the greatest danger to the South lies not in what the Yankees are doing, but in what the secessionists are urging upon us! I tell you that *the only earthly chance* to preserve *both* the Union *and* the Southern way of life is to *gain time!* Whether the future holds war or peaceful compromise, the South is ill prepared in every respect save the inherent valor of her sons.

"But the whole Southern mind is inflamed to the highest pitch and the voices of disunion scorn every suggestion of compromise. Why are they acting with such ruinous and indecent haste? Are they absolute fools? No, my friends, they are instinctively very cunning. They are precipitating our people into a revolution without giving them time to *think!* The truth of the matter is this: *they are afraid lest the people shall think clearly!* Hence the hasty action of South Carolina, Georgia, and several other states in calling august conventions while leaving only a brief time for the election of delegates.

"But the people *must* think! And when they do begin to think and hear the matter properly discussed, they will, I am convinced, think long and soberly before they tear down this noble fabric of nationhood, and invite anarchy and confusion, carnage and civil strife, not to mention financial ruin. And they do this with the breathless hurry of men flying from a pestilence. If we gain time, however, we get the advantage of sober reflection and second thought, and no people on God's earth have this in a greater degree than ours. Merely by *waiting*, which is after all a very simple thing to do, we also gain the advantage of developments in Congress which I believe will prove favorable. Eminent and patriotic men of all parties are maturing plans of compromise, which will be offered soon, and I will not allow myself to believe that *all* of them will fail.

"But if they do, and we should be forced to go out at last, what difference, in the name of common sense, could a few months make? I have met Mister Lincoln, and took his measure as a sane and cautious man. To assume that his ascent to office is by itself a reason for fear is perfect humbuggery. If we go out now, we cannot take the army and navy with us, but will have to form our own, starting from scratch. Mister Lincoln, make no mistake, has the power to prevent our going out, or to force us back if we do go out. That is the fact of things!

"I tell you this great rashness which burns in the public mind *must* and *will* burn out, and cooler councils rule the day. But for this to happen, we must gain time—'Make haste slowly' should be our motto. We have everything to gain and nothing on earth to lose, by caution and delay. On the other hand, if we take too hasty action, we may be taking a fatal step, which we can never retrace—may lose a heritage, which we can never regain, though we seek it 'earnestly and with tears.' I tell you that we must . . . "

Vance stopped in midsentence. Beyond the walls of the meeting hall, a great tumult suddenly swept the street, a discordant sound comprising both anger and jubilation. Shots rang out as people discharged their firearms toward the sky. Vance felt a thrill of dread coursing through his nerves. He beheld a disheveled and sweat-streaked man elbowing his way through the crowd, waving a sealed document in his hand, and clearing a passage by crying out: "Make way! Urgent dispatch for Congressman Vance! Make way, I implore you!"

The man staggered to the podium, saluted, and handed his message to Vance.

Zeb unfolded the document and read it through twice, while a tense silence cloaked the room, heavy and restless, like the air before a violent thunderstorm. Once he had digested the import, he stepped back to the pulpit and raised his hands for silence.

"My friends . . . fellow citizens of North Carolina . . . this news is momentous and grave. Two days ago, in order to forestall its reinforcement, the secessionists of Charleston opened fire on Fort Sumter. In response, President Lincoln has issued a call for seventy-five thousand volunteers to put down, by force of arms, the rebellious states of the South. It is invasion! It is war, all but openly declared!"

Zebulon Vance would never forget that moment. The very air vibrated with consequence, as though this instant were ripped from the continuity of normal time and set aside as a separate reality. In the churning silence, Vance turned toward Sheriff Dugger, who had greeted the announcement with a feral smile of vindication. This debate, at least, was over. Vance stepped up to the trembling secessionist and embraced him, marveling at the sensation of fever that rose from the sheriff's skin. The two men held on to each other for a timeless interval. Then Vance returned to the podium.

"The course of the world has been altered, and all that I have told you is swept away. I must call upon every man here to volunteer, not to fight *against* South Carolina, but to fight *for* her! If war must come, as now seems certain, then I prefer to be with my own people. And if blood must be shed, let it be Northern blood! If we must slay, I had rather slay strangers than my own kindred and neighbors! Right or wrong, the Southern states must now go forward together and face the horrors of war as a body—sharing a common fate, and with the help of Almighty God, prevailing for the common good!"

Moved to chills by the import of the moment, Vance felt tears come to his eyes. He could say nothing more. With wavering vision, he saw Sheriff Dugger rise from his seat, throw his hands into the air, and shout: "Hurrah! Hurrah for Jefferson Davis and the Southern Confederacy!" Then Dugger pulled out a flask and emptied it, his face turning beet-red as the whiskey beat its fiery drum. Shouting incoherently, Dugger leaped off the podium and plowed his way through the crowd and out into the warm spring day. Fully half the audience, infected with the same fever, surged after him.

As the hall slowly emptied of the remaining, and presumably pro-Union, spectators, Vance, his massive shoulders sagging under a new weight, sat down next to his old friend Dr. Swain.

"Well, Zeb," muttered Swain, taking a swig from his own bottle, "I have never before seen you bested in a debate."

Vance said nothing; he slouched forward, his big-boned hands knotted and his brow deeply scored. Swain handed him the almost-empty bottle and Vance drained the last of its contents.

"We have been trampled by History itself," he said.

"Not as severely as we will be trampled by the mob outside," said Swain. "Just listen to them howl!"

Vance cocked his head toward the open window. He heard cheers, oaths, and the occasional pistol shot.

"Perhaps our presence out there would help restore order," said Vance, standing and sucking in a great draft of air.

"Just as likely, our presence will bring forth tar and feathers," growled Swain. "Half of Buncombe County is for the Union. The first battle of the war could erupt right here. Nevertheless, you are right: we must do what we can to cool things down."

But when they stepped outside, they found pandemonium. Nearly every man they saw, be he a wealthy farmer from the prime bottomlands or a hardscrabble hillbilly from the remotest cove, brandished a weapon, and many were clearly drunk. Sheriff Dugger, already working on a new jug of liquor, waved his revolver and kept shouting, "Huzzah for Jeff Davis! All true Southern men should volunteer to fight!"

A wild-eyed knot of men had gathered around the sheriff, cheering lustily along with him. As Vance and Swain watched from the steps of the church, an invisible boundary seemed to form between those who echoed Dugger's bellicose ravings and those who were either pro-Union or simply shocked into silence by the gravity of events. But as Dugger and his fired-up rebel recruits began to taunt the Unionists, the Unionists began to taunt them back with shouts of, "Hurrah for Washington and Honest Abe Lincoln!"

After a few moments of mutual antagonism, the two halves of the crowd faced each other like contending armies, their faces contorted with passion and rage. To Vance, Sheriff Dugger looked unmistakably like a man who was determined, before the day was out, to shoot somebody.

"Come, Edward, let's do whatever we can to keep these fools from tearing into each other." Vance moved to station himself in front of the rebel faction, while Swain, who had long ago declared his neutrality as a physician, moved to calm the Unionists. Neither man, however, had time to do more than clear his throat before the situation exploded.

From the "Union" side of the street, a trio of burly, dirt-stained farmers stepped forward provocatively. "This is a rich man's war," cried the man in front, fiercely clutching a well-honed sickle in his hand, "and I say let the rich men do the fighting!"

Sheriff Dugger, who had been elected by the wealthier citizens and who considered himself to be far superior in station to these rural clodhoppers, placed his whiskey jug upon the ground and with cold deliberation aimed his pistol at the tall farmer. Acting on well-meant impulse, Dr. Swain threw himself between the sheriff and his target just as the big cap-and-ball weapon fired. The ball ripped through the meat of Swain's left arm, flinging a geyser of blood into the air. White-faced, Swain clutched at his wound and slowly sank to his knees.

From the Unionists, there arose a wild scream of anger. One shot had turned them into a bloodthirsty mob. Vance moved quickly to

Swain's side and used the doctor's own belt to form a tourniquet. Sheriff Dugger, meanwhile, seemed suddenly to understand that he was confronted by many more presumed enemies than his pistol had shots. Before anyone could follow him, he bolted into the sheriff's office and slammed the door behind him. An instant later, Vance heard the sound of breaking glass and beheld Dugger's demented face looming behind the hammers of a double-barreled shotgun.

"Any of you damned Black Republicans want to take a shot at me, by God I will oblige you!" he shouted. Evidently, there were many in the street who were happy to accept that challenge—as he bent protectively over his friend, Vance heard a dozen hammers cock. The fusillade peppered the windowsill and shattered the remaining glass. Dugger yelped, struck either by a ball or by flying shards. His face a mask of blood, the sheriff fired both barrels in the general direction of the crowd. But everyone who still retained a lick of sense had fanned out on either side of Dugger's arc of fire, and the blast succeeded only in peppering the sign above the barbershop across the way.

Before the pain-maddened Dugger could reload, the tall farmer and his companions swarmed forward, their teeth bared. Using a heavy pine bench as a battering ram, they quickly demolished the door and vanished inside the sheriff's office. The now-silent crowd heard shouts of rage, a single pistol shot, and a drawn-out scream. A moment later, the savagely lacerated body of Sheriff Dugger came flying through the window and collapsed in the dusty street like a torn-open sack of feed.

Vance remembered little of the riot that followed. Rebels and Unionists waded into each other with fists and clubs and farming tools. Women gathered their children and tried to flee. "Look at them, the goddamned fools!" said Swain through gritted teeth.

"Can you stand, Edward?"

"It's my arm that's busted, Zeb, not my legs."

Suddenly, Swain began to laugh.

"What is so damned funny?"

"Just the fact that I'm the only doctor in town! Who's going to dress my arm?"

"I will," said Vance grimly. "We'll go to your office and you can talk me through the steps."

"Bring some more whiskey, then. Of all our times together, my friend, this day is the most memorable!"

Two days later, when Swain's wound had begun to heal and Zeb

Vance was packing for his return to Raleigh, Vance learned an interesting thing: the farmer whom Dugger had shot at had fled to Kentucky with the intention of enlisting in the Federal army, and had taken two strapping sons with him. *Our loss, their gain.*

A few hours later, Zebulon Vance learned an even more interesting thing: he had been elected captain of the regional militia company, the Buncombe Rough and Readies. His return to Raleigh, then, would not be solitary, but at the head of more than one hundred men. He was honored, of course, but apprehensive; rough, they certainly were—but they were a long way from ready.

Rebel Jews

AMPUTATING INSTRUMENTS—Any medical gentleman having a case of amputating instruments to dispose of, should promptly communicate with Dr. J. A. Miller, Surgeon, Eight Regiment of N.C. Volunteers, now training at Camp Wyatt near Wilmington.

—The Wilmington Journal, August 30 1861

For Sergeant Frederick Reilly, the morning of April 16, 1861, began just like every other morning of his tenure as fort keeper. At half past eight, the sun's rays slanted through the window above his cot, stroked his face, and woke him. While coffee came to a boil, Sergeant Reilly donned his uniform and indulged in some luxurious stretching. He was in no hurry. Aside from making a routine log entry, there was nothing much for him to do; there never was.

Another man might have been driven mad by the solitude and quiet, but Reilly rather liked it. He had plenty of time to read, to comb the beaches for interesting shells to add to the collection he had started during the long bleak days of winter, to write letters to his parents and siblings in Maryland.

The post of fort keeper was a fairly recent bureaucratic innovation, dating back to the years following the Mexican War. Because the United States's standing army was so small, and the cost of maintaining even a skeleton garrison so high, almost every coastal fort except those protecting New York, Baltimore, and Washington was presided over, in peacetime, by a single noncommissioned officer. Ostensibly, the fort keeper's job was to secure his post against vandalism and to maintain a symbolic presence of Federal authority. Fort

Caswell was so isolated, however, that Reilly's most demanding task had been the collection of small user fees from surf-fishers who came out by boat from Smithville and Wilmington.

Regulations required the sergeant to undertake one daily inspection of the fort, a single perambulation around the walls, during which he was supposed to note any deficiencies in the fort's ordnance or construction. A summary of such matters formed the basis of his monthly reports, taken back to civilization—and apparently into limbo—on the same packet boat that brought him supplies, mail, and news of the outside world.

Reilly's world was not small. As he paced the stone parapets after breakfast, he visited in turn each of his favorite vantage points and savored the view. Fort Caswell stood on the easternmost arm of Oak Island, hard against the Old Inlet to the mighty Cape Fear River. A mile to the east, across a narrow channel of deep water, lay the sprawling marshy triangle of Bald Head Island, tapering southeast to Cape Fear itself, where the treacherous Frying Pan Shoals, a maelstrom of powerful conflicting currents, shrouded the hulks of a hundred sunken ships—the name "Cape Fear" had not been chosen lightly. Old Inlet was one of only two navigable channels opening from the sea into the Cape Fear River and thence to the docks of Wilmington. Its course was easily traced by the calm green color of its waters, in marked contrast to the sandy turbulence of the surf on either side. A mile or so to the northwest, Reilly could see smoke rising from the chimneys of tiny Smithville. Through his spyglass, he saw a small flotilla of boats stirring at the village docks.

One of these mornings, he knew, just such a modest armada would herald a rebel operation against the fort. In theory, in time of national crisis, all forts under the care of solitary sergeants were supposed to be reinforced by full garrisons and brought to a state of readiness. Reilly smiled to himself—he had been in the army since 1856, there *had* been a national crisis for about three of those five years, and he had yet to receive a single reinforcement. Not that it would have made much difference. In the twenty-five years since it was built, Fort Caswell had slid into decrepitude. There were cracks in its masonry walls; windblown sand and tidal surges from storms had filled up most of the protective moat, and the barracks had been taken over by spiders and mildew. Although it was ideally sited to cork up the Old Inlet, the fort mounted only two cannons: 24-pounder smoothbores whose wooden carriages were so rotted from exposure that they would probably disintegrate with the first shot.

After making his required circuit of the walls, he once more lifted his glass toward Smithville and saw that the flotilla he had spotted earlier was now halfway across the distance between the fort and the village. He counted seven small steam launches, each carrying about a dozen men, all clad in a motley of uniforms. Sunlight winked on bayonets and from the sword blade held aloft by a man standing in the bow of the foremost boat. Reilly recognized John Cantwell, commander of the local militia regiment, a likeable fellow with whom he had discussed, on several occasions, the fine points of surf-casting.

Ah, thought Reilly, lowering his spyglass, so today is the day. *As well this morning as any other.* He had time, he figured, to change into his dress uniform and buckle on his salt-pitted sword before the boats arrived. If the thing had to be done, it was best to do it decorously.

Cantwell's boat crunched into the sand just as Reilly emerged in his somewhat bedraggled uniform. Spying him, Cantwell saluted.

"Good morning, Frederick. I presume you know why we are here."

Reilly returned the salute. "I assume, John, that it is not for a day of fishing."

Cantwell tried to suppress a grin. He sucked himself into a ramrod-straight posture and announced, as though reading the words from an unseen script, that he was here, along with members of the Wilmington Light Infantry, the Cape Fear Light Artillery, the German Volunteers, and the Wilmington Rifle Guards, to seize Fort Caswell for the Confederacy.

"Has North Carolina gone out, then?" asked Reilly.

"Not officially, but it is only a matter of time. Say, Frederick, you don't have any reinforcements lurking about, do you? A surprise ambush while my men are disembarking?"

"No, John, I am alone and quite outnumbered."

"Quite. Well, I suppose this is the moment when you offer me your sword."

Sergeant Reilly stepped forward, drew his blade, and handed it pommel-first to the militia commander. Then, with considerable jingling, he also handed over a large iron key-ring.

"My sword, sir, and the keys to the fort. I'll need a proper receipt, of course."

Cantwell saluted and handed the sword back while stuffing the keys into his belt. "Do you wish to make a formal statement of parole, Sergeant? I've already arranged a train ticket for you back to

Maryland, and the rail lines are still open to the North. You can take the receipt with you."

Reilly thrust his sword back into its scabbard.

"As a matter of fact, John, I would prefer to throw in with you gentlemen, for I am a friend of the Southern cause, as are the members of my family back home. I'll send the receipt in the mail along with my letter of resignation. Have you any need for another artilleryman?"

Cantwell clapped him on the shoulder and said, "We will likely need every gunner we can lay hands on, Frederick. Can you show us around the fort, then?"

Reilly smiled ruefully. "I will, but you won't like what you see. I hope you brought a lot of shovels."

Largo Landau carefully tied the final ribbon in her hair and fluffed her ringlets until they bounced. Two months past her nineteenth birthday, she was acutely conscious of her appearance and still learning the arcane procedures required to enhance it. She wondered, as she scrutinized her lightly powdered cheeks in the mirror, what young women had done in the days before gaslight; even a flock of candles would not have been sufficient to view oneself with clarity. On the other hand, candlelight must have made it easier to hide small imperfections. Like that small mole on her right cheek. When her mother, Rachel, was still alive, she had insisted that it was a beauty mark and not a flaw, but in the five years since Rachel's passing, Largo had become uncertain. Should she dab it with powder or wear it proudly? After viewing herself from as many angles as she could manage, with the gas both high and low, she finally concluded that the mole helped draw attention to her eyes, which everyone agreed were her best feature. From her mother's Sephardic ancestors, she had inherited a smooth dusky complexion, shining hair the color of india ink, a full "gypsy" mouth, and eyes as black and flashing as lacquered ebonite, with pupils whose depth had captured and drowned, like fierce tiny whirlpools, the flirting, reconnoitering gazes of the young men who had begun to appraise her with speculative interest when she was only fifteen. The sons of Wilmington's elite now made her welcome at their dances and soirees even if their parents still harbored some touch of diffidence about her Israelite heritage.

Downstairs, Jacob Landau called to her. "Are you ready, my dear? We do not want to be late for this dinner!"

No, indeed not. Largo knew how important this event was to her father. Jacob had always let Rachel carry the religious burden for the family when she was alive. They had immigrated from Munich in 1840, fed up with residence quotas and political oppression, lured by utopian accounts of the New World's economic opportunities and relative liberalism. Once settled in Wilmington, Jacob had opened the Cape Fear Dry Goods and Fashion Emporium, on the corner of Front and Dock Streets, proximate to both the waterfront and the bustling city market. An earnestly sociable, if not exactly gregarious, young man, with a true Bavarian's love of food, drink, and conversation, Jacob had quickly taken the measure of his new community and befriended many of the shipowners whose vessels were the fulcrum of Wilmington's prosperity. In order to do that, he had blended in, rapidly assuming Southern attitudes and habits of speech, working with an elocution teacher to perfect his English and soften the hard edges of his German accent. This campaign of assimilation paid off handsomely: Jacob's store often got the first and best pick of luxury items brought in from Europe, the Caribbean, and England. "The finest selection at the fairest price" was his motto, and the city's well-to-do citizens rewarded him with steady patronage, even if some of them did refer to his establishment, among themselves, as the Jew Store.

While Jacob focused on building his market, Rachel, by default as much as inclination, assumed the task of keeping alive their religious identity. In their home, the Sabbath was kept and the High Holy Days duly celebrated. Over the years, as the Jewish population of Wilmington grew to a hundred or so, Rachel's house became the informal center of spiritual gravity for that community. The closest synagogue was in Charleston, and its rabbi always seemed too busy to visit Wilmington, although he did send cheery letters from time to time. At the time she became ill, Rachel had been dreaming about founding a synagogue and had been in correspondence with communities in Richmond, Baltimore, and New York, gathering information and exchanging views, even though—as a woman—there was nothing concrete she could do. Jacob appreciated her idealism, but did not share it. If there were serious undercurrents of prejudice in Wilmington, he reasoned, nothing would bring them faster to the surface than the public dedication of a Jewish house of worship.

The malaria, when it struck, ravaged Rachel quickly. Jacob summoned Wilmington's most renowned physician, Dr. Baccus Satchwell—whose wife and daughters were frequent customers of his store. Satchwell had wrestled with the disease, administering decoctions of Peruvian cinchona bark and increasingly potent emetics, but these treatments did not arrest Rachel's decline. There were two kinds of malaria, Satchwell explained, the periodic, which caused great suffering for four or five days then gradually faded, and the continued fever, which caused irreparable "degeneration of the spleen." Jacob was quite distraught by this time; it took him a while to realize that the doctor was telling him discreetly that his wife was dying.

The imminent death of his spouse rekindled in Jacob's breast all the love he had once felt for Rachel, which he had sometimes been too busy to demonstrate properly in recent years. He stayed by her bed around the clock, wiping her molten face with cool compresses and, in the final stages, administering the recommended dose of laudanum to ease her suffering. In a searing moment of clarity, just before she lapsed into penultimate unconsciousness, Rachel opened her eyes, clasped her husband's hands fiercely, and charged him to fulfill her dream of creating a synagogue in Wilmington. Of course Jacob swore that he would, and as soon as the words left his lips, he was filled with a surge of righteousness—as though her spirit were passing from her flesh to his. Satisfied, she smiled lovingly and went to sleep, dying peacefully two hours later.

Since Rachel's death, Jacob Landau was a changed man. A prophetic fire burned in him. From New York he obtained a Torah scroll (although his knowledge of written Hebrew was rudimentary), a fine silver-plated menorah, and a large shofar, which he sometimes sounded, just to remind himself, and presumably several of his neighbors, what a ram's horn sounded like. He began correspondence with representatives of older, more established Jewish communities, seeking advice and support. The war had interrupted most of that, but in the interregnum he became much more active in Wilmington's minuscule Jewish population. He attended, and often hosted, informal minyanim—in the absence of a proper synagogue, any place where ten or more adult male Jews congregated to worship was considered a de facto Jewish house of worship; and in the absence of an ordained rabbi, a layman could preside over such congregations as a hazzan, a kind of rabbinical deputy. The God of Israel, he learned, was not dogmatic but very practical, even as His people had learned to be during their centuries of wandering. A proper synagogue was certainly to God's liking, but until such a building existed, He was content to visit any dwelling, however humble, where His people gathered to worship Him.

Largo watched her father's transformation with sadness and wonder. Instead of trying to erase the cultural boundaries between him and the Gentile community, Jacob now embraced them. A few of Wilmington's more devout Jews had gravitated to their new hazzan, while a recently arrived Polish immigrant was now instructing Jacob in Hebrew. Funds collected for the synagogue were held in escrow in the Bank of the Cape Fear. The amount so far was modest, but Jacob was convinced that the nascent civil war would generate business on an unprecedented scale. If the Jews of Wilmington could convince the Confederate authorities of their loyalty and worth, the synagogue fund would grow accordingly.

That was what made tonight's dinner so important to Jacob. The occasion was a visit by the new Confederate attorney general, Judah P. Benjamin, a Louisiana Jew who had served with distinction in the U.S. Senate until his state went out. It was said that Jefferson Davis thought highly of Benjamin and sought his advice on many matters. If Jacob could only gain Benjamin's ear and ignite his interest in the synagogue project, unpredictable benefits would surely flow from that connection with Richmond.

"Please, daughter! We shall be late!"

"Only a minute longer, Father. You don't want me to look like a witch, do you?"

From the foot of the stairs, Jacob laughed. "You would still look like an angel, even if you tried to be a witch."

Largo had chosen satin and lavender, texture and color that complimented her hair and eyes. She wore fewer petticoats than was fashionable, which called discreet attention to her slender waist, and perhaps—if the viewer were so inclined—hinted at the shapeliness of her legs. Her bosom was modest, about average she guessed, and she could do nothing to accentuate it without causing eyebrows to rise. But the slopes of her shoulders were fashionably bare and the magnolia corsage on her left breast she considered to be a subtle advertisement for what she did have. As a final touch—suggested by her father—she carried a fan decorated with an engraving of Jefferson Davis. Such accessories were "all the rage" among Wilmington's belles and Jacob, with his usual perspicacity, had been the first merchant to stock them.

Jacob took her arm at the foot of the stairs. He was formally and conservatively dressed in black and carried an elegant top hat and a walking cane topped with mother-of-pearl, gentle indications of wealth and dignity. The butler, a salaried free man named Wellington, opened the door for them and they strode proudly into the amethyst twilight painting the river.

The Landaus' house was on Walnut Street, between Third and Fourth. As they walked outside, Largo observed that the nearby Cotton Exchange, despite the late hour, was still open and crowded, as planters, shippers, and speculators bargained and schemed under the urgent spur of impending war. Largo was struck by the contrast between the soft languorous twilight, so typically Wilmingtonian in its suggestion of slow days and gracious ways, and the hard-edged tumult of commerce. She supposed that this dichotomy would only grow as the summer drew near. She liked the whiff of excitement in the air, the nebulous promise of great events yet unknown. As much as she loved her father, she longed to be something more than the daughter of a prominent merchant, to gravitate toward the far horizons of experience. Tonight's dinner party, she thought, might well constitute the overture to an opera about to unfold. She actually knew a bit about opera. When she was but ten, Rachel and Jacob had taken her to the Thalian Hall to hear the legendary soprano Jenny Lind, the "Swedish Nightingale." Miss Lind's performance was so rapturously received that after her triumph every opera troupe touring the East added Wilmington to its itinerary. "I have known larger cities in Europe with less kultur than here," Jacob used to avow. Until Largo turned sixteen, she was not allowed to attend performances of Shakespeare, whose works, though heavily censored for American consumption, were still considered too bawdy and profane for youthful ears. But she had supplemented her formal education with a feast of recitals, monologues, operettas, farces, and the exotic entertainments offered by P. T. Barnum and his imitators. From Tippo Sahib the Hindoo Contortionist to Professor Barrow's Sable Serenaders and Minstrel Review, she tried to see everything that came through town. To Largo, who had never traveled farther than Charleston in one direction and Raleigh in the other, it seemed as though the whole world passed through Wilmington.

As they walked south on Front Street, a wide macadamized thoroughfare well lit by gas lamps, they passed the post office on their left, and tarried there to exchange pleasantries with some acquaintances. One block farther south, on the river side, they passed the hulking platform and trading booths of the slave market, not much used in recent years, not since the African trade had been suppressed and most slave trading was done between cities, families, and estates within the Deep South. Nevertheless, it was still a popular public meeting place. Only a few months after Largo's parents arrived from Germany, there had been a brutal slave uprising on the plantations in Dare and Brunswick Counties. Militia companies from Wilmington had joined with vigilante bands to track down the fugitives, and fourteen men and boys had been summarily hanged from the selling platforms of the slave market. Their bodies had been left dangling, as a warning to all Negroes, but after two days the resulting clouds of seagulls became too noxious, in both their feeding and their by-products, for the citizens to tolerate. So the half-eaten corpses were cut down and tossed into the river. Alligators attracted from the upriver marshes—rarely seen this close to the city—turned the water into a loathsome froth as they feasted.

Just after her eighteenth birthday, Largo sneaked away to witness a big auction. From her reading and general knowledge, she expected to see a cruel, almost Roman, spectacle, with clanking chains and cracking whips, wailing women and growling bucks. Instead, the entire proceeding had been orderly and businesslike, even during the most spirited bidding. Each Negro was clothed to the extent of abbreviated modesty, and displayed like prime livestock, his or her physical attributes and docile attitudes extolled fulsomely. She saw no whips, nor any marks upon their dark mysterious flesh, although when she looked more closely, she did see pistols in the belts of some traders and overseers. Conversation among the bidders was brisk and knowledgeable, and they all seemed to have sharp eyes for a bargain. The prices asked and bid—often $1,000 or more—surprised her. There were, she supposed, brutal and inhumane slave-owners, but it did not seem logical to her that planters would willingly damage an asset in which they had invested such sums. She left the auction more puzzled than offended.

On the next Sabbath observance, Largo asked her father if there was not a disturbing resemblance between the South's Negroes and the Hebrews in Egypt. Jacob's response had been ambiguous, and not altogether comfortable. The similarities, he averred, were superficial. On a well-run plantation, the blacks lived better than they had in the jungles whence they came. The more enlightened citizens of Wilmington understood that slavery as an institution must inevitably evolve beyond mere bondage—were there not hundreds of free Negroes in the city, working as shipwrights, carpenters, stevedores, groomsmen, and the like? Even the Southerners who were most uncomfortable with slavery understood that it could not be abolished suddenly without causing economic ruin to people of all colors.

"But as Jews, Father, are we not obligated to oppose human bondage, even if it is benign?"

"As Jews," Jacob sternly replied, "we have been persecuted and restricted all over Europe. Here in the South, we have been made welcome. We do not have Palestine, only a fantasy based on ancient history, but we have made the South our country instead. In time, we will do our part to transform this society, but we cannot do that by making trouble and calling attention to ourselves. In this house, at least, we employ only free Negroes. We pay them a fair wage and they work willingly and hard. We are therefore setting an example as to how things *might* be, if the North only gives us time to make the slow transition. Besides, daughter, the African and the West Indian are still half-pagan. If the Negroes worshiped the God of Israel, perhaps He would intervene on their behalf as he did for the Hebrews in Egypt."

Largo had been puzzling over that discussion ever since. But when the deserted slave market—now acquiring a sinister aspect as darkness flowed up from the river and drowned it in shadow—passed beyond their view, she returned to the moment. If there was to be war, the matter would be resolved, one way or another. And if God were willing to give the South more time than Abe Lincoln was, then surely He would also bless the arms of the Confederacy.

They turned left on Market Street and walked toward the landmark steeple of St. James Episcopal Church. There was still considerable traffic: men on horseback, couples in carriages, servants on errands, peddlers vending their wares. On this street, at this hour, Wilmington seemed like any other cosmopolitan place in America, and prettier than most. Ten thousand people lived here, but few of them were hungry and fewer still were criminals. Largo was glad her parents had settled here, rather than in New York, with its slums and gangs, its white slavers and perpetually drunken Irishmen.

Their destination was the elegant Burgwyn-White house on the southwest corner of Third and Market. Even by American standards, it was an "historic" residence, a two-story Georgian mansion graced with wide verandas and framed by a six-tiered formal garden, built in 1770. In 1781, Lord Cornwallis had stayed there as a welcome guest while his troops recuperated from the bloody nose they had received at the Battle of Guilford Courthouse. One of his lieutenants, a dashing young warrior who rode with Tarleton's dreaded cavalry, had fallen in love with one of John Burgwyn's daughters, and she with him; their conjoined initials were still visible, carved into the frame of a parlor window. Now owned by the prosperous Wright family, second-generation descendants of another of old Burgwyn's daughters, the house was a center of Wilmington's social life.

Inside were Wilmington's elite. Gaslights vied with crystal chandeliers to create a brightness not much less than daylight. In the ballroom, a string quartet played waltzes and quadrilles. Many of the men strutted about in new military uniforms, each apparently designed according to the owner's whim—Largo beheld so many epaulets, stars, and scabbards that she wondered how anyone could tell a man's rank without asking. Every officer in the region, it seemed, had turned out for this event. That was only logical, for the occasion of Judah Benjamin's visit was to solemnize the appointment of Major Chase Whiting as inspector general of coastal defenses. Given the fact that North Carolina had not yet gone out of the Union, Whiting's appointment under such a title seemed, to Largo, both premature and somewhat provocative, but no one else seemed bothered by the anomaly. Everyone here seemed to assume that the Old North State would soon be Confederate and therefore would soon be at war.

Jacob handed his daughter a cup of punch, lifted from a silver tray carried by a passing Negro in formal attire. For himself, he fetched a glass of sherry. Gesturing across the ballroom, he said, "There is our stalwart defender, I believe." She turned to look.

Major Chase Whiting was a man of graying visage, though he was but thirty-seven, dapper though somber of mien; his features—dominated by dark brooding eyes—reminded Largo of the writer Edgar Allan Poe, whose fanciful stories were popular among Wilmington's young intelligentsia and whose portrait she had seen in *Blackwood's Magazine*. Whiting's family hailed from Massachusetts, but Chase had been born in Biloxi; after graduating first in the West Point class of 1841, he had spent most of his career as a coast-defense engineer at various Southern posts. One of his assignments took him to Wilmington, where he courted and married a prominent local beauty named Katherine Davis Walker. Although Whiting disapproved of slavery, he found Southern life, with its leisurely pace and decorous manners, far more congenial than the raw-edged commercialism of Yankee cities. The proud but anachronistic romanticism of the planter-aristocrats sustained a culture far superior, to his tastes, to the rowdy immigrant-plagued societies of New York and Baltimore. In

February, he had resigned his Federal commission and offered his services to the Confederacy. When he was promoted to major and assigned to the Cape Fear district, Wilmington rejoiced. Despite his Yankee roots, Chase Whiting loved the South. "His blood is all meridian," claimed his friends.

Upon noticing Jacob's arrival, several guests gravitated in his direction. Largo recognized James Fulton, editor of the *Wilmington Daily Journal;* William Beery, owner of the shipyard on Eagle Island; and the irascible Dr. Baccus Satchwell. After Fulton shook hands with Jacob and gallantly bowed to Largo, he smiled conspiratorially and said, "Are we still awaiting the arrival of the occult Jew?"

"I thought that was *my* distinction," replied Jacob, affecting a tone of banter.

Fulton chortled—clearly the journalist had consumed more than a token glass of champagne—and clapped Jacob on the shoulder.

"No, my friend, you are the Reasonable Jew! Which is a good thing, too, as most of the people in this room have credit at your establishment and I'll wager that some of them are dilatory in settling their accounts. Dr. Satchwell's fashionable wife, for instance."

"Mrs. Satchwell is an esteemed patron and a lady of high taste," Jacob responded. "I may even extend her line of credit, seeing as how the good doctor's fortune will surely increase as soon as a battle or two is fought."

Satchwell made a gesture of ironic self-deprecation. "You would be surprised, gentlemen, at the irregularity of my income. I have often thought it strange that a man will willingly pay his lawyer a hundred dollars to secure his property, but dawdles reluctantly when asked to pay fifty dollars to a physician for saving his life. My new wartime policy will be to accept payment in the form of chickens, cotton shares, and barrels of gunpowder—I can speculate on the side and become as prosperous in fact as you imagine me to be!"

Editor Fulton glanced at the ballroom entrance. A short, rotund man with a florid, clean-shaven countenance had arrived in their midst, flanked by two unfamiliar officers whose dapper air of self-importance spoke of Richmond.

"There he is, Jacob—your coreligionist, the honorable Judah Benjamin, attorney general of the Confederate states. He is here to demonstrate President Davis's concern for the Cape Fear region. I had rather Mister Davis send us the same weight in the form of artillery, but we must be grateful for what we receive."

"Remember your promise, James," said Jacob to the editor.

"I shall arrange an introduction, Jacob, just as soon as Mister Benjamin has been suitably plied with flattery and unction. But I would not get my hopes up with regard to the synagogue project—Mister Benjamin is a politician first and always, but a Jew only on rare occasions, or so I am told. How could it be otherwise?"

Largo knew she was expected to be present when her father met Judah Benjamin, to ally her charm with his eloquence. But her gaze had quickly gone beyond the portly dignitary and had focused instead on a tall elegant young man in some sort of nautical uniform. He was unfamiliar and striking, and he bore himself with the confidence of a man who was equal in rank or stature to anyone else in the room, even if his dress did not proclaim as much. Evidently, he was known to most of the other young women for he was soon surrounded by a half-dozen of the prettiest, most eligible girls in Wilmington. He seemed perfectly at ease with their attention and accepted their flattery as his due. There was something exotic and compelling about him and Largo, much to her own surprise, wanted very much to meet him.

"Father, gentlemen, please excuse me for a moment so I can pay my respects to some of my friends. I do not wish to bore you with women's talk." The faint irony of that remark was lost on Jacob and his companions—it would never have occurred to them that anyone could be equally bored by "men's talk."

She drifted through the ballroom, greeting acquaintances, exchanging pleasantries, seeming to move at random yet seeking gradually to place herself near the unknown guest. Fragments of conversation swirled around her ears, a kaleidoscope of sounds touched with the urgency of great external events:

"Our boys will knock the doodle out of the Yankee!"

"Oh, if we could but hear the roar of the British lion."

"Free love is a Yankee predilection—we have never introduced it in the South and never shall."

"Observe how she flirts! What a little puff of vanity!"

"His manners are too frenchy for me."

"A march on Washington would settle the business promptly."

"I understand their 'honeymoon' was not successful—I did not inquire further."

"Pure filibuster, that speech!"

"But our Negroes are so well behaved and affectionate—a little lazy perhaps, but that is no crime and we do not require unreasonable diligence from them."

"It well becomes the just to be thankful."

"Surely, Ivanhoe's Rebecca was not more fair—"

Without consciously willing it, Largo had come to a halt before the elegant stranger. A few seconds passed awkwardly before she realized that he had been speaking to, and about, her—in the cultured tones of an English gentleman. At least, this was how she imagined English gentlemen would speak, for until this moment she had never actually met one, but only read dreamily about them in romances. Rallying her wits, she flashed her eyes from behind the cover of her fan.

"You have read Sir Walter Scott, sir?"

"Indeed, madam. And Byron and Shelley and Shakespeare."

"Lord Byron was a wicked man, or so I have heard."

"My father knew him and testified to his wickedness in very colorful language."

"Your father was a poet, too?"

The young man laughed. "Oh, no! But he was a bit of a rake, in his youth, when he first served in Parliament. I have the honor to bear his name: Captain Augustus Hobart-Hampden, at your service, on extended leave from Her Majesty's Royal Navy."

"And I am Largo Landau. Which name shall I call you by, sir?"

"Which name?"

"Hobart or Hampden? In the South, we seldom hyphenate."

"You may call me Augustus; in fact, I insist upon it."

He kissed her hand with practiced suavity. He was slender but broad-shouldered, with a fine, slightly dimpled chin, a tart but merry mouth, strong gray eyes, and a splendid mahogany moustache, curled up toward his cheeks and waxed to vigorous points.

"Largo is an unusual name," the Englishman said, as though savoring the two syllables. "A musical term, is it not?"

"Yes. It means 'slow,' 'flowing,' 'restful.' My mother loved music and played the violin quite well. My father used to joke that he had to argue her out of naming me *Allegro,* which means . . . "

"I *know* what the terms mean, Miss Landau. My grandfather was a patron of the great Haydn, when that composer resided in London. I was surrounded by music from birth."

Their eyes held for a moment; the moment extended until Largo broke the mood with the quickest conversational cliché that came to mind.

"What brings you to Wilmington, Captain?"

"Curiosity, Miss Landau. The scent of adventure. And a quest for beauty, which until now has been in vain."

"You are forward, sir."

"I am direct, madam, as naval officers tend to be."

"But you are not in naval uniform . . . Augustus."

"As I stated: I am on leave, although still technically an officer. I wear the clothes of a merchant captain, for I expect to be sailing on merchant vessels, not warships."

He was easy to talk to, and in his company Largo felt none of the fumbling constraints she experienced when bantering with the young men of her usual acquaintance. A captain of the Royal Navy! He must have seen a lot of the world, infinitely more than she had even read about. With his wavy hair, bold yet graceful manner, and dashing features, he must have conversed with many women, or even . . . Largo blushed at the thought as it took shape in her mind, and hid her cheeks, for a few seconds, behind the fan-pleated visage of Jefferson Davis. Noble English women, seductive French ladies possessed of erotic secrets, hot-eyed Spanish courtesans, houris of Persia, princesses of India, wanton South Sea islanders who danced naked . . . So worldly a man that he could spot her instantly for a Jewess, and just as quickly compliment her from that very angle by referring to Ivanhoe's secret love, Rebecca, who happened to be the literary character with whom Largo most closely identified.

"In other words, Captain, you too see the coming war as a business opportunity?"

"Doesn't everyone in this city? What better place could I find from which to observe the workings of the Confederate economy?"

On a sudden whim, Largo wagged her fan teasingly and said, "I know, now! You are a spy!"

For an instant, Hobart-Hampden's face froze, and she knew she had instinctively hit the mark, or close to it.

"Nothing so romantic, I assure you! And certainly nothing so secretive! The Confederacy needs English support and England needs cotton for her mills. Her Majesty's government, in consequence, needs eyes and ears on this side of the ocean. Fortunately, the queen has no objections if I make myself rich in the process of serving as her agent. I am hoping to gain command of a fast ship and I have letters of credit on file here, in Nassau, and in Bermuda. I intend to be successful in a variety of roles, and to have a damned fine time while I am at it!"

Largo knew she ought to object to his language and to the familiarity it implied, but his eyes burned with such earnest intensity when he spoke that she could not muster genuine indignation. Besides, her father, who was about to be introduced to Judah Benjamin, was making frantic signals for her to join him.

"Excuse me, but I think I should rejoin my father now. Perhaps you will come introduce yourself when he has finished his business with Mister Benjamin."

"I would be honored to meet Jacob Landau. Do not look surprised—your father is well regarded by the community and will certainly play a central role in wartime commerce, whatever forms it takes."

"Well, Captain, I am glad to know that people speak well of my father. Truth to tell, I have sometimes found it hard to relate to his accounts of the repression and prejudice he experienced in Europe. I have always been encouraged to think of myself, first and foremost, as a citizen of Wilmington."

"I am certainly sure that you were also taught not to strike up conversations with naval officers unless you were properly introduced—I detect a glance of disapproval being shot in our direction by your father. Perhaps you had better rejoin him before he challenges me to a duel." Hobart-Hampden bowed respectfully, but rolled his eyes insistently to speed her on her way back to the spheres of propriety.

"We will speak again, Captain . . . I mean, Augustus?"

"You may count on it."

Largo nodded to the Englishman, then turned reluctantly from his company and steered a purposeful course toward her father and the cluster of prominent men now gathered around the evening's most important guest.

Plump, florid, clean-shaven, both self-conscious and self-assured, Judah P. Benjamin had the hearty manner of a politician who was always "on the stump." His wide, all-encompassing gestures had the style of a large but somehow vague embrace, as though he sought to enfold everyone within the ambit of his voice but at the same time to keep a certain distance from them. Jacob Landau had cornered the Confederate attorney general, after being introduced by Editor Fulton—who now stood to one side, wryly observing the Encounter of the Israelites as though it were a secret Masonic ritual suddenly revealed in the full light of day. When Largo reached her father's side, she curtsied deeply and received in return an openly frank scrutiny that seemed equal to the detached passion of a jeweler appraising a precious stone whose exact value challenged his judgment. *"Enchanté!"*

crooned Mr. Benjamin as he bowed and brushed his hot full lips across her extended hand.

"I was just inviting Mister Benjamin to celebrate the Sabbath at our house," said Jacob.

"And I was about to explain the reasons why I cannot do that," replied Benjamin with practiced unction. "Miss Landau, perhaps you can understand, a trifle better than your esteemed father, why it is incumbent upon Southern Jewry to refrain, at least for the duration of the coming war, from calling attention to our differentness."

Largo blinked in surprise—she was not used to being asked about her political opinions and indeed was not altogether sure what they were; the very society she had grown up in was reforming itself on a daily basis. As an attractive young woman, *and* as a Jew, she felt doubly constrained within the roiling flux of that process.

"In Wilmington, Mister Benjamin, our differentness does not seem to matter all that much."

"Perhaps not now, not yet, not upon the surface of things," crooned the politician. "We rank higher than Negroes and Yankees, and we shall continue to enjoy that status as long as we demonstrate Southern patriotism. Indeed, we Israelites know something of bondage and oppression, and we instinctively understand that the status of our African population is already superior to that of many factory workers in the North. A slave who is treated decently by his owner enjoys more self-respect than the white immigrant enslaved to wages. I have learned, during my years of prominence, that most far-seeing Southerners know full well that slavery as an institution must yield, in time, to something less odious in the eyes of the world. But we must be free to create that new system from our own cultural realities—in other words, we must not yield to coercion or force."

"Indeed we must not," seconded Jacob. "But can we not do that while still observing our own religious customs?"

"Perhaps, if it were only a matter of *that*. As long as we are seen to be Southern patriots first, and Jews discreetly second, we will continue to enjoy tolerance. But I fear this war will be neither short nor easily won, and if the South suffers reverses, and hardships descend on our civilian population, the oldest and deepest forms of anti-Semitism could easily boil up again. If we prosper as individuals when the South as a whole endures suffering, we might again be singled out as grasping Shylocks, aliens, potential subversives, drinkers of infants' blood, and all the other hoary accusations that have hounded us since the Diaspora. If things go badly for the South—may God forbid—those who suffer the most will need to find someone else to blame. By process of elimination: they could not blame God without risking His displeasure; they could not blame the Negroes, because the Negroes have no power to shape events; but they could, very easily, turn upon the Jews. It has happened a thousand times in Europe and Russia, and it could happen here."

Largo tried to follow this serpentine reasoning. *Is this how all politicians think?* Aloud, she responded, "In essence, then, you do not approve of my father's efforts to organize a synagogue?" Instantly, she knew she had broached the matter prematurely; Benjamin's eyebrows lifted and a flush of embarrassment colored Jacob's cheeks.

"Ah, yes. I understand the need of Wilmington's Jews to band together in a time of crisis. But surely, my dear Mister Landau, you cannot succeed in such a costly enterprise without the support—and even the financial blessing—of the Gentile community. I must advise you to do what I have done: subordinate your racial concerns to the cause of the Confederacy. Demonstrate zeal, loyalty, and courage. Take up the musket if you can, support the cause spiritually and economically if you cannot fight. The equation is brutally simple: if the South prevails, your contribution to the victory will assure continued tolerance. *Then* your synagogue can be built. But if the South goes down, you must share in full the hardship of defeat or you may find yourselves being *blamed for it!*"

As he reached this conclusion, a change came over Benjamin's face and for an instant the bland, affable politician's mask slipped away and revealed the passionate man beneath. Mr. Benjamin, it seemed clear to her, had not reached his stated equilibrium without long, hard thought and no small degree of anguish.

"But, sir . . . !" Jacob started to protest; this was not what he had wanted to hear. Largo intervened, stepping slightly between the two men, interrupting her father's importuning reach with her own hand, which she placed compassionately on Benjamin's sleeve.

"Father, there is wisdom in what the attorney general says, and he has broader insights into the matter than we. He has traveled widely, and resided in high places. If we must set aside our dreams for the sake of victory, I am sure God will understand."

Judah Benjamin looked at Largo with new interest and respect, and with furtive gratitude. "You are fortunate, Jacob, to have such an insightful daughter. Her sensitivity is equal to her beauty. If God had granted me such a daughter . . . but He has not, and at my age it is wise to banish regrets."

With a bow and a brisk handshake, the politician excused himself and gravitated to the company of Fulton, Major Whiting, and Dr. Satchwell, who had gathered about the nearest bowl of fortified punch and were rapidly diminishing its contents.

Jacob remained only as long as decorum required. On the walk home, Largo found him sulky at first, but soon resigned. Jacob would never say it aloud, but Largo could tell that Benjamin's advice had temporarily absolved Jacob of the obligation he felt toward his dying wife's request. In time, certainly, Wilmington would have a synagogue; but first, there was a war to fight. By the time Jacob had consumed a large prebedtime brandy, he seemed to have girded on an invisible sword, so fervently did he speak of the Confederate cause. Let him roar like the Lion of Judah, she thought. *But thank you, God, that he is too old to enlist!*

As she drifted into sleep, with images of the gallant Hobart-Hampden already lining up to populate her dreams, she heard her father walking restlessly downstairs, and then a quiet, melancholy toot of the shofar, like the day's final signal sounded by a watchman on the walls of Jerusalem.

Governor John Ellis mopped his brow. Despite the fact that his rank entitled him to a place near an open window, he was sweltering. The weather was more like that of midsummer than late spring: thick muggy air, resistant to any breeze, sunlight that hammered the ground until those subjected to it felt light-headed. The delegates who had crowded into the North Carolina House of Commons on this twentieth day of May, 1861, waved their fans so vigorously that the instruments made a soft susurrus not unlike that of coastal surf.

Since Lincoln's call for troops, on April 15, the secessionist cause had evolved from an option to a matter of practical debate, and finally into an emotional juggernaut. Ellis knew that secession was a foregone conclusion, but he had insisted that the process be accomplished in measured parliamentary steps. He had called the General Assembly into special session on May 1, and today, on May 20, the matter would be resolved. The delegates' mood was ardent and no longer bipartisan; Virginia had gone out exactly two weeks earlier, and North Carolina seemed caught up in the powerful undertow generated by that event. By one o'clock in the afternoon, the parade of speakers had exhausted their blasts of rhetoric; even men who had urged moderation only a month before were caught in the undertow and declared themselves, one after the other, for the cause. During most of the morning, Ellis had been too distracted by the heat to pay much attention to the speechifying; he did not feel well—there was a tightness in his chest that made the humid air indigestible to his lungs. Waves of dizziness came and went, and his right hand ached from hours of fanning. He would surely be glad when this day's business was over.

And now the only question that remained was the wording of the ordinance of secession. The president of the assembly, a prominent Warren County planter named Weldon Edwards, read out the agreed-upon phrases:

> "*We, the people of the State of North Carolina in Convention assembled, do declare and ordain, and it is hereby declared and ordained, that the ordinance adopted by the State Convention in 1789, whereby the Constitution of the United States was ratified and adopted; and all acts and parts of acts of the General Assembly, ratifying and adopting amendments to said Constitution, are hereby repealed, rescinded, and abrogated!*
>
> "*We do further declare and ordain, that the Union now subsisting between the State of North Carolina and the other States, under the title of 'The United States of America,' is hereby dissolved . . .* "

Only one ballot was needed to pass the resolution. From his vantage point on the speakers' platform, Ellis saw only a few dissenting hands signifying "Nay!" Indeed, the vote was so lopsided that a number of men, seized by the passion of the moment, did not linger for the official tally, but ran pell-mell from the room to spread the news. Ellis watched them scatter across the green lawns, waving and gesticulating to the crowds that had gathered soon after dawn and grown hourly since. From the topmost cupola of the capitol building, someone waved a crude, homemade Confederate flag. A group of cheering men ran to the flagpole and roughly lowered the Stars and Stripes.

By the time John Ellis could disengage himself from the mob that had swarmed onto the stage as soon as the votes were counted, he was half faint from lack of air, almost as though he were beset by a sudden fever. Another, much vaster, fever gripped the city of Raleigh—as Ellis slowly trudged back toward his office, he could hear cannons blasting, church bells ringing, brass bands blaring, and volleys being fired into the air.

Ellis saw total strangers embracing, men and women singing and shouting, bottles of whiskey passed from hand to hand. Here and there on the fringes of the celebrant mob, Ellis saw small groups of Unionists, many with their heads bowed and some openly weeping. The governor understood the emotions on both sides. Where the secessionists saw the start of a wild and romantic crusade, an adventure beyond compare, and expressed their feelings with naive bloodthirstiness, the more thoughtful citizens surely realized that, win or lose, the day also marked the end of something: the genteel, decent, slow yet gradually progressive way of life that had characterized North Carolina's culture since the end of the Revolution. Yet Ellis was sure that those men, too, would take up the gun and fight; the loyalties born of blood and the stern obligations of pride would demand it. And the sword, once drawn with such bloodthirsty alacrity, would not so easily be returned to its scabbard.

Halfway back to his office, not far from the flagpole where only one banner now hung, Ellis felt a strong breeze coming across the shaded grounds, as though the concussion of saluting guns had stirred the very air to excitement. At first he reveled in the sudden coolness, but after a few deeply contented breaths, he wrinkled his face in disgust at the unmistakable odor of human waste. For an instant he was puzzled, and then he understood: the wind was coming from the direction of Camp Ellis, two miles west—a raw expanse of trampled-down cornfield, named one week ago in the governor's honor, where militia companies from all over the state were mustering, drilling, and coagulating into regiments. Ellis grimaced as the cloacal reek intensified on the freshening breeze. If five thousand men can generate such a stink in only one week, he thought, what appalling odors would taint the wind when that number doubled, tripled, as companies from the more distant counties arrived?

Two days earlier—partly to absent himself from the political tension that simmered in the capital—Ellis had ridden out to the encampment to see and be seen by the new recruits. He found conditions there to be much more primitive than his aides had reported: what had been described to him as "barracks" turned out to be nothing more than crude huts and lean-tos cobbled together from raw splintery pineboards. The men slept either on the ground itself or on planks; no mattresses were in evidence—the only concession to basic comfort was a thin scatter of straw. When it rained, the men got soaked; when it was dry, they coughed and choked on clouds of fine red-clay dust. One soldier, accosted at random by the governor, complained that he and his hut-mates shared one tin pail among them, and used it for shaving, baking cornbread, boiling coffee, cleaning dishes, and washing their feet after a hard day's drill. Not long after Ellis heard this distressing report, he witnessed the arrival of a company designated the Warren County Guards. Gaudily overdressed, the men marched smartly into bivouac at the head of an outlandish baggage train composed of pack mules, farm wagons, carriages, and what appeared to be an antique stagecoach. Instead of powder, rations, and blankets, however, the vehicles were crammed with heavy camp chests, bedsteads, quilts, oil lamps, kettles, banjos, fiddles, and a variety of farming implements whose military utility was esoteric at best.

Ellis had hoped his impromptu visit would be a welcome recess from the political vortex that surrounded him at the state capitol; instead, he returned from his tour of inspection even more depressed than before. The men were eager, excited, even boastful; but they had few modern weapons and no apparent grasp of basic sanitation. On this fateful and muggy day, Ellis reflected, the main product of all their bravado and enthusiasm was the smell of shit. One of the foremost by-products of any army, he supposed. The stench clung to him like an invisible film as he entered the capitol.

That evening, Governor Ellis dined quietly with his friend Henry T. Clark, Speaker of the Senate. Halfway through his second after-dinner cognac, John Ellis grew pale, then flushed, panting for breath. Clutching at his chest, he whispered "Oh God!" and toppled forward. Clark rushed to his side. Ellis gathered his last strength and said: "You are my successor, Henry. If North Carolina is to survive the coming trial, you must move Heaven and Earth to mobilize her people and resources. We have discussed what needs to be done and . . . " Ellis trembled and slumped heavily into his colleague's arms. Before he lost consciousness, he managed to say one more thing: "Make sure those fine young men at least have enough straw to sleep on."

He went into a coma and died quietly two days later. Henry Clark was duly sworn in as governor and moved swiftly to implement the statewide actions Ellis had already adumbrated in a lengthy memo to the legislature.

Lamb's First Fort

A MANLY WEAPON—In looking at the stalwart frames and resolute faces of the Southern troops, it is evident at a glance that, where they do not have sword-bayonets, they ought to have Bowie knives—so beautiful and effective is a Bowie knife that, no matter what other weapons they have, or even if they have no other weapons at all, every son of the South ought to be armed with one. Nothing tests the metal of a man like the taste of cold steel in a close hug! Our enemies are great at showering bullets at long range; but it should be our policy to avoid the long taw and bring them into that close embrace which can alone express the strength of our brotherly love.

—The Wilmington Journal, April 16 1861

Two weeks after Virginia's secession, Norfolk was gripped by a mood of crisis. The clash of priorities—strengthening the coastal defenses, building shallow-draft gunboats, establishing chains of command for both land and naval forces—had revealed just how woefully unprepared the South was for the stringent realities of conflict. Even the simplest tasks were girdled by confusion and redundancy of effort. Commander Samuel H. Parker, a career naval officer who had resigned his lieutenant's commission on the day Virginia went out, was recommissioned—and promoted by one grade—expeditiously enough, and given a clear, unambiguous set of orders: take command of the tug *Beaufort*, convert her into a gunboat, sail her south through the Great Dismal Swamp Canal, and report to Elizabeth City, North Carolina, where—he was assured—the Confederacy was massing "a fleet capable of controlling the waters of Albemarle Sound."

When Parker located the *Beaufort* amid the chaotic scatter and noise of the Norfolk docks, the first thing he noticed was that both the boiler and the compartment best suited to serve as the powder magazine were situated above the waterline, where they were almost certain to be hit during any serious engagement. Parker immediately requisitioned a supply of quarter-inch iron plate from a warehouse not more than a half-mile from where the tug was moored. A week went by, while Parker and his crew busied themselves strengthening the forward bulwarks so that neither the weight nor the recoil of a rifled 32-pounder would split the hull, and there was no sign of the iron. When Parker, now greatly aggravated by the seemingly pointless delay, went to headquarters and inquired about his requisition, the clerks on duty could find no trace of the document and could only suggest that Parker write another requisition and deliver it by hand instead of by messenger.

That night, Parker and ten of his crewmen disguised themselves with kerchiefs, "borrowed" two wagons, and confronted the warehouse sentries with drawn pistols. Then they helped themselves to all the iron they might need, and by morning they were well into the Dismal Swamp Canal and beyond the reach of any reprimand. Stripped to the waist under the hot May sun, Parker's men punched holes in the iron plates and hung them over the hull to shield the most vulnerable spots.

Aside from Parker and his pilot, a leathery old salt named Archibald Gordon who had spent years traveling the canal, not a man among the thirty-five who made up the crew had any nautical experience. They were farmers and tradesmen and students. But they were zealous, and they drilled on the 32-pounder until they were proficient. If their gunnery matched their boastfulness, Parker mused, they might actually hit something . . . sooner or later.

Once the impromptu armor had been mounted, and the basics of loading the cannon engraved on their minds, the crew had nothing else to do but watch the scenery drift by. To a man, they agreed that the Great Dismal Swamp lived up to its name. In the six hours since their predawn departure from Norfolk, they had not seen a sign of human habitation. On either side, the marsh stretched to the horizon, vast and desolate. The canal averaged twenty feet in width; the *Beaufort* was seventeen feet wide, so both sides of the hull were regularly scrubbed by dense walls of sharp-edged savanna grass—one crewman, idly reaching out to stroke the passing vegetation, suffered a three-inch cut on his palm. From the elevation of the pilothouse, Commander Parker enjoyed a much wider view: beyond the grassy embankments, he saw black-water lakes, their surfaces pocked with the stumps of rotted trees. A solitary chalk-white egret pecked at an unseen meal—one of the few birds Parker saw all day. Between the monotonous chug of the steam engine and the heavy cloak of the air, rich with odors of decay, Parker felt inclined to drowse. There was no real reason why he could not nap—the pilot was fully capable of navigating all the way to Elizabeth City—but he did not want to set a poor example for the crew. So he amused himself by keeping a mental catalogue of the vegetation they passed; he noted longleaf and scrub pines, turkey oaks, wax myrtle, bald cypress, and tupelo gum trees. For every species he could identify, however, there were several he could not. The tugboat was moving fast enough to create its own breeze, so they were spared the attention of the local mosquito population, which the pilot described as both large and ravenous.

At four o'clock in the afternoon, they sailed past the tiny fishing village of South Mills, where the inhabitants turned out to cheer. A few miles below South Mills, the canal widened into a regular channel and through his spyglass Parker could see the great coppery glare of Albemarle Sound. Just at sunset, with the docks of Elizabeth City now in view, the *Beaufort* chugged past a huge bull alligator who scrutinized the boat with black, unblinking eyes and sublime indifference, a reptilian Cerebus on guard at the entrance to a theater of war. As the *Beaufort* drew abreast of the monster, one of the crew ducked into the bunkhouse and grabbed a rifle. Urged on with shouts of encouragement from his bored comrades, the man braced his weapon on the port gunwale and took aim at the great scaly snout just visible above the reeds. Before he could cock the hammer, Parker barked a warning: "Belay there, private! Belay, I say! That 'gator's a Rebel if ever I saw one. I'll wager he's waiting patiently for the chance to sink his teeth into some Yankee meat!"

Abashed, the private lowered his rifle and swung his cap, dancing an impromptu jig. "Huzzah for the Rebel 'gator!" The men joined in with a welcome round of laughter, backslapping, and high spirits that did much to relieve the tedium of the voyage from Norfolk. Parker smiled to himself. Perhaps they could be made into sailors after all. He wished at that moment for a keg of rum—a good healthy dram would keep their spirits high until they docked. But rum, like good gunpowder, was a scarce commodity in the fledgling Confederate navy.

Elizabeth City might not be much of a port, but if there were sailors present in any number, there were bound to be shopkeepers ready to sell them liquor.

The pilot altered course to the southwest, aiming toward the dim scatter of lights that defined their destination, just as the last molten rind of sun disappeared behind the trees of the coastal forest. Refracted from the undersides of towering clouds, a rich saffron light tinted the lake-smooth waters of Albemarle Sound. Parker climbed onto the timbered pedestal that anchored the 32-pounder to the bow and addressed his crew. Once they were docked, he told them, he would report to the local naval commander and ascertain the whereabouts of their sleeping quarters; after that, the men were free to avail themselves of local amenities until the hour of eleven o'clock.

"Any man not accounted for after that time will face punishment, and, while I do not expect most of you to abstain from drink, I do expect you to comport yourselves like gentlemen. Remember: we are the first line of defense for these people, and nothing will more certainly undermine their confidence in us than coarse, lewd, drunken behavior. Now men, let's dock this ship smartly, like real sailors!"

But none of Parker's men had ever docked a ninety-two-foot vessel before, smartly or otherwise, and their debut performance was greeted with hoots of derision from those ashore who gathered to watch it. Two men in the bow, tasked with slowing the *Beaufort*'s momentum by means of a stout pole, missed the pilings altogether and the tug crunched sharply into the wharf, knocking half the crew off their feet. Embarrassed and enraged, Parker bellowed orders, but only succeeded in confusing the men further. In response to his command to "make fast that bowline!," the hapless fellow holding the rope managed to loop both his own legs in a hangman's noose of two-inch hemp. By the time some helpful onlookers, wheezing with laughter, leaped on board to render assistance, the *Beaufort* had scraped forward the entire length of the dock and buried her bow in a tangle of nets that had been hung out to dry on the pilings.

Parker gathered what was left of his dignity and climbed onto the dock. He approached the first man he saw whose sleeves displayed the single stripe of an ensign. Parker stopped, glaring, and waited for his due salute. The ensign struggled to suppress his laughter and managed to come more or less to attention.

"Ensign O'Hara, Confederate navy, attached to the North Carolina Department, sir!"

"Commander Samuel Parker, reporting as ordered with the auxiliary gunboat CSS *Beaufort.* If you can contain your mirth long enough, Ensign, perhaps you'll be able to direct me to your commanding officer and after that, make sure my crew gets fed and shown to their quarters."

Something in Parker's tone made the young officer momentarily glad that flogging had been abolished as the standard naval punishment. Now the picture of disciplined rectitude, he pointed to a ramshackle chandler's shop across the street from the docks. "Right in there, sir. Captain Branch is expecting you."

Parker raked the young man with one final broadside of a stare, then strode off. He had only gone a few feet before Ensign O'Hara called out. "Umm, sir? Commander Parker, sir?"

Pivoting sternly, Parker said, "What is it, Ensign?"

Beneath his sparse red whiskers, the young man flashed another smile. "I just wanted to tell you, sir, that the men who were laughing tonight did an even worse job when they got here last week—they managed to ram and sink the mayor's favorite fishing boat. Real sailors are in short supply, sir."

"Well, we shall have to make 'real sailors' out of the men we've got."

Parker resumed his walk. Night had fallen and the flickering oil lamps hung from nails here and there revealed few details of the tiny port. He dimly perceived the shapes of several other large craft docked on either side of his own ship; canvas-shrouded cannon loomed on their bows. Circumventing a large fresh pile of horse droppings, Parker saw a sudden rectangle of light wash over the packed clay road, and at the same time heard a hearty voice call out in greeting.

"Sam Parker, you survived the treacherous passage, I see!"

"Ah, William! I had hoped you were the 'Captain Branch' referred to. It is good to see you again!"

The two officers shook hands, then embraced warmly. Branch opened the creaking door to his temporary headquarters. The place looked and smelled like every other dockside store, albeit on a small and shabby scale in keeping with the size of the port it served. In shadowed piles in the corners were barrels of flour and hardtack, coils of rope, oddments of tackle, rolls of sail canvas, crab traps, and netting. Nearer to the desk where Branch had spread a map of coastal North Carolina, Parker spied a glinting bouquet of cutlasses, a stand of rifles, and a wicked but anachronistic cluster of what appeared to be sixteenth-century pikes. Useful for repelling boarders, he surmised, or for harpooning any stray whales that wandered in from the Gulf Stream. Gunpowder, of course, would be stored elsewhere, away from the combustible flicker of oil lamps, candles, and carelessly thrown cigar butts.

Branch held a chair for Parker, offered him a cheroot, and poured brandy into a dented pewter mug. "Here, Samuel. Good English stuff and very nearly the last of it to be found on these barren shores!" Branch hoisted his own cup and offered a toast: "To all the brave captains!"

"Hear, hear!" responded Parker, allowing the brandy's heat to open the portals of memory.

Only a short span of seniority separated the two men: Parker was twenty-eight, and Branch thirty. The older man was a native of these waters, from New Bern, and the younger was a Virginian, not born to the sea but powerfully drawn to it from his youth. Both had enlisted in the U.S. Navy eleven years ago and fate had thrown them together in the same class of midshipmen. In addition to their shared youth and genteel backgrounds, both had been starry-eyed romantics at the time—dreaming of Decatur-like exploits against Barbary pirates, or gallant broadside duels in which they would be given the chance to utter some ringing imperishable phrase in the manner of John Paul Jones's reply to the captain of the more powerful *Seraphis:* "Surrender, sir? Never! I have not yet begun to fight!"

Instead, they found themselves marking time in a service calcified by long years of peace and bureaucratic inertia. Promotions had been parsimoniously doled out on the basis of seniority, which by 1860 was very senior indeed. Vigorous and imaginative young officers remained frozen in subordinate rank for years, sometimes decades, until their best and keenest qualities had been dulled. The system was choked at the top with superannuated gold braid; any officer who simply lived long enough, unless he was an outright criminal or a scandalous degenerate, could be sure of reaching the topmost rungs of the promotional ladder. Initiative, familiarity with changing technology, these counted for nothing. When war finally came, the high command of the U.S. Navy was fossilized. In a decade of loyal service, both Parker and Branch had moved from ensigns to lieutenants, a single advancement in rank, and until the war came along, both men had fully expected to be middle-aged before ascending to a captaincy.

In stark contrast, the infant navy of the Confederate states was starting from scratch and from very far behind. Industry and imagination were welcomed; indeed, they were the only two commodities abundantly present. Simply by resigning from one navy and volunteering for another, both men had leaped forward to flag rank—Branch in overall naval command of the whole North Carolina coast, and Parker in command of the *Beaufort.*

"It isn't much of a ship, I grant you," said Branch, leaning forward to light Parker's cigar. "But it is, by a matter of two or three feet, the largest in the fleet."

Parker noted the wry smile on Branch's thin, ascetic lips as he uttered the word "fleet." William still looked like a corsair, Parker reflected: a rakish upturned moustache waxed to a pair of needle points, a trim goatee, sunken cheeks, and smoldering brown eyes. He was a man prepared to seize the best destiny available.

"Exactly what sort of 'fleet' have we got?" Parker asked.

"A veritable armada: five, counting your own ship. The best and fastest is the side-wheeler *Winslow,* formerly a coastal trading vessel; the other three are the *Oregon,* named after a local inlet, the *Ellis,* named in honor of the late governor, and the *Raleigh.* The *Winslow* mounts a thirty-two-pounder on the bow and a rifled twenty-four-pounder on the stern. All the rest carry a single cannon apiece. Six guns on five ships."

"And the smallest ship in the U.S. Navy mounts a dozen. I begin to see the situation. No fast and powerful frigates, eh?"

Branch laughed, almost choking on a swallow of brandy. "Perhaps in time, Samuel. There are a couple of yards in Wilmington capable of turning out such a ship, although under the circumstances, I would trade a pair of frigates for a dozen shallow-draft gunboats. We have what we have, and must make the best of it. The inhabitants have already dubbed us the 'Mosquito Fleet,' and as far as the state newspapers are concerned, the laugh of the satirist has already driven us from these waters. Come look at the map, and I'll show you what's what."

For the next half-hour, the two officers studied the coast of North Carolina. Parker was impressed with the degree of study Branch had given to strategic matters, despite the ludicrous imbalance between the naval resources available to the contending sides. The coastline of North Carolina seemed almost designed by Nature to provide a defensive bastion. The Outer Banks—that long thin necklace of barrier islands that protected the sounds and riverine estuaries from the ravages of the Atlantic—served as an outer wall, and the two great sounds, Albemarle to the north and Pamlico to the south, acted as vast moats. The true coastline began on the western shores of the sounds, where several small ports (New Bern, Beaufort, Morehead City, and Edenton) and one large port (Wilmington) lay athwart the channels of mighty rivers—the Cape Fear, the Neuse, the Pasquotank, the Roanoke, the Chowan, and the Tar—which were navigable so far inland as to give access to fully one-third of the state's interior, as well as the main north-south railhead at Goldsboro. From the strategic point of view, a powerful Federal invasion, staged from the coastal ports, could drive inland, supported most of the way by river gunboats, sever the rail connection with Virginia, and, without much difficulty under present circumstances, threaten Raleigh itself.

"Fortunately, the defense enjoys at least as much advantage," said Branch, tapping a tobacco-stained finger against the crenellations of the Outer Banks. "In order to reach anything worth capturing, the invaders must first penetrate into the sounds, and there are only a handful of inlets along the entire coast deep enough for ocean-going vessels to pass." Branch proceeded to adumbrate them, from north to south: Oregon, Hatteras, Beaufort, and the two inlets leading to Wilmington. To secure the entire coast, it was necessary only to fortify these choke points with heavy seacoast artillery and maintain a strong infantry reserve, based in the sound-side ports, which could be rushed to reinforce any threatened location.

"Surely, these precautions have been given the highest priority in Richmond."

Again Branch laughed, but this time sourly. "Oh, yes, Samuel, you would think so, wouldn't you? Any fool of a midshipman can see what needs to be done. It will take months for Lincoln to field a serious army against Virginia, but he already has the resources to mount a naval operation. I and every other Confederate officer in this region have repeatedly telegraphed the capital, requesting adequate artillery and engineers to build the necessary works. But so far, actual construction has begun only at Hatteras, Ocracoke, and Oregon inlets. We have occupied old Fort Macon, guarding the passage to Beaufort and Morehead City, as well as Fort Caswell, below Wilmington. But the artillery we've been sent is inadequate and Richmond insists that we parcel out the guns equally among the various works—which means none of them are really well defended. The gunners are poorly trained militia, their powder is scandalously bad, and some of the guns are so old that they're more dangerous to their crews than to anyone in front of them! To speed up construction, at least, we have attempted to lease large numbers of slaves from the local planters—whose property we are, after all, protecting—but so far their response has been both meager and grudging."

This review of the situation seemed to have sapped some of Branch's characteristic ebullience. His shoulders were slumped as he bent to refill their glasses, and as his face moved through the brightest corona of lamplight, Parker saw shadows of weariness under his friend's eyes.

"Not every prospect is so discouraging, Samuel." Branch thumped his cup against the map's barren depiction of the Atlantic. "Not far off the Outer Banks lie the main trade routes between the northern ports and the Indies. Teak, rum, sugar, tobacco, finished goods from England all pass within easy striking distance of these inlets, many of them along routes that can be observed from the lighthouse on Cape Hatteras. Commercial vessels, Samuel, and none of them armed! These inlets can also serve as sally ports, from which sufficiently bold and skillful seamen might dash out when the opportunity presents itself, and capture valuable goods by means of simple intimidation. It is what the French loftily describe as *guerre de course*, but you and I would prefer to call by its more romantic name: privateering.

"Three weeks ago, on the strength of a memorandum largely drafted by myself, President Davis authorized the Confederate Congress to issue letters of marque. Any captain who applies for one, and who is willing to arm his vessel at his own expense, can legally attack Yankee ships on the high seas. The word is spreading down the coast. I understand ships from Charleston, Savannah, and Saint Augustine are already heading this way. If we add to them the support of the Mosquito Fleet . . . well, I read somewhere that even an elephant can be driven mad by enough mosquito bites."

Branch sat down again and stared moodily into his drink. Veils of smoke eddied slowly in the close and humid air. In the marshy forest outside, nocturnal insects buzzed and chittered in counterpoint to Branch's last remarks. The captain wiped a film of sweat from his wide sun-browned forehead and looked up at his old friend. A slow, almost feral smile crept across his lips and his eyes began to burn with the zeal that Parker remembered from their midshipman days.

"You know what gave me the idea, Samuel? *Blackbeard!* Aye, Edward Teach, the cruelest and craftiest of pirates! He used to frequent these waters in the *Queen Anne's Revenge.* He'd lay to behind the Banks until his lookouts spotted a sail out to sea, then he'd crowd on the canvas and sprint out to investigate. Many a French and Spanish ship were plundered only a day's sail from where we sit tonight. Of course, when it no longer became politically expedient to attack French and Spanish ships, the British tried to rein him in. He responded by plundering English ships as well, and eventually they hanged him for it."

Parker reassuringly said, "Whatever our fate, William, it will surely not be the gallows."

After some additional conversation about their families, the two officers parted for the night. Despite the heaviness of drink and the fatigues of the day, Parker tossed for a long time before succumbing to sleep, his mind on fire with visions of gallant adventure on the high seas, of prizes taken amid the ring of blades and the roar of pistols. Together, by God—he vowed as he turned in his hammock to catch a faint breeze slithering through the insect netting—he and Branch would make their mosquitoes bite hard enough to madden the Yankee elephant.

Rarely had Daisy Lamb seen her husband so agitated. Anger was not a Christian response to the misdeeds of any other Christian person, but, as William had growled during supper, "There are times when the other cheek simply cannot be turned!" Unaccustomed to such a tone from their father, the children looked up anxiously, fearing themselves somehow to be the cause.

"Ssshh, William," chided Daisy. "Whatever the matter is, we can discuss it after the children are asleep." Chastened, Lamb flashed a smile of reassurance at his babies, then commenced sullenly to finish his meal.

Later, when the parents were alone, Daisy learned that William Lamb had on that day survived his first two skirmishes: one with a Federal gunboat and the other with the Confederate hierarchy. From the manner of his recounting, it was clear that he would sooner undergo the former again and again than the latter experience one more time.

At ten o'clock on that sunny morning in early May, William Lamb and the men of the Woodis Rifles, hastily retrained as gunners, had been manning the fortifications on Seabird Point, near the confluence of the James River and the Chesapeake Bay. Masked by the dazzle of the sun, a Federal gunboat had sallied out from Hampton Roads, northeast of Lamb's battery, and opened fire upon them from long range. Lamb's weapons were elderly 32-pounders, which had been crudely rifled and scantily supplied with shells that only approximately fit the barrel grooves. One did not *aim* such guns, William told his wife, one simply *pointed* them in the enemy's general direction and hoped for the best. The cannon were mounted *en barbette,* which was to say they were sited to fire over their cover rather than through it, by means of less vulnerable embrasures. Those defensive works had been sketched out and their construction overseen by some newly commissioned Rebel major who designated himself an engineer. Since the man kept referring to the drawings in an old West Point textbook, Lamb and his men thought his engineering qualifications rather dubious.

As a result, the Seabird Point works comprised a single row of gabions, open-ended baskets woven from slats of wood and filled with rocks and earth; stacked together, they looked not unlike a line of giant thimbles. On the sea face of this "rampart," the overseeing "engineer"—once more referring to his textbook—had ordered the emplacement of a slanted row of wooden railroad ties, like a half-collapsed fence. The crowning touch was the seemingly random distribution of odd bits of iron on top of the wood. After three days of backbreaking toil, aided only by a handful of sullen Negroes mobilized from God knew where, Lamb and his men had created a fortification that looked as though it might wash away with the next floodtide. But the "engineer" had pronounced the works sound, then departed, never to be seen again.

"Too bad," growled William. "Oh, too bad that man was not here today!"

Sore from their labors, his men had slept late that morning, as had William himself. Instead of relieving the nighttime sentries promptly at eight, the garrison had straggled in by twos and threes, groggy and moaning for coffee. They were scattered about, leaning on the newly built walls and slouching over the gunmounts, or tossing crusts to "Jeff Davis," the mongrel dog they had adopted as mascot, when the first Yankee shell whistled in, followed a few seconds later by the report of a very large naval gun.

Instead of the more familiar *swoosh* of roundshot, this projectile screeched its way overhead with the sound of an angry bobcat. Startled men scalded themselves with spilled coffee and turned in abrupt horror in the middle of their parade ground to see the shell explode fifty yards away: a dirty gray cotton-ball spewing big ugly chunks of iron over a thirty-foot radius. The dog, who happened to be relieving himself on a patch of weeds, lost all four legs to a single piece of shrapnel and rolled howling for a moment, a spurting red-and-brown lozenge, before mercifully expiring.

To their credit, Lamb recounted to Daisy, his men had sprung instantly into action, ramming home powder-bags and their untried shells. Lamb grabbed a spyglass and focused on the Union ship, estimated the range, then called out a fuse length to his gunners. Three of the six 32-pounders roared together, the other three fired in staggered afterthought, making an altogether satisfying and thunderous blast. But the poorly made shells did not, in fact, fit snugly into the impromptu rifling and they left the barrels so slow, fat, and wobbly that Lamb could see them arcing east with his naked eyes. Feathers of water spurted when they landed, a good one hundred yards short of their target.

"Raise those guns!" cried Lamb, just before he was knocked off his feet by the concussion of a second Yankee shell, this one smashing into the sand at the foot of the gabions. Spitting and wiping his eyes, Lamb staggered to his feet, choking on his first deep breath of angry powder smoke.

For the next fifteen minutes, the unequal duel continued: methodical aimed fire from the ship, answered by energetic but utterly ineffectual salvoes from the land. This Yankee skipper was no fool: instead of anchoring to give his gunners a steady platform, he was using his steam engine to cruise in figure-eight loops, maintaining just enough headway to present an ever-changing range yet not so fast as to upset his own gunners' aim. Shell after shell pounded the sand around Lamb's batteries; three gouged out huge splintery wounds in the seaward planks, and two shattered the patches of iron as though they were tin plates.

"You see, Daisy," he said as he bent over a napkin with his pencil, "in older times, when ships attacked a fort, the fort had all the advantage. It was a stable platform and any sailing ship that challenged it had to close the range perilously, just to smother the works with solid shot. But now, with steam instead of sails, and big rifled guns, the advantage lies with the ship, unless it is faced with heavier ordnance, which was definitely not the case this morning!" Daisy watched with genuine interest as Lamb drew a representation of the two different tactics and she thought: Well, yes, that is clear enough, a matter of elementary geometry.

After the Union ship had finished making its statement and steamed insolently back toward Hampton Roads, Lamb went out to inspect the damage closely. The gabions had been moderately effective, although two of them were split open like seedpods, but the wooden wall and the haphazard ironworks had broken like twigs. A dud shell confirmed his initial guess: they had been fired on by a pair of 11-inch Parrott rifles.

Pondering the equation between fortress design and damage, he reasoned that such large, heavy shells, with their unprecedentedly powerful bursting-charges, could only be nullified if they struck a *yielding* surface rather than a brittle one, which would only transmit the shock of their impact, not absorb it. The dirt-filled baskets had done a reasonable job of that. Lamb envisioned a double row of gabions, like halves of a sandwich, with four or five feet of densely packed sand between them. Yes, that should work, and also minimize the danger from shell splinters.

Again he sketched, and again Daisy could see the clarity of his thinking. Big shells were a new weapon in this war, not the short-range and unreliable novelties they had been in previous conflicts, and so a new response was required. Daisy suspected that the war would provide many such examples of new techniques and new machinery.

"Did you tell anyone of your idea?" she asked.

But she was unprepared for the vehemence of his reaction. He slammed down his coffee cup and glowered.

"As soon as the danger was over, I went directly to the commandant of Norfolk."

Who happened to be the newly appointed general Benjamin Huger, a political ally of Jefferson Davis, and a man who combined arrogance with complacency. General Huger had interpreted the morning's skirmish as a probe heralding a massive Federal assault across the water from the huge anchorage at Hampton Roads, a possibility that obsessed him, even though, from what Lamb understood, it would be months, if ever, before the Union navy could manage such an operation; the navy had not attempted so large an operation since the landings at Vera Cruz, during the Mexican War a quarter-century before. There was plenty of time, in Lamb's opinion, to strengthen Norfolk with more modern cannon and redesigned fortifications. He explained all this to Huger, who watched him with a bland equanimity that could not help but grate on the nerves of a soldier who has just been shot at and who assumes, with some logic, that the experience has imparted a certain practical wisdom.

When Lamb finished his report and recommendations, Huger merely smiled patronizingly, tapped a quill pen on a stack of administrative papers, and replied: "Tut-tut-tut, Captain Lamb! Tut-tut, I say. Our leaders in Richmond are doing everything in their power, sir, everything in their considerable wisdom, to defend the Southern nation. As soon as they can send more artillery, they will. One cannot conjure Parrott rifles out of thin air!" Amused by the profundity of this observation, Huger gave a wet little snort of a laugh.

"No, one cannot," said Lamb through tightened lips. "But until these elusive cannons make their appearance, can we not at least rebuild our current works to withstand the sort of punishment the navy is capable of throwing at us?"

"I have been assured that our defenses are adequate," Huger bristled.

"General, the man who designed them was reading instructions from a textbook!"

"See here, Captain, if Richmond sends us an engineer, we must do as he advises! I cannot turn around and wire President Davis for another one!"

Lamb imitated Huger, pulling his nostrils apart and snarling like a boar. Daisy laughed. Lamb smiled wryly. "Indeed, it would be comical if this man were not in charge of the finest port in Virginia."

"Oh, William, he won't last long—he's only warming the chair for someone better. President Davis is no fool."

"Perhaps not, but he often seems content to take fools' advice."

Daisy pushed aside the dishes and moved around to sit in his lap. She kissed his cheek and nuzzled his sparse ginger-colored moustache. "The children are fast asleep, Young Soldier of the Lord. And my defenses are willing to be breached."

Since his appointment on March 1 as Secretary of the Union navy, the Honorable Gideon Welles had acquired two nicknames. To the more critical and impatient Northern papers, he was Rip Van Winkle, the prickly old gentleman whose Navy, in the four-and-a-half months since Fort Sumter's capitulation, had done nothing discernible to interfere with Confederate movements or commerce. At the start of his tenure, Welles had attempted to reason with reporters, explaining that a modern fleet could not be conjured from a sleepy peacetime service in a matter of weeks, but the only word that stuck in the editors' minds was "sleepy"; hence the opprobrious Rip van Winkle. Throughout May, those same newspapers had openly discussed possible strategies, publicly announced the strength of every force Lincoln had put into the field, and repeatedly chastised Welles and his officers for not "putting teeth" into the blockade, as though the boastful proclamation of it, on April 19, could turn it into a fact.

At that time, a mere six weeks after his appointment as secretary, Welles already knew the navy was utterly unprepared to mount any sort of blockade, never mind an offensive operation. On paper, the navy counted ninety ships, but only thirty-eight of those were steam powered. Of that number, five were undergoing repairs, one was patrolling the Great Lakes, and three others—on close inspection—proved to be structurally or mechanically unsound. Most of the seaworthy vessels were scattered abroad, showing the flag or guarding trade routes. Thus, on the day when Lincoln proclaimed his blockade, the number of ships immediately available to patrol an enemy coastline almost four thousand miles long was three, mounting a total of twenty-four guns. No wonder the newspapers, Northern and Southern alike, scoffed at the proclamation.

Welles had taken immediate steps to curb the scandalous amount of sensitive information appearing in the papers; he himself no longer spoke to the press, and all public statements from his subordinates had to be cleared with him in advance. Welles's testiness had not endeared him to journalists, and his physical appearance invited lampoons almost as frequently as the gawky visage of President Lincoln.

At age fifty-nine, Welles cultivated what he regarded as a dignified style, though uncharitable associates sometimes referred to him as the Undertaker. His customary attire consisted of formal trousers, a double-breasted black waistcoat, and a somber black frock coat. His salt-and-pepper eyebrows seemed perpetually raised in skeptical surprise, even as his thin, sharply incised mouth seemed always poised on a grimace of distaste. His head in its entirety was framed by a wide half-moon of snow-white whiskers, covering everything from his earlobes down, except for his upper lip, which he kept clean shaven. His one concession to vanity was a luxuriously curled wig, chestnut brown except for a few artful streaks of gray.

If hostile editors and cartoonists had chosen to transform his appearance into that of Rip van Winkle, President Lincoln had studied those same features and seen in them loyalty, resilience, and dogged determination. To the president, Gideon Welles was Father Neptune and Welles secretly cherished the appellation.

As he strode from the White House lawn to Pennsylvania Avenue, steering a course toward the frumpy brown-brick hulk that housed the Navy Department, Welles marveled at the feverish bustle that gripped the city of Washington. Regiments marched through in clouds of dust, heading for McDowell's growing army. Merchants, speculators, political hangers-on of every stripe, spies, harlots, vagabonds, and swaggering newly commissioned officers beyond counting—never had the city throbbed with such energy. Never mind the drumming heat of August and the floods of perspiration it unleashed, everyone was in a hurry to go *somewhere* and do some*thing.* Halfway to the Navy Department, Welles felt a welcome breeze off the Potomac, then wrinkled his nose at the fecund aroma of the immense horse pens down by the river.

Welles nodded to the sentries at the door and consulted his watch as he walked briskly down the main corridor toward his office. Waiting inside were the assistant secretary, the capable Gustavus Fox, Commodore Silas Stringham, and General Benjamin Butler. It was not, Welles reflected, the handsomest gathering of men in Washington. Stringham was a bony, hollow-eyed New Englander whose head and neck seemed inflated by the stiff celluloid collar he affected even on days as stifling as this; one had only to look at him to see the end product of the navy's hallowed seniority system. There were other, younger, more energetic officers Welles would have preferred, but he could not very well replace Stringham until the commodore demonstrated either physical infirmity or gross incompetence.

Next to Ben Butler, Stringham looked like Adonis. Butler loved the pomp of military rank, and usually appeared in full dress uniform, including pistol, saber, and kepi. One knew when Butler entered a room, all a-jingle, without looking up to see him. Indeed, Welles avoided looking at Butler whenever possible, for Butler was uncommonly and disconcertingly ugly. His sagging, overstuffed face bobbed like a white balloon atop an obese torso. Forehead and skull were completely bald and somewhat liver-spotted, while the back and sides were draped with a long greasy tonsure of thin hair. His moustache, too, was sparse and poorly groomed and did little to hide his fat moist lips. His cheeks formed two quivering fleshy dewlaps that eventually merged with the topmost of his several chins. His eyes were small and beady, ringed with puffy, dissolute-looking pouches of flesh, and the right eye, afflicted by some sort of muscular disorder, wandered independently of the left—like a white marble rolling in a pool of oil.

Back in his native Massachusetts, however, Benjamin Butler was regarded as a very successful man. His law practice and his business dealings—the envious suggested that the two were often too closely intertwined—had made him rich, and he had risen to national prominence in the Democratic Party by carefully nurturing alliances and doing favors. So powerful were his supporters that Lincoln had no choice but to appoint him a major general, if only for the sake of political harmony. As commander of the Fort Monroe garrison, Butler had impetuously mounted an attack on Jeb McGruder's Rebel force at Bethel, Virginia, on the tenth of June and had been soundly trounced—the first Federal commander to be beaten in the field. Ever since then, Butler had been yapping for a chance to redeem his "reputation" and his cronies had brought such pressure on Lincoln that the president, much against his better judgment, yielded once again.

As Welles shook hands all around, another officer came in, smartly clad in a captain's uniform. Welles put a hand on the young officer's arm and propelled him in front of the others.

"Gentlemen, may I introduce Captain Charles Hobson, commanding the sloop *Cumberland* and recently returned from a vigorous reconnaissance of the North Carolina coast. Captain, please repeat for these gentlemen the gist of your report."

Without consulting any notes, Hobson summarized things neatly. "We cruised offshore, from the Virginia state line to Cape Lookout, observing, taking notes, and interrogating a number of fishermen whom we intercepted at various points. Not surprisingly, since they were floating directly beneath our guns, all of them protested enthusiasm for the Union. Some of them meant it—they are simple, uneducated men, and the lofty principles articulated by Jefferson Davis have no real bearing on their lives. In any case, we heard enough consistent information to sketch a roughly accurate picture.

"As we suspected, the Rebels have erected two fortifications at Hatteras Inlet, Fort Clark on the eastern side of the island and Fort Hatteras on the western side. They are built from sand and sod, and appear to be weakly garrisoned."

"What guns do they mount?" interrupted Butler.

"We endeavored to find out by closing to within two thousand yards and trading a few broadsides with Fort Clark. Their return fire was slow and erratic, and few of the balls carried that distance. I estimate their guns to be smoothbore thirty-two-pounders, probably no more than eight in each position. More and better cannons are said to be coming, however."

"Then we must strike now!" cried Butler, slapping his meaty thighs.

Gideon Welles held up his hand and quietly asked, "And what about the privateers, Captain? Did you catch any of them?"

"No, sir. From the lighthouse on Cape Hatteras, the Rebel lookouts have a grand view out to sea. They signal the privateers whenever a Federal warship shows its masts, and none will emerge until the coast is again clear. Hatteras Inlet is certainly the main rendezvous for these brigands, since it is centrally located and fortified."

After a few more remarks, Welles dismissed the captain and waved a document at the other three men.

"I was asked this morning to meet with President Lincoln. He was concerned about this letter, signed by the heads of the five largest maritime insurance companies in Philadelphia, Boston, and New York. The depredations of these Carolina pirates have caused a panic all out of proportion to their numbers. If something is not done to curb them, insurance rates will go sky-high and commerce will suffer—not to mention the bank accounts of the gentlemen who importune us so urgently.

"Commodore Stringham, General Butler, please prepare an operational plan for a landing on Hatteras Island and the capture of its fortifications. That will put a cork in the bottle! And a victory of any kind, coming after our recent defeats in the field, will greatly stir the public's enthusiasm." Welles glanced up and saw Butler's cheeks spotted with red; he had not missed the inference. *Given sufficient troops and guns, even this poltroon should be able to subdue two small forts made from sand.*

Lincoln had asked Father Neptune to provide a quick, cheap victory, and Neptune had set his myrmidons in motion.

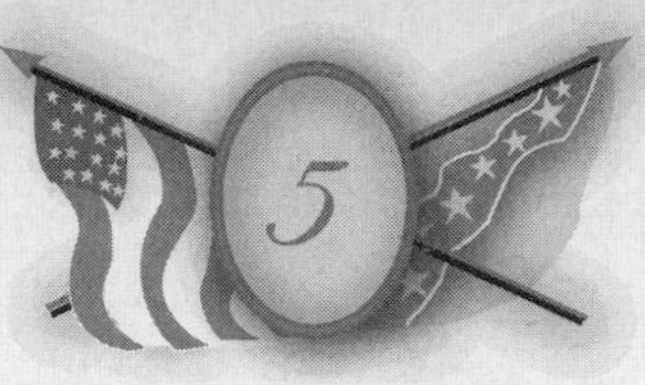

5 The Bite of the Mosquito Fleet

LUBRICATING OIL—We have been using all this week, on all of our machinery, lubricating oil expressed from the humble ground-pea, and find it to work admirably, with no more tendency to gum up than the best sperm or olive oil. We think that it will become a valuable element in the commercial independence of the South, now that we have become blockaded.

—The Wilmington Journal, November 17 1861

Will Cushing did not stay long in Fredonia. Two weeks after he gave his mother a dress, and three weeks after his resignation from the Naval Academy, came word of the attack on Fort Sumter. He packed hurriedly and returned to Washington, where he presented himself at Commodore Smith's front door, feeling rather like the Prodigal Nephew, and all but begged for shelter. To his aunt, he looked like a wounded sparrow, nervous, agitated, and in pain.

When the commodore came home from the Navy Department, two hours past dinnertime, he took one look at his skinny, hand-wringing nineteen-year-old nephew and instantly sized up the situation.

"Back so soon, William? Well, I suppose we should discuss your situation anew, in light of the grave events that have occurred since you left the service. Wait for me in the study while I have a bite to eat. You may help yourself to a glass of brandy, if you like, but only one. There is no time, not anymore, for you to indulge in cloudy thinking."

After a perfunctory meal of cold chicken and dumplings, Commodore Smith went to his study, nodded sternly at Will, and closed the door. Will saw at once that his uncle was tired, that his days had become long and his duties more strenuous than either man would have believed possible only a week ago. Smith poured a drink for himself and sat down, motioning for Will to do the same.

"Commodore, I . . . "

"Hush, boy! Three weeks ago, you were rash enough to get yourself expelled from the academy, but now that the shooting has started, you are all fired up again. Had you been more patient, not to say prudent, you would already be on your way to active service, and with a midshipman's rank."

"Sir, my worst grade was in Spanish. We are not at war with Spain!"

"Spanish has nothing to do with it. You repeatedly demonstrated a lack of respect for your superiors, and therefore a lack of respect for the navy itself. Why should the navy take you back?"

"Because I am a good sailor, a brave man, and a natural-born leader!"

Cushing pounded fist into palm as he grated out the words. Commodore Smith studied him for a moment: so young, so passionate, so wrought-up that his thin-boned shoulders were trembling. Smith took a long, slow drink and while he did so his expression remained righteous and unforgiving. Then, as he lowered his glass, he permitted his features to soften, almost to the point of a smile.

"To be frank with you, William, I rather expected to see you here again, as soon as the news reached you about Fort Sumter. I have taken another look at your files, spoken to a few academy men who think more highly of you than did Superintendent Blake. It seems to me that, aside from a youthful disposition to commit mischief, your shortcomings were more scholastic than naval. As you pointed out, fluency in Spanish is hardly helpful under present circumstances."

Suddenly changing course, Smith leaned forward and spoke with melodramatic emphasis:

"So, tell me, Will Cushing—will we whip these damned Rebels in three months, as everyone in Washington seems to think?"

Cushing hesitated before replying, not at all sure what his uncle wanted to hear, then spoke soberly.

"Sir, I trained with Southerners for four years. I think, during that time, I learned something true about their character. They are valiant, proud people; not only shall we not whip them in three months, but it may be that three *years* will not suffice to conquer them. If my opinion offends you, Uncle, I am heartily sorry."

"Honesty and good sense are not offensive. They are also in short supply at the moment. Anyone who says we can lick this rebellion in ninety days is a damned fool."

Smith rose and smiled reassuringly at his nephew. "The quickest way to handle this is to plead your case to Gideon Welles himself. As you can imagine, he has weightier issues on his mind than the fate of one ex-midshipman, but if I can catch him at the right moment, he might take an interest, if only as a favor to me. I cannot promise anything, and it may be days before I have an opportunity to broach the subject. Be patient, Will, and feel free to come and go as you like until I have some news for you."

Four days passed, during which Cushing scarcely saw his uncle again. Restlessly, he revisited the places he had frequented during his days as a congressional page, but encountered few of his former colleagues; all those old enough and fit enough had gone into service, on one side or the other. He resisted the temptation to loiter near the Navy Department, where he would surely encounter men he had known at the academy—such chance reunions would be awkward if not painful.

On Sunday night, five days after his return to Washington, he chose to dine alone in a small restaurant familiar to him from pleasanter days. He was morosely reading a newspaper and drinking an afterdinner coffee when he was approached by a well-dressed young man who moved and spoke in the manner of someone who did not wish to attract attention.

"Excuse me, sir, but aren't you Midshipman William Cushing, Class of Sixty-one?"

"I *was*," replied Cushing, scowling at the reminder. "And you are . . . ?"

"Jones. Edwin Jones. From Baltimore. I'm a journalist."

Cushing thought the man's accent was more upper-class Virginia than middle-class Maryland, and there was definitely something furtive in his glance. Curious, he shook the stranger's hand and gestured for him to take a seat.

"Have we met before, Mister Jones?"

"No, sir, we have not, but we have some mutual friends. Former classmates from Annapolis. Fine young men who send their greetings and their respect."

"It is always pleasant to hear from former classmates. Would you care to name them specifically?"

"That would not be prudent, Mister Cushing. I am merely, as it were, a messenger."

"And what is the message?"

"Several of your close classmates, as you know, followed their conscience and chose to serve the South. They believe that you were unfairly treated by the United States Navy and wish to assure you that a place of honor awaits you if you choose to turn your gaze in a Southern direction. A new and progressive kind of navy is being created by the Confederacy. Opportunities abound for fame and glory, for the companionship of men who admire your professional qualities and would have you treated accordingly. A lieutenant's commission is yours, sir, the instant you change from blue uniform to gray. And a command of your own. A *ship,* Mister Cushing! Perhaps even an ironclad. You look surprised? I tell you, the Confederate navy welcomes innovation. Meet me later tonight and we can be safe in Richmond before the sun sets tomorrow. The front lines are very porous, and I have passes."

For a feverish moment, Cushing felt the wicked appeal of the proposition. *That will show the bastards!* Then he thought of the shame such an act would bring to his uncle, his beloved mother, and his older brother Alonzo, who had graduated from West Point in June and who had been commissioned, only days ago, as captain in command of the Fourth New York Artillery, on its way to join McDowell's army this very night.

"Mister Jones," he finally said, "the Southern men I served with at the academy would never stain their honor, nor make insult to my own, by suggesting that I commit an act of treason. Nor would they employ a human weasel such as you to be their errand boy. If you are not gone utterly from my sight within fifteen seconds, I shall denounce you as a spy and you will be giving your next 'message' to a party of Union soldiers. *Do I make myself perfectly clear?"*

So comical was "Jones's" panicky retreat that Cushing laughed himself into a coughing spasm.

At nine-thirty the next morning, a courier rapped on the Smiths' front door and handed Cushing a note signed by Secretary of the Navy Gideon Welles. Could Mr. Cushing meet with the Secretary, in his office, at eleven o'clock sharp?

Cushing was fifteen minutes early. While he waited in the secretary's anteroom, dozens of young navy officers came through, delivering or picking up documents. Inevitably, one of them was a former Annapolis classmate. Resplendent in his new uniform, the midshipman picked up a packet of memoranda from the desk of Welles's adjutant, then paused long enough to mouth the words "Welcome back, Will!" before resuming his urgent journey through the bureaucratic maze.

At precisely eleven, Cushing was escorted into Welles's office. In person, the secretary looked every bit as biblical as he did in the newspaper engravings. He shook hands with the impersonal firmness of a mortician, then got straight to the point.

"Commodore Smith tells me you are ready to come back into the fold. Your academic records, however, tell me that you were an erratic student and a troublemaker of the first order. To complicate matters further, your former commanding officer aboard the *Plymouth* tells me stories of bravery and resourcefulness. Pray, whom shall I believe?"

"Believe this, sir: the navy is my life—I was, and I still am, determined to serve in it, even if I have to enlist as an ordinary seaman."

Welles stroked his chin meditatively.

"Mister Cushing, the navy is about to expand beyond anything you, or even I, can imagine. We have been charged with the task of choking off an enemy coastline almost four thousand miles long, not counting a few minor inland waterways such as the Mississippi River. The Union needs good officers, men capable of conducting operations on a scale never before seen in naval history. Those officers must be able to follow orders as well as give them—*even if those orders are given by a stuttering old fool.* Are you the kind of man the navy needs or not?"

Although he was not in uniform, Cushing braced himself ramrod-straight and replied, "Just give me a chance to prove it, sir."

Welles picked up a folded document and weighed it with his fingertips, his Old Testament brows furrowed sternly.

"Very well, Mister Cushing. Against the better judgment of several senior officers, I'm going to do that. You have zeal and enthusiasm, and even some of your critics admit as much. Temper those qualities with some self-discipline and you can go far. Here is your new appointment: master's mate aboard the *Minnesota.* She's being refitted in Boston Harbor at the moment."

Cushing took the document reverently, but with a puzzled expression.

"A simple 'thank-you' might be in order, son . . . "

"I'm sorry, Secretary Welles, but I did not know such a rank as master's mate existed."

"Used to, back around the Mexican War. The navy did away with it after the academy opened in Annapolis. Now that we are commissioning so many new men who did not graduate from the academy, the rank of midshipman no longer carries the prestige it should, or so all the Annapolis men seem to feel, so we have reinstated the rank of master's mate to distinguish a 'lesser' type of officer than the academy graduates. And they have a point—they *should* be distinguished from men who did not put in four years of hard work to earn the rank of midshipman. You, Mister Cushing, did not graduate, so if you want to be a midshipman again, you have to earn it. Until that time, the only slot open for you is that of master's mate, which is admittedly a kind of limbo. Take it or leave it."

With a bold flourish, Will Cushing signed the papers reinstating him to naval service, gave Gideon Welles a proper Annapolis salute, and went back out into the bustling corridors, where he broke into a jig of pure delight.

Two days later, wearing a new uniform and more bemused than humbled by his unfamiliar rank, he reported for duty aboard the steam frigate *Minnesota*, in Boston Harbor. In this, he was well pleased, for there was no handsomer ship in the fleet. Commissioned in 1857, displacing almost five thousand tons, the *Minnesota* was home to a crew of 640. Although her chief means of propulsion derived from a screw propeller driven by a pair of horizontal trunk engines—each rated at five hundred horsepower—she still retained three lofty auxiliary masts and her graceful lines were those of a sailing ship. If you ignored the squat black smokestack amidships, you could see her bloodline all the way back to the legendary *Constitution*. And despite her trim, compact layout, she carried a formidable suite of armament: forty-seven 8-, 9-, and 10-inch cannon.

When Cushing first came aboard, the frigate was a beehive of activity, swarming with carpenters, iron fitters, woodworkers, and ordnance officers overseeing the storage of powder and shot. The decks were an obstacle course of ropes, crates, cargo nets, barrels of salt pork, knots of heavy chain, and tools of all kinds. After a perfunctory welcome by his captain, a leathery old salt named Van Brunt whose commission dated back to 1814, Cushing was put immediately to work, alongside the other four masters' mates who had already come aboard. They were all young and all green except for Cushing, and they were assigned to every foul, sweaty task that the frigate's six lieutenants (all middle-aged and encrusted with seniority) disdained to dirty their hands with. Cushing did not mind: he was once again serving on a man-of-war, and all other considerations were secondary.

On May 8, the *Minnesota* was ready for sea duty with Admiral Stringham's blockading squadron. At half past nine, her mighty boilers seething with steam pressure, the frigate slipped her cables and majestically threaded her way through Boston's crowded harbor and toward the open sea. The docks were crowded with spectators, many of them there to bid farewell to husbands, brothers, and sons, while the shroud lines of every other big ship in the harbor were lined with cheering crewmen. Steam whistles tooted deliriously, and the great coastal guns of Fort Independence fired a thunderous salute. In reply, the *Minnesota* unleashed two full broadsides.

Thus did Will Cushing set forth on his first wartime cruise, his skin tingling from the spectacle of the moment, wreathed in powder smoke, head proudly turned into the wind.

A long, plodding time would go by before he smelled gunpowder again. From Boston, the *Minnesota* went on blockade duty at the mouth of the Chesapeake Bay. After five uneventful days of monotonous patrolling, the frigate did intercept a schooner filled with contraband tobacco trying to sneak from Richmond to Baltimore. In June, she sailed to the waters off Charleston and fruitlessly scoured the South Carolina coast. Heat, boredom, and monotonous, barely edible food were his main enemies, abetted by the cruel irony that the citizens of Charleston, who were ostensibly being blockaded, continued to lead their prosperous, well-fed lives without any comparable hardships.

Cushing's day began at five-thirty A.M. Between reveille and breakfast, at eight o'clock, he and the other masters' mates oversaw routine maintenance: sweeping, polishing, and holystoning the decks; buffing the brass fittings to a spotless gloss; splicing ropes; mending sails; sewing clothes. After breakfast, the crew was given a half hour to attend to their personal toilettes. For a time, Cushing contemplated trying to grow a beard, since his daily shave was always accomplished in a bucket of cold salt water, but his facial hair proved laughably sparse. The rest of the day—every day—was taken up with alternating watches and drills.

Two months and a week passed in this manner. Late in July, a packet steamer brought news of the big fight at Manassas. Cushing writhed with frustration. His brother Alonzo had certainly been in the fight. And if *two* Cushings had been on the field that day, surely the Union would have been victorious. Cushing brooded for days and began fantasizing about resigning his navy commission and enlisting in the army instead.

In mid-August, when the *Minnesota*'s crew, stupefied equally by boredom and heat, had lapsed into dull-witted apathy, new orders arrived. After reading them in the privacy of his cabin, and dashing off a response for the picketboat to carry back, Captain Van Brunt summoned all officers to a conference and informed them the frigate was ordered back to Hampton Roads to be refitted and resupplied so it could take part in a major amphibious operation against the coast of North Carolina.

On the afternoon of August 26, 1861, Samuel Parker and the crew of the *Beaufort* made a long, slow passage from New Bern to the rickety dock that served both Fort Hatteras and Fort Clark, a voyage of ninety miles across the glassy furnace of Pamlico Sound. Behind her, the tug hauled a wooden barge riding low in the water from the weight of a 32-pounder smoothbore and the subassemblies of its wooden carriage. It had taken all morning to load the weapon. Mount and barrel, it weighed seven thousand pounds, and the process of shipping, transferring, ferrying, and remounting it in a fort was every bit as slow, tedious, and labor-intensive as it had been during George Washington's day.

Once they were under way, Parker seated himself in the shade and perused a two-day-old newspaper from Richmond. The crew idled or trailed fishing lines baited with hunks of crab in the calm, blue-green water. At least they were beginning to look like sailors. Tanned and lean, they no longer made a spectacle when they attempted to dock or cast off. They had picked up a smattering of nautical jargon, learned to tie a few basic knots, and memorized the difference between "port" and "starboard."

During the weeks since Captain Branch had inaugurated his commerce raiding campaign, the Mosquito Fleet had enjoyed considerable success, capturing a dozen small merchantmen under sail and seizing cargoes of sugarcane from Cuba, porcelain dinnerware from Bermuda, and outbound loads of lumber and cloth from New England. In the course of unloading their prizes, before sending the empty-handed crews on their way and under parole, the *Beaufort*'s crew had helped themselves to various atmospheric articles of clothing and naval accoutrements: berets, scarves, cutlasses, pipes, and tunics. Some of them now affected "sailors' beards," bristly coxcombs of whiskers trained to encircle their otherwise clean-shaven faces. Parker did not think their appearance would have frightened Blackbeard, but he had no doubt now as to their spirits. The whole business, so far, had been rather a lark.

For the garrisons of the two Cape Hatteras forts, however, the war had produced tedium, squalor, and discomfort. Aside from the big guns, which were sent by rail at the rate of one or two a week, the *Beaufort* also brought mail, hardtack, powder, and fresh water to those barren and windswept outposts. To a man, the crew pitied the troops they serviced.

Now, as the afternoon waned, a sweet little breeze fluffed the waters of Pamlico Sound. Parker could see the closer of the works, Fort Hatteras, looming sullenly on the shallow dunes ahead. Fort Clark, the smaller of the two works, was discernible a quarter mile east, on the seaward side of Hatteras Inlet. From any distance, neither work was very impressive: low quadrangles of coarse gray sand faced with timbers and sod. Three hundred and fifty men, drawn from the untested ranks of the Seventh North Carolina, were imprisoned within those mud-pie bastions. Since most of the heavy spade-turning labor was done by rotating consignments of Negroes from the mainland, who clearly considered this assignment to be a form of particularly wicked torture, the garrisons spent most of their time stunned into torpor by the heat, or tormented to the brink of madness by sand fleas, fat green bottle-flies, and the ubiquitous mosquitoes who claimed the region whenever the sea breeze abated. Since there was not enough gunpowder to permit actual target practice, the men drilled "dry" in the mornings, before the relentless heat began to hammer against hats and caps that soon became too hot to wear.

Otherwise, men and officers alike whiled away the days by burrowing for shade, practicing immobility, and drinking. Or fishing and drinking. Or playing cards and drinking. Or trying to get sand crabs to compete in races, with extra drink as the tender of all wagers. Every week, a handful of soldiers were given overnight leave to avail themselves of the amenities in the tiny fishing village of Portsmouth, near Ocracoke Inlet, a wretchedly impoverished enclave whose citizens alternately profited and suffered from their visits. Only a man sick enough to be at death's portal could anticipate transfer to the mainland. From their commanding officer on down, all were convinced that Richmond had forgotten their very existence. Colonel William

Martin, who had been given command of the forts in May, had his hands full with routine repairs and chronic discontent. After a week's heroic but foredoomed efforts to smarten up the troops, Martin had himself yielded to ennui and was now usually well into his cups by midafternoon. Parker did not judge his fellow officer too harshly: tasked with guarding the most strategically important location between Norfolk and Wilmington, Martin had been given a skeleton force of green recruits and some venerable artillery dating from the War of 1812, and ordered to hold a pair of pestilential pigsties against the might of the U.S. Navy. Under the circumstances, Parker reflected, he too would have sought consolation from the bottle. At least the *Beaufort* was bringing another cannon.

Colonel Martin hailed the tug as it drew near. He was stripped to the waist, armed with a dented pail and some kind of implement resembling a hoe, and was industriously combing the sound-side shore for clams.

"Got another thirty-two-pounder for you, Colonel!" shouted Parker above the racket of the steam engine. Martin waved nonchalantly and pointed to a patch of sand already deeply rutted.

"Run it aground in the usual spot, Captain. We have a bunch of niggers comin' out tomorrow to pull it into the fort."

Parker gave a signal, and the helmsman cut the tug sharply to starboard while another man slipped the hawser ropes connecting the *Beaufort* to the wallowing cargo barge. One man rode the raft into shore, sluggishly propelled by brute momentum, and cast a rope to a group of half-naked soldiers who made it fast to some pilings.

Satisfied that the cannon was safely aground, Colonel Martin waved his men away and strode out to the *Beaufort*. Two of Parker's men helped him climb aboard and for a moment, as he stood there with sunlight glinting on the sweat and brine that matted his chest hairs, he looked like a wet hunting dog preparing to shake. As he leaned forward to shake Parker's hand, he deposited his clam bucket on the deck. Peering over, Parker counted four shellfish, matted with sand and algae, clumped in the bottom.

"Scrawny things, aren't they?" mused Martin. "I don't fancy them myself, but one of the niggers showed our cook a way to steam them properly, so those who do find them edible can have their fill."

"But surely, Colonel, you don't have to dig them yourself!" teased Parker.

"It gives me something to do, Mister Parker, besides writing reports to Richmond which never get acknowledged, much less acted upon. You don't by any chance have a bit of good news in that regard?" Martin's eyes pleaded. Parker had to look away before delivering the routine and too predictable reply.

"Not much, I'm afraid. Two hundred men have been ordered to build an earthwork near Portsmouth, but on the mainland, there are no organized reserves, just aimless clumps of miltiamen puttering about and waiting for orders. Captain Branch informed me last night that Richmond may reorganize and put us in the same district as Norfolk."

Martin snorted and spat over the side. "The damned fools can 'reorganize' until the cows come home, and it makes no difference! We need heavy guns, shells, reliable powder, and some trained gunners instead of bumpkins posing as soldiers!"

"That may not be the worst of it," Parker said. "Rumor has it that our next commander will be Benjamin Huger."

Martin sputtered with disbelief. In the peacetime army, Huger had been an object of contempt. Sour-faced and indolent, an opinionated martinet who always managed, through political connections, to weasel out of strenuous duty, Huger had brought inertia and near paralysis to a number of drab administrative posts.

"Ben Huger is a barnacle on the ship of state!" growled Martin. He looked for a moment as though he were about to kick his bucket over the side. He was working himself into a righteous tirade when one of his men appeared at the water's edge, cupping his hands and hollering.

"Message for Commander Parker, sir!"

Parker crooked one arm over the barrel of the 32-pounder and leaned over as far as he dared. The soldier gestured vaguely in the direction of the lighthouse. "Signal flags from the lookouts, sir! Merchant ship in sight, two miles east of the cape, heading north!"

Parker's men cheered the news and two of them immediately started throwing pine logs into the firebox. The *Beaufort* began to vibrate as steam pressure accumulated.

"Sorry to leave you so abruptly, Colonel. If you have any dispatches for us to take back, I'll try to pick them up later."

Martin flung his pail onto the beach and started to climb back into the languid water. "Dispatches? What's the point, Mister Parker? I am tired of yelling at the deaf and pointing out the obvious to the blind. If Ben Huger does take command in Norfolk, I'd be better off writing an appeal to Abe Lincoln—at least I'd know someone would *read* it. Every time you boys go out and take a merchantman, you just focus more Yankee attention on this spot. Too many mosquito bites, and the dumbest ox will learn to bite back!"

Anxious to get up steam and be off, Parker nevertheless understood the colonel's point. All he could say in response, as the *Beaufort* backed away from the beach, was both obvious and banal: "I have my orders, Colonel, as you have yours."

Martin did not reply. He merely stood in the water, his homemade trident resting on one bony, sunburned shoulder, and glowered after the departing boat like Robinson Crusoe, freshly marooned.

Parker's mood brightened as the *Beaufort* gained speed and steered an arrow-straight course for the inlet. As she passed over the swash—the turbulent throat of the channel where tidal rips and submarine convections roiled the water into froth—the boat bounded high and crashed hard, throwing a brilliant fan of spray from her bow. Above, the afternoon sky glowed vast and vaulted, and the stiffening wind seemed to carry the scent of prey. Parker could almost imagine himself aboard a real man-of-war instead of a converted tugboat, and his men—to judge from their excitement and the bloodthirsty way they flashed their swords and clutched their rifles, straining for a glimpse of their target—seemed to fancy themselves Blackbeard's own devils. *This is more like it! Whatever else happens, we'll remember moments like this for the rest of our days.*

When they were clear of the swash and the boat stopped rocking and settled into a steady rhythm, Parker climbed to the top of the deckhouse and extended his telescope. At first he could see only the wavering unstable line of the horizon, but when his eyes adjusted he spotted a mast, five points off the port bow. He leaned his head into the pilothouse and ordered an interception course.

Suddenly, an eager brown face popped into view, startling him. It belonged to Able Seaman Spratley, a Georgia volunteer who had proved himself a natural gunner and who could often be found fussing with his beloved 32-pounder, polishing the already-polished aiming tackle, tightening ropes already taut, counting ammunition already tallied. Hot for the chase, Spratley bobbed up and down like a jack-in-the-box.

"Permission to load cannon, sir?"

Parker ruminated for a moment. They could not possibly haul into range for another half hour, but the sea was favorable and the powder unlikely to get wet.

"Permission granted, Seaman Spratley. Solid shot to begin with, if you please."

Parker knew Spratley and his crew would have preferred to lob exploding shells—in this regard, they were like boys playing with fireworks—but shells were hard to come by and solid shot ought to suffice. Registering a flicker of disappointment, Sprately saluted and vanished once more beneath the deckhouse roof. Soon Parker could hear the drill being executed with more enthusiasm than expertise. He was rather proud of the way these amateur militiamen had shaped up into a real crew, but there remained in the back of his mind a nagging awareness that they had not yet been in a real fight.

Their prey turned out to be the sailing brig *William McGilvery*, inward bound to Bangor, Maine, according to the lettering on her stern. Her skipper was making a bold run for it, crowding on every inch of canvas and hoping that the wind would last longer than the *Beaufort*'s supply of firewood. Parker was watching the fuel consumption closely. He estimated that if he could not intimidate the brig into stopping within the next twenty minutes, he might well have to give up the chase. When the range closed below two thousand yards, he gave permission for Spratley's crew to fire. Since the 32-pounder was rifled, it could reach that distance with some degree of accuracy. Parker ducked and covered his ears as the cannon boomed and hot reeking smoke blew back over his head. His gunners cheered, as they did whenever they fired the piece, without waiting to see the results.

Thanks to the mellow sunset-tinted light and pellucid air, Parker could see the ball arcing away. Seconds later, he saw a graceful plume of white rise about a hundred yards ahead of the fleeing brig. That might be enough to do it: a classic shot across the bow. If the *William McGilvery*'s captain had any lingering doubts as to the nature of the situation, he would have them no longer.

Parker watched through his glass, close enough now to see the minute shapes of the brig's crewmen running to and fro like disturbed ants. Not only did she not drop sail and come about, but she seemed to gain a knot or two as her helmsman steered toward the place where the cannonball had landed.

"By God, sir, he's making a run for it!"

"Commendable but futile. Another shot, Mister Sprately, whenever you please."

This time, the projectile tore a ragged furrow in the water only a ship's length from the brig. Still, it plowed on. Parker cursed. He was reaching the halfway point in his fuel and daylight was ebbing.

"All right, Mr. Spratley, try to get his attention with a shell. Four-second fuse, I should think."

Yelping like pups, the gunners switched to fused ammunition. After a moment's delay while the gun barrel was swabbed free of any lingering sparks, the rough iron wad, spitting fire, was rammed home. Flash and bang! Parker could hear the lumpy projectile hum in the air and could trace its sparkling path until it whistled between the brig's foresail and mainstays and burst close enough to shred canvas.

Now, at last, the merchantman hove to and the crew began dipping its sails. Parker unholstered his Colt and checked each of the loaded cylinders to make sure no spray had landed on the caps. Then he leaped back to the deck and congratulated the gun crew. A seven-man boarding party was already assembled, straining for their taste of action. They were well armed, although resistance was unlikely. A show of force, backed by the big gun's proximity, had always proved sufficient.

This time, Parker and his boarding party were greeted with a broadside of invective. The brig's captain, Master Hiram Carlisle, was a tough, stringy old seabird with sparse white whiskers and an Adam's apple that bobbed like a fishing cork. Somewhat to the consternation of his frightened sailors, Master Carlisle shook a knobby fist in Parker's face, cursed him for a "Damned Rebel!" and stamped on the decks like a man verging on seizure. Tobacco-brown spittle bubbled on the old man's lips. Only the tip of Parker's cutlass, unwaveringly held a few inches from his heart, seemed to restrain the New Englander from physically lashing out. Indeed, so prolonged and so overwrought was Master Carlisle's tirade that Parker began to suspect some motive other than honest pique. When Carlisle finally paused to draw breath, Parker suddenly heard a faint but regular *thump-thump!* from below, accompanied by a slight rhythmic vibration. Carlisle heard it too, and his eyes flashed with apprehension. Parker whirled about and pointed to two of his men.

"Get below and stop those men from scuttling the ship!"

A moment later, the chopping noises ceased, replaced by muffled cries. Then two Yankee sailors, prodded by bayonets, emerged from the aft cargo hatch. They were drenched in seawater and sweat, and one of them nursed a swelling cut on his forehead. One of the guards brandished an axe.

"They was knockin' holes in the hull, Cap'n Parker!"

Master Carlisle leered defiantly. "I'll give her to Davy Jones before I'll yield to you!" he sputtered.

Parker was torn between vexation at the old sailor's guile and admiration for his grit. He ordered Carlisle and his crew transferred to the *Beaufort*, where they were locked in the confines of the hold. Then he mustered every man he could spare and set about trying to save his prize.

The brig's cargo hold was ankle-deep in rising water. By following bubbling paths of turbulence, Parker located four ragged plate-sized holes in the bottom. Fortunately, the cargo consisted mainly of heavy tuns of Cuban molasses that, when manhandled onto their sides, proved adequate to plug the leaks. After an hour of heavy labor, with water now lapping at his shins, Parker was satisfied that the *William McGilvery* would stay afloat. He located the ship's pump, but found that it too had been mangled by the axe and was useless.

Night had fallen while he was below; the humid darkness surprised him when he returned to the open deck. Although the brig was now heavy and unwieldy, the sea was calm. Tow lines were rigged, and the *Beaufort* strained to achieve a modest headway of two or three knots, her waterlogged prize reluctantly following. Parker stationed a man on the stern with an axe, ready to cut the tow if the brig started taking on more water. At this rate, the return voyage would take all night, but after the excitement of the afternoon's chase and the hard work of salvage, he was damned if he would return empty-handed. After determining that all was well, Parker set the watch schedule, then went to his modest cabin and, fully dressed in his salt-stiff uniform, flopped down into a deep and righteous sleep.

He awoke, with great reluctance, when Seaman Spratley shook him. "Cap'n Parker, sir, you'd better come on deck and see this!"

It was the last hour of night on the sea around them. Like the whisper of a conspiracy, some faint diffusion of predawn murk gave definition to a heavy glove of fog. Even the sound of the *Beaufort*'s engine was muffled and furtive. At first, following where his men so anxiously pointed, Parker could see nothing but sluggish banks of gray smoke. Then, as if conjured by a sorcerer's spell, great black wedges materialized, knifing into a waveless oily swell, the nearest barely a cable's length away from the tugboat's starboard side. Beneath his feet, a dull steady vibration beat like the ocean's secret heart.

"Dear God Almighty," breathed Samuel Parker. "It's the U.S. Navy!"

Olympian and majestic, disdainful of the low and insignificant

Beaufort, the squadron lumbered past at moderate speed. The great dark cannon-studded bulks faded in and out of sight, spectral leviathans locked in purpose. From their ponderous side-wheels spread wakes tall enough to slosh water over the tug's gunwales. Straining his sight, Parker identified a steam frigate (the *Wabash* or the *Minnesota,* perhaps), a seemingly gigantic long-range side-wheel cruiser (the *Susquehanna,* he was certain, having once served aboard her), an indeterminate and ghostly number of medium-sized gunboats, and at least two enormous transports. Parker extrapolated the firepower he knew these vessels carried: 9- and 11-inch rifles, 100-pounders, Parrotts and Dahlgrens, at least one hundred guns. And in the transports, a thousand men.

Why no one aboard that grand and powerful fleet spotted the *Beaufort* and its wallowing charge, Parker could not guess: carelessness, low visibility, inexperienced lookouts, or arrogant disdain. Perhaps—and this was even more frightening—they *had* been spotted but deemed unworthy of a broadside. By this hour, the *Beaufort* was within a few miles of the Outer Banks. That seemed the most logical explanation: this fleet was under orders not to fire, not to reveal its presence.

Majestic and indifferent, the black shapes plowed on, steering south-southwest, until they were lost to sight. Aboard the *Beaufort,* men began to breathe again. Parker felt his stomach unknot as the last vessel disappeared into the landward gloom. Beside him, frozen to the railing, stood gunner Spratley, muttering a prayer. When he spoke, it was an awestruck whisper.

"Cap'n Parker, sir, where are they going?"

"Can't you guess, Mister Spratley? Can't you guess?"

Spratley bowed his head and murmured, "God have mercy on the men at Hatteras."

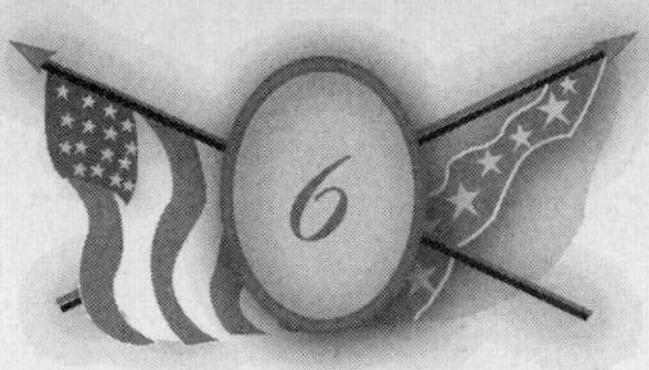

"Once More, Boys, for Twice the Glory!"

SMALL FAVORS THANKFULLY RECEIVED, LARGER ONES IN PROPORTION—The fall of the Hatteras forts will have the effect of detaining certain regiments to guard the state's inner coasts against Butler's hen-house-robbing, home-burning, negro-thieving troops, but it will hardly require more men to guard the inland shores than the Outer Banks. With any alertness and preparation, no Yankee force need ever be allowed to penetrate Albemarle Sound.

—The Wilmington Journal, September 5 1861

Old Popeye Butler is not so big a fool as he appears, thought Colonel Rush Hawkins, commander of the Ninth New York Infantry. General Butler's conversation could be lively and the man himself quite engaging—as long as you avoided becoming mesmerized by the rolling of his defective eye. And the moist heavy truculence of his lips. And the way his triple jowls trembled like jelly when he made one of his numerous emphatic gestures or laughed at one of his own coarse jokes.

Butler and Hawkins had never met before, but the forced companionship of the voyage on Commodore Stringham's flagship, the USS *Minnesota*—and the undertone of tension surrounding this first Federal amphibious operation of the war—had caused them to strike up a friendship. They had things in common, despite the fourteen years that separated their ages. Both men hungered, unabashedly, for martial glory, and both had donned uniforms directly from civilian occupations of some importance. Both were lawyers with a taste for political power. At age twenty-nine, Hawkins was on leave from a New York firm that specialized in the legal problems of the rich, and he knew that Butler could teach him a lot about ambition, influence, and the steady acquisition of wealth.

Of course, long before he ever met Butler, Rush Hawkins had known those things about the general; anyone who read the newspapers knew them. What surprised Hawkins was Butler's intense, almost childlike fascination with military technology. The night before they sailed, Hawkins and Colonel Max Weber, commander of the mostly German-speaking Twentieth New York, had dined with Commodore Stringham and his subordinates in the upholstered comfort of the *Minnesota*'s wardroom. Inevitably, there was much talk about their objectives, the two forts guarding Hatteras Inlet, and about how to subdue them. The naval officers radiated optimism: the fleet carried 149 guns, at least two-thirds of which were heavier and longer-ranged than the old 32-pounders presumed to be the Rebels' heaviest ordnance. Deploying metaphors of tempest and tidal wave, the navy men seemed certain that the enemy works would evaporate like a child's sandcastle in heavy surf—all that their army colleagues need do was wade ashore and accept the Rebels' surrender. While the discussion waxed sanguine, Butler busied himself, between gulps of sherry, by making curious geometrical sketches on the pages of a dispatch notebook. Intrigued, Hawkins bent sideways to get a better view, and became even more mystified when he beheld not only tangents, angles, and cosines, but several rather arcane mathematical equations. After contemplating his notes for a few minutes, Butler raised his big bulbous head, his eyes protruding as though the skull behind them were filled with pressured air.

"Tell me, Commodore Stringham, how do you plan to form and maneuver your ships?"

Stringham's hollow-cheeked face bobbed for a moment on the gristle stalk of his neck, like a poorly tethered balloon. Then he forced his puritanical features into a thin and slightly condescending smile.

"General Butler, I don't propose to 'maneuver' the ships at all. We'll form a line abreast of the forts, drop anchor, and open fire. When the Rebel guns are silenced, you and Colonel Weber can disembark your men and round up the prisoners. I don't expect there will be anymore to it than that."

Stringham turned back to his navy colleagues and was about to resume his interrupted conversation. Butler forestalled this with a heavy, insistent, prefatory cough. Then, while Hawkins watched in quiet surprise, Butler began a lengthy and highly technical discourse on the current state of naval and coastal ordnance, punctuating his remarks by jabbing a pudgy index finger at the arcane scribbles he had drawn. Hawkins several times lost the thread of Butler's reasoning, but after numerous digressions into the fields of metallurgy, steam mechanics, nautical engineering, chemistry, physics, and contemporary military history (an impassioned summary of the lessons to be learned from the recent Crimean War), he seemed to be propounding a comprehensive set of tactics for ship-to-shore bombardment. He rattled on about facing angles, penetration coefficients, propellant charges, fuse lengths, air friction, and the relative efficacy of various calibers and configurations of cannons. For all his bombast and irritating self-satisfaction, it was clear to Hawkins that this ungainly toad of a politician-turned-soldier had educated himself zealously in the science of modern warfare. While Butler pontificated, Stringham and his officers sat with glazed, impervious faces and thin, empty smiles of bored indulgence. When Butler finally ran out of steam, his quivering cheeks dappled with red splotches, Stringham nodded curtly in his direction.

"All well and good, General Butler, but quite beside the point. I shall attack those forts the way ships have been attacking forts for the last three hundred years. Nothing more is required."

First Hawkins, then a couple of the younger naval officers, tried to steer the conversation away from the shoals on which it had run aground, but both Butler and Stringham had become sulky and remote. A sullen and brittle mood settled over the table, quite dispelling the earlier comraderie, and when Butler excused himself, on the pretext of sudden indigestion, no one urged him to stay for another round of toasts. In the awkward silence attending his retirement, Butler managed to have the last word, in a manner of speaking. He waddled through the swinging saloon doors; just before he opened the hatchway to the outside deck, he paused long enough to break wind, producing a serpentine sonority that reminded Hawkins of a spit-clogged trombone.

Not long afterward, Hawkins also took his leave; even though he was wrought-up by the prospect of action, he wanted to be fresh and rested in the morning. On his way back to his bunk, Hawkins passed General Butler's cabin and saw that the lights were still on. From within, he heard the rumbling cough of a heavy cigar-smoker. On impulse, he knocked.

Butler seemed surprised and genuinely pleased to see Hawkins.

After a few awkward seconds, he invited the colonel inside, thrust a cigar into his hand, and dispensed a generous portion of brandy from a well-stocked bar. Soon, the two officers were deep in conversation. Butler's interest in military science, Hawkins soon learned, was both genuine and passionate. In fact, the general considered himself something of a visionary, especially in contrast to such traditional conservatives as Stringham, whom he referred to once as "a moss-backed old snapping turtle." One drink led to another, and before long, the mood between the two officers became one of mutual interest and regard, if not exactly of nascent friendship. Hawkins realized that Ben Butler was no idiot, and that Butler's unapologetic drive for self-advancement, along with his ruthless instinct for seizing and manipulating political advantage, were at least in part motivated by the sad but ineluctable fact of his physical repulsiveness. Those same qualities, had they been manifested in a dashing man of handsome physique, would have made Butler the object of masculine envy and female attentiveness.

At one point, after the two men had emptied their glasses several times, Butler took Hawkins into his confidence by showing him a private journal, bound in wine-red leather, in which Butler routinely jotted down notes and notions about modern warfare. He flipped the pages for Hawkins with the enthusiasm of a little boy showing off a collection of exotic marbles. In quick procession, Hawkins saw a hot-air balloon with a wicker gondola capable of carrying three men—one to steer, one to observe with a telescope, and one to unleash the several explosive shells that dangled from the keel on long hawser ropes (a "bombing machine" said Butler); a breech-loading rifled cannon topped with a strange iron box—"a magazine-fed artillery piece, capable of firing four shots with a single loading," Butler said; a long cylindrical iron tube powered by a small steam engine and steered with metal vanes—"a self-propelled torpedo," said Butler, which could be launched from forts against blockading ships; braided strands of wire studded with double-headed nails—"a barbed fence," said Butler, for protecting entrenchments. As the general explained each of these marvels, Hawkins's appreciation grew.

"Alas," said Butler finally, as he closed the journal and returned it to a drawer beneath his bunk, "too many of my ideas require engineering skills and mechanical devices that have not yet been perfected, or even invented. Still, what is modern warfare but a vast working laboratory? If the war lasts long enough, I shall find scientists and inventors who share my visions. One way or another, I shall patent enough designs to emerge from the war a wealthy and respected man. The conflict is too large and too diverse to be left to the narrow vision of the 'professionals,' Colonel Hawkins. Most of them, like old Stringham, are focused on the next rung of their promotion, bound by old habits, shackled by traditions. This is a war that needs the vision, the enthusiasm, of the informed and passionate amateur!"

" 'Amateur,' General? You rate yourself too humbly!" Both men recognized the unction in Hawkins's choice of words, but Butler, who was well schooled in the uses of flattery, received it as his due; Hawkins, whose ambitions were as driving as Butler's, though less clear-focused because of his youth, came to polite pandering quite naturally. In this regard, they were kindred spirits.

"I mean 'amateur' in the original Latin sense of the word: 'one who loves a thing.' You know, Colonel, *amo-amas-amat*? There is enough glory to go around, if you know how to conjure it."

Butler smiled like a Borgia pope contemplating a roomful of suborned cardinals. "Tomorrow morning, Colonel Hawkins, you and your regiment will be the vanguard of the first amphibious operation launched by the United States Navy since the invasion of Mexico. Succeed, and your name will be in headlines."

"And so will yours, General."

The two men eyed each other with wary understanding. Then Butler raised his glass in a toast. "To glory!"

By the time Hawkins lurched back to his cabin, it was two o'clock in the morning and he was decidedly drunk. He lay down on his bunk fully dressed, draping his sash and sword belt over a chair. His last waking thoughts were about the future. He *would* find fame and glory, and he would discreetly follow Butler's lead. It was not necessary—perhaps not even desirable and maybe impossible—to like him. Lincoln, it was said, positively loathed Ben Butler, but dared not oppose him because of the general's web of political connections. There was much that an ambitious young officer could learn from such a mentor. *As long as I keep my gaze averted from that damned dead-cuttlefish of an eyeball.*

When an orderly woke Hawkins at seven o'clock, he faced God's own wrath of a headache. But even as he donned his sword, Hawkins felt the pain recede, replaced or at least submerged beneath a new sensation: a fist of fearful excitement that clenched in his stomach. I am about to go into battle, he thought. What a wonder that is! *Dear God, please show me the hilt of Glory's sword, that I may grasp it and hold it aloft for all to see.*

He left the flagship at eight o'clock, in company with Colonel Weber. Two sailors rowed the officers to the transports where their respective regiments were mustered on deck. Hawkins's second-in-command, Major Junius Brown, welcomed him aboard with a parade-ground salute and the ringing words: "Ninth New York Infantry all present and accounted for, sir! Will you inspect the troops?"

Indeed he would, and with a preening sense of pride. There was no sharper-looking regiment in the Union army. For some reason unconnected with actual military prowess, the haute couture of military dress in 1860 was patterned after the French Algerian regiments, the Zouaves. Drawing on public subscription and, to a limited extent, his own funds, Hawkins had taken care that the Ninth New York should be more Zouave than all the other Zouave regiments he had seen. Each man wore loose, ballooned powder-blue trousers with bright magenta stripes down the outer seams, tucked snugly into high black boots polished to a fine gloss; loose waistcoat-style jackets trimmed with matching magenta whorls and edged all around with dark maroon; a scarlet sash wide enough to cover the abdomen, so that even a stout man appeared fit and flat-stomached; on the head, a matching scarlet fez with dark blue tassel. By now, many of the men had grown facial hair to match Hawkins's own: long pomaded curls in back, an aggressive wedge of chin whiskers as sharply trimmed as prized topiary, and an extravagant moustache curving upward in waxed points. *Oh, but they are natty and handsome!* Hawkins felt a tingle of pride as he inspected each company of the four-hundred-man unit. *Let me inspire them to fight as keenly as they drill.*

His Zouaves. His peacock-proud and ever-so-stylish men. What officer could boast a finer-looking command?

Not that he actually knew many of them well on a personal level, of course. Not even Major Junius Brown, who had served as the Ninth New York's second-in-command since the regiment had mustered at White Plains. Hawkins discouraged familiarity, having read somewhere that it was "bad for discipline" and having likewise formed a belief that an aloof commander was more respected than a backslapper. He knew that Brown was from Albany and had been a minor railroad executive before the war; he also knew that Brown discharged his duties punctually, maintained a proper professional attitude toward his superiors, and was capable of handling the vast amount of paperwork generated by a regiment in wartime—an aspect of command that Hawkins found extremely onerous. Brown was also a good intermediary between Hawkins and his various company commanders, most of whom were, to their colonel, just names on the muster roll.

Hawkins scanned the ranks and spotted one man he did know by name and whose welfare was a concern. Alfred Dunn, the color sergeant of Company A, was a great white oak of a man whose majestic beard seemed thick enough to stop a minié ball. Dunn had been a Hudson Valley dairy farmer for more than forty years, but he still spoke with a rough working-class English accent. He could not have been less than sixty-five years old, and would certainly have been rejected for service, in spite of his remarkable vigor, had it not been for one incredible fact: Dunn had served as a drummer boy at the Battle of Waterloo, and he had the papers to prove it. His story quite overawed the enlistment board and his sharpness at drill soon earned him promotion to sergeant. You need only look at him to feel his massive confidence and inner strength. The young soldiers in his company worshiped him, and Rush Hawkins had on several occasions questioned the old man closely about his youthful adventures. After a glass or two of whiskey, old Dunn could talk for hours about the things he had seen on that incredible day, and sometimes, when Hawkins was feeling melancholy, he would summon the sergeant to his quarters and ask him to describe, one more time, the charge of the Scots Grays or the Old Guard's Last Stand.

Hawkins observed the color sergeant now, youthfully erect, and wondered once again if there were not some less dangerous duty to which he could assign the old warrior, without offending his dignity. But you only had to look into Alfred Dunn's eyes to know that he would reject any such suggestion.

Moved to oratory, Hawkins mounted a supply crate and spoke briefly to his men, reminding them that they would be the first Federal soldiers to set foot on a Rebel shore, and that the eyes of their wives and sweethearts, indeed the eyes of the nation, would be upon them this day. When he finished, he drew his sword and cried: "Let me hear your battle cry, men!" and four hundred voices responded in full-throated unison: "*Zou-zou-zou! Zou-zou-zou!*"

By this time, hard summer sunlight had wiped away all but a few scraps of mist. The day would be sultry. Standing with his officers at the starboard rail, Hawkins could see the top of the Hatteras lighthouse, and through his telescope he could see some Confederate signalers urgently waving flags of alarm. The shape of the nearest Rebel bastion, Fort Clark, was still dim and blurred, but its garrison would have seen the fleet materializing out of the morning haze and would be counting its masts: three modern steam frigates, the *Wabash, Cumberland,* and *Minnesota*; a big side-wheel steamer, the *Monticello*; and three medium-sized gunboats. Behind the combatant ships, two large transports and a gaggle of landing boats were strung out behind a half-dozen auxiliary tugs.

For the next hour, the infantry could only watch as the North Carolina coastline grew solid and more defined: long ridges of sand bewhiskered with sea oats and clumps of gnarled, wind-sculpted brush, not a tree in sight, nor any other mark of human habitation save the low gray walls of the two forts and the Rebel flags hanging limply above the ramparts. Ponderously but with admirable precision, Stringham's warships maneuvered into line about two thousand yards from Fort Clark, dropped anchors, and waited for the commodore's signal. He gave it at precisely 10:05 A.M.

Every starboard gun in the fleet discharged at once, sending a heavy slap of vibration through the air and causing many of the infantry to cringe involuntarily. At the first taste of drifting powder-smoke, Hawkins's men began yelling "Huzzah! Huzzah!" The first broadsides spattered all around the target—some balls lashed the surf; some smacked into the beach and bounced inland, spewing fans of sandy spray until they lost momentum and buried themselves in the dunes. Some shells shrieked over the fort; some exploded above it, pocking the sky with white chalky clouds and yellow flashes. About one-third of the projectiles struck Fort Clark fair and hard, furrowing its sod-covered walls and uprooting great fountains of muck whose particles hung in the air like smears of ink before raining back down onto the sweating heads and backs of the Rebel gun crews.

Of course the fort replied, as best it could. Hawkins was amazed to see a half-dozen black dots curving out toward the ships, so slow and deliberate in their flight that one officer remarked, "I declare, I do believe you could extend your arms and catch them," to which Hawkins replied, "Yes, but you would only do that once and then you would have no arms left to catch another." None of the Rebel balls landed within a hundred feet of Stringham's line. Observing this shortfall, the sailors cheered and redoubled their efforts at their cannon.

By eleven o'clock, the whole landscape of Hatteras Inlet was so obscured by a huge gritty muddle of smoke and roiling sand that nothing could be seen of the Confederates' fortifications. But the Union gun crews already had the range and continued methodically to lob salvo after salvo into the murk. The Rebels no longer replied; they had seen the futility of trying to hit Stringham's ships and were obviously conserving ammunition for the Federal landing. Either that, or Stringham's fire, which Hawkins estimated at approximately one thousand rounds per hour, had already wrecked the Rebel guns. Hawkins fervently hoped so. Even a single surviving 32-pounder could wreak havoc among the landing boats, and for all their puffed-up zeal, he did not know how much of a shelling his untried men could really handle.

At noon, the Federal landing boats went in; not a shot was fired at Hawkins and the three hundred men who landed in the first hour. But with typical Hatteras perversity, the wind suddenly shifted and strengthened into strong southerly gusts. Previously tranquil surf turned rough, rolling up turbulent white-fanged waves that capsized two of the empty boats heading back out to ferry the final one-hundred-man installment of the Ninth New York. Stringham ordered a temporary halt in landing operations.

By early afternoon, weather conditions were so bad that Stringham was compelled to order his ships to steam farther out from shore. Rush Hawkins and three-fourths of his command were stranded on the beach, nine hundred yards north of Fort Clark, with no food or water except for what they carried, no ammunition for their two little howitzers, and much of their rifle powder too damp to use. Taking stock of his situation, Hawkins felt a tickle of dread; what had started as a grand and bloodless adventure had quickly turned into a serious predicament. During their first hour under the August sun, confident that additional supplies would soon be landed, his men had drunk liberally from their canteens. In their woolen uniforms they sweated like mules, and some were already complaining of heat exhaustion. The Zouaves looked to Hawkins for instruction, for direction, for a purpose more productive than merely standing about in salt-stiff shoes, their eyes smarting and lips cracking.

What to do? Where to start untying the elusive knot of glory? Hawkins shook his own canteen and discovered that it was half-empty; he did not remember drinking from it, but he must have. He rationed himself to a single hot gulp, then began to issue orders. He bade the troops to form up by companies and told the officers to make sure the men's rifles held dry charges. Then he slogged to the top of a sand dune and waved his sword to gain their attention.

"Men of the Ninth Zouaves! The sea has taken sides against us! I will not minimize our plight: we are alone on a hostile shore. Neither the rest of our regiment nor any of Colonel Weber's Twentieth New York can be landed under these conditions. We are short of food and water, and half our ammunition is wet. If we want more provisions, we will have to take them from the Rebels! After the pounding they have taken this morning, the Rebs can't have much stomach left for a real fight. We will advance toward the enemy by companies, and halt at my command when we're close enough to see what their condition is. Slow march! Follow me! Let's hear the battle cry!"

"*Zou! Zou! Zou!*" the men responded, albeit without their earlier enthusiasm. Hawkins detailed ten men to stay behind and guard the howitzers, then led the rest south, toward the boiling tip of the island, where smoke and spraying sand from Stringham's renewed bombardment obscured all sight of their objectives.

As they marched, the men's spirits improved. They had covered half the distance from their landing site to Fort Clark, close enough to feel the thump of exploding shells, when a panic-stricken cry went up from the rear of the column. "Cavalry!" someone cried. Hawkins turned about and saw a cloud of powdery sand scrolling in their direction and, wraithlike within it, the shapes of galloping horses.

"Signal the gunboats to fire at them!" he yelled, and a signalman stepped out to the water's edge and waved his banners accordingly.

But the Rebel "cavalry," as it drew closer, proved to be a small herd of wild ponies. Hawkins wondered where they came from. Had they swum ashore from some Elizabethan shipwreck? Had they been bred by the pirates who once haunted these waters? Had any man ever ridden one?

"Stop the shelling!" he called to the signalman, but the first salvo was already on its way. A curtain of sand slashed up in front of the herd and one of the lead ponies, a handsome brown-and-white colt, was grazed in the stomach as he ran. Keening with pain, the animal ran right past Hawkins, teeth bared and eyes aflame, intestines unwinding like a long purple snake from its cut-open belly. Still screaming, the horse plunged ahead and vanished into the shroud of shellfire near the fort.

The sudden and terrible sight stopped the Ninth New York in its tracks, as though an angel of woe had flown above their heads and covered them with its cold shadow. Hawkins called for a ten-minute rest, then he scurried to the crest of a waist-high dune, extended his spyglass, and rested his elbows against the scorching sand. Stringham's bombardment was desultory now and a southerly wind had cleared some of the smoke. Through the glass, the northern face of Fort Clark looked as though it had been furrowed by a giant tiller: scorched and flayed wedges of sod were flung all about and the parapet seemed to have been bitten into by a large rabid animal. Hawkins saw what appeared to be the muzzle of a cannon pointing at the sky, the stump of a shattered flagpole, a smear of ruptured sandbags and splintered planks. Refocusing to a slightly greater depth, he saw a ragged group of men staggering from a sally port on the bastion's western side and running pell-mell across a marshy causeway leading to Fort Hatteras, just barely visible through the haze and lingering smoke.

"They are running, boys!" he cried. "We'll storm the place with cold steel! Zouaves, fix bayonets!"

Despite their thirst and discomfort and exhaustion, the men cheered and snapped steel onto their rifles with parade-ground smartness, then launched a spontaneous charge before Hawkins could bark the order. Pleased by their spirit, he waved his sword and stumbled forward through the ankle-deep sand. Observing the Zouaves's attack, Stringham ordered his gunners to cease firing. Now that he had lurched close enough to see details of Fort Clark's mauled embrasures and dismounted cannon, Hawkins fervently hoped he was not running straight into a trap—a couple of field pieces crammed with grapeshot would have stopped his charge like a brick wall. But no resistance of any kind met the New Yorkers as they scrambled up the ramparts on hands and knees, shouting wildly.

In no aspect was Fort Clark impressive. Several of its guns had been dismounted by the Navy's fire and the rest had been spiked. A methodical search revealed two musty barrels of powder, but not a single shell or cannonball—the Rebs had run out of ammunition hours ago. The garrison had lived in oven-hot tin-roofed shacks and slept on piles of weeds. From an open latrine rose abominable odors—the castings of fear-churned bowels. Indeed, the fort's whole interior resembled a pig sty more than a military installation: torn boxes, papers, scraps of uniforms, broken ramrods, stove-in buckets, a pair of eyeglasses, and an empty holster, a bugle cut in half by shell fragments—the place was an ungodly mess. Hawkins's men found bloodstains fading into the sand, but no bodies; clearly the retreating men had taken their wounded and dead, if any, with them. What they did *not* find were any traces of food or fresh water; the water barrels had been hacked open and drained, and cartons of hardtack had been drenched with seawater. It was one o'clock in the afternoon, and the sun pounded straight down into the squalid rectangle, amplifying the stench and causing the victors to stagger beneath its bronze oppression.

Perhaps Fort Clark was not much of a prize, reflected Rush Hawkins, but by God it was the first Confederate work to be captured in battle anywhere in North America. And *he* had done it, leading a valiant assault. Never mind that the charge had been unopposed—to the men watching offshore, it must have looked gallant indeed. Hawkins fancied he could actually taste the glory: sharp, metallic, astringent. Next week—he would bet money on it—this charge would be immortalized by a front-page engraving in *Harper's Weekly*. He would be famous, perhaps even decorated, as the first successful commander in the whole Federal army. Unable to contain his joy, he flung his arms wide beneath the raging sun and howled triumphantly.

Two hours later he was barely able to stand and his breathing was scorched and labored. He spat until he ran out of saliva but could not rid his mouth entirely of sand; and his men were coated with it on every sweat-soaked inch of their bodies. They had searched every corner of the fort, desperately seeking food and water, but had found no trace of either. Their own canteens were dry. Ominously dangerous surf told them that no supply boats would come ashore this day. In the flats between dunes, knots of desperately thirsty men scraped holes in the sand, hoping to find potable water. A few—tougher or more tormented than the rest—actually leaned down into these pits and sucked on the brackish slush that collected in the bottom. The lucky ones vomited up this vile liquid before it could work into their guts; the ones who managed to keep it down now lay in whatever shade was available, their stomachs bloated and cramped, moaning with pain.

At twilight—after a patrol failed to locate the dead horse—someone shot a large seagull, butchered the filthy thing with a bayonet, and tried to roast it over a driftwood fire. The meat was gray and stringy and cooked up like clots of blackened phlegm. Only the man who had shot the bird actually tried to eat some of it and he only kept it down for a minute or two.

With darkness, the offshore wind died and the damp air within the fort thickened, heavy with sickly odor. Utterly drained, the men of the Ninth New York lay sprawled in wretchedness all about, too miserable even to complain and too weary to do more than paw feebly at the big hungry mosquitoes that buzzed tormentingly in their ears and fattened impudently on their exposed flesh. Hawkins posted sentries, but he knew they would fall asleep. Given the condition of the Ninth New York, a single fresh company of Rebels, armed with nothing more than rocks and clubs, could recapture the fort with ease, and there was nothing Hawkins could do to stop them. The last thing he heard before dozing off was a brave but despairing bit of doggerel intoned by a Long Island corporal: "*Now I lay me down to sleep, in muck that's many fathoms deep. If I should die before I wake, just hunt me up with an oyster rake.*"

Thunder woke them. At 7:30, Stringham's flotilla formed a crescent around Fort Hatteras and began a blistering bombardment. Hawkins's men, most of them unable to speak above a raw croak, dragged crates and stools to the south wall and became spectators, seeking to distract themselves from the torments of hunger and thirst and insect bites. Emboldened by yesterday's one-sided victory, Stringham had stationed his ships closer inshore today. The shorter range and calmer seas dramatically improved the fleet's gunnery. Using his watch, a pencil stub, and a message pad, Hawkins did some calculations. He found that, on average, the navy was hitting Hatteras with twenty-eight rounds every minute. Yet the Rebs fought back, as best they could. At 8:14, a round of solid shot struck the *Monticello*, smashing her boat davits and tearing a big splintery gash in her deck. Over the next three hours, the defenders scored other hits, cutting some rigging, perforating a couple of smokestacks, chopping off spars, and—he learned later—damaging the *Monticello*'s galley. But the Rebels' fire soon grew ragged and by eleven o'clock it ceased altogether. Shortly thereafter, a little band of confederates stood up on the sagging ramparts and waved a tattered white sheet. By that time, the fleet had lowered its landing boats and the men of Weber's Twentieth New York were filling them with blue uniforms. The sight stirred resentment in Hawkins's breast. Struggling to moisten his tongue, he turned to the men nearest him and croaked, "They're surrendering, boys! The damned Rebs are giving up! And Weber's men are coming ashore to take the fort. After all we have suffered, it is we who should have that honor! If we hurry, we can get there first! Can you make one more effort, boys? For twice the glory?"

The singing corporal from Long Island, who happened to be standing next to Hawkins, peered at him with undisguised astonishment. Hawkins turned upon the man and grasped his jacket lapels, flushed with a sudden energy that came from some mysterious depth of ambition and desire. Incredulous bloodshot eyes stared back at him from under salt-encrusted brows. The corporal's cheeks were like parchment; he was dehydrated, sweated out, and his jaw worked side to side as though his tongue were too swollen to find accommodation. Livid red bite-marks covered him like a pox.

"Are you with me, man?" Hawkins shouted.

The corporal peered anxiously around, acutely aware that he had suddenly become the spokesman for the entire regiment. No ripple of inspiration or renewed vigor passed through the other men gathered nearby—their faces were sullen and drawn. Then the corporal turned back and faced Hawkins, who was choleric with emotion and who had once more drawn his completely useless sword. With the eternal instinct of the infantryman, the corporal understood that here was an officer who would inflict any hardship on his men, if doing so brought him another dollop of "glory"; and any man who opposed him, whether from common sense or sheer exhaustion, was likely to be brought up on charges. Something in the corporal's gaze hinted at the imminence of mutiny and Hawkins drew back from that dagger-flick of rage. Then a tall shadow fell over both men and Color Sergeant Dunn appeared, glaring down at the corporal, making a low growling sound in his throat and humbling him with an expression of contempt, as if to say: *I am three times your age, but I am ready to go where my commander sends me.* Drawing his breath in very slowly, the corporal finally replied, "I reckon we can give it one more push, Colonel Hawkins, as long as them Rebels aren't shooting at us."

"Good man!" boomed Hawkins, thrusting his sword in the general direction of their smoldering objective. "Zouaves, quick march!" Without glancing back to see how many followed him, Hawkins stumbled awkwardly down the shell-pocked face of the southern wall, splashed through a scum-covered tidal pond, and lurched stiffly across the intervening dunes. Perhaps a third of his command came staggering after him, some of them limping and using their rifles for support, others growling curses from sun-cracked lips, in no order whatever, a mob more than a unit, half-leprous in appearance and showing the trapped but determined expression of men who know that the only way to end their agony is to press on and endure one last round of suffering. Shamed by the sight of Sergeant Dunn stoically advancing, they staggered forward.

Fresh and riled up, the men of Weber's regiment leaped from their boats as soon as the keels grated on bottom-sand. Burdened by packs and weapons, a few of them were knocked down by waves and came up sputtering. While Weber's companies formed ranks on the beach, Hawkins staggered on, following the point of his own sword, never looking back. When he reached the gate of Fort Hatteras, he was greeted by a grimy knot of Confederate officers, fidgeting uneasily beneath their flag of surrender. To them, Hawkins looked like a madman, his hair and beard white with salt, his lips blistered, his eyes feverish. He sounded like a madman, too, when he drew himself erect in front of the Confederates, saluted them with his sword, and tried to draw enough breath to accept their surrender in the name of . . . something or other. What actually came from his mouth was almost unintelligible.

"AYE . . . ha' . . . HONOR . . . to . . . cep . . . yer . . . S'RENDER . . . ghennelmen."

Then he fainted into the arms of a Rebel lieutenant who stank of sweat and mildew. And strewn behind him, fallen or kneeling or twitching helplessly on their backs like upended turtles, moaning under the pitiless glare of the sky, were 148 men of the Ninth New York.

Two men later died of sunstroke. They were the only Federal fatalities of the battle. When some of Hawkins's subordinates filed a written protest regarding his callous and vainglorious behavior, Hawkins's new patron, General Benjamin Butler, made sure the petition was squelched. As the originator of the first successful Northern operation of the war, Butler was feted and praised when he returned to Washington. Rush Hawkins was promoted to command the entire Outer Banks garrison, leaping ahead of the senior and incredulous Colonel Weber. Two weeks later, courtesy of Ben Butler, Hawkins received a fresh copy of *Harper's Weekly,* and there on the front page was the very engraving he had fantasized: the gallant Rush Hawkins charging with drawn sword in front of a phalanx of valiant Zouaves, while shot and shell rained down on them from an imaginary fortress that bore virtually no resemblance to the real Hatteras works. For days thereafter, Hawkins proudly showed the image to anyone of any rank who came within range.

August 30, 1861
Aboard the USS Minnesota
Off Hatteras Inlet, North Carolina
Dearest Mother—

Two days ago, I participated in the largest Naval operation since the War with Mexico, and I want to jot down a few lines about it for you while the excitement still runs in my veins. This was my first experience with real Action, and I must say that in terms of spectacle and stirring gratification, it was all I could have wished!

Our fleet was given the task of providing covering fire for an assault on two strategic Rebel forts guarding the mouth of the Inlet, from which in recent weeks so many privateers have sallied forth to raid our merchant ships. Under the command of the weather-beaten old Flag Officer Stringham (or, as we like to call him, "Old Sting-em," for his rough tongue and dictatorial manner), our ship was third in line, behind the Wabash *and the* Cumberland. *Those two ships reached their assigned stations at about 10 o'clock and began the shelling. My ship reached station about fifteen minutes later, and joined in.*

Oh, Mother, words cannot describe the pleasure and excitement of the moment when we fired our first broadside! Our whole line erupted into a mass of flame and smoke. Very soon we had the range of the closest fort and through my glass I could see tents and huts torn apart, and Rebel bodies flying through the air. Three times the Secessionist flag was shot down, and three times replaced by the gallant defenders until a shot struck that banner square and blew it to threads.

My gun crew maintained a hot and steady fire, until, at the bombardment's height, one of the sailors got so excited that he dropped the sponger overboard! It was unthinkable that my cannon alone should fall silent, so I yelled at the man to dive in and retrieve the impliment. "Oh, Master Cushing, I cannot swim!" pleaded the fellow, his eyes wide with distress. No time could be wasted, so I dropped my sword on the deck, tossed my cap to the nearest man, and plunged into the sea, which was about eighteen feet below. I grasped the sponger without difficulty and handed it to a seaman who had clambered down on a ratline. Then I took the same rope and scrambled back on deck. From start to finish, the whole incident occupied only a few moments, and we quickly resumed fire as though nothing had happened. But our captain had observed it, and instead of chastising me for my crewman's carelessness, he has praised me by name in his official report and recommended me for promotion! At this rate, a few more battles should see me elevated to Admiral!

Your loving son,
Will

The Banshee Sails (Without an Alligator)

A DANGEROUS NEGRO—On Thursday last, Mr. E. McBride, a resident of neighboring Onslow County and the town of Jacksonville, was killed by a negro, under the following circumstances: For some outrageous conduct, he thought it his duty to punish the negro, and so sent him to the corn crib on the pretext of gathering corn, while Mr. McBride summoned a neighbor to assist him in subduing the negro, who was a strong and wilful young buck. When the neighbor came up, Mr. McBride prepared to enter the corn crib. As he stooped for that purpose, the negro smote him a dastardly blow with a plank, then fled headlong into the woods. Mr. McBride died the same night, never speaking a word after receipt of the blow. It is supposed that his murderer will try to reach Yankee lines near Morehead City. We have no further description of him than his name, which is "Amos." <u>Look out for him</u> (and for all other suspicious persons, black or white).

—The Wilmington Journal, January 3 1861

In late July, Major Harry Burgwyn, scion of a prominent East Coast clan, assumed the duties of executive officer of the Twenty-sixth North Carolina. Burgwyn was a graduate of Virginia Military Institue, where he had studied under Stonewall Jackson and some other now-famous confederate leaders; he looked, acted, and thought like a professional soldier. A beardless, slender, tight-wound youth fresh from celebrating his twentieth birthday at home, he was an unknown quantity to the men of his new regiment, most of whom found him rigid to the point of priggishness. In the beginning, Burgwyn's relations with Zeb Vance were strained, and his relations with the rank and file often bordered on mutual hostility. Vance had dutifully studied the official field regulations, but made no secret of how boring and picky he thought many of them were. On the morning after Burgwyn's arrival in camp, Harry had watched with growing impatience while Vance tried to hold a routine drill exercise. Vance more or less made up the commands as he went along, and the men responded with sloppy indifference.

Finally, Harry could not stand it any longer. He stepped forward angrily and fairly shouted, "Colonel Vance, sir, you cannot order 'right-shoulder arms' from 'present arms' without first ordering 'port arms'!"

Vance looked puzzled, or perhaps just sublimely disingenuous—Burgwyn could not tell which.

"Why not? I have just done it."

"Because . . . because *that's not the proper way!*"

Vance shrugged. The assembled infantrymen struggled to suppress their grins.

"The men had no trouble doing it, Major. But perhaps you discerned some subtle problem that escaped my attention. So why don't *you* take over this drill, while I observe *the proper way of doing things* from under the shade of yonder walnut tree?"

Since then, the two officers had worked out a modus operandi that suited their disparate personalities. Burgwyn had come to realize that Vance was a natural-born leader, and enormously popular with the rank and file, but he was easygoing to a fault and never pretended to be anything but an amateur soldier. He was happy to turn over the formal details to Harry, intervening only when he thought the major was being unduly harsh.

September brought no respite from the heat and wet-wool humidity of the dog days—so called by North Carolinians because they hammered even the hardiest soul into the sullen lethargy of an old hound sprawled on a cabin porch, too stupefied by the weather even to gnaw at its fleas. During the brutal hours of midday, the men of the Twenty-sixth North Carolina followed the example of their commander and languished under whatever shade was available. They drilled after breakfast, when it was still possible to move without lathering like a blown horse, or in the shadowed respite of late afternoon.

They were encamped near Kinston, on the edge of a large, pestilential bog named Gum Swamp, ostensibly guarding the railroad that ran southeast between the port of Morehead City and the vital junction at Goldsboro, where regional tracks fed into the main supply artery for eastern Virginia. Exactly what they were guarding against was unclear, but as the simmering weeks crawled by, new companies arrived to flesh out the regiment's strength. Vance's original unit, the Buncombe Rough and Readies, had been absorbed into the larger formation in June, and Vance had been elected regimental commander. When word came, on the last day of August, that Forts Hatteras and Clark had fallen, the men tried to shake off their lassitude, just in case the Yankee expeditionary force should make a stab for the inland railroads, but nothing happened and boredom soon returned. Today, however, as if to signal new urgency, a wagon had arrived from Raleigh bearing newly printed pamphlets entitled "A Soldier's Guide to Good Health." After lunch, Zeb Vance spent a while leafing through this curious document, in the company of his executive officer.

"Well, Harry, this *is* enlightening! To avoid the irritation caused by mosquitoes, we should all sleep under insect netting. Of course, we *have* no proper netting and any man who sleeps under heavier protection will most likely suffocate before dawn. And to avoid stomach ailments, we are sternly lectured about drinking from the same streams in which we defecate! Medical science marches on!"

Harry Burgwyn did not think such commonsense advice was entirely amiss. Until he had taken control of camp discipline and constructed proper latrines, Vance's men had shat wherever the mood came upon them, including the creeks whose water was now used for washing and cooking.

"Here's something for you, Zebulon. Under the heading of 'Beards,' on page thirty-one: '*As for the beard, let it grow, but not longer than three inches. This strengthens and thickens its growth and thus makes it a more perfect protection for the lungs against dirt, and of the throat against cold and winds in winter . . .* 'Among the bearded men of this regiment, do you know any who would willingly stop at three inches?"

Vance thoughtfully rubbed his own smooth chin. "Hmmm. Whiskers, whiskers . . . I am reminded of something!"

Propelled by sudden energy, Vance strode out of their tent and into the glaring sunlight. Pausing in midstride, he threw Burgwyn an explanation: "The band got new music yesterday, something about beards. Supposed to be jolly. I am going to have them play that, and a few other tunes. It'll take the boys' minds off their boredom."

Burgwyn shook his head as Vance scampered off in search of his musicians. Among the men who had joined the Twenty-sixth in recent weeks were several well-schooled Moravian instrumentalists, men accustomed to ensemble playing. Vance, who had a natural ear for music and was passionate about it as only a true amateur can be, had decreed a regimental band. Unofficially, the group was called Zeb's Band-a-monium, although their playing was in fact quite polished. Starved for entertainment of any kind, the men gladly exempted the bandsmen from most nonessential work details. Word got around, and a few more musicians showed up, with instruments, from other eastern-county regiments. As a result, the Twenty-sixth North Carolina now boasted the largest and most popular band in the state, perhaps in the whole Confederacy. Their repertoire was constantly expanding, as new hymns, dance tunes, and patriotic ditties rolled off Confederate printing presses and were forwarded to Kinston by music printers eager to publicize their newest offerings.

Burgwyn returned to the pile of paperwork on his desk, initialing roll calls, sick lists, commissary requisitions, and quartermaster inventories. He had barely started when Vance returned, out of breath and gleeful of countenance.

"Ufff! Hoo! They need another half hour to practice the new song. Quick, Harry, have we got any task on today's docket that can be dispatched so quickly?"

Burgwyn shuffled documents. A proper army, he knew, would not deviate from strict routine for the sake of an impromptu band concert, but the Confederate army was writing its own rules these days. He held up a document for Vance's appraisal.

"The matter of Private Blaylock, Colonel. The surgeon reports no improvement in his condition, and I've taken the liberty of drawing up his discharge papers."

"Well, fetch him in, Harry, and we will dispose of it expeditiously."

Five minutes later, an orderly returned with Private Lawrence Blaylock, of Company F—a tall, rawboned man in his midtwenties from Watauga County in the mountainous northwest corner of the state. Blaylock had recently contracted a mysterious skin ailment: every visible part of his flesh was covered with crusty, boil-red sores whose painful itching caused the unfortunate man to twitch and wince even when standing at attention. A few steps behind Keith Blaylock was his younger brother, Sam, a quiet and soft-featured lad who seemed inseparable from his sibling.

"Private Lawrence McKesson Blaylock reporting as ordered, sir."

Vance looked up from Blaylock's service record with a bemused expression.

"I knew a gent named Austin Blaylock, runs a livery stable over in Madison. Nice fellow—swears he voted for me."

"One of my uncles, Colonel. We're a powerful large family."

"You come from good stock, lad. And it is a pity for the regiment to lose such a man, but according to the surgeon's report, you have contracted an unknown skin disease, which may well be contagious. He urges me to give you a medical discharge, for the good of the regiment as a whole. I've already signed the papers, and Major Burgwyn will witness—just sign or make your mark here, and you are free to return to the moutains."

Blaylock scratched a symbol that might have been his name or an Egyptian hieroglyph. Then he gestured somewhat timidly toward his brother, Sam.

"Uh, Colonel Vance, as long as we are doing this, I think you might want to draw up another paper for Sam."

Vance looked up, nibbling on the end of his pen in puzzlement. "Why so? Has Sam also contracted this same mysterious ailment? If so, I see no signs of it on his body."

"Perhaps, Colonel, you had best take another look at that body."

Sam stepped forward and somberly unbuttoned his jacket, holding open both lapels so that the two officers could enjoy an unobstructed view.

"My God! Look at those brown-nosed puppies!" exclaimed Zeb Vance. "He has boobies! I mean, *she* . . . I mean . . . What in thunder *do* I mean?"

"Sam" stepped closer and saluted, making no effort to recover "his" splendid pair of crab-apple breasts.

"I am Matilda Blaylock, Colonel Vance, seventeen years old and a bride for the past six months. When Keith joined up, I followed, so we might continue to live together without interrupting the course of our wedded bliss."

Then it must be the quietest "wedded bliss" conceivable! No one had thought it strange when two brothers lodged together. No one thought it strange that "Sam" spoke only in monosyllables and only in response to a direct order. No one even thought it strange that Sam was never seen to bathe or answer Nature's call when other men were around—that could be attributed to some quirk of personal hygiene or simply to hillbilly reticence. As a mountain man himself, Vance knew that other North Carolinians regarded their western counterparts as natural-born eccentrics. And in this case, he reflected, they were right.

Smiling slyly, Vance leaned over to Burgwyn and muttered: "Well, Harry, is there anything in official regulations which covers this contingency?"

"I think I can say, without looking, that there is not."

"In that case, we must choose exactly the right words. When the history of this war comes to be written, the Twenty-sixth North Carolina will, at the very least, provide a unique footnote."

Vance scribbled hastily on a fresh sheet of foolscap. He handed the document to Matilda Blaylock, who stared at it blankly. "You will have to read it to me, Colonel, for I do not know much about letters."

"It says that Mrs. J. M. Blaylock is hereby lawfully discharged from Confederate service on account of being a woman. I think that covers your situation as succinctly as any words can. And if anyone questions you, my dear young woman, you can always 'prove' your status to them as you have proven it to us. Now, both of you, pack up and go home."

The newlyweds saluted and mumbled their thanks. When they were gone, Harry Burgwyn buried his face in his hands, not knowing whether to laugh or weep with exasperation. "By God," he finally said, "has there ever been such an army in all of history?"

Vance slapped his thigh and guffawed. "No, sir, there has not! And that fact will either be our salvation or our downfall! At least our regiment can boast not only the best band in the state, but the sweetest pair of titties in the entire Confederate army!"

Their laughter was interrupted by the growling blats and phlegmy wheezes of the band tuning their instruments. The regiment gathered to listen, even the sentries—Burgwyn made a note to insist, once again, that sentries were *not* permitted to leave their posts for a concert, but he doubted that Vance would back him up with any disciplinary action. One of the bandsmen handed the two officers a copy of the new sheet music, inviting them to sing along as soon as the tune became familiar. Vance himself gave the downbeat, and the brass came in together, creating a bronzen wall of stirring sound.

As they marched through the town with their banners so gay,
I ran to the window to hear the band play;
I peeped through the blinds very cautiously then,
Lest the neighbors should say I was gazing at men.
Oh, I heard the drums beat, and the music so sweet,
But my eyes at the time caught a much greater treat;

The troops were the finest I ever did see,
And the Captain with his whiskers took a sly glance at me.

Suddenly, Zeb Vance doubled over with laughter. Burgwyn stared at him—the incident with Mrs. Blaylock was droll, but not *that* amusing. Vance just waved him away, not wanting to spoil the joke by sharing it with a man who might not see the humor in it. Zeb Vance was a country boy; he knew full well that Keith Blaylock did not suffer from some loathsome unknown contagion, but from the worst case of self-inflicted poison oak imaginable. Vance was picturing the young recruit rolling naked in the stuff somewhere out in Gum Swamp, and he figured that any man so determined to get out of service as to embrace such suffering might as well be sent home.

Besides, what man would not prefer the tender companionship of a high-breasted seventeen-year-old lass to the rough, unsavory life of this encampment?

Remembering the sight of those breasts, Vance stirred restlessly, his mind wandering from the music.

I could use a helping of that. So could we all.

"Where is Bright?" chafed Matthew Sloane. "The boilers are hot, the pressure up, and I am ready to weigh anchor!"

"Ironic name for a man so afflicted with . . . linguistic peculiarities," muttered Augustus Hobart-Hampden, raising a moistened finger to test the wind.

"So I have often thought," nodded Matthew, "but he knows these waters like the palm of his hand and he has spent weeks down here learning the mechanics of this newfangled engine. We really cannot make our maiden voyage without him."

"Maybe he's getting some last-minute advice from the alligators," said Mary Harper, leaning along the portside rail and placing her hand on her husband's shoulder. Both Matthew and the Englishman looked at her blankly, but Largo Landau laughed quietly—Mary Harper had told her the story of Bright and his wise old 'gator, and the tale was now one of the growing number of private amusements they shared.

Evidently, the fact of war made many things possible that would have been unlikely in times of peace—how else could Mary Harper explain the group of disparate people now gathered by the *Banshee*'s wheelhouse? The friendship that had grown between herself and the vivacious young Largo might be attributable to the fact that neither woman had grown up with a sister, and both had always lamented the absence of a confidant of the same gender. The bond between Matthew and Jacob Landau, though affable enough on a personal level, was clearly that of two entrepreneurs drawn together by the excitement of a bold new business venture—Matthew and his steamer as the source of goods, and Jacob as the commercial genius who could best transform those goods into profit. And Fitz-John Bright, when and if he deigned to join them, was the fulcrum on which the physical success of the venture—those aspects of it that involved propulsion, navigation, and eluding the Yankee blockaders—might be said to pivot.

The common ingredient for all of them was Augustus Hobart-Hampden, who seemed to know everything and everybody in Wilmington, who had instigated discussions between Matthew and Jacob, and who had been unstinting with both his interest and Her Majesty's money during the early, faltering stages of the enterprise. H-H, as Matthew had taken to calling him, was a remarkable *facilitator.*

Hobart-Hampden had first entered the picture back in May, when Matthew had dry-docked the *Banshee* in James Cassidey's shipyard at the foot of Church Street only to learn that the steam engine he had ordered from Baltimore, a week before the attack on Fort Sumter, had been confiscated at the Virginia-Maryland border and impounded by the Federal government. An official telegram had coldly informed him that he could reclaim it after the cessation of hostilities. Matthew had spent the next five days—while the immobilized *Banshee* was running up a dockage fee of $20 a day—importuning bankers, importers, wholesalers, shipwrights, and any other citizens who might know where an up-to-date steam engine could be bought. None did, of course, and several of them were impolite enough to laugh in his face when he asked.

On the evening of the fifth day, Matthew was sitting alone in a waterfront tavern, quietly getting drunk so that he could face the inevitable: for him, there would be no grand and profitable career as a blockade-runner. He could sail the *Banshee* back to Pine Haven and continue to use her for occasional intracoastal voyages on the Cape Fear, or he could sell her outright to the Confederacy for much less than she was worth. The first alternative was a dull and dubious prospect, but the second was emotionally wrenching. Next to Pine Haven itself, the ship was his proudest possession, and by removing her from the slave trade, Matthew had redeemed the vessel's soul. Not for several years had the cargo holds smelled *black.*

It was at this moment, like an elegant pomaded angel, that Hobart-Hampden appeared at Matthew's table and introduced himself. Her Brittainic Majesty paid for the next two rounds of drink, and before long Matthew was unloading his problems on the affable and sympathetic Englishman. Surprisingly, H-H already knew of Matthew's plight, and he had inspected the *Banshee* with a sharp professional eye. With a few modifications, he averred, the ship could be turned into a first-class blockade-runner, and the man—or "*men*," he was careful to add—who owned her could more than pay for the conversion from the profits of the first successful voyage. All subsequent round-trips would reap an even bigger profit on everything from Enfield rifles to the odd crates of luxury goods tucked here and there, which need not appear on the official cargo manifest, if Mr. Sloane caught the drift.

Mr. Sloane most certainly did; Hobart-Hampden had even given some thought to which trinkets—silks and perfumes and sweets, for instance—might bring the highest price while occupying the smallest space. As it happened, the captain suavely continued, he knew there were a few brand-new steam engines warehoused in Nassau, fresh from the renowned shipyards of Liverpool. Given the scarcity and value of those machines, they would not remain on the market for long.

Yes, Matthew Sloane agreed, that was an opportunity quickly to be seized; but he had no contacts in the Bahamas, and probably could not afford to commission someone to travel there and handle the transaction, which was bound to be complicated and shrouded in bureaucratic obstructions.

True, the Englishman nodded; but the thing could be done, and the steam engine brought to Wilmington on the first available ship large enough to carry it. It was all a matter of money and connections. He knew a customs official in Nassau who was sympathetic to the South and who would cut through the formalities for a price that was not unreasonable, given the modicum of risk involved. In return for a reasonable share of the profits, Hobart-Hampden would book passage on the next blockade-runner heading out to Nassau and would bring back the engine when he returned. He would also supervise its installation as well as some other desirable modifications to the *Banshee*. No formal contract would be necessary, he stated; when doing business with a gentleman of Mr. Sloane's reputation, a handshake was sufficient. It would also obviate, thought Matthew, the need for any documents to be signed by a representative of the Crown. Fair enough, he supposed, considering the ambiguity of H-H's official status and the freewheeling style of his activities.

True to his word, the Royal Navy man bought passage to Nassau on a runner that would leave on the next moonless tide. The night before he was scheduled to leave, he hosted a small dinner party at a large, sprawling, yellow house on Market Street that was already becoming known as Buckingham Palace because of the growing number of Englishmen who leased quarters and conducted business there. Matthew had sent for Mary Harper to join him in Wilmington, while they waited for the steam engine to arrive, both so that she could share in the excitement and perhaps so that she could provide a levelheaded counterweight to his own impulsive style of doing business. They made a striking couple: Matthew in a new white cotton shirt, striped cravat, and a waistcoat of embossed maroon silk, and Mary Harper demonstratively patriotic in an O-shaped bodice of dove-gray cotton, pagoda sleeves that subtly emphasized the graceful curve of her arms, a full skirt pleated at the waist, the whole ensemble trimmed with a fichu of soft and gauzy green. Hobart-Hampden looked dashing in a royal-blue merchant captain's uniform and with a ceremonial-looking sword jingling from a tight black satin sash.

Two other people were on hand when the Sloanes arrived: Jacob Landau and his daughter, so musically named yet so un-largo-like in spirit and tempo, or so it seemed to Mary Harper when she first met the younger woman. H-H had invited them, drawn them into "the circle of overlapping interests" as he called it, because a blockade-running venture, to reap maximum success, required a sharp mercantile mind on the shore as well as a bold captain at the helm. That was his explanation, as he introduced the two families, but Mary Harper saw the way his glance kept returning to Largo and hers to him. This mutual interest, Mary Harper surmised, had not yet become an open flirtation—and might *not* become "open" at all, considering how protective Jacob was—but there was a hint of the romantic hovering over those two, like a teasing scent of magnolias. Mary Harper found the situation interesting, even as she found Largo uncommonly well-read and quick-witted.

Before leaving for Nassau, H-H led Matthew on a tour of the drydocked *Banshee*, pointing out a number of modifications that could be undertaken immediately, before the power plant was even installed. The two auxiliary masts would be trimmed to reduce visibility, and hinged appropriately so they could be tucked out of the way when the ship was running on steam alone. Likewise, the deckhouses and pilot-house should be reduced to minimal size and all extraneous trim removed, both to further lower the ship's silhouette and to lighten her overall weight. Matthew had drawn up plans for a coal bunker large enough to hold 300 tons—more than ample for a round-trip to either Nassau or Bermuda; Hobart-Hampden suggested reconfiguring for two symmetrical bunkers, each capable of holding 250 tons.

"But why?" protested Matthew, who was worried that the cost of these structural changes was approaching that of the engine itself. "One-way to Nassau only requires one hundred and twenty-five tons."

"Yes, but that's one hundred and twenty-five tons of first-rate coal. What makes you so certain you will always have that at your disposal? Think bituminous as well as anthracite, Mister Sloane, and poor-grade bituminous at that. Besides, we ought to have room in the fuel bunkers for an emergency supply of cotton bales. The Yankee blockade is laughably inefficient for the moment, but it will gradually grow tighter and more effective—there will inevitably be times when a quick burst of speed is necessary, and nothing boosts steam pressure faster than a few bales of turpentine-soaked cotton thrown into the fire."

"Won't that cause the engine to blow up?"

"Theoretically, after a certain time. We shall have to experiment at leisure to find out what the practical limits are. Better to do that *before* they start shooting at us, eh?"

Matthew wondered, not for the first time, just why Hobart-Hampden was so keen on the tactics of blockade-running, and where his theoretical ideas came from. This time, he asked the questions outright; the *Banshee* was, after all, his property, not that of Queen Victoria.

Hobart-Hampden slung a brotherly arm over Matthew's shoulder and gestured toward the tin-bright expanse of the Cape Fear River.

"Believe me when I say that the Royal Navy has given some thought to these matters—there is a committee of venerable gentlemen who have been pondering the pros and cons of blockade strategy ever since Napoleon first toyed with the idea. Various contingencies have been adumbrated and various expedients suggested to improve a blockade-runner's chances. England is an island, Matthew, and almost as dependent on imported goods as the Confederacy. At the moment, the French lack the strength or the motive for imposing a blockade—I suppose Trafalgar taught them a thing or two—but who knows what powers might arise on the Continent between now and the turn of the century? Russia might ally with the Prussians, for instance. New technologies—steam-powered torpedoes, for example—are bound to change things. And the South, having no standing navy of its own, is more likely to embrace new and radical ideas. You see the outlines of the picture, do you not?"

Matthew laughed uneasily. "In other words, our civil war is a laboratory where the Royal Navy can observe the outcome of various 'experiments' without risking English lives or English treasure?"

Hobart-Hampden became slightly indignant. "Considering how much money I have already invested in this project, and considering the fact that I am about to risk at least *one* English life—my own—by sailing to Nassau to purchase a steam engine, I really ought to take offense."

"Augustus, what motivates you?"

"It is really simple, old boy: patriotism, greed, and a lust for adventure. Whilst serving as the eyes and ears of Her Majesty's Navy, I am also in the right place, at the right time, to make myself very rich—and have a jolly good time in the bargain!"

Matthew could not stay vexed with H-H for long. And when the Englishman sailed for Nassau, on the first moonless high tide of July, Matthew joined Mary Harper in saying a prayer for Hobart-Hampden's safe return. Jacob and Largo did the same, or so they told the Sloanes, and burned candles or sacrificed a goat or whatever the Hebrews did to curry God's favor on a dangerous undertaking. Perhaps, Matthew reasoned, God paid more attention when addressed from both a New and an Old Testament platform simultaneously.

At the time Hobart-Hampden sailed back to Wilmington, there were only four Union vessels assigned to the Wilmington blockade: two off the Old Inlet, one off the New, and another limping back to Hampton Roads with boiler trouble. The *City of Glasgow* therefore had no trouble eluding capture; she approached the coast slowly, inside a fog bank, then turned southeast and made the final run at top speed, in the clear, until she was safely past the new batteries Chase Whiting had emplaced on Confederate Point, guarding the New Inlet.

Thus did Matthew Sloane become the owner of a shiny new Trenholm & Bulloch double-boiler oscillating steam engine, each boiler rated at 260 horsepower. Though more mechanically complex than the older side-lever or walking-beam engines, the oscillating engine was more compact—it could be mounted below the *Banshee*'s waterline and no part of it extended higher or wider than the side-wheel paddles themselves. The only way Yankee gunners could hit it was by sheer luck.

Now, on the morning of August 30, 1861, the *Banshee* was ready for her first cruise out to sea—a quick morning run down the Cape Fear to the Old Inlet, a cautious cruise around Bald Head Island, to get an idea of how well and how fast she could move on open water, then a furtive run back in through the New Inlet, all safely inside the patrol radius of the blockaders. A festive mood prevailed on the bridge, where the three men who owned pieces of the venture were eager to cast off, and the wife and daughter, radiant in new sun bonnets, excitedly pointed out to each other the waterfront's colorful sights.

Hobart-Hampden swung his telescope so he could peer straight up Castle Street. "There is our man Bright now, I believe. And he is not alone. He's leading a band of rather agitated Negroes who are pulling what appears to be a circus wagon."

"What *now*?" sighed Mary Harper.

The vehicle in question was indeed a circus wagon, or had been at some uncertain time in the past, for it had not seen a paintbrush or an oilcan for quite some time. Inside the rusted cage, held vertical by four muscular, sweat-filmed blacks whose eyes kept rolling apprehensively, was a seven-foot bull alligator, sunk lethargically in a pile of wet straw. Fitz-John Bright doffed his cap, bowed toward the bridge, and made a grand sweeping gesture at the beast.

"Mez-DAMs and M'SURES, allow me to present our mas-COT!"

The alligator snorted and flicked his massive tail against the bars. Observing the incredulous expressions on the bridge, Bright hurried up the gangplank and plunged into an explanation: "Mister Sloane, suh, every ship needs a mas-COT. And what better ani-MAL than a true-blue Rebel al-li-GAH-tor? And BE-sides, did you not tell me that block-KADE runners are not allowed to be armed?"

"Indeed so, Mister Bright, for then we could legally be classified as pirates and subject to hanging."

Bright gestured again at the reptile, as though it were a relative whom he was recommending for employment. "Ya see, suh, if the YAN-kees was to board us on the HIGH SEAS, we could not RE-pel them with pistols and swords, but if we let ole Beauregard out of his cage, they will clear the decks in no TIME!"

" 'Beauregard,' did you say?"

"He AN-swers to that name, suh."

"Excuse me, Mister Bright," said Mary Harper, "but is that the same alligator you were talking to last spring, on the night of our party?"

"Yessum. That, or one of his cousins. Ah sent some niggers into the swamps to CATCH him in June, found that ole cage fer sale, been keepin' him 'specially for this DAY. Trained him up right good, too."

"Trained him?" scoffed Jacob. "To do what, recite Shakespeare?"

"Just you watch, Mister Lan-DOW!" Bright signaled one of the Negroes standing uneasily around the cage. The man took a heavy sack from his shoulder, rested it on the ground, and opened it, carefully averting his nostrils.

"*Mein Gott!*" cried Jacob. "What is that stench?"

"Dead mullet wrapped in horsemeat. Smells a mite ripe to us, maybe, but to ole Beau, it's AM-brow-see-ya!" The Negro gingerly held up a ten-pound slab of offal. Everyone noticed at once that the 'gator food was wrapped in cheap blue cloth—Yankee-uniform-blue. Bright opened a trapdoor in the top of the cage. At the first scent of meat, the alligator came swiftly to life, thrashing his tail, hissing, and opening his primordial jaws to reveal what seemed like hundreds of spiky teeth. When the food parcel landed in that red gleaming maw, the jaws clapped shut like guillotine blades and rancid sanguine juices spurted out their sides.

"Um, very impressive," said Matthew. "How are we supposed to keep him fed during a voyage?"

"Fish will do just fine."

"How many pounds of fish does Beauregard eat per diem?"

Bright scratched his head. "Who is PERDIUM, suh?"

"How much does the alligator eat in a single day!" Matthew was growing impatient with this farce, his emotions divided between peevish anger and uproarious laughter.

"Oh, 'bout FIF-ty pounds, I reckon. Anything less, he gets a mite sulky."

"In other words, on a six-day run to Bermuda, we would have to carry three hundred pounds of dead fish? Mister Bright, this is a commercial venture. Do you have any idea how much three hundred pounds of coffee, or chocolate, or perfume, or even sewing needles is worth these days?"

"No suh."

"Well, neither do I, yet, but I am sure the value far outweighs any possible worth your reptile might have as a deterrent to a Yankee boarding party! I appreciate your, um, creative thinking, Mister Bright, but I am afraid the alligator cannot go."

Bright looked crestfallen for a moment, then shrugged and drew from inside his jacket a compact pistol and pointed it at the cage. The Negroes scattered. The alligator looked up, its eyes as unreadable as black glass beads, sublimely indifferent.

"Don't kill him, for God's sake!" cried Jacob. "Just open the cage and dump him back into the river."

Bright uncocked the revolver and looked at his master for confirmation. Matthew nodded emphatically. "Mister Landau is right. It's only a defenseless brute, but it is one of God's creatures."

"Ah would not call him defenseless, exactly," muttered Bright. As if to reinforce the comment, Beauregard yawned languidly and sunlight sparkled on his teeth. Bright gestured to his Negroes, who could not resist insolently rolling their eyes at the futility of their previous labors, and they pushed the cage to the edge of the dock. Even after the cage door was opened, the alligator had to be prodded from its postprandial stupor with a sharp stick before it got the idea. Without looking back, it waddled to the edge of the dock and flopped heavily into the river.

Fitz-John Bright dusted his hands and muttered, "That is THAT." Largo whispered something in Mary Harper's ear; she nodded.

"Matthew, give the hands a little money for their efforts."

"Hmph. Well, that seems only fair." He strode down the gangplank and put a few coins into the hands of each Negro. "You boys be back here at sunset and we'll take you back to Pine Haven. Do not spend this money on drink. If anyone questions you, just tell them who your master is." He turned to Bright and put a hand on his shoulder. "I am sorry, Bright, but we cannot take passengers who consume fifty pounds of food per day."

"Just an EYE-deah, suh. I reckon I should get to the wheel now."

"Yes. The day is advancing."

Matthew rang the ship's bell festively; Bright tugged a lanyard and the steam whistle blared with pent-up energy. From up and down the waterfront other vessels replied, saluting the newest addition to Wilmington's fleet. Workers, crewmen, and pedestrians flowed to the waterfront, waving handkerchiefs and cheering as the *Banshee* slowly steered past the channel markers and into deep water. She was a proud sight, and all five people who had a stake in her knew it and shared that pride.

Once they cleared the dockside congestion, Bright turned the vessel south, passing Eagles Island on the starboard side, where Beery's shipyard teemed with activity and work gangs of Rebel recruits toiled shirtless under the broiling sun, unloading wagons and boxcars and barges and building from their cargoes small mountains of barrels and crates. As the island slipped behind the *Banshee*'s murmuring wake, the river gradually broadened. Mister Bright rang on another knot or two and in moments they had passed beyond all the docks and machinery and bustle of the city. They were alone on the Cape Fear River, the horizons widening into sandy, partly forested wilderness on either side and the sky enormous, vaulted, disdainfully aloof to all who came and went on the great river. Two miles below Eagles Island, they passed the Dram Tree—a noble antique cypress shaped like a **Y** and bearded with whisps of Spanish moss. Largo Landau pointed it out to Augustus Hobart-Hampden, who had not strayed far from her side.

"It is called that because when sailors see it, they know safe harbor is only a few miles away. They can relax and pass out a glass of rum, happy to have survived the passage."

"Are the waters off the Cape as dangerous as the sailors claim?"

Oh, yes, Largo assured him, and as they steamed south toward the Old Inlet she told him more about the land and the river. When he settled in Wilmington, Jacob had diligently studied its history, with a sincerity that impressed even the city's resident antiquarians. Jacob in turn had passed his curiosity and knowledge on to Largo. The process helped the Landaus to take root quickly in this new soil.

The first European to see and describe the region was Giovanni da Verrazano, in 1524. Despite his favorable verdict ("a sandy shore filled with many faire fields and plaines, full of mightie greate woods, replenished with divers sorts of trees, as pleasant and delectable to behold as it were possible to imagine"), more than a hundred years passed before the English actually tried to settle here. First (Largo pointed to the west) they tried on the landward shore, with a settlement named Charles Town, in 1660. But they pulled out again seven years later, bedeviled by pirates, unfriendly Indians, and voracious mosquitoes, and moved both themselves and the name to South Carolina instead. Over the next fifty years, various other settlements sprang up on the higher, healthier eastern bank and clung there tenaciously, under various names—New Liverpool, New Carthage, New Towne, Newton—until 1740, when the town was incorporated and a new governor appointed, a man so grateful to receive the job that he renamed the settlement for his patron, Spencer Compton, the Earl of Wilmington.

The place was defined more by the river than by the sea, Largo said. A thousand streams, fed by runoff from the eastern slopes of the Appalachian Mountains, meandered downhill through the Piedmont to form the Cape Fear Basin. Gathering size and strength, creeks joined to become streams, streams merged into rivers, and many rivers eventually merged to form the mighty Cape Fear. Until it reached full flow some thirty miles north of Wilmington, where its mass was given one final boost by the numberless black-water creeks that seeped from the unmapped and mostly uninhabited swamps, the river was narrow but deep—navigable by merchant vessels as far as 150 miles inland, an artery into the state's fertile heart. The river was cold-looking even in summer, but its color was a rich dark olive green, swirled as it neared the coast with veins of tar-brown tannin leeched from the jungly vegetation of the marshes.

The *Banshee* gained a knot or two as the channel widened. Far away off the starboard bow her passengers now saw the peaceful hamlet of Smithville. Both land and sky seemed to pull back to a vaster reach, and it was possible to smell the sea, now only ten miles away.

"Now," Largo told her English friend, "now you will see—if you but open your imagination to it—why men named this place Cape Fear."

Behold its vastness. Feel the untamed wildness of its wind. Lift your face into the torrents of its light. Look up and lose yourself in contemplation of the towers and crenellations of its immeasurable clouds. For we are about to reach the concept and reason for its name: the bleak and naked elbow of Bald Head Island, thrusting out far into the sea, demarcating a place where land and water strive warlike for domination—that terror of mariners and wrecker-of-great-ships named Frying Pan Shoals because the shallow reef-strewn water spits and bubbles there like hot grease in a skillet. Taken as a whole, this is a place of warning and woe; this is where the great waves born in the Arctic reach the end of their majestic thousand-mile voyages, carrying with them the sweep and power of all that emptiness and hurling it against the last outpost of land. It is the playground of tempests. It is a kingdom of silence and awe, where the only sounds are the shriek of gulls, the roar of breakers, and the dirge hymn of the endless wind. Its whole aspect is suggestive, not of beauty and repose, but of desolation and wildness. Imagination cannot adorn it. Romance cannot sanctify it. No human emotion can soften it.

"Is it not grand, Augustus!" cried Largo at the end of her description. He replied by reaching, very discreetly, for her hand, and for a moment they shared a warmth made sweeter by the cold immensity of the elements it defied.

As they traversed the Old Inlet and steamed south into the open sea, the mood brightened and a warm, gentle wind embraced them so that everyone on the bridge unconsciously leaned forward. A line of demarcation passed under the bow: cloudy mud from the turbulent shoal waters gave way to the vivid blue-green that heralded the nearness of the Gulf Stream. Ruffled by the wind, yet relaxed and benevolent of aspect, the water sported whitecaps as frisky as rabbits.

"The WHIND and WAH-vees seem ideal, Captain!" said Mr. Bright. "Shall we open up the THRODDLE and see what she can do?"

Matthew nodded, his eyes bright as a boy's, then he coughed a few times, clearing his throat as though searching for the proper intonation of command. "You may take her to three-quarters speed, Mister Bright, and if she is still intact after five minutes, lay the throttle wide open."

"Aye, suh!"

Like the mythical spirit that was her namesake, the *Banshee* growled as pent-up pressure jetted into the pistons driving the wheels. She vibrated harshly for a moment, gaining traction on the obdurate waters, bending them to the will of Trenholm & Bulloch's engineers, then surged forward smoothly, like a thoroughbred finding its race, and drew a cheer from passengers and crew alike. Ten . . . twelve . . . fifteen and a half knots, and every rivet, bulkhead, and stanchion vibrated confidently, as if to say: There is a bit more in reserve, which you may call upon if you are in peril. Fine, but not today, mused Matthew Sloane.

"Take her back to three-fourths throttle, Mister Bright. Let's not put undue strain on the engines until we must."

"She's a fine steamship, Matthew!" said Hobart-Hampden, clapping him on the back.

"Oh my, yes!" exclaimed Mary Harper. "That was *most* exhilarating, Matthew!" A private communicative twinkle in her eyes informed him that she had become excited in *that* way, too, as certain women were said to become after riding a fine stallion. Matthew automatically winked back at her, then turned his head as embarrassment colored his cheeks. Marital intimacy had been a surprising pleasure between them until Mary Harper became too frail to have more children. Perhaps "frail" was not the accurate word (although it was the first that came to his mind), for she seemed physically robust and she certainly seemed to welcome their now-infrequent episodes of congress. Indeed, his *desire* for her was as vigorous as ever, but his terror of impregnating her and possibly endangering her life had made of him a wary, self-conscious, awkward lover; it seemed cruel to ignite a fire in each other that could not burn to its conclusive heat for both. Still—he knew it—he would come to her bed that night, for the steamer's maiden voyage had been so perfect, so exhilarating, as to kindle arousal in him as well. Perhaps, through luck or serendipitous discovery, they might yet find a formula for intimacy that did not leave one, or the other, or sometimes both, frustrated and unfulfilled. If only he knew more of such worldly matters.

Then it occurred to him that he was, henceforth, a *sea captain*, destined to spend much time in the company of sailors. And sailors *knew things* that gentlemen of his class did not. Surely he was not the first husband to suffer this quandary. The trick would be to find the proper moment to bring it up. Perhaps in a foreign port, where people had a more down-to-earth attitude toward matters . . . well . . . *sexual.* Again, he bared his smile to the wind and his face to the summer sun.

The paddles' steady heartbeat discouraged conversation, leaving each of the others solitary in thought, while Matthew was savoring the chance to take out a second mortgage on his manhood. For Jacob Landau, the *Banshee* was no virility symbol, but a means to a practical end. It was the lever for unprecedented wealth, and his faith was the fulcrum—if he attained that wealth, he could keep his deathbed promise to Rachel. For a large enough bounty, he could lure a rabbi from as far away as Warsaw to the new synagogue in Wilmington.

Largo, for her part, basked in a new feeling of closeness to the handsome Englishman whom she had already marked out to be her first real lover.

Mary Harper Sloane marveled at a feeling she had not known since just before her marriage. She was a mature woman, no romantic adolescent, yet she felt again as though she were a butterfly ripening in a cocoon. Whatever the war might bring, she would become a different, wiser, more self-aware woman during its course; and because she was fairly well satisfied with who she had *been,* she faced the prospect of *becoming* with curiosity, eagerness, and grace.

Augustus Hobart-Hampden, as usual, kept inscrutably to himself. He seemed to relish the voyage—the separate and the blended sensations of it—on a primal, physical, sensual level—which was of course one reason why Largo took every decent or clandestine opportunity to touch his hand and revel in the virile energy that radiated from his body.

Thus did they complete a two-hour voyage from the Old Inlet to the New, and as they sailed back into the Cape Fear—past the primitive earthworks on Confederate Point—they were cheered by a thin line of Rebel soldiers, who paused in their digging and heaping long enough to salute the newest blockade-runner. Bright pulled his lanyard and the steamship gave a mighty *toot!* as she crossed the last sandbar and entered the river's calm embrace. When the Dram Tree hove into sight, Jacob uncovered a large wicker picnic basket—imported from London—within which nested fine china, silver utensils, and two bottles of champagne, all secured with brass-buckled leather straps. Separate tins held tea biscuits, candied fruit, and a Gouda cheese as big as a small pumpkin. Toasts were proposed and consumed, the glasses ringing together as they sailed past the venerable cypress. Excitement and sea air had sharpened appetites, so the celebrants piled their plates and ate without stint. It had been a fine outing: the ship proved more than satisfactory, the weather had been balmy, and not once had they sighted so much as a smoke trail from the Yankee blockaders.

While they ate and drank, the only somber note was sounded by Hobart-Hampden, who glanced down at his plate full of delicacies and his glass full of good champagne and mused: "Hard to imagine, I suppose, but in a year or two the delicacies I am holding might literally be worth their weight in gold. On the open market, of course. As the importers, we will suffer no scarcities."

Leaving Bright to oversee preparations for the morning voyage back to Pine Haven, the others sauntered into town, thinking to drop by the Cotton Exchange before retiring for an afternoon nap. Both Jacob and Matthew agreed that the next order of business was to learn the state of the market, so that they could purchase their first cargo according to the optimum blend of price and quality.

They spent an hour in the Cotton Exchange, learning what was for sale and where and for how much. By the time twilight was painting the river, the cargo manifest for the *Banshee*'s first run was itemized. She would leave on the next moonless night, twelve days hence.

Their business concluded, Hobart-Hampden thanked them for a

splendid day, shook hands with the men, gallantly kissed the hands of the ladies—lingering, perhaps, on Largo's hand just a bit longer than etiquette dictated—then vanished into the crowded streets, intent on yet another of his mysterious errands.

Then the Landaus walked home and the Sloanes walked toward their lodgings.

"It is still early for supper, my dear," said Matthew.

"Can you think of some way to fill the next hour or two?"

"I believe I can," he said, linking arms with his wife and affecting just a bit of swagger, if only to mask the unease in his heart. *Let it be all right this time*, he prayed, but he was not at all certain that God entertained prayers of this sort.

The Cannons of General Huger

NEW STUDY OF MORBIDITY—One of our most esteemed physicians, Dr. Baccus Satchwell, reports to us that a new medical study from Great Britain—a copy of which was delivered to him by a recently-arrived blockade-runner captain—indicates that many sudden deaths usually attributed to heart failure are instead caused by <u>*blood congestion in the lungs.*</u> *Some of the causes adumbrated, he reports, are: cold feet, over-tight shoes, restrictive clothing, costivness, sitting still until chilled after being warmed by strenuous labor; going too suddenly from a close heated room into frigid air, especially after prolonged public speaking; and sudden depressing news impacting on the blood's circulation. We agree with Dr. Satchwell that these findings are, in themselves, "sudden depressing news," given that it is virtually impossible for any person to avoid most, or* <u>*any,*</u> *of these causes unless he spends his entire waking life in a state of mute immobility.*

—The Wilmington Journal, December 21 1861

General Chase Whiting was so tired that he slept through most of the boat ride from Wilmington to his downriver headquarters at Smithville. His wife, Katherine, had prepared a welcome-home meal of roasted lamb, hot biscuits, rice with gravy, and fresh green beans, and after he had satisfied the initial roar of his appetite, he had almost dozed at the table. Katherine had made herself especially pretty, thinking to welcome him into her bed, and Whiting appreciated the gesture but could not entertain any thought of acting on it. Fortunately, she understood—as a soldier's wife must—and sent him to bed as soon as he had eaten his fill. The meal weighed in his stomach like a cannonball. He had only the strength to remove his boots before sleep came on like a wave, submerging him just seconds after his head touched the pillow.

He awakened fully and instantly when the parlor clock struck three A.M. Each chime—icy and desolate within the warm darkness of his home—cracked against his ears like the percussion of an implacable tocsin. Whiting lay still for a moment, hoping that sleep would pull him under again, but it did not; instead, his mind was inundated not with renewed weariness but with a caustic flood of statistics, measurements, topographical sketches, and data.

Accepting wakefulness as one more of duty's imperatives, Whiting eased out of bed, tugged on his boots, and made his way quietly down the stairs. He paused in the foyer, wondering whether or not to don his coat, but decided against it. Although the coastal nights had grown perceptibly cooler with the coming of October, they had not yet acquired the crystalline edge of true autumn. He stepped outside and was enveloped in a thin chilly mist washing up from the river. It wrapped the street lamps with gauze and lent a certain fairy-tale ambience to the village. Hunching his shoulders, Whiting strode off toward his headquarters.

If the two inlets were the highways leading through the Cape Fear estuary, then Smithville was the gatekeeper's house for Wilmington. Snug against the western shore, roughly two miles north of Old Inlet, Smithville was metamorphosing from the rustic fishing village it had been earlier in the year. New telegraph lines tied it to Wilmington; an enlarged customshouse by the main wharf was increasingly busy as the pace of the blockade-running trade picked up; a new half-formed crescent of earthworks rose slowly on the highest bluff commanding the river, but many more weeks had to pass before it could be considered a "fort"—right now, it was just a raw fieldwork housing a battery of elderly smoothbore Napoleons.

Chase Whiting had thought himself well rid of this thankless job when General Johnston transferred him to Harper's Ferry in May, describing Whiting to one Richmond correspondent as "the sort of engineer whom God, not West Point, creates." Whiting soon found himself overseeing the complicated transfer, by railroad, of scattered Confederate units to the rallying point of Manassas. That assignment had stimulated his intellect, challenged him as no other ever had, and although he longed for a field command, he understood how vital his logistical skills had been to the ultimate Southern victory. Evidently, so did Richmond, for no less a personage than Jefferson Davis had awarded Whiting a battlefield promotion to brigadier general. Joe Johnston promised him command of a division.

Then, eight weeks later, Whiting found himself back in Wilmington, charged once more with overseeing the defense of the whole North Carolina coastline. This unexpected turnabout could be regarded either as a compliment to his sagacity as an engineer or as a sign that, for some occult reason, he was no longer in Richmond's good graces. Well, he thought, I am a soldier and I will obey my orders. *But I am surely destined for something grander than this.*

His record certainly indicated as much. If ever a man had been born to be a soldier, it was Chase Whiting. His grandfather had fought in the Revolution, and his father Levi had served from 1812 to his death in 1853, achieving the rank of lieutenant colonel. Chase unhesitatingly picked up the patriotic torch and worked hard to prove himself worthy. He excelled in academics, entering Georgetown University at the age of fourteen and completing the four-year curriculum in only two, graduating second in his class. West Point was the next logical step, and his father secured an appointment for Chase in 1841. He graduated at the head of his class and was honored by a commission in the Engineers, the most elite branch of the peacetime army. He supervised construction projects in Baltimore, Savannah, Pensacola, and San Francisco; he also laid out a supply road from San Antonio to El Paso and fought in skirmishes against the Comanches. By the standards of peacetime service, his rise was commensurate with his reputation, and when he resigned to fight for the South, on February 20, 1861, he had attained the rank of captain. Richmond had made him a major, a colonel, then a general, in less than six months. That, surely, was a sign of confidence in his ability to create a coherent defense where now there was disorganization, confusion, and a chronic shortage of everything required for the protection of a long, vulnerable coastline. His obsession with the assignment, his endless schemes for improving the effectiveness of what little he did have, had become a kind of brain fever. What the Confederacy had asked him to do was, on the face of it, quite impossible. He had understood as much, in a theoretical way, before embarking on a three-week inspection tour of the coast. Now that he had seen things with his own eyes, he was close to despair.

"Halt! Who goes there?" The voice penetrated the fog—a youthful voice straining for a tone of authority still beyond its grasp. Whiting dutifully halted and identified himself, adding: "Good work, son. If the Yankees ever decided to raid us, this is the sort of night they would choose. Carry on." He exchanged salutes with the teenaged sentry and went inside. No one was on duty except the telegraphist, who had probably been dozing until he heard the general's voice but who now looked keen and alert. The telegraph key was silent at this hour, but with woeful predictability its operators had transcribed a mountain of messages during Whiting's absence. He gathered them in two hands, crossed the hall, and shut himself in his office, beneath the maps and hydrographic charts that decorated its walls.

Before wading through the messages, he poured three fingers of good bourbon into a chipped tumbler and lightened its hue with a dollop of water. As usual, the first detonation of warmth in his belly seemed to cleanse and sharpen his mind. The fact was curious to those who knew him well, but he seldom drank in a public, social setting. Good whiskey, in Whiting's opinion, was an adjunct to private contemplation, whether it be analytical or poetic, and he knew there were some people who already believed he drank too much. Plainly, he did not agree with them. If he did have enemies in high places, he would not give them any satisfaction by becoming tipsy at a ball, a dinner, or a reception. No indeed. His relationship with bourbon was a private partnership, as though the whiskey sensed his appreciation of its beneficent qualities and granted him, in benign return for his respect, the best notions, the most heightened degree of reflection, it could impart. *Good bourbon is as faithful a companion as a good dog,* his father used to say, and Whiting had adopted that maxim early in his adulthood.

Certainly, the situation in which he found himself required both clarity and a considerable degree of inspiration.

Whiting's first task, after he was reappointed to oversee the state's coastal defenses, had been to gather, study, and correlate all available information about the progress that had been made since his departure for the Manassas campaign. His conclusion: not much. Thank God the Yankees had taken a breather after capturing the Hatteras works, settling into an apparent state of strategic lethargy. If they had moved quickly, using their momentum, they could have taken some mainland ports, thrust inland and probably cut the railroad line at Goldsboro. A bolder commander than Butler might have driven all the way to Raleigh and cut the Confederacy in two. But, having been granted this reprieve, Richmond had done almost nothing to prevent another Yankee commander from doing the same thing.

Oh, there had been a lot of administrative shuffling, some more raw and poorly armed regiments had entered the state's rolls, and many reports had been written, but no coherent strategy had emerged for improving the situation. That chore was apparently left to him.

The distance from the Virginia border to that of South Carolina—if measured along the parabolic curve of the Outer Banks—was approximately three hundred miles. On paper, that distance was defended by 6,387 men. On the actual ground, Whiting estimated, the total number of men present and fit for duty on any given day was probably less than 5,000. Lines of authority and responsibility, zones of command, and routes of supply, all were tangled, obscured, and tended to blur when subjected to scrutiny.

After this preliminary study, Whiting had concluded that the only way to learn the truth of the matter was by personal inspection. Before he left, however, he pressed upon Richmond, by means of an urgent and closely reasoned memorandum, the necessity of dividing the coastal command along logical geographical lines—*"no officer, however diligent and well served by his subordinates, can reasonably be expected to mount a successful defense of the entire North Carolina coast. The theater is too vast, communications too unreliable, and the circumstances from place to place too varied. The configuration and strategic options applicable in the Albemarle Sound region are markedly different from those obtaining in the Cape Fear River delta."* He had concluded by urging that the coast be divided into three separate commands: from the Virginia line to Cape Hatteras, comprising the Albemarle Sound District; from Hatteras to Fort Macon, comprising the Pamlico Sound District; and everything south of Fort Macon, comprising the Cape Fear District. Whiting would retain overall command, but would exert operational authority only in the latter district, while two other capable officers should be placed in tactical command of the two northerly districts. He had appended a list of men whom he regarded as suitable for the posts, and he had closed by attaching some affidavits supporting his conclusions, signed by respected general officers who knew the region well enough to comprehend the impracticality of the existing situation. Some of those signatures carried weight: Generals P. T. Beauregard, Joseph E. Johnston, D. H. Hill, and Henry A. Wise.

Once this report was on the wire to Richmond, Whiting figured he had done all he could do from a distance, and set forth on a grueling tour of inspection. He had expected to be gone for ten days. Instead, it required twenty-one days of hard travel by horseback, steamer, and occasionally rowboat, just to get a brief impression of all the sites shown on his most up-to-date map.

He was not optimistic at the start of his journey; by the end of it, he was appalled.

He first visited Fort Macon, purportedly the strongest Rebel position in the state, which guarded the ports of Beaufort and Morehead City, the eastern terminus of the vital Atlantic and North Carolina Railroad. As a former U.S. Army engineer, Whiting knew that the place had been neglected in prewar budgets, but he was quite unprepared for the extent of its deterioration. As he approached on the waters of Bogue Sound, the fort looked massive and formidable. Inside the ramparts, things were very different: woodwork bleached and cracked from exposure, ironwork covered with a pox of rust, the masonry walls powdery and flaking. Only four of Macon's fifty-odd cannons were long-range enough to engage Federal steamers at sea and those were mounted on carriages so ramshackle they appeared ready to crumble from the recoil of the first shot.

From there, Whiting's route bent inland, zigzagging long distances between deeply indented crossings of the major rivers. He visited New Bern on the Neuse River, "Little" Washington on the Pamlico River, Plymouth and Edenton on the Chowan River. Military readiness varied wildly from place to place. New Bern at least had a tolerable battery, decent earthworks, and the protection of an infantry regiment—the Twenty-sixth North Carolina, led by a full-of-himself mountaineer politician named Vance. A hundred miles north, however, the inhabitants of Plymouth and Edenton proved surly and almost criminally indifferent to their security; the small garrisons in those towns, paralyzed by a lack of supplies, artillery, and clear direction, had become indolent and resigned. Whiting tongue-lashed their officers into action and by the time he departed, the spade had once again been set a-turning in both places. At Elizabeth City, the only sizeable town in the northeastern corner of the state, he found a contrasting smugness due to the proximity of the so-called Mosquito Fleet. Whiting admired the bellicose zeal of the ships' officers, especially Branch and Parker; he acknowledged their early successes as commerce raiders and praised their nettlesome sporadic shelling of the Union lodgments on the Outer Banks, but the ragtag assortment of ships was farcically unfit to oppose any serious enemy naval incursion.

Worst of all, however, was the state of things on Roanoke Island. There simply *was* no more strategically vital location on these waters—any fool could see that by glancing at a map. Roanoke Island was the cork in the bottleneck that blocked any Federal moves inland from the captured bases on Hatteras and the adjacent barrier islands. Possession of it would give the enemy easy access not only to several navigable rivers, but also to the Dismal Swamp Canal leading to Norfolk. If adequately reinforced, Whiting believed, it could also serve as a sally port for counterattacks against the exposed western flanks of the existing Yankee footholds. And if it fell . . . every place on Albemarle Sound would be rendered instantly indefensible.

When the island's new commander, fifty-five-year-old Brigadier General Henry A. Wise, led Whiting on a tour of inspection, he did so with apologies and obvious chagrin. In contrast to the windswept and sparklingly clean barrier islands of the Outer Banks, Roanoke Island was a swampy pesthole and the fifteen hundred men stationed there were poorly trained, fed worse, clothed in rags, and pathetically armed with a motley of shotguns, fowling pieces, varmint rifles, and family-heirloom muskets. The only weapons he saw in abundance were hundreds of Bowie knives, which the men brandished with the bloodthirsty enthusiasm of children waving wooden swords. They had the bravado of troops who have never been under fire, and like Indians daubing war paint, they had graced their scarecrow companies with ferocious names: the Hatteras Avengers, the Yankee Killers, the Fayetteville Spartans, the Goldsboro Grizzlies . . .

Whiting was aghast, while quickly assuring Wise that he could not be held responsible for a situation he had inherited only two weeks before. Wise was a politically appointed general, but he was not stupid. He had an instinctive eye for terrain and a sound grasp of tactical principles. And he had a quick answer to Whiting's most urgent question: "Why are there no heavy guns yet mounted?"

"Because General Huger in Norfolk has laid claim to them, insisting that he must have them to repel an imminent invasion across the Chesapeake Bay. Until Richmond disposes of the matter, hopefully in our favor, most of our heavy guns remain on railroad cars or canal barges. It is really very vexing, General. As for the handful of batteries I possess, their ammunition is scant and the boys crewing them scarcely know a lanyard from a plow handle. And that's not the worst of it."

"Go on."

"Well, sir, General Huger has given orders that top priority be given to constructing fortifications on the *northern* half of the island."

"What in God's name *for?* The enemy lies to the south!"

"He is obsessed with Norfolk and has some plan to fall back here should the Yankees drive him from that place. He is hoarding barges and boats for that eventuality—and I am forbidden to divert any manpower to build works covering the southern end of the island until the northward-facing positions are finished. General Whiting, I only have a handful of shovels and picks—the work progresses slowly and the men, frankly, consider it a waste of time. As you pointed out, the only way the enemy can attack this place is from the bases he already has on the Outer Banks."

"I cannot fathom General Huger's reasoning," scowled Whiting. "If my information is correct, Norfolk already has more guns and men than any place except Richmond. Surely the enemy knows that, too. Well, General Wise, knowing Ben Huger as I do and knowing Richmond's inefficiency better with every passing day, I cannot promise you miracles. But I will intervene as urgently as possible. You have done as much as you can in a short time, and at least your men have high spirits . . . if little else."

Wise bowed courteously. "You may rely upon a hard fight, sir, when the time comes. But without significant reinforcements, I fear it will be a short one."

Wise did have a scheme to drive belts of pilings into the Sound, athwart the Yankees' most likely routes. Whiting concurred—that would keep the garrison busy and might have some utility in battle. He drew up a document giving Wise the power to requisition Negro labor and pile-driving equipment anywhere he could find it—there was nothing else of practical value he could do for the time being.

On the long sad-hearted journey back to Smithville, Whiting strove to get a mental grip on the situation, but no matter how he reviewed the things he had seen and reports he had heard, his options always seemed very circumscribed. It had taken him three days to reach some vulnerable positions that the Yankees could strike, by water, in a matter of hours. Nothing held them back except inertia on the part of the high command in Washington. Whiting knew he could not count on that for long—rumors abounded that overall command of the Federal forces was about to pass into the capable hands of George McClellan, one of the best organizers and soundest technical minds in the U.S. Army. "Little Mac" would get things rolling.

By the time he reached home, Whiting had formulated a strategy predicated on geographical reality and optimism. The most forward, exposed, and valuable locations—Fort Macon, New Bern, and Roanoke Island—should be made strong enough to pin down any

Federal landings for a period of seventy-two hours—that was the first priority. Second, he wanted to establish a strong theaterwide reserve, four to six regiments, in Goldsboro—the only real communications hub north of Wilmington. When the Yankees tipped their hand, the reinforced bastions would hold them in place and the Confederate reserve would strike them from the flank or rear.

This reorganization would require time, trained troops, more guns, and above all else the cooperation of the Confederate government. Now that he had seen things with his own eyes, Whiting thought the urgency of the situation was crystal clear. He would first read through the messages accumulated during his absence, then spend the rest of the day going through his extensive notes and drafting a strong, thorough, and specific report to the secretary of war.

But first, he must read through the messages, for they might contain some clues as to how things stood in Richmond. The war was only eight months old, but already the Southern military effort was wrapped in the tentacles of politics.

The first dozen telegrams were routine, concerned with the to-and-fro transfer of individual officers and minor units, a company here and a battery there. Whiting read them, initialed them, and piled them to one side so they could be filed later by his aide-de-camp. Then he refilled his glass with bourbon; he would nurse this second drink, for dawn was not that far away and he forbade himself any beverage but coffee after the bugle sounded reveille at six o'clock.

He took a big swallow and grunted with appreciation when the whiskey boomed in his stomach like a stirring drum. Then he read the next and so far longest message. Then read it again, his blood pressure rising. Then he banged a fist against the table, sloshing drops of bourbon on the telegrams.

"By God, this is intolerable!"

In response to your request . . . the northern sector of the North Carolina coast had been made a separate entity, renamed the Albemarle Sound District, and placed under the tactical command of Henry A. Wise. The new district, however, was hereby incorporated into the "Norfolk Department" and *overall* command was transferred to General Benjamin Huger. The orders were signed by the new secretary of war, Judah P. Benjamin.

Whiting finished his drink and without conscious thought poured another. Three weeks ago, when he had departed for his tour of inspection, Judah Benjamin was attorney general. Now, as if by magic, he was secretary of war. As far as Whiting could tell, from reports and his own limited personal contact with Benjamin, the bland, affable, moonfaced Jew had absolutely no qualifications for managing an army. *Politics again! He knows nothing about war except how to use it for political advantage!* Had Davis taken leave of his senses, or had he shuffled the Cabinet in order to placate his vociferous critics in the Georgia, Alabama, and Louisiana legislatures? If nothing else, Judah Benjamin was innocuous; his appointment was as bland a compromise as could be imagined. No state would feel slighted, although all the states might be puzzled. The real strategic decisions, Whiting guessed, were being made by Davis's trusted friend General Braxton Bragg, with Benjamin passively signing documents.

That was bad enough, Whiting thought. He had served with Bragg and found him to be contentious, abrasive, and soured by chronic dyspepsia. But to take the Albemarle Sound District away from Whiting's command and give it to Huger? When it was Huger who held hostage the cannons that might save Roanoke Island? It was unfathomable, beyond logic or reason. And it had already been done (*In response to your request . . .*), sneaked into place, before Whiting could protest.

He was so angry that he did not feel the effects of the third drink. He stuck his head outside the office and ordered anyone within hearing to bring coffee.

An angry telegram would do no good. Huger was the sort of bureaucratic general who thrived on telegrams, minutes, and memoranda. His tactical skills with pen and paper had no doubt helped him secure his current prestigious post in the first place. The amount of leverage one might exert on him depended on who wielded the most power in Richmond on any given day, Huger's patrons or one's own. And Huger was much better acquainted with those shifting tides than Whiting ever wanted to be. Whiting tallied up the things he knew for sure:

1. There was some long-simmering rancor between Jefferson Davis and his chief field commander, Joseph E. Johnston, reportedly dating from a romantic rivalry during their days as West Point cadets.
2. Joe Johnston had probably done more to generate the victory at Bull Run than any other man, but when Davis handed out promotions after the victory, Johnston was last on the list, an affront that drew a formal protest from the touchy Johnston. The Richmond

papers had gotten hold of a copy and editorialized on Johnston's behalf. Davis was predictably furious and accused Johnston of giving private information to the press. Johnston denied it in tones of fullest umbrage.

3. Whiting's strategy for the North Carolina coast had been reviewed and approved by Johnston, Hill, and Beauregard. Benjamin Huger might not know that.

4. Davis was also at loggerheads with Beauregard, whose swaggering personal style the dour president found obnoxious. Both Beauregard and Johnston had spoken disparagingly and publicly about Judah Benjamin's fitness to be secretary of war.

5. The one general who consistently had the president's ear as well as his full support, Braxton Bragg, might very well be using Benjamin as a cat's paw to influence Confederate strategy as Bragg thought it should go.

6. Ben Huger was an avowed Bragg partisan and one of the few officers who could stand being in the same room with Bragg for more than fifteen minutes.

At this point, Whiting stopped trying to figure things out. The Confederacy was not yet one year old, and while its primary objective—survival—was crystal clear, everything between good intentions and the achievement of that objective was already hopelessly befogged. The whole labyrinthine structure was dizzying. Not since the generals of post-Caesarian Rome, thought Whiting, have brave, clearheaded soldiers been forced to perform their duties in the depths of such political murk.

He wadded up the sheet of foolscap he had scribbled on and threw it angrily across his office. No, indeed; nothing could be done with words on paper, and certainly not at a distance. There were too many arcane obstructions, too many quicksand pits. But in person, man to man, Ben Huger could be intimidated—*that much,* Whiting knew. There seemed only one course of action open to Whiting: he must confront Huger in person, as a battlefield general squaring off against a paper-pusher, and browbeat him into acquiescence.

So Chase Whiting would not acknowledge this directive from Richmond, and he would not telegraph Huger in advance. He would simply go to Norfolk and *appear* in full dress uniform. As weary as he was, he kept remembering the naive patriotism of those ragged young men on Roanoke Island, and knew that his conscience would not rest until he had done everything in his power to give them a fighting chance.

Chase Whiting's anger began to simmer again as soon as his train slowed down to negotiate the Norfolk switching yard. A string of flatcars was parked on a spur line curving east toward a complex of storage sheds and warehouses. Some of the cargo was still shrouded in tarpaulins, but several cars lay open to the elements, obviously awaiting the crews and machinery needed to transfer their heavy loads.

"Good God!" gasped Whiting, causing several nearby passengers to turn their heads in his direction. He could not quite believe it, but there, not forty yards from where he sat, was God's own plenty of artillery. During the brief interval when the flatcars were visible, he saw three 8-inch columbiads, a pair of 42-pounder naval guns, a 7-inch Blakely and, most tantalizing of all, an entire battery of 6.4-inch seacoast Parrott rifles that could hurl shells out to sixty-eight hundred yards and solid shot to eight thousand yards, equaling or surpassing the range of any U.S. Navy ship capable of negotiating the passage into Pamlico Sound. Then the track curved and Whiting obtained a brief glimpse of a warehouse interior stacked with iron cylinders and wooden carriages—field guns, he guessed, at least thirty of them. It was as if Norfolk were a gigantic magnet whose pull drew hither every piece of artillery within a hundred-mile radius. How many of those weapons were intended for Wise's forces on Roanoke? If General Huger's need was so great, why were these guns sitting idle?

Whiting vowed grimly that he would not leave Norfolk without answers. He was quite prepared to throw the weight of his expertise at Benjamin Huger, even if the result was an unseemly quarrel and the eventual displeasure of Jefferson Davis.

Despite his slight stature, Whiting cut an imposing figure in his finest uniform. The first sentry he encountered, at the gate to the rail yard, snapped to attention and gave a parade-ground salute. Whiting asked directions to General Huger's headquarters. If General Whiting needed a horse, the sentry promised, one would be found, for the distance was about a mile. Whiting shook his head; the walk would give him time to compose his thoughts—although at that moment he felt quite capable of wringing Huger's fat neck, he did not want to barge in looking for a fight.

Huger's headquarters was located in a stout, two-story brick building from whose upper windows one could enjoy a sweeping view of the harbor and the broad silvery bay beyond. The view from the bottom story was severely limited, however, because the building's outer walls had been fortified—up to the middle of the window frames—with a massive sloping dike of sandbags, rather as though General Huger were anticipating a flood of biblical proportions. The front entrance was guarded by two sentries who carried, in addition to bayoneted rifles, a brace of revolvers stuck through their belts. Off to one side, aiming in the general direction of Maryland, was a 12-pounder howitzer well supplied with cases of grapeshot.

After Whiting had introduced himself and stated his business, one sentry ducked inside to announce the visitor. The remaining guard remained stiffly braced at attention. He looked so uncomfortable that Whiting took pity; the private was just a boy. "As you were, son, I'm not here to see how well your buttons are polished." Whiting gestured at the gun and the sandbags and said, "Is General Huger expecting the enemy to lay siege to this location?"

A quick insubordinate flicker of disdain twisted the sentry's mouth as he replied, in the tone of a man answering the same question for the one-hundredth time: "General Huger believes in being prepared for any possible contingency, sir."

This morning, thought Whiting, I am a contingency he is not counting on.

The other sentry now returned, looking somewhat flustered.

"General Huger sends his compliments, sir, and his apologies. He is dictating some important dispatches to Richmond and does not want his train of thought interrupted. Could the general please return in one hour? General Huger will be happy to see you at that time."

Whiting felt his cheeks flush. "When a general comes calling on another general, the dictation of memoranda is customarily set aside."

Obviously uncomfortable with the message he was sent to convey, the private forged ahead. "General Huger says, you being an engineer and all, why not take a walk down by the shore and inspect our defenses?"

"Very well. I shall return in one hour."

Under other circumstances, Whiting would have enjoyed his walk to the coastal batteries—the day was bright with the particular quality of light that only comes at the end of autumn. At least he could see for himself whether or not Norfolk's security required so many cannons.

He scrutinized the defenses with an engineer's eye: they were uniformly constructed and sited logically, as though someone had studied a map of the coast, stuck pins in the likeliest spots, and then commenced to fortify them all according to the same pattern. In fact, Norfolk's defenses looked as though they had been *assembled* from one huge box full of uniform components. No matter what the angle of slope, the fluctuations of tide, the natural cover or lack of it, from place to place the batteries were identical, as though each one had been forged serially by a vast tool-and-die stamper. Every place the same: the guns were all mounted *en barbette*, so they could fire over the top of earthen ramparts, their ammunition neatly stacked in pyramids, their powder protected by small semicircular *ravelins* that might absorb a few cannonballs but offered no defense against plunging fire except for canvas tarpaulins shielding them from rain. The gun crews lived in small tin-roofed huts about fifty yards behind their pieces and a hundred yards from their outhouses, and the ground between their quarters and their weapons was bare trampled sea-grass and sand.

As Whiting strode past one battery after another, he felt a growing unease. These defenses appeared to have been copied directly from a textbook dating back to the Mexican War. Against a foe armed with short-range smoothbores firing solid shot, they were adequate. Against a steam frigate firing powerful shells from 11-inch Dahlgrens, they would not last long. Whoever had been in charge of the work had simply studied a diagram and reproduced it without the slightest regard for terrain or changing technology. Almost to a man, the crews looked bored and listless, and the officers he spoke to were no keener than the men serving under them. A common thread ran through their remarks: not one of them believed there was the remotest chance of the enemy launching a frontal amphibious assault on Norfolk, not when the port could be outflanked at numerous points along this side of the James River. As for the uninspired uniformity of the works, that was the way they had been sketched out by someone sent from Richmond and that was the way General Huger wanted them to be. And although Huger seldom left the security of his brick bastion to actually visit the batteries, no officer wanted to risk his wrath by deviating from the original configuration. "Just in case he *does* make a surprise inspection," as one rather shamefaced lieutenant told Whiting, who only shook his head in dismay before walking off to inspect the next position.

Lost in maudlin contemplation, Whiting used up half of his idle hour and was on the verge of returning to Huger's little castle when he topped a large sand dune and came within sight of Seabird Point, a strategically vital bluff overlooking the confluence of the James River and the Chesapeake Bay. What he saw when he topped the dune was so strikingly different from any other position that he muttered, "Now *that's* more like it!"

Whoever had laid out this position knew his business. In conformance with the terrain—a broad wedge of elevated dunes that undulated in several natural lines, forming a low bluff that afforded excellent observation—the battery had been shaped into a classic arrowhead *redan.* Ships firing at it would strike it at an angle, which would greatly weaken the effect of their shells. The tip of the arrow had been left blunt, however—a configuration the French called *pan coupé*—so that one of the battery's guns could fire straight out.

The walls of the *redan* were massive and tremendously thick, girded with huge gabions filled with sand. They would absorb rather than transmit the impact of both roundshot and pointed shells. Each gun pit was roofed with logs and sand, then covered with slabs of sod from which quick-growing sea grass had sprouted. Not only were the gunners shielded from overhead bursts, but their very positions would appear, from any distance greater than a few hundred yards, to be ordinary dunes. The men's quarters had been designed with similar care: the basic huts had been covered over to look like weed-strewn mounds. The entrances faced *away* from the beach and the crews could move from their sleeping quarters to their battle stations by means of deep zigzag trenches.

Powder and ammunition were dispersed so that each weapon had its own magazine—reinforced bunkers dug into the back side of the ramparts, which appeared to Whiting to be invulnerable to anything except an incredibly lucky random shot. To complete the arrangement, a thick abatis of fallen trees, their outward-facing limbs whittled to sharp points, had been emplaced on the beach, on both flanks, for a length of at least one hundred yards.

His thoughts focused on professional admiration, Whiting jumped when something exploded on his right, where the coastal bluffs tapered off into shallow gullies. Turning in that direction, he saw a small sandy cloud of smoke rising into the wind. As soon as the smoke dissipated, a group of soldiers, led by a dapper young officer, came out of cover to inspect the site of the detonation. Intensely curious, Whiting walked in their direction, halting only when one of the men spotted his rank and called everyone to attention. Salutes were exchanged and the young officer in charge strode forward with his hand outstretched. Whiting judged the fellow to be in his midtwenties; he was inordinately handsome, with a warm gaze, wavy hair, and a profile that looked as though it was waiting to be stamped on a Roman coin.

"Captain William Lamb, at your service!"

Whiting pointed to the small scorched crater and saw, for the first time, strands of copper wire extending back to an occult-looking contraption of Leyden jars, magnetic coils, and levers.

"Is this some sort of secret weapon, Captain Lamb?"

The young man smiled and nodded proudly. "Indeed it is, sir. We are trying to perfect a galvanic torpedo, actuated by electrical current. The idea is to surround our position with a field of them and detonate them, in relative safety, from inside the battery if the enemy should launch an infantry attack."

"Ingenious!" Whiting was genuinely impressed. "The idea seems to work."

Lamb shook his head. "In theory and with small amounts of powder, yes. But it is far from reliable—the detonating devices are cumbersome and fragile, and if we bury the wires deep enough to protect them from shellfire, they inevitably become corroded by the groundwater beneath us. I am considering coating the wires with gutta-percha, but so far I have not found a source for it. Perhaps I could send a blockade-runner to Malaya."

Whiting enjoyed his first laugh in many days. Not only was this young man resourceful and technically skilled, he radiated optimism and good humor. His gunners moved and spoke with a palpable energy he had not seen anywhere else that morning. He asked Lamb what class he had graduated with.

"Class, General? What sort of class?" Lamb appeared genuinely puzzled.

"West Point, of course! You don't learn this kind of engineering skill in a seminary!"

"I am not a West Point man, sir. But I am fascinated by heavy guns and the art of fortification—for I regard it as nothing less than an art. Why, you have only to study the works of Vauban to see an exquisite combination of strength and aesthetic symmetry. As for this position, I have designed it to replicate, on a very small scale, the Great Redan of Sevastopol, which was a masterpiece!"

"You have a natural talent, Captain Lamb—I would have supposed this work to be the design of a very experienced engineer."

"I am complimented, sir. Would you like a guided tour?"

"I would indeed, but it will have to wait until after I meet with General Huger. I fear I shall be somewhat late as it is, but since he has already kept *me* waiting, I have no compunction about the matter. We will speak again, Captain."

Whiting was, in fact, only ten minutes late for his appointment; the return walk was much brisker, for he did not need to observe anything more. If Huger really anticipated an invasion, he needed more men like Lamb instead of more guns, which he already had in plenty.

When he reached Huger's headquarters, one of the sentries stopped him and requested, with some embarrassment, that the general please wipe the sand from his boots before entering. Then he proffered a dingy towel that was evidently kept nearby for just that purpose. Whiting was too flabbergasted to protest.

Inside the building, an aide escorted him to Huger's office and opened the door for him. The two generals saluted and exchanged formal greetings. Benjamin Huger looked exactly as Whiting remembered him: pudgy and florid, beardless, and quick to perspire. A well-fed stove made the room suffocatingly hot, so that Huger's head gleamed as though he had rubbed it with oil. Periodically, he took out an immense checkered handkerchief and mopped his brow. Whiting wondered why the man simply did not open his window and temper the atmosphere with a draft of brisk sea air.

Without preamble, Whiting reported the deplorable condition of the coastal defenses and pointed out that Norfolk was garrisoned by fifteen thousand idle troops. Huger took offense.

"Idle, sir? When the enemy's largest naval base lies right across the bay? It is only a matter of time before Norfolk is invaded from the water! When that happens, I shall need every man and every gun."

"Including the cannons sitting uselessly in the rail yard? General, the real danger to Norfolk lies to the south, where the enemy already has a foothold. If Roanoke Island falls, what's to stop the Yankees from sailing up the Dismal Swamp Canal and taking Norfolk from the rear? At the moment, there is nothing at all to prevent that. Do you have any evidence that this massive invasion is actually imminent?"

"Indeed I do, sir! My agents have sent numerous articles from the Northern press, hinting that such an action is being planned."

"Did these same agents actually *see* preparations being made?"

"How could they? Hampton Roads is always full of ships, and units of troops are always marching through. I suspect the preparations are being made in some secret place along the Chesapeake shore, troops arriving by night and hiding by day."

Whiting did not point out that there was no place on that coast "secret" enough to hide the massive buildup that would have to presage any amphibious operation of the size Huger envisioned. Instead, he tried more indirect reasoning.

"Does it not seem likely that those newspaper accounts were purposefully planted, to keep attention focused on Norfolk while the enemy actually prepares to invade North Carolina? Besides, sir, I am not asking you to strip Norfolk of its defenses, just to part with a few thousand men and some suitable guns. My state lies open to the enemy, whenever and wherever he chooses to move!"

Huger's complexion reddened even more and he balled his right hand into a fist, stopping just short of pounding the desk.

"Your state, sir, is forever whining and complaining for more than its fair share! To be candid, I do not entirely trust the citizens of North Carolina and neither does President Davis—they were the last to secede and did so reluctantly. You want cooler heads and harder work from the men you do have, instead of more troops. Show them an example, General—nothing is more tonic for dispirited troops than a commanding presence."

"Those are strange words coming from an officer who seldom leaves his fortress to spend time among his own men."

Huger's fist now came down and he rose in anger, stung by the rebuke. A fine cloud of spittle issued from his quivering, fleshy lips.

"See here, General Whiting! I run my command as I see fit, and my plans have been approved by no less a personage than Braxton Bragg. *My old friend*, Braxton Bragg. The northern coast of Carolina was made a separate district at your own request and you no longer have command over it. I do!"

A vulpine smile stretched Huger's mouth. "You can, of course, take this dispute to Richmond for adjudication, but I think you already know the futility of that."

"Yes," said Whiting, tasting bitterness. "*Your friend* Braxton Bragg. I am sure he would take your side in this quarrel."

"No one has the president's ear more closely." Huger's expression turned smug. Now that he held the high cards, he shifted into a conciliatory mood, knowing full well that many other reputable officers held him in less esteem than Bragg, and knowing that Bragg, even though he would side with Huger, might well be angered by such a distraction.

"Come, come, General Whiting. Our defenses are almost complete, and when the last works are finished, I'll see to it that Roanoke Island gets some of the leftover guns. Meantime, light a fire under this fellow Wise and see if he can't raise the fighting spirit of the men he already has, rather than constantly bombarding me with pleas for more of everything."

Whiting would have to be content with that vague promise, for he sensed the gray stony weight of the Richmond bureaucracy shoring up Ben Huger. He rose and nodded coldly.

"There is one small favor I ask of you, one officer to another, informally."

Huger looked at him with eyes like a badger's.

"And what is that, sir?"

"Can you not spare me one man? I met an officer today who impressed me with his spirit and imagination. A young fellow named Lamb. I could make good use of him down at Wilmington."

"Spare him? Why, I shall be happy to be rid of him! A damned insubordinate troublemaker. I'll have him transferred as soon as a suitable replacement can be found. Is there anything else?"

"No, General Huger, I suppose there is not. Good day."

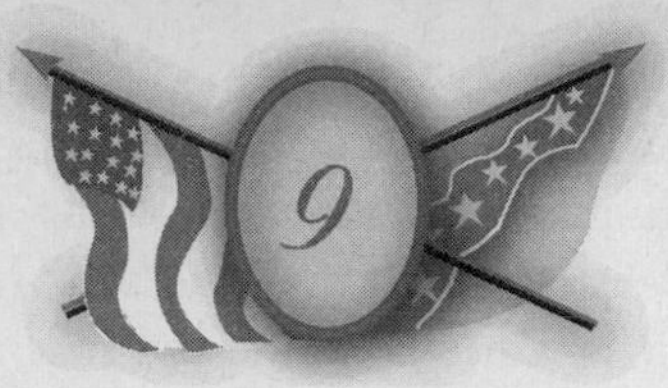

High Tides and Moonless Nights

AT THE THEATRE:

Wednesday Evening, January 8, 1862

THE FAMOUS THESPIAN FAMILY "THE QUEEN SISTERS"
Of Charleston, S.C., whose performances in all the principal Southern cities have elicited the highest encomiums of the Press And the Public, will make their first local appearance in the Amazing piece, written expressly for them, entitled:

THE VIGILANCE COMMITTEE
Or
A LOVER IN A BOX

Which gives an amusing sketch of the principal events of Secession, culminating in a grand tableau depicting the Yankee rout at Bull Run and a droll parody of "Honest Abe's Worst Nightmare." This lavish production features Much Singing and Dancing. Music by THE PALMETTO BAND!

Doors open at 7 o'clock, to commence at 7:30. Admission to Parquette and Dress Circle: 50 cents. Gallery: 25 cents.

—The Wilmington Journal, January 9 1862

October in Washington had been dry and unseasonably hot and perpetual dust clouds coated the shriveling leaves and caused pedestrians to wheeze and cough. But on the last day of the month came autumn rain in abundance. The capital's boulevards quickly turned into canals of mire and the trees dripped mud until the downpour scoured them clean of dust and beat their leaves to the ground, where they formed treacherous, hard-to-see hazards and caused many people to slip.

In the office of Secretary of the Navy Gideon Welles, a strategy conference convened at ten o'clock in the morning. Present were Welles, General Ambrose Burnside, Commodore Louis M. Goldsborough, and three brigade commanders: Brigadiers John G. Foster, Jesse Reno, and John Parke; the role of each man was clearly understood by all. Less definite was the role of Colonel Rush Hawkins and General Benjamin Butler. One could speculate about Hawkins—as commander of the Union troops on the Outer Banks, he was there, presumably, to contribute fresh information about the state of things on that coast. But no one, not even Welles, knew why Ben Butler was here. Butler sometimes showed up unexpectedly at important meetings, even when he had no logical interest in the matters under discussion—nor, for that matter, any contribution to make. Usually, he just stayed in the background and observed the proceedings with the patient, hooded gaze of a crocodile. Everyone knew Butler was politically very powerful and that unpleasant things sometimes happened to men who opposed him. Surely, someone very high in the Lincoln administration knew where Butler went and approved of his habitual eavesdropping. He was an éminence gris whom no one wished either to acknowledge or to ignore. His presence at the Navy Department, however, was almost certainly connected with Colonel Hawkins, who was rumored to be Butler's protégé and whom Butler had promoted—over the head of at least one senior officer—after the capture of the Hatteras forts.

One important person should have been present—it was his strategy at the top of the agenda, after all—and that was General George McClellan. But everyone knew that on the next morning, November 1, 1961, McClellan would assume command of the entire Federal military establishment, replacing the stouthearted but superannuated Winfield Scott, who had lost his mental equilibrium after the debacle of Manassas. In McClellan were vested the hopes and passions of the Northern public and the press. Vain and arrogant he might be, but there was no more progressive mind in the army, and no better organizer. Everyone who had been frightened and stung by the Rebel victory could now rest more easily at night; "Little Mac" would set things right.

Of course, Welles was informed about the new commander's strategy and supported it wholeheartedly, but the one man in the room who truly knew McClellan's mind was Ambrose Burnside. The two men were old friends. In 1852, Burnside had staked most of his personal wealth on a breech-loading carbine he had invented, manufactured in token quantities, and hoped to sell to the government in great numbers. When the government declined and Burnside found himself in serious financial trouble, McClellan, who was then an executive with the Illinois Central Railroad, stepped in and offered his friend a high-paying job with the firm. Burnside did well in the railroad business and soon rose to become treasurer of the corporation.

Burnside was also a West Point man, Class of '47, and when war broke out, he was a natural candidate for command. Appointed leader of the First Rhode Island, he got a taste of combat at Manassas. His performance in that engagement was undistinguished, but since so many Federal officers had done as badly or worse, no one paid much attention. In August, he had been promoted to general.

He was thirty-seven years old and a man of impressive countenance. He had a bald, lofty cranium whose wispy fringe of top hair was turned into a bristling statement of virility by the bushy muttonchop whiskers that hung from his cheeks, arched over his clean-shaven chin, and met like an exclamation point at the philtrum of his nose. His gaze was stern and penetrating, his brows beetling and aggressive, and his most habitual expression was a ferocious scowl.

Since late September, he was commander in chief of a force known as Burnside's Coastal Division. His assignment was to bring the war to the Rebels by implementing concepts McClellan had developed during his many sessions with the Blockade Strategy Board. There, McClellan had found young, energetic officers who shared his appreciation of modern technology instead of being mystified by it, as were the elderly cronies of Winfield Scott. Where those mens' imaginations were held captive by their memories of the Mexican War, McClellan surveyed things from the much more up-to-date perspective of the Crimean conflict, a pivotally transitional war that he had observed closely while serving in a U.S. Army delegation sent overseas to report on new military technology and its impact on operations and tactics. The Crimean campaigns proved that rifled weapons gave a massive advantage to the defense, rendering the traditional Napoleonic frontal assault a very costly, if not entirely futile, proposition. McClellan's insight went deeper, however. Almost as important as modern firepower, he theorized, were the twin inventions of the telegraph and the railroad.

For an army operating on internals lines—for example, the Confederates—those two innovations offered tremendous advantages. The telegraph communicated fresh information about enemy movements, and the railroads permitted the rapid concentration of men and supplies to counter those moves with localized superiority. The telegraph and the railroad, McClellan argued, were the reasons behind the South's stunning victory at Manassas, not some mythical quality of battlefield invincibility. If the South's rail junctions, bridges, and telegraph stations could be neutralized even partly, the Confederate field armies would be left blind, hungry, and immobilized. Moreover, the enemy's war effort was absolutely dependent upon only two rail networks: the lines going east through the Mississippi Valley and those running south to north along the Atlantic seaboard. To utterly paralyze the Confederacy, he reasoned, you needed only to seize the critical rail junctions: Jackson, Corinth, Nashville, Knoxville, Decatur, Selma, Montgomery, Charleston, and Goldsboro, North Carolina. If even half of those objectives could be taken swiftly, the Confederacy would be fragmented and forced either to recapture them or to surrender. McClellan did not count on a quick surrender, but he did reckon on decimating the Rebels' counterattacks with his well-entrenched weaponry. The resulting bloodbath, he believed, would ultimately lead to their capitulation.

He could easily see from his maps that all of those rail junctions except Knoxville could be reached by water. It would require months of planning, training, and logistical stockpiling before the Union army could hope to overwhelm the defenses of Richmond in one grand climactic campaign, but in the meantime, the Union did have a powerful navy and the capacity to conduct swift, stunning, amphibious thrusts, at virtually any point it chose along the vast Rebel coastline. Once McClellan knew he would be placed in full command, he authorized the formation of two amphibious forces: Burnside's fifteen-thousand-man division, supported by Commodore Goldsborough's fleet, and a similar legion, led by Commodore DuPont, tasked with capturing Port Royal, South Carolina, and turning it into the primary supply depot for the entire blockade fleet.

DuPont's force was already in motion, and on this rainy morning, Burnside's division would officially be activated. It would not be able to sail, however, until January 1862 at the earliest. The biggest delay was caused by the lack of suitable transports.

The gruff, pipe-smoking Goldsborough made that plain in a gravelly voice: "Gentlemen, I have just returned from a personal inspection of the auxiliary vessels that have been purchased by General Burnside's agents and sailed—or in some cases *towed*—to Hampton Roads. There are fifty-five ships in all, and of that number perhaps a dozen are truly seaworthy. I have clambered over, in, and around vessels of every size, description, and state of decrepitude. We have a fleet composed of worn-out passenger ferries, tugs, fishing boats, mail packets, a former slave-ship, and at least three craft which, from their appearance and odor, served until recently as garbage scows."

Burnside interjected, his side-whiskers bristling: "Commodore, I dispatched for this purpose some experienced New England officers. The need was great and time was pressing. No doubt some advantage was taken by waterfront sharpies to unload vessels no longer in their prime, but I could not very well order my men to dive in and make an underwater inspection of each ship. If it floated, could move under its own power, and was large enough to hold men, horses, and powder, it was purchased. I did not have a mogul's treasury at my disposal. And I do realize that several of these craft broke down on their way from Boston, New York, and wherever else they were starting from, but . . ."

"Six of them broke down, to be exact," huffed Goldsborough, jetting pipe smoke from his mouth. "The fault lies not with your agents, General, but with the scoundrels who took advantage of them. *My point* is that I must now detach a large number of carpenters and shipfitters to plug the leaks, shore up the hulls, and repair the steam engines. Consequently, we cannot hope to assemble the full armada until Christmas at the earliest.

"As for the navy's part, we will have all our ships assembled and fully supplied on or about December first. The fleet will comprise twenty ships, mounting a total of sixty-four guns. Fifteen of those are the new nine-inch Dahlgrens, which are potent weapons indeed. Ammunition and victuals are fully loaded. You may count on the navy, gentlemen."

Gideon Welles looked up from the notes he was scratching and nodded to Burnside, who then rose and nodded to each of the generals present, with the pointed exception of Ben Butler and his young sycophant Hawkins. Observing the slight, Butler tugged nervously at one of his chins.

"Organization of the Coastal Division has been made final, and our orders have officially been issued. Generals Foster, Reno, and Clarke command three brigades of infantry, sixteen regiments, twelve thousand men in all.

"Our objectives, in order of priority, are as follows: one—the capture of Roanoke Island; two—the capture of New Bern and Beaufort, which will then be transformed into coaling stations and supply depots; three—the capture or neutralization of Fort Macon. If circumstances seem favorable after these operations have been completed, we have discretionary permission to launch a raid against the important rail junction at Goldsboro and to destroy as much of the Wilmington and Weldon Railroad as we can."

General Foster, a solidly built man with luxurious whiskers and a reputation for quiet competence, raised his hand.

"If we meet with extraordinary success, might we move also against Raleigh or Wilmington?"

"I know how strongly you support that strategy, John, but McClellan has a wait-and-see opinion. On paper, those plans look promising, but on the ground they may prove too risky. The Rebs might fold up and run away, or they may react to our attacks like angry hornets. By all means, continue to develop your idea, but do not get your hopes up."

Butler raised a meaty hand and waved it like a schoolboy seeking the teacher's attention.

"Yes, General Butler?"

"General Burnside, you have read the reports of Colonel Rush Hawkins"—he patted Hawkins on the shoulder with an avuncular touch that made Hawkins's eyes widen in surprise—"who is the only senior officer with firsthand knowledge of conditions on the North Carolina coast. His bravery in storming the Hatteras forts is a matter of record, and he is eager to lead his regiment, the Ninth New York, in the coming campaign. In view of his experience and the sterling nature of his character, for which I can vouch most heartily, I'd like to submit a request that he be promoted to brigadier general, and be appointed second-in-command of the First Brigade, authorized to take over should General Foster be wounded or become otherwise indisposed. Here is the document—signed by a number of prominent senators and officers."

Rush Hawkins felt his cheeks flush. Butler had often spoke of "giving him a hand up," but this request was highly irregular and more than a bit embarrassing. During the next few seconds, Hawkins could feel the temperature fall several degrees. Butler remained standing, hand outstretched, the petition wavering in his pudgy fingers like a loose shutter that was irritatingly out of reach. Gideon Welles stared at Butler with open incredulity, his jaw clenched and nostrils wide. Generals Reno, Foster, and Parke exchanged uneasy glances. Burnside looked as though he were struggling to suppress a raucous laugh. Finally, after clearing his throat elaborately, he took the paper from Butler's hand and made a demonstration of glancing over it.

"Mmm, yes. Impressive names, these. Unfortunately, I do not see either President Lincoln's signature or that of General McClellan. I do, however, have documents authorizing the current structure of command and approving the operation *as I have just described it.* To which, I can assure you, McClellan's signature is appended. If you wish to submit your memorandum as a formal proposal, we can do so very quickly—a telegram to McClellan's headquarters describing your proposal should bring a prompt response."

Butler weighed the full implications; he knew men who, at the moment, were more influential and even more politically powerful than George McClellan. But if McClellan *did* take Richmond the following spring, he would almost certainly become the next president of the United States. If so, he would not look kindly upon any man who had distracted him on his march to victory.

Butler folded his papers, cleared his throat, and dipped his head in acknowledgment of the awkwardness he had injected into an otherwise smooth conference.

"Gentlemen, it's not my intention to distract you, and certainly not my wish to annoy General McClellan. I merely wanted to make sure that Colonel Hawkins is given responsibilities commensurate with his proven abilities."

John Foster lifted his gaze toward Hawkins, not even deigning to glance at Butler. "Colonel Hawkins, you will have ample chance to prove your worth as a loyal regimental commander. And don't worry: should I be killed or wounded, my replacement will reward you—or not, as he sees fit. I'll see to it that he keeps a close eye on you."

Hawkins looked so uncomfortable that it was hard not to feel pity for him.

"I understand, sir," he stammered. "I will be that loyal regimental commander and will follow you to the gates of Hell if you so order."

"The beaches of Roanoke Island will be far enough, thank you," rumbled Foster. "Now, if you two gentlemen have nothing further to contribute . . . we have much work to do." Hawkins saluted with the prim rectitude of a West Point plebe, turned smartly on his heel, and opened the conference-room door for Butler.

When the interlopers had gone, Burnside shook his head ruefully. "That man Butler is a bloated tick on the body politic. And Colonel Hawkins . . . "

"Is the parasite who lives on the tick's back," chuckled Foster. "Don't worry, Ambrose. I shall make sure Hawkins gets his chance to be valorous. And it won't be like Fort Hatteras—this time, people will be shooting at him."

November 7th, 1861
Aboard the USS Cambridge
At the mouth of the Rappahannock River
Dearest Mother—
Forgive the long interruption between my letters and rest assured that it was caused by no grievous wound. About two weeks ago, I contracted Typhus Fever, which illness necessitated a lengthy recuperation at the main Navy hospital in Hampton Roads. Due to the high fever, I remember little of the first week, indeed sometimes it seems that delirium can be a merciful state! But when I regained awareness, I discovered that I had lost fifteen pounds of body weight, and as you know, I am skinny to begin with and can ill afford to lose an ounce. My chief attendant, a gruff Rhode Island physician aptly named "Dr. Cutter," described my recovery as "remarkable".

On the tenth day of my recuperation, I received a surprise visit from an old Annapolis mate, Lieutenant Charles Flusser, who graduated one class ahead of me and has advanced farther in rank as a consequence of that and of his generally good behavior. He brought news that I have been assigned to a new ship, the Cambridge, *which he describes wryly as "a very sharp little vessel."*

"It is good to see you, William," he said, shaking my hand. He sat by my bed and for a while we reminisced about jolly times and common friends. After a time, he remarked, "Aside from being pale and wan, you look to be on the mend. The doctors told me you were nearing the end of your stay here, but I wanted to look at you closely before making you this

proposition." I caught the scent of action and immediately gave him my full attention. He had recently learned that there was a loaded blockade-runner anchored near the mouth of the Curatoma branch of the river, which is to say about twenty-six miles from the Rappahannock's mouth. He had proposed to take a small vessel up and cut that ship out. When he learned that I was idle in my bed, he thought, "It would be a shame for Will Cushing to miss out on this!" *and so came to see for himself whether or not I was fit to accompany him.*

Well, Mother, the very idea acted on me like a tonic. Two days later, I discharged myself from the hospital, donned my uniform, and followed old Flusser to a warehouse where I was outfitted with a cutlass, a revolver, and a Sharp's Rifle. We sailed in a converted tug, the USS Rescue *armed with a 32pdr. I was placed in command of that weapon.*

We steamed without incident up the river, and found a schooner of some 120 tons, fully loaded with lumber and wheat, whose crew, apparently, had hurriedly abandoned ship when they saw us approaching. There being no Rebel troops about to dispute us, we put the runner to the torch and remained long enough to make sure she burned to the waterline.

Our return trip was certainly lively. Having been caught napping, the local Confederates now sought to cut us off and repay us in kind. When we were abreast of a place called Mary's Point, we came under a brisk fire from a field piece and some riflemen, estimated at 30 or so. The first shot from the shore was well-laid, as it carried away the davits on our port side. Struck once! *I thought, then turned to my crew and ordered them, "Load canister, boys, and aim just below that large patch of drifting smoke!" We drove the Rebel gunners away quickly, then took our time about targeting their cannon. One shell was enough to dismount the weapon, and I caught a glimpse of its barrel as it tumbled down and raised a great splash in the water.*

Despite a perfect rain of balls, we suffered only two men wounded before sailing out of rifle range. When we returned, we received hearty congratulations. I came through safely, although my coat did not, for a deckhouse splinter torn off by one of the Rebels' roundshots struck that useful garment, but knowing that it is impossible to kill a midshipman, it only tore the coat and lodged in the vest, where I found it. It was not over-large, no bigger than my fist, but I have kept it as a memento and plan to send it to you as soon as the next mail leaves the Cambridge, *where I am now fully returned to normal and tedious blockade patrols.*

Things grew lively again last Sunday, however, as we intercepted two boatloads of contraband Negroes who had been watching our route from the shore and risked their all to steal the boats and reach us. They are all stout and healthy, and would likely have been worth many tens of thousands of dollars to their previous owners. They are now happy as flies in a sugar bowl. They dance and sing every night, till my sides ache with laughter.

No place in Wilmington symbolized normalcy more than the grand and gilded Thalian Hall, whose columned entrance faced busy Princess Street, on the southern flank of City Hall. Indeed, the conjoining of those two facilities proclaimed to every visitor that this was a city where culture was honored, inextricably woven into the fabric of everyday life.

On this brisk November evening, one day after a rather jolly Thanksgiving feast laid on at Hobart-Hampton's headquarters in the big Yellow House on Market Street, the Wilmington gentry were flocking to the Thalian as though nothing at all had changed in their world. Gaslights danced in their fixtures, illuminating the bonnets and shawls of the women, the top hats, watch fobs, and rings of the men. Vehicles of all sorts and classes filled the street, their drivers jostling for positions as close to the entrance as possible. All that distinguished this evening from its antebellum equivalents was the unusual percentage of uniforms. That, and a subtle forced gaiety in the tone of conversation, as though everyone were trying very hard to reassure everyone else that such a display of fashion and civility, in and of itself, formed a bulwark strong enough to fend off the coming tempest. To Mary Harper Sloane, the mood of the other revelers seemed both brave and melancholy. But we too, she reflected, are behaving the same way, even though we have more reason than most to feel the imminence of some vast, dark, unpredictable tide. *We, too, are smiling our brightest smiles, and dressed for display. And despite the grave import of the night, we speak in gay and witty voices, seeking to charm, impress, and reassure. Is the real play inside, upon the stage, or out here in the street?*

Certainly, no man inside the theater or out was playing his part with more zest than Augustus Hobart-Hampden, who led the Sloanes and Landaus confidently through the crowd, clearing a path—by means of some palpable projection of authority—like Moses parting the waters. Although both Matthew and Jacob were dressed very well and very formally, H-H seemed radiant with virile authority, like a European dictator of fashion intent on bringing new paradigms of finery to the laggard provinces. Above a shirt of the best Lancastershire cotton he sported a glossy silk cravat, colored a subdued red with thin yet bold stripes of contrasting scarlet; his tone-on-tone waistcoat was woven from the costliest brocade, the neckline cut dashingly low; his frock coat, impeccably tailored to match his frame, was of the finest woolen broadcloth. Its color was a dark not-quite-black that verged on charcoal, and it was trimmed with velvet collars and buttoned, cuff-link style, with jeweled studs. As if to confirm that, yes indeed, this coat was the acme of the London tailor's craft, he wore in the single-notched lapel a small gold pin in the shape of the British lion. Completing this ensemble was a low-crowned, medium-brimmed Panama hat and well-made shoes trimmed with snow-white spats that seemed magically to repel all the random contaminants of the environment. In his right hand he carried a beautifully polished walking stick of Hindu teak, topped with a heavy, many-faceted knob of what certainly appeared to be pure silver. On a man of lesser self-assurance, such a turnout might have seemed gaudy, even dandified, but Hobart-Hampden simply made of his attire a bold and utterly individual statement. Men looked at him with envy; women just looked at him, often and speculatively.

The play this evening was an historical melodrama called *Brutus, or the Fall of Tarquin* by the once-popular John Howard Payne. The actors were capable and well-versed, but the dialogue seemed to Mary Harper to be overflorid and already archaic, despite the fact that the drama was scarcely twenty years old. More to the point, there seemed a disturbing incongruity between the pasteboard armor and wooden swords of the Romans strutting the stage and the cold, all-too-real glint of the swords worn by at least one-third of the men in the hall. Not long into the first act, her mind began to turn from the play to the more somber drama that would be enacted later that night, at one A.M., when the sickle moon crept from the sea and hung low above the horizon for a few hours, just long enough for the *Banshee* to clear New Inlet on her maiden voyage to Nassau.

Ever since the *Banshee*'s successful trials, Matthew had been impatient to load her up and go. But Hobart-Hampden counciled patience—matters were complicated, he said. Throughout October, the blockade was proven repeatedly to be a sham. So few Federal ships were on station at any one time that skippers running goods into

Savannah, Charleston, or Wilmington had a much greater risk of running aground than of running into a warship. So porous was the blockade off both the Atlantic and the Gulf ports that even sailing ships came and went more or less at their masters' pleasure. Cotton prices in Nassau and Bermuda were already so high that a schooner could haul enough bales to make her crewmen wealthy. Such vessels came into Wilmington at the rate of four or five a week and auctioned off their modest cargoes of luxury goods at quadruple the price they would have fetched in the spring.

A new sense of urgency altered the picture on November 7, when news came that a Federal expedition, under Commodore DuPont, had captured Port Royal, a previously unimportant harbor that was potentially the best supply base between Savannah and Charleston. Once that base became fully operational, the blockade ships would no longer have to steam back to Hampton Roads for revictualing and repair—which meant that each blockading vessel could stay on station for a much longer time. The net effect would be tantamount to doubling the number of available Yankee ships.

Such a bold and intelligent operation, H-H told them, signaled a much more serious approach to the blockade strategy. It was reasonable to assume that enemy spies now roamed the streets of Wilmington, keeping a sharp eye on the blockade-runners' comings and goings.

For this reason Matthew and Hobart-Hampden made preparations slowly and secretively for the all-important maiden voyage of the "Anglo-Confederate Trading Company," as their enterprise was now legally registered in both Nassau and Liverpool. In the weeks before Thanksgiving, the *Banshee* was gone on frequent short trips up and down the Cape Fear River and its tributaries, quietly and under cover of night taking on numerous small loads of pressed baled cotton along with barrels of naval stores and odd quantities of good tobacco. At one of those places, Matthew rendezvoused with a Confederate agent who contracted, with a down payment in gold eagles, for as much military cargo as the ship might bring back. And now the *Banshee* lay at the foot of Chestnut Street, low in the water, fully manned by close-mouthed sailors whom Hobart-Hampden had recruited, and watched over by an excited Fitz-John Bright, who paced the quarterdeck in full nautical dress, a brace of loaded pistols thrust, in the best piratical style, through his sash.

The visit to the Thalian had been Matthew's scheme—let the

cream of Wilmington society along with any Yankee spies now mingling with that part of the population see the Sloanes and the Landaus in formal attire, enjoying an evening at the theater. Neither Matthew nor Hobart-Hampden looked at all like men about to embark on a perilous voyage. At intermission, they mingled gaily with the rest of the audience, and when the play was finally over, they took their time about leaving. They planned to walk to Jacob's address and be publicly seen entering the house and extinguishing the lamp above the door.

They were forced, however, to make a considerable detour. A hard fast autumn rain had come down while they were in the theater and the city's numerous tiny creeks, called dry ponds by the inhabitants, were in full brief flood. Nowhere was the water so wide as to prevent the men from simply jumping over, but the two ladies, in their layered hoop skirts, could not be so athletic. Jacob scurried off to find a dry route and returned a moment later with news of a passable alley between First and Second Streets, which came out somewhere near the post office. The way proved dry, but dark and narrow. The men automatically assumed a protective formation, with Jacob and Matthew in front of the ladies and Hobart-Hampden, a lighted cheroot clamped in his teeth, bringing up the rear.

They had gone perhaps one-third of the distance when Mary Harper heard a faint splash, its volume multiplied by the walls, exactly as though someone had trodden into the rain pond behind them. A prickling went down her arms. Instinctively, she tightened her grip on Largo's hand and whispered to Hobart-Hampden, "H-H, I think we're being followed."

Hobart-Hampden knocked the ash from his cigar, smiled thinly, and said: "I know. They've been on our trail since we left the Thalian."

"They?"

Very firmly, the Englishman pushed Largo forward. "I'll explain later. Go on without me for the moment."

Her heart now thumping like a drum, Mary Harper lifted her skirts and increased her pace, while Largo did the same. Matthew shepherded Jacob and the ladies out into the lighted expanse of First Street, then turned back to render assistance to Hobart-Hampden. He barely had time to reenter the alley before the violence erupted.

It all happened very quickly: from the far end of the passage loomed two ragged men, one carrying a club and the other a long, curiously curved knife. As they launched themselves at Hobart-Hampden (one of them screaming "*Perfidious Albion!*" with a heavy barbarous accent), he leaped back like a panther and filled the distance between himself and the nearest assailant with a vicious swipe of his cane. The ruffian with the club went down, but the other redoubled his efforts to stab the Englishman, who backed up again, and with a motion so swift it registered as a blur, drew a sword from his cane. He parried—effortlessly, it seemed to the onlookers—several rough and clumsy thrusts, then leaped back once more to give himself room for an overhead cut that terminated in a solid crunch of bone and cartilage and a wail of agony. The second ertswhile assassin clutched at his right arm and ran away as fast as he could. Hobart-Hampden stooped and looked at something, then took out his pocket handkerchief and picked it up.

When he emerged into the streetlights, Mary Harper yelped and Largo gasped. Hobart-Hampden was holding the attacker's dagger with three of the assassin's fingers still wrapped around the hilt. After examining the style and workmanship of the scimitar, he nodded in satisfaction, then tossed weapon, fingers, and blood-spotted handkerchief back into the alley.

"*Lieber Gott!*" cried Jacob. "Were those Yankee agents?"

The Englishman chuckled and plunged his hands into a nearby watering trough.

"Hardly! If I had to venture a guess, I would say that they were agents of the sultan of Khorasan. He placed a huge bounty on my head after a bit of unpleasantness several years ago in Turkestan. Persistent blighters, I must say. Thought I'd given them the slip in Calcutta."

At Jacob's house, after a brief walk in utter silence, Matthew and Hobart-Hampden hurriedly changed into very different clothing. At midnight, a covered hansom stopped at the house and the five of them piled in and lowered the shades. The distance from the Landau house to the dock was not far, but this means of travel was more discreet than a stroll, and safer, too, as the earlier incident had proven.

By the time they disembarked at the foot of Chestnut Street, the runners-to-be did not need to watch for the moon. It was obscured by low black clouds and gusts of cold rain. The wharf smelled of tar and wet hemp, and the misty river smelled of marsh and reeds and tidal wrack.

Even from this close a distance, the *Banshee* was hard to see, her color not far removed from that of the clouds beyond the wheelhouse.

Her auxiliary masts had been folded away, to reduce both friction and visibility, and she rode very low. Inside her capacious holds were 740 bales of compressed cotton, each weighing 450 pounds, thirty-six barrels of turpentine, pitch, and tar, and a few hundredweight of tobacco, stored in bundles wherever there was room. From her stack drifted only the thinnest ribbon of coal smoke. Aside from the lantern being held at the top of the gangway by Mister Bright, not a glimmer of light showed; even to those viewing it from the dock, on such a night as this, it *crouched* more than "loomed," a massive and substantial darkness shrouded in several shades of moonless, rainswept night.

The actual moment of parting was brief. After embracing her husband with all her strength, Mary Harper grabbed Hobart-Hampden's hand and said, "Take good care of him, dear Augustus." He gallantly kissed her hand and replied: "Dear lady, he will return to you an even better man than he is now. You have my word on it."

There was little ceremony to the actual departure: all but two of the mooring lines had already been loosened. Steam pressure was sufficient to ease them down the river until they felt secure in firing up the boilers for the open sea. Ponderously, starboard bow first, the *Banshee* turned from the land and sought the river's embrace. A quick whisk of rain made the spectators duck their heads for a moment, and when they looked again, the *Banshee* was gone and all that remained of her presence was the fading heartbeat of her paddle wheels.

It had been arranged for Mary Harper to stay overnight in the Landaus' guest room; tomorrow, weather permitting, she would go home on one of Pine Haven's launches.

After a large glass of brandy, to ward off any ill effects from the weather, Jacob excused himself and climbed the stairs, leaving the two women alone in the parlor. Neither wanted to retire quite yet—both of them had just bid farewell to the men they loved (one of whom had nearly been skewered by a sinister *thugee* only an hour before) and both sought comfort in conversation. They might well have been sisters. Mary Harper saw in Largo both the energy and the boldness of youth, as well as a hungry curiosity for the world, a joy for pure experience. Largo's spirit has taken flight, thought Mary Harper, and she wished for her young companion an odyssey both high and wondrous . . . before she was compelled to return to earth, as all women are, sooner or later.

Largo gestured at the rain spots and mud stains on her gown. "We are both a mess, aren't we? Let's go upstairs and change into night clothes and then we can talk awhile in my room. And bring your glass and that bottle of brandy—I fear that after tonight's events, a glass of sherry simply will not do the trick."

"Won't your father know we've been drinking from it?"

Largo laughed dryly. "There are other bottles where that came from." Then, with a mighty rustling of petticoats, she whirled about and made for the stairs.

Mary Harper was shown into her room and once the door was closed, she eagerly stripped off the wilted layers of her finery, shook the rain from her hair, and took from her valise a long cotton nightdress. Then she walked over to the nightstand, where a large pitcher of water, a washcloth, and a towel had been laid out for her. She washed her critical parts vigorously, the rough cloth and cold water reddening her skin. As she scrubbed the intimate perspiration from between her thighs, she experienced a surprising sting of physical desire. It was very curious, she thought, that danger, excitement, and even the stress of parting should enflame the coarser emotions, and even stranger that the sensations should be so sweet. As though the Lord had concentrated all the contradictions of human feelings in just three places: heart and head and loins. There were profound but mysterious connections binding each place to the others, but a person could live a long life without ever mapping their courses. In the space of an hour, she had experienced the heightened awareness that comes when one is preparing to do something secretive and risky, the lightning strike of excitement that comes from sudden violence, and the deep shudder of anxiety that comes from saying farewell to a loved one who conceivably might not return . . . and through God knew what convolutions of the nerves, all these things might be resolved, or at least reconciled, by a twisting spasm of erotic sensation. If she still felt this way later, if the brandy worked to stimulate rather than to soothe, she would take care of the matter. Over recent years, and always with a combined feeling of secret glee and blushing shame, she had learned how to give herself pleasure, and how to do it quietly.

She dried herself thoroughly and slid into her nightdress. She sat down at the dressing table, facing a large but plain mirror, and began combing the tangles from her hair. After a few strokes, she realized that another woman was staring at her, as though a miniature head had popped out of a tiny door in the mirror's surface. But the face was only a reflection from a framed daguerreotype turned backward, so that the subject of the portrait seemed to be looking at herself, replicating on a smaller scale the very expression on Mary Harper's face. This woman had robust features made gentle by large dark eyes that seemed to contain all softness, all comfort, all desire. Her hair hung down free and very long. Her clothing was subtly unfamiliar—European, perhaps, and somewhat old-fashioned. She was not a great natural beauty, but in a somber and lyrical way, she held one's attention and rewarded it fully—she had obviously been one of those fortunate women who retain, well into middle age, some seasoned measure of the full beauty they had in youth. And those deep, exotic, intelligent eyes—they would never age at all. The man who wed such a woman was be fortunate indeed.

It was then that Mary Harper understood she was looking at Largo's mother, Rachel. This portrait must have been made during the too-brief interlude between the day she arrived in Wilmington and the night she died of malaria. Mary Harper almost turned the picture around, then realized that there was some significance—for Jacob or Largo or both—to the mirror-facing arrangement. Hurriedly, Mary Harper finished brushing her hair, tied it back with a lavender ribbon, donned her bedroom slippers, and went next door to Largo's room. The door was open and she felt no compunction about walking in without a knock.

Upon looking at one another, both women laughed: in their ankle-length white cotton nightdresses—identical except for their makers' whims of lace ruching and touches of embroidery—they truly did look like sisters.

And like sisters, they talked into the night, fueling their companionship with sips of brandy—two headstrong girls doing something naughty while their parents were away. By unspoken agreement they did not review the events of this evening—both women had seen and felt the same things. Instead, they filled in the details of their lives, each to the other, in a way they had not had time to do before. Mary Harper described a life of privilege and comfort, circumscription and boring predictability; Largo told what she knew of the Landaus' Bavarian roots and of the various persecutions that caused Jacob and Rachel to seek their fortunes in America. She described her mother's sudden death, and how it had been preceded by her father's promise to build a synagogue, a tale that Mary Harper found both sweet and stirring.

Once the past had been dealt with, and the brandy bottle made considerably lighter, they spoke of the men they loved, now somewhere near the New Inlet, steaming closer to the guns of any Yankee ship that might be prowling.

Largo admitted what Mary Harper already knew: that she was in love with the handsome Hobart-Hampden and that she would give herself to him at the first opportunity. Ordinarily, Mary Harper would have made a display of disapproval, but considering what she had felt earlier, she waived the sham of hypocrisy. To a sister, this would surely have been a topic of frequent conversation.

"Well, he *is* a fine-looking man, Largo, but you must know in your heart that such a man is most unlikely to propose marriage. People may notice, and people will talk."

Largo tossed her mane of glowing hair, black as squid ink, and the points of her breasts rose bravely against the cotton cloth. "People will notice as they like and say what they want. I am a Jew, Mary, and quite accustomed to being stared at as though I had horns and a tail. When the war truly comes home to us, as I fear it must, people will have more urgent things on their minds than my private life. Besides, I don't want to *marry* him—as his wife, I would never be free from jealousy, and I would be left alone to diddle myself while he is off on secret missions to Timbuktu. I want to give myself not only to a man whom I love, but also to one who is a skilled lover. I do not want my defloration to be an experience to be *gotten over,* but one to savor!"

"Well, yes, it does only happen once. But, my dear, you must not become pregnant!"

Largo's eyes glittered with mischief. "I have prepared for that. Last week, I went down to one of the whorehouses in Paddy's Hollow and offered to pay one of the madams a full day's wages if she would instruct me in certain practical—and theoretical—matters. How to give pleasure . . . how to avoid becoming, as she colorfully put it, 'knocked up.' "

"I know about syringes and hot water—they are notoriously unreliable."

"Not if you use a mixture of alum and sulphate of zinc. But there is another method less extreme and more, um, *natural.* A sponge *pessairre.*"

Largo explained the shape and purpose of the device, adding that these things could be purchased at any well-stocked pharmacy simply by asking for a "female preventative."

"Have you acquired one?"

For the first time, Largo blushed. "There are limits to my

boldness. I would perish of embarrassment if I ran into someone we knew. But surely H-H would do it as brazenly as you please."

Mary Harper took her hand and gave a tiny hiccup as the brandy changed positions.

"I am a married woman and wear the ring to prove it. Tomorrow, before I go back to Pine Haven, I will go to a druggist and buy one for you."

As an equally tipsy Largo leaned over and gave her a grateful hug, Mary Harper thought: And while I'm at it, I shall buy one for myself, too.

Dawn was not far off when they parted. Mary Harper asked for directions to the "necessary" and was directed to a closet at the far end of the hall. As she tiptoed in that direction, she saw a bright flickering light through a doorway that was ajar—presumably the door to Jacob's bedroom. Curious, and emboldened by the brandy, she paused and peeked in.

A golden seven-branched candelabra flared on the mantelpiece, and Jacob Landau knelt beneath its somewhat lurid glow, a skullcap precariously balanced atop his head. Before him was a portrait of Largo's mother. At Jacob's knees was an open book, and as he rocked back and forth, murmuring quietly and rhythmically, Mary Harper assumed he was saying prayers. Only when the chanting turned into a long dark moan and Jacob's shoulders began to quake did she realize that he was also crying.

From Gentleman Farmer to Dashing Buccaneer

COLD WEATHER—The Charlotte, N.C., Bulletin of yesterday, says that the weather there during the last three days has been most awful. Icicles unto nine inches long adorn the eaves of every roof.

It may be "cold comfort" for us to suggest that even this is not an unmitigated evil:—That there is both money and patriotism, the one to be made and the other to be served, by saving this ice for next summer. We speak not simply of ice as a matter of luxury or comfort, and long use has made it seem almost a necessary to many; but it may also be the last hope of the wounded, racked with pain and parched with thirst; or of the invalids whose pulses throb with fever, who may find in it coolness and perhaps safety.

Save the ice, wherever it can be saved, for it will all be needed.

—The Wilmington Journal, January 7 1862

General Chase Whiting had made thorough preparations to receive his young protégé, and when the Lambs got off the train from Norfolk, on the afternoon of November 24, Whiting had been there to greet them, with a wagon for their luggage, two husky male servants to tote their baggage, small candy boxes for the three children, and the key to the house he had leased at the corner of Church and Third Streets. With his courtly manners, Whiting instantly charmed Daisy; with his sweets, he endeared himself to Dick, Ria, and little Sallie, who promptly dubbed him Uncle General, much to Whiting's evident delight. And Daisy impulsively hugged the general when she saw the house.

Surrounded by gardens made private by an elegant brick wall, and shaded by sycamore trees garbed in twining ivy, the house was surely the handsomest residence the Lambs had known since their marriage.

The downstairs rooms were lit by many plate-glass windows and floored with velvet carpets of maroon and oyster-shell white. There were well-stocked bookcases and a fine German piano and all the fireplaces had bumpers of polished brass. China, crystal, damask napkins, and silver bowls glowed on the pantry shelves, and the storeroom off the detached kitchen was amply stocked.

From the day they moved in, the Lambs were treated as honorary Wilmingtonians. There was a steady parade of callers, military and civilian, men and women, and each one, it seemed, brought something tasty: pies, fried chicken, eggs, cakes. So ample were these hospitality offerings that the Lambs' servants only cooked for themselves during the first week of occupancy.

Daisy found the city itself to be as congenial as its inhabitants. As a native of dour but cultured Providence, Rhode Island, Daisy appreciated the attractions at the Thalian, the robust religious life that had sewn the city thickly with steeples, and the bookshop she found on Front Street, which was surprisingly well stocked with novels and periodicals from the Continent. On most days, William left early, sailing downriver in a little steamer that flew an outsize Rebel flag; he did not return until after dark. Daisy therefore had plenty of time to explore the city and cultivate new friendships.

William had been on duty since the morning after they arrived. He took the steamer down to Smithville, where Whiting had established his headquarters. Whiting gave him some maps and an engineer's drafting kit, then sent him upriver again to the sparsely inhabited site of Olde Brunswick Towne. His orders were to study the ground thoroughly for a week, then present Whiting with a master plan for fortifying the place. "You see," Whiting said, gesturing at the big wall map of the Cape Fear estuary, "we need to make this whole region, from the sea to the railroad crossing north of Wilmington, into one gigantic bastion. We are not so easily blockaded here as is the case in Charleston, Savannah, and Mobile. But we can be taken by amphibious assault whenever the Yankees make up their minds to do it. So we need strong works and plenty of them—and we need them as quickly as possible."

Every day since, Lamb and a small escort of surveyors had prowled the historic site of Olde Brunswick Towne, once a thriving colonial port and now deserted save for a few fishermen and their families, who had taken residence in some of the old weather-battered buildings. The first thing Lamb did was to befriend these impoverished squatters, a matter easily accomplished by ordering down from Wilmington a boatload of store-bought food and some wine. In return for Lamb's largesse, the inhabitants gladly shared their knowledge of the local land and water.

They also shared their knowledge of local history, which was more colorful and prosperous than the half-ruined buildings suggested. Brunswick had been founded in 1729 by some entrepreneurs who took advantage of the Tuscarora War to relieve the local Indians of a vast tract of real estate. For decades, the little port thrived, until some local patriots rioted against the Stamp Act almost ten years before the Battle of Lexington. To repay their rebelliousness the British sacked and burned the town in 1776. Brunswick never recovered. The upstart port of Wilmington—which offered a far more sheltered anchorage during the hurricane season from June to November—grew rapidly and aggressively, leaving little Brunswick to a prolonged and genteel decline.

Lamb's favorite view was to the southwest, where a huge lake, modestly named Orton Pond, served as a moat for Orton Plantation, a lofty and regal fiefdom originally laid out by one of Brunswick's founding fathers. Orton was, by far, the biggest and wealthiest plantation in the whole Cape Fear region. Viewed from across the lake, it dominated the landscape like a Southern version of Olympus: proud white Doric pillars rising from manicured lawns dotted with gardens and speckled with ostentatious topiary.

His favorite location, though, was the old graveyard behind the walls of Saint Philip's Church. Here he found some measure of poetry in the mossy obelisks and slanted headstones. Names and dates and inscriptions evoked the realities of the past: memorials to drowned pilots, statues honoring entire crews who had perished at sea, plaques commemorating the brief flickering existence of children slain by yellow fever, bas-reliefs of cannons and flags honoring the remains of the soldiers—British and Patriot alike—who had found their final resting place here beneath gray-bearded oaks.

For seven days, Lamb and his party surveyed the region, took fresh soundings of the river bottom, measured the depth and current of the larger creeks, and tested the composition of the soil. On December 8, he presented General Whiting with a complete plan for a defensive work to be named Fort Anderson. He proposed to anchor the entire position on the four-foot-thick stone walls of the church. From there, he envisioned a massive wall of sand and tarred sandbags, reinforced with timbers and covered with growing turf, that curved from the riverbank, where the added height of the bluffs gave a total and commanding elevation of twenty-four feet, to the marshy end of Orton Pond, which completely protected the right flank. He made room for nine guns of the heaviest available caliber and designed thick sand revetments for their protection. Restored buildings in Brunswick proper would serve as barracks, commissary, and hospital. There would be a central, strategic magazine behind the church and smaller "ready" magazines buried in the mounds that separated each gun emplacement from its neighbors. Finally, he had found suitable locations on the western part of the river itself, where massive wooden pilings could be driven in belts twenty to thirty feet wide, to impede any landing by the enemy. Sprinkled around the pilings, like deadly lobster pots, would be torpedo mines, both free-floating and attached to spars. In a sheaf of separate calculations, Lamb had projected the needed strength of the garrison, the approximate tonnage of quartermaster stores needed to sustain it for each month, and the number of Negro laborers required to move the earth and drive the pilings.

Whiting found nothing in this scheme that could be improved upon and assured Lamb that he would start rounding up workers and tools. "The hardest part will be finding the proper guns, unless you can send a raiding party to Norfolk to purloin some of those weapons presently being hoarded by General Huger."

So when William Lamb returned to Wilmington at sunset, on December 8, 1861, he was elated with the happiness of a man who has just passed his first important test. There was, by common agreement, no finer engineer in the army than Chase Whiting—with the possible exception of Robert E. Lee—and he did not bestow his approval lightly, especially not in the realm of fortifications.

Daisy was waiting on the wharf, holding hands with Ria and Dick. In their carriage, in a snug basket nestled in the ample lap of a servant, baby Sallie rested with her head on a rag doll, staring wide-eyed and bemused at the gas lamps just starting to flare overhead, wondrous as comets to her freshening senses. Lamb waved as the launch drifted in and was made fast by a Confederate private. Daisy had foregone her usual hairstyle—two tight buns severely pulled back and parted in the center by a line of chalk-white skin—in favor of a bouquet of ringlets. Her warm eyes reflected the last scarlet wash of sunset and her welcoming smile was like a beacon. *I will build my fort to protect these loved ones, and any foe who tries to sail up this river will have to do it over my lifeless corpse.*

"Who is coming to dinner?" he asked, after embracing her and kissing her cheek.

"Why, no one, William. Is there someone you wanted to invite?"

"I don't *know* anyone, except for that private guarding the launch, who has not either dined or taken tea with us at least once since the day we moved in!"

"Then isn't it time we dined alone?"

There might be a hint of intimacy-to-come in the sly tilt of her smile.

"I certainly agree. But be warned: I am ravenous from tramping the swamps and making secret military plans!"

She had laid out quite a spread for him: fried chicken and sliced ham, Irish potatoes, pickled snap-beans, and pumpkin pie for dessert. After the children went to bed, she joined him in the parlor where he poured a sherry for her and a robust brandy for himself. Daisy told him about her day and he told her about his satisfactory meeting with Whiting—at least as much he thought might be of interest. Although the night was more brisk than cold, she had ordered a small fire laid, more for the atmosphere it generated than for the heat it produced.

"You do seem happy here, Daisy. I worried about that, you know, before we left Norfolk."

"I like it here, dearest, truly I do. The people are warmhearted and the city feels . . . so *remote* from the war. I'll be sad to leave, when the time comes."

"When what time comes?"

"Darling Will, we're going to have another child." She laughed nervously. "I thought it might be best to tell you after stuffing you with a big meal. I would feel much safer if I were at home in Providence, under the care of the same doctor who delivered the other three babies. I shall not go until the new year, but it seems I am already two months into my term. If only I did not feel somehow like a *deserter* . . . "

Instantly he was at her side, grasping her hands joyfully.

"I'll hear no more of that, Daisy Lamb! Right now, there is much greater danger in Wilmington than in Rhode Island. Our defenses are weak and scattered, and until we make them strong and coordinated, the Yankees can come ashore anywhere they like and capture this place without anything more than a skirmish. Believe me, although I will miss you and the children with all my heart, I will rest more easily knowing you are all out of harm's way."

Daisy regarded him with an expression of mingled relief and skepticism. *While that may well be true, what else* would *you say?*

In truth, William Lamb's emotions were mixed. He would, of course, miss Daisy and the children, and most of all he would miss the luxury of coming home each night as he had done today. At the same time, he felt a conviction that the planning and construction of Fort Anderson was only the first of many important tasks he would be called on to perform in this war, in this place. He would need all his concentration and energy, of that he was certain. For within his breast there burned a new and fierce infatuation: the Young Soldier of the Lord had fallen in love with his fort.

Matthew Sloane had much to think about on the afternoon of December 24, 1861, so he left the piloting in Fitz-Bright's capable hands while the *Banshee* made the two-hour voyage upriver from Wilmington to Pine Haven. Damp, earth-smelling fog choked the channel and the water was up from winter rains. Fitz-Bright maintained a dead-slow headway and had stationed hands on the bow to watch for tree limbs. Over the swamps to the east, where the mist finally faded in the treetops, the sun showed pale and weak, like a dirty pearl.

Matthew had deliberately not told Mary Harper when he expected to return. The actual run to Nassau took only three days each way and two of those days were spent in British waters, thanks to the way the Bahamas angled toward the American coast. Because this whole blockade-running business was still such a new phenomenon, not even Hobart-Hampden could guess how long it would take to sell their cotton and reload the ship with her mingled cargo of military wares and civilian luxuries. "I will need a couple of days to snoop around," he told Matthew, in his usual cryptic manner, on the day they spotted Nassau, a bright semitropical splash of color on the horizon. The process of cargo exchange had in fact required nearly a week, and a stubborn nor'easter had kept ships bottled up in the harbor for another week. Mary Harper would be worried, of course, but she would put a brave face on things, as she always did.

Matthew Sloane was a man reenergized. The actual runs through the blockade zone had been, in Hobart-Hampden's words, "a piece of bloody cake," and the only sign of a Yankee ship was a brief trail of smoke they spotted on the first day of the homeward leg; the ship that produced it never came above the horizon, and the *Banshee*'s anthracite coal gave off too faint a trail for her to be seen in turn.

But even though the two voyages had been without incident, for Matthew they had been rendered vivid by the tonic of proximate danger. His senses had quickened; his body felt lithe and coiled, ready to respond to any contingency. The dash out of the New Inlet into the teeth of cold rain and moderate chop, the ship throbbing beneath him like a thoroughbred horse, the stars winking on and off as ragged bands of cloud, hard-driven by the wind, sailed across the sky, had kindled in his heart a consuming, virile excitement.

"I feel seized by destiny!" he confided in Hobart-Hampden as they reached the open sea and picked up speed.

"Just as long as you don't get seized by the U.S. Navy," the Englishman replied, struggling to light a cheroot from the binnacle lamp.

Nassau only deepened Matthew's intoxication: the glaring white of its colonial buildings, the waxy saturated greens of its foliage, the buzz and tumult of the docks, where dozens of ships great and small were discharging or loading cargo—it was a sight that hinted of the days of piracy and lawless adventure. This moment, he knew, was as close as he would ever get to that swashbuckling life and for a moment he regretted that runners had to sail unarmed. A commerce-raiding cruiser, now that would be the thing!

As they drew into the harbor, Matthew was dazzled by whiteness, as though mounds of snow lay all around: King Cotton. In stacks and pyramids, its whiteness washing out the other colors, vivid though they were; cotton on the docks, cotton on ramps, cotton bulging out of cargo slings, cotton on wagons, cotton being hauled by glistening bare-chested blacks into warehouses whose entrances were guarded by hirsute ruffians armed with shotguns. Suddenly a scarlet parrot glided by, like a stroke of red paint, breaking Matthew out of his snow-blind trance.

"It appears that things have started bustling without us," he observed.

"Give it a year," said Hobart-Hampden, "and you won't recognize this place."

"Will it last as long as a year?"

"The war? Yes, Matthew, it will. It's barely warmed up as yet."

From the teeming waterfront came a perfect Babel of tongues: from men in various uniforms, in sailors' stripes, in business suits, in white Panama jackets with broad straw hats; men in turbans and small, gaily colored square caps; men who tried to look like wolves and men content to skulk like ferrets; men who moved, gestured, spoke, like they were *involved.* Scanning the harbor, Matthew identified Mexicans, Orientals, Frenchmen, dandified Spaniards, a couple of rotund Dutchmen, and large numbers of the seemingly ubiquitous Irish.

"Are there spies about, do you think?"

"Oh, yes, Matthew, behind every closed shutter and under every bed! This is where the war's pulse beats loudest, so this is where they gather. All in the name of patriotism, of course, but every one of them looking to make a few pounds on the side, too."

After hiring some dockside lackeys to carry their bags, Hobart-Hampden led Matthew through the raucous and frequently noisome crowd to the high white stucco pile of the Royal Victoria Hotel. The porch and lobby were so crowded that Matthew did not think much of their chance of getting accommodations. But when Hobart-Hampden reached the registration desk, he was greeted fawningly by the harried-looking clerk.

"Ah, Captain Roberts! How good to see you again. Your usual rooms, sir?"

"Quite."

Matthew looked around in puzzlement, for he could see no one standing near who might answer to the name Captain Roberts. But at that instant, a dapper British officer in a tight beribboned red tunic saw them and changed course, extending his hand past Matthew and flashing a toothy smile.

"Roberts, old fellow! How splendid to see you again!"

"Yes, of course. Matthew Sloane, may I present Leftenant Carruthers of Her Majesty's West India Regiment, quartered here, I believe, for the duration of your civil war." As he made the introduction, "Roberts" trod rather firmly on Matthew's foot.

"Mister Sloane is a gentleman farmer turned merchant captain."

Matthew shook hands with the red-faced officer—a bit old to be a lieutenant and decorated about the nose and cheeks with the faint blue capillaries that denoted too much fondness for the bottle. Having briefly acknowledged Matthew's existence, Leftenant Carruthers clapped "Roberts" on the shoulder.

"I say, Roberts, if it's entertainment you want, you have come to the right place! Cockfights, horse races, boxing matches, games of chance beyond counting, and doxies of every color—as long as you like brown! Haw, haw!"

"Most enticing. Well, Leftenant, it is a pleasure to see you again, but now we must refresh ourselves from our travels and keep some business appointments with impatient men. Perhaps we can meet you on the hotel veranda after dinner—have a few gin rickeys for old times' sake, eh?"

"Oh yes, at least a few. I'll see you later, then."

"Not if I can possibly avoid it," muttered Hobart-Hampden as the redcoat officer sauntered toward the nearest bar. Matthew tapped him on the shoulder and grinned mischievously.

"*Captain Roberts?* Explain yourself Augustus, if *that* is your Christian name."

Hobart-Hampden shrugged. "A *nom de guerre* I have used on previous assignments. Keeps people guessing, that sort of thing, and since everyone in Nassau seems to recognize me by it, can you remember to call me 'Roberts' in public, Matthew? It's a petty vanity, I know, but it helps to reinforce my image as a dashing buccaneer."

"If that's the impression you want to give, why not get yourself outfitted with a wooden leg and a parrot? Surely you don't expect your Wilmington friends to suddenly start calling you 'Captain Roberts'?"

"You have a point, althought it might have some limited value as camouflage."

"If I may say so, it seems rather a transparent dodge. Would it really convey anonymity?"

"*Anonymity* has never been my goal! But it might cause a moment's confusion on the part of our enemies."

"*Our* enemies? I'm not the man who was almost skewered by a homicidal thug last week across from the Wilmington post office."

Hobart-Hampden put a fatherly arm around Matthew's shoulder and gestured toward the crowded waterfront. "It all looks exciting and colorful and jolly, doesn't it? Let me tell you, though, that what you see is only the first and most polite wave of this gold rush. Where there are great fortunes to be made, you will find more bad men than good. And if this war drags on, as I fear it will, then men will die because of words overheard here, and ships will sink, and widows sob because of deeds plotted in places like this. What we do does not take place in a vacuum."

For Matthew, the next three days went by in a blur. They met with bankers and clerks, warehouse owners, cotton factors, shipping agents, and minor diplomats, men whose trust and cooperation were vital, or so Hobart-Hampden informed him. Money and credit letters changed hands and, as they did so, the *Banshee* disgorged her cotton bales and floated high in the water, then began to sink once more as heavier goods, in crates labeled INDUSTRIAL MACHINERY and FARMING IMPLEMENTS began to replace the cotton. Matthew did his best to remember the names and stations of the men they dealt with, and strove to establish a rapport with each of them. That was made easier because of the intermediacy of "Captain Roberts," whom everyone seemed either to know or to have heard favorably about.

When a sudden gale came up and dangerous seas delayed their departure, Hobart-Hampden took it as a sign from God that he and Matthew should make the most of enforced leisure. So for several nights, while the storm howled around the harbor, they went forth to gamble and carouse. Matthew discovered that he could handle strong Jamaican rum rather better than he would have guessed based on his considerable experience with plantation parties; he learned two new card games at the cost of twenty pounds, then won back thirty at a cockfight.

On the last night in Nassau, as the gale faded and the stars reappeared, Hobert-Hampden invited Matthew to accompany him to a brothel on the outskirts of town where, he promised, "gentlemen of every conceivable taste might find discreet and sanitary companionship. Not a pox-box in the lot! I have that on the sworn word of the regimental surgeon of the West India lads."

Matthew blushed and stammered. The newborn adventurer wanted to swagger forth and wallow guiltlessly; the faithful husband did not.

"I cannot, Augustus. I must remain loyal to Mary Harper."

Hobart-Hampden lifted his eyebrows and said, "Suit yourself. But you might learn a thing or two that your dear wife would enjoy learning about as well. Ah! I see by your inadvertent wince that I have hit a tender target. Well, don't wait up for me."

But Matthew did, and he drank a good bit while he waited. He was sprawled disconsolately in his half of the suite, bottle in hand, when Hobart-Hampden reeled in sometime after two o'clock, his cravat untied, wine stains on his shirt, smelling of gin and sweat and common perfume.

"Why so forlorn, my friend?" He shed his coat, rolled up his sleeves, and offered Matthew a cheroot while helping himself to the contents of the bottle.

"Oh, Augustus, it is as you surmised! When we were younger, my wife and I knew mutual passion and knew it well, but since she was forbidden to bear more children, I feel constrained to approach her as though she were made of fragile china!" Wringing his hands, Matthew pored out his feelings to the older man, with a frankness he would never have employed when sober. The Englishman meditatively smoked, broke out another bottle of wine, and nodded his head in all the right, brotherly places until Matthew finally ran out of steam and began gently to weep. Hobart-Hampden embraced him and drunkenly tried to reassure him.

"Come, now, my friend, this situation is not uncommon, nor by any means hopeless, although I am constantly amazed that American gentlemen of your rank are so pig-ignorant regarding any level of sexual activity more sophisticated than what they witness in the barnyard. Here, refill your glass, and I shall begin your instruction. Let's see how well you remember your Latin."

Matthew's "instruction" continued during the homeward voyage, whenever there was a moment of privacy. Armed with new knowledge, as well as a new and far more worldly attitude, Matthew returned to Wilmington standing taller, in his own eyes at least, than when he departed.

Dawn found the *Banshee* docked again in Wilmington. Sunset found Matthew, Jacob, and Hobart-Hampden each $5,000 richer from turning over their cargo to Confederate agents who were waiting with gold in hand: two thousand Enfield rifles, 250 pigs of lead, twenty thousand percussion caps, thirty-five hundred overcoats, and several casks of ether. Mr. Bright, as pilot and helmsman, pocketed $600, and even the lowliest deckhand received more than he would have from six months of peacetime work.

They sold all the luxury goods at auction, the general opinion among the shareholders being that competitive bidding would fetch more than retail sales from Jacob's store. The idea proved to be a shrewd one. In just four hours of lively bidding, the three shipowners made profits of sixty percent or more on limited quantities of wine, thread, coffee, tea, stationery, soap, and other sundries.

At the end of day, after toting up their profits in the office behind Jacob's store, they were more than satisfied—this runner business was proving more lucrative than even Hobart-Hampden had envisioned. After solemnly shaking hands with the other two men, Jacob Landau hefted his share and said: "I am pleased that you gentlemen have been so successful. As for myself and my daughter, we already have enough for our foreseeable needs, so this money is for God's house." He placed the funds inside his safe and twirled the dial.

The morning of Christmas Eve was spent making arrangements for a second voyage as soon as possible in the new year. "Captain Roberts" went off to do whatever it was he did when he was not smuggling weapons or cutting the fingers off thugs. Matthew bought toys and candy for the children and made sure his private share of contraband treasures was Christmas-wrapped for Mary Harper. Then, with Mr. Bright singing jauntily in several unknown keys, he ordered the *Banshee* to Pine Haven.

When he and Mary Harper finally embraced, it was an event. Each thought the other had never looked more desirable, and each had surprises in store for the other when the children were asleep and the servants dismissed. Both husband and wife were delighted with those surprises, and neither asked, nor very much cared, where the other had learned such things.

For, as Hobart-Hampden had said back in Nassau: "On the morning after her wedding night with Prince Albert, the queen is supposed to have remarked: 'If that is what *sex* is all about, then it really is too good for the common people.' "

General Chase Whiting received a Christmas present from his old friend and comrade-in-arms, General Joseph E. Johnston, now commanding the Army of Northern Virginia. If Benjamin Huger, and by extension Jefferson Davis, regarded Whiting as a bureaucratic thorn in Richmond's complacent hide, Old Joe knew Whiting's worth and valued him appropriately. Since the two men had last shared drinks, during the halcyon glow that followed the victory at Bull Run, Whiting had gently but repeatedly importuned Johnston for a field command and Johnston had always responded with assurances that such a command would devolve to Whiting "when the political climate was more favorable," which was a polite way of reminding Whiting that President Davis bore Johnston scant goodwill and would happily include all of Johnston's friends under the somber umbrella of his prejudice.

But McClellan's appointment as commander in chief of the Army of the Potomac, in November, signaled to every one on both sides of the Potomac that a great Napoleonic campaign against Richmond was as inevitable a part of the coming spring as the blossoms on honeysuckle. Grudges or no, Davis now had no alternative but to put the defense of Richmond into Johnston's capable hands and Johnston wanted his favorite officers in the field when McClellan moved. Military exigencies, for the moment, overrode political ones, so Davis deferred to Johnston's wishes.

Joe Johnston could therefore request the services of any officer he favored, and those requests were, for the time being, routinely approved. General Whiting had been ordered to report to Johnston, at the latter's field headquarters in Centreville, Virginia, on January 20, 1862, to assume command of a division. Command of the Department of North Carolina would then devolve to the already overworked D. H. Hill, whom Chase Whiting had always found sympathetic to the idea of strong coastal defenses. Whether Hill would be any more successful in procuring heavy guns for Roanoke Island remained to be seen.

Whiting yearned to be free of the encumbrances and frustrations of his Carolina command. He had done everything in his circumscribed power to bring order and coherence to this far-flung region. He had devised a good strategy, and his personal physical exertions while touring the coast had won him, he believed, the loyalty of the men on the ground. His only regrets were personal: he loved Wilmington and so did his wife, Katherine. She would not be happy in Richmond, with its tidal undertows of rumor and its airless mood of intrigue. He therefore insisted that she *stay* in Wilmington at least through the summer—if McClellan succeeded and Richmond came under attack, she would be safe and well attended by her many friends.

As for the Cape Fear defenses, Whiting was relatively certain that the river fortifications would be completed on schedule, and the ongoing refurbishment of Fort Caswell, augmented by smaller ancillary batteries on Oak and Bald Head Islands, had made the Old Inlet relatively secure. He felt less sanguine about New Inlet, however; isolated batteries had been erected there during the summer and Richmond had promised more and larger weapons, but as yet there was no comprehensive scheme for the sort of mammoth works required to protect that place. Already, the burgeoning traffic of blockade-runners had given unprecedented importance to New Inlet. Whiting had ruminated considerably, and made sketches, but other priorities had pressed too close for him to give New Inlet the attention it must soon have. As an engineer, he was attracted by the challenge; as a pragmatist, he knew that the project required a special kind of vision, something of conceptual grandeur—and the only other Confederate engineer of sufficient rank who could provide that was Robert E. Lee, who was decidedly unavailable.

Whiting poured another whiskey and pondered the big map of the Cape Fear estuary on the far wall of his office. If there was no other general officer both suitable and available, then the job must perforce go to a younger man of lesser rank. Whiting smiled. The work young William Lamb had done in surveying and designing Fort Anderson, the new bastion guarding the Cape Fear's western bank, indicated not only a natural genius for the art of fortification, but also a brightness of spirit that was worth more than a hundred big guns. That particular kind of inspiration was a gift from the god of war, and Whiting was self-critical enough to know that he did not have it. It was almost a quality of grace, and it stood apart from any professional education. Lamb would be preoccupied with Fort Anderson for several months, but once that project was completed, any competent officer could take over the post. Lamb's qualities demanded a larger theater, one commensurate with possible greatness.

Savoring the whiskey's glow, and happy in the knowledge that he would soon be commanding a division in what promised to be this war's greatest campaign, Chase Whiting wrote the appropriate orders.

1862

11

Dinner with General Butler

EARLY BREAKFAST—Breakfast should be eaten in the morning, before leaving the house for labor of any description; those who do it will be able to perform more work, and with greater efficiency and alacrity, than those who work an hour or two before breakfast. Besides this, the average duration of the life of those who take exercise or work will be a number of years greater than those who do otherwise. Most persons begin to feel weak after having been engaged five or six hours in their ordinary avocation. A good meal invigorates; but from the last meal of the day until the next morning, there is an interval of some twelve hours; hence, the body in a sense is weak, especially the stomach, and in proportion cannot resist deleterious agencies, whether of the fierce cold of mid-winter or of the poisonous miasma which rests upon the surface of the Earth, whenever the sun shines on a blade of vegetation or a heap of offal. This miasma is more solid, more concentrated, and hence more malignant about sunrise and sunset, than at any other hour of the twenty-four, because the cold of night condenses it, and it is on the first few inches above the soil in its most solid form; but as the sun rises, it warms and expands and ascends to a point higher enough to be breathed, and being taken into the lungs with the air, and swallowed with the saliva into the stomach, all weak and empty as it is, it is greedily drunk in, thrown immediately into the circulation of the blood, and carried to every part of the body, depositing its most poisonous influence at the fountain-head of essential bile.

—The Wilmington Journal, February 1 1862

At precisely seven-thirty in the morning, January 9, 1862, General Ambrose Burnside took his place on the foredeck of the small fast steamer *Picket,* spanking fresh with new paint and polished brass, and sailed out to review the ships and men of his Coastal Division. Intermittent spits of light rain did not obscure the spectacle or dampen the enthusiasm of the spectators, none of whom had ever seen an armada of such size and power. As vast as was the sheltered anchorage of Hampton Roads, it was on this morning crowded almost to its limits by eighty vessels: warships of several classes, tugs, barges, floating batteries under tow, and transports containing twelve thousand men and two thousand horses. So numerous were the mastheads all around that they obscured large swaths of the gray and lowering sky.

All the crews and troops had already been mustered and they crowded the rails of every ship like garlands of blue flowers. As Burnside steamed back and forth, he was greeted with lusty cheers. The general responded with all the theatricality of an opera star milking a standing ovation. As he neared each ship in turn, he removed his trademark hat—a jaunty black bowl-shaped thing that might have looked slightly ridiculous on a man of lesser confidence—and waved it vigorously, summoning loud huzzahs, shrieking steam whistles, and thunderous cannon salutes that rattled the windows of Fort Monroe's barracks, eight miles away.

From his splendid vantage point on the quarterdeck of the screw steamer *Comstock,* Colonel Rush Hawkins reveled in the ceremony and felt his skin prickle as it always did when glory was in the air. When Burnside's boat came abreast of the *Comstock,* Hawkins brandished his highly polished sword and led the Ninth New York Zouaves in three cheers. Burnside pointed approvingly at Hawkins—or so Hawkins interpreted the gesture—and tossed off a casual salute, which Hawkins returned with all the parade-ground snap he could muster.

But the excitement proved anticlimactic. Instead of the stately noon departure that had been planned, the fleet soon found itself wrapped in fog and immobilized for at least another day. While his frustrated men killed time by gambling, writing letters, and consuming all the fresh food they had brought aboard in their knapsacks, Hawkins paced nervously in his cabin, unwilling to doff his dress uniform and sword in case the sun should suddenly break out and the ship weigh anchor and another picturesque appearance become necessary. When he did, finally, accept the delay and remove his woolen coat, gloves, pistol, and sword belt, he suffered a sudden chill and summoned an orderly to light the coal fire already laid in the cabin's tiny stove.

He kept to himself all afternoon and evening, even taking his meal in the cabin. He tried to read a Baltimore newspaper, but could not concentrate; tried to write letters, but could think of nothing worth saying; meticulously cleaned and oiled his revolver for the third time in as many days. All the while, his mind kept repeating, like a magic-lantern show, scenes from the previous night's dinner ashore with General Benjamin Butler.

Butler had no official role to play in Burnside's expedition—as Burnside himself had made caustically clear during that embarrassing conference with Secretary Welles—and the unexpected invitation to dine with him ("alone," the message stipulated) seemed to mean that the general had journeyed here for the specific purpose of visiting his protégé. When Hawkins rode up to the given address, he found a comfortable white frame dwelling in one of the raw mud-road neighborhoods that had sprung up around Fort Monroe since the war began. Not until two smirking sentries ushered him through the front door and into a dimly lit hallway that reeked of perfume—in the recesses of which he spotted several giggling young women darting through doorways, their petticoats rustling like a flock of startled pigeons—did Hawkins realize it was a whorehouse.

"There you are!" Butler's croaky voice boomed from the parlor. Hawkins did a smart left-face and automatically saluted the strange tableau before him: Butler reclining on a massive overstuffed horsehair sofa, a frilly antimacassar bunched up behind his ponderous head, and a dining table fairly moaning under its burden of meat, fruit, bread, cheese, potatoes, gravies, wines, brandies, and heavy silver soup tureens. On the general's left was a concupiscent, big-breasted young woman with long hennaed hair and a cigar clamped provocatively in her full lips, her hand frozen in the act of delivering to Butler's open mouth a tea biscuit trimmed with a wedge of Gouda. On his right was a svelte, almost serpentine brunette with swan-white skin, darkly smoldering eyes, and an impudent scarlet slash of a mouth. In a quick and businesslike flutter, she danced across the room and gave Hawkins a sharp nipping kiss on the mouth.

"Eat, drink, and be merry," chortled Butler, indicating that Hawkins should take a seat on a vacant sofa opposite the one he occupied. "This will be your last decent meal for God knows how long,

Colonel. *And* your last chance to enjoy some feminine companionship before entering the hairy embrace of Mars. Do sit down and take your fill. We can discuss business afterward, over brandy and cigars, as befits men of destiny."

While Hawkins ate, Butler recounted the latest Washington gossip, flavoring the soliloquy with scandalously coarse jokes, sending the red-haired doxie into convulsions of tipsy laughter, and punctuating it with unsuppressed belches and poorly stifled farts. When the parlor clock struck eight, however, Butler's demeanor changed abruptly. The slur went out of his voice, his mouth became tight, and his shoulders straightened.

"Leave us now, ladies. We have business to discuss. I'll call for you later."

Obediently, the girls scampered into the hall, closing the door as they left.

In the sudden silence, the clocked ticked very loudly. For two long minutes Butler did not speak or even move, although one eyelid began to twitch vigorously. Hawkins tried not to stare at it.

"I am glad we had a chance to meet before you embarked on this new campaign, Colonel. May you emerge from it both victorious and unharmed. Do you expect the Rebels to fight hard for their island?"

"They will fight like the very devil for it, sir. It is the most important position they hold between Norfolk and Wilmington. And they've had all winter to bring heavy guns down from Norfolk."

Butler smiled and lifted his eyebrows.

"*Some* guns have been sent from Norfolk, that is true. All the cannon in the world, however, won't do the Rebs any good if they are short of ammunition."

"Are they?"

Butler nodded. "Yes, quite short. And most of what they have is solid shot. They have very few shells."

Hawkins had the feeling that Butler was toying with him—not unkindly, but with the coyness of a man who knows much more than he can say and wants you to know it, too. Where *did* he get such information? How far and just how powerful *was* his reach?

"But let us move on beyond tactics to matters of grand strategy. I have taken a liking to you, Hawkins, as you must know by now. We have much in common, I think. Pride, ambition, a thirst for glory. I wonder, though, if you are the kind of man who can take the *long* view of something as dramatic as this war. It won't last forever, you know, and our side will eventually win. It is a matter of cold economic fact: we have all the factories, which means that not only can we mobilize more men, but we can supply them more lavishly with arms and equipment. The South has an agrarian economy, so every man they put in the field reduces the wealth of that economy."

"You have certainly thought this out, General. You have a lot of strategic sense."

"Yes, and even my enemies acknowledge the fact. But there are spheres of strategy, Colonel, of greater and lesser circumference. Sometimes, those spheres overlap and it takes a sharp man to see the larger shape of things."

Hawkins was baffled—was this a discussion of strategy or a geometry lesson? Sensing his confusion, Butler made an impatient gesture.

"Let me get to the point, Hawkins. The South holds one important economic card and one only. Can you name it?"

"Cotton."

"Exactly! The Union army needs uniforms, but the Northern mills cannot manufacture uniforms without cotton. At present, and for the foreseeable future, the supply is tightly regulated by the government and the men who run those mills are forced to pay an exorbitant price, because Southern cotton is contraband and all the other cotton has to be imported. It is very complicated, what with tariffs and import duties and licenses. By the time the raw material reaches a uniform factory, or a flag factory, or a blanket factory, the accumulated costs have all but eaten up the legitimate profit the factory owners are entitled to. This in turn hurts the Northern economy and that, in its turn, will prolong the war. Would it not make things better all around, not to say more profitable, if the factories could obtain their raw materials directly from the South?"

"Of course, General. But it would also be illegal."

Butler scowled. "Only in the most technical sense, I assure you. But if you find the idea morally repugnant, perhaps I have misjudged your character. In which case, I bid you good evening and wish you luck." Butler rose and stuck out his hand. Hawkins felt sweat running down his neck. He did not shake the proffered hand.

"What role can I play, General? I am only an infantry officer."

Butler smiled like a proud parent. "You are also the man on the spot—which is to say the coast of North Carolina. You see, I am empowered to speak for a group of very wealthy and influential businessmen. I am, so to speak, their eyes and ears in Washington, where I have enough friends to nudge things in suitable directions from time to time. These men will be very grateful, after the war is over, to those who have helped them.

"You are aware of the increase in blockade-running? Do you think most of the captains of those vessels are acting from patriotism? Bosh! There are fortunes to be made, and made fast—*that* is what it all boils down to, Colonel. Why should not some of that cotton go straight to the North instead of to England? Why should there be a shortage either of blue uniforms or of profit for the men who manufacture them?"

"But those blockade-runners return with military supplies. By furthering their activities, you would be aiding the enemy."

"Why should *our* ships carry a lot of strategic goods, for God's sake? Once the blockade really starts to pinch and the other Southern ports are captured, a pound of coffee sold in Wilmington will be worth more than a barrel of gunpowder. How could any of our soldiers be harmed by a bag of coffee?"

"Excuse me, sir, but am I right in assuming that there is some connection between my assignment in North Carolina and the proximity of Wilmington?"

"Ah! I marked you for a man of acumen and now you prove it! One cannot with any certainty predict how military operations will develop, but I rather think that Wilmington will be the *last* Rebel port to fall. The men I represent have a vested interest in keeping it open, or will have as soon as we finish outfitting our ships and find trustworthy men to crew them."

"What is to prevent one of 'our' ships from getting blown to pieces by a Federal frigate?"

"The risks of war cannot be done away with altogether, Hawkins. All the blockade-runners must take that chance. But for our ships, the risk is minimal. We have men in positions of command on the blockade line, men who know how to demonstrate zeal in their task without actually being successful at it."

Rush Hawkins felt dizzy. The scope and audacity of the scheme were breathtaking. As he reviewed each dovetailing segment of the operation, he could not see that any *harm* would be done to the Union cause or to its troops. He could serve Lincoln and serve Butler—or the shadowy entrepreneurs who stood behind him—simultaneously. Quietly, he told Butler that he was in. Then he asked once more what his role would be.

"We need a small, out-of-the-way, but not utterly primitive location where cargo from the big runners can be transferred to smaller vessels for the final trip north, or, perhaps, where the runner ships themselves can be cosmetically altered to look like legitimate Yankee merchantmen—the final shape of the scheme will be defined by events and opportunities. Up in the northeast corner of North Carolina, along one of those numerous rivers, there must be a suitable place, a fishing village or something. We must have it under Union control as soon as possible, even if the plans don't call for it actually to be captured. Scout around, Colonel, and find me such a place. When you have, concoct some plausible reason to capture it. I leave that part of it to your imagination. Send me a written report when it is done."

Butler now relaxed again and refilled his wineglass. "Now that our business is concluded, we can bring the whores back in." He reached for a dinner bell. Just before he rang, Hawkins reached out and gripped his arm.

"Just tell me one thing, General Butler. How did you know that the guns on Roanoke Island are short of ammunition?"

"I have another associate in Norfolk, Colonel, who has made certain of it."

Hawkins stayed long enough to enjoy a quick but not altogether perfunctory coupling in the brunette's tiny bedroom, but he drank no more alcohol and by the time he bade farewell to the general, he was fairly well recovered from the effects of what he had drunk earlier.

Now, of course, he was doubly glad for that decision. The whole regiment had turned out before dawn to prepare for Burnside's inspection and Hawkins tended to be extremely choleric when he was wakened early after a serious bout of drinking.

In the snug privacy of his cabin, he sought the council of his Christian upbringing, realizing after a fidgety hour that it was his meeting with Butler, and not apprehension of the imminent campaign, that made him so restless. He went over and over his recollections of what had been said and *implied,* and still he could not find dishonor in his decision. He was not, after all, committing *treason,* or selling tainted meat to the army, or any other wicked thing. His patriotism was unblemished, his confidence in his own valor unshaken. With a distinguished war record, sufficient financial resources, and Ben Butler's patronage, he could reenter civilian life with every prospect of happiness and security. Perhaps a career in politics. A seat in Congress would not be out of reach.

Then he was jolted from his reverie by a sudden cold thought: to *enjoy* such a future, he would first have to survive the war. He had stormed the Hatteras forts boldly enough, but that was action against a foe already beaten and ready to surrender. Ammunition shortage or not, the Rebels defending Roanoke Island were likely to make a real fight of it. Martial glory usually came to men who had been shot at repeatedly. How many heroes of the Mexican War had traded an arm, a leg, an eye, or even—dear Christ!—a testicle for their honors? In the wake of this disturbing thought came another, far more comforting. If he became truly valuable to Butler—an important cog in the general's vast machine—would not Butler keep him out of harm's way? All he had to do, really, was to survive this one coming battle, then carry out the general's wishes. He would become *indispensable.* He would survive. He would not be touched by ball or fragment. God had already shown His favor to Rush Hawkins. With this final thought came serenity. He donned his nightshirt and climbed into his bunk

At noon the next day, in clear cold weather, the ships of Burnside's Coastal Division slipped their cables, weighed their anchors, and departed. Order was fairly kept until they reached open sea, off Cape Henry, Virginia. Even under the calmest, most benign conditions, it would have been difficult to keep formation with such a sprawling, polyglot armada; under a stiff wind and on moderate seas, the task proved impossible, no matter how many frantic and eventually threatening orders were sent up the halyards of Admiral Goldsborough's flagship. There were too many vessels; some were powered by steam, while others still hauled under canvas, and all with divergent seakeeping characteristics.

Hawkins had looked forward to a swift, untroubled passage to the Carolina shore, during which he could divert himself by playing cards with Major Brown, his second-in-command, or absorbing nautical wisdom from the *Comstock*'s grizzled and picturesque skipper. But that individual made no appearance at all during the first day of the voyage, neither on the bridge nor anywhere else. He was finally discovered, by the steward, sprawled on the floor of his cabin, stupefied by drink and half-drowned in a pool of vomit. When this news was semaphored to Goldsborough, the order came back for Hawkins to clap the man in irons and replace him with the first officer, an affable but apparently slow-witted fellow who inspired no confidence. Thereafter and for the remainder of the voyage, Hawkins found himself bombarded by all the myriad troublesome responsibilities of command, a Gordian knot of mundane, vexatious, and downright unpleasant demands upon his time.

Conditions worsened as the fleet sailed south, and Cape Hatteras welcomed them to Carolina waters with a howling nor'easter. Towering seas pounded the ships without letup for two full days, making it impossible even to think about crossing the bar from open sea to the sheltered waters of Pamlico Sound. Goldsborough could do nothing but order his ships to drop anchor and ride it out.

Hawkins had never been seasick a day in his life, and suspected that those who did succumb harbored some defect of character that rendered them weak and susceptible to that malady. Eight hours into the storm, this point of view was dramatically and permanently altered. On every ship in sight, gray-faced soldiers lined the rails day and night, producing a veritable Niagara of puke. No sooner had Hawkins started to recover than he was besieged by company commanders who ventured topside and brought reports of worsening conditions belowdecks. The men's quarters were dirtier than most stables, they complained; icy water sloshed ankle-deep in some compartments, bearing the occasional dead rat; for those men still able to contemplate food, there was nothing to eat but boiled pork that was beginning to turn sour and moldy in its barrels. By the second and worst day of the storm, there was a desperate shortage of potable water—soldiers fortunate enough to own tin cups came creeping out on the deck, filled them with rainwater, and sold them below to the highest bidder. Hawkins understood, in some vague way, that as the regimental commander he was supposed to either alleviate these sufferings or make some spirit-raising gesture of sympathy by going below and pretending to share the soldiers' misery. Finally, at the urging of Major Brown and a committee of lesser officers, he accepted the necessity of doing this, but he got no farther than the first open hatchway before the medieval stench from below flipped his stomach over once again and rendered him helpless with retching.

Goldsborough lost five ships to the gale, grounded or simply battered to pieces by the waves, along with several men and more than one hundred horses. Even after the weather moderated and the thin wintry sun came out again, his troubles were not over. Many of the ships Burnside had purchased in New York—from salesmen who assured his agents that the vessels drew only six feet of water—turned out to have drafts of eight, nine, even ten feet. Moreover, the gale had rucked up the sandbars under the swash, so that the average depth of Hatteras Inlet now measured seven and a half feet. For most of one day, consternation paralyzed everything—rumors flourished among the infantry that the entire expedition would have to be scrapped. But Goldsborough, in a state of near-volcanic rage, ordered his staff to come up with a solution and eventually they did. Several of the very biggest transports were deliberately rammed into the swash at full speed, then fixed in place by tugs and kedge anchors while the ebbing tide rolled beneath their keels and scooped out enormous amounts of sand. When they were once more afloat, the big ships got up steam and charged forward again until they were stuck fast. Yard by yard, over the course of six tidal cycles, the transports repeated this process until they had cleared the channel; then the ships of lesser draft followed them. Not until February 5 was this Herculean task completed and all the transports reassembled in Pamlico Sound, escorted by all of the warships except for the largest and heaviest frigates, which were unable to risk the crossing.

Burnside's armada made a brave and stately sight as it steamed into the mouth of Croatan Sound, the three-mile-wide channel that separated the western side of Roanoke Island from the mainland. At sunset, the ships anchored off the southwest corner of the island. For the next two days, a soupy swirling fog cloaked the water, too dense for any military action to be practicable. At four o'clock in the afternoon, February 7, Captain William Branch, commander of the Mosquito Fleet, dispatched the lightly armed but relatively fast CSS *Appomattox* to reconnoiter the Federal anchorage and bring back what information she could.

Despite the fog, Burnside's picketboats spotted the *Appomattox* as it slowed and twisted to find a clear path through the pilings and sunken hulks Branch had emplaced across Croatan Sound, with the intention of bottling up the Union ships in a place where they could be fired upon, to maximum effect, by the combined guns of the Mosquito Fleet and those of the land fortifications. Acting under orders from Admiral Goldsborough, the picketboats did not fire on the little scout, but retired quietly into the fog, luring the *Appomattox* closer to the main fleet. "They will probably send a boat to scout us out," Goldsborough had said during the morning conference with his skippers, Burnside, and Burnside's three brigade commanders—"Don't fire upon it. Let them get close and take a good hard look at what opposes them, and carry the intelligence back to the Rebel ships. If their commander has any sense, he'll steam away during the night and that will be one less thing to worry about in the morning."

Indeed, as the *Appomattox* drew near enough to count the fog-shrouded hulls and smokestacks arrayed before her, one of the Federal gunboats flashed its signal light: *Is this the best you can send against us?* to which the Confederate crew replied: *Don't be impudent, or we will blow you out of the water.* And as darkness settled over the sound and the scout ship retired, its mission as complete as visibility allowed, there was a murmur of laughter from those Federal seamen who had witnessed the exchange.

For Captain Branch, aboard his flagship CSS *Ellis,* there was no cause for humor in the report brought back by the *Appomattox.* Her skipper had counted at least fifteen warships and had jotted down the names of most of them. Branch knew the presumed armament of each class of Federal warship, so it did not take him long to calculate the odds. Discounting the big frigates, which he was sure drew too much water to pass the swash at Hatteras, Goldsborough still commanded at least fifty guns, some of which would be 100-pounders and 9-inch rifles. All of Branch's ships combined carried nine cannons, the largest of which were 32-pounders. It was as bad as he had feared. He saw no point in sharing these numbers with his captains—they already knew they were vastly outnumbered and hopelessly outgunned. Like him, they all seemed resigned to doing their duty, and he would say nothing to them that might conjure in their breasts the acidity of despair that now scorched his own.

Besides, his plans were made and coordinated with the Confederate gunners on shore, and there was nothing more to be done until tomorrow. Then he joined his ships' officers for a somber meal of corn dodgers, coffee, and the roasted breast of a migrating duck that one of his men had shot that afternoon when it landed within range. As the postprandial brandy and cigars went 'round the tiny wardroom table, Branch contemplated making some kind of stirring Shakespearean speech, but his heart was not in it and after a few self-conscious toasts to Jeff Davis and the Rebel flag, they all retired to their respective ships.

Branch took half a bottle of brandy and a pair of cigars back to his cabin, changed into a quilted dressing gown, turned up the lamps, then settled down with a copy of *Ivanhoe.* He only had time to read a few pages, however, when someone knocked on his door. Hoping this intrusion did not herald more bad news, he bade the visitor entry, whereupon he was both surprised and delighted to see his old friend and comrade, Commander Samuel Parker, who had rowed himself over from the *Beaufort.* Parker had brought more brandy and a handsomely bound copy of Sir Walter Scott's *Quentin Durwood.*

"For your collection, William," Parker said, handing over the book. "I found it in a shop in Elizabeth City, of all places. Knowing your fondness for Scott's romances, I thought you might enjoy it."

"This is very thoughtful of you, Sam. And wonderfully coincident—you see what I am reading tonight."

"*Ivanhoe* is your favorite, I remember. How many times have you read it?"

"Since I discovered it as a lad? Oh, a dozen or more. I can recite whole pages from memory, but there is something soothing about the ritual of reading them from the text . . . a permanence of beauty that stands forever opposed to the brutalities of fortune. Life deals us blows and sorrows, loved ones betray us, friends become enemies, black becomes white—but the music in these pages remains faithful and forever. It is reassuring to know that something beautiful can indeed be incorruptible."

For the next two hours, they discussed literature, comparing their favorite episodes and characters from the novels of Scott, the plays of Shakespeare, the epic musings of Milton and Goethe. By doing so, they succeeded, for a time, in removing themselves from the grim realities that confronted them. The spell was broken when the ship's bell tolled midnight.

"I had better row back to the *Beaufort,*" said Parker upon the last reverberation of the twelfth tone.

"And I had better get some sleep. I *am* glad you came tonight, Sam. Who knows when our next visit will be?"

Parker paused with his hand on the cabin door. "I see no way we can win this battle. But perhaps we can salvage our honor."

"Yes. There is a spiritual victory in that, I suppose. Come, let me walk you back to your boat."

As Parker tucked himself into his skiff, he shook his head in weary amusement. "What strangely constituted beings we are! Two men looking forward to death in less than twenty-four hours—and death in defeat, too, not in victory—and still we are able to lose ourselves in great literature."

"It is a wonder, is it not? Well, good-bye, my friend, and good luck tomorrow. Ah, God, if we could only hope for a victory! But never mind—come again when you can!"

Headquarters of Forces on Roanoke Island
February 6, 1862

I have the honor to report that the enemy fleet has crossed the bar at Hatteras Inlet and is at this moment steaming unopposed toward Roanoke Island. From the number and size of transports reported to me, I estimate the landing force to be not fewer than ten thousand men. They are strongly escorted, moreover, by numerous heavily armed gunboats, any one of which alone can hurl a heavier broadside than all of our little ships combined.

The situation on the island remains highly unfavorable. The bomb-proof quarters which I ordered constructed two weeks ago at Fort Bartow remain unbuilt due to a shortage of negroe labor, tools, and heavy timbers, all of which I have repeatedly requisitioned from your Department. Several of the guns which have been dispatched since mid-January arrived without sights and remain so hampered to this day, a situation which could be corrected by the labors of a single artisan in a single day. For the 32-pounders that are my heaviest weapons, I have approximately 1,000 rounds of shot, but only 150 shells. I have a total of 1,822 men under my command, but of that number, one-fifth are sick on any given day, one-third are still armed with flint and steel rifles, one-half are clad in rags, and all are exhausted and malnourished.

It is not too late, General Huger. A regiment of good infantry and a few batteries of field guns could reach us from Norfolk before the enemy has completed his landings. With these modest reinforcements, I would have enough men to attack them at the water's edge, where they dare not direct their naval gunfire without hitting their own troops. As matters stand now, I can only man the earth redoubt across the Island's only road and await the pleasure of the enemy.

Very respectfully, your obedient servant,
Henry A. Wise, Brigadier General

Headquarters of the Department of Norfolk
February 7, 1862

I have the honor to reply to your dispatch of the 6th instant. As I have repeatedly stated, the artillery previously dispatched from here should, if properly sited, be sufficient to repel the enemy's gunboats, and that in turn will give his infantry no opportunity to land. I do not consider large infantry forces necessary for the defense of the island.

If your men stand by the guns and remain cool, all will be well. Nevertheless, I am prepared to send you another three companies of infantry and some howitzers, but due to a shortage of suitable vessels in this city, their transfer will be greatly expedited if you can send to Norfolk all the steamers you can spare.

I am, sir, very respectfully yours.
Benjamin Huger, Major General

The fog was gone in the morning, but otherwise the weather remained poor. Cold rain squalls dimpled the water and gusty winds roughened it. At the morning conference between Burnside and Goldsborough, there had been some discussion of postponing the landing for another day, but that was rejected because it might give the defenders a chance to summon reinforcements from the mainland and to fortify the chosen landing beach, a gently sloping indentation decorated with rusting crab traps and weather-beaten fishing shacks, known locally and somewhat pretentiously as Ashby's Harbor. The distance from the farthest transports to the beach was not great and the infantry commanders reported that their men were fired up and eager to get ashore—a mood that might not survive another night of cold rations and wet straw mattresses.

Once the decision had been made, everyone got down to business. After the morning coffee was boiled and distributed, all cooking fires were extinguished, sawdust was spread upon the decks to soak up any blood, and the infantry mustered on deck by companies. At nine o'clock, a set of damp signal flags rasped up the halyards of Goldsborough's flagship: *Today the country expects every man to do his duty.*

"Appropriate," muttered Major Junius Brown, "but not very original."

Rush Hawkins agreed—what was needed, he thought, was something more akin to Henry the Fifth's Agincourt speech. But he was not so sure that Brown's observation was proper, either. Goldsborough was a fighting sailor, not a poet.

Now Brown tapped Hawkins on the shoulder. "Look there, sir! The gunboats are moving up." Threading their way around the transports, moving with stately deliberation, nineteen warships headed north. Cold wet light shimmered on the barrels of their guns and the infantry in the closest transports gave three cheers for the bluejackets manning those weapons.

Hawkins knew where the warships were going, having seen the dispositions marked on a map: they would form a crescent just south of the line of Confederate obstacles and would steam back and forth across Croatan Sound, engaging land batteries as they revealed their positions, and any naval units the enemy was reckless enough to send out. Two miles below the firing line lay the transports, guarded by a pair of shallow-draft gunboats in case the landing was opposed by field artillery. Between the landing beach and the obstacles, there were no Confederate forts. Burnside had questioned several contraband Negroes and a handful of Union sympathizers, all of whom knew the island well and had observed Rebel activity there; all agreed that the closest guns to the landing were mounted in Fort Bartow, a massive but half-finished earthwork covering the left side of the obstacle line from a low scrubby bluff. All other fortifications, the informants agreed, were located on the northern third of the island, a scheme so irrational that some naval officers feared they were sailing into a very subtle trap.

Well, thought Rush Hawkins, they would find out very soon.

"Out of the way, there! Rope ladders coming up!"

Already, other regiments were climbing down the side of their transports and filling up the long lines of landing craft that filed slowly by on their towlines. There were enough boats, Burnside had estimated, to land four thousand men and two batteries of guns every six hours. Since the *Comstock* was closer to shore than most of the transports, its troops would be among the first to land. Every officer of the Ninth Zouaves who possessed a spyglass or binoculars was intently studying the enemy shore. They were within range of a 12-pounder, should the Rebels have one pointed at them, and every man was braced for the sound of enemy fire.

At ten-thirty A.M., when they heard the first dull *thump* of a 32-pounder, they jumped. And then they laughed nervously, because the fire was distant and could not possibly be aimed at them.

Fort Bartow fired the first shot and Samuel Parker noted the time. Smoke from the 32-pounder's muzzle hung in the damp air, dissipating slowly at the edges, gray scarves peeling off one by one and drifting over the earthen parapets and falling slowly to the dark waters of the sound. For a long moment following that first shot, there was silence; Parker could hear reverberations of the blast bouncing back in faint echoes from the mainland forests and the countless coves indenting the shoreline. The silence attenuated, became an ominous vacuum that demanded to be filled. Then a ripple of fire slashed across the arc of the Yankee fleet, and a few seconds later the air was filled with thunder and iron.

In accordance to the tactics worked out between Branch and his captains, two Mosquito Fleet vessels steamed south and threaded their way between the pilings and the masts of sunken blockships, hoping to entice pursuit and thereby lead a detached Yankee ship or two into closer, more narrow waters, where fire could be massed against it. But Goldsborough's men would not take the bait—his ships remained anchored in a disciplined crescent, methodically ranging on their targets. As Parker watched, the nimble CSS *Forrest* turned back through the obstacles, bravely but ineffectually popping off shots from her stern-mounted 24-pounder. Just as the *Forrest* was about to rejoin the rest of the Mosquito Fleet, a big Federal shell, 9-inch at the least, detonated above the deckhouse. As if by magic, the smokestack was peppered with daylight and one of the gunners reeled around with his hands over his face and a gleaming bib of scarlet flowing down his chest from the shell fragment that had scalped him.

Overhead and all around, the density of Federal fire formed a solid vault of noise: smoothbore balls huffed like locomotives, shells from the big rifled guns whirred like giant partridges, and their cast-iron bolts moaned a long dismal wail of lamentation. Powder smoke, keen and caustic to the nostrils, curdled and thickened, buffeted into shapes as fantastic as those of storm clouds viewed by poets. Whenever the nearby ships fired, Parker felt his chest compress like a bellows. All along the frontage of the Mosquito Fleet, the water was stippled and spiked and roweled by iron, and shell fragments sizzled like bacon when they were quenched striking the water. Parker was spellbound by the sight—this was a naval battle as he had imagined one to be, a spectacle both grand and terrifying. Through his glass, he saw a Federal ship that had become detached from the main squadron and was now a hundred yards closer than the rest. He could not make out her name, but she was either the *Commodore Perry* or a newly built gunboat of the same class. Cupping his hands, he yelled down to his own gunners to aim at the gunboat's waterline. When no one responded, Parker peered down at the foredeck.

Spratley and his gun crew were now cringing behind their gun's massive wooden carriage, clutching their sponges and aiming spikes, their eyes either tightly shut or rolling in terror. Parker could see a fan-shaped scorch on the deck beside the mount, where hot fragments had landed close, and he understood full well that this experience was vastly and fearfully different from anything he and they had ever imagined. They looked like nothing so much as a bunch of turtles trying to crawl into their shells. *Damn them! I have every right to be just as scared as they are!* Parker drew his Colt, pointed it at Spratley, and called out: "Able Seaman Spratley, if you do not man your gun and commence firing on this instant, I will kill you myself!"

Spratley stared up in confusion. Not only had he never been shot at before, but his captain had never before addressed him in such a manner. The pistol barrel did not waver, and Parker's eyes held no pity. When he cocked the hammer, the sound was amazingly loud and distinct, demoting the cannons' roar to a sullen rumble of background noise. Spratley shook his head, raised his hands in supplication, then in submission. Shame reddened his cheeks. He stood up and took a deep breath. Snarling and cursing, he kicked the other cowering gunners until they too were on their feet and at their posts.

"You heard the captain, you dogs! Aim for that arrogant son-of-a-bitchin' gunboat out in front!"

Parker was only too happy to reholster his revolver, and doubly glad that the gun crew had not seen how his legs had trembled during the confrontation. Spratley's boys sponged the barrel, rammed home the powder cartridge and wadding, trimmed the fuse of a shell to match the range of the target, then stood at attention, hands over their ears and mouths agape to equalize the air pressure, while Spratley himself pulled the greasy lanyard and fired the piece. Shock waves from the muzzle blast buffeted Parker as he tried to focus on the Federal gunboat. Though she was partly obscured by the smoke of her own salvos, she was beam on and as good a target as they were likely to get. Unheard above the other racket, the *Beaufort*'s shell flashed and some bits of rope and railing spun into the air.

"That's the way, men! Another shell in the same spot!"

Spratley turned toward the ammunition locker and did some quick finger-counting.

"No more shells, Captain. We'll do our best with roundshot."

Two times, possibly three, the *Beaufort*'s gunners struck the *Commodore Perry* with cannonballs, punching plate-sized holes in her hull just at the waterline. Paddle wheels frothing, the gunboat retreated. If those had been shells, Parker lamented, we would have sunk the bastard. Nevertheless, it was damned good shooting, considering how shaky the gunners had been only fifteen minutes earlier.

"Well done, Mr. Spratley. You gave the Yankees something to think about, at least."

As they reloaded, and Parker took the *Beaufort* through a starboard turn and back again—just to confuse anyone trying to draw a bead on them—the gun crew chattered busily among themselves. When the 32-pounder was again ready to fire, Spratley took a few steps toward the bridge, took off his cap, and said: "Cap'n Parker, sir, about that incident earlier . . . me and the boys wanted to apologize. It won't happen again."

"What incident? This was your first time under serious fire" (*and mine, too!*), "and it is no picnic."

"Aye, sir. But just like anything else that calls you out hard, it's all a matter of getting used to it."

For the next two hours, the Mosquito Fleet continued to trade shots with the Federal gunboats, without apparent effect on either side, until a 9-inch shell plunged through the deck of the CSS *Winslow,* tearing out her bottom. Her crew managed to beach her in a swampy cove a hundred yards north of Fort Bartow, where she settled so deep in the bottom mud that only her wheelhouse and smokestack remained above water.

For most of the afternoon, however, the Federal warships concentrated their fire on Fort Bartow, which was clearly a much greater danger to them than Branch's hapless flotilla. From the Mosquito Fleet's point of view, the fort appeared to be disintegrating. Hundred-pound and 9-inch rounds plowed into the ramparts at the rate of three per minute; columns of sand, sod, and marsh grass spouted forty feet high and rained back down on the backs and heads of the sweating, deafened gun crews. Shell flashes stalked back and forth, bursting high and bursting low, bursting inside the walls and in the tangled swamps beyond, and clotting the air above the works with dirty splotches. But the actual damage must have been less than an observer might conclude from all the flash and fury, for the fort's 32-pounders maintained a slow but steady fire throughout the day and every now and then one of the Federal gunboats would cough up a wad of splinters and rigging where roundshot scored a hit.

At four-thirty, Branch ordered the Mosquitoes back to Elizabeth City to recoal and replenish their ammunition. The *Winslow* had been sunk, four other vessels damaged to some extent, and a dozen men had been wounded. As they sailed away, the sun broke through a narrow gap in the clouds and briefly poured a sulfurous yellow light across the great pall of gun smoke that hung over Pamlico Sound. Sam Parker reckoned they had done everything possible with the puny resources at their disposal. "Honor" had been satisfied, whatever *that* amounted to under such hopeless circumstances, and things might have gone much worse for the little Rebel fleet. Indeed, things surely *would* have been much, much worse if the Yankees hadn't focused most of their attention on Fort Bartow, pausing only now and then to take a swat at the Mosquitoes as though they were no more of a nuisance than the insects for whom they were named.

The next time the two fleets met in battle, Parker reflected, the enemy's attention would not be divided. But that time was still in the future, by a matter of days at least, and for the moment Parker gave thanks to God that his ship and his outmatched but gallant crew had come through their trial-by-fire unscathed.

While the naval engagement thudded and growled off to the north, Burnside's amphibious landing went off as smoothly as a well-rehearsed training exercise. Not so much as a rifle shot was fired as the crowded and vulnerable boats wallowed into the shallows and disgorged their loads of infantry. The Ninth New York came ashore without getting wet above the shins. Burnside landed five thousand men and six fieldpieces during the day and all the rest were ashore by midnight. Intermittent rainsqualls turned much of the ground into mire, so the three brigade commanders were content to pitch camp and let their men take whatever rest and sustenance they could. Things would be sorted out in the morning, after scouts had gone out and taken the measure of both the land and the Rebels' defensive positions.

During the night, however, several local self-proclaimed Unionists hailed the anchored transports from a rowboat. These individuals were duly brought before General Burnside, who questioned them thoroughly, then sent them ashore, accompanied by an aide-de-camp, so they could share their intelligence with the commanders of the three infantry brigades. Rush Hawkins had just fallen asleep, sometime after one A.M., when he was awakened by one of General Foster's couriers and summoned to a conference at First Brigade headquarters. Puffy-eyed and half-dressed, Hawkins stumbled awkwardly through wet sand and tangled underbrush until he could see Foster's tent. Inside were Foster and his staff along with all five of the brigade's regimental commanders. Hawkins sidled up to a big map, held down at the corners by a lantern and some cartridge boxes, that seemed to have captured everyone's attention. Standing diffidently off to one side were three raggedly dressed civilians, two middle-aged men and an apparently dim-witted boy, all of whom smelled of fish. From time to time, Foster pointed to the map and asked a question of the trio's apparent leader, a sunburned, rawboned man with the deeply lined face of a fisherman who kept twisting the brim of his straw hat while he attempted to answer Foster's questions.

"Are you certain that the swamps on either side of the road are impassable?"

"Yessir, Ah am. When one of the local cows gets lost in there, we just leave her be, 'cause they ain't no gettin' her back."

Another civilian, an elderly man with patches of rash on his withered forearms and virtually no remaining teeth, spoke in confirmation: "Gen'ral, I done fit in the Seminole Wars, and hit's worse in them swamps than it was in the Everglades."

After a few more questions, Foster dismissed the three and sent them, under guard, to get some food. Then he summarized for the newcomers what he had learned: On all of Roanoke Island, there was only one road larger than a cow path, a deeply rutted wagon track that ran north to south from the fishing villages on the island's northern coast to an abandoned turpentine plantation near the other end. The road followed a narrow hump of elevated land, some natural and some man-made, and on either side were bogs, moribund black ponds, cypress groves shrouded in vines and decorated with thorns an inch long. The Rebels had thrown up an earthwork across the road, anchored on either side by the swamps; directly athwart the road itself, they had constructed a triangular bastion mounting at least two and possibly three fieldpieces, caliber unknown. Burnside's plan of attack was brutally simple—given the nature of the terrain, it had to be. Foster's brigade would lead, General Reno's brigade would follow at a five-hundred-yard interval, and General Parke's brigade would be in reserve. "The Tenth Connecticut will lead the assault, flanked west of the road by the Twenty-first Massachusetts and to the east of the road by the Twenty-third Massachusetts." Foster nodded in turn to the commanders of those regiments. "Colonel Hawkins, your men will support the Tenth Connecticut and be ready to advance through it, if it gets stuck or if the Rebels start to waver. I will send a runner with orders to that effect. Please do not advance until I tell you to."

The colonel of the Twenty-first Massachusetts stepped forward and thumped the map. "General Foster, you're putting us right into those swamps."

"Yes, I am, and for two reasons. One is that our Unionist friends might actually be Confederate agents sent here to spread false information, in which case those swamps might not be as dense as they told us. The second is that the swamps really are bad, but not so bad as to preclude a slow advance that exerts pressure on the enemy's flanks. If the latter is true, well, more than one commander has come to grief because he entrusted his flanks to ground that *someone else* assured him was 'impenetrable.' "

As he watched Burnside's field artillery struggle to reach its supporting positions, Rush Hawkins decided that the adjective "impenetrable" was a very relative term. From what the Ninth New York had seen of it this morning, *all* of Roanoke Island—or at least those parts of it not underwater—was covered by foliage of an almost tropical density. Even though the companies of the Tenth Connecticut had blazed the trail before them, the Zouaves still found the going rough. The ground was spongy and corrugated and a careless step could turn a man's ankle and send him sprawling. As the regiment slogged through a maritime forest of tangled, wind-sculpted pines, hidden creepers wrapped around their feet and thorn-covered vines ripped at their uniforms and clutched at their packs and rifle slings. By the time they reached the road and turned left to follow the Tenth Connecticut, Hawkins's men were sweat-soaked and plastered with bits of vegetation while their hands and faces were red with scratches. Half a mile north of the spot where they had met the road, they halted. Sergeant Dunn planted the regimental colors firmly in the sand about a hundred yards behind the rearmost rank of their Connecticut comrades.

There they waited, kneeling or sitting, while the guns came up, their approach heralded by the teamsters' furious oaths. "Gee up there, you lop-eared son of a bitch!" being one of the more common. Finally, the Napoleons and the stubby howitzers came into view, half-dragged and half-pushed by man and mule, their wheels slick with muck and their ammunition caissons lurching over stumps and fallen limbs. Slowly, and with much more swearing, the batteries crept along the road's shoulders and passed out of sight on the left side of the Connecticut men. A half hour later, a runner came to Hawkins from the front and informed him that the Tenth Connecticut was prepared to launch an assault as soon as the artillery could give support.

Hawkins spent the next fifteen minutes trying to dig a pestiferous sand flea from beneath the flaring cuff of his Zouave trousers. He almost had the insect in his grasp when the Union cannons began firing. He could see a ripple of tension pass through the massed shoulders of the Connecticut men as they braced for the signal to attack. A bugle sounded, officers yelled, and the Connecticut regiment began to unwind forward in a stumbling run. Almost immediately, the air above the roadbed was alive with the hissing, clattering ruckus of grapeshot and minié balls.

In effect, and by defensive design, the road was like an elevated causeway leading straight into the mouth of the Rebel guns that commanded its length for a quarter mile. Added to the cannons' thunder was the constant crackle of musketry. A storm of lead swept the roadway like a broom, causing the sand to writhe and spit beneath the feet of the Connecticut men, whose assault was stopped stone-cold just seconds after it began. Dropping prone, they tried to return fire. After the first exchange of volleys, smoke closed in so fast and so thick that neither side could see the other. This worked to the Rebels' advantage, since they had only to keep firing down the road; when some order was restored to the attackers, they replied by firing high, firing low, and firing obliquely, hoping to cover as much of the defenders' line as possible. To stand upright for an aimed shot was to be hit. Here and there, lashed on by the curses of their sergeants, some of the Connecticut soldiers tried to advance by crawling forward a short distance, reloading while prone, then rising to one knee to fire, then dropping down and crawling again. It was slow work and largely futile, but they kept at it with great courage, sometimes taunting the Confederates with shouts of "No Bull Run here!"

Aside from the leaf-clipping crackle of misdirected grapeshot far overhead and the occasional *vvvmmmm!* made by a half-spent minié ball, the Ninth New York was not yet really under fire. But that could change quickly if the men in front of them should break or be ordered to withdraw. Every few minutes, a wounded man came lurching through the smoke, on his own or slung between two comrades who looked quite eager to carry their burden as far to the rear as necessary. The New Yorkers could not help but gawk at these powder-grimed phantoms, for they had seen nothing like this at Fort Hatteras. When one Connecticut corporal came shambling down the road, clutching in gray-faced silence the severed remnant of his own right arm, some of Hawkins's men started to waver and one young fellow heaved up what was left of his breakfast. Observing this crack in discipline, Color Sergeant Dunn sidled over to the panicky soldiers and began talking to them calmly. He was too far away and the ambient noise was too loud for Hawkins to hear what the old trooper said, but there was something massively reassuring in his very presence. I lived through Waterloo, his gestures said, and you can live through this little skirmish. *And it does no good to stare at the wounded—they are in another world from yours and they cannot or will not impart any useful wisdom.*

After another hour of grinding punishment, the Tenth Connecticut was given permission to withdraw and a runner came to Hawkins bearing a message.

"General Foster's compliments, sir. He instructs you to advance two hundred yards and be prepared to support the Twenty-first Massachusetts, who are attempting to turn the enemy's right flank by advancing through the swamp. If they succeed, you are to pour rifle fire at the Rebel position, but not to charge unless so ordered by General Foster."

"Evidently, the swamp is not so 'impassable' after all."

"Well, we are in the process of finding out, Colonel."

The aide saluted and scurried back into the trees. Hawkins sent word to his companies to clear a path for the Tenth Connecticut, then close ranks and advance to occupy their former position.

This was not an easy process, nor a swift one. Almost another hour went by before the last stragglers passed to the rear and the Ninth New York could crawl forward. From the altered volume and density of the fire, it seemed that the Confederates were trying to conserve their ammunition, but the smoke was as thick as ever and all that could be seen of their position were sporadic stabs of light. Scattered like rag dolls across the road were dead Connecticut soldiers and every time Hawkins saw some particularly ghastly injury, he felt his nerves grow tighter by a notch. Death and glory were balanced on the sword's edge in this place. Most of the enemy's rifle fire was high, so as long as the New Yorkers stayed prone, and the smoke remained opaque, they would probably be all right. They suffered only one fatality during this period of waiting—a Confederate roundshot, weakly delivered by bad powder or a short charge, came *thump-thumping* like a bowling ball out of the smoke and down the middle of the road, losing velocity each time it skipped on the sand and so harmless, indeed comical, did it seem, that one young man, despite the horrified warnings of more experienced comrades, reached out to catch it and for his stupidity suffered a surgically precise decapitation, after which the cannonball continued to skip merrily down the road while the poor man's head flew off to one side and landed faceup in a pool of scum-covered swamp water.

Now there was movement, a lot of it, off to the right. General Foster and his staff came forward, as though tracking something, pointing and gesticulating toward the undergrowth. Now Hawkins could see them, the men of the Twenty-first Massachusetts, as they staggered and lurched and hacked their way through waist-deep water, their fixed bayonets festooned with muck and garlands of foliage. There was no order to their formation any longer—they were a howling mob with briar-torn hands and heavy wet boots, but they had momentum and they seemed ready to make the Rebs pay for every particle of discomfort and misery they had suffered while traversing the wilderness. Just then, a cold wind pushed some of the smoke into the trees and Hawkins could see the relative geometry of converging forces. The Twenty-first was going to hit the Rebel flank at a favorably oblique angle and the Rebels, still preoccupied with shooting up the roadway, did not see it coming and had no time to turn their cannons in a new direction. But now, with the nearest charging Yankee only fifty yards away and the underbrush thinning out, some Rebel infantry heard the cheers, turned, saw that blue steel-tipped wave bearing down on them, and began to point, yell a warning, and turn their rifles around.

Unconsciously, Rush Hawkins had been making his way forward, until he stood between his own men and the vantage point of the cheering and visibly agitated General Foster. With preternatural calm and the sort of highly charged combat vision that makes everything, however chaotic, appear to be unfolding very slowly, Hawkins calculated time, distance, and vectors. No doubt about it: the Massachusetts regiment would strike the Rebel line first and their charge looked to be unstoppable. Already, some of the defenders were wavering. If the Rebels broke now, they would flee like rabbits, swept before the ferocious swamp-chargers like so much chaff. But there was still time for a share of glory.

Hawkins ran over to General Foster, who swiveled to look at him with an expression of utter mystification coupled with irritation at having his attention diverted from the battle's climax. Drawing his sword, Hawkins gestured wildly at the Rebel breastworks, where the volume of rifle fire had suddenly diminished quite markedly, and screamed something incoherent about launching a charge.

"There is no need, Colonel Hawkins! Just support the Twenty-first with rifle fire, as you were ordered to do!"

But in the turbulent, reeking, bullet-boiling air between them, Foster's admonition somehow turned inside out and by the time his words reached Hawkins's ears, they rang out nobly and clarion-bright. "*You are the very man and this is the very moment! Zouaves, charge that battery!*"

So filled with pent-up tension were his men that they needed no encouragement. When they saw their colonel's sword go forward, they leveled their bayonets and followed, screaming their battle cry: "*Zou-zou-zou!*"

By this time, the Twenty-first Massachusetts had crashed into the Confederate right and shattered it, the scratched, mud-caked, boot-sloshing furiously *angry* New Englanders swarming irresistibly up and over the earthworks. The Rebel defenders suddenly realized they had been thunderstruck from the depths of the supposedly impassable swamp. Seized by panic and despair, they turned around and fled down the road, into the pines, splashing into the bogs, the Devil at their heels, their cause and prospects utterly undone.

When Hawkins reached the Rebel guns, he realized that the issue was already decided. The Zouaves swept over the earthworks and found no one left to fight. Some of them fired halfheartedly at the fleeing enemy; others just stared dumbfounded at their self-satisfied comrades from Massachusetts, who clearly believed they had just won the battle with their own gallant charge.

Hawkins stood distractedly beside one of the captured Rebel guns, sword drooping, so choked with frustration and bile that he trembled and shook and blew foam like a man verging on a seizure.

Puffing hard, Color Sergeant Dunn, who, despite his age, would have charged anyway, even if Hawkins had ordered him not to, posed dramatically on the parapet, waving the flag from side to side, savoring the moment.

This was not right! The battle could not be over! The charge of the Zouaves could not be so superfluous and barren of consequence! His own valor and audacity could not be so mocked! He swiveled his head in a fever of desperate searching. Surely, there was *some* resistance to be overcome, *some* Rebel soldiers who would fight to the bitter end!

Yes, by God! There! Two Confederate privates, gunners by the look of them, popped up from a hidey-hole dug into the embankment behind their abandoned field piece. One was a gruff gray-bearded older man, wearing a dirty butternut coat and a red-checked bandanna and clutching to his waistband a knife the size of a Roman short-sword; the other was a powder-filthy youth, no more than sixteen, trembling with fright but resolutely clutching a bell-mouthed scattergun of antique vintage. The older man stepped protectively in front of the boy, as though to shield him from the bayonets poised all about, and made a motion with his hand that Hawkins's fevered senses interpreted as a threat, although others, later, insisted the old fellow was just trying to hand over the weapon as a gesture of capitulation. Hawkins's nerves were primed and overwrought and he reacted swiftly to his perception, leaping down from the embankment and taking a great sweeping hack with his sword, burying its blade deep into the meat of the old man's thigh. The Rebel grunted in surprise as a geyser of blood shot up from his severed femoral artery. He opened his mouth and might have said something, but whatever it was disappeared beneath the boy's terrified shriek of *"Poppa!"* and was totally obliterated by the grating roar of the old fowling piece, whose barrel he had crammed with rocks, nails, and scraps of iron.

Sergeant Dunn, old soldier to the last, leaped in front of Hawkins when he saw the muzzle coming up and took the full charge in his bowels. A flurry of rifle balls tore into the boy, spinning him like a shredded top. As the sound of the last shot died away, Hawkins felt a red prickly mist rising from his head, replaced by a wave of pitiless cold. Flinging away his sword as though the pommel had become red-hot, he knelt beside the color sergeant, whose hands knotted fiercely in an unthinking effort to keep the flag from being soiled by his leaking innards. Dimly he heard men bawling for a surgeon.

When he arrived, the doctor took one look and shook his head. Word of Dunn's condition spread quickly through the regiment and many of the young men who had fallen under the spell of the old warrior's tales came forward to shake his hand until he was too faint to make the effort and seemed to lapse into unconsciousness. Inevitably, someone passed forward an almost full bottle of whiskey and asked the surgeon if Dunn could drink from it. "Why not? Nothing can harm him or help him now. He won't last until dark."

At that remark, old Dunn's eyes fluttered open and he raised himself a few inches on one elbow, extending a clawlike hand toward the bottle. "I've seen men get well from worse than this," he croaked. "But I thank you for your opinion, doctor, as long as it gives me the whiskey." He upended the bottle and drank a long pull. Then he smiled and lay back down. He made a sound somewhere between a moan and a sigh and, as the whiskey began to bubble evilly out through the holes in his abdomen, he died.

When Hawkins finally ordered up a burial detail, he could hear the sounds of acrimonious debate starting to rise into the twilight sky—already, the men of the two regiments were starting to argue about whose victory this had been.

That night, in General Foster's tent, Hawkins was given a severe tongue-lashing for his impetuosity, but Foster stopped short of a written rebuke—after all, a victory was a victory, and the Zouaves's charge, though utterly unnecessary, had been spirited.

February 10, 1862
The Roanoke Island Battlefield
Dearest Mother—

My ship, the USS Cambridge, *being too large to cross the swash at Hatteras, I was forced to miss the action of two days ago. Indeed, I spent the day as I had several previous days, overseeing the unloading of supplies. This morning, however, a request came from General Foster stating that his men needed food (there being scarcely anything edible left from the captured Rebel stores), and so I volunteered to command a shallow-draft barge laden with rations and medicine. After depositing our cargo with Foster's quartermasters, we were charged with bringing off wounded men to one of the hospital ships, along with some sacks of mail. While we waited, I decided to go ashore and poke around.*

The battle for Roanoke Island was the largest yet fought in these waters, involving a fierce exchange of naval gunnery on the 7th and a hard-fought land engagement on the 8th. Until the enemy ran short of ammunition and could be assaulted, there was a bloody stalemate in front of his works. I am told that General Foster's brigade alone suffered about 35 men killed and more than 200 men wounded. Rebel casualties are variously reported, but when their main works were outflanked and overrun, they were quick to surrender and the tally of prisoners must be close to two thousand.

I was naturally curious to get a close look at these fellows. They are a motley-looking set, mostly clothed (I can hardly call it uniformed) in a dirty-looking homespun gray cloth. Every man seemed to have cut his attire from a design of his own. Some wore what was probably meant for a frock coat, others wore jackets or roundabouts; some of the coats were long skirted, some short; some tight fitting, others baggy and loose; and no two men dressed alike. Their head coverings matched the rest of their rig, from stovepipe hats to coonskin caps, and for blankets they clutched everything from old bedquilts to cotton bagging to strips of carpet, and in several cases old Buffalo robes, derived from God knows where.

Now that the fighting is over, there appears to be remarkably little animosity between the two sides, save for a certain understandable measure of gloating from Burnside's men and a commensurate sullenness on the part of the captured Southerners. A more lasting impression is made from the many casual friendships commonly struck.

I struck up a conversation with a young man from Raleigh; he was smart appearing and loquacious and he said: "This has turned out not as I wished, but not different from what I expected when we saw the force you had. I accept the situation and am glad it is no worse. I am 'Secesh' clear through, and after I am exchanged, I warrant I shall be after you again. But when this little dispute is finally settled, if you should ever come to Raleigh, please hunt me up. If I am still alive by then, you will be welcome for as long as you choose to stay, and when you leave, if you don't say you've had as right smart a time as you ever had, why call me a liar and I will call you a gentleman!"

Some of the soldiers I talked to expressed surprise over the number of fearsome bowie knives they found littering the battlefield. They asked some of the ex-slaves about the Rebels' preference for carrying that kind of weapon. The Negroes said that the Rebs had cut many a fine caper with those knives before awestruck Darkies, but that they had quickly discovered once the fighting started that a man waving a knife—however large and sharp—does not much intimidate a man with a loaded musket, standing fifty feet away. As you may imagine, though, there is a brisk trade in these blades, for whatever their shortcomings as weapons, they make colorful and bloodthirsty souvenirs.

This morning, our squadron of gunboats went off to the north, toward the Rebel base at Elizabeth City, where the so-called Mosquito Fleet is said to be regrouping for a last stand. My friend Charles Flusser is there, aboard the Commodore Perry, *and I envy him the chance to see a real naval battle.*

If at all possible, Mother, I shall trade some rum and tobacco for one of those bowie knives, and send it to you in the same package as this letter.

Your loving (and healthy!) son,
Will

Jefferson Davis Takes the Oath

A MONSTER BABY—The Greenville (Tenn) Banner *gives the following account of a baby in that vicinity: It is only 13 months old on the 26th instant, and weighs about 50 pounds. It is a female, has a well-balanced round head covered with beautiful black hair; its eyes are gray, keen, and intelligent. It is sprightly, full of play and mischief. It measures three inches wider around the waist than its mother, and weighs twice as much as its brother, who is three years old. Its flesh is soft as silk and the amount of fat is such that it can be rolled around an adult's forearm. If you plan to travel in this part of Tennessee, it is worth going to see!*

—The Wilmington Journal, February 10 1862

After shooting off all his ammunition during the battle on February 7, Captain Branch led his battered little armada back to Elizabeth City, where he regrouped them, affected such repairs as were possible, divided all available ammunition equally among the ships, and prepared as best he could to meet the inevitable Federal attack.

There was a small fort, mounting four guns, at Cobb's Point, a half mile downstream from Elizabeth City. Fire from that position, Branch hoped, would delay and disorganize the enemy gunboats and perhaps cause them some damage. The rest of the Mosquito Fleet was stationed in a line adjacent to the town: the *Seabird, Ellis, Appomattox, Beaufort, Fanny,* and the *Oregon.* Using his emergency authority, Branch ordered out the local militia; a few dozen old men and boys answered the call, badly armed and shaking with fear, but when he ordered them to go and man the battery at Cobb's Point, they went. Not until dawn of February 10 could he spare the time to inspect that position, so crucial to his defensive plans. He found four guns, just as he been told, but only six militiamen on hand to work them. Sputtering with rage, he grabbed the nearest young man and threatened him with blows.

"Where are the men I ordered here yesterday?"

The lad cringed in anticipation of Branch's wrath, a snail trail of snot running from one nostril.

"Come sunup, they all absquatulated, sir! Run off while we was asleep."

"By God!" cried Branch to the unanswering heavens. "Are these the men with whom I am to defend this place against the U.S. Navy?" Then, to the trembling boy again, "Do any of you know how to load, aim, and fire these cannons?"

The militiamen hung their heads and scuffed their feet. "Somebody was supposed to come show us that stuff, Admiral," whimpered another boy, "only nobody ever did."

Realizing that anger would only cause these wretches to bolt the minute his back was turned, Branch tried an appeal to their patriotism. "Men, if the Yankees get past this fort without being punished by its guns, they will roll right over us and capture the town. I will send some gunners to you from my ships, but you must stand fast and obey their orders without hesitation. You can fire down upon the Yankees, but they cannot raise their guns to fire back at you, so there is really very little danger."

Observing the modest elevation of the earthworks, Branch was not at all sure that statement was accurate, but it seemed to put some spine in these dispirited wretches. On impulse, he deputized the runny-nosed boy as brevet corporal and left him in charge; then he rowed back to the Mosquito Fleet as fast as he could and hailed each ship in turn, ordering their captains to detach two or three gun-trained sailors, place them under command of Sam Parker on the *Beaufort,* and reinforce the land battery as quickly as possible.

Parker thought it might be too late, but he promised to do his best, because he knew that without supporting fire from the land guns, Branch's ships did not have a prayer of mounting effective resistance. Able Seaman Spratley immediately volunteered, as did his entire gun crew, but Parker turned him down.

"Give me two good men and that will do, Mister Spratley. I need you here, aboard the *Beaufort,* and I'm placing you in command during my absence—you know her moods and her abilities." The lank Georgia farmer drew himself taller with pride, for this gesture of trust proved that Parker had truly forgiven him for his moment of funk during the earlier battle.

"You can rely on me, sir! We'll fight her bravely and make you proud!"

"I am certain you will. But if and when resistance becomes hopeless, don't risk your lives pointlessly—spike the gun, beach the ship, then set fire to her and get away as best you can. This will not be the last battle we fight."

Four guns on the Point—three trained men to work each one at moderate efficiency—and the militiamen to lift the powder and shot. A dozen sailors, Parker figured, would be the minimum to man the battery and the maximum that could be spared from the ships. He split the force between two boats and ordered both crews to row hard. The Yankee gunboats had departed the waters around Roanoke Island early that morning—the news had been signaled up the coast with fires and flags—and even at a leisurely pace, they should arrive soon. Meanwhile, a glazed silence descended over the Pasquotank River, intensified by the measured splash of Parker's oarsmen. The Mosquito Fleet's ships were cleared for action, with maneuvering speed stoked in their boilers; the calm gray wintry morning held its breath.

When Parker's boats were within twenty feet of the shore, the first Union ships hove into view around a distant wooded bend, in scrupulous formation, unhurried, deliberate, projecting an air of certainty, as though the outcome of the day's events were a foregone conclusion. Parker felt furiously angry—it need not have turned out this way. Richmond had known Burnside was coming and there had been no doubt as to where he would strike. There had been more than enough time to turn this part of North Carolina into a formidable bastion, and to rush to completion the emergency plan Branch had submitted back in August for a fleet of cheap, shallow-draft gunboats capable of waging nautical guerrilla war. But nothing had been done that was not halfhearted, incomplete, or far too late. And who would be blamed for the disaster, once its full dire measure had been taken? To ask that question was to answer it.

Parker led his men from the boats to the earthworks and was not at all surprised to find there a single sniffling militia boy, rubbing his nose on the back of his cuff, half petrified with shame and fear.

"Where the hell are the men who were here an hour ago?"

"All run away, sir. When I tried to stop them, they threatened to throw me into the river."

There was no time for recriminations. Parker detailed three men to each gun and trained the whole battery on the Union flotilla, now scarcely a mile away. Even as he shouted orders, he saw the enemy ships pick up speed and with his glass he read the signal hoisted from their flagship: *Dash at the enemy!* He calculated quickly: one salvo as they drew abreast of Cobb's Point, then independent fire as they passed at close range—they would still be within easy range when they slowed down to engage the Mosquitoes, so perhaps all was not yet lost.

All four guns fired more or less together, causing the sand parapet to collapse, so indifferent and ignorant was the workmanship of those who had built it. Parker saw four columns of water rise near the Federal ships and he was pleased. The next time his gunners fired, the enemy vessels would be broadside at a flat angle and a comfortable range, and they would suffer.

But instead of the expected gun-drill commands, he heard only an explosion of profanity. The sailors gestured wildly at the gun mounts. Suddenly Parker understood. The guns had been sited so they could only fire *downstream*; they could not pivot to the left and follow the enemy fleet upstream. Already, the Yankee gunboats were moving beyond the muzzles' restricted arc. Everyone seemed to realize the situation at once, and the whole detachment, including—to his undying credit—the forlorn militia lad, swarmed over the left-most gun and tried to turn it a few degrees by sheer brute force. But the weapon was too heavy and the Yankee ships moving too briskly. Both angle and distance opened quickly, so Parker yelled for the crews to take cover, fully anticipationg a blistering fire from the enemy's stern mounts. None came. Unharmed, untroubled, and apparently uninterested in their puny display of resistance, the Federal squadron steamed past serenely and bore down on the hapless remnanats of the Mosquito Fleet.

Parker and his men were now mere spectators, and despite their bitterness and frustration they were mesmerized by the scene. Advancing in a great iron wedge, cleaving angry white wakes from their bows, the gunboats surged forward at full throttle, spooling out behind them long black ribbons of funnel smoke. It was a slashing attack by powerful ships and well-trained crews, and it stirred in Parker's breast a bittersweet feeling of professional pride—what naval officer would not be thrilled by this spectacle? Fortunate was the sailor who saw such a thing even once in his career.

From the Rebel line came a ragged salvo fired by seven guns, and from the charging enemy blazed a cataclysmic reply from six times that number. Through his glass, Parker clearly saw Able Seaman Spratley coolly giving orders to the crew of the *Beaufort*'s 32-pounder while steering the little warship in a twisting path intended to present the smallest possible target. The Yankee ships ripped through the churning white wall of their own gunsmoke, their prows emerging like blood-wet axe blades. Roundshot from a Rebel gun—it could have been the *Beaufort*'s and Parker silently cheered that it was—peeled the roof from the USS *Ceres*'s pilothouse and for an instant, before smoke once more obscured the scene, Parker could see her startled helmsman peering up at the open sky and reaching for his hat, which had been plucked neatly off by the cannonball's suction. At the same time, the CSS *Oregon* shuddered from multiple shell strikes, her paddle box pounded to splinters, her boiler venting steam with the howl of a scalded dog, her forward gun dismounted and all the crew strewn about, stunned or dead or wounded, and fires washing through the deckhouse.

Whatever order there might have been to the Confederate formation, it was all lost after the first ninety seconds. Each captain fought as best he could from the exigencies of his own situation. The *Ellis,* one of the few Rebel ships that mounted more than one gun, turned hard a-starboard to bring its stern 12-pounder to bear on the hard-charging *Commodore Perry* and succeeded in raking the latter's bow with canister, killing or maiming everyone within the balls' murderous arc. Then the *Perry* rammed the *Ellis* amidships and broke her in two. The next Confederate ship in line, the *Seabird,* was so badly mangled that no structure above her deck was readily identifiable—burning like a torch, she drifted out of line and used the last of her power to run herself aground.

Now the remaining ships on both sides were intermingled in a smoke-shrouded, flame-stabbed tangle of hulls and paddle wheels and rigging. When Parker finally caught a glimpse of the *Beaufort,* he was thrilled to see her emerge from the melee at flank speed, her 32-pounder still firing, bearing down on the USS *Wabash* with the clear intent of laying alongside her and boarding. Beside the wheelhouse, he saw Spratley at the head of twenty men, all armed with cutlasses and pistols. It was the bravest, and yet the most futile, act he had ever seen. The *Wabash* nimbly turned away and, when the *Beaufort* drew abreast, pivoted her 9-inch rifle and sent a shell crashing into the hull, where it exploded deep in the ship's bowels and touched off the boiler. Parker saw Seaman Spratley rise majestically on top of the boiling detonation, his hair and clothing streaming flames and his cutlass still pointed valorously at the enemy. Then, perhaps mercifully, the *Beaufort*'s magazine blew up and when the smoke and debris finally cleared, there was nothing left of her but a few smoldering planks on the water.

In the confusion, one Confederate ship, the *Appomattox,* succeeded in picking up some survivors, including Captain Branch, and escaping up the Pasquotank River and thence into the Dismal Swamp Canal. Just below the South Mills locks, however, it was discovered that the *Appomattox* was four inches too wide to make the passage to Norfolk, so she, too, was abandoned and burned. The locks themselves were then destroyed to thwart any pursuit or thrust at Norfolk.

From first shot to last, the Battle of Elizabeth City had lasted just twenty-one minutes. Helpless to affect the outcome, Parker and his detachment watched it all from their ringside seats at Cobb's Point and more than one man wept. The only thing they could do, finally, was to spike the guns, roll the powder and shot into the river, and make their escape by rowboat when darkness fell.

From the *Richmond Examiner,* March 2, 1862:

> *. . . the affair at Roanoke Island was as outrageous as it was incomprehensible. When I read in this and other Southern papers about our valor, I wonder if they are describing the same battle as I witnessed. Not outside the annals of Greece and Rome, we are told, can such tales of heroism be found! Whole regiments of Yankees were defeated by companies, and the defenders finally yielded only to death. Yet what was the actual loss? In the Forty-fifth Virginia, three were killed and eight wounded; in the Thirty-first North Carolina, one was killed and eleven wounded, and so on through the entire roster of units present. We yielded, quite simply, because we ran out of ammunition at the crux of the engagement. And this engagement need not have been fought, but for the fact that most of the heavy guns on the Island were pointed* away *from the enemy's landing boats. Ninety percent of the troops defending Roanoke Island were in the wrong place, and the remaining ten percent were critically deficient in ammunition, as well as every other Thing required for success.*
>
> *If the hand of treason be found in this matter, then let justice be brought swiftly against the traitors* no matter what their rank. *But if this disaster was brought about by sheer incompetence, then our Army had better surrender now, for the Confederacy is a gone coon.*
>
> *I am, sir, etc., "A Loyal Officer."*

General Chase Whiting was chilled to the bone. And bored. Like everything else the Richmond government tried to accomplish, the inauguration ceremony of Jefferson Davis was late getting started and dilatory in execution. The morning of February 22, 1862, offered no better prospects than most of the wintry days preceding it. Somber clouds hung like funeral crepe over the spires of Richmond, and a cold steady drizzle had been falling since dawn. Mud rose in the already liquefied streets and, from the crowd assembled to watch the historic occasion, one heard more curses than cheers. On this day, as on so many others Chase Whiting had endured since reporting to Virginia, the sun definitely was not shining upon the Cause.

Many of the dignified gentlemen standing on the reviewing platform had already uncorked their pocket flasks and taken a nip or two for the sake of internal warmth. Under the circumstances, Whiting thought he might be excused for doing the same. He took a healthy swallow of bourbon from his own flask and rejoiced at the sudden blooming heat that spread throughout his slight body. His companion—the two men were sharing the same umbrella—seemingly did not mind, or even notice, so Whiting handed the flask over to his old friend and mentor, General Joseph Eggleston Johnston. Old Joe looked down in surprise, then smiled absently and accepted the flask, permitting himself a pair of moderate sips before handing it back to Whiting.

Even after standing in the damp for an hour, after days and weeks of tension and exertion, Joe Johnston looked like a soldier. No, a *commander*. Whiting felt shabby as well as miserably dank, and his woolen uniform itched and his nose kept threatening to run, but Johnston looked smart and crisp in full ceremonial dress. Like Whiting, he was a man of modest stature and no great weight, maybe 140 pounds if you added the sword and revolver. Somehow, though, Johnston always *seemed* taller, by virtue of his habitually erect carriage. His strong gray eyes seemed ever alert, and the neatly trimmed thatch of his grizzled moustache, goatee, and side-whiskers gave him a bristling and bellicose appearance, even when he stood in repose. At fifty-four, he possessed a deep fund of energy and maintained a daily schedule that would have exhausted many younger men. If he often struck subordinates as being preoccupied, there were plenty of reasons for it.

Since the end of August, Johnston had struggled mightily to turn the ragtag Confederate army into a disciplined and decently equipped force. From the beginning of his tenure, however, he had been plagued not only by vile weather and chronic shortages of every basic commodity, but also by the incessant yapping of the Richmond press. The week after the fortuitous victory at Bull Run, Johnston had been castigated for not following up with a triumphant march on Washington—an operation that, had he undertaken it, would have qualified him for a lunatic asylum. Johnston could not respond publicly to this deranged clamor without letting the enemy know just how weak and disorganized the Rebel army really was.

When the Confederate government promulgated its first list of promotions, on August 31, Johnston took umbrage at the fact that General Beauregard was ranked higher than he—a slight made more galling by the fact that Beauregard had claimed more credit for the Bull Run victory than he deserved. Whiting had planned the logistics for that battle, and he knew that Johnston's decisions had set the stage for victory to a much greater extent than Beauregard's exaggerated battlefield heroics. Johnston had written an intemperate letter of protest, which chanced to arrive in Davis's hands when the president was sick and feverish, and Davis had snapped back angrily with a letter of his own, fairly slapping Johnston down for insubordination. Although the two men had worked in harness since then, and neither of them had ever spoken of the incident to the other, Whiting felt certain that neither man had ever quite forgiven the other.

When he arrived in Virginia, on the last day of the old year, Chase Whiting had been given command of a seventy-five-hundred-man division on the southern bank of the Potomac River. His zone of responsibility stretched ten miles eastward, from Aquia Creek, almost due south of Washington. His assignment was to guard against any sudden amphibious attacks and to deny the enemy free passage along that stretch of the river. Consequently, he inherited a significant portion of the entire Confederate inventory of heavy guns. There was a singular irony here, considering how hard Whiting had worked to obtain even a few such weapons for Roanoke Island, but even here, so close to Richmond, Whiting did not have enough guns to do the job assigned to him. To maintain at least the illusion of strength, Whiting had filled empty revetments with "Quaker Guns"—black-painted logs mounted on dummy carriages, which might give a casual enemy observer the impression of bristling ramparts where few yet existed. In January and February, a dozen brand-new guns had come up from the Tredegar Iron Works in Richmond, but two of those had burst on their first shot and Whiting's gunners had naturally grown skittish about serving them unless it were to repel a full-scale Federal assault.

Nor were the older, better-cast weapons entirely reliable—to stretch the available ammunition supply, Richmond had started mixing ordinary blasting powder with proper gunpowder, so that no two consecutive rounds behaved alike; some shots plunked absurdly into the river, a hundred yards from the muzzle, while others sailed majestically in the general direction of Washington and landed God knew where.

It had been a miserable winter for the men of the Department of Northern Virginia, and Whiting was not sorry to have missed the December portion. The troops from Deep South states had never experienced *real* winter before and were stunned by the persistent bone-brittling cold, the howling subarctic winds, the sleety rain, and the occasional outright snowstorm. Tents were few and every cabin was stuffed with wretched, hacking men and the lice that suckled on them; those who could find no other shelter dwelled under leaky lean-tos of rough pine and warmed themselves by the acrid smoke of damp wood scraps and oddments of combustible trash. In some regiments, one-third of the men were too sick to stand muster on any given day. Their diet was monotonous and unhealthy—fresh vegetables were rare, and antiscurvy fruits almost nonexistent. In mid-January, Whiting was forced to put his men on half-rations for almost a week, even though his headquarters was only twenty miles from the main Confederate supply depot at Manassas.

Johnston had worked mightily to keep his army intact and raise morale, but it was quickly apparent to Whiting that Johnston had to contend with *two* enemies: McClellan's forces across the Potomac and the bureaucracy in Richmond. President Davis had, as usual, made politically expedient choices to head the Quartermaster and Commissary Departments, men of limited competence who acted as though their authority had come from God instead of Jeff Davis. When Johnston wrote imploringly to obtain more forage for his weak and spindly transport animals, Adjutant General Samuel Cooper blithely responded that "considerable savings could be realized if the animals could be subsisted without hay," suggesting that Johnston feed them with a mixture of "corn shucks and wheat chaff."

As Whiting might have predicted, the clumsiest and most infuriating obstructionism originated from Judah Benjamin's War Department. Benjamin often sent orders to Johnston's subordinate commanders without bothering to send copies to Johnston. It was the War Department bureaucrats, not the divisional or regimental commanders, who approved the lists of names for furloughs. Only a week after Whiting arrived in Virginia, Johnston received an order requiring him to send back to Richmond all the rifles of the sick and furloughed, so the weapons could be distributed to newly arrived regiments. Johnston balked—how, then, was he supposed to *rearm* the men who came back from the hospitals and from their visits home?

Whiting hoped he could avoid becoming embroiled in the constant bickering, but that was not to be. In mid-January, he and all the other brigade commanders received orders from the War Department that they should reorganize the entire army so that men from the same state all served together in homogenous brigades. The purpose of this drastic restructuring, according to Benjamin's order, was "to gratify state pride and keep up that healthful and valuable emulation which forms so important an element in military affairs." Leaving aside the fact that Judah Benjamin knew nothing about "military affairs" save what he had read in books, the very notion was ludicrous and its deeper motive quite transparent: Jefferson Davis was under desperate pressure to create command openings for important political allies who were presently cooling their heels in dull, obscure administrative posts within their own states.

Dutifully, and without editorial comment, Joseph Johnston sent copies of this order to every division and brigade commander. To a man, they were outraged, and Whiting's written response was typical of their sentiments: *"The men are proud of their intermingled companies and draw strength from the fact that Georgians, Carolinians, and Alabamans serve together side by side. They are used to my command, and I to them, and we are now accustomed to acting together. This policy is as suicidal as it is foolish and I will not do it!"* Somehow, a copy of Whiting's memo ended up landing on President Davis's desk, and Jefferson Davis did not appreciate being called a fool, even by implication.

"I fear he will now consider you an enemy," Johnston wrote to Whiting. Whiting replied: "I have enjoyed that distinction already, for some months, since I picked a fight with Ben Huger in Norfolk. Let us both grow stronger under his enmity." Faced with unanimous opposition, Davis did not press the scheme, but every officer who opposed it on record knew that the president was unlikely to forget their lack of cooperation.

On February 18, Davis summoned Joe Johnston to Richmond to discuss "serious matters." The tone of the telegram was that of a command, so Johnston made ready for his first trip to the capital since July. He also rode over to Whiting's headquarters and asked if Whiting would accompany him. As it happened, Whiting was considering a trip to Richmond anyway—he had heard rumors that a shipment of prime English powder had arrived from Wilmington, via the blockade-runners, and he wanted to be the first general in line for some of it.

On the following morning, he and Johnston boarded the train at Centreville, conversed amiably on the trip, and reached Richmond six hours later. Richmond was bursting at the seams, its peacetime population of thirty-eight thousand more than doubled by the arrival of new regiments, contractors, refugees, recuperating wounded, deserters, tourists who wanted to witness the inauguration, newspaper reporters, and idle men on furlough. The two generals walked up Broad Street and turned past Capital Square, making directly for Davis's offices at the Customs House. Johnston had made arrangements for them to stay in a private home during their visit, for there simply were no vacant hotel rooms, even for generals.

From the moment they passed the sentries, the two officers could feel tension in the very air. The president's secretary seemed dumbfounded by their sudden appearance. Johnston handed the man a copy of Davis's telegram and waited with scowling impatience while the man read it.

"General Johnston, I'm afraid the Cabinet is in emergency session at the moment and I have orders not to interrupt the meeting for any reason."

Johnston's brow furrowed more deeply—he had caught the scent of something gone awry.

"What crisis has arisen?" he asked.

"You haven't heard the news, then?"

"No, sir. We have been on the morning train and have only just arrived in the city."

"Well, sir, the news has not been made public yet, but you are entitled to hear it. Word came this morning that Fort Donelson has fallen."

Something like a soft moan passed from Whiting's lips. The South had just lost control of northern Tennessee. It was not a mortal blow, but it was a deep and crippling wound. Color drained from Joe Johnston's cheeks. He took a *carte de visit* from his jacket and wrote on it before handing it to the secretary.

"Here is the address where General Whiting and I can be found. Tell President Davis that we are available, at his pleasure, when circumstances permit."

Davis sent for Johnston early the next morning. Chase Whiting, rather pointedly, was not invited to the meeting. He spent the day trying in vain to locate the British gunpowder of which he had heard report. He went from office to office, speaking to one factotum after another, without encountering any concrete information. He even swallowed his pride and attempted to pay a courtesy call on Judah Benjamin, only to learn that Benjamin, too, was closeted with Davis, Johnston, and the rest of the Cabinet. No doubt remained: something big was up. Curious to learn what it might be, Whiting returned to his lodgings to nervously await Joe Johnston's return.

When Johnston appeared, late in the afternoon, he looked weary. Whiting could well imagine how airless and stressful the Cabinet meeting must have been, and he could tell right away that Johnston was bursting to share information. Johnston located their host and requested a private room where he and Whiting could confer without anyone overhearing them. The two officers were duly ushered into a small parlor where a fire blazed cheerily in the hearth and a large bottle of excellent sherry decorated the largest table.

When the doors were closed and the first glasses poured, Johnston came right to the point: "We're pulling back. All except for Jackson up in the Shenandoah and a token garrison at Fredericksburg. The president has concluded that our forces are too extended and too detached from one another. He already had this scheme in mind, but the fall of Fort Donelson has fixed it. The strategy is one of concentration, so that we may take more rapid advantage of any opening McClellan shows us when he advances. He intends to strip Florida, Georgia, and South Carolina of every available company. I'm afraid that means your friends in North Carolina will receive no reinforcements, and may even be required to give up some of the men they already have. He is also bringing Robert Lee back from Georgia to coordinate military affairs—that, at least, is good news. I would much prefer to deal with Lee than with anyone in the present War Department."

"How far will this retrograde movement extend and when are we supposed to start?" Whiting asked glumly.

"In general, I think the south bank of the Rappahannock will make a suitable line. As for the timing, the president leaves that to me. I am instructed to keep him informed, but not to commit any particulars to paper, in the interests of security."

"What about Norfolk?"

"We will hold it as long as we can—it is, after all, the only first-class navy yard in the South. The ironclad *Virginia* is almost ready, and it may prove sufficiently frightening to keep the enemy away from the city. I would of course feel better if someone other than General Huger were in charge of that place."

"So would I," muttered Whiting. Suddenly, a deeply disturbing thought flashed through Whiting's mind.

"What about my heavy guns, Joseph? I don't have enough horses even for the field artillery, never mind a piece that weighs seventeen thousand pounds. And the roads are quagmires without bottom."

Johnston looked at his old friend sadly.

"If the means cannot be found to move the heavy weapons, then they must be wrecked and left behind."

Whiting hurriedly poured another glass and downed it quickly.

"Is this a sound strategy, Joseph?"

"It will be seen as such, if McClellan is kind enough to give us an opportunity to make the most of it. As long as we're stuck in Richmond for the next two days, we may as well begin developing plans. I'll summon the division commanders for a council of war as soon as we return to Centreville."

"Is there any compelling reason why we are, as you say, 'stuck in Richmond' for the next two days?"

Johnston smiled wryly.

"Yes, Chase. President Davis has invited us both to attend his inauguration. In view of the friction that has occurred in the past, it would behoove us to show at least that token of respect."

But the next morning, as the cold rain drummed above their heads and the appointed time came and went, both generals now wished they had made excuses and returned to their respective commands. The crowd below the reviewing stand was sullen and silent; they had come to witness a rare moment of history, but many were doubtless wondering if that privilege was worth a case of pneumonia. Without realizing it, Whiting finished off the contents of his flask, and when Johnston motioned for another drink, he fumbled in his pockets with embarrassment. Then a civilian dignitary tapped him on the arm and extended a much larger flask, half full.

"Here, generals, a bit of warmth from the fine state of Tennessee!" said the fellow.

"Just a sip, sir," smiled Johnston. "We don't want to be hogs."

The man waved with inebriated gallantry. "Keep it, gentlemen, with my compliments. I have another in my pocket just like it. By

God, the Yankees may have more guns than we do, but they can't make sipping whiskey worth a parson's fart!"

"Indeed not, sir," chuckled Whiting. "It is a valuable secret weapon!"

Twenty minutes later, and far behind schedule, Jefferson Davis and his entourage strode from the capitol to the podium, stationing themselves close to the statute of George Washington. Negroes in funereal black scampered behind the politicians, trying to keep them dry with umbrellas. After a soggy fanfare from the assembled musicians, Davis stepped forward and began his speech.

Chase Whiting did not hear a word of it above the rain, and neither did anyone else who was more than twenty feet from the president. Predictably, however, the address went on far too long, and by the end of it small groups of citizens could be seen melting away. The crowd's apathy was as palpable as their physical discomfort—over the past year, they had heard quite enough speeches. Whiting nursed the whiskey, taking surreptitious nips every now and then. He might someday tell his grandchildren, "I was there when Davis took the oath," but his immediate and overriding concern was for his precious heavy guns. There along the riverbank, *under his hand and control,* were enough big-caliber weapons—rifled as well as smoothbore—to make Roanoke Island impregnable, with enough left over to double the strength of the works at Wilmington. But Roanoke Island was already lost, having fallen in February, and New Bern in mid-March, and there was nothing Chase Whiting could have done to prevent those twin disasters. He was reconciled to these events by the belief that his cannons were at least protecting Richmond. Now, they probably would not have a chance to fire so much as a single shell at the enemy. The simple futility of it galled him beyond measure.

Whiting understood, and had ultimately come to accept, that Davis's strategy during the first year of conflict had necessarily been one of bluff, of defending—or giving the appearance of defending—every important location on the outer boundaries of the Confederacy; at least the president had bought time for new regiments to be formed, new cannons to be forged at Tredegar, gleaming new British Enfields to be funneled through the blockade. Clearly, the unbelievably quick capitulation of Fort Donelson had changed the strategic focus to one of *concentration* and Joe Johnston was ready to embrace the concept, for all winter long he had fretted about how overextended and potentially vulnerable his forces were.

But this was a massive change, and the more Whiting considered it, the less confident he was that it could be done. Johnston's personal staff was composed of earnest and competent young officers, but like everyone else, they were learning as they went along. No one had trained them to conduct this kind of operation because no American army of this size had ever attempted one before. As for the men in the ranks, they were cocksure because about half of them had fought in one relatively short battle and all of them had spent a hard winter drilling and coping with shortages of all kinds. They *thought* they were hard-bitten veterans, but they had not yet fought a real campaign, nor had they ever faced an enemy as numerous and well-equipped as the force McClellan was grooming on the other side of the Potomac. If Johnston ordered them to shed every accumulated item not required for "light marching order," they would have no idea what to do. Whiting could visualize the chaos: did that mean you should leave the iron skillet behind but take the coffee mug? If you had two blankets, did you discard one?

Halfway through the president's speech, a barrage of sodden thunder rolled over the city and the rain fell harder in its wake. By now, the only people who could hear what Davis was saying were the Cabinet, the attendant Negroes, and George Washington. Whiting grew more depressed with each leaden moment. If McClellan got wind of the retrograde and moved aggressively while Johnston's divisions were strung out and in the open, the result would be catastrophic. Shuddering, Whiting took a big gulp of Tennessee Sunshine—there were times when even the steadiest soldier needed a jolt of "Dutch Courage" to peer into the abyss of worst possibilities. Thankfully, as it sometimes did, that extra dollop of bourbon brought renewed clarity: this was George McClellan, after all, and while Little Mac might dress and strut like his idol Napoleon, there was no trace in his character of the Corsican's killer instinct, nothing but lip service paid to the maxim of "*toujours l'audace!*" Whiting smiled at the mood change. He returned the almost empty flask to the florid Tennesseean standing at his shoulder. He was on the verge of really feeling the whiskey, and that was where he should stop consuming it. He might brood over a few more glasses tonight, while he poured over his maps and tried to formulate some deus ex machina plan to save some of his big guns, but the rest of the day would be a *political* event and until he and Joe Johnston were safely on the train back to Centreville, they would both be walking on glass.

Suddenly there was a scattering of applause and a rain-soaked battery of 12-pounders began firing the presidential salute. A band began to play, and some die-hard Rebels in the crowd, or what was left of it, began to throw their hats and shout the obligatory huzzahs. President Davis waved in response, still carrying himself with dignity despite the soaking he had received. Give him credit for that, thought Whiting; the man tries to inhabit the role thrust upon him. In truth, there were few Southern leaders who could have done as well and many who would have done far worse.

In such a newfound mood of charity, Whiting dutifully followed two paces behind Johnston as they moved under the welcome cover of the capitol portico and joined the throng of people swarming to congratulate President Davis. Whiting was amazed to see how Johnston's figure dominated the area where they stood, despite the fact that many men were taller and many of them wore stovepipe hats. There had been speculation among the many disaffected officers who chaffed under Richmond's bungling interference, that Johnston himself should be made president, or, for that matter, military dictator. If God favored Old Joe with a victory in the weeks to come, such disaffection might grow into a genuine movement. Whiting knew where his loyalties would fall in that eventuality.

Slowly the two generals edged their way closer to President Davis. The air under the cupola was steamy and dank, and to judge from the passing fumes, more than a few of the spectators had warded off the chill in the same manner as Whiting and Johnston. Whiting found himself breathing deeply, through his mouth; it was one thing to enjoy your own whiskey, and quite another to ingest the multiplied echoes of it wafted about on the exhalations of other men, especially men who had been sweating for two hours inside wet woolen clothes. Out of the rain finally, many of the attendees lit cigars, and the smoke hung in torpid clouds, adding to the muddled stink. Suddenly, Whiting felt nauseated.

Just as he was wondering whether or not he should quietly excuse himself from the reception line and seek a private corner in which to be sick, Whiting felt Joe Johnston tugging on his sleeve. Queasily, he responded, planting a smile on his face and thrusting out his hand toward Jeff Davis.

"Sincerest congratulations, Mister President," he stammered, and just as he took the presidential hand, someone right behind him emitted a huge, silent belch, filling Whiting's nostrils with the stench of tobacco, whiskey, and a breakfast that had apparently included a large portion of pickled herring.

"General Whiting, are you ill, sir?" inquired Davis, frowning in concern and no small amount of distaste.

"Acute indigestion," suggested Johnston, with a look of consternation.

Chase Whiting knew that if he attempted to say one more word to Jefferson Davis, he was very likely going to be sick all over the man's boots. Bowing and waving his hands apologetically, he spun away and lurched through the crowd, seeking the nearest place where he could throw up in some degree of privacy. As he retreated, he heard Davis say to Johnston: "Is General Whiting drunk, sir? He certainly seems to be!" He passed out of earshot before he could hear Johnston's reply.

On the slow, rackety train back to Centreville, Johnston tried to calm his friend. "I assured him it was only a brief case of stomach fever brought on by too much good Richmond food poured upon two months' worth of field rations. That *was* the truth, wasn't it, Chase?"

"General, I had a few more sips than you did, to ward off the chill, but I was in no way inebriated. Just dizzy from the sudden closeness of the air. The timing was unfortunate, and I fear the president took offense."

"I wouldn't worry about that, Chase. President Davis makes a habit of taking offense at something or someone at least five times a day before lunch. He has surely forgotten about the incident by now."

Somehow Whiting doubted that. But his protestations were interrupted by the appearance of a well-dressed civilian who rudely intruded upon the officers' privacy and introduced himself as an agent of the Commissary Department.

"Is it true, gentlemen, that the whole army is planning to withdraw from the lines around Manassass?"

Appalled, Johnston scowled furiously at the man and snapped, "Where on earth did you hear that ridiculous rumor, sir?"

"Oh, last night at dinner, General, from the wife of someone in President Davis's Cabinet."

"I cannot discuss such matters, sir."

Observing Johnston's icy expression, the civilian at last realized that he had presumed too much. Muttering apologies, he backed off, but not before giving a conspiratorial wink that infuriated both officers. After he went away, Joe Johnston shook his grizzled head wearily and snarled, "Now the cat is out of the goddamned bag!"

13

Jack Fairless Never Owned a Slave

BEWARE THE SPECULATOR—Speculation in times like these is awful. It is like dancing over a volcano or playing bluff in the sanctuary. Speculation and alcoholic spirits have done us more harm than the enemy. One has crippled our resources; the other has lulled our vigilance and prevented our working diligently and clear-mindedly. We are learning in a hard school. We ought to learn our lessons, or we will be made to suffer keenly, and more keenly yet.

—The Wilmington Journal, March 15 1862

Jack Fairless had never owned a slave, never expected to, and did not have much use for the people he knew who did. Nevertheless, when the war came along, he suddenly felt mighty Southern—especially when he heard that the Secesh recruiting officers in Asheville were offering a bounty of $50 for any man who enlisted for twelve months. Fifty dollars would pay his family's debts with enough left over to see them through a year. When his enlistment was up—if the war lasted that long—he could come home a respected and traveled man, presumably carrying another bonus from the grateful Confederate government in far-off Richmond and, if he was lucky, a pack full of Yankee plunder. He could buy a few acres of good bottomland and, with hard work and the blessing of God, he would be able to raise his family above the circumstances that had entrapped them for two generations.

Things had not always been that way. Jack's great-great-grandfather Isaiah had been a prosperous Pennsylvania farmer of hardy Scottish lineage, a man of piety and standing, admired by all who knew him. Until he made the mistake of proclaiming loyalty to King George. A less principled man would have bent with the political wind when the Tory cause began to wane, but Isaiah was too proud or too stubborn. When the Revolution was an accomplished fact, he found himself friendless and his children the object of abuse, verbal and otherwise. Vindictive laws were passed against propertied ex-Tories and Isaiah found himself both burdensomely taxed and unable to sell his produce. In 1790, he abruptly decided to liquidate all his remaining property and move to western North Carolina. He had heard reports that a man could buy land there for two shillings an acre.

But Isaiah Fairless did not find the promised land in those mountains. It was true that men could buy land cheap, but only if they could prove their service in the American army. Isaiah had no discharge papers and as he pushed deeper into the frontier, from Alleghany County on the Virginia line two hundred miles southwest to Buncombe County, he discovered that all the good riverside bottomland—those long, dark-loamed ribbons of well-watered soil where corn grew heavy overnight—had already been bought up by the first wave of settlers. The most desirable parcels still on the market belonged to real estate speculators, who either shunned ex-Tories or took gross advantage of them by selling them mediocre land at usurious prices. Isaiah was left with three choices: he could lie about his beliefs, he could swallow the humiliation of working another man's good soil as a tenant farmer, or he could keep moving.

He would not lie, because lies were an affront to his stern and unforgiving God, and he would not take on the shackles of tenancy—his own forebears had left Great Britain to escape that same pernicious system of bondage. Unyielding as stone, his meager resources dwindling week by week, he had no choice but to push on, ever deeper into the forest-clad wilderness, until he found some land that belonged to no one, some rough and rock-strewn coves watered by the lesser creeks. He found such a place in the folded high country west of Asheville, where several other families had already settled and bestowed the name of Spillcorn Creek. For a few generations, life in that rude and scattered community was quite tolerable. The land was not prime, but there was a sufficiency of it to provide for one's family, when its grudging yield was added to the wild game abundant in the vicinity. Neighbors were few, but when the families got together, they were mighty sociable. All of them shared one special quality: a defiant left-aloneness toward the increasingly alien world of the town dwellers and the wealthy bottomland farmers. The folks in Spillcorn Creek did not have much, but by Almighty God, what they had was *theirs.*

By the time Jack Fairless was born, in 1836, privacy had become isolation, ignorance of the outside world had become a virtue, and pride had become sheer cussedness. Most of the game had been exterminated and the soil had grown weary and children just kept being born. The Fairless family still owned a patchwork of breaky-back cornfields, a grove of persimmon trees, and a couple of spavined mules that could be loaned to other families at planting time, in exchange for eggs and molasses and homemade whiskey, but mostly the clan raised hogs, and as soon as Jack was old enough to share the work, he helped to drive the surplus pigs to Asheville, where they were sold to buy salt to preserve, through the long iron winter, the meat of the pigs held back for family consumption.

Fully half the children born in Spillcorn Creek did not live past sixteen, and that may have been a backhanded mercy, given the paper-thin margin between chronic poverty and actual brute starvation. Theirs was a circular, precarious existence. Too much bad weather, too much sickness, one broken plow too many, and the whole structure of it rattled under the strain and sometimes verged on collapse. Two adverse winters in a row had brought hard times to the Fairless family and despite the gall of it to their pride, they had been forced to buy a winter's worth of salt on credit, a low and humiliating circumstance that placed them—in their own eyes, at least—in a whole new category of poor. For two generations, their subsistence had been marginal—no one alive could remember when things were otherwise—but they had never ever been in debt before. So when news of the war trickled out from Asheville into the hardscrabble backwoods, along with the rumor of a $50 enlistment bounty, the opportunity seemed a godsend.

Jack Fairless was the most suitable male, by virtue of age and general health, so off he went, assuming the role of soldier-provider with no more forethought than he would have given to a routine hog drive. He would go to Asheville, seek out the recruiting post, make his mark, and take his oath. Then he would pay the family's debts and send back to them enough real money to see them through the year of his enlistment.

Jack was not comfortable when dealing with townsfolk; their prejudices and greed were legendary among the poor farmers. There was an old Dutch mirror in the Fairless cabin, one of the few heirlooms that had survived since Isaiah's day, and Jack was shrewd enough to know how he must look to the well-dressed citizens of Asheville: the very embodiment of a hillbilly. He was six-two high, pale and spotted on the face with large pink freckles; he had water-blue eyes and thin rangy shoulders, and his lank sandy hair just fell wherever it pleased; he could not grow a respectable beard and so his mouth looked thin and bitter, his lower lip pressed up over the upper so that, unless he were smiling, his features always looked pinched. Using the mirror, he had tried to make himself more presentable, but his fair skin turned red beneath a razor and although he slicked back his hair with ample bear grease, by the time he reached Asheville, it looked like a wind-tossed haystack.

He was therefore unprepared for, and more than a little taken in by, the hearty welcome he received at the recruiting station of the Twenty-sixth North Carolina. Officers in splendid uniforms clasped his hand and told him what a fine-looking fellow he was, a real potential Yankee-killer, a true Son of the South. The examining physician complimented him on strong limbs, clear lungs, and for having sufficient natural teeth to tear open a rifle cartridge. He made his mark on a document, swore an oath, and was officially transformed into Private Jack Fairless.

And then he asked about his bounty. The question was received with a moment of awkward silence, then the swearing-in officer doubled up with laughter and cried, "Ye gods, here's another one! That is one hell of a rumor, ain't it boys?"

Then the man shook his head with an expression that blended sympathy and amusement, as if to say, "These clodhoppers will believe any damn thing." There was no enlistment bounty. As a private soldier, he would be paid $5 a month in Confederate scrip; he would be fed, clothed, and doctored. That was the extent of Richmond's obligation to Jack Fairless and his family. He should be proud, the recruiting officers told him, to be doing his patriotic duty. Jack's understanding of the word "patriot" was dim and encrusted with family lore about the Revolutionary War, when "patriots" were persecuting his ancestors. As the reality of his situation sank in, he went from stunned incredulity to outrage at being swindled. He tried to tear up the enlistment document, but when he lunged for it, the officer behind the desk—who had seen this sort of thing before—pulled it away, drew his pistol, and called for an armed guard to take Jack Fairless away. During the next few weeks, while the new batch of recruits was preparing to march, he tried to escape three times and ended up making the march to Raleigh in chains and covered with bruises. Once the Twenty-sixth went into training bivouac, he was left pretty much alone—penniless and two hundred miles from home, there was not much chance of escape and the certainty of a firing squad if he tried and got caught. He subsided into sullen acceptance, made easier by the comradeship of many other mountain boys and by the sense of adventure that attended their drill. When he got paid, he dutifully sent most of the cash to his family, with the help of an educated sergeant who knew how to write and send letters.

There *were* some good things about soldiering. While many of the men in his company complained that the food was "so bad a nigger wouldn't eat it," Jack found it not much different from what he had eaten all his life. The brogans on his feet were better than any shoes he had ever worn, and he was already—like every other man and boy in Spillcorn Creek—an excellent rifle shot.

Once his basic training was complete and the regiment encamped at Gum Swamp, near Kinston, guarding the first railroad he had ever laid eyes on, boredom quickly took possession of him. He balked at petty discipline, hated sentry duty, and could not for the life of him understand why he had to show respect for a man just because he had stripes on his sleeves. By the time the regiment moved into the line protecting New Bern, in February, he had not been paid at all for three months. As far as he was concerned, that was the last straw. He had been in Rebel service for seven months and he had never even seen a Yankee, much less fired his rifle at one. Increasingly, he wondered why he should *want to.* Rumor had it that Yankee soldiers, at least, got paid on time. If that turned out to be the case, Jack reasoned, a man would have to be dumber than a Chinaman's earwig to prefer a gray uniform to a blue. He knew there would be a battle soon—Colonel Vance and the other officers spoke of little else—and there was bound to be a passel of confusion. In all the smoke and ruction, a clever man could slip away into the woods, hide out until the fighting was over, then make his way to Yankee lines and give himself up. All he had to do was be patient, and any man who had hunted wild turkeys knew how to do that.

One morning in early March, Jack and ten other men were ordered out to gather firewood. There was plenty of it in the surrounding piney woods, but every day you had to go farther to find it. There were now some forty-five hundred men encamped southeast of New Bern and they consumed wood in prodigious amounts. Just before the forage detail marched out, Lieutenant Colonel Harry Burgwyn, the recently promoted second-in-command of the Twenty-sixth, cantered up with the welcome news that several railcars full of sawn wood had been delivered the night before. It seemed that the next regiment in line to the east, the Thirty-fifth North Carolina, was composed mostly of men from this part of the state, one of whose uncles owned a sawmill in New Bern. Since the commander of that regiment, Colonel John Cantwell of Wilmington, was a political crony of Colonel Vance, he had generously offered to share the bounty with Vance's unit. "You men round up some wagons," ordered Burgwyn, "ride over there, find the woodpile, and bring back our share."

Jack Fairless was constantly surprised by the contrast between March weather in the mountains and March weather on the coast. Up in Buncombe County, you could still get a passel of snow all the way through the month, and the days were often low-skied, cold-winded, and blurred by fog. Around here, though, the midday sun already carried enough weight to make a body sweat like a mule. By the time he and the others finished chucking a few cords of firewood into these wagons, they would all smell like mules, too.

Since the Kinston–to–Morehead City rail line ran arrow-straight through the middle of the Thirty-fifth's position, they had no trouble finding the firewood. Three hours later, all the wagons were full and Jack Fairless was every bit as sweaty and fragrant as he had expected to be, and itchy-scratchy all over where pieces of bark, pine needles, and splinters were plastered to his skin. He and his wagon-mates took turns swigging tepid branch water from the big teamster's canteen stored under the driver's seat, brushed themselves off as best they could, and allowed as how they would dearly love a drink of good whiskey. Even a drink of bad whiskey, thought Fairless. It was funny how something you'd never thought much about suddenly became important when you couldn't get it anymore. Some of the thirstier men in Jack's company complained endlessly about the lack and eagerly volunteered for any duty that brought them closer to New Bern, where a man might be able to buy an overpriced jar of cornlikker from enterprising civilians—provided there were no officers around and he was willing to run the risk of field punishment if he was caught out. Two weeks ago, some ignorant jackass from Company B had been gulled into paying $5 for what turned out to be a bottle of turpentine, but that hadn't stopped him from drinking a few swallows, with predictably dire results.

Creaking and groaning, the wagon lurched over pine stumps while the driver tried to steer around the worst patches of mud. They were about halfway through the Thirty-fifth's encampment, rumbling through a clearing where the midday sun was downright burdensome, when Jack saw something he had never seen before.

Not far off, in the exact sun-beaten center of the clearing, beneath the bored gaze of a sentry leaning on a bayoneted rifle, sat a man trussed up so tight the veins in his temples seemed about to burst. Fairless told the driver to stop, which the man did without question, since the sight was so unusual. Jack hopped down and strode over for a closer look. Somebody had done a real job on this fellow: he was bent forward toward his thighs, ankles and wrists tightly bound; his hands, splotched and swollen from lack of circulation, had been forced out and down, almost to his shins, and a stout three-inch pole had been forced through the space between the backs of his knees and his elbows. He had also been gagged with a thick leather strap that forced his jaws open as wide as a scream. His dark, smooth skin was glazed with sweat and the exposed portions of it were tormented by insects. His guard was a beardless teenager who began to fidget when Fairless drew near and towered over him.

"What did this man do?"

"Drunk and disorderly, attempting to strike an officer. He is what you might call a habitual offender. This time, he didn't get off lightly—Colonel Cantwell ordered him bucked and gagged."

"How long has he been tied up like this?"

"Oh, a smidgen over an hour."

"How long a spell does he have to go?"

"Two more hours."

"He won't be able to walk."

"Not for a while, that's for dang sure, and when the blood comes back into his arms and legs, he will whimper like a dog."

"It ain't right to do a body this way, I don't care how damn drunk he was."

"Well, ol' Cyrus here—that's his name, Cyrus Bone—he comes from around these parts, and I reckon his kinfolk keep sneaking him whiskey, 'cause he drinks more of it than any man in the regiment. If he was to get caught every time he got drunk, they'd've hung his worthless ass by now. He's mean as a snake even when he's sober, but he is death-and-Jesus when he gets aholt of a bottle."

Upon hearing himself discussed, the bound man slowly raised his head, blinking red-eyed in the glare, to see who belonged to the unfamiliar voice. Jack Fairless had expected to see a villainous and dissolute beast, but instead he saw a dark angel. Cyrus Bone had a mass of curly black hair, a thick curly beard, and the most piercingly intense eyes Jack Fairless had ever seen, eyes the color of a black-water creek. Despite the agony he was in, Bone's broad features had a cold serenity about them, just as his body, even though it was knotted up like a hoe-chopped worm, still radiated an aura of immense coiled energy.

"Where's he from?"

"Some puke-hole village up on the Tar River, if I recollect rightly."

Jack Fairless felt a sudden rage. He drew closer to the guard and stared down at him, his fists clenched.

"Son, you ought not to insult a man when he's helpless and in pain, nor his kin, nor the place he comes from neither. From the look of him, Mister Bone here could snap your scrawny chicken-neck with one hand, if he was of a mind."

The guard looked away awkwardly.

Jack Fairless knelt beside the man, so close he could smell the stink of his cramps. A trickle of blood ran down Cyrus Bone's jaw from where the gag sawed into his lips, and his breathing was hoarse and raw. Jack knew how dry a man could get on the morning after a good drunk, so he turned to the guard and said, "Can't you at least give him some water?"

"I ain't supposed to give him nothin'."

"Well, by God, I don't answer to your colonel."

Jack strode furiously back to the wagon and brought back the canteen. Not really caring who saw him, he loosened the cords on the ends of the gag, pried it away from the man's mouth, and poured a long thin stream of water into the opening. Cyrus Bone swallowed it with such ravenous pleasure that his shoulders trembled. Then he looked Jack Fairless full in the eyes and whispered: "Thank you, brother. What is your name?"

"Private Jack Fairless, Twenty-sixth North Carolina."

"Well, Jack, I will seek you out when I can and repay this kindness."

"Where I come from, we don't even truss a hog like this before we butcher him."

The sentry, appalled to think that an officer might come by and hold him responsible for interfering with a prescribed field punishment, now regained his nerve and lowered his bayonet until it was almost touching Jack's ribs.

"You better put his gag back in, good and tight, and clear out right now."

"Or you'll do what?" growled Jack. With all his rangy strength, he reached out his free hand and made a fist around the blade. Then he slowly and contemptuously pushed it aside, not even flinching when it cut into his palm and sent blood rivering down the knotted tendons of his forearm.

"You want that gag back in his mouth, put it in yourself. But be careful he don't bite off a finger or two when you do it."

Then he strode away, gratified to hear a rumble of laughter from the tortured mouth of Cyrus Bone, while the guard tried to figure things out.

Two nights later, when Jack was standing guard on the night's first watch, Cyrus Bone appeared by his side, materializing out of the shadows so silently that Jack nearly dropped his rifle when a hand suddenly appeared in front of his face, waving a glazed half-gallon jug. Signaling for stealth, Bone led Jack into a small gully, uncorked the jug, and handed it over with a smile so sweet and affable that it seemed to be made from sunshine.

"Cyrus Bone remembers his friends. Few pulls off-a this jug and you won't mind standing around in the cold nearly so much."

"What if I get caught?"

Bone handed him a large shag of chewing tobacco. "After you've drunk your fill, just pop a plug of this into your mouth and chaw on it some. That way, ain't nobody can smell it on your breath. Anybody comes to your post to check up on you, just hide the jug in here, step back out in a lively manner, and tell 'em you were takin' a piss. How they gonna prove you wrong?"

No one came to check, so during the two hours remaining to his watch, Jack Fairless drank whiskey with his new friend. For Jack, it had been a long while between drinks, and Bone's liquor was smooth, store-bought-tasting. In whispers, they told each other about their lives and how they had come to be in this place, in this army. Cyrus Bone was twenty-eight, four years older than Jack, and he had plied the trade of coastal pilot, up and down the breadth of North Carolina, for ten years. "What I don't know about it ain't worth knowing," he boasted. "And when I'm sober, I'm the best pilot between Norfolk and Wilmington."

The trouble was, Cyrus Bone did not particularly like being sober. He preferred to let good whiskey soften the edges of his reality, and when a sufficiency of it had gotten him where he wanted to be, he tended to get very angry when someone intruded. He had a bad temper, he knew, and quick fists, and he had seen the inside of the jails in six different counties. Most of the fights he had been in were triggered by insinuations that he was part Negro, but, he insisted, his dark complexion came instead from "Injun" blood, three or four generations back. And he was aggressively proud of that. His family was poor, numerous, scattered up and down the rivers, and fiercely loyal to one another. That, Bone explained, was why he always had access to good whiskey. "Cousins all over the place, Jack! Kin helps out kin! Ain't that the way it works?"

Fairless knew for a fact that it did, and he too had God's own plenty of cousins. In Cyrus's account of his background, Jack recognized many of the same qualities of fierce independence that characterized his mountain neighbors, the same deep innate distrust of city dwellers and authority figures. Why, then, was Cyrus Bone serving in the Rebel army? Bone stifled a loud guffaw as he replied.

"The last jedge I went up before, he gave me a choice: three years in jail or a year in the army."

"That ain't much of a choice, I reckon."

"Oh yes, it is. 'Cause it is a hell of a lot easier to get out of this army than it is to get out of jail. I got it all planned. When the battle starts, I'll jest hide in the smoke until the Yankees get close, then put up my hands and surrender. I heard tell that General Burnside is looking for Union men who know this coast. I know of some old-time Buffaloes who have already gone over."

"Buffaloes," Jack learned, was regional slang for people who had supported Millard Fillmore in the elections of 1856. Presumably, the lowly bison had a reputation for being lazy, dirty, and stupid, which was why the wealthy secessionists had chosen that label for the poor whites who did not have any economic stake in secession.

By the time the jug was empty, the two men were fast friends, and both were resolved to desert at the first opportunity. Bone would scout around for a good hiding place near the front lines, and the two of them could meet there while the battle raged. Neither of them doubted for a minute that Burnside would overwhelm the New Bern defenses. Just before Cyrus melted back into the darkness, silent as a swamp panther, he promised to bring more whiskey in two nights, when Jack was not on duty—he knew an old turpentine warehouse deep in the woods, where they could finalize their plans in seclusion.

Not until Jack Fairless stood up and tried to walk back to his sentry post did he realize just how hard the whiskey had hit him. His long legs felt wobbly and his rifle felt buttery and cumbersome. He was awash with warm good feeling and he could not help but chuckle at the thought of skedaddling in the middle of a battle. Why not toss his lot in with Cyrus Bone's? He would never make it back to the mountains on his own. He was sorry there was nothing more he could do for his family in Spillcorn Creek, but they would get by. They always did. And when the war was over, he could go back with a saddlebag full of Yankee money and nobody would be the wiser.

After some deep breaths and stern words of self-admonition, Jack managed to regain his balance and to resume pacing off his assigned route. Just in time, too, because here came that stiff-backed Harry Burgwyn, out to make a surprise inspection of the perimeter. Jack fumbled for the tobacco Cyrus had given him, hoping it would indeed mask the smell of whiskey. Unfortunately, his coordination was not quite as good as he thought it was and while he patted himself down to find the tobacco, he dropped his rifle and the goddamned thing went off. Lieutenant Colonel Burgwyn ran up to him and found him gaping in disbelief at the cloud of smoke wrapping his legs, the unbitten tobacco halfway to his mouth.

Right after breakfast the next morning, Jack Fairless went before the regimental officers for a disciplinary hearing. The charge was "Being Intoxicated While on Guard Duty." Harry Burgwyn wanted to "make an example" of Jack by subjecting him to the same bucking-and-gagging torture that had been inflicted on Cyrus Bone. Colonel Vance, on the other hand, was much more forgiving. With Burnside's armada just across Pamlico Sound, preparing to ascend the Neuse River for its attack on New Bern, Vance did not want to take the chance of injuring a healthy rifleman. Zeb Vance was a mountain man himself, Jack knew, and repeatedly had shown his reluctance to step on the mountaineers' spirits with overly harsh discipline. For a while, the two officers engaged in a spirited argument, while Jack struggled with a parched mouth and a thundering headache. He was resolved: he would kill with his bare hands any man who tried to hog-tie him and gladly hang for it, rather than endure so much as an hour of what he had seen done to Cyrus Bone. After one particularly acrimonious exchange, Colonel Vance struck the table before him and said: "Harry, God damn it, the man was not asleep at his post, just a little tipsy. I know his people and where he comes from, and if you try to break their pride, you lose them forever. My decision is made: Private

Fairless is hereby sentenced to one hour of wearing the barrel-shirt and three passes through the company gauntlet."

If Vance had truly sought to assuage Jack's pride, he failed. The barrel-shirt was not designed to inflict pain so much as utter humiliation. A hole was cut in the bottom of a flour barrel, just big enough for Jack's head, and after the barrel passed around his shoulders, he could make no motion other than a stiff-legged hobble. Then the other men in his company armed themselves with various cudgels and formed two lines. Jack was ordered to slow-march three times down the middle, while everyone else beat on the barrel with their clubs and sticks. Whether by accident or intent, of course, several of the blows landed on his unprotected head. But the worst bruises were on his spirit and the most powerful emotion he felt was not shame but hatred.

Even after the punishment was over, he sulked all day beneath the scorn, pity, and contempt of his "comrades," mulling over desperate schemes for deserting that very night. He knew that without the geographical knowledge and personal connections of his friend Cyrus Bone, he stood very little chance of getting as far as New Bern, and beyond that place, his knowledge of the land was limited to the railroad line itself, where Confederate patrols would be thickest and most vigilant. Late that afternoon, however, came word that Burnside's fleet had embarked and would reach the mouth of the Neuse River by nightfall. In a day or two, there would be a battle; if Jack could only be patient until then, his chance would come. Still sore from his earlier drubbing, he went to sleep that night with some new peace of mind; from a welter of confusion, a clear path had emerged.

He was not surprised when Cyrus Bone crept noiselessly into his tent several hours before dawn. When they were alone together in the same thicket where they had shared whiskey, Bone clasped his hand and said: "I heard what the sum-bitches did to you, Jack. I ought not to have given you that whiskey."

"Hell, no. Been a long time since I tasted anything that good. I reckon they done worse to you, and I don't figure on giving 'em a chance to do *anything* to me again."

"So we are still of the same mind about our future plans?"

"More strong than ever."

"Good man. Then here's what I propose: on the east side of the railroad tracks, just off my regiment's right flank, there's a big ol' brickyard. Some fool general gave that spot to a militia battalion—

all green and scared shitless. That's where the Yanks will break our line, I'd bet my life on it, so that's where the fighting will be over first. You lay low, wait for a chance, then sneak over and meet me there by the kiln with the big chimbley. We'll surrender to the first calm-looking Yankee officer that comes along, then we will make ourselves so useful to ol' Burnside that we'll end up being promoted instead of shot."

"How can you be so sure we'll lose?"

Bone laughed and hawked a disdainful gob into the pine scrub.

"'Cause they got three times as many soljers as we got, plus a slew of gunboats with nine-inch rifles fore and aft, that's why. How long you think this collection of redneck trash can stand up to that?"

Jack supposed that *was* the question, even though he was sure that Cyrus Bone had been called redneck trash on some occasions. Just as Jack himself had been.

"All right, Cyrus. I will see you at the brickyard."

The Battle of New Bern played out very much as Lieutenant Colonel Harry Burgwyn predicted it would exactly one week before it took place. On March 7, with a punctiliousness that Zeb Vance thought bordered on smugness, the restless Burgwyn had gone out early in the morning and actually measured every foot of the Confederate line. He started on the banks of the Neuse—the Rebels' extreme left flank—where a diamond-shaped earthwork had been erected and dubbed Fort Thompson. There he found eleven guns of various marque and potency, only three of which could be swiveled to fire at Union ground troops. As for the waterfront weapons, intended to fend off Burnside's powerful squadron of gunboats, they happened to be engaged in a practice shoot when Burgwyn arrived—banging away at some empty barrels that had been dumped into the river a mile or two upstream—and the results were not encouraging. Despite the slow current and short range, not to mention the fact that the barrels were not shooting back, Fort Thompson's gunners displayed remarkable consistency in not hitting a single target. Moreover, to Harry's disgust, the crews' drill was lethargic and bereft of the crisp snap that marked a sharp battery. Their officers, to a man, seemed unconcerned. When Harry questioned them, they shrugged and mouthed ignorant platitudes about how one Rebel could outfight five Yankees six days from Sunday, and besides, the gunboats would be bigger than the barrels, and therefore much easier to hit. Plainly, no one in the fort had learned a thing from the defeats at

Hatteras Inlet and Roanoke Island. The fort's commander displayed a nonchalance that Harry found infuriating: he sat on a camp stool, placidly puffing on his pipe, and responded to Burgwyn's sharp questions with the observation that "as long as the infantry lines hold, we will support them. If they break, well, we are not too far from the bridge into New Bern, so we should have plenty of time to spike the guns and retire in safety. As for the gunboats . . . I don't expect them to fight at close range because the river gets pretty shallow here. Why should we anticipate the worst when there is nothing we can do to affect the course of events?"

Dumbfounded by this response, Burgwyn sputtered: "The eyes of the whole Confederacy are on us, sir! If New Bern falls without at least a valiant defense, the newspapers will trumpet our cowardice to the world!"

"That may be so, Lieutenant Colonel Burgwyn, but I would rather have my name fill twenty newspapers than have it decorate one tombstone."

Harry stalked away and continued his tour of inspection, taking notes along the way. From Fort Thompson on the Neuse, the Confederate line extended westward to a large deep stream known as Bryce's Creek. Earthworks covered the whole front except in the exact center, where the train tracks intersected the abandoned brickyard and the line bent northward for 150 yards perpendicular to the rails. The Twenty-sixth North Carolina's entrenchments followed an elevated creek bank from that point over to Bryce's Creek. Any officer with half a brain could see how dangerous this gap would become once Burnside found it, but the strength of the brickworks' buildings had been deemed sufficient to multiply the effectiveness of the raw militia battalion stationed there. The defenders' sole reserve regiment, the Thirty-third North Carolina, was massed half a mile north of the gap, where, in theory, it could be rushed forward down the rails to counterattack any Union penetration. The Rebel commanders thought this scheme was actually a clever way to turn a weakness into an advantage, by luring the enemy into the gap and smiting him when he was disorganized. Harry Burgwyn thought the plan was sheer idiocy and could work only in the unlikely event of the militia putting up such a spirited resistance as to give the reserves plenty of time to get in place for their counterattack.

When Harry returned to headquarters, footsore and sullen, he shared his calculations with Zeb Vance. To defend the existing line, he declared, would require an absolute minimum of sixty-two hundred men, drawn up in two ranks, each man one yard apart from the other, and backed by a tactical reserve of at least fifteen hundred well-trained infantry and several horse-drawn batteries. The total number of men on hand was about four thousand, at least five hundred of whom were sick on any given day, and there were a grand total of two 24-pounders in reserve, stationed so far in the rear that they could not possibly be brought into action in less than thirty minutes. "New Bern," he concluded angrily, "is virtually defenseless! And the newspapers prattle on about how it will become 'a second Sevastopol'! The damnable part of it, Zebulon, is that we have had time and warning enough to do that."

Vance had no ready answer and did not want to insult Burgwyn's professionalism by mouthing platitudes about how the Southerners' innate valor and ferocity would compensate for inferior numbers, half-finished fortifications, and limited ammunition. Maybe those in Virginia who had witnessed the Yankees routing at Bull Run could take comfort in that mythology, but nothing had yet occurred on the coast of North Carolina that added one shred of credence to this notion.

So Vance had sought to placate his fiery subordinate with phlegmatic stoicism. "It may not be so bad, Harry. The men are ready to fight and the Yankees are not ten feet tall. Great victories have been won against greater odds, you know."

"Oh, really? Can you name one?"

"Umm, not offhand. You know military history much better than I, Harry."

Burgwyn glared back with just a trace of smugness. "Well enough to know that all such victories were won with swords, spears, and bayonets, in the days when great commanders led their men into battle by personal example and the tide could turn on the inspiration or willpower of the moment. I know of no such victories since the adoption of the rifled musket."

"Perhaps, in that case, we shall have the honor of setting a precedent."

But when the day of battle came, things developed rather as Harry Burgwyn had predicted, although neither man understood that until days afterward, when the pattern of the whole engagement became clear. Burnside embarked his invasion force—approximately eleven thousand men—from Roanoke Island on March 11. When Burnside's ships anchored at Slocum's Creek, just after dark on March 12, he was only seventeen overland miles from New Bern. His troops were ordered to march fast and light, carrying only blanket rolls, haversacks, canteens, and sixty rounds per man. March 13 was spent getting the whole force ashore, organized, and in motion. But two days of torrential rains had turned the soil into thick, glutinous, boot-sucking mud and caused some of the men's rifle stocks to swell up so badly that they could not extract the ramrods until they had laboriously dried the weapons by their campfires.

At dawn on March 14, the Twenty-sixth North Carolina stood to at first light and made ready, with grim innocence, to face its first battle. Daylight revealed heavy mist shrouding the pine forest and casting the whole landscape into a weird and mournful aspect. For the first hour, the loudest sound Vance heard was the hammering of a woodpecker. He had somehow expected the land to look different on the morning of a battle, but except for the fog, it was the same dismal gray-green countryside as before. He and Harry Burgwyn positioned their horses near the center of the regiment on a slight elevation. Beyond the makeshift trenches and pine-tree abatis, the piled-up stones and clay-packed sandbags and the tense restless rows of riflemen, stretched a broad swath of weedy marsh threaded with creeks. Any Yankees stupid enough or unlucky enough to attack across that ground, would find the going hard and slow. Elsewhere along the Rebel line, the land was more open, and on the axis of the railroad tracks it was almost inviting. Vance could not see beyond his own left flank, but he kept throwing glances in that direction, as though casting a spell of resolution on the militia troops who held the brickyard.

An hour dragged by without significant event. Harry Burgwyn kept consulting his watch, as though impatient for the show to begin. Equipment clanked and jingled as restless men shifted position. The sun climbed, the mist melted away. Everyone jumped when the distinctive *bang!* of a Parrott rifle blew the silence away from the direction of Fort Thompson. "Ah! Eight-fifteen!" called Harry Burgwyn, snapping his watch shut, like a man approving of some great act of promptitude.

Firing grew general rather quickly, starting far off on the left near the river and gradually seeping westward until it crackled in front of the brickyard. After a while, smoke began to drift over Vance's lines and the keen scent of powder rode every breath, but in front of the regiment nothing changed and nothing stirred. Rifle volleys crackled like distant wildfire from the brickyard to the river, but except for an occasional stray minié ball clacking through the trees, not a bullet or a shell came anywhere near the Twenty-sixth.

Things got busier thirty minutes later, when a dispatch rider galloped up, saluted, and blurted out: "Colonel Vance, the enemy are pushing hard into the brickyard and may overrun it soon! Refuse your left flank and prepare to attack them if the opportunity arises!"

"Now we'll see action!" cried Harry Burgwyn, slapping his horse and riding off toward the loudest volume of firing. Vance followed him, eager to see at last some stirring tableaux of battle. But when they reached the left flank, they found those companies already steeped back in echelon, as though the very volume and fury of the musketry to their left had inexorably shoved them in the proper direction.

Now Vance could at last see something, but the density of smoke and the roiling confusion made it difficult to know what it was. Muzzle flashes and moving men seethed inside the smoke, and the attackers shouted and cheered, so he could tell how close the Yankees were even though he could not, reliably, observe them. Agitated, Vance dismounted and paced around, squinting intently into the smoke. Then, out of sheer frustration, he drew his revolver, aimed it at a skyward angle, and emptied the cylinder. Burgwyn looked at him in astonishment, and Vance cried out: "If my bullets reach their apogee right over the Yankees' heads, I may hit one of the bastards! You know, Harry, like a mortar!"

Burgwyn just shook his head and handed Vance a freshly loaded cylinder from the spare ones he carried in a leather pouch. Somewhat sheepishly, Vance busied himself reloading. He had just finished reseating the loaded cylinder when the ground on the regiment's left front exploded like water in a hot skillet. Desperate-looking men in butternut came running out of the smoke, some without rifles, some hobbling and lurching from injuries real or feigned. But like a wavelet hitting a sandbar, the running men came up against another line of gray-clad soldiers, these standing firm and resolute.

"Carmichael's men from the Thirty-third!" said Burgwyn. Officers with drawn swords leaped forward and grasped at the fleeing militiamen. Some few of them shook off their panic, squared their shoulders, and joined the ranks. Most, however, just plunged ahead, roiling the lines as they plowed through, oblivious to the taunts and curses and rifle butts thrown at them.

"Goddamighty *damn!*" shouted a private off to Vance's immediate right. "Thar come the Yankees!"

Now that the broken militia had vanished in the general direction of New Bern, a curious and glassy silence graced the moment. Yes, Vance could see them now: too winded to yell, the Federals halted and re-formed as coolly as though they were on a drill field. Sergeants dressed their ranks, restoring some measure of control and giving their men a precious moment to catch their breaths—hundreds of men in blue charged with an aura of momentum that Vance could actually feel. It was *here,* then, on Vance's portion of the ground, that the battle would be decided. The Twenty-six and Thirty-third North Carolina, now formed up like a giant **L**, were the last bulwark. For the duration of that hard crystalline moment, the battle *looked* like a battle should, in Vance's mind: ranks and flags and formations, vectors of advance and lines of resistance.

"Men of the Twenty-sixth! " he cried. Then, quite suddenly, his mind went blank. What were the commands he was supposed to give? Jesus knew, he had memorized them back in May and rehearsed them through week after week of enervating drill, and now that his brain was bubbling like a stewpot, his tongue clove to the parched roof of his mouth. Harry Burgwyn was peering up at him, ready to jump in. So Vance finished up with the first words that came roaring up: "*Shoot those blue-coated bastards!*"

Both sides volleyed simultaneously and that moment of clarity, when Zeb Vance saw the battle whole and frozen, shattered forever. His regiment fired, the Yankees fired, the lines of the Thirty-third fired, and everything once more became obscure, chaotic. Vance was beside himself, jumping up and down in his saddle and swearing as only a frustrated mountaineer could swear. This was formless insanity—where were the clear dramatic progressions of the history books and the newspaper engravings? The stroke and riposte, the wheel and volley, the climactic charges? Vance felt himself suspended in a vortex of electrically charged frustration: serious fighting roared and blazed out there, not much more than a hundred yards away, but all he could *see* was thick coiling smoke, spikes of fire, and grainy shadows jerking along like poorly controlled marionettes.

Surely, any second now, the Yankees would materialize out of the smoke and he could—at long last—fire his revolver at something besides the sky. But that did not happen. His men kept firing volleys into the smoke, but hardly a shot came back. The Federal attack was coiling around them like a great snake, still following its original line of momentum down the Beaufort road and the railroad embankment, and never offering them more than a suggestive glimpse of its true nature.

"Is it always like this, Harry?"

"I would not presume to know, Colonel Vance—this is my first engagement, too."

Gradually, the mass of firing moved away and to the north. The day grew muggy and the men's canteens went dry. When the smoke began to dissipate, all Vance could see were some scattered bodies, a riderless horse snuffling among the fallen, and a few forlorn wounded men picking their way back to whatever primitive comfort waited for them.

Harry Burgwyn scowled. "Colonel, it does appear that we may be the only intact Confederate regiment left on the field. If the Yankees have not attacked us directly, the only logical explanation is that they don't need to. I think we had best make a plan for withdrawal."

"Lieutenant Colonel Burgwyn, we were ordered to hold this line and we have received no contrary order."

"Damn it, Zebulon, there may not be anybody left to give us an order."

At that moment, a haggard powder-stained lieutenant rode up from the northwest, saluted, and gasped: "Colonel Vance, you must retreat and keep your regiment intact. There are five thousand Yankees moving up the Beaufort road between you and the New Bern bridge. I believe the way is still open to the northwest, across Bryce's Creek. You must move at once, sir, for as soon as the enemy realizes you are still on the field, he will try to bag your entire regiment."

Then the man spurred his horse around and galloped away into the pines.

Harry Burgwyn was already studying his map and dictating notes to the company commanders. Trembling with nervous exhaustion, Vance could only nod his agreement. The Twenty-sixth would pull back like a collapsing bag, one company at a time, and march due northwest to Bryce's Creek. The first men on the scene would scout for a suitable fording place. The pace would be slow and methodical and a full company would guard the rear and give warning of pursuit.

For Zeb Vance, the next two hours passed like a fever dream. A "battle" had happened; he had been there; his men had performed well and fired their rifles as ordered; and yet nothing made any sense. He had witnessed no acts of gallantry—indeed, aside from the firing of a few volleys at a distant and mostly invisible enemy, he had seen no conspicuous act of any kind. Distant spatters of rifle fire broke out periodically, but never directed at them. Still, as the retreat progressed, the men lost cohesion amid the tangled brush and treacherous bogs, and their imaginations flamed with images of triumphant Yankees, their ranks tipped with naked steel, suddenly materializing behind them. By the time the regiment reached Bryce's Creek, it had become something very much like a mob.

But two days of heavy rain had turned the stream into a foaming river. Of the first five men who ran headlong into the water, three were instantly swept away and drowned, and the other two barely escaped. Zeb Vance knew well the vagaries of flooded creeks, for the mountains were veined with them and every spring when the snow melted on the higher peaks, there were some branches you simply did not try to cross. While Burgwyn and the other officers tried to re-form the mass of fleeing men into companies, Vance rode ahead, in the direction of New Bern, and found a place where the stream looked fordable. Impulsively, he rode in, and just as quickly fell off into the freezing water, for the horse in its wisdom had managed to find the one deep hole Vance had overlooked. He sputtered for air, shocked into clarity by the chill, and found the presence of mind to wrap both hands around the reins. The animal was not injured, just indignant, and he obediently dragged the colonel of the Twenty-sixth North Carolina back to shallow water.

By the time Vance had recovered his dignity and his teeth had stopped chattering, Harry Burgwyn had found a wide calm stretch of water and his scouts had found three flat-bottomed fishing pirogues. Eighteen men at a time, the regiment crossed, in good order and with no further incidents. Vance stayed with Harry and the rear guard and went across in the last boat.

By nightfall, they rejoined the remnants of the Confederate force at their encampment north of the smoldering stumps of the New Bern bridge. A palpable funk of defeat and weariness rose from the huddled survivors. As Vance's men straggled past the railroad tracks, they were subjected to derisive catcalls from a clean, well-rested company of Virginian regulars, the advance unit of a regiment that had been dispatched, days too late, to bolster the line below New Bern.

"Whooo-eee! You Carolina tar-tappers! Next time you get set to fight, put some of that tar on your heels, so you'll stick until we get there to win it for you!"

One of Vance's soldiers, hobbling on a twisted ankle, snarled back at the mocking Virginian, "Maybe if you'd'a scraped the tar off your own damned heels, you'd have been there this morning in time to put your arse where your mouth is, you swamp-rat."

Wisely, the officers in charge of this Virginia unit decided to bivouac them at a great remove from the sullen, whipped-dog Carolinians.

John Cantwell's preemptive "capture" of Fort Caswell had made him and his Cape Fear Minutemen the heroes of the hour back in April of '61. When he led his colorful militia company into active service with the newly formed Thirty-fifth North Carolina, his honorary rank of colonel had been made official. Social prominence and good political connections had done the rest, and by midsummer he was elevated to command the entire regiment. Unlike Zeb Vance, Cantwell had formal military training: two years at Virginia Military Institute, where he had studied under the dour and humorless Stonewall Jackson before he resigned to take over the Wilmington business affairs of his recently deceased father. During their tedious months of drill, and their boring tour of duty guarding the railroad at Kinston, his soldiers discovered him to be a tight, highly strung martinet and some of them compared him, unfavorably, to the affable Zebulon Vance, whose own regiment was often encamped in the same general vicinity.

Private Cyrus Bone had shown up on the muster role of Company A in mid-September, when the Thirty-fifth was digging entrenchments on the mainland near Morehead City. Within a matter of weeks, Private Bone had begun to earn a reputation for being a hard case, and the commander of Company A confessed to Cantwell that he did not know how to handle the man. Bone followed the orders he found congenial, and disregarded those he did not—an attitude that gradually began to infect other members of his company. At first, Cantwell was merely irritated by these complaints and curtly tossed the responsibility back to the captain of Company A, who supposedly had all the authority needed to bring one recalcitrant private to heel.

By January, however, when the regiment arrived at New Bern and began constructing earthworks along the banks of the Neuse River, it had become obvious to Cantwell that the captain of Company A was shamelessly and profoundly *afraid* of Cyrus Bone. So Cantwell had taken it upon himself to check on Bone's record; when sober, Cyrus Bone was one of the best pilots and navigators on the coast. He was also known as a hell-raiser; put him together with a demijohn of whiskey, and some kind of trouble usually ensued. He had been hauled before the law in at least five counties, for petty theft, public brawling, aggravated assault, and once for "inciting a riot," whatever that meant. Bone's last encounter with a judge had resulted in his coerced enlistment. This information gave Cantwell come insight into Company A's problem. It also indicated to him that, properly motivated, Cyrus Bone had the potential to be a good infantryman. He had the rough but powerful charisma of a gang leader; in battle, such a man could exert a steadying influence on those around him. John Cantwell decided that Cyrus Bone was a professional challenge, and he pondered the man's case accordingly. Discipline was needed, certainly, and if Bone's captain was unwilling or unable to provide that, Cantwell wanted to understand why.

So he had Private Bone brought to his tent one bitterly cold night in late January, so that he might take the man's measure for himself. The interview had not gone as Cantwell thought it would. For one thing, Bone was not a grunting sullen thug. He proved to be articulate, quick-witted, and capable of exuding a strange kind of charm. He made no secret of the fact that he was no Confederate patriot, that he was in Cantwell's regiment only as an alternative to a hard-labor sentence in the state penitentiary, and that he despised authority, no matter what color uniform it wore. As he affirmed all these things, he favored Cantwell with a smile so disarming and manly that Cantwell's emotions became more confused. He found himself almost liking the man.

Except for one thing: for all that Bone was handsome, confident, and strong, there was a darkness in the depths of his eyes so hard and cold that Cantwell had difficulty meeting their gaze. John Cantwell loved the uniform and trappings of rank, and felt himself naturally born to command men in battle. Orders snapped from his tongue with whip-crack precision. He had not, of course, actually led his men into battle, not yet, but he had always been absolutely confident that he *could,* when the time came. The compacted, coiled-spring intensity behind Cyrus Bone's gaze somehow drilled right through Cantwell's confidence. Although there were no charges of attempted murder in Bone's record, Cantwell simply knew, after thirty minutes of conversation, that Bone either had killed men, or could have killed them, without hesitation, remorse, or mercy. This man carried in his breast such a capacity for violence that the muted vibrations of it reached across the space separating the two men and placed upon John Cantwell's heart the chill of a skeleton's touch. It had nothing to do with rank, or station in life, or religion, or politics, or even the circumstances of a great war. It was a statement of fact: the man standing in John Cantwell's tent was a killer; born to it; comfortable with it. Yet, "killing" was what soldiers, ultimately, *did.* Killing Yankees was what Cantwell had been training his regiment to do. But out of all the soldiers Cantwell had commanded, this was the only man he had met who was perfectly prepared to do it, without any training, without a shred of Rebel patriotism, without coercion, without any motivation at all except for Cyrus Bone's pleasure and convenience At that moment, Cantwell understood why the captain of Company A was afraid of Private Bone—in the heat of battle, you did not want Cyrus Bone behind you with a loaded musket and a grudge.

Cantwell was so disturbed, by the end of this man-to-man interview, that he finally blurted out, "Do you intend to desert this army, Private Bone?"

Bone's sensual mouth formed a wide, lazy smile, and Cantwell once more felt a skeletal finger prodding the bones that shielded his heart.

"At the first chance I get, Colonel."

"I could have you shot, if you so much as try."

"I ain't tried yet, sir. When I make up my mind to it, you are welcome to take a shot at me. I will even let you take a shot. Just one. But you will never stand me in front of a firing squad."

Cantwell squirmed, furiously confused, and finally lashed out with all the ostensible power of his rank.

"No, Private Bone, but if you do not start acting like a goddamned soldier and show some respect for your company commander, I will by God break you!"

"Well," Bone whispered dryly, "you can certainly try."

Cantwell had tried. He ordered Company A's captain to report any infraction, however minor, and he had ordered field punishments to be carried out by members of his own headquarters staff. For weeks, Bone had played a sly, mocking, private game with Cantwell. Starting with minor acts of insubordination, committed with such casual indifference to their consequences that Bone's fellow soldiers were both entertained and filled with admiration for his cunning, there had been a gradual, cat-and-mouse escalation. Bone made his move and Cantwell responded, while the men of Company A followed every nuance of this contest of wills. How far would each man go? Bets were made. Stories spread throughout the regiment, embellished with each telling. Instead of wearing down Cyrus Bone's recalcitrant will, Cantwell's increasingly ferocious punishments seemed rather to hone and refine it. Instead of making an example of Bone, Cantwell was slowly turning him into a legend. Cantwell knew what was happening, and by the eve of the battle he had become furiously distracted, shrill, and neuraesthenic in the conduct of his own duties.

He was certain, for instance, that Bone had deliberately gotten himself drunk and taken a swing at his captain, just to see how far Cantwell would go, this close to his first battle. So Cantwell ordered him bucked and gagged, which was the most severe field punishment allowed, now that flogging was no longer permitted. But Cyrus Bone's spirit had only been hardened by the pain and humiliation; when he staggered back to his company after the torture, his mouth bleeding, forehead blistered, and his cramped leg muscles trembling so violently that he could barely walk, the men actually cheered him.

John Cantwell therefore entered his first battle in a state of high agitation and scorched nerves. He was concerned with the defensive tactics of his own men and the actions of the enemy, but he was also obsessed by the knowledge that Cyrus Bone was going to desert, under fire, and that act would give John Cantwell the right, indeed the *obligation,* to shoot him on the spot. If he killed no other man on this day, even if he did not slay a single Yankee soldier, he was going to kill Private Bone. Because if he did not, he was sure that Private Bone would come back some night and kill him.

So Cantwell led his regiment through the day with one eye on the Yankees and one eye on Company A, and he took the greatest care never to position himself in front of Cyrus Bone's musket. When the militia holding the brickyard gave way and the enemy swept up along the railroad tracks, he strove mightily to restore order, to swing his right-flank companies around, even rouse them to counterattack the flank of the enemy penetration. But the panicked militiamen ran in all directions, and they swept around John Cantwell like a herd of wild-eyed animals. He cursed, he shouted, he beat on running men with the flat of his sword, but to no avail. Only one of his fleeing men paid any attention to him—pausing just long enough to crack Cantwell smartly on the head with his rifle butt. The last thing he saw before he lost consciousness was Private Cyrus Bone—a hundred yards away—calmly shouldering his weapon and walking off into the woods. Bone turned, just before he vanished into the pines, and glared at Cantwell, and even at such a distance, even through the scrim of smoke and the confused movement of many men, his eyes stabbed like ice picks.

An hour later, when the Twenty-sixth North Carolina began its withdrawal, Jack Fairless had no trouble hanging back and initiating his own desertion. No one missed him. He ditched his weapon and pack, then scuttled around among the fallen until he found a dead Massachusetts man with a white handkerchief in his pocket. Holding this surrender token in full view, ready to wave it at any Yankee he encountered, Jack cautiously made his way east until he found the railroad tracks. Then he turned right and followed them, knowing they would lead him straight to the brickyard. Wounded men stumbled along the same general route, some in gray and some in blue. A few Yankee stragglers passed him, going the opposite direction toward New Bern, but all they did was glance at him and wave him along in the same direction he was already headed.

He reached the brickyard in midafternoon, and by then the battlefield was mostly quiet except for the moans and pleas of the wounded. Jack began to search for Cyrus Bone. Bone was near. Jack was sure he could feel his presence. But he was startled, frozen in his tracks, when he heard his friend's voice, just around the other side of a shed whose bullet-pocked brick walls oozed red powder.

"I promised you a shot, Colonel. You gonna take it or not?"

Jack peered around the shed and was astonished to see a Confederate colonel standing nearby, legs spread, both hands gripping his pistol, and even more astonished to see Cyrus Bone, sitting placidly atop a low brick wall with his trousers down, obviously midway through taking a shit.

"Finish what you're doing, Private Bone, and pull your pants up. I will not demean myself by shooting a man in . . . in . . . your condition."

"My condition?" Bone chuckled. "Why, Colonel Cantwell, this here's the most satisfying shit I've taken in months. And you know why, sir? It's the first shit I've taken as a free man."

"And the last you shall ever take, you brute."

But the officer's hands were shaking. Jack Fairless had no earthly idea how this bizarre confrontation had come about, but his new friend looked to be in the most vulnerable of human postures, and apparently unarmed.

"Tell me, Colonel, did you kill any Yankees today with that revolver? I didn't think so. Well, I reckon they'll make you a general, now. You don't mind if I wipe myself before you shoot me, do you?"

"Don't try any tricks, Bone. I will blow your head off at this range."

Bone moved his left hand slowly out of sight, then displayed a fluffy branch of soft green pine needles and began wiping himself.

"Man, that sure is better'n usin' a corncob."

Bone had spotted Jack, peering incredulously around the corner of the shed, and communicated it to Jack with one quick shift of his blazing eyes. He tossed the smeared pine branch aside, cool and casual, and hooked his thumbs into his belt.

"I would say, Colonel, that if you're going to shoot, the time for it would be *now*."

Jack Fairless leaped out and struck the officer's head with a brickbat. The man wobbled and tried to turn, but he was slow and dazed, and Jack had no trouble knocking the pistol from his hand.

Cantwell groaned and sank to his knees, then fell over on his back. Now Jack could see an angry swelling bruise on the man's cheek, a fresh wound from the recent fighting. Cantwell's eyes rolled, as though he were trying to bring the sky into focus. Jack stood aside and glanced around. For the moment, the three of them were alone. He knew Cyrus Bone was going to kill this man. The interesting question was *how*.

Bone finished hitching up his trousers and calmly retrieved his rifle from behind the wall, where he had put it down to answer nature's call, presuming Cantwell to be long gone, when John Cantwell caught him at such an inconvenient moment. Now he walked over and prodded the stunned man with his foot, speaking to Jack in a calm, slow voice that made Jack shiver.

"Remember when you gave me water, Jack? This here's the man who did that to me. And now he is delivered under my hand. I think it is only fair that his death should last as long as my punishment, don't you? So that he might have plenty of time to reflect on his cruelty and repent."

Bone detached the bayonet from his rifle and held it into the afternoon sunlight, examining it with exaggerated thoroughness.

"I am told that the worst of all wounds is a perforation of the bowels, which in this case would be almost comical, considering the situation he found me in. But it's possible for a man to recover from a bayonet thrust in those parts. Not likely, but possible, provided the blade was clean and the wound did not mortify. Oh, but if it does, Jack, if the wound does turn black and festers, then it's a different story altogether. The man so afflicted cannot be helped. He will die slowly, tormented by thirst, raving with pain."

Cyrus Bone went back to the brick wall, leaned over it, and smeared the bayonet with a thick coating of his own excrement. Then he bent over John Cantwell and very slowly pushed the blade into his groin, all the way through, pinning him to the ground, working the steel back and forth.

Jack Fairless had never heard a man scream the way John Cantwell did—the wordless wail of a beast driven mad by pain and incomprehensible horror. It went on and on until, abruptly, Cantwell's vocal cords could no longer sustain it and all that issued from his yawning mouth was a thin, high-pitched whistle. Cyrus Bone dusted off his hands, threw a companionable arm around Jack's shoulder, and led him away. Instead of being shocked and revolted, Jack was impressed with the power and decisiveness of Bone's act: retribution so inhuman, dealt out with such disdain for every civilized custom and restraint, that it seemed to him a godlike act. Perhaps Cyrus Bone was one of Satan's angels; perhaps God had averted His eyes from this whole war—certainly Jack had seen no evidence of His alleged mercy, justice, and compassion. If any man alive was destined to survive this conflict, it was Cyrus Bone, and as long as Jack was under Bone's protection, no man would ever mock or mistreat him again.

Jack looked back only once, and saw Cantwell writhing like an insect. Then he pulled out the white handkerchief and the two friends walked away, searching for the nearest Yankee officer to whom they might surrender. Jack felt, on the whole, rather good. He had a friend now, for the first time since he had enlisted, and together they would share a whole new life.

Zouaves Amok—the Looting of Shelborne's Point

THE SOLDIERS AT KINSTON—We have received a very liberal contribution of fifty dollars from a citizen of this town who has a brother among the sufferers, who writes as follows under date of the 21st instant:—

Dear Brother: I have just returned from a scout. Serg't Eldere, two privates and myself brought in three prisoners. We got the drop on them about three miles from New Bern. You said: "Do your duty." Well, you can rely on that or I am deceived in myself.

When we retreated from New Bern we saved nothing. All I have in the world is on my back. When we were whipped out of New Bern, I marched six days, and a worse used up man than I was would be hard to find. I wish you would send me some drawers and socks, and a handkerchief. I will pay you for these things as soon as WE are paid. Just now, we are faring awful. No blankets, filthy clothes, and all of us just in a huddle of misery and tiredness.

When I get time, I will send you ALL the particulars of the disaster that befell us. I fought hard until we ran out of ammunition and the Yankees flanked us—all the men around me fought hard. But we were promised reinforcements, cannon, and supplies, and NONE were sent even though we had more than sufficient warning of Burnside's attack and many days during which we could have made New Bern too strong for him to take.

But now I will not write of these things, for I have had enough of despair to last a lifetime and it avails nothing to become angry about the way we were left hung out to dry.

Yr. Loving Brother, "A.H.B."

This newspaper will be pleased to receive any contributions immediately, for the relief of these ill-used men, and will promptly send to them whatever our readers can donate.

The matters described in this soldier's letter must be addressed. Action is called for—Instant action.

—The Wilmington Journal, March 26 1862

Three days after the battle of New Bern, Rush Hawkins found what he was looking for. Because his unwritten orders from Ben Butler were only roughly congruent to the Burnside Expedition's formal agenda, Hawkins took care to create a foundation of plausibility. After the downcast Rebel prisoners had been rounded up, he summoned Major Junius Brown and told him to pick several trustworthy men—not officers, for the Rebel soldiers would be less frank and forthcoming when confronted with authority—and send them ambling through the ranks of the prisoners, striking up friendly conversation, handing out the odd plug of tobacco or a bit of coffee. General Burnside needed intelligence of a specific and local kind, he told Brown. The commander in chief was looking for a small, out-of-the-way, easily defensible port, a place easily reached by water but not so close to the enemy railroad as to provoke an angry response. Elaborate facilities were not needed: decent wharfage, a warehouse or two, and some buildings suitable for housing a small administrative staff—anything else that might be required could be developed as needed. Brown was shrewd enough to ask what the purpose of this incursion might be, since General Burnside already controlled every port of any size north of Wilmington. Hawkins was prepared for the question: the thinly populated counties between the Pamlico River and Albemarle Sound were reportedly home to many Union sympathizers, and Burnside wanted to establish a safe haven for them.

That much was certainly true. If Burnside could recruit even one skimpy battalion of North Carolina Unionists, the Northern press would inflate it into a veritable legion and Burnside's superiors would be mightily pleased. Junius Brown accepted that explanation without question and went off, with his usual dispatch, to make things happen.

Two days later, he brought into Hawkins's tent a pair of ragged men as different from one another as salt and pepper. Private Fairless was thin and gangly, with arms and legs too long for his uniform, and water-blue eyes that seemed to float restlessly in the pale flat pan of his face; his companion, Private Cyrus Bone, was shorter, dark skinned, brawny in the arms, and blessed with features of remarkable manly beauty. Bone did the talking for both of them.

Yessir, they wuz both Union men from way back. They had not fired a shot during the recent battle, but had sought the first opportunity to turn themselves in. Nothing would make them happier than to serve the Union.

Yes, there were many Union men in these parts, but they were keeping low at the moment. Bone had cousins or friends in every county along the coast, all the way down to the Cape Fear, or so he claimed.

As to the matter of a small local port, why Cyrus Bone knew just the place: Shelborne's Point, the county seat of Hyde County, all by its lonesome at the end of a deepwater indentation on the Pamlico River, just before it narrowed to become the South Roanoke River. The population was about four hundred, and half of them, at least, were Union sympathizers who would welcome the protection of a blue-coat garrison.

After dismissing the two men, Hawkins studied the map. There was no village marked at the spot Bone had pointed out, but that was not unusual, given the near-Elizabethan inaccuracies of the maps Burnside was forced to use. It was centrally located, about ninety miles northwest of Cape Hatteras, but far enough from any established Union bases so that vessels might come and go without being seen. Equally as important, it was too remote from any important strategic objective for the Rebels to care very much about the place. All things considered, Shelborne's Point might be just the place General Butler was looking for.

Hawkins had no trouble gaining Burnside's permission to mount an expedition. By all means, he told Hawkins, take a detachment upriver and liberate this hotbed of Unionism. Hell, take the whole regiment. Burnside's naval advisor, Commander Stephen Rowan, having swept the waters clean of all enemy vessels and still puffed up from his grand naval charge at Elizabeth City, would be delighted to cooperate in any amphibious operation that offered even a remote chance of action. Indeed Rowan was eager, when Burnside summoned him and explained the nature of the operation. As the two officers left Burnside's tent, Rowan even clapped Hawkins on the shoulder and thanked him for devising the plan.

The Ninth New York was also eager, once Hawkins issued the orders. The regiment had taken only a peripheral part in the New Bern battle—most of their day had been spent in reserve on Burnside's right flank, within sight of the Neuse River, where they had suffered more casualties from poorly aimed naval rounds lobbed over their heads by Rowan's zealous gun crews than they had from Rebel fire. Now that the fighting was over, they were locked once more into camp routine: drilling, polishing, digging fieldworks around New

Bern to defend against an enemy whom everyone knew lacked utterly any capacity to bother them; they had become sullen and bored and, in the eyes of their commander, a sharp keen instrument already spotted with rust.

So on the morning of March 20, when they were drawn up in ranks to board the vessels waiting to transport them, they cheered Hawkins lustily when he reviewed them. Then they filed aboard the eight gunboats Rowan had assigned to the mission and made themselves as comfortable as possible. Rush Hawkins and his staff joined Commander Rowan on his flagship, the *Delaware.* The voyage down the Neuse, then northeast on Pamlico Sound, then northwest on the river leading to Shelborne's Point, was an all-day cruise. Clear, brisk weather and the gathering colors of spring gave a pastoral charm to the surroundings. Hawkins felt invigorated and extremely pleased with himself; after all, he was doing a signal service for General Burnside while simultaneously carrying out the unwritten orders of his even more powerful patron, General Butler.

Bone and Fairless, the two deserters whose tale had set the whole affair in motion, were now clad in new Federal uniforms, but they wore no insignia of rank and Hawkins had not yet entrusted them with rifles. Despite the convincing amount of detail Mr. Bone had put forth—even down to a rough sketch of the town's layout—there was a slightly dubious, ruffianly air about the two men. Fairless, the long-limbed mountaineer, never said much, but there was something disturbing about his gaze, some tension between the piercing intensity of it and the watery blue prisms through which that gaze was focused. Bone was stronger, more articulate, and clearly more versed in the ways of the world, and Fairless obviously worshiped him, but Hawkins sensed that, of the two, Jack Fairless might ultimately be the more dangerous man. Bone was a boastful, swaggering rogue, all right, but his emotions were all on display and his guile had an almost playful edge to it. In olden times, Hawkins thought, Cyrus Bone would have found his calling as a bosun's mate on Blackbeard's flagship. Fairless, however, was somehow unformed—he was an ungainly vessel whose character was a blank page on which the war itself would write the particulars. *When you first meet him, you might think him a simpleton; but that would be a mistake.*

When the flotilla reached the Pamlico River, in midafternoon, the men lining the ships' railings began to see occasional signs of human habitation: small cabins surrounded by tobacco fields, a few flat-bottomed fishing boats, some laden with rusting crab pots and nets, and, once, a weather-worn woman of indeterminate age, clad in faded calico, who watched the passing fleet with blank impassivity. A sad air of desolation hung over these hardscrabble farms and not once did Hawkins's men see a white male of conscriptable age. As they drew closer to Shelborne's Point, however, they saw a few black people, all of whom ran eagerly to the shore and waved and hollered.

"Mister Bone, exactly what exercises those Negroes so wildly?"

"Why, Colonel, it is merely the sight of our flag and our blue uniforms. Them poor niggers think we represent *Massa Bobolition,* come to set them free."

"And so we shall, sooner or later." It pleased Hawkins to think of himself as a liberator, even though he personally had no use for colored people and thought there was something morally queasy about wealthy whites who professed the abolitionist passion. They had always reminded him of people who perform their acts of charity in public, as though they were accumulating merit points for admission to Heaven.

"How far to the village now, Mister Bone?"

"No more'n an hour at this pace, Colonel. It'll heave into sight off the port bow after we round a long red-clay bluff. You'll see the dock before you see any buildings."

Only an hour . . . Jack Fairless licked his sun-chapped lips and tried to imitate his friend's nonchalance, but he knew what Bone had schemed and he understood that a lot—a *whole damn lot*—could go wrong. The night after Bone had first talked to Colonel Hawkins, he confided in Fairless his chain of reasoning. He knew Hyde County well, and he knew for damn-sure that most of its dirt-poor inhabitants did not give a mule's pecker about this war, or had even the vaguest understanding of the issues that had set it off. He knew that only the wealthier of Shelborne Point's four hundred inhabitants were dedicated Confederates and he knew their leader, Judge Rufus Murdock, all too well. Cyrus Bone had served a number of minor sentences in Murdock's jail, a gloomy chamber beneath the county courthouse, where waterbugs crawled over him at night. He been awaiting trial there on a charge of aggravated assault when the war broke out. The judge gave Cyrus a chance between "working out his violence upon the Yankees" by enlisting, or rotting in jail until the next county assize and, after that, pulling at least six months' hard labor at the penitentiary in Raleigh. Cyrus had, upon the instant, felt mighty Southern, and went along docilely with the recruiters. Murdock admonished him to "fight honorably" if he wanted his criminal record expunged. Then the good judge set about recruiting his own company, the Hyde County Bobcats. Cyrus had no idea where that outfit was now stationed, or even if Judge Murdock had found enough volunteers actually to *make* a company, but he did know that his criminal records were on file in that courthouse, and if something should happen to them during the town's occupation by Hawkins's regiment, well, sir, that would be a stroke of luck indeed.

At four in the afternoon, a thin mist began to veil portions of the river, interlaced with slanting filigrees of sunlight. Rush Hawkins, unable to contain his restlessness, climbed the *Delaware*'s mast and attached himself to the crosstree, peering intently at the rising, pine-topped bluff that loomed on the port side. Everything seemed peaceful. The loudest sound was the leisurely *whump* of the gunboat's paddle. Now Hawkins could see the end of the dock, and on it he saw a large black woman in a kerchief vigorously waving a piece of white cloth. *Hold your horses, Mammy—here comes Massa Bobolition.*

"We have a welcoming committee," he called down.

Cyrus Bone looked where Hawkins was pointing and he too saw the colored woman on the dock. There was something disturbingly familiar about her. Then recognition struck him like a galvanic shock: she was Judge Murdock's favorite house-slave. He cupped his hands and started to warn Hawkins, but he was a fraction of a second too late because Hawkins had just seen the glint of sunlight on rifle barrels amid the thickets atop the red-clay bluff, not more than fifty yards away.

"Sheer off!" he screamed. "Rebels on the shore! Ring on and sheer off!" Stunned, the pilot automatically threw the wheel hard to starboard and Rush Hawkins tumbled down from his perch just before a half-dozen minié balls gouged splinters from the wood he had been braced against.

A sheet of rifle fire poured out from the top of the bluff. Balls whanged and clanged and zinged and beat like hailstones and one of Rowan's sailors doubled over screaming. As the gunboat continued to turn, Hawkins's men returned fire as best they could with the angle constantly changing. Already, the smokestack was dimpled all down its length, a binnacle light was smashed, and several New Yorkers wounded. The Rebel ambush also included a couple of small cannons, but they could not depress sufficiently to hit the *Delaware* and their balls zoomed whistling overhead and threw up graceful fountains of riverwater in midstream. Neither could Rowan's armament be elevated sufficiently to return fire. Cyrus Bone pulled Jack Fairless under cover and snarled, "God damn it, we're in trouble now!"

The next gunboat in line, whose skipper clearly saw the situation as it was, quickly turned into midstream and just as soon as his aft Parrott rifle could bear on the bluff, began vigorously shelling the Rebel position. There was room on this part of the river for two more gunboats to bring their fire to bear, and soon the bluff was disintegrating in red chunks and clumps of foliage. The Rebels withstood the barrage long enough to fire a 12-pound solid shot into the hull of the second gunboat in line, wounding two men with splinters, and then prudently withdrew. Cascades of earth from the shattered embankment stained the river like tanner's dye.

Commander Rowan signaled for the entire flotilla to withdraw half a mile downstream, where the river widened greatly and anyone firing on them from the shore would in return feel the broadside weight of eighteen naval guns.

Once the firing died down, Rush Hawkins realized that he had twisted an ankle when he fell from the mast. The first thing he did after he staggered to his feet was to kick Cyrus Bone in the buttocks, yelling: "You treacherous cur! You led us into that ambush! I'll have you shot before the sun goes down!"

A shadow fell across Hawkins's choleric face and he turned from the crouching Bone to find himself staring upward into the cold pale pools of Jack Fairless's eyes. Somehow, during the confusion, Fairless had acquired a pistol; he had enough sense not to point it at Hawkins, but the weapon was lightly tucked into his trousers and his rawboned hand was inches from the butt.

"No, Colonel," Fairless said, "Cyrus tried to warn you about it. He knew that darkie woman on the dock and he smelled a trap. He just didn't have time to get the words out before them Rebs cut loose."

"It's true, sir," echoed Bone, rising to his feet and casting a quick, grateful look at his friend. "Nigger-woman belongs to Judge Murdock, and he is the hottest Confederate in Hyde County. I reckon it was his company that bushwhacked us, just as I reckon it was his idea to make her wave that white flag and lure us in."

Hawkins swiveled his gaze from one man to the other. He was furiously angry—as much because of his undignified tumble as anything else—and wanted to take that anger out on *someone.* Just then,

Major Brown touched his shoulder and spoke some words of caution: "Colonel, if these boys are telling the truth, they can still be mighty useful to us. If they are lying, we should be able to determine that after we have taken the town and interrogated the citizens. It can all be straightened out later."

Hawkins nodded, tight-lipped. "Very well. Until we can get to the bottom of things, I want these two men under guard at all times. And I want this man disarmed!"

Major Brown reached out and took the pistol from Jack Fairless, who made no move against him, but stood impassively, with a small smile on his face. He had spoken up and helped his friend out of trouble, and he felt extremely pleased with himself.

On their second approach to Shelborne's Point, the gunboats steered close to the east bank of the river, so their guns could reach the far side. As each boat approached the dock and began disgorging its troops, at least two others stood off and gave cover. Not a shot was fired and the Negro woman who had waved the white flag was nowhere to be seen. A few dozen townspeople, mostly women and the elderly, gathered in frightened curiosity as the Zouaves trooped ashore and formed ranks. With their colorful uniforms, stern faces, and fixed bayonets, they were an intimidating sight. Hawkins flourished his sword and prepared to march down the gangplank. Just before he could do so, however, Cyrus Bone called out, "Colonel Hawkins? Might I have a brief word with you in private?"

Angry at the interruption, Hawkins almost ignored the request, then thought better of it. Suppose there was another ambush planned, inside the town? Perhaps this ruffian knew something more than he had so far divulged.

"Make it quick, Mister Bone."

"Well, sir"—Bone leaned forward and lowered his voice to a conspiratorial register that Hawkins, to his surprise, found almost seductive—"what I have to say is for your ears only." He nodded at the two men who had been ordered to guard him and Jack Fairless. Hawkins grew suspicious. Bone bent even closer and his voice became like the tone of a cello. "Colonel, you may bind my hands if you wish, or draw your Colt and hold it on me. I mean you anything but harm."

Intrigued now, Hawkins waved away the sentries. If Bone were stupid enough to attack him, there were a dozen of Rowan's sailors loitering nearby, each one armed with a cutlass and all of them riled up because of the recent ambush.

"Very well, Mister Bone, I am listening."

"You strike me, sir, as a man of ambition. And if I may say so, ambition cannot easily be satisfied on an officer's salary. I can show you a place where there is gold and silver."

"I am not a thief, sir!"

"And I am not suggesting that you are, Colonel. What you are, as soon as you set foot on that landing, is the *conqueror* of this enemy town. To the victor belong the spoils, I've heard it said."

Hawkins considered the matter. He had already decided to turn his men loose for a time, to repay the Rebs for their treachery earlier in the day. While it would surely look bad to Commander Rowan if the colonel of the Ninth New York came back aboard his ship with pieces of silverware falling out of his pockets, there was no necessity for that. The regiment was here to stay and its commander would need a headquarters, preferably a large and well-appointed residence. And in such a residence, a great deal of wealth could be kept safe and far removed from official scrutiny.

"All right, Mister Bone. You and your friend may come ashore and when I have finished addressing the townspeople, I will take a look at whatever you have to show me. You will walk ten paces before me and my pistol will be aimed at your back every step of the way."

Hawkins ordered a wagon brought up to the front of the regiment and from that platform he harangued the cowering spectators: "I will not mince words—this afternoon, my men were fired upon while *a flag of truce* was being displayed from this very dock. By this barbarous act, this town forfeited the right to be treated in accordance with the established rules of war! My men are ready to burn this place to ashes—I need only hand them a torch. It is plain to see that someone among you knows who baited this trap, and many of you must have a good idea of where the bushwhackers have fled. If we learn where they are, then we will take the fight to them, musket and sword! If someone provides me with that intelligence, we will go in hot pursuit and I will leave you be in all other respects. If not, then the consequences will be on your own heads. I will wait for two minutes for someone to volunteer the information."

With an operatic flourish, Hawkins drew forth his watch and nailed it with his stare. Some of the civilians exchanged nervous glances, a few whispered to those around them, but no one spoke up or stepped forward. At the end of two minutes, Hawkins closed his watch with a snap as harsh as the click of a cocked hammer.

"So be it." He turned to face the regiment. "Men of the Ninth New York! In retaliation for a cowardly and dastardly violation of a flag of truce, you may inflict a lesson on these Rebels that they shall not forget no matter how long we occupy this place. There will be no arson, for we ourselves will need many of these buildings, and any man who molests a woman or a child will face the severest field punishment. Otherwise, from now until dark, this town is yours by right of conquest!"

It took a few seconds for the import of his words to sink in, but when the men realized that he had just given them license to plunder, they gave a ferocious cheer and got down to the job smartly. Hawkins watched them stream up the lanes and into homes and sheds and stores, nodding in satisfaction at the just reckoning he had unleashed. When he stepped down from the wagon, however, Major Junius Brown was standing before him with mouth agape and all the color drained from his cheeks.

"Good Lord, Colonel, what purpose will this gain? If these people harbored Unionist sympathies before today, they are surely changing sides right now!"

"Damn your milk-fed sensibilities, Major Brown! I intend to put the fear of God and the Ninth Zouaves into these scoundrels, and if you do not have the stomach to watch, you have my permission to retire to the ship and avoid the sight!"

Brown saluted and said from clenched jaws: "No, Colonel. I am staying right here and doing whatever I can to keep these men from turning into savages."

"Suit yourself," growled Hawkins. Then he motioned to Fairless and Bone, who obediently walked ten paces ahead and showed no distress when they heard Hawkins draw back the hammer on his Colt.

"Gentlemen, lead the way. And do not even think about overpowering me, for at the first hint of treachery, I shall blow your brains out."

As the trio strode off, Hawkins eyed the town calculatingly. It was a plain but orderly place, more like a New England village than he had expected. The town square was shaded by a venerable oak and beneath its leaves stood a bronze statue of George Washington. Off to Washington's left was an empty pedestal decorated with a plaque that said: "Twelve-pounder cannon employed by the Patriots at Yorktown." Probably the same piece that punched a hole in one of Rowan's gunboats, mused Hawkins. If the Rebs were reduced already to stripping antique fieldpieces from historical monuments, perhaps this war would end sooner than most people expected.

While the turmoil and shouting grew louder behind them, the three men left the center of the village and walked north, angling away from the river, on a narrow but well-maintained wagon road. Once they passed beyond sight of the town, Hawkins scanned both sides of the track, suddenly fearful that the riverbank ambush had been only one part of a subtler ruse to entrap his whole command. By now, to judge from the shots being fired (into the air, he hoped), the vengeful howls of the Zouaves, and the lamentations of their victims, the Ninth New York was about as disorganized as a regiment could be. What if the enemy had a brigade of cavalry secreted in the woods? He pondered the elegance of the scheme, then dismissed it as fantastically unlikely. In the whole of eastern North Carolina, the Rebels could not scrape together a brigade of cavalry. No, he was sure of it: the ambush had been the work of a local company, probably not one-tenth the strength of the Zouaves, and any attacking force that penetrated the town would run headlong into the concentrated fire of Rowan's ships.

Besides, he could see no sizable cover on either hand. Wooden fences lined the track and the thick forest near the river had been replaced by broad and orderly fields where spring corn nodded silkily in the breeze and the slightly metallic odor of tobacco plants mixed with the perfume of early flowers. This was a prosperous farm, he thought, and the war had not brought it low, for he could see more than a dozen blacks working in the fields. That was fortunate, for if he did choose Shelborne's Point to be Ben Butler's private fiefdom, its garrison would need to be kept so happy and so well fed that no sane man would want to trade duty here for a spot in the front lines around Richmond. Fresh vegetables, sweet corn, plenty of tobacco, and what was that patch? Yes, by God, it was *watermelon.* Whiskey and whores could be imported later. It might not be very exciting to spend the rest of the war here, but it would certainly be pleasant, compared to the alternatives.

"Yonder 'tis, Colonel," said Cyrus Bone, pointing to an open wrought-iron gate flanked by a pair of majestic magnolia trees.

"Yonder is *what,* Mr. Bone?"

"Why, Jedge Murdock's plantation, sir! Fanciest house in the county. If ol' Murdock was commanding them bushwhackers today, I reckon his house is enemy territory. You won't find a nicer headquarters between here and Wilmington."

Indeed, as Hawkins saw when they passed through the gate, the prospect was suddenly mighty appealing. He admired the graceful lines of the white two-story home, especially its broad and well-shaded veranda and the fan-shaped expanse of beveled glass that capped the front door. He was, however, momentarily nonplussed as to how he should proceed. It was one thing to let the troops vent some steam by looting a few trinkets and stealing some chickens. But as a uniformed officer of the United States Army, he could hardly barge in, accompanied by two rough men, and help himself to whatever caught his eye. Perhaps the judge was *not* off campaigning, but peacefully preparing for his supper? As they drew near the hitching post below the front steps, a Negro woman suddenly appeared, walking around the porch corner balancing a wicker basket of laundry on her head. Hawkins and Bone instantly recognized her as the person who had waved the bogus white flag from the dock. The woman's head was bent beneath her load and she did not see the three Yankees until she was close enough to feel the sudden coolness of their shadows. As she looked up, pop-eyed, Cyrus Bone dove forward and grasped her arms, causing the laundry basket to spill its contents around her feet.

"This here's the one, Colonel Hawkins! I bet there ain't much she cannot tell us about this afternoon's fracas. What's your name, you black bitch?"

"Missuz Keen, your honor, and Massa Murdock, he calls me Calliope. I didn't have no selection in that matter, sir, 'cause the jedge, he say he gwine ta have me whupped if I did not do what he wanted."

She went to her knees in supplication, a large ebony woman with gleaming teeth and eyes as wide as those of a jig-dancer in a minstrel show. Rush Hawkins turned his pistol toward the slave—tacitly signaling a newfound faith in Cyrus Bone's loyalties.

"Under the laws of war, I have the right to hang you for what you did this morning. But if you tell me where the judge and his company have gone, I will spare you and take out my vengeance on him."

Now Calliope Keen writhed with indecision. She had known about the ambush, and she must therefore know where the judge and his Hyde County Bobcats planned to go if and when the Yankees captured Shelborne's Point. But Murdock was her master; she had grown up on this plantation and obedience to his will was deeply ingrained.

"Massa, I ran back here as soon as the firing started. I ain't seen where they went, but I heard the jedge say they was supposed to re-lay or sumpthin' north of here, acrosst Pocatasi Creek."

"You mean '*rally*,' I think. How far is that and how many men are with him?"

"No more'n sixty, sir. And hit's about three mile in that direction."

Suddenly, Jack Fairless muttered, "Sheee-it!" then stepped forward and tugged on Hawkins's sleeve. "Lookee yonder, Colonel."

Protruding from the pile of sheets, pillow cases, towels, and aprons was one trouser leg of Confederate gray. Grasping the cuff, Fairless pulled the whole garment forth and held it out for inspection. Although it had been diligently scrubbed and soaked and pounded, there was a jagged six-inch tear just above the left knee and surrounding it was the faint corona of a bloodstain.

Calliope Keen began to wail and wring her hands. Leaving her there to writhe with guilt and shame and fear, Hawkins motioned for the two deserters to follow him. As they saluted and said "Yes sir!" in unison, Cyrus Bone winked at Jack Fairless as if to say: *We are in the clear now, my friend. And we have a patron to boot. Good times may lie ahead!*

Hawkins found more blood on the porch, small spidery blotches of it, where someone with a fair to middling wound had dragged himself into the house. Warily, they tried the door, which was unlocked. Inside, the house smelled clean and polished, as though the owner could not tolerate a speck of dust in any corner. As they stood in the hallway, uncertain about what to do next, Cyrus again tugged on Hawkins's sleeve and nodded toward the spacious parlor that opened off the right side of the hallway. "*In there!*" Hawkins responded with a quizzical look, then he recalled what the real purpose of this reconnaissance was and he went with Bone into the room so indicated.

The furnishings were elegant, a mixture of richly polished walnut American Empire, massive and clean-lined, and more delicate and costly Hepplewhite pieces. Occupying one entire wall was a huge breakfront cabinet, and behind the glass gleamed heaps of silver: utensils, platters, candlesticks, and a great heavy tureen, big enough to hold a full-grown sea turtle. Hawkins understood at once that the contents of this one cabinet were worth several thousand dollars. And if the rest of the house were furnished on a commensurately ostentatious scale, there would be more silver, some gold, and jewels. Judge Murdock was obviously a man of high-flown taste and considerable wealth.

"How did you know to come here?" he said to Cyrus Bone.

"Hell, Colonel, I robbed bits and pieces from the old bastard three times without getting caught. I got greedy on the fourth trip, though, and the jedge got the drop on me with a scattergun."

"He's here, isn't he?"

"I reckon so. Wounded in the leg like that, he could not keep up with his men when they withdrew. A man's first instinct would be to return home, if'n he was in pain and need of care."

"Then we had best search upstairs in the bedrooms. Be wary, though, because he may be armed."

Cyrus Bone extended his hand and looked Hawkins squarely in the eyes. "Sir, if that be true, perhaps you should give me the Colt, for I am skilled with a pistol and I would not hesitate a second to shoot, whereas you might."

Grinning, Hawkins reached into his right boot and took out a single-shot derringer. He showed it to Bone, who smiled back in appreciation. Hawkins transferred the big Colt to Bone, butt first, then cocked the smaller weapon and motioned for Bone to proceed back into the hallway and up the stairs. "Colonel, you are a man after my own heart," laughed Bone.

There were more blood spots on the graceful curving staircase. They climbed silently, and had spoken only in whispers since entering the house. When they reached the top of the stairs, a manservant, clad in a fancy ruffled outfit that was both impractical and archaic, emerged from a doorway on the left. He was carrying an enameled basin full of water and blood-soiled linen. When he saw the three blue-coats on the stairs, he shrieked and dropped the basin, flinging pinkish water over Cyrus Bone's head.

Bone lunged forward, past the open doorway, roughly knocking the darkie aside. From within came a blast of buckshot, splintering the door frame. Hawkins ran into the room, pistol extended, before the occupant had time to reload. Judge Murdock lay in his own bed, pale and sweating, covered with a sticky sheet except for his left leg, which poked out, white and hairy and crowned with a thick wad of bandages. A half-empty bottle of whiskey stood on the bedside table. He was a man of graying years, decorated with fierce boar's-bristle chin whiskers. While he fumbled to reload his shotgun, he stared contemptuously at Hawkins's derringer.

"You do not frighten me with that popgun, sir!"

Then Cyrus Bone came through the doorway and leveled the big revolver, a feral grin cutting across his dark features.

"How about this gun, Jedge? Mighty pleased to meet you again under these circumstances."

Murdock threw the shotgun at Bone, who knocked it aside easily and kept moving until he was close enough to pistol-whip the judge's right hand. The sound of splintering bone was gruesomely loud and Murdock could not help but scream.

"Let's see you shoot anything now, *Your Honor*!"

"That's enough, Mister Bone! I want this man conscious when I hang him for his treachery."

"It'll be nearly dark by the time we get back to town," muttered Jack Fairless, who was observing the scene with all the riveted gusto of a spectator at a good cockfight.

"Let him spend the night in his own jail, then," growled Bone.

"That would be fitting," agreed Hawkins, uncocking the derringer and taking back the Colt from Bone's hand. "You men go downstairs, find some niggers, and have them prepare a wagon or a buckboard. This house is now officially the headquarters of the Ninth New York."

Judge Murdock tried to spit at Hawkins, but all he could manage was some dribble that landed mostly on his own chest. "Take it and be damned, sir!"

"Now, Judge, you ought to have known better than to use a white flag to launch your scheme. That puts you in a category quite distinct from that of a prisoner of war. I intend to garrison this town, and I intend to make an example of you before the citizens. Of course, if you should tell me the whereabouts of your company and its strength, I might relent."

"I would not tell you that if the second coming of Jesus depended on it. You may hang me ten times over and I will spit in your eye each time you do. Just tell me one thing before I die: how many of you did we kill this afternoon?"

"Not a man," lied Hawkins smoothly, relishing the disappointment on the older man's face. "A few nicks and scratches, perhaps, but nothing serious. Your whole devious scheme went for naught, you old bastard."

By the time they had loaded their prisoner onto the back of a carryall and driven back to Shelborne's Point, night was falling rapidly. But there was no darkness, for, contrary to Hawkins's orders, several buildings were ablaze, their former inhabitants watching helplessly, wrapped in blankets and clutching whatever pitiful belongings they had been able to rescue. By the flames' mounting light, the scene might fairly be described as *infernal.* Obviously some of the Zouaves had discovered and consumed a considerable amount of spirits. The wilder men capered and whooped, dragging velvet drapes through the mud, brandishing candlesticks, clocks, hat racks and watches, chamber pots and framed lithographs, decking themselves out in jewelry both common and valuable. Piles of loot lay everywhere: toys, dolls, daguerrotypes, dresses, boots, vases, every variety of object that might catch the fancy of a drunken lout. A corporal lurched by with no less than four hats teetering on his head. Another wild-eyed trooper ran past holding his rifle like a lance, a squawking blood-flinging rooster skewered on his bayonet, flapping its wings in futile desperation. Dead dogs spotted the yards, and terrified pigs squealed as stumbling cursing men chased them down.

Rush Hawkins felt himself go cold as he observed the madness: by authorizing this, he realized, he had made the kind of mistake most officers make only once in their careers. To their credit, many of the Zouaves had refused to join in these depredations and they had formed sullen ranks around Major Brown, whose normally stolid features were contorted now with impotent fury. Farther back, behind the infantry, Hawkins saw Commander Rowan himself aiding a party of sailors who were manhandling a small howitzer down the wharf. When Brown spied Hawkins, he left the ranks and ran across the square to confront him, without the courtesy of a salute.

"Colonel Hawkins, do you command soldiers or a horde of Visigoths? This atrocity is your doing, sir, and yours alone! Both Commander Rowan and I intend to file a full report to General Burnside about what has happened here. But for the moment, this madness must be stopped. With or without your permission, I am about to order the responsible and sober men of the regiment to fire a warning volley over the looters' heads, and if *that* does not sober them up fast enough, Commander Rowan is fully prepared to clear the streets with grapeshot!"

Hawkins thought he heard a low rumbling chuckle from Cyrus Bone, but he gave it no thought. His career, quite literally, was going up in flames, and he cursed himself for being a greedy fool and Ben Butler for putting him in this position to begin with. It was a good thing he had chosen to leave the judge's silver for another visit.

Drawing his Colt, he jumped from the carryall and loped across the square. He did not have to pretend to be appalled, although his reasons were very different from those of Rowan and Brown. Snapping out commands, he ordered the disciplined soldiers to fire over the heads of the rampagers. Three hundred rifles discharged as one, creating God's own wrath of a thunderclap, and when the smoke cleared, the miscreants stood frozen and, to some extent at least, shamefaced.

"You men form ranks! Drop your plunder and consider yourselves under field arrest. Any man too drunk to follow this order *will* face corporal punishment, I promise you!"

By this time Commander Rowan had arrived, panting from exertion and splotched with rage. "Hawkins, this is an outrage! Order your men to fall out and help extinguish those fires. General Burnside will hear of this, oh, yes, and you will face the severest kind of inquiry. Personally, sir, I hope to see you flogged!"

Suddenly, Rowan spotted the wounded man in the back of the carryall.

"And who is this, pray tell?"

"This is Judge Rufus Murdock, late of the Confederate army, and the man responsible for peppering your ships while displaying a flag of truce. For that, I intend to hang him in the morning from that tree yonder, as an example to all Rebel sympathizers."

Rowan gaped in disbelief. "Colonel Hawkins, you have done more to fuel Rebel sympathies today than Abe Lincoln managed to do in a year. Major Brown, fetch a stretcher and have this man taken aboard the *Delaware*. Then find my surgeon and have those wounds tended to."

All around the square, raw emotion crackled like the very flames that fueled it. Slowly, the looters shook off their berserker trances, dropped their plunder, and staggered back to their companies. It was, by then, too late to extinguish any of the fires. Four homes and a livery stable burned to the ground. Rowan stationed a heavy guard of sailors throughout the town, with orders to shoot on sight any more Zouaves found looting or committing arson. The surgeon who examined the half-conscious Murdock concluded that both the shrapnel-smashed thigh and the hand Cyrus Bone had crushed were beyond saving. This was the doctor's first double amputation, however, and he measured out only enough chloroform for one. Halfway through the second procedure—with the saw rasping through thighbone—*grutz! grutz!*—Murdock regained consciousness long enough to utter a heart-stopping scream. The sound reverberated hauntingly over the river and the wide and verdant fields.

Otherwise, the night was tense but quiet, at least until one o'clock, when a violent conflagration exploded in the county courthouse.

From the fury and rapidity of the blaze, it was obvious that some powerful accelerant had been used; indeed, when the ashes were examined the next morning, there was a pervasive reek of turpentine tainting the air. One sentry claimed to have seen two men—one stocky and one gangling-thin—hightailing it away from the building just before the initial blast, but he could not identify them. Whoever they were, whatever their obscure motivation, the perpetrators might as well have been phantoms.

The Siege of Fort Macon

OLD BOSSY'S LOOKIN' MIGHTY NERVOUS—It is really becoming a serious quandary as to what we shall eat and what we shall drink and wherewithal we shall fill that internal cavity. Beef, there is none. Mutton is a forgotten thing. And as for poultry, well, we doubt that half the people in town can recollect whether a turkey has two legs or four.

There is a right decent looking old cow of our acquaintance, who begins to exhibit unmistakable signs of uneasiness if any body gazes at her too long or too earnestly. She is getting thin either from mental anxiety or from a determination to reduce her flesh and with it the temptation of erst-while butchers to make beef of her. So suspicious indeed has she become that although we have known her from the days when she was a young mother with her firstborn infant trotting after her, she will shake her head angrily and walk off in the sulks if we but look at her carnivorously.

—The Wilmington Journal, April 10 1862

If war brought nothing else, thought Captain Frederick Reilly, it certainly brought swift promotion. Especially if you joined an army that had a chronic need for good artillerists. After years of contemplative boredom as the caretaker ordinance sergeant of various coastal forts, Reilly had jumped rank to lieutenant only a month after his ceremonial surrender of Fort Caswell to Cantwell's impetuous Rebel militia of Wilmington. During the war's first months, Reilly had been dispatched hither and yon, from Virginia to South Carolina, assisting in the organization and equipage of various batteries of field artillery. He had performed those duties with exemplary professionalism, but his real expertise was in the realm of coastal defense, and he was baffled when his repeated requests for transfer to that arm seemingly went unheeded, while, one by one, the enemy besieged and captured, with almost contemptuous ease, the ill-prepared bastions that guarded the North Carolina coast. Finally, in February 1862, orders had come through posting him urgently to Fort Macon. With the fall of New Bern on March 14, Fort Macon became the *only* significant Rebel strong point left between Wilmington and Norfolk.

To the eyes of the nervous civilians who watched through telescopes from Beaufort and Morehead City, the fort looked impressive, solid, defiant; as long as the Confederate flag flew above its ramparts, no Yankee vessel could approach them. Indeed, when Reilly—now a captain and charged with commanding the fort's puissant battery of columbiads—had crossed Bogue Bank in a small supply-steamer, Fort Macon did look powerful, almost majestic. But if there was one thing Reilly knew well it was the history and condition of the South's coastal forts. After introducing himself to Fort Macon's commander, Colonel Moses J. White, a twenty-seven-year-old Vicksburg native, Reilly had inspected the work with a keen professional eye. What he saw and learned was not encouraging.

Nowhere else were the Outer Banks so close to the mainland as they were here, where Bogue and Shackleford Banks guarded the approaches to Beaufort and Morehead City—the waters of Bogue Bank were only two miles wide, and from either port, it was a short, straight run through Beaufort Inlet to the open sea. General Burnside surely knew that; Beaufort would make an excellent satellite base to augment the larger facility now under construction at Port Royal, South Carolina; and Morehead City was the terminus of the North Carolina and Atlantic Railroad. With those two places under his control, Burnside would have a first-rate supply line running to his main base at New Bern. But first he would have to subdue Fort Macon, for its big guns effectively closed Beaufort Inlet to Union traffic.

Reilly quickly learned that the garrison took fierce pride in their strategic importance. Never mind that the other coastal defenses works had fallen so ignominiously; Fort Macon was, in their minds at least, the equivalent of Gibraltar. As they went about their daily drill, Reilly's gun crews could be heard chanting, to the approximate tune of "Dixie," a bit of patriotic doggerel that included the chorus:

If Lincoln wants to save his bacon,
He'd better stay away from old Fort Macon!

Poor men, thought Reilly. They simply do not understand. But if Fort Macon were to have even the slightest chance of surviving the tempest that would soon descend upon it, the men would need every ounce of that optimism to sustain them.

Reilly knew that the need for some kind of defensive works on this part of the coast had been recognized since colonial times. Beaufort had always been one of the busiest official ports of entry on the continent, and as such it was a tempting target for enemies and brigands. The Spanish had given the place a good plundering in 1747, and shortly thereafter the first, primitive fortifications had been erected on the tip of Bogue Bank. Following the War of 1812, which revealed in the starkest terms America's vulnerability to seaborne attack, Washington had developed a comprehensive program for the nation's seacoast defenses. Plans were drawn up for Fort Macon, in 1824, construction began in 1826 and continued, in a rather desultory manner, until 1834, when the fort received its first garrison. But it was fully manned only during times of international tension; in between, it fell under the care of another ordinance sergeant whose tour of duty was surely as lonesome and pointless as Reilly's own had been down at Fort Caswell.

When seen from a distance, as Reilly had seen it on the day he was ferried out to report for duty, Fort Macon was a handsome and formidable-looking work: pentagonal symmetry and smooth thick masonry walls gave it an aura of latent power. Viewed against the backdrop of wide undulant sand and flat distant ocean, a Rebel flag straining taut in the constant wind, it positively *loomed.* To the anxious crowds of civilians watching from the rooftops of Beaufort, the black spikes of cannon barrels that crowned the work like an iron wreath made it also seem to *bristle.*

But Frederick Reilly knew that was an illusion. Engineers had stopped building inland forts of brick and stone sometime during the late Renaissance, after the giant siege guns of the Medicis had proven capable of hammering such walls into dust. Seacoast fortifications, however, continued to be built of masonry well into the present century. Masonry provided a simple, economical, and functionally elegant way of constructing a fort, and as long as that fort was not expected to come under fire from the landward side, it served well enough. This was due to the more or less random quality of naval gunnery at the time. To punch through a stout masonry wall with roundshot, it was necessary to hit the same spot over and over again until the bricks and stones were crushed and dislodged. But broadsides fired from moving wooden ships, their decks rolling and pitching, could be aimed only in a general way; accurate sustained fire against a small section of wall was virtually impossible. Ships could neutralize forts only by ganging up on them in sufficient numbers to literally smother the walls with shot. As long as that equation held, masonry walls sufficed.

But modern technology had shattered that equation forever. The superiority of rifles over smoothbore muskets had been known for a century: a gun barrel with a spiral-grooved bore imparted a stabilizing spin to its projectiles, which yielded greater range and accuracy. But well into the present century, armies had still fought mainly with smoothbores—rifles were expensive to manufacture, and had a markedly slower rate of fire than the short-ranged flintlock. That changed in 1848, when French army captain Claude Minié invented a one-piece, powder and ball cartridge that revolutionized land warfare by enabling rifled muskets to be fired and reloaded very quickly. As with infantry muskets, rifling significantly increased both the range and accuracy of shipboard ordnance and made it possible to replace roundshot with pointed, elongated projectiles—shells and solid "bolts"—that had much greater mass than a spherical cannonball and encountered far less air resistance in flight. Steam-powered ships also made for much more stable firing platforms, indifferent to wind and current. These changes were not exactly trade secrets among the armies of Europe and the Americas, and field engineers had long since abandoned maronary in favor of massive earthen walls, which tended to absorb rather than transmit the energy of rifled projectiles. When its ordeal began, Fort Macon would have to endure with defensive engineering that was a generation out-of-date.

It would begin soon, Reilly reflected, as he worked by lantern light on his cherished schematic drawings for a new type of coastal defense vessel. And matters were going to be made worse by the presence of a commander who was manifestly unfit to lead twenty-two officers and 419 enlisted men through a siege. Colonel Moses J. White—Vicksburg born and raised, West Point Class of '58—was a tall, beardless, dark-complected man of twenty-nine. He wore his hair unfashionably short, a vanity that gave him an unfortunate resemblance to one of the tar-stained scavenger birds that darted endlessly to and fro at the line of the surf, pecking incessantly for gritty morsels of food not even the gulls would deign to eat. Loud noises made White jump and, in Reilly's experience, there was no more disconcerting habit for, of all things, an artilleryman. Every time Fort Macon's gun crews held a live-fire exercise, White would twitch and hop about with every blast, giving his men the unfair but disturbing impression that he was terrified of his own guns. White's obvious neurasthenia went beyond mere reflexive twitches—he also suffered from periodic seizures of grand mal, and was forced to remain in his quarters for their duration, attended by the fort's surgeon, who could barely hide his disgust at having to mop the drool from his commanding officer's chin while poking into his mouth with a leather-covered stick to prevent the helpless colonel from choking on his own tongue.

By mid-March, it was clear that a siege was coming. Picketboats filled with Yankee officers crisscrossed the waters of Bogue Sound; detailed observations of the fort were being made, notes taken, plans discussed. It would have been gratifying to lob a shot at those irritating little boats, but none of the fort's cannons could bear on that quadrant. At about the same time, the taller buildings on shore sprouted Union flags; no doubt signalmen were beneath them, ready to correct the fall of shot, by heliograph, when the battle commenced. Next came boatloads of infantry, who went ashore south of the fort, just beyond the maximum range of its heaviest guns, and established a huge encampment covering the sands as far as Reilly could peer into the southerly mist. White sent out spies, of course, and soon learned that he faced two full regiments—the Fourth Rhode Island and the Eighth Connecticut—commanded by the highly able General John G. Parke. Last, but most ominously, came wallowing barges pulled by straining tugboats, laden with heavy ordnance shrouded in canvas. When the weapons were emplaced, behind massive sand revetments, they were revealed to be a powerful mix of 8-inch Parrott rifles, augmented by 8- and 10-inch siege mortars.

Colonel White, for all his failings, was no fool—he could see exactly what was going on and could feel the invisible noose tightening around his fort. There just wasn't much of anything he could do about it. Lacking sufficient infantry to challenge the Federals with a surprise attack, there was only one type of weapon that could enable the garrison to neutralize Parke's siege batteries: mortars, which could shoot over the sandhill revetments and smite the Yankee gunners sheltering behind them. Despite ample warning and increasingly desperate pleas to Richmond, White had not received a single such weapon—such mortars as the Confederates had, he was testily informed, were needed in the permanent ring of defenses now being erected around the capital.

The siege formally opened on the morning of March 23, when a dispatch rider approached the fort's main gate under flag of truce and delivered to Colonel White a pro forma request:

Sir:

In order to save the unnecessary effusion of blood I have the honor to demand the evacuation of the fort and the surrender of the forces under your command.

Having intimate knowledge of the entire work, and having an overwhelming force at my command, with all necessary means at hand to reduce the work, its fall is inevitable.

On condition that no damage be done to the fortifications or armaments, your command will be released as prisoners of war on parole.

Very respectfully yours &c.
Jon. G. Parke

Now Reilly stood at attention on this clean, brisk seaside morning, in front of his columbiad gunners, and listened while White read both Parke's demand and his own reply:

"Men, I have sent the following reply to General Parke: '*Sir: Your request is received and I have the honor to decline it in all particulars. If you want Fort Macon, you must come and take it.'* Three cheers for old Fort Macon!"

While the garrison dutifully voiced their huzzahs, Reilly fought down a sense of futility. These men really had little idea what Parke's guns could do to the place, and no idea whatsoever how little their own guns could do in return. Without mortars, their only recourse was simply to smother the Yankee batteries with a hailstorm of shot and shell, in the hope that a certain percentage of rounds would do them harm. But Reilly knew that the fort's magazine contained only thirty-five thousand pounds of powder, much of it substandard and past its prime, enough for three days of sustained firing. The fort's best weapons were Reilly's columbiads, brawny weapons weighing fifteen thousand pounds and capable of accurate shooting out to five thousand five hundred yards. Predictably, there was less ammunition for them than for the older 32-pounders. Reilly was a *gunner;* he would make the most of the cannons God had placed under his command—both pride and duty demanded as much—but he had no intention of ending his Confederate career on this bleak sandspit. When the fort capitulated, as it must, Reilly intended to descend a rope from the window of his quarters and make straight for the sun-bleached old rowboat he had hidden beneath the sand near the marshy tip of Bogue Bank. He had expertise that would be valuable to the South and, more than that, he had a head full of ideas and a sheaf of schematic drawings wrapped in a waterproof cocoon of oiled paper. Let Colonel White and his hapless men sign away their freedom on documents of parole. Reilly intended to carry on. It was more than duty; it seemed to be his calling.

Since adolescence, Reilly had been fascinated by the topic of siege warfare, and during his long solitary days as a fort keeper, he had accumulated a fairly comprehensive library of history books and professional studies. But reading about siege warfare was one thing; participating in it was quite another. No matter how busy he was or how stressful his duties, part of Reilly's mind remained detached, coolly observant, measuring each new experience against that fund of data, ordnance theory, and historical exegesis. Despite the implied personal danger of his situation, he was grimly satisfied to learn that his imaginings of what a real siege might be like conformed rather closely to the real thing.

The opening moves were slow, measured, and rather stately—Reilly likened them to a courtly masque at the Sun King's palace. Every day the Federal works grew more elaborate, almost ceremonially so. He watched the enemy engineers erect huge wooden pylons and decorate them with wrist-thick chains and tackle, then operate them to lift the great gleaming Parrott rifles onto their carriages, the barrels trembling on their chains like beasts restrained, then slowly vanishing behind their protective revetments. Other artillerists paced off specified distances, stopping near the limit of the fort's effective range to set up aiming stakes. Several times each day, the Yankee lines sparkled with flaring light as the signalmen tested their heliographs—and after a moment, like a melody reprised, came tiny answering flashes from church steeples and observation towers on the mainland. There was a symmetry in the process that was close to elegance, for those observers would be able to see, and correct, the fall of shot from their distant comrades more quickly than a telegraphist. Every day, the besiegers' labyrinth of trenches and bombproofs inched closer. There was no disturbing them, for Parke had positioned a full regiment of infantry to guard the workers against any sortie the defenders might be tempted to make. By April 8 the whole Yankee position, when viewed from Reilly's post on the parapets, resembled a vast gray-and-ochre quilt, studded with iron and decorated with windblown pennants. The closest trenches were a mere thirteen hundred yards from the sand-drifted moat; behind them were Parke's 8-inch mortars. Two hundred yards behind them were the Parrott guns; and two hundred yards behind *them* were the squat, brutal-looking 10-inch mortars.

Beginning on April 10, Colonel White ordered each of Fort Macon's guns to fire two rounds daily at the siege works; he did not have enough powder for a saturation bombardment, but at least this gesture of defiance raised the garrison's spirits and gave the gunners some practice in setting fuse lengths of a more or less correct duration. Each day, the Rebel cannon fired at different times, at different intervals, hoping thereby to harass the enemy. But Parke's guns remained ominously silent, almost disdainfully so.

Reilly preoccupied himself by implementing a fairly desperate scheme, one that met with Colonel White's equally desperate approval. Reilly selected four of the older and more worn out 32-pounders, had them winched off their trunions and remounted atop makeshift wedges of stone and earth, which gave the barrels 40 to 50 degrees of elevation. In this way did he give Fort Macon a homemade battery of mortars. By carefully experimenting with different powder charges and fuses, the converted weapons could indeed put their shells above the enemy gunners' heads. When he tried them out, they did work more or less as intended, but precise aiming was impossible, and for all of Reilly's ingenuity, their random sprinkling of explosions amounted to nothing more than a nuisance for Parke's men.

By April 24, all of Parke's preparations were complete. Once more, a dispatch rider cantered up with a flag of truce and delivered a courteous but firm demand for surrender, this one signed by General Burnside himself, who had come down from New Bern to witness the operation. This time, White was clearly tempted; his position was hopeless and everyone knew it. But Fort Macon still had the capacity to resist, and honor demanded its forfeit in Rebel blood. As he watched the Yankee messenger ride back to the siege lines, Reilly knew for a certainty: tomorrow the curtain would rise and the tempest be unleashed.

March 10, 1862
Aboard the USS Cambridge
With the North Atlantic Blockade Squadron, North Carolina
Dearest Mother—

It is blowing as if all the nor'westers in the world had been tied up for the last twenty years and had just broken loose. The waves have been rolling twenty feet high all afternoon, dashing against us, making the old ship shiver like a freezing giant. Just now, a huge roaring foam-crested mass of water comes crashing over the bow and sweeping the decks. Yet here I am, comfortably writing to you, with only six inches of planking between myself and the wild, sublime wrath of Nature. If there is one time more than another when one realizes God's greatness and His mercy, it is such a moment as this. A man who has a Christian heart must think of the time when Christ said to such a sea, "Peace! Be still!" and so I feel safe in the hand of God.

Yet fearful as this gale may be, it is but a poor footnote to what I witnessed two days ago. On that morning, we were keeping station off Fortress Monroe, awaiting orders, when one of the Cambridge's *lookouts spotted a low, massive, iron-clad ram steaming with unruffled majesty around the Rebel forts protecting Norfolk harbor. It was the former USS* Merrimac, *now renamed the* Virginia, *which the enemy captured early in the war and about which we had heard many rumors. Escorted only by two small gunboats, this curious, geometrical-looking vessel now made bold to challenge the entire Union fleet in Hampton Roads.*

As the Cambridge *is but a modest screw steamer mounting five guns, we were hardly a fitting adversary, and were ordered alongside the* St. Lawrence, *an Old Navy sailing frigate mounting fifty-two guns and large enough to shield us. We were ordered to take the frigate in tow, and haul her about so that she could deliver a huge broadside. But between the smallness of our engine, the vast weight of the* St. Lawrence, *and the necessity to keep both vessels away from the* Merrimac's *great ram, the battle was nearly over by the time we accomplished this task. The* Cumberland *was rammed and sunk, the* Congress *was severely battered and had to strike her colors, and my beloved old ship, the* Minnesota, *ran aground whilst evading the Rebel ram and was in danger of being pounded to scrap by the* Merrimac's *heavy rifles. We did some good fighting, even though it appeared that our heaviest solid shots did no more than make dimples on the ironclad's plate. With sunset, the Rebel juggernaut retired and we aided in getting the* Minnesota *refloated. By that time, we had been informed that a new Union ironclad had just arrived in Hampton Roads—a ship of the most unconventional design—and it is likely that a great duel was fought between the two iron giants on the following day. We, alas, did not witness it, having been ordered back to blockade duty as soon as our commanders learned that the* Cambridge *had suffered only superficial splinter damage.*

I am proud to state, however, that I was the only ship's officer to receive a wound during this historic engagement, which must surely mark the terminus of the age of wooden ships. A hundred-pound shell burst over our decks late in the day, and a fragment from it has taken out an inch of flesh. It is a slight injury, but it bled considerably, as scalp wounds usually do. I do indeed look like a hero with my bandages, but the only lasting effect was a severe throbbing in my temples, which the surgeon dutifully medicated with a ration of rum, liberally enhanced by laudanum. Perhaps it is the latter ingredient which keeps my stomach calm during the present gale.

I am hoping for some good hunting when the weather abates. Now that Burnside has taken New Bern and so many other locations, we may bag a blockade-runner or two who are trying to make a last dash out before the inevitable fall of Fort Macon. I have yet to experience a good sea-chase, and I look forward to it keenly.

I will send this letter on the next available dispatch boat, and I pray that it finds you in good health and continued pride in . . .

Your loving son,
Will

Just before dawn on the morning of April 25, 1862, General Ambrose Burnside and his staff assembled on the upper piazza of the Atlantic Hotel in Beaufort to witness the final act of Burnside's Carolina campaign. The general looked sleek and prosperous, as indeed he had cause to be. In four months and at a cost of less than one thousand casualties—the majority of them from illness, accident, and shipwreck rather than enemy fire—Ambrose Burnside had subjugated thirteen North Carolina counties and removed from production some 2.5 million acres of prime agricultural soil. From this vast region the Confederates would not only get no more supplies, but would also collect no more taxes and obtain no more recruits. Cities and towns lost to the enemy included New Bern, Elizabeth City, Beaufort, Morehead City, Plymouth, Washington, and two dozen lesser localities. In consequence, blockade-runners could no longer make for safety in Beaufort or the sounds, but were forced to make Wilmington their only haven; this narrowing of options would henceforth make the U.S. Navy's blockade much easier to enforce. And finally, on the eve of McClellan's massive Peninsula campaign, large numbers of Confederate regulars and militia would be permanently tied down in the region, guarding the critical railroad junction at Goldsboro, that precious fount of victuals, ammunition, and reinforcements for the Rebel armies in Virginia. The scope of Burnside's successes had shifted his eager mind into a strategic mode—he saw no reason why he should not move east and cut those rails. Patrols and informants agreed that organized resistance was, for the time being, feeble. That would not last. But once he had Goldsboro, why stop there? Why not a bold strike all the way to Raleigh? Cut the Confederacy in two on an east-west axis? Isolate Richmond? End the whole bloody business in one magnificent thrust? Ah, well, *that* was the rub. Little Mac would never acquiesce and he could be eternally unforgiving to any subordinate who stole the limelight. So Ambrose Burnside had, by this morning, phlegmatically accepted the notion that today's bombardment of Fort Macon would probably be the climax of his Carolina campaign; he was resolved to savor it as a grand tableau, a martial spectacle of the first order.

So, too, were the thousands of ordinary soldiers and civilians who had thronged to every vantage point during the night, bearing picnic baskets and champagne and opera glasses, dressed in finery as though attending the theater; blue-coats mingled freely with unregenerate Rebel patriots, both sides amicably resolved on a grand day's entertainment. Indeed, many good-natured wagers were laid on as to how long the fort would hold out—two days was the mean estimation, but dedicated gamblers were handicapping everything from the exact hour of surrender to the percentage of casualties each side might suffer. Some few true-blue Rebels even boasted that the work was "impregnable" and bet accordingly, a chimerical wager eagerly accepted by any Federal gambler to whom it was offered.

In truth, the fort looked mighty grand in the first clean, mild light of dawn, its dark and lowering mass framed by the glassy calm of the sound and the great pearlescent vault of the seaward heavens. As the light grew more ample, a fortuitous-seeming breeze uncurled the Stars and Bars from its flagstaff. Caught up in the theater of the moment, the spectators of both sides greeted this event with applause. On hearing this demonstration, however, Burnside scowled thunderously and muttered: "That is distasteful! Very soon now, those poor bastards will be dying, and for no better reason than stiff-necked Rebel pride."

Within the walls of Fort Macon, the morning began routinely, with reveille at five A.M. and roll call twenty minutes later. The numbers were not auspicious: of the 453 men comprising the garrison, only 263 were reported as present and fit for duty—all the others were indisposed from measles, diarrhea, and the usual assortment of "fevers."

Though Captain Frederick Reilly had not slept well, the restlessness was caused by nervous excitement rather than fear—or so he convinced himself, although he suspected that on the eve of battle there might not be much distinction. He was resolved to fight his guns smartly and valorously for as long as could be done, and then, when defeat became inevitable and surrender loomed, he was equally resolved to escape before he could be ensnared in the protocols of prisoner paroles. After a quick spartan breakfast of corn dodgers and molasses, washed down with bitter coffee, he made his final preparations. He unrolled a rope ladder through the window and anchored one end of it to his bed, the heaviest item of furniture in the room. The loose end dangled five or six feet above the sandy bottom of the moat. Against the wall, he placed his waterproofed satchel, containing his proposed design for an ironclad ram of advanced design, a change of underclothing, and his identity papers. A hundred feet from the rope's bottom rung, his tiny rowboat waited, covered with tarp, sand, and sea oats, invisible from all but the closest distance. He had caulked it with tar-impregnated cotton and fashioned an oar from a plank of yellow pine. He had also studied the local tides and currents. If he launched at early dark and caught the incoming tide, he should be very close to shore, some miles south of Morehead City, by full daylight. He did not doubt that, if he succeeded in that first stage, he could eventually make his way to Wilmington and reenter Confederate service. For added insurance, there was another waterproofed box stowed under the boat's thwarts, containing hardtack biscuits, a canteen, and a loaded revolver.

Satisfied, Reilly strode to the parapets and bid his columbiad gunners a good morning. The weapons were well maintained and finely polished, and the crews seemed as well prepared as they could be. On either side, there were no better smoothbores than these 10- and 8-inch weapons, each capable of throwing a heavy round, with high elevation and impressive reach. Their shells and balls did not achieve, and could not be made to achieve, the vicious velocity of a rifled projectile, but they said their piece with puissance and staggering blasts.

"When will it begin, sir?" asked a lanky young corporal named Combs, his sleeves already splashed with water from the tall sponge he carried.

"Any minute, Mister Combs. The day is fair, the light will soon be perfect, and the enemy's preparations are more than complete. Just remember what I told you—what I told all of you."

"Aye, sir. That there will be terrible noise and smoke and stink, but little danger to any one man except through sheer bad luck. Remember your drill and serve your gun like a soldier. All else is up to Providence."

"Good lad. You'll do well, I am sure."

Just then: a flash—a gasp from all the men at all the guns—and the sharp *cra-blam!* from a Parrott rifle, smiting their ears just before its 30-pound cast-iron bolt slammed into Fort Macon's upper wall and gouged out a geyser of brick dust, some of which drifted over Reilly and his gunners, giving them a taste of disintegration, powdery and raw against the mucous membranes. Then all the Union guns joined in and the fort's twenty-seven guns replied with vigor and steadiness, lavishly expending ammunition. Concussion hammered Reilly's muscles and after the first moment or two his throat felt scorched from powder smoke. He had stuffed his own ears with cotton and suggested his crews do the same, and this measure seemed, in practice, to impart just a bit of comforting distance between his skull and the immediacy of the cannons' thunder, so that the sound became more jellied than abrasive. The gun crews seemed to swim inside the noise and veils of grit.

His columbiads were already aimed; deflection and fuse lengths had been calculated to a nicety over many days' practice. All that was necessary was to focus on the drill, oblivious to any large, heavy, fire-spitting objects that might plow the air nearby. Each man's movements were finely choreographed, the end of one procedure meshing finely with the start of another. After the cannon creates fire, those who served it must extinguish all traces of one round before being able safely to fire another: hence the long ash staff of the sponge, crowned at one end with a wool-covered cylinder just slightly smaller in diameter than the barrel's bore. Combs, as number one in the gun crew, was responsible for making sure that the sponge head was damp enough to quench any glowing particles left over from the shot just fired, yet not so dripping wet as to convert stray fibers and powder grains into a foul accumulation of paste. Combs and number two gunner shoved the sponge into the smoking muzzle and gave it three clockwise turns and three more counterclockwise, while number three placed his buckskin-covered thumb over the firing vent, so no air would whistle about inside and move any potentially dangerous embers beyond the cooling touch of the sponge.

Number four gunner bent down behind the mount and loaded the designated powder cartridge into a pass box, stoutly made from pine and fitted with solid brass handles. As soon as the begrimed sponge head made its final cleansing twist, the pass box was carried forward and its powder bag lodged in the muzzle's mouth, where Combs and number two rotated the sponger so that its dry end became the ramrod. Gently, they fitted the powder bag inside the barrel, making sure it was both intact and snug; then Combs and number two rammed the charge home, seating it firmly at the base of the barrel. Next came a wad of hay or rags, sealing the powder charge airtight so that the intended round would leave the gun with maximum velocity. Then came "the business," as Reilly liked to say: either a ponderous solid cannonball or an explosive shell banded to a wooden sabot plug, fuse end forward so it would not explode before reaching the general vicinity of the enemy. Number three scuttled forward and thrust a thick, sharp wire down the vent, piercing the powder bag below. The final step required the introduction of a friction primer, really nothing more than a fancy match, into the same vent. A firm but steady tug on the lanyard—a deceptively puny spark from the primer, like flint striking steel—and the columbiad bellowed to life. Its sole purpose for existing consummated in one gigantic and violent second, fire from the muzzle fractured the air, which virtually collapsed in upon its own molecules. This was the age-old chemical apocalypse of sulfur, charcoal, and potassium nitrate, replicated uncountable times over the centuries. This explosive fist of fire and brimstone was the culmination of the alchemists' dream—instead of turning base metal into gold, base metal, hurtling at four hundred feet per second, could turn not only gold, but marble and granite and anything else in its path, into rubble.

At least we make a valiant noise, thought Reilly. From the shore, the fort must have appeared formidable in its wrath—great coils of white and gray smoke whipped violently in the sea breeze, and fearsome lances of flame spurted from the parapets. The ground trembled. Roundshot struck the dunes, throwing up huge rooster tails of sand, then bounced almost playfully from hummock to hummock until all their velocity was spent. Every time a Parrott bolt hit the walls, Reilly could feel the slap through the soles of his feet, could almost feel the walls shudder as their masonry absorbed the crushing impact and vomited forth the blood-colored powder of shattered brick. Overhead, the enemy's mortar shells traced sparkling arcs across the calm blue morning sky. For the first ten minutes, the majority of mortar rounds fell short, while many of the Parrott shells zoomed overhead and landed harmlessly in the waters of Bogue Inlet. Then, quite suddenly, the enemy's fire became focused and much more accurate—the amount of time, Reilly conjectured, it had taken for the signalmen on shore to relay corrections and for the Yankee gunners to fine-tune the elevation and deflection of their pieces.

This newfound precision was demonstrated when an 8-inch mortar shell dropped squarely into the columbiad battery. "*Cover, men!*" Reilly screamed, and the crews scampered to the side of their guns, putting the massive mounts and barrels between themselves and the hot iron kettle that rolled around on the parapet floor like some living thing, fire spitting from its fuse with a high, nerve-twisting shriek.

All of Reilly's men sought cover except for Combs, who had the heroic impulse to use his ramrod as a lever and thereby tip the sizzling bomb over the parapet's inner face, so that it might explode harmlessly on the parade ground below. But the instant Combs made his move, the shell went off. Fragments sliced open his scalp, flinging a great quantity of cranial blood into the air, and other fragments tore his trousers to shreds and flayed his calves, and one large chunk of iron struck him full in the chest, shattering his ribs and driving the jagged bones into his lungs. By all rights, he should have died instantly, but he did not. Instead, he fell on his back, rib bones sticking out like antlers, and he began to scream and writhe helplessly.

"Take him to the infirmary," Reilly ordered, stabbing a powder-blackened finger at the two nearest gunners.

"I ain't touchin' him, Captain Reilly!" croaked one of the horrified men. "He's liable to come apart in my hands!"

"God damn you, either carry that man to the surgeon or shoot him dead! That's an order! Do it, you two men, one thing or the other." To drive home the point, Reilly held out his own pistol.

White-faced and cursing, the two men grasped Combs and lifted him. Reilly could hear bones snapping and organs slopping in torrents of blood, and now he was grateful for the bombardment's horrific noise because it masked the wounded man's howls, which rose to an inhuman pitch as he was carried, none too gently, down the nearest steps and across the parade ground to the place where the fort's surgeon plied his grisly trade. As he watched Combs's shattered body descend into the cool shadows below, Reilly caught a glimpse of Colonel White, over by a battery of 32-pounders, hopping frenziedly up and down, waving his sword uselessly at the Yankees. *If he has one of his fits now, I will drop a cannonball on his head just to spare us the spectacle.*

"Back to your guns," ordered Reilly. But the rhythm of the drill had been broken, the protective veil of business as usual ripped away along with Combs's rib cage. Now, in order to "serve" their guns, the men had to step over and around a big scorch mark where the mortar shell had exploded, leaving a great bruise, lumpy with human tissue, on the very stones of the fort, so the gun crew moved with the jerky self-consciousness of men who half expected an enemy shell to land between their shoulder blades. Every time a shell burst anywhere near the battery, everyone flinched as though anticipating a blow from a whip. Reilly glanced at his watch: they had been firing for more than an hour, along with the 32- and 24-pounders, making a sizable dent in the fort's ammunition supply.

There was another lull at 9:30, when the Yankees adjusted their fire once more. While it lasted, Reilly ordered his men to stand down and drink some water, for they were lathered like blown horses now, their faces streaked with powder, heads aching, and ears ringing. Reilly was washing down, with some difficulty, a piece of hardtack, knowing that it might be a long time before he had a proper meal again, when Colonel White ran over to the columbiads. The man was clearly at the end of his tether, grinding his jaws and repeatedly twisting his hands together. In this brief interlude of silence, down in the surgery, Combs began to scream again, and White's face turned ashen at the sound.

"Captain Reilly, are your men holding up? Are you doing any hurt to the enemy?"

"We are placing our shots well, Colonel, but I fear the enemy's emplacements are too well protected for us to really get at them. At best, we're causing them some inconvenience. As for my men, they are doing their duty."

"They must continue to do so, Captain. I cannot yield with honor while so much of our powder remains unfired."

Combs screamed again, like a dog whose hindquarters had been crushed by a passing wagon. Reilly gestured in that direction.

"Colonel White, *that* is the sound of 'honor' being satisfied."

White flinched as though Reilly had slapped him. He worked his mouth open and shut, rummaging with his tongue for the proper response. Whatever he was going to say, however, was drowned out in a sudden wave of explosions, punctuated by the freight-train rush of Parrott bolts sailing over the parapets. The besiegers had refined their aim once more and now sent a perfect rain of fire against the fort. Mortar shells whistled down like giant hailstones, peppering the parapets and scattering the gun crews. Solid shot bit into the walls, gouging great black pits in the masonry. Some rounds fell inside the walls and caromed around from angle to angle, plowing furrows in the parade ground, knocking down tents and huts. Even as Reilly watched, a Parrott bolt dropped full into the latrine pit, throwing up a vile fountain of shit. Colonel White rushed back to his former position near the 32-pounders, waving his arms and exhorting the crews to perform unspecified acts of valor.

For three more hours, the bombardment continued without pause. At 1:30 P.M. the Yankee gunners scored their deadliest single hit: an 8-inch Parrott bolt split the carriage of a columbiad, dismounting the gun and hideously wounding two of its crew. Then, its velocity seemingly undiminished, it glanced off at an oblique angle and crashed into a 32-pounder, cracking its barrel with such force that the entire crew was blown to the ground. Still unspent, the bolt sizzled across the parapet like a serpent and finally came to rest in a rain gutter. Return fire from the fort had become scattered and feeble—Reilly's men were getting off one or two shots every five minutes and the other batteries were doing no better. Six weapons had been disabled or smashed.

In what proved to be a climax of sorts, the besiegers then concentrated all their Parrott fire on a single masonry wall, each strike grinding deeper into the bricks, creating an ominous tunnel, a relentless hammering that reverberated through the earth. Reilly, although exhausted and somewhat dazed, suddenly understood what was happening. It made sense—after all, the enemy knew everything there was to know about the fort's design. Seized with urgency and fear, Reilly tucked his head down and ran over to Colonel White's position. He did not bother to salute, but grabbed the officer by his lapels and turned him in the direction of the nearest steps.

"Come with me, sir! I fear we are in grave danger."

"What? What? Of course we're in danger, man!"

"No time to explain, Colonel. God damn it, just follow me!"

Irritated but too weary to object, White rose from his crouch, dusted the brick powder from his shoulders, and followed Reilly down to the parade ground. Dodging mortar shells, they ran across a scorched plain littered with what looked like broken crockery and came to a halt before the massive bombproof doors of the powder magazine. *Thump! Thump!* The sound of the Parrott bolts was close. Comprehension dawned in White's eyes. Together they entered the magazine, still loaded with fifteen thousand pounds of powder. Every time a Parrott round smote the external wall, huge tongues of dust poured down. And through the haze, they could see daylight—the first small crack opened by those repeated hits on the same section of wall.

"Dear God, we are done for!" cried the colonel.

"Yes, we are—if one lucky shell punches through that hole. It's only a matter of time, sir—they know perfectly well where our magazine is located."

"Ah, God, this is intolerable!"

For a moment, Reilly thought the man was just going to stand there, wringing his hands and cursing the Fates, until his whole fort blew up in one gigantic blast. Then he saw the colonel's eyes begin to roll loosely in their sockets, while his whole body shook in spasms of delirium. White's jaws worked up and down, uttering nothing but gabbling nonsense, and flecks of foam danced on his lips. Cursing him, Reilly ran back to the parapets and straight up to the most senior officer he could find. He explained the situation, and when he described the crack in the magazine's outer wall, the man at once ordered a white flag to be hoisted above the parapets.

"I'll send the surgeon to look after Colonel White," said Reilly, trembling with relief.

And that he would, before ducking into his quarters and making his escape. But the surgeon, his leather apron smeared with gore, was almost insensibly drunk. The wounded shrank from his touch as he bent to examine them, peppering their injuries with cigar ash and slurring his words. Bloody saws and probes littered the operating table. By dint of sheer repetition, Reilly finally convinced the besotted physician to go look after Colonel White.

Alone now in the company of fourteen grievously wounded men, in the sudden quiet of a cease-fire, Reilly heard a terrible phlegm-clotted moan. One of the wounded raised himself on an elbow and made a supplicating gesture. "Captain Reilly, you must do something about poor Combs! Some of us tried, but the doctor is too drunk to think straight. Said he couldn't do anything for Combs except stop him from screaming. So he gagged him and rolled him back into the darkness to die."

Reilly stepped further into the reeking shadows and found that this was the case. Poor Combs lay twitching in his own blood, his one good hand bound to the stretcher handle and a wad of leather stuffed in his mouth. His shattered ribs trembled as he fought for breath with tortured, lacerated lungs. His eyes were glassy and his head tossed feverishly. He did not appear cognizant of anything external to his own agony. *Could a man be driven mad by pain?*

"Why wasn't this man given chloroform?" asked Reilly to the wounded.

"Doctor said it would be a waste—Combs was as good as dead, anyhow."

Reilly wondered if he had enough time to locate the doctor and shoot him down like the dog he was. Instead, he rummaged through the medical supplies and found a half-empty jar of chloroform—at least the doctor had given some to the other wounded men, which explained why half of them were unconscious and the other half too dazed to take action on their own. Reilly did not know how much chloroform it would take to kill a man, but he sopped a generous dollop of it onto a wad of cotton and gently placed it over Combs's face. The man bucked involuntarily, for the sensation must have been akin to drowning, but then, when he felt the fumes carrying him away, his moans changed into a great sigh of relief and his eyes gave passing thanks to Reilly for his mercy. Holding his breath against the smell, Reilly poured still more anaesthetic into the cotton, and felt Combs's shattered body go limp. Dizzied by the fumes, Reilly continued to press the reeking mask against Combs's face until, with a peaceful shudder of relinquishment, the man stopped breathing.

"God bless you, Captain Reilly," said one of the wounded.

As he turned to leave this chamber of horrors, Reilly paused to say: "You men bring charges against that butcher. Testify to his dereliction. The Yankee commander, General Parke, is a civilized man, and I am sure he will be as outraged as I am."

Then he strode briskly into the sunlight, kicking at pieces of cold shrapnel, and turned his back forever on Fort Macon.

Zeb Vance and the Half-a-Man

FROM ROANOKE ISLAND—Ten free negroes recently reached Perquiman's County, from Roanoke Island, who report that the Federals are heavily fortifying the place. These negroes were furnished with passes for the purpose of visiting their families on the mainland and inducing them to return to Federal territory.

They say, however, that now that they have reached home, that no inducement would compel them to go back to their would-be "liberators." The experience they have already had among the Yankees satisfied them that it is misfortune of the direst character to fall into their hands; and they say that, though worked excessively, they received but a scanty allotment of food and not enough money in wages to purchase even a decent shirt to cover their backs.

Perhaps the State could organize a tour of these unfortunates, so that they could relate their experiences to the widest possible audience of their ebony brethren.

—The Wilmington Journal, April 13 1862

On May 31 1862, the Army of Northern Virginia was larger and better supplied than it had ever been. McClellan had finally made his move, landing sixty thousand men at Fort Monroe during the last week in March and ponderously advancing them up the Peninsula, between the York and James Rivers, until he confronted prepared Confederate defenses thrown up across his path on a line that stretched southwest from old Yorktown. Facing him was a single division of ten thousand men under Jeb Magruder. A determined thunderbolt assault could have swept Magruder's men like windblown chaff, but such was McClellan's caution that he halted before the half-finished Rebel earthworks and prepared a methodical siege, scheduled to open with a stupendous artillery bombardment on April 3. Johnston gave him the slip, however, and staged a general withdrawal two days earlier, catching McClellan off balance. McClellan again paused to "consolidate" while Johnston withdrew once more to the prepared defenses on the south bank of the Rappahannock, the last and strongest line before Richmond itself. Norfolk, outflanked and now as vulnerable to amphibious assault as Benjamin Huger had long dreaded, was abandoned soon thereafter; the shipyard, and with it the ironclad *Virginia* (née *Merrimac*) were put to the torch. Huger was ordered first to Petersburg, and then to join the main force outside Richmond. The other division commanders greeted the news of his arrival with something less than wild enthusiasm. Johnston gathered every company he could and watched for an opportunity to strike some portion of the Federal horde under conditions that would give him at least local superiority. Meanwhile, McClellan dithered and seemed to be intimidated to excess caution by his own grossly exaggerated estimates of the size of Johnston's force.

For Chase Whiting, the nine weeks since Davis's inauguration had been tense and emotional. With a heart heavy as lead, Whiting dutifully spiked his heavy artillery on the night of March 11 and withdrew his men and field guns to the new line on the Rappahannock. Since the start of McClellan's offensive, Whiting's men had fought only once, a covering action during which they had handily repelled a half-hearted Federal amphibious probe on Johnston's left flank. The rest of the time, they had marched and countermarched and dug so many entrenchments north and east of Richmond that they began referring to Robert E. Lee, who had laid out the defensive plan with his engineer's eye, as the King of Spades.

Eventually, on May 20, McClellan did exactly what Johnston and Lee were hoping he would do: he detached his entire Fourth Corps and advanced it to the village of Seven Pines, opening a gap of five miles between that force and three other corps encamped on the north bank of the Chickahominy River. A few days later, he pushed another corps forward on the north bank of the river, chasing a Rebel rear guard out of Mechanicsville, only five miles from Richmond. From there, McClellan's scouts could see the distant spires of the city and when the wind was right could hear the church bells. Johnston spent a few days making sure that this blunder was not a feint, and when he was convinced that it was not, he made plans to spring a trap.

When Whiting rode over to Johnston's headquarters on the night of May 30, near Old Tavern on Nine Mile Road, he was agitated by the certain knowledge that the time of retreats was over; that, like a coiled spring under pressure, the Army of Northern Virginia was compressed, physically and spiritually, to the limit and was ready to snap back in the faces of its tormentors. When the summons came from Johnston, Whiting guessed that the counterstroke was about to be launched. As he reined in outside headquarters, just before twilight, he saw the big, bluff figure of James Longstreet coming out. If Longstreet were excited by the plan he had just been made privy to, the man did not show it. Behind his grand spade-shaped whiskers, Longstreet's mouth was tight and dour. He barely acknowledged Whiting as the two generals passed on the stairs, nodding and growling something that might have been "Good evening," then strode slowly to his horse. A palpable wave of indifference extended like a ship's wake behind his massive shoulders. In late February, Whiting knew, three of Longstreet's children had died of fever in Richmond, and when Longstreet returned to the army from burying them, he was no longer the bluff and hearty man he had been. Every time Whiting had seen him in the intervening weeks, Longstreet had appeared wrapped in gloom and silence, speaking only when he had to and then saying as little as possible. As Whiting removed his gloves and announced himself to Johnston's aide-de-camp, he hoped that Longstreet's demeanor would not rub off on his division. Whatever Joe Johnston was planning, Longstreet's brigades would surely be in the thick of it.

Johnston welcomed Whiting warmly and offered him hot coffee, which Whiting politely accepted; he had resolved to drink nothing stronger for the duration of the coming engagement.

When Johnston explained his plan and pointed out its main elements on the map, Whiting felt his admiration grow. Old Joe intended to throw two-thirds of his army against the isolated Federal Fourth Corps, marching the divisions of Longstreet, Huger, and D. H. Hill along parallel roads so they would converge on the enemy simultaneously from the front and both flanks. The rest of his force, principally the veteran brigades under Magruder, would remain in place along the south bank of the Chickahominy, to protect the rear and left flank from any interference by the three Yankee corps strung out in a southeasterly line from Mechanicsville. Whiting's division would be stationed between Magruder's line and Longstreet's left, as a tactical reserve. If the enemy crossed the river south of Magruder,

Whiting was to block the move with as many regiments as he deemed necessary; he must also be prepared to reinforce the main Rebel thrust should Longstreet require additional weight to break the Federal line near Fair Oaks Station. As he studied the map, Whiting saw only one dark contingency. He tapped his finger on the Grapevine Bridge across the Chickahominy, some three miles east of Old Tavern.

"General Johnston, my scouts inform me that this bridge has been fully repaired. McClellan's entire Second Corps is massed on the other side. Their commander, General Sumner, is an impulsive man. If he marches to the sound of the guns and crosses in strength while my brigades are in motion, he could strike us a hard blow."

For the first time in their long relationship, Johnston snapped at Whiting, revealing for an instant the incredible stress of his situation.

"Come, come, General Whiting! You are much too cautious! By the time they realize what is happening, we will have routed their forces on this side of the river."

Taken aback by his friend's display of temper, Whiting blurted out: "Perhaps so, if things go as planned."

"They *will*, sir! *They must!*"

But as Whiting rode back to his division later that night, he was not wholly convinced. No army in the world had tried such a phased, parallel-convergence of divisions since the days of Napoleon. And however neat the movements might seem on the map, Whiting knew the landscape on this part of the Peninsula could be confusing; between the neat lines of the major roads, which were themselves deeply rutted and broken up after the spring rains, lay a bewildering maze of cow paths and snaky bogs, briar-choked thickets and nameless meandering creeks. Visibility was limited; units would be hard-pressed to maintain contact with whoever was on their flanks. Add on to these facts the inevitable confusion and noise and emotions of battle, and anything could go wrong. *We don't yet know how to translate the neatness of a map-planned maneuver into the reality of the field. The regimental commanders don't know, the brigade commanders don't know, and neither do Johnston and Lee. For all the months we have been under arms, we are still an amateur army. Our best hope lies in the fact that the Yankees are the same.*

It was close to midnight by the time Whiting had briefed his brigade commanders. When he was at last alone in his quarters, he found himself longing for a drink. Just one. His nerves were already raw and he knew that sleep would be elusive. Very well, then. It was his duty to get some rest, and he would flush out the scent and residue of the bourbon with extra coffee in the morning. He did not, in fact, get to sleep until almost two o'clock in the morning, and as he was pouring the third of the five stiff drinks he would eventually consume, a thunderstorm broke loose over the Peninsula that sounded like the firing of Hell's own batteries. Yes, of course, he reflected; now the roads would be knee-deep in mud in the morning. Well, there was nothing he could do about the whims of providence—and the same rain would swell the Chickahominy and flood the fords and, with any luck, submerge or wash away that pesky Grapevine Bridge that worried him so much.

He was awakened at five and immediately regretted his indulgence of the night before. His mouth tasted—or so he imagined—like the floor of a stable, and his head ached fiercely. The first news he received, while pouring coffee down his throat as fast as he could, was that two men from Pettigrew's brigade had been killed by lightning during the storm. Whiting tried not to consider that as an omen. He refused to go into the biggest battle of his career weighted down with superstition.

By six A.M. Whiting was at his post, a mile north of Nine Mile Road, and his head was clear. But instead of glimpsing Longstreet's men heading east along that route, he found some of Longstreet's regiments marching *south* at right angles to their supposed axis of advance and completely blocking Whiting's path. After nervously observing this parade for twenty minutes, Whiting sent a courier to the commander in chief, inquiring if Johnston had ordered such a last-minute change of plan. Shortly after seven o'clock the courier returned. General Whiting was not to worry—Longstreet's left wing was *supposed* to precede Whiting's division on the Nine Mile Road.

"Did you not inform General Johnston that at least part of General Longstreet's division is marching south, *away* from Nine Mile Road?"

"I did, General. He did not seem concerned."

"Did he *explain* the reason for his lack of consternation?"

"No, General, he did not."

Whiting felt the first worm of dread stirring in his unsettled stomach.

"Kindly ride back and find General Longstreet himself. Give him my compliments and ask what his intentions are with regard to this new deployment."

Even as the courier galloped off again, Whiting thought he knew. Longstreet had decided, for God knew what reason, to shift his advance to a more southerly route, which would place his division behind that of D. H. Hill rather than beside it, on Hill's left, which was where Johnston wanted it to be. Had Johnston's orders been unclear? Or had Longstreet simply decided to run the battle according to his own whims?

Whiting never found out. He subsequently learned that the courier he sent to find Longstreet got lost in the White Oak Swamp, took a wrong turn, and rode east until he was captured by Yankee pickets belonging to Phillip Kearny's brigade, three miles behind enemy lines. Whiting knew that his own division was where it was supposed to be and that Hill's division was supposed to open the attack at eight o'clock, to be followed almost immediately by Longstreet's and Huger's divisions. But eight o'clock came and the loudest thing Whiting heard was a teamster swearing at a mud-stuck team of mules. At nine o'clock, Whiting ordered his brigades to stand at ease until further notice. By eleven o'clock, Whiting was beside himself with fret. Turning temporary command over to Wade Hampton, he rode off to the farmhouse where Johnston—presumably—still had his headquarters. He found Old Joe stamping back and forth on the porch, so wrought up he was gnawing on the whiskers beneath his lower lip. Seeing him dismount, Johnston ran up to Whiting and grabbed his shoulders.

"General Whiting, I hope you bring news!"

"No, General, I've come in search of it. Since part of Longstreet's left wing marched across my front this morning, I have been completely in the dark."

"My God, what's happening? Hill has not initiated the attack, Longstreet seems to have vanished, and the last man I sent to find Huger reported that Huger had only just gotten out of bed! Christ and blue lightning, are these the men with whom I am to redeem the Confederacy?"

In all the years he had known Johnston, Whiting had never seen him in such a state of nerves. On the map, his plan had looked logical, simple, eminently sound. We need to have it spelled out for us, in every *written* particular, thought Whiting; it is not enough, at this stage, for the commander to give verbal instructions while pointing at a map, however clear those instructions might be in his own mind. Longstreet was sullen and willful, Huger lazy and incompetent, and the short-tempered Harvey Hill was probably foaming at the mouth because he was under orders not to start the battle until he knew Longstreet and Huger were in position on his flanks, which, clearly, they were not.

Just as Whiting moved to Johnston's side and bent over the map, he heard cheers in the direction of Richmond. Johnston straightened himself and shielded his eyes with one gloved hand to ascertain the source of the commotion. Whiting was astonished to see Robert E. Lee and his retinue come riding into view. An expression of acute vexation twisted Johnston's face for one long minute; then the general mastered his composure and strode forth to meet his old colleague.

Whiting empathized with Johnston's discomfort. While Johnston retained operational command of the army, Lee had gradually assumed more and more day-to-day power since he had arrived in Richmond to "coordinate" the campaign. On this of all days, "Marse Robert" was not going to sit at a desk in Richmond and read telegrams. Lee was constitutionally incapable of staying away from the field, no matter what funds of confidence he still retained toward Joe Johnston. Whiting could understand: the first eleven months of the war had been a cycle of frustration and bitterness for Lee. After surveying what would become the innermost defensive lines around Richmond, Lee had been sent, last August, to salvage Confederate fortunes in West Virginia, and he had failed dismally. Never mind that he had been given dullards for subordinates and pathetically inadequate resources for the task, the Richmond papers had heaped scorn upon him, christening him Granny Lee. After that failed campaign, Lee was sent, in a state of semidisgrace, to oversee the coastal defenses from South Carolina to Florida, a task that he had found every bit as thankless and onerous as Whiting had found it to be in North Carolina. When Lee came back to Richmond, in March, Johnston accepted the command restructuring with apparent good grace, for his friendship with Lee had been forged in fire at Buena Vista and Cerro Gordo during the war with Mexico.

An aide ran forth to take the reins of Lee's horse, Traveler, and Lee dismounted with an energetic bound. He practically leaped up the stairs to shake Johnston's hand, then Whiting's.

"General, I am not here to interfere or usurp your authority. I simply could not sit idly in Richmond while this battle was fought. If you wish my advice, I shall give it—otherwise, please ignore me."

Lee's disingenuousness, thought Whiting, is flabbergasting. One thing Joe Johnston did not need at that moment was to have Robert

E. Lee hovering like an anxious nanny on the periphery of his vision. How could he admit to Lee that his whole plan seemed to have miscarried? Johnston made a brave effort to seem calm and in control as he ushered Lee into the farmhouse, but Whiting knew Old Joe's innards must have been churning. The whole situation was one of excruciating embarrassment, and Whiting did not care to suffer the mood any longer. He rode back to his own division and waited for orders or enlightenment, whichever came first.

Not until much later did Chase Whiting piece together what happened on that day, and even after he understood the chronology, he could not for the life of him understand *how* Joe Johnston's perfectly sound plan had fallen apart so completely. Johnston had achieved numerical superiority south of the Chickahominy—fifty-two thousand men against thirty-three thousand—and had the plan come to fruition, he would have struck the exposed Federal Fourth Corps from three directions with twenty-two brigades, an overwhelming blow. But Longstreet took the wrong road . . . and Ben Huger slept late . . . and somehow thirteen brigades got hopelessly jammed up on the Williamsburg Road; seven of them never saw action at all, and no more than four were ever engaged at one time, on their own, with little or no support from the others.

Five hours after the scheduled starting time, at one in the afternoon, Harvey Hill's fury boiled over and, acting on his own initiative, he sent his men forward against the Federal left wing. The assault began furiously, but lost impetus quickly as the men struggled through bogs and briar patches, hammered at long range by rifled artillery. By sheer determination some of Hill's men broke portions of the Federal line but, by the time they did so, they were too winded and too savaged by casualties to press on. Had even a portion of Longstreet's division been on hand to relieve them, a Rebel victory would still have been possible. But by the time Longstreet's brigades got sorted out from the confusion on the Williamsburg Road, they too went into action piecemeal.

Joe Johnston kept listening for the sounds of pitched battle, but because of some acoustic anomaly, born of wind and weather conditions, all he heard was cannon fire, no musketry, no cheers. Not until four o'clock did he finally receive a message from Longstreet, indicating a hard-fought engagement in the center, heavy casualties, and the prospect of delayed success if Whiting's division should attack on his left and throw additional pressure against the Yankees. Gentleman that he was, Robert Lee had stayed discreetly in the background and had not asked probing questions, which Johnston obviously could not have answered anyway. After reading Longstreet's dispatch, Johnston drafted an order directing Whiting to make a general attack. Before the ink was dry, however, someone burst into the room and announced that President Davis had been spotted on Nine Mile Road, riding toward Johnston's headquarters. The very last thing Joe Johnston needed at that moment was the gimlet-eyed stare of Jeff Davis and the unanswerable questions the president was certain to ask. Johnston suddenly decided to supervise Whiting's attack in person—he simply could not stand the thought of yet another confrontation with Davis. He galloped off just as the president came into sight at the far end of a cornfield.

Chase Whiting felt enormously relieved when Johnston arrived, just before five o'clock, and he lost no time forming his brigades for the attack. Whiting did not know that the sounds of heavy combat were clearly audible to the Federal officers on the far bank of the Chickahominy and that the commander of the Union Second Corps, General Edwin Sumner, had funneled an entire division across the Grapevine Bridge along with considerable artillery. Instead of delivering a flanking attack against the already hard-pressed Fourth Corps, Whiting was about to launch a frontal assault against a fresh division.

Whiting watched the attack from a wooded knoll about two hundred yards north of Fair Oaks Station, placing himself to the right of Johnston and a jumpy young aide who was feverishly excited by his first battle and who kept standing up on his stirrups to get a better view until Johnson growled: "Colonel, please either stand or sit. It is very distracting to have you popping up and down like a jack-in-the-box."

Whiting ordered all four of his brigades to advance in line abreast, but as the men encountered streams and woods, rail fences and ravines, the line inevitably bent, then came apart. General Law's brigade, on the right, covered the smoothest ground and so was five hundred yards ahead of the other three brigades when it ran headlong into the well-concealed Federal line. Whiting gasped when it happened: one moment, Law's men were advancing up a slight, grassy incline toward what appeared to be an empty, lightly wooded meadow. Suddenly, a double rank of bluecoats rose up in front of them, bayonets rippling like silver minnows in a turbulent pond, and a murderous sheet of fire swept across Law's foremost companies, cutting men down like a scythe. At the same time, several batteries, hidden in the trees a hundred yards behind the Federal infantry, opened up with canister. Through his telescope, Whiting could see clumps of infantry dissolve into clouds of red grit as the canister balls ripped through their flesh. Law's men reeled but they did not break, and Whiting was fiercely proud to see how they closed ranks, delivered a return volley, then charged. They got to within twenty yards of the Yankee line before the defenders could reload and fire a second massive volley, then many of Law's Confederates—*Oh, too many!*—went down hard, the impact of minié balls at such close range causing their bodies to leap and spin and convulse.

Then Pettigrew's brigade came up, on Law's left, and joined the fray, and Whiting realized that he now faced at least as many men as he commanded, possibly more, for now some additional, hitherto concealed, Federal brigades stood up, a wall of steel-tipped blue that stretched at least a mile in the direction of the Chickahominy. There was no way to flank them. Hatton's brigade came up on Pettigrew's left, and big Wade Hampton's brigade came up last, on Hatton's left. By that time, so much smoke lay across the field that Whiting could no longer make out details.

"Your men are fighting well, Chase," complimented Joe Johnston.

"Thank you, General, " said Whiting, *but they are not fighting the battle they were supposed to fight.*

And they were not winning the fight they were in. Between six and six-thirty, Whiting received news that General Hatton had been killed, General Pettigrew had been wounded and captured, and Wade Hampton had taken a ball in the foot. Casualties among the rank and file, of course, would not be known until the fighting sputtered out with the coming of darkness but, from the way things were going, Whiting estimated that he was losing three men for every one lost to the defenders.

Gray dusk seeped down from an overcast sky as Whiting recalled his men. To continue the attack in darkness would have been worse than fruitless. There was still scattered firing for a while, and at one time a stray minié ball carried over the officers' position with a sound like a large slow hornet. The young aide on Johnston's left side instinctively ducked.

"Colonel, there is no use of dodging," chided Old Joe. "By the time you can hear them, they've already passed."

Scarcely had Johnston finished speaking when Whiting heard a sound like the flat of an axe striking a log. Johnston's body rocked back in the saddle and a mushroom of blood spouted from a ragged hole in the cloth covering his right shoulder.

"God damn," said Old Joe. Whiting and the nervous young aide sprang from their saddles and rushed to Johnston's side, propping him up and struggling to pry his boots from the stirrups. At that moment, a Federal shell—probably a random stray round not even aimed at them—exploded twenty feet in front of the three officers, momentarily blinding and deafening Chase Whiting. Neither the aide nor Whiting suffered a scratch, but one big fragment, a smoking lump of iron about the size of a cantaloupe, bounced up and smote Johnston flush in the chest, then dropped harmlessly into the grass. Had the fragment been jagged, it would have cut off the top half of Johnston's body, but it still had enough kinetic energy to hurl Johnston out of their grasp. He sailed off his horse as though yanked by a giant invisibly hook. By the time Whiting and the young colonel reached his side, Johnston lay flat on his back, utterly stunned and gasping wildly for breath with lungs that had been punched flat and momentarily had stopped working. With admirably quick thinking, the young colonel bent over Johnston's gaping mouth and began forcing air into the general's windpipe. Johnston writhed and choked, insensible to what was happening, a man on the verge of drowning. Whiting held the general's flailing arms while the aide continued to pump air like a bellows. After a tense couple of minutes, Johnston's lungs began functioning again and his eyes stopped rolling in their sockets. Whiting cradled his injured friend, shielding him with his own body, while the aide ran off to find some stretcher-bearers.

It was almost full dark by the time Joe Johnston was carried from the field and into a surgeon's tent. Whiting stayed on the line and made sure his men were properly encamped for the night, and fed, and the wounded given care or carried to the nearest field hospital. One by one, the regimental roles were called, but even before the final tally Whiting knew he had lost more than a thousand men. At eight o'clock, after a spartan meal and two cups of tepid coffee, he remounted and rode back down Nine Mile Road to see how Joe Johnston was doing.

Whiting was weary down to his marrow, and as his horse slowly plodded along, he fell into a state of semiconsciousness. When a well-dressed civilian in a top hat cantered past, it seemed to Whiting more dream than real. Then, as the hoofbeats receded, he came alert with a cold sense of alarm. He had not seen the rider's face, but belatedly he recognized the horse. Cursing, Whiting turned his animal back and urged it into a gallop.

No question about it: the phantom rider was Jefferson Davis. Either the president had grown so restless waiting to learn more about the battle that he had ridden off to see the tail end of it himself, or he had gotten word of Johnston's wounding and was hastening to ascertain the general's condition. Either way, thought Whiting, the damned fool is heading straight for Yankee lines. Oh, he could see it now, blazed across the front page of the Richmond papers: CONFEDERATE PRESIDENT SLAIN/CAPTURED/WOUNDED IN HEINOUS AMBUSH!!

He dared not yell the man's name, in case there were enemy soldiers prowling about in the blasted, corpse-strewn zone between the two armies. Finally, he caught sight of Davis, still cantering briskly in the general direction of McClellan's headquarters. Whiting spurred his mount and the poor beast responded with a shudder of resignation—the day had been long for him as well. When he was within hailing distance, Whiting called out the most suitable words that came to mind: "Halt, there! Please halt!" and when Davis seemed not to hear him, "For God's sake, Your Excellency, *stop!*"

When he drew near and saluted, Davis recognized him.

"General Whiting. Good evening, sir. I am searching for General Johnston. I must know what happened today!"

"Mister President, General Johnston lies grievously wounded in the hospital at Old Tavern, and you, sir, are riding straight toward Yankee lines."

"Good lord, was I really?" It was the first and only time Whiting saw Jefferson Davis with a look of chagrin, like a truant boy who has just been caught out. "I suppose I owe you my thanks, General Whiting. The old soldier in my blood got the better of my prudence, and all I could think of was riding to the guns."

"That's just some blind shelling up ahead sir. All the serious fighting is finished."

"Well, did we win?"

"We surely gave them a rough time, from what I could see. But I do not think we won, sir. They put a fresh division across the river and stopped my brigade cold. I cannot vouch for what happened on Longstreet's front, or Huger's, or General Hill's. I do not think the attack was coordinated as General Johnston planned it."

Davis chewed on the information as though it were a hard biscuit. "That is bad news, sir, bad news indeed. Well, perhaps we shall do better tomorrow. I should pay my respects to General Johnston, now. Will you ride with me?"

Whiting did want to visit Joe Johnston, but he did not particularly want to make conversation with President Davis. He honestly could not explain the battle, but that would not stop Davis from asking questions. Fortunately, the president rode in sulky silence for most of the journey, so Whiting was spared the extra strain of being diplomatic. Only once did Davis venture a significant remark.

"Active command will devolve to General Lee now, I expect."

"Yes, sir. He is a good man, and the army will quickly learn to respect him."

"But will they love him, sir, as they love Johnston? If the love of one's troops were the largest measure of generalship, then Johnston would be another Bonaparte. But he retreated, and retreated, and now, today, when he had McClellan at the disadvantage, he botched the opportunity. I am of course saddened by the news of his injury, but the end result may prove to be fortuitous for our cause."

They could hear and smell the big hospital at Old Tavern long before its cluster of lanterns came into view. There was a westerly wind now, and the screams carried far, as did the faint odor of necrotic flesh. Both Whiting and Davis, however, were veterans of the Mexican War, and no strangers to the carnage that followed a battle. They tethered their mounts and picked their way through rows of wounded men. Those still conscious, startled by the sudden appearance of the president, followed them with fire-red eyes, like the eyes of demons. General Johnston, they learned, had been taken to a bedroom on the second floor of the tavern. Whiting stood aside to let Davis make the first visit. Joe Johnston never repeated what the president had said during the ten minutes he was in the room. Davis reemerged with ashen cheeks and said to Whiting: "They have removed the ball and stanched the blood, but the impact broke his shoulder. He will be out of action for a long, long time." Davis shook hands with Whiting and walked down the stairs, bearing the expression of a man who still had many pressing errands to tend to.

Whiting opened the door and stepped into Johnston's room. The general lay half covered with a linen sheet, two pillows beneath his grizzled head. His thin right shoulder was packed with rusty bandages and there was a terrible purple bruise centered on his shaggy breast. At first Whiting thought the general had fallen asleep but, when he turned to go, Joe Johnston stirred and spoke.

"Chase . . . I am glad to see you. Do you know who was just here? President Davis, by heaven! Did you see him on your way up?"

"More than that, Joseph. I escorted him here, after I chanced upon him riding merrily toward enemy lines in the dark. If I had not caught up with him, he would surely have been killed or made prisoner."

Johnston managed a faint chuckle. "And the papers would no doubt blame it on *me.* Along with today's debacle. I should have known better than to give verbal orders to someone as headstrong as Pete Longstreet and someone as lazy as Ben Huger. Next time, I will take great pains to spell everything out in writing, to the finest detail . . . if there is a next time."

"Don't say so, Joseph. You have many good battles still to fight."

"Yes, but not tomorrow's. Command will go to Lee now, and it may prove so that the bullet which struck me down was the luckiest thing that ever happened to our cause. Well, at least it is harder to think badly of a wounded general than a whole one. Now, my friend, I think I shall sleep—I am still groggy from the chloroform. Your men behaved splendidly today, General Whiting."

"I'm proud of them, sir. If courage alone could guarantee victory, we should have swept the enemy from the field."

"Yes. But courage alone seldom does."

Johnston seemed to be drifting off. His breathing grew heavy and his eyes closed. Whiting stood and turned to go.

"One more thing, Chase."

"Yes, Joseph?"

"Don't expect Jefferson Davis to like you now just because you saved his bacon tonight. A man of ordinary grace would be forever grateful—but Jeff Davis has never forgotten a slight or forgiven an opponent and he suckles grudges like a sow does piglets. He believes you are disloyal to him, obstinately opposed to his will, and that you drink too damned much."

"He may be right, in all three cases. Sleep well, General."

Zebulon Vance could not remember a time in his life when he was hotter, stickier, or thirstier than he was at six o'clock on the first afternoon of July. If the dog days of North Carolina were a trial to body and spirit, the depths of midsummer in tidewater Virginia were a foretaste of Hell. Even the fitful breeze, when it deigned to breathe at all, was baking hot and woolly against his sweat-glazed skin. Every soldier near Vance, officer or private, smelled of armpit and crotch. They moved as little as possible, trying to conserve their strength before the inevitable order to attack. The grass all around was dry and sun-bleached to a pale and juiceless shade of tan; if you crushed it by moving about, it released faint clouds of dusty spoors that scratched the nostrils and caused some of the men to sneeze repeatedly and convulsively. Half the men of the Twenty-sixth North Carolina were already chigger-bit and all of them were adrift in a semiconscious state of fear-heavy torpor. They had not moved for ninety minutes, but every enemy cannon whose crew did not have a more urgent target was methodically sprinkling shells in their general direction.

Every time a Federal battery roared from the crest of Malvern Hill, the long, shallow, sixty-foot elevation in front of them, the entire regiment cringed and shriveled, shoulder blades constricting, buttocks clamping, arms above their heads, kissing and nuzzling the ground.

Like a sudden tempest, the roar and thump and musket crackle of pitched combat rose to a crescendo off to the east, where Huger's and Hill's divisions were attacking. More faintly, during the lulls between attacks, Vance could hear a continual mumble of distant artillery from a mile to the northeast, where Stonewall Jackson's division was supposed to be plowing into McClellan's right flank. But if Jackson had been successful, then the enemy troops in front of Vance's regiment should already be pulling back, and there was no slackening of their fire as the day wore on toward dusk. This would not be the first time Jackson had failed since force-marching his men back from the Shenandoah Valley; according to countless rumors and anecdotes, the supposedly fire-breathing Stonewall had burned himself out in the Valley campaign and was for the moment imprisoned in a strange envelope of lethargy brought about by absolute physical and emotional exhaustion. Harry Burgwyn, for one, thought Jackson's legend was grossly inflated and, over campfire brandy with Vance, had described him as "the Mad Presbyterian," averring that, sooner or later, "the God of the Calvinists" would grow tired of bestowing good luck on Jackson and some unfazed Yankee opponent would "tar the living daylights out of him." As it happened, Vance encountered a young captain the very next day who had been serving with Stonewall since December, and when Vance asked *his* opinion of Jackson, the fellow had unhesitatingly replied, "Colonel, he's crazier than a shit-house rat."

If Jackson had misfired once again, Vance thought, Lee's "grand attack" on Malvern Hill had probably degenerated into a slugging match, and the enemy had good high ground and four times as many cannons as Lee had been able to muster on this day. If that were indeed the case, Vance rather hoped the darkness would fall before his regiment was ordered forward.

The Twenty-sixth had seen little action since the retreat from New Bern. From March 16 to June 20, it was encamped near Kinston again, guarding the railroad into Virginia against an inland thrust by Burnside. But Burnside turned his attention to Fort Macon. Shortly after that inadequate bastion fell, he was ordered to detach about half of his troops for duty with McClellan. Except for minor skirmishing, and a few riverine probes by Yankee gunboats, the North Carolina coast grew quiet. What excitement there was proved to be political rather than military. The Twenty-sixth was a "twelve-month" regiment, and when its tour of duty was involuntarily extended by another year, its members conducted a raucous election of officers, as did the men in every other year-old unit. Zeb Vance was handily reelected—only seven votes against him, in fact—and Harry Burgwyn won enough votes to remain as second-in-command. If the vote had been held before the New Bern battle—where the previously grumbling soldiers had learned the value of Harry's discipline and the metal of his courage—Burgwyn would surely have been sent packing. At about the same time as the elections, the regiment was incorporated into a new brigade, under the command of Brigadier General Robert Ransom, a much younger and more respected officer than the superannuated Theophilus Holmes, whom Ransom replaced.

Ransom's brigade arrived on the Peninsula on June 24, but until today, the Twenty-sixth had only exchanged sporadic fire with Yankee pickets. Today would bring the regiment's first real combat since New Bern, and from all that Vance knew and could see, the attack on Malvern Hill promised to be something vastly different, and more deadly by several orders of magnitude.

Vance glanced at his pocket watch once more: six forty-five and the shadows were growing longer. If the order to attack did not come soon, darkness would save both blood and honor. He rather hoped that he and his men might be excused from this one, for he had listened to Harry's explanation of Lee's strategy and followed it on a map; even though his military expertise was limited, Vance agreed with Burgwyn that Lee's primary motivation for staging this attack must have been wild impatience instead of cool reason. McClellan *was* retreating to his bases on the James River; Richmond *had* been saved; in twenty-four hours, the Yankees would have skedaddled off Malvern

Hill of their own accord and some fancy marching by Lee's units might yet offer a chance to strike them while their artillery was limbered up and their infantry columns strung out. Instead, Lee had chosen to throw everything he had against Malvern Hill, where McClellan's artillery was massed on a broad plateau averaging sixty feet in elevation above the surrounding swampland and approachable only by a frontal uphill march in every direction except the northeast, where Jackson was supposed to be clawing into the enemy's flank. But the infantry and batteries in front of Vance's lines seemed unperturbed and there had been no change in the leisurely, evenly paced rhythm of their fire.

They know we are here. They're waiting for us. When we cover the last hundred yards, we'll be close enough for their guns to fire a double load of canister. It will be like charging into a wall of giant shotguns. Dear Jesus. For the first time that day, real fear punched Zeb Vance in the stomach and he fought down the urge to vomit, knowing that if he did so, he would be even drier, emptier, and more foul-smelling than he already was. After all, he reasoned, he had stood for reelection as colonel in command, and it was his job as well as his duty to lead these men into the storm. A shell flew overhead, spitting like a clogged steam valve, and burst harmlessly in the trees behind them. Off to the left, the sounds of combat were growing less intense. Maybe Huger's brigades had taken the enemy line after all . . . or maybe they were falling back. Either outcome would explain the gradual diminuendo of musketry, like wildfire dying down on the edge of a creek.

All of a sudden, a large gray rabbit hopped out of the grass right in front of them. "There's my supper!" said one man, lancing out at the animal with his fixed bayonet. The rabbit jumped in alarm and hightailed it straight across the front of the regiment.

"Go it, cottontail!" shouted Zeb Vance. "If I had no more reputation to lose than you have, I'd run, too!" The men laughed uproariously and Vance suddenly felt calm and unafraid. He had voiced the sentiments of everyone. Harry Burgwyn called out from his place in the line, "I see the colonel has not lost his genius for stump speeches!" And that, too, was the right thing for Harry to say—it reminded them once more that they were a *unit,* not just a collection of tired, hot, terrified individuals.

Just as well, thought Vance, when the order to advance reached him only seconds later. He acted: he drew his sword and held it aloft for all to see, then stabbed it out toward the hill. "Forward, Twenty-sixth! Quick march!"

Then they all stood up into the sudden cool of the twilight, their own shadows thrown far ahead up the slope by the lowering sun. Three hundred yards to the crest. It would be nearly dark when they closed with the enemy. If they made it that far. Five North Carolina regiments in line, the whole brigade, rising like a vast butternut-robed choir holding rifles instead of hymnals, and each man with a prayer on his lips. The flags went up, and the last rusty light of the sun bathed those standards in ruddy glory while the men holding them remained gloomed in shadow. Forward, all, with measured drill-field tread, all yet in silence save for the jangle of equipment. No increase yet in fire from the hill, just the same scattered thundery bursts as before. Maybe the Yanks *have* pulled back. After the first one hundred yards, a slight flat dip in the land, like an overgrown wagon road. Halting for a moment to re-dress their lines, the company commanders rushing to and fro, holding their swords out two-handed at arm's length like rulers measuring the straightness of a Euclidean exercise. Men breathing hard, but so far still through their noses, so they still have plenty of wind. And they need it when the order changes to "At the double-quick!" Impossible for the enemy not to see them now, if he is still there above them, so Vance calls out, "Let 'em know we're coming, boys!" and the Twenty-sixth responds with a hair-raising banshee wail, venting their hours of fear and discomfort like overloaded steam engines.

Then into the cool shade of scattered trees, the crest of Malvern Hill intermittently in sight, and on the right where the trees thin out, a long column of blue soldiers, moving off the plateau in the direction of the James River. This might work! thinks Vance—we might hit them while they're in marching order—might roll right over the bastards! But no, they are no longer moving—they have halted, coolly dressing their formation, and at some unheard command, they turn and face the North Carolinians at a range of one hundred yards and deliver a stupendous volley, and for that instant, it seems the very hill has been split apart by a volcanic cataclysm. Now the cannons open fire and the clover field dimples with puffs of dirt and grass where the canister balls rake the earth, and so violent is the combined blast of a thousand rifles and at least a dozen guns that the very air quakes in their faces, jarring them like a slap. All along the brigade front, men go down and flags waver. Some of them, caught full by the canister charges, are simply *erased,* vanishing in ghastly red sprays of meat and cloth. Others stare, openmouthed and stupefied, at the crimson fountains that have replaced their arms or legs or hands, and only begin to scream when their brains finally process the awful information their eyes report. It is almost dark now, and some of Ransom's men have survived the wave of iron and gotten to within fifty yards of the enemy, and beyond that they cannot advance, so they drop down and shoot at the great spears of flame and gouts of smoke. Those who still attempt to charge make themselves perfect targets against the hard orange sunset and so die quickly, jerking and thrashing from the impact of a perfect rain of minié balls, pieces of their flesh swarming about them like nocturnal insects in frenzy 'round a blazing lamp.

Zeb Vance felt as though he were wading through molasses, as though gravity itself had multiplied its pull in response to all the noise and flame and powder reek. The attack was as good as over three minutes after the first Union volley, so what point was there to waving his sword again, especially since the sword weighed like railroad iron and he was gasping like a landed fish, unable to find enough oxygen in the harsh grit of gunsmoke that enveloped his head. Mere flesh, he thought; that is all we are, and the only way we could stop those guns is by masking their fire with our shattered bodies. Until this moment, thanks to the ambiguity of his experiences in the Battle of New Bern, he had reserved judgment on war itself, but now in the stench and chaos and blind howling terror of the last attack on Malvern Hill, he saw the leering skull of its face, stripped of "glory," making of pride and courage a grisly mockery. A blast of canister passed his head so close he could feel it suck the air behind it, and the soldier in front of him took a glancing blow from a few of the balls. The right side of his head vanished in a wet gush, showering Vance with brains and bits of cranium, and as the man flew back, he spun around from the impact and the stock of his rifle cracked Vance smartly on the temple. I'm hit, he thought, and right in the noggin. Then he fell senseless into the blood-soaked grass.

He woke to moonlight, eyelids teary with dew and head throbbing like a badly set bone. He had a searing memory of blood, but his hands found nothing but a wincing lump on his temple. His muscles ached from uncoiled tension and sheer physical exertion, and several joints cracked as he rose to a crouch, still instinctively bending over to present a smaller target. But there was no firing now. McClellan's men had moved on, and Lee's men had gone back to camp for the sorrowful night. Vance stood erect and took deep breaths against a sudden wave of dizziness. Clear skies and low summer stars framed a three-quarter moon as bright as sunlit mercury. The field now belonged to the dead, the helplessly maimed, and the lost.

At his feet lay the soldier with half a head, surrounded by a congealed and gleaming puddle of black jelly. As Vance rose to his full height, he saw more and more of the slopes of Malvern Hill, the moonlit grass spotted with dark, still shapes. He peered in the direction he assumed his regiment had gone in retreat, hoping to see their campfires. But the woods were dotted with fires set by exploding shells, and he did not see a clear path that way. So he walked down to the narrow level stretch where they had halted before the charge and began stumbling toward the swampy plains, hoping sooner or later to strike the Darbytown Road. At first, he managed to steer a zigzag path around the dead but, as he drew closer to the place where Huger's and D. H. Hill's men had launched their piecemeal attacks earlier in the day, the corpses were sewn so thickly that he sometimes trod upon them and beneath his boots their splayed limbs and inert torsos felt as irregular and grindingly firm as bags of sand. If he had the choice, he steered his way over the men felled by bullets and avoided the dreadful lumpy shapes of those cut down by shells and grapeshot. He tramped past half a company of men cut down in a neat precise row, their outflung bayonets gleaming like icicles in the direction of the summit. The men who had fallen forward still retained some shred of dignity, but those who had been hurled onto their backs presented a ghastly face to the stars: already stiff and swollen—some of them had lain thus through the whole hot afternoon—their faces were dark as minstrels' from biting open black-powder cartridges and flinching against the snap of percussion caps just inches from their eyes, and most of them had their mouths open in an oval rictus of surprise. A row of those upturned faces looked like a display of black jack-o'-lanterns all carved from the same pattern, all their mouths forming the same startled bone-white *Oh!* Where the Rebel dead lay thickest, the air was already starting to char and thicken from their corruption. When he entered this miasmic zone, Vance wrapped his handkerchief around his nose and mouth, wishing rather ludicrously for a dollop of cologne.

Not until he stepped on one corpse who suddenly sprang to life and cursed him for a ghoul did Vance realize that there were still living men among the dead. He knelt beside the wounded man and apologized, asking if there was anything he could do.

"Why, yes, Colonel," the man croaked, his white cracked lips trembling like a pair of worms. "Some water."

Vance fumbled for his own canteen, remembered that it was dry, and rummaged among the nearest bodies until he found one that sloshed. As he knelt to give the wounded man a drink, Vance observed for the first time that although the fellow had a full compliment of arms and hands, his whole body was gone from the groin on down. How was it possible, he marveled, for a man to sustain such a truncation and yet remain alive, and conscious, and now that he had drunk his fill of water, astoundingly calm? Even as Vance took back the empty canteen, he saw the water trickling out from the man's pulverized guts and forming a pool in the moonlight.

"Thank you, sir."

"Can I . . . er . . . do anything else for you, son?"

"Yes, sir. You can shoot me. I know the extent of my injuries, and I would be better off. Before the numbness wears off, you understand."

Vance felt a cold snake of horror unwinding in his bowels.

"I . . . I don't think I can do that."

"Ah, yes, of course not. Though when you think about it, shooting me is not all that different from ordering me into that wall of fire yesterday. Seems only fair that officers who can order men to their deaths ought to be responsible for finishing the job."

"I understand why you feel that way. God help me, I cannot just shoot you."

The half-man gave Vance a calm, sympathetic smile.

"No, sir, I suppose you can't. In that case, however, will you do me the favor of finding a loaded musket and placing it in my hands? I've tried dragging myself. As long as I lie still I can bear the pain, but when I move, it hurts so bad it makes me faint. Just find me a loaded rifle, Colonel, and leave me be. I'll make my peace with God and wait until you are safely gone."

His mind almost shut down with emotion, Vance probed around until he found two rifles still primed with copper caps. He placed them gently in the half-man's embrace and said, "I brought you a pair, in case one misfires."

"God bless you, sir. And one more thing, if you'd be so kind: in my breast pocket you will find a letter to my mother. I'd be most obliged if you could send it on for me."

Vance took the document and bent down to kiss the man on his forehead. Unable to speak for the tears welling in his throat, he resumed his lonely walk. Three minutes later he heard a stark and solitary shot. As though that noise were some kind of cock's crow for the unconscious, other wounded men now began to call out. Filled with shame as well as horror, Vance steered his erratic course away from them, but their imprecations followed him through the dark.

"Fourth Louisiana! Where are you boys? It's ol' Beauchamp here! Come and get me, boys, for the love of God!"

"Water! I'm on fire! Water! Over near the dead horses!"

"Mother? Please come for me, Mother! I've been a good boy, like you told me to be! Come take me home!"

"My eyes! Somebody help me! I'm blind!"

Followed by this chorus of the damned, Vance finally reached the road and started trudging toward friendly lines. After a while, he reached the picket lines and got directions to Ransom's encampment. Just before dawn, he finally found the Twenty-sixth, and one of the first men he encountered was Harry Burgwyn. *Doesn't he ever sleep?*

"My God, Colonel Vance! We thought you had been killed or captured! You, there, fetch a surgeon at once! And some whiskey!"

"Just get the whiskey, Private," Vance countered. "Aside from a lump on the head, I'm fine."

Vance pulled a folding stool from his tent and gratefully drank some bourbon while Harry brought him up to date on the news. From all indications, the attack had done little more than put a bump in McClellan's road to the James. Stonewall Jackson had failed utterly to deliver his attack, leaving D. H. Hill to take on the whole Yankee line with one division. In some places, it was said, Hill's men got to within twenty feet of the enemy guns before being cut down. Ben Huger's division was late starting and lost all coherence under the heavy artillery fire; his regiments attacked, some of them anyhow, but did so one at a time, and so were defeated easily. Rumor already told how Lee had sacked Huger on the spot, transferring him to an administrative job in the West and commanding that he never again be allowed to lead men in battle. Magruder's brigades made the bravest showing, but they too were unsupported and could make no headway in the face of stout resistance and failing light. It had been a day of useless, pointless slaughter. The North Carolina regiments in Ransom's brigade had suffered six hundred dead, wounded, and missing. The Twenty-sixth had come off easier than most, because it had been recalled only a few minutes into its charge, but even so had lost fifty men or more, including four company commanders. Vance listened and drank, knowing he was just minutes away from collapsing. He wanted to tell Harry about the moonlit black-faced dead with gaping white holes for mouths, and about the half-man who by all reason and mercy should have died instantly but had not. But there were no words to describe these things; the only sound that would have come from his mouth, if he had tried, was a scream.

"Harry, I am going to resign my commission. As soon as the paperwork can be completed, the regiment is yours. I am no coward—I went forward with everyone else when ordered to. But I cannot, and will not, order other men into another such holocaust ever again. And so I am finished as a battlefield officer. The men have come to respect you, now, and will serve you loyally. You have been trained to it, while I am still only an amateur warrior. In time, I would learn the profession, but I no longer want to."

"What will you do now, Colonel?"

"Return to public service, where I belong. The South has more than enough fair to middlin' colonels, Harry, but damned few governors who are not either rogues or poltroons."

" 'Governor Vance,' eh?"

"Well, why not? Governor Clark will not stand for reelection, although he has done an honest, hardworking job of filling in since John Ellis died. Only two months ago, the Confederate Congress enacted conscription—someone must see that the policy is carried out fairly in North Carolina. Someone must see to it, as the war drags on, that the rights of the people are not trampled by a tyranny in Richmond, perhaps even worse than they ever were from the government in Washington. If this war is about one thing above all others, it is the rights of each state's citizens to live as they choose. Whether the South wins or loses, Harry, the great state of North Carolina will go on. I believe in my heart that I can lead her people wisely."

Burgwyn chuckled and shook his head.

"You don't have to make a speech to me, Colonel Vance. If there was ever a man born and groomed to be governor, it's you."

Reeling a little bit from both whiskey and exhaustion, Vance clapped Harry on the back and poured another liberal dollop into the lieutenant colonel's cup.

"Come on now, Harry, admit it: you'd be much happier knowing

I was *behind* you in Raleigh than having me in front of you waving my sword!"

"Well, sir, let me say that I would be the first to vote for you."

Vance nodded and downed the last of his drink. Then, without another word, he went into his tent, flopped down on his cot, and began to snore.

The Merchant Princes of Wilmington

GUERRILLA COMPANIES—We need more independent guerrilla companies to hang about the invaders of our homes and pick them off as opportunity offers. Morgan and Ashby are doing great work in this way, and just such men are needed in every State. On the Carolina coast, such a man as Morgan would find a rich field for operations. And we are surprised that the citizens of the counties infested with the marauders, and those threatened, do not form independent companies and detachments and annoy the enemy in every way possible. While the Yankees remained on the sand banks of Hatteras and on Roanoke Island, it was not easy to get at them, but New Bern, Beaufort and all the other occupied points around the coast should be made most uncomfortable to the invaders. These men come to enslave us and ruin us, and should be killed in every way possible. The people of the South must determine to be free, and freedom can only be retained by whipping the Yankees, so let us fight them in every way possible.

—The Wilmington Journal, April 17 1862

Since the *Banshee*'s maiden voyage, in November 1861, the U.S. Navy's original gaggle of patrol ships had acquired a formal name—the North Atlantic Blockading Squadron—and a much improved state of efficiency. The balance began to tilt, ever so slowly, at about the same time Matthew and Hobart-Hampden returned from that first, enormously profitable round-trip to Nassau.

Admiral DuPont's capture of Port Royal, South Carolina, in that same month of November 1861, and energetic development of that place into a major supply and repair facility equidistant from both Charleston and Savannah, changed the strategic situation profoundly. No longer did the blockading ships have to make the long voyage back to the Chesapeake Bay harbors in order to recoal or affect repairs. By the start of 1862, both Savannah and Charleston were so closely invested that only small intracoastal runners could risk making for those ports with any chance of success. New Orleans had fallen to Admiral Farragut's fleet in April 1862, which in turn freed more Union ships for duty on the Atlantic coast. By June of that year—aside from some small, remote harbors in Florida and Texas, Wilmington was the Confederacy's only remaining port of entry for the European supplies that were so vital to the war's continued prosecution.

But still, the blockaders' vigilance was, at times, astonishingly lax, and the runners dashing in and out of Wilmington had perfected their tactics and camouflage to a degree that, so far, seemed to offset the numerical odds against them.

Not until the *Banshee*'s fourth return voyage did Matthew Sloane have a really close encounter with the blockading squadron. A strong head wind kept pushing the runner away from shore, and several times during the night Matthew was forced to execute evasive detours to avoid detection by the increased number of patrol vessels. By the time the eastern sky acquired the definition and color of encroaching dawn, the *Banshee* was still almost thirty miles north of New Inlet, near the reefy shores of Masonboro Inlet where fingers of watery smoke marked the location of the Confederate saltworks. There was no time to slip back over the horizon, so Matthew had no choice but to order full speed, turn hard to port, and hope that the ship's low profile and smoke-gray camouflage would blend in with the blurry mist of surf and render her invisible.

Fitz-John Bright became energized by the challenge, shouting orders down at the engine stokers and gripping the wheel with white-knuckled concentration: "You men give me COAL and do not STINT! Higher REV-o-lu-SHUNS, if you PLEASE, and keep it UP until the pre-SHURE gauge pops like a BROW-ken watch-glass!"

By the time the ship had made its turn and was running due south, parallel with the surf, the boilers were hissing, the paddle wheels slapping water in one continuous sound, *Whop-whop-whop!* Standing on the low-slung bridge just to the right of Master Bright, Matthew was compelled to gyrate through a number of uncaptainly contortions so he could remain upright and dignified as the vessel lurched beyond her maximum safe speed of fifteen knots. He felt the bow lift as the paddles dug deeper and he once more dispatched to

Heaven a silent prayer of gratitude that Mister Bright, for all his eccentricities, was an instinctively brilliant pilot, for at this speed there was no way to take depth-soundings and the bottom ruck along this part of the coast changed like the pleats of an accordion with every squall and the tides of every full moon. Matthew had by now become a capable seaman, but he did not possess, and probably never would, Mister Bright's uncanny ability to read depth and current from the color of water and the streaks of foam upon the looming surface. It was as though a sensitive lead-line ran through Bright's spine and down through his shoes, the deck, and the hull, and thence down into the currents, sniffing them like a proboscis and sending information back up to the pilot's brain by means of vibrations too subtle for anyone else to interpret.

If the remaining coal had been of good quality, the *Banshee* would have made a quick clean dash through New Inlet, protected from close pursuit by the Rebel batteries guarding the channel. But already, not quite a year into the organized blockade-running trade, high-grade anthracite coal was becoming scarce and expensive, with much of the limited supply being siphoned off by the railroads. What remained in the ship's fuel bunkers was poor, crumbly stuff that burned dirty and dark. Matthew happened to glance up at the smokestacks at just the moment when the stokers switched from the last of the good coal to the smutty dregs on the bottom of the heap. Boilers, keel, and deck, the *Banshee* registered the change by convulsing with a huge belch of pressure change and a great coughing discharge of gritty black soot.

"Damn that filthy stuff!" cried Matthew.

Seemingly unconcerned and not breaking his fixed glare at the water ahead, Mister Bright replied: "Aye, it's dirty as a mad-MAN's drawers, that it IS! But, you SEE, Captain Sloane, the BER-lures *hate* to burn the stuff and so will EX-pell it all the faster. Like a man sputting up a good PUKE!" And, true, by the time Matthew figured out that "BER-lores" meant "boilers," the engines had made some sort of peace with the inferior coal and were grinding out another half-knot or so. The bow wake fairly sizzled, arcing high on either side of the bowsprit like fountain water.

Matthew was so enveloped with sensations of speed and thrusting excitement, almost embarrassingly sensual at such a moment, that several crystalline seconds went by before he realized that the *Banshee* was under fire. As the sea alongside spat and columned, alarmingly close, Matthew turned his telescope aft and saw a Yankee frigate about a mile away, wreathed in tattered smoke as she fired at the runner with her big rifled bow-chaser. The pursuing captain had a bone in his teeth, for he was not only running with engines wide open but had crowded on all his auxiliary canvas as well. Flame blossomed from the blockader's bow—so quickly that Matthew felt a rush of admiration for the speed of her gun crew—and a shell banged close enough to ping the *Banshee's* stack with fragments. Simultaneously, signal rockets zoomed up to alert the ships patrolling closer to New Inlet. Several of the crew flinched and crouched, and Mister Bright scornfully addressed them: "Gentlemen, a pro-JEC-tile has a thing called a 'line of TRA-ject-or-y,' and all you NEED to do, in OR-der to RE-main PURR-fect-ly safe, is to stand to the LEFT or the RIGHT of that line!"

Perhaps ten miles remained to New Inlet, and with any luck, Confederate spotters had already signaled an alert to the covering batteries. Responding to the signal rockets, three more Union vessels hove into view, converging on the *Banshee* at an oblique angle, and the foremost of them turned to starboard and fired a broadside. But the water around the runner was not disturbed, for they had not spotted her gull's-belly color against the smudge of surf and were instead opening fire on the original pursuer. Straddled by shell splashes, that vessel altered course and promptly ran up the Union ensign, which was the only thing her captain could do, but that created a new element of uncertainty since more than one runner skipper had escaped capture by suddenly raising the Stars and Stripes at just such a critical juncture.

By now, however, the *Banshee* was belching out such a streamer of foul bituminous smoke that a blind man could have spotted her by the stench alone. After a few moments of frenzied back-and-forth signaling, all four of the Yankee ships began to act in concert and the sea four cable-lengths in front of the runner erupted in a wild froth as roundshot struck like hail. Matthew Sloane grasped the railing and clenched his teeth, certain that the next broadside would drop right upon their heads.

Just then, he heard a couple of freight trains rushing overhead and saw the widening embrace of New Inlet, guarded by sand castles topped with spikes of flame. Swiveling his head to the left, he saw a pair of massive waterspouts fling up just fifty yards in front of the closest Yankee steamer, signaling unmistakably that they were about to steam into range of the heavy coastal guns that had been tracking them since the *Banshee* was spotted. Abruptly, the pursuers turned aside, and through his glass Matthew could see some of the enemy sailors cheering, like good sports after losing a close race. Four minutes later, as the *Banshee* sped through New Inlet and reached the safe embrace of the river, the Confederate gunners were cheering as well and waving their hats, so Mister Bright vented from the overheated boilers a wild shriek of triumph.

They were home and unscathed. And in a short while, they would all—from the captain to the lowliest coal dust covered engine-stoker—be considerably richer. Matthew Sloane had never felt more vibrantly alive. The first thing he would do after docking in Wilmington would be to dispatch Mister Bright upriver to fetch Mary Harper down from Pine Haven. He wanted her by his side during the exciting days ahead. He wanted her, period.

When they came abreast of the Dram Tree, Matthew ceremoniously unbunged a suitably large cask of rum and drew the first, captain's, cup, followed eagerly by the rest of the officers and crew, not in descending order but in a now-traditional democratic surge of first-come-first-served. Matthew was finishing his third cup as the *Banshee* turned northeast to pass Eagles Island, where Beery's Shipyard swarmed with activity: runners and intracoastal steamers laid up to have their bottoms scraped, boilers cleaned, and routine damage repaired, and where a large new keel had just been laid in a separate, guarded slip, the foundation, so rumor had it, of a mighty new Confederate ironclad, as yet unnamed.

Now Wilmington itself came into view—white and green and sharp beyond a forest of masts and smokestacks, all framed by the turbid brown artery of the river. Each landmark had become a friend: the plain white cupola of the Methodist church on Front Street; the brawny square tower of old Saint John's Episcopal; the taller, upstart, holier-than-thou spire of First Presbyterian; the dun-colored bulk of the Customs House; the distant authority of Town Hall's Corinthian columns; and the turbulent waterfront itself, aswarm with agents, wholesalers, roistering stevedores, tipsy sailors, pickpockets, whores, and spies, and the throng of the just-plain-curious, eager to partake of the excitement and hoping to learn what new goods might be arriving.

Matthew had learned to read their faces. Those with a lot of money in their pockets had flushed, eager countenances, glazed with a spending fever they could barely contain; those with little to spend looked on with expressions of anxious longing—to these less affluent would go the gleanings after each big auction: thimbles and buttons and scraps of ordinary ribbon. Thus did the *Banshee* come under passionate, many-eyed scrutiny as she tamped down her engines and glided into harbor, low in the water from her cargo's weight, pregnant with the heavy stuff of war, yet gorged as well with the gentler ballast of consumer goods. As soon as the ship was made fast and the gangplank extended, florid men in top hats swarmed aboard, glasses of champagne extended before them, each one vying with the others to give the runner's officers such an indelible memory of welcome that the welcomers' faces might stand out in the crowd when the choicest civilian goods went up for auction.

Matthew politely evaded most of the handshakes and proffered glasses and threaded his way ashore, then across Water Street to the corner where Jacob and Largo Landau customarily waited on the estimated days of the *Banshee*'s return. When they saw him, they waved and surged forward to greet their friend and business partner. Jacob looked robust and prosperous—as well he might, considering the profits that were about to be made—and Largo was a dusky vision of big vivid eyes, white shoulders, and berry-red lips. Behind them, smiling almost paternally, was Hobart-Hampden, who had chosen to stay behind on this particular voyage, for inscrutable reasons of his own. Matthew suspected that the sensuous young Jewess might have been one of them. As usual, the Englishman was elegantly turned out and had stationed himself just behind Largo's silken neck, where he could imbibe her scented warmth. Before more gentlemanly thoughts could fill his head, Matthew Sloane could not help but wonder: Had they done it yet? *Has the watchful old Jew let her out of sight long enough for an opportunity to arise? Or, practical man that he is, has he just accepted his daughter's infatuation and factored in the labyrinthine moral equation already imposed upon him by the war?*

First they dealt with agents of the Confederate government, who assembled in Jacob's office at the rear of his store, while the clerks out front distributed leaflets about Monday's auction. The men from Richmond had already gone through the *Banshee*'s holds and inspected the military goods within, so there was little haggling as the items were ticked off on the bills of lading and the sales transactions completed. Unto these worthies, the stockholders in the Anglo-Confederate Trading Company rendered up: eighteen crates of knapsacks, 250 bags of saltpeter, fourteen cases of blankets and shoes, three hundred pigs of lead, fifty cases of .54-caliber Austrian rifles, one hundred crates of sheet tin, and two cases of first-quality

Sheffield cavalry sabers, ordered by Jefferson Davis personally so that he might distribute them to victorious officers as tokens of honor. "*Two cases?*" quipped Hobart-Hampden when that item was read aloud. "There aren't that many good cavalry generals in the whole of both armies!" This bon mot elicited small, pained smiles from the Rebel purchasing agents.

All weekend, crates of civilian goods were transferred from the *Banshee* to Jacob's warehouse, adjacent to the main showroom. Each wagon load was guarded by a pair of waterfront toughs armed with cudgels and revolvers, and other rough men stood sentry around the warehouse at night. The auction was scheduled to begin at ten o'clock Monday morning, July 2. By eight o'clock the street was full, and by nine Hobart-Hampden had to insert armed men between the store and the crowd, lest some person of quality be accidentally shoved through the plate-glass window, behind which now sparkled samples of the cargo recently smuggled past the collective nose of the U.S. Navy. Such scenes had become common now; speculators from all over the South had descended on Wilmington as word of the blockade-runners' successes spread. An enterprising fellow might purchase a load of luxury goods at auction for 500 percent more than their prewar value, then resell them in Arkansas or Alabama—if he could manage to convey them such a distance—for 1,000 percent above that same point of economic reference. The city's population had grown by several thousand, and there was much loose comparison being made between the new "Merchant Princes" of the Cape Fear and the doges of Renaissance Venice. Those who already had sufficient goods for their own immediate use continued to purchase more whenever a cargo went up for auction, either as an investment, or simply because they were possessed by a fever of acquisition. Those who already had the most wanted more. Those of middling means wanted whatever they could afford, whether the goods in question were of immediate use to them or not. Those of limited means still came flocking to the weekly runners' auctions, whether held in a store or in the covered market or simply out on the docks, hoping to parlay a relationship or a familial tie into a serendipitous acquisition, or merely to savor the heady excitement and pick up a few odds and ends after the affluent had hauled away their costlier purchases.

Since Jacob Landau was uncomfortable in the role of huckster, and understandably wished to put a protective layer between his cut of the proceeds and the stereotype of the grasping Jew, he engaged a veteran auctioneer to handle the actual bidding, a man who knew, as *Journal* editor James Fulton tellingly observed, "how to bring the rubes into the tent." All the investors stayed discreetly in the background, adopting the guise of disinterested spectators. They were joined on this occasion by Mary Harper, who had come down from Pine Haven the night before, and who, to judge from her radiant complexion and sparkling eyes, had enjoyed a highly satisfactory reunion the previous night with her swashbuckling husband.

When the doors were opened at ten, Jacob's store filled quickly to capacity. The auctioneer cleverly allowed a few moments of suspense, so that the first wave of bidders might observe the full panoply of goods laid out for inspection and vent some of their emotions with suitable exclamations, gasps, and squeals of delight. Once this overture was concluded, the bidding began.

On this voyage, the *Banshee* had been stuffed to the gunwales with desirable goods, for the importers at Nassau had made heroic efforts to match supply and demand. Surveying the radiant display, some of the bidders averred that God must truly be on the side of the Rebellion if He could provide such munificence, conveniently forgetting that all of these items, and many more besides, could easily be purchased from any well-stocked store in New York or Philadelphia, at uninflated prices just pennies over what they had been before the war. However the bidders wished to view the auction, whatever their political or theological tenants, their mood was such that they would have bought gaily painted rocks if nothing better were available. The bidding, from opening gavel to hoarse termination four hours later, was frenzied. Coffee, oranges, bolts of silk, costume jewelry, gloves, scented candles, thread and needles, toys, brandy, potted meat, quinine packets, stationery, ladies' hats and parasols, chocolates and hard candies, tea, tinned biscuits, hard-rinded cheeses, buttons and geegaws . . . whatever the commodity was, it sold for triple or quadruple what the *Banshee*'s owners had paid for it in Nassau.

By three in the afternoon, the last reluctant customers had been shooed out of the store. Jacob locked the doors and drew curtains across the display windows so that the consortium might count their profits in decorous privacy. The *Banshee* had paid for its own renovations after the second voyage, and Matthew had been smart enough to make sure that all the hands, from Mister Bright on down, received not only a fair share of the take but a generous one. The crew had proven reliable, and he wanted to keep them together as a loyal team.

After the third voyage, even the ordinary seamen pocketed more money from that single trip than they could have earned in a year of peacetime service. As for the primary investors, the proceeds from this fourth voyage had put them securely over the line from "prosperous" into "rich."

To the surprise of his daughter, and the wry amusement of Hobart-Hampden and the Sloanes, Jacob Landau had started to enjoy the game for its own sake. To be sure, he still talked about using his money to build a synagogue, but now that he had amassed enough profit to build several of them, his instinct for pure commerce had reasserted itself. Among the multitude of newcomers to Wilmington were a sprinkling of Jews from other Southern cities, all of whom dutifully introduced themselves to Jacob. But he did not go out of his way to socialize with them or lend his ear to their schemes. Old prejudices were simmering again. Many of these "New Jews" had escaped conscription into the Rebel army by hiring poor gentile substitutes to serve in their stead, and their presence was tolerated rather than welcomed. After almost a year in the runner trade, however, Jacob Landau had become as zealous a Confederate patriot as any man in Wilmington. The Confederacy was now his country, his fatherland, his Second Israel. Thanks to its very existence, he had prospered beyond his dreams, and he had become so vocal in his zeal to defend the rebellious entity that he had won the grudging admiration of even so rabid a secessionist as James Fulton. When Jacob had donated several thousand dollars to the Soldiers' and Sailors' Benevolent Society, Fulton had sung his praises on the front page of the *Journal* and the ladies who administered that charity had thrown a well-attended party in his honor. Largo found this transformation understandable, but there were private moments when she wondered her if father was really as stable and focused as he seemed to be outwardly. He still prayed every night, holding his private colloquies with Jehovah, but now he began and ended this ritual with a mighty toot on the shofar, which gave his prayers a militant punctuation, as though he were Joshua stirring his men for battle with the Canaanites. Largo was not absolutely sure about it, but she understood that the ram's horn was reserved for the High Holy Days, and for Rosh Hashanah in particular. It might not exactly be heresy to blow the thing every night, but it did not seem entirely proper, either.

Something else bothered Largo, too. Gradually, over the course of the war's first year, Jacob had stopped addressing subvocal comments to the spirit of his dead wife. His preoccupation with the Confederate cause, and the wealth he was accumulating by virtue of the Confederacy's very existence, seemed to have drawn him more deeply into the hard-edged here and now. Rachel's memory, and the fantasy of her spiritual presence, seemed to have receded, or at least assumed a lesser priority. Largo now lived with her father in a state of fluctuating ambiguity. He was the same dear man, yet he was different. The fact that he no longer rolled his eyes Heavenward and spoke intimately to a dead woman could surely be interpreted as a sign of robust mental health; but Largo worried that it was also a sign of a more callous heart. She loved him as always, and worried about him, but there were times when she felt a bit stifled by him. He was so intensely preoccupied—with his business ventures, his dedication to Rachel's memory, and with his newfound zeal for the Confederate cause—that his presence soaked up too much air from the rooms through which he passed.

On the afternoon following the auction, Jacob was practically ebullient. After toting up the sales and estimating the profits, which verged on astronomical, he impulsively invited everyone to dinner at one of the city's finest hotels. In the midst of their celebration, a messenger arrived bearing an invitation addressed to all the occupants at their table. A great party was to be held on the following night, July 3, to celebrate the return of General Chase Whiting, newly reappointed as commander of the Cape Fear District.

When Robert E. Lee requested a private meeting with Chase Whiting, several days after Joe Johnston had fallen gravely wounded at the Battle of Seven Pines, he did not exactly *sack* Whiting from his field command with the Army of Northern Virginia. Instead, he served Whiting a splendid dinner, plied him with good wine—although Whiting could not help but notice that whiskey was not on the table—and slowly directed their conversation to the subject of Wilmington and its ever-growing importance to the Confederate cause. With Charleston virtually sealed off, Norfolk in ashes, and New Orleans gone since the end of April, Wilmington and its blockade-runners had become the most vital source of supply on both the Atlantic and Gulf coasts. Lee's army could not stay in the field if Wilmington fell, too. A great engineer was needed to coordinate and strengthen the Cape Fear defenses, and Lee knew there was no finer engineer in the South—with the possible but unspoken exception of himself—than Chase Whiting. By all reports,

Lee continued in his most soothing, bourbon-mellow Virginia accent, Whiting had made an excellent start on the necessary works, and during Whiting's term of service in Virginia a dreary succession of second-rate commanders had come and gone in the Cape Fear District, throwing up a battery here and there, but doing little to weave a coherent master plan. Whiting knew the region, and its citizens knew and trusted him. And finally, over postprandial brandies, Lee stated that "it was the president's wish" that Whiting return to the Cape Fear and transform it into an impregnable bastion. Lee gave his word that Whiting's requests for cannons and other resources would be given "a high priority."

So there it was. Whiting bade farewell to his men, now encamped near Mechanicsville and recuperating from their exertions during the Peninsula battles, and packed his bags. Whiting planned to slip in and out of Wilmington by night, reoccupy his former headquarters at Smithville, and avoid the humiliation of public discourse until he was emotionally reconciled to what he regarded as a new state of exile. Such a private, clandestine journey was not his lot, however, for the word of his reappointment had already reached Wilmington and when his train pulled in, there was a large and enthusiastic crowd, led as usual by Editor Fulton, and the warmth of their welcome proved to be a balm to Whiting's bruised self-esteem rather than the embarrassment he had dreaded. On reflection, he was relieved to be far away from the intrigues of Richmond, back among people he knew and cared for, in a land whose wide-horizoned beauty had always stirred him, and posted to a command that was virtually autonomous. When he learned that a full-scale party was being thrown in honor of his return, he actually started looking forward to it. *At least I can drink a glass of good whiskey among these people and not be blamed for the collapse of the Confederacy as a result of it.* And his wife, Katherine, who was a native of Smithville, and who had been widely regarded as one of the prettiest belles in the Cape Fear region when she had married him in 1857, was overjoyed to be reunited with her husband. By the night of the party, Whiting had managed to convince himself that the occasion marked a new beginning rather than a banishment from the bull's-eye of things in Virginia. Virginia could go hang and be damned—Marse Robert's whole army would collapse in a matter of months if Wilmington were captured.

Although the day had been typically hot, twilight conjured a breeze strong enough to push across the dunes, on toward the river. Through a slow lavender twilight, the Whitings steamed north to the city on the evening ferry from Smithville, which docked at the base of Market Street, and from there were conveyed to their destination aboard a relatively clean phaeton provided by the mayor.

Wilmington was sprinkled with regal homes, but by local custom all save one were referred to simply as the Savage House or the McGowan House; only one dwelling had earned the title of "mansion"—the enormous and architecturally eccentric home of Dr. John Dillard Bellamy, on the corner of Market and North Fifth Street. Bellamy may have hung out his shingle as a physician, many years earlier, but his abiding expertise was in the field of land speculation and he had become one of the city's wealthiest men. He, too, had seen the potential profits to be made from running the blockade and he was a known investor in at least three successful ships. At the start of the new year, he had sent his large family to the safety of one of his upriver farms for the war's duration, and he now dwelt in regal solitude, attended by a large retinue of servants who were housed in a commodious brick structure whose solidity and comforts made a mockery of the term "slaves' quarters." The Bellamy Mansion, with its substantial air of unruffled majesty, had become a semiofficial Confederate headquarters. It was here that visiting generals, dignitaries, and variously ranked foreign emissaries preferred to take lodgings when they were in town—for the mansion's serenity, grace, and opulence made even the best of the city's hotel suites seem common and low-rent by comparison. To reflect this proud new status, a great Confederate flag now hung from the right-hand balcony on the second floor, and an equally large state flag draped from the matching balcony on the left. Atop the vast, pedimented, gabled roof loomed a cupola as big as a small house. The view from that spot was reported to be unexcelled, so there was a permanent observation post in the cupola, manned by shifts of lookouts who probed the far horizons by means of a ponderous brass Nelsonian telescope mounted on a mahogany tripod.

Bellamy's yard was so large, a regiment of men could have camped in it if they could find room to pitch their tents among the manicured gardens and huge magnolia trees. The mansion sat on a high raised basement outlined with thick brick pedestals that seemed deeply rooted in the earth. Their vertical lines were carried soaring upward by colossal, free-standing Corinthian columns. A broad covered porch defined the second of the structure's three full stories, creating a handsome promenade around three of its four coequal sides. A magnificent wrought-iron fence, decorated with the most elaborate Italianate patterns and whorls, surrounded the entire property. One approached the front door by climbing a staircase wide enough to accommodate a locomotive, and entered beneath a richly carved segmented entablature made resonant by tall flanking Palladian windows. By the time the Whitings arrived, the party in their honor was well under way. Groups of guests, balancing punch cups and small plates of hors d'oeuvres, strolled the porch, the women in their hoop skirts looking like floating gardenias. Word of the Whitings' arrival spread quickly as they were spotted climbing the steps, and by the time they reached the landing, their path to the door was lined on both sides with well-wishers. They strode through a corridor lined with applause, salutes, bows, and glasses raised in honor. Whiting paused to acknowledge the demonstration. He was back in the sultry embrace of the society he had chosen above all others. These people looked upon him as their guardian, their shield and buckler. And his pride, which had been so roughly bruised by the recent events in Virginia, came fully back to life. As he escorted Katherine down the aisle formed by rows of celebrants, he felt his stride grow more assured, his shoulders broaden, his body charged with energy. At that moment, he would have died to protect the people of Wilmington.

Dr. Bellamy's mansion was designed to accommodate balls and dinner parties on the biggest scale. By opening or closing some unobtrusive partitions, the servants could create a wide bright arena for dancing, a banquet hall big enough to seat fifty diners, or any number of smaller, more intimate spaces where business might be conducted, cigars smoked, and courtships advanced. Strategically placed tables displayed a fund of delicacies, from broiled shrimp and wafer-thin slices of ham, to sweetbreads and bowls of fruit. Waiters in brocaded livery passed gracefully through each room and hall and along each side of the great porch, bearing goblets of champagne and wine. In the library, framed by the deep civilized glow of gaslight on leather bindings, two Negro bartenders dispensed juleps, whiskey sours, and tumblers of unadulterated liquor; for the ladies and the adolescents, there were bowls of punch and jugs of sweetened tea in the ballroom and on both sides of the grand central hallway. After paying their respects to Dr. Bellamy, the Whitings followed separate paths, for Chase had worked up a go-to-meeting thirst and his wife understood that, even now, General Whiting was on duty and must be available to any man soliciting his company and conversation.

For Chase Whiting, this was a homecoming, and on every hand

he encountered old friends and some nodding acquaintances who, by virtue of their deeds or eccentricities, had become living icons of Wilmington's society. In the main hall, he saw and greeted: Old Silas Martin, retired sea captain (salty as a slab of driftwood, with bristling snow-white brows and rheumy blue eyes), ear trumpet jammed to his head, rotating in place like some curious nautical instrument, who thirty years ago had taken his only daughter on a cruise to Italy, where she died, and then preserved her body in a barrel of rum until he could reach Wilmington and give her a proper Christian burial in Oakdale Cemetery . . . and Captain Henry Savage, newly appointed collector of customs, who was explaining to several interested people the various techniques he used to smoke out stowaways . . . and the Reverend Robert Dane, pastor of Saint James Episcopal, delicately sipping tea and nipping at canapés with precise little bites of his prominent slanted yellowish teeth, solemnly talking shop with Landau, the prominent Hebrew (*"But if your faith decrees that you can worship Jehovah in any place and under any circumstances, why not attend some of our services in lieu of a proper Jewish tabernacle?"*—*"Because I believe that God wants me to store up my prayers until I can build him a proper House, so that my faith might gather spiritual interest, as it were, and emerge both larger and more powerful when it is finally unfurled in the proper setting . . . "*) . . . and behind the merchant, his raven-haired, dusky-eyed daughter, as tall as the father was short, as exotic as he was ordinary, whose gaze kept darting boldly in the direction of a roguishly handsome young gentleman who spoke with a cultured British accent . . . and Dr. Baccus Satchwell, who had probably delivered more than half of the younger guests . . . and James Fulton, the irascible, pontificating editor of the *Wilmington Journal* . . . and the portly Mister Beery, whose shipyard was a veritable hive of wartime activity.

When Whiting paused to speak with those two men, at least long enough to finish his drink, Fulton importuned him with a conspiratorial tug on the sleeve, saying: "Ah, General, I hope you will attend my announcement later in the evening. It concerns a matter of vital interest to the defense of our city."

"Why, yes, of course, Mister Fulton. Can you give me a hint as to what that might be?"

Fulton winked, obviously enjoying himself. "Why spoil the effect, sir? I want to unleash my subject like a Jovian thunderbolt, striking everyone simultaneously!" . . . so Whiting merely nodded (thinking: *What a puffed-up little humbug he can be!*), then walked away and into the library, in search of a refill. As he entered that leather-bound oasis of masculine asceticism, he spied one of the men he had been searching for most diligently.

Captain William Lamb—the dashing Young Soldier of the Lord, whom Whiting had last seen on the eve of his departure for Virginia, and to whom Whiting had entrusted the fortification of New Inlet—was standing with three other officers, two of them wearing the dress uniform of the Confederate navy and the other, an army captain with a reddish beard, boyish freckles, and penetrating blue eyes. These gentlemen tendered warm greetings to Whiting when he joined them, followed by the necessary introductions. The tallest man, a dour-looking fellow with a brittle, almost academic air about him, was Flag Officer (né Captain) William Branch, and the other sailor was Captain (né Commander) Samuel Parker, and the blue-eyed army man was Captain Frederick Reilly. Whiting learned Reilly's story first, since that was the topic of discussion when he approached the group: Reilly had endured the bombardment of Fort Macon, made a valiant escape before the garrison's surrender, and spent the intervening weeks making his way to Wilmington, where he sought out Flag Officer Branch, now the senior Confederate navy officer in the Cape Fear District, in order to present to him a sheaf of drawings for the construction of a simple, practical, relatively inexpensive, but potentially quite formidable armored ram, designed from the keel up to fit the circumstances of North Carolina's rivers and sounds. Whiting filed away this information for later examination and, as soon as it was polite for him to do so, asked Captain Lamb about his progress on the works at New Inlet.

But Lamb could tell him only rumors and fragments. Instead of being promoted and assigned to the New Inlet works, as Whiting had desired and recommended to Richmond, Lamb was passed over no less than four times and remained in his former place, as commander of Fort Anderson on the west bank of the river, halfway between Wilmington and Smithville. In April, Lamb's men had elected him to command the Thirty-sixth North Carolina, as their regiment was now designated, so the young Virginian was now a colonel. Otherwise, for both Lamb and his men, the period from Christmas until the end of June had been a time of unrelieved tedium. During that same time, several other commanding officers had come and gone from New Inlet, and while each of them was doubtless worthy and well-intentioned, not one of them had remained in place long enough to become intimate with the landscape, much less devise a master plan for its defense.

As far as Lamb knew, some more sand had been thrown up and a handful of additional cannons had been shipped in, but whatever work had been done, it was haphazard and sporadic in nature. The last Richmond appointee had stayed only three weeks before being ordered somewhere else; at the moment, there simply was no senior officer in charge of Confederate Point.

"That situation will change as of tomorrow morning, Colonel Lamb. I am in command now, and I will write the order first thing. You go over to Confederate Point in the morning and take command of whatever troops are already there. I'll send the rest of your regiment across as soon as I can transfer some of those new conscript companies into a garrison for Fort Anderson. Be at my headquarters in Smithville at ten o'clock, and we shall cut the Gordian knot with the stroke of a single decree. Now then, tell me about your wife and darling children."

Daisy Lamb was with her family in Rhode Island, eight months along and able to communicate only through coded letters that were routed through Nassau and thence, via blockade-runners, to her beloved husband, whose enforced idleness had given him plenty of time and opportunity to fret about her and his three children. Poor man, thought Whiting; even if the birth went well, it would be no easy task to get Daisy Lamb and her offspring back through enemy lines, for the regulations concerning civilian travel had become much stricter since Daisy went north, and the blockade's noose much tighter. Whiting had always thought of the Lambs' marriage as a strong and vibrant union of kindred souls, and Daisy Lamb as the sort of wife who would endure any hardship to be close to her mate. He that knew the woman had grit, and that she loved the South as much as anyone born to it. Whatever the difficulties ahead, Daisy Lamb was equal to their demands—of that, Whiting was certain.

Now the five officers turned their conversation toward professional matters; the talk became livelier and more lubricated, for the bar was almost within arm's reach and they had only to extend an empty glass to find it magically refilled again by an affable Negro. Branch and Parker, Whiting learned, had fought a valiant but hopeless battle against Burnside's gunboats, and both men had watched their doughty little fleet annihilated one day later at the Battle of Elizabeth City. As the two sailors answered Whiting's questions, the general began to sense that the debacle on Albemarle Sound had affected them in very different ways.

Branch seemed by far the more bitter about the experience, and when he spoke of the Mosquito Fleet, his body became so stiff that he seemed less *in uniform* than stuffed into a scabbard. Perhaps he felt uneasy because his promotion had come hard upon the heels of an absolute defeat, although from what Whiting had heard, Branch had led his little ships with much courage and determination. Perhaps it was the hollowness of his new command—except for a handful of tugs and coastal steamers being modified at Beery's Shipyard so they could carry a cannon or two without capsizing, there *was* no "Confederate navy" in these waters. If the big ship recently laid down at Beery's was indeed an ironclad, it was at present nothing more than a rough wooden keel. Most likely, Whiting reasoned, Branch was an officer haunted by defeat, unlikely ever to find a chance to avenge that defeat, and frozen in bureaucratic Purgatory as a mere figurehead, burdened by immense responsibilities but lacking every resource needed to take action; a locomotive with a full head of steam condemned to spin its wheels in place because the track behind it was broken and the track in front was slick with grease. Branch might be the biggest frog in the puddle, but the puddle was mighty shallow.

Captain Sam Parker, by contrast, seemed optimistic as well as bellicose. It was he, rather than Branch, who voiced the greatest enthusiasm about Reilly's ironclad design, averring that all Wilmington needed, in order to become impregnable, was a flotilla of smaller *Merrimacs* acting in concert with powerful shore batteries. Parker spoke as if those vessels could be conjured from thin air in a matter of months. The resources could be found, he said; iron plate could be imported from Great Britain, along with enough puissant Armstrong guns to give each ram the strongest possible armament; eager crews could be found; the necessary funds could be obtained by local subscription if Richmond could not or would not provide the money. "The Mosquito Fleet can be reborn," he declared, "and the men who gave their lives at Elizabeth City will be avenged many times over!"

Whiting promised he would cooperate fully with the navy in every possible way, but even as he spoke the words he wished that Parker, rather than the taciturn Branch, had been placed in overall command. For all their misfortunes with the Mosquito Fleet, neither of these good men had any real idea of how chronic and pervasive was the Confederacy's shortage of resources, how slow and inefficient was Richmond's administration. Passion, drive, and energy would be needed—the very qualities Parker exhibited abundantly—rather than the caution, pessimism, and gloom that enshrouded Flag Officer Branch.

Just then, an equerry approached and requested the officers' attendance in the ballroom, where an important announcement was about to be made. Lamb shot an inquiring look at Whiting, who could only reply with a shrug. "Any idea what this is about?" Whiting asked Branch.

"Ram fever," Branch intoned lugubriously. "Mister Fulton has contracted a severe case of it."

Guests filed into the ballroom until it was full. Dr. Bellamy rapped spoon on glass to get everyone's attention, then turned the floor over to James Fulton, who seemed somewhat flushed for drink and who hooked his thumbs under his suspenders like a door-to-door drummer about to make his pitch.

"Ladies and gentlemen, officers and runner captains! Last spring, the Confederate navy revolutionized the art of warfare when the *Merrimac* sallied into Hampton Roads and sank a splendid frigate in fifteen minutes. The Yankees at once grasped the importance of this lesson and have acted upon it with all the energy which their desire to gain the mastery of our harbors can inspire. And since that day, the keels of dozens of *Merrimacs* have been hewn in northern shipyards, and ten thousand anvils have rung with the shaping of armor plates designed to ward off our batteries. Now, it is a fact that ironclad vessels cannot be built in a day, and it is also a fact, however lamentable, that the South can never hope to match the enemy ship for ship.

"But we do not need to do that, my friends, for we have no intention of attacking New York or Baltimore. We wish only to defend ourselves and keep the vital supplies of war flowing freely from our docks to the far-flung battlefields. We need few ships, but in order for us to meet iron with iron, those ships must be so powerful that their very existence will act as a deterrent. If we can defend the waters of the Cape Fear with a small fleet of well-armed shallow draft ironclads, we can meet an invading force on equal terms, for in these waters there is room enough only for a squadron, not a whole armada. Therefore, I say to you: unless we mean to give up our city to the invader, we must build our own *Merrimacs*. And we must begin their construction with all possible dispatch. If we do not, then we have only ourselves to blame, months or years hence, when the Yankees launch their mailed fleets against us and we are unprepared.

"To further this vital project, myself and a number of other prominent citizens have launched a subscription drive for the construction of the first Cape Fear ironclad ram in Mister Beery's shipyard. The fund will be held in trust by the Bank of the Cape Fear, of which our esteemed host, Dr. Bellamy, is a director. Beginning with tomorrow's edition, the *Journal* will solicit contributions from the general populace. We will say to our readers: Give money if you have it. If you have no money, give iron. If you have no iron, give wood and tools and food for the construction crews. I have in my hand a bank draft from Dr. Bellamy for three thousand dollars, and a draft from my newspaper for another fifteen hundred. After the party, there will be an organizational meeting in the parlor, and I urge every man to join us. I most earnestly exhort, however, the captains, agents, and merchants who have profited so greatly from the blockade-runners' successes. You gentlemen now enjoy a prosperity that can end as quickly as it began, should the Yankees force a passage into the river, or capture the fortifications that guard the two inlets."

Fulton stepped back and Dr. Bellamy practically leaped forward, arms open as though embracing his guests. "Thank you for your attention, and thank you in advance for your patriotic generosity. The meeting will begin at eleven o'clock sharp, but until then, please enjoy yourselves without stint or hesitation."

Something about that announcement struck a chord of excitement in Jacob Landau and for the next half hour he moved eagerly through the crowd, visiting one group of men then another, fetching drinks, gesturing vigorously. Largo observed her father with a mixture of amusement and concern; she had no idea how well Jacob could hold his liquor in such a setting, for at home he rarely partook of anything other than his customary bedtime brandies. But tonight, his emotional identification with the cause seemed to have reached a fever pitch, and he was uncharacteristically loquacious, transparently eager for signs of the total acceptance that had always been withheld, however subtly and decorously—by Wilmington's social elite. In between bursts of conversation, he checked in with his daughter, as though fulfilling some needful obligation, but he did not tarry, for Largo was always well attended by young women who were drawn to her aura of independence and young men who were compelled to pay court to her exotic beauty even if that same invisible envelope of reticence stopped them short of outright flirtation. Perhaps Jacob was reassured by the proximity of Hobart-Hampden, who always seemed to be protectively aware of Largo's location and circumstances, even if he were on the far side of the room. Every Wilmingtonian of consequence knew that the Englishman was part of the consortium that owned the *Banshee,* and that he had made another new fortune on top of the mysterious fortune he already had before the war broke out. Whenever the Landaus and the Sloanes were seen together, the Englishman was not far away. This alignment was now a permanent constellation in the skies of wartime commerce, and Hobart-Hampden's role was interpreted as that of a concerned, protective investor. His behavior, as always, was impeccable and slightly aloof; if the gossips had formerly speculated on the entertaining possibility that the dashing Englishman might actually be sparking with the Jewess, they had long since turned their attention elsewhere. It was known that Hobart-Hampden had formally leased the big Yellow House on upper Market Street and turned it into an unofficial British consulate, renting out its rooms and suites to the other equally colorful English adventurers who had descended on the city since the runner trade had become so lucrative. Every night, at that address, there were parties and games of chance, and people had grown used to the sight of women, escorted or not, coming and going. Pious citizens professed indignation that such a "sink of iniquity" had appeared in a proper neighborhood, far removed from the gin shops and whorehouses of Paddy's Hollow; but the prevailing sentiment among Wilmington's gentlemen was one of tolerance, envy, and titillation. Let the Britishers have their fun, as long as it did not spill out into the streets, for in their wake came a worldly prosperity and sophistication that seemed both a catalyst and a tonic. If the formidable Hobart-Hampden indulged himself in venery—and what red-blooded swashbuckler did not?—then he did not have to leave his residence to find it. Having thus entertained and then ruled out the idea that his interest in Largo Landau was predatory or lecherous, most observers simply accepted the appearance of things: Hobart-Hampden merely kept an eye on Largo so that her father would not be distracted from business, would not have to hover protectively, would not have to play the role of her absent mother on top of all of his other responsibilities.

As the eleventh hour approached, the guests began a complicated shuffle. Husbands and brothers and sweethearts escorted their ladies home or to some safe conveyance, then regrouped for the "Ironclad Meeting." Jacob wanted to stay; indeed, he was flushed with excitement at the thought. Largo should not wait up for him, he insisted, for this gathering would surely continue into the wee hours. Would it be an imposition on Hobart-Hampden if he escorted her safely home?

"Why, not at all, sir," replied Hobart-Hampden, bowing slightly. "I would be honored."

Few people paid much attention when Largo and Hobart-Hampden left the Bellamy Mansion together. An obsequious young man in sailor's garb immediately ran off and came back moments later at the reins of a two-seater runabout decorated on both sides with the British lion. The driver hopped down, saluted, handed the reins to Hobart-Hampden, then scurried off into the darkness, clutching his gratuity. Once they had negotiated the crowd of pedestrians and conveyances, they drove for several blocks in the direction of the Landaus' house. As soon as Hobart-Hampden felt certain no one was watching them, he turned the horses into a side street, then doubled back up Grace Street in the general direction of the Yellow House.

Let him kiss me with the kisses of his mouth—
For thy love is better than wine.
Thine ointments have a goodly fragrance;
Thy name is an ointment poured forth;
Therefore do the maidens love thee;
The king hath brought me into his chambers;
We will be glad and rejoice in thee,
We will find thy love more fragrant than wine!

It was not often possible for them to be together here, in the Yellow House where Hobart-Hampden was both landlord and minister-without-portfolio; before tonight, only four times since Largo had first given herself to him in early spring. But because of all the rowdy activity inside the place, Hobart-Hampden had secured a private entrance at the rear of the house, carefully chosen so that comings and goings, be they amorous or diplomatic, might not be observed from any neighbor's window. His suite of rooms was furnished in a style both masculine and comfortable: in the parlor, a pair of upholstered wingback chairs with Ottoman footstools, a writing desk (always piled with rolled-up charts and correspondence files tied with ribbons), a rosewood dining table where he might entertain, conspire, or enjoy a secluded private dinner, a locked breakfront bookcase (Scott, Shakespeare, Dickens, Byron, and an interesting collection of Gothic romances, including two scandalous novels by Mister Lewis,

The Monk and *The Bravo of Venice*); and in the bedroom, a four-poster big enough for three large adults, shrouded in fine damask mosquito netting and crowned with a goosedown mattress fine-tuned to a perfect balance between healthful firmness and sensuous yield. No cold floors here, in wintertime, thanks to a Norwegian tile stove and a thick-piled Turkoman carpet. In a spacious alcove behind a lacquered Chinoise screen stood a comfortable necessary that could be flushed with water on demand (the first such contrivance Largo had ever seen), and a large porcelain bathtub on lion's-claw legs, which could be filled with hot water piped from a storage tank warmed by the kitchen stove. These sanitary fixtures, so progressive and commodious, were not the only innovations H-H had installed. Behind the obligatory portrait of Queen Victoria was a large wall safe in which he kept . . . what? Treasure maps? Cypher books? A horde of golden guineas? Largo could only guess; she had seen him open and close the vault, but he had never invited her to examine its contents. And both rooms were ventilated by cleverly placed wall and ceiling louvers that could be opened wide to admit the full nocturnal breeze, or closed to preserve the heat in winter. There were few windows and these were always tightly shuttered, a fact that Largo attributed to her lover's need for absolute security, but the rooms never felt stuffy or cavelike.

They scurried inside on this night, her fifth visit to his sanctum sanctorum, and after their first long embrace, Largo observed with some surprise that in the interval since her last rendezvous, the walls had been lined entirely with panels of cork. While Hobart-Hampden poured sherry into a pair of crystal goblets engraved with the crest of the royal yacht ("When my tour of duty on that ship was finished, Her Majesty gave me a silver watch, in gratitude, I suppose, for my discretion, but I wanted something more suitable as a keepsake, so I helped myself to a few nice things. She'll never miss them."), Largo ran her hands over the cork walls and poked at them with a finger. Slowly, a flush of embarrassment colored her cheeks. She glanced over her shoulder, smiling with mischief.

"Really, Augustus, am I *that* loud?"

For an instant he glanced at her blankly, then he caught her meaning and laughed in appreciation.

"No, my dear, you are not. At least, not as a rule. But some of the other lodgers can be, especially when there is a party going on. I don't often seek extended periods of peace and quiet, but when I do, I want to be utterly undisturbed. Besides, if I cannot hear what goes on in the rest of the house, then no one can hear what goes on in here. And contrary to your lascivious grin, I am primarily speaking of *conversations,* not, um, other sorts of activity. Here, O daughter of Zion, let's drink a toast to the unbuilt ironclad which has given us this opportunity."

They touched glasses and the fine crystal chimed sweetly.

Behold thou art fair, my love; behold thou art *fair;*
Thine eyes are as doves.
Behold thou art fair, my beloved;
Also our couch is leafy.
The beams of our houses are cedars,
And our panels are cypresses.
I am a rose of Sharon,
A lily of the valleys.

"Be mindful of your father, Largo. I fear that, in his mind, that whole business about founding a Jewish church has become too closely wrapped inside the Confederate patriotism that now seizes him. He believes he has found a homeland, a cause, a means to enter fully into society, Aladdin's gold, and the Fountain of Youth, all rolled into one rare and surely temporary set of historical circumstances. The men who are on top of things today will welcome his enthusiasm, and his gold, and share their whiskey and cigars with him, but mark my words: if this war goes irrevocably against them, he will once again be the outsider, the grasping Jew, the scapegoat. Jacob will listen to you—and you must be 'the still small voice' that helps him stay on course. Do not, for example, let him pledge too generously for these chimerical warships. I do not think anyone in that room tonight, including Flag Officer Branch or the ingenious Captain Reilly, who really has come up with a first-rate design, has the slightest idea of how expensive and difficult this undertaking will be. And perhaps even more to the point, the very idea that a handful of vessels, no matter how powerful, can deter the whole United States Navy is simply ludicrous."

"I will speak to him, Augustus. He knows much about commerce, but nothing about warships. He only wants to *help.*"

She made a gesture of impatience, for she had not come here to discuss strategy. She drained her glass and held it out for more. Her gaze was steady and unequivocal.

"We only have two hours, Augustus. Pour me another drink and bring forth your magical pipe. Who knows when we will have another opportunity?"

He raised his eyebrows in appreciation of her forwardness. "I shall probably roast in Hell for turning you into a debauched woman." Handing her a full glass, he rose and strode to the locked bookcase. He returned to the sofa a moment later, bearing an ornate case from which he removed a small water pipe with two serpentine mouthpieces, a box of matches, and a small flat fragrant block of hashish wrapped in butcher's paper.

"Ah, yes," she murmured. "That would be just the thing."

To his credit, he had not forced the opiate upon her; she had only learned about his own occasional indulgence during a long postcoital conversation on her second and so far longest visit to his rooms—while Jacob was away in Raleigh on business. She had spent the whole night here on that occasion, and it had been a bacchanalia, a banquete, a scouring whirlwind. During the mellow interval between their first and second bouts of lovemaking, he had refreshed himself with a few puffs on the hubble-bubble, producing the apparatus without preamble and carefully watching her to gauge her reaction. Largo rather liked the earthy, slightly sweet aroma, and she was sophisticated enough to realize at once that it came from something other than tobacco. Was it opium? No, he replied. Opium inspired a dreamy lethargy, which was its most insidious and addictive trait, while hashish, smoked in moderation, served primarily to enhance the senses. It was a reliable adjunct to meditation, or to the contemplation of an artwork, or to really serious lovemaking. The danger of addiction was greatly exaggerated, he assured her, and its sinister reputation came mostly from the hysterical ravings of missionaries who either had no firsthand knowledge of its effects, or who had tried it and were aghast at the lascivious thoughts that were let out of the cage when the drug blew away their inhibitions. Hobart-Hampden had acquired a taste for it during a sensitive mission to Afghanistan.

Largo suppressed the desire to ask how many other women he had smoked it with. Rather to her surprise, she really did not care. Carefully, and with much coughing and sputtering until she got the hang of it, she shared a bowl with him, the two of them sucking on the mouthpieces while gazing at each other across the smoldering nugget. At first she felt nothing but dizziness, not unlike the head-spinning lurch she had experienced when she tried to smoke one of Jacob's cigars years ago. But when he put away the pipe and began caressing her again, this time slowly and gently, her flesh responded in new and altogether delightful ways. Time dilated around them, and she gave herself over to sensations that were as delicate as the quiver of a dreaming eyelid, until her whole body swooned like butter in a churn. Each kiss, as his mouth descended from her engorged nipples to her belly to the silkiness of her inner thighs, was a symphony of sensations. She drifted on the lawless currents of renegade pleasure, and when at length he opened her legs like a Bible and began softly kissing and tonguing her most intimate place, she was already trembling at the margins of Heaven. Even then, he took a long sweet time, allowing her to explore this new and seductive terrain of the senses, building a crescendo, then suddenly going from slow and soft to vigorous and insistent, and when she was spent, surprised and excited by the sounds that rose from her own throat, she arched her back and clawed at his shoulders and soared into a realm where suns exploded behind her eyes.

Now, when he brought out the pipe, she felt no hesitation about smoking it. So what if they only had two hours? How much could they do with each other in that time? That seemed to pose a stirring challenge, once they had inhaled an appropriate amount of this aphrodisiac. This interval would be a shared exploration. To signal as much, Largo began to sway and undulate, and to tantalize him by slowly peeling away her layers of clothing. Hobart-Hampden watched with obvious appreciation, like a conquistador about to open a chest of Aztec gold.

"I do this for the adventure of it," Largo had said on their first night of intimacy, by way of explaining why she had chosen him to be the instrument of her defloration—a process he had accomplished with sensitivity, skill, and surprising delicacy, so that the quick rip of pain was soothed and largely submerged by gratifying sensations of pleasure. "I cannot command a ship, I cannot serve a cannon, and I cannot charge the enemy at the head of gallant horsemen, although I believe my spirit is fully equal to any of those tasks. I have always been restless with the role I was expected to play. When the time was considered right, I would play host to a number of proper courtiers—Jewish, if Poppa could round up the right sort of fellow; gentile, I suppose, if the advantage to be gained were commensurate with the break in tradition. I was schooled to choose a man of property and status—whether he excited either my loins or my intellect was of no consequence. From the moment I acquiesced, every subsequent thing was laid out like granite milestones: I would become a dutiful and supportive helpmeet, make sure the house was clean and the food was served properly, and all the guests had a good time at my parties. And I would bear children at predictable intervals and make sure they learned good manners and studied their lessons and made good matches when their turn came. Honestly, Augustus, can you imagine a duller or more stifling fate?"

"As a man, I can only agree. But surely, my dear, that is a woman's lot in life, and most women seem content enough with it."

"Yes, they *seem* content, but what choice do they have? How many of them bring passion to their husband's bed instead of obligation?"

"Our friends, the Sloanes, seem genuinely fond of each other, in 'that' way, I mean."

"Indeed they do, now that the war has broken apart their old routine! Matthew has been transformed from a gentleman farmer into a dashing blockade-runner, so he is not the same man at all. His gaze is more confident, his stride more virile, and when he returns to Mary Harper's arms after a successful voyage, he brings with him the myrrh and frankincense of danger! The perfume of gunpowder and canvas and coal smoke! And because he is away so much, many of the daily responsibilities of running Pine Haven have fallen on her shoulders. Sometimes I think she is stimulated by these new challenges, but at other times I sense that they oppress her by their weight and sheer variety. This expanded role—Southern women of her class were not bred to be *masters* of a plantation as well as being Mistress of the Big House. I would not trade her 'adventure' for mine, but I watch the transformation with great fascination. She has great strength of character, I think, and depths that have never been sounded before. So, for better or worse, she, too, is marching toward new horizons.

"It is the war, Augustus. Whatever the ultimate outcome, this event has turned our assumptions topsy-turvy. All of a sudden, life is a banquet of *possibilities* for men and women alike, and nothing will ever be the same again. You, dear Augustus, you are my first great adventure."

Not on that night, nor on any other, had they professed "love" in the valentine-shaped phrases of popular fiction or greeting-card poetry. Such flowery sentiments, with all their smug implications of eternal wedded bliss, had no place in their mutual attraction. Largo gave herself to him like an explorer setting forth on a voyage whose destination was less important than the wonders and risks to be experienced along the way. She was as aroused by all that he embodied—his culture, his worldliness, his centaurlike zest for life itself—as she was by his assured, attentive lovemaking. She wanted to be woman enough to match him appetite for appetite, jest for jest, pleasure for pleasure.

Awake, O north wind;
And come, thou south;
Blow upon my garden,
That the spices thereof may flow out.
Let my beloved come into his garden,
And eat his precious fruits.

And on this night, while the officers and gentlemen of Wilmington laid at least the financial keel of their great warships, Largo and her lover went about their pleasures with such hammer-and-tongs enthusiasm that, by the end of their allotted two hours, they both had reason to be glad the walls were lined with cork.

18

Red Over Green—What Does It Mean

GENERAL BENJAMIN BUTLER—The reader will find under this morning's telegraphic columns brief but true autobiography of the "three-day's-wonder" whose name heads this article. That it is genuine, we know, because it is true to life. We have seen the author, and if Heaven ever expended more of labor and energy in framing one man over another, surely the finishing touch was given in writing VILLAIN on the brow of General Benjamin Butler.

We saw him in person at the Charleston Convention in May 1860, and of all that assemblage of sharpers, inside and outside of the Convention hall, there was no countenance that could approach his in all that makes men hate his race. He seemed to be a "man" only because he could talk. His smile was a ghastly scowl; his looks greedy and devouring; his eye like a serpent's but without its charm; his nose mounting the air sniffing for prey; his forehead low, skulking, and brutal. Instantly, we thought of the line: "A man may smile and smile, and be a villain still." But seeing that this creature could not form a human-looking smile, our loathing was turned to pity, to think he was so blasted by Nature in his making.

When we heard that he was appointed to the command of the Federal forces in the Gulf, we were convinced more than ever of the malignity and abandonment of Northern rule. Nothing but the deepest hatred for a chivalrous people, nothing but the most artful and ingenious cruelty; nothing but the most reckless desperation, could have suggested the appointment of such a <u>*thing*</u> *to bear rule, even for a brief day, over a generous and high-minded populace.*

—The Wilmington Journal, May 23 1862

Life is good, thought newly promoted brigadier general Rush Hawkins, as he settled into a cane-backed chair on the porch of what used to be Judge Murdock's home, on the outskirts of Shelborne's Point, and surveyed the pleasing breakfast that had been spread out for him by Calliope Keen, the head House Nigger, in antebellum parlance. Ol' Calliope had been sullen at first, for she had been genuinely fond of Judge Murdock, by all accounts a firm but fair master, but Hawkins had gradually gained her trust by treating her, and all the other Negroes on the place, with an attitude of noblesse oblige that the simple darkies interpreted as respect. He always took care to address Calliope as Mrs. Keen, and to make sure his commands took the form of polite requests. Hawkins assured Judge Murdock's slaves that they had been "liberated," even though their lives remained essentially the same as before. Now they waited on Hawkins hand and foot, with big toothy smiles and such eagerness to please that it stopped just short of fawning. On Hawkins's part, the whole thing had been a studied performance; personally, he had no philosophical truck with abolitionism and no great fondness for black people. When the war was over, he rather hoped they would all stay in the South.

Hawkins spread over his lap a fine damask napkin and dug hungrily into robust portions of eggs and grits, biscuits and honey, washing down the first vivifying mouthful with a gulp of excellent coffee, just recently shipped down to Shelborne's Point from Norfolk via the Dismal Swamp Canal. Lord, but these people knew how to make good biscuits! Neatly folded next to the table setting was a stack of fairly recent Confederate newspapers. Hawkins read them whenever he could, mainly to find out if anyone in power had taken any notice of the transformation of this sleepy little fishing village into a fortified Union port. So far, no one had. Even so, there was plenty of interesting news, some of which bore indirectly on Hawkins's situation. And much of it concerned Ben Butler, who had really stirred up a ruckus during the two months he had been military governor of New Orleans.

Butler had governed the newly conquered city—if "governed" was the word for it—as though it were his personal satrap. Pompous orations had been followed swiftly by outrageous acts. When a die-hard Rebel citizen publicly tore up an American flag, Butler had him arrested, tried for treason, and hanged. When a woman emptied her chamber pot on Admiral Farragut's head, Butler issued a proclamation stating that any woman who showed "disrespect" for the occupying authorities could be jailed as a common whore. This slander on Southern womanhood had generated choleric outrage throughout the Confederacy. Jefferson Davis branded Butler an outlaw and vowed to hang him without a trial if the general ever came under his hand—a prospect that was about as likely as a visit to Richmond by the emperor of China. "Beast Butler" was now the pop-eyed general's title in all the Southern papers. In the Union army, however, he had come to be known as Spoons Butler because, it was said, he had amassed whole warehouses full of silverware from the outraged gentry of Louisiana. Not surprisingly, Butler's popularity in the Northern states had never been higher—reports of his boorish tyranny were fed to the more vengeful Rebel-haters like gobbets of red meat. *That was the way to treat 'em, Uncle Ben!*

Sure enough, there Butler was again, on the front page of a week-old edition of the *Raleigh Standard*: a scabrous caricature depicted a waddling simian Ben Butler being led to the gallows by a mob identified as "Defenders of Our Womens' Honor," and beneath the cartoon was the ripest specimen Hawkins had yet seen of the seed-spitting poems people were scribbling about the Massachusetts general:

Brutal and vulgar, a coward and Knave;
Famed for no action, noble or brave;
Beastly by instinct, a drunkard and sot;
Ugly and venomous, on Mankind a blot;
Thief, liar, and scoundrel in highest degree;
Let Yankeedom boast of such heroes as thee;
Every woman and child shall ages to come,
Remember thee, monster, thou vilest of scum.

Hawkins chuckled; that covered just about everything, and if Uncle Ben had read it, he would have savored every rancorous word. Hell, he probably had it cut out and framed. Rush Hawkins had indeed come to have an avuncular fondness for his gross and unrepentant benefactor—especially now that Butler was settled in a distant fiefdom and was not able to make a sudden personal appearance in Shelborne's Point. Butler had certainly looked after his protégé. Not only had Hawkins received a general's star, but he now enjoyed the luxury of what seemed to be a totally autonomous command. He wasn't even sure *who* his immediate superior was. The orders that had come down to him in the same packet with his promotion had originated directly in the War Department and bore the signature of some major general of whom Hawkins had never heard, most likely a high-level bureaucrat who was also in Butler's pocket. Burnside was still nominally in command of all the Federal troops in North Carolina, but he had been ordered to take some of his best regiments and go back to join McClellan. Command would probably devolve to John G. Foster, but so far Hawkins had received no orders at all from either officer. Administratively, his little command seemed to be on its own.

Butler had not forgotten him, though. Two days after his promotion, Hawkins had turned over command of the Ninth New York to Junius Brown, whose first responsibility was to load the New Yorkers on transports and take them back to Fortress Monroe at Hampton Roads, presumably for service with McClellan. The same transports had brought four companies, some 550 men, from Butler's original command, the Sixth Massachusetts. They were raw recruits led by equally inexperienced officers, and the implication of their innocence was that Hawkins could shape them into whatever sort of force he needed to keep things running smoothly at Shelborne's Point. Officially, they were here to support a new force known as the First Carolina Unionist Volunteers, which at present comprised about eighty ruffians, deserters, and outliers on the dodge from Rebel conscription, an astonishing number of whom were apparently "cousins" of Cyrus Bone, who was now a brevet captain, with Jack Fairless as his second-in-command.

Things had shaken down nicely after that transfer of power. Butler had sent, or had caused to be sent, a number of supply vessels containing construction materials, carpenters, blacksmiths, two surgeons, a quartermaster who could seemingly conjure any needed supplies out of thin air simply by dispatching a request up the Dismal Swamp Canal to Norfolk, and seven hardworking whores from Annapolis, including the two ladies Hawkins had already met during his last conference with Butler. In a matter of weeks, the little town had been transformed. Docking facilities were enlarged, two spacious warehouses erected, and a tall fence thrown up in a semicircle around the whole complex, so that no one on the land side could observe what went on. The landward approaches to the town had been fortified strongly and bristled with field artillery. All of this work was accomplished by the fresh recruits, most of whom seemed quite happy to be here and not marching with McClellan. Hawkins had cemented their loyalty by making sure each boy got an occasional turn with one of the whores—a new experience for most of the lads and one that caused some of them spontaneously to cheer Hawkins when he appeared.

When there was sterner work to be done, or a lesson to be administered, Hawkins relied on Cyrus Bone and his Buffaloes, as they insisted on calling themselves. In late May, for instance, a small force of ragtag Rebel cavalry had been spotted in the swampy woods outside of town. Bone and his men had backtracked the horsemen's trail and discovered that they had been sheltered for several nights by a tobacco farmer named Jackson. Bone had interrogated the man roughly but effectively, by crushing his thumbs between two fence rails, and when he was satisfied that the patrol in question was too weak to be more than a scouting party, he had confiscated everything of value on the place, then burned it to the ground. Any remaining Rebel sympathizers in the surrounding countryside got the intended message. So had the draft dodgers, Unionists, and opportunistic riffraff throughout this part of North Carolina—hardly a day went without a couple of new Buffalo recruits showing up, on foot, on mules, or on dingy little pirogues they had poled and paddled up the Pamlico River from God knew where. Hawkins had given Bone full discretion to impose discipline on his outliers, but did require him to keep them encamped outside of town so they would not molest the cowed civilians.

Hawkins had, in short, carried out all of Butler's wishes, both spoken and implied. Shelborne's Point was a going concern. While Butler had not yet implemented his grand scheme of two-faced blockade-running, Hawkins knew the operation would begin soon. To judge from the accounts in Rebel newspapers, McClellan was beaten to pieces already, and reeling back down the Peninsula in disarray, "Marse Robert" nipping at his heels. Surprisingly, though, the Northern newspapers forwarded from Norfolk contained much the same news, although couched in less hyperbolic and apocalyptic verbiage. Hawkins had met McClellan once and thought him a vain, fussy, overstuffed little tyrant. It was unfortunate, of course, that nothing had changed as a result of his elephantine campaign except the population of the United States, but all things considered, Rush Hawkins was not unhappy with the prospect of a longer and more profitable war. Perhaps *that* was why Butler had not yet begun his clandestine operations—he had prudently waited to see if McClellan might actually capture Richmond before fully committing to such an expensive investment. And meantime, just in case the war did suddenly end, Butler was sucking New Orleans dry. Shrewd.

Hawkins's full-bellied reverie was interrupted by the sound of a rider galloping up the road from town. The man dismounted at the foot of the porch, saluted, and breathlessly announced that there was a gunboat anchored at the dock, and that its commander bore urgent dispatches for General Hawkins. Hawkins called out to the nearest Negro and ordered his own mount saddled and brought round. Twenty minutes later, he was shaking the hand of Lieutenant Jeremiah Stonecipher ("United States Naval Academy, Class of Sixty-Two!"), skipper of the USS *Trenton,* a trim side-wheeler mounting a pair of long-range 5.3-inch Parrott rifles, bow and stern, and a 10-inch mortar in an armored well amidships.

"A handsome gunboat, Lieutenant. Your first command?"

"Yes sir, General. The ship came off the ways the same week I graduated from the Academy. Such a coincidence is surely the mark of Destiny, don't you think?"

Hawkins suppressed a grin at the young officer's bubbling enthusiasm. In the peacetime navy, this lad would have remained an ensign until Hell froze over or every man senior to him retired or died.

"Are you stationed with the blockading squadron?"

Stonecipher toed the dock with one glossy boot and glanced nervously about.

"Not exactly, General. My orders are to attach my ship to your command, either to defend this base or to support any offensive actions you might wish to mount of an amphibious nature."

"For how long a time?"

"Until I receive orders from the navy to go elsewhere."

Hawkins looked at the *Trenton* with new interest. Those Parrotts could far outrange any field guns the Rebels might deploy against Shelborne's Point. Butler had, in effect, given Hawkins his own private naval squadron.

"And I must say, General Hawkins, that I am deeply honored, sir, to be made a part of such an important and sensitive operation."

How much does he know? The eager young lieutenant was too fresh, too pumped with patriotic zeal, to be already in cahoots with what was really happening here.

"I see. Well, I am glad you feel that way, son. Now, I believe you have dispatches for me."

Stonecipher blushed and whapped his forehead in a gesture of contrition.

"Yes, yes, of course. If you will accompany me to my cabin, sir, where we can discuss things in private."

His cabin was as newly minted and well scrubbed as its occupant. It was also swelteringly hot. Hawkins unbuttoned his jacket and fanned himself with a handy copy of *Frank Leslie's Illustrated Newspaper,* on the cover of which, appropriately, was a stirring woodcut depicting George McClellan reviewing his troops "on the outskirts of Richmond." Lieutenant Stonecipher did not loosen any buttons or fan himself, but briskly produced a leather pouch full of maps and documents. He spread some of these on the little table, arranging them just so, with gestures and appropriate throat clearings that had obviously been rehearsed. He certainly is *keen,* thought Hawkins, and so full of boyish excitement that they might well be planning a raid to capture Jeff Davis himself. All the same, Hawkins was impressed by the young man's succinct presentation.

"Here, sir, is the port of Wilmington. On the night of June the twentieth, when the moon will be at quarter and will not rise until after midnight, a ship named the *Columbine,* a single-screw freighter displacing three hundred tons, and stuffed with prime cotton, will make a dash out of Old Inlet, then assume a heading east-by-north-east, a course which will bring it to the blockade line in a place that is patrolled by a frigate whose engine will have suffered a convenient mechanical breakdown, so that it cannot pursue the *Columbine* even if the lookouts see her coming. Once the runner is beyond the outer line of blockaders—approximately *here*—she will come about north-east and steam parallel to the Outer Banks until she reaches a point—*here*—opposite Ocracoke Inlet, at about one A.M. on the morning of the twenty-first. As you know, most of our blockading ships are concentrated in two rings around Wilmington, so there will be only one ship patrolling off that portion of the coast, the USS *Cambridge,* whose captain is privy to the operational details. The *Columbine* will display the proper signal lights, red over green, and the *Cambridge* will make a display of giving chase, but without success. Once through the inlet, the *Columbine* will scoot across Pamlico Sound and make straight for Shelborne's Point.

"When she ties up in your secluded area, we will quickly transform her appearance by building a false deckhouse and a second, dummy, smokestack. We'll paint over her misty gray camouflage with the bold, honest colors of a New England merchantman, and rename her, quite fittingly I think, the *Chameleon,* out of Plymouth, Massachusetts, and rig her out with recognition flags suitable for her new role. Do you think we can accomplish all that in twenty-four hours, General?"

"Yes, Lieutenant. The paint and lumber and such have been stored here for some time, and my men will turn to with a will. Pray continue; this plan grows more fascinating by the moment."

"Hrumph. Well, if we can transform the ship in that time, it can sail boldly out through the same inlet—the *Cambridge* is due to head for Beaufort that day for refueling and supplies, and the ship assigned to relieve her won't arrive on station until the twenty-second. Meanwhile, the good ship *Chameleon* will steam to New York, where she will be but one ship among hundreds, and there unload her cotton. Now, sir, here is where the plan becomes truly ingenious! That cotton will go straight to the mills of New England, to be made into uniforms for the Union army, and the vessel will return here and be converted back into its original color and configuration. It will then return to Wilmington just as it left, and everyone will think it has just completed an ordinary run to Nassau. The military stores will be sold to Confederate agents, and the proceeds will pay for another shipment of prime cotton!"

"Wait, wait, please. I followed everything clearly except that business about 'military stores.' Will the ship in fact be carrying the same sort of things a *real* runner would bring back from Nassau?"

"Ah, General, that is the subtlest and most delightful part of the scheme! While the ship is docked in New York, it will indeed be loaded with military stores. But the rifles are defective—either they won't shoot at all or they will explode in the faces of the Rebel soldiers who fire them! Not *all* of them, of course, or someone would smell a rat. Just enough of them to sew the seeds of fear and doubt among the troops to whom they are issued! Likewise, the ship will carry kegs of gunpowder that *look* exactly like good English powder, but that has been adulterated with inert chemicals so that it will fizzle instead of fire! And the blankets, uniforms, and trousers have already been impregnated with lice! And as for the tinned beef, well, sir, any Rebel who partakes of it will be spending more time evacuating his bowels than fighting. The mills of New England get fine Southern cotton for their needs, and the damned Rebels get useless rifles, tainted food, worthless powder, and verminous blankets in return! I tell you, sir, whoever thought up this scheme deserves a medal!"

It was all Hawkins could do not to burst out laughing. Truly, Butler and his shadowy conspirators were inspired. Such elegant symmetry verged upon Art! To young Lieutenant Stonecipher, the plot was a grand and patriotic design. The mills of New England got the cotton they needed, and the Union forces got their uniforms, and the enemy received in exchange a lot of dangerous rubbish. Best of all, everyone who understood what was really going on stood to make an obscene amount of money from the scheme, both coming and going. The ill-gotten profits from the whole elaborate system would reach the right pockets in ways so devious that no one could ever untangle the paperwork. Hawkins's share of the take would probably arrive inside one of these same diplomatic pouches, and the naïve Lieutenant Stonecipher would proudly pass the cash into Hawkins's hands, believing all the while that he was delivering secret orders or other documents of great importance. Obviously, the voyage of the *Columbine/Chameleon* was a trial run, to see if the thing could be done according to plan. Hawkins knew something about the price of cotton, and he estimated that this one shipload might well net a profit of $70,000, discounting the incidental profit accruing to the men who sold the rifles, blankets, and potted meat. Butler had offered Hawkins a 6 percent cut on every shipload, and if this first venture went off successfully, there was no reason why Shelborne's Point might not process two or three "blockade-runners" per week. By God, it was brilliant! At the conclusion of Stonecipher's briefing, Hawkins could not refrain from jumping up and grasping the young man's hand.

"Excellent, sir! You have it all down! We shall do good work here, Lieutenant! Thank you for a clear and stimulating presentation. Now, I think this calls for a toast. Break out the whiskey, son."

Stonecipher blushed again. "I don't drink spirits, General, nor do I permit my crew to consume anything stronger than tea or coffee."

"No rum? A naval ship without grog?"

"Not aboard the *Trenton,* sir! My father founded the local Temperance League in East Orange, New Jersey."

Hawkins peered at the young officer with open disbelief. This would have to be changed, or the crew would surely mutiny. *They are technically under my command, after all.*

For the moment, however, he did not want to insult young Stonecipher's faith in sobriety. Instead, he clapped a fatherly arm around the lieutenant's shoulder and said, "Well, if I cannot interest you in a drink, how about a quick trip to the local *belles de jour* to get your ashes hauled?"

Stonecipher looked at Hawkins with an expression of utter incomprehension. He obviously had no idea what the general was talking about. Such innocence was astonishing, but it would not last long, not if Hawkins could help it. A teetotaler *and* a virgin? Things must have changed a great deal at the Naval Academy.

"I'll wager fifty cents on Lord Nelson," said Will Cushing. He had been studying the rats carefully during the preliminary races. Lord Nelson was a slow starter and had tied for last place in the first race, but the lean piebald rodent shed his sleepy-eyed look in the second race and nosed out Achilles for next-to-last place. In the next three races, Cushing's favorite became more and more aggressive, beating John Paul Jones, Beauregard, and Little Mac. Now only two contestants remained: Lord Nelson and Honest Abe, a plump, foul-tempered gray who looked as though he would just as soon devour the competition as he would the rock-hard lump of cheese that served as bait. Betting was brisk and generally favored Honest Abe, but Cushing saw a fierce gleam in Lord Nelson's beady eyes—indicative, he thought, of both the rodent's sporting instinct and his consuming hunger.

Rat-racing was a bit more complicated than one might think. If the winners of each heat actually got to devour the bait, they started losing their competitive edge, so one sailor always snatched the cheese out of the twelve-foot-long box just before the winner could sink his teeth into it. By the time only two rodents remained, they were both so energized by frustration that a splendid, and sometimes bloody, contest was all but certain. There was also a great deal of interest in the rat owners' various training regimens; some men rewarded their pets with extra food if they did well, while others preferred to keep their rodents on half-rations in between these events. Perhaps the most curious aspect of the whole diversion was the affection some men felt for their rats. After the rodent of choice had been captured, tamed, and somewhat trained, its owner usually strove to keep the beast clean and happy. It was not unusual to see men stroking their vermin like cats, feeding them by hand, or actually talking to them. One engineer had actually trained his rat to dance on its hind legs, which of course made the creature too valuable for racing.

Three officers and twenty-odd sailors standing or squatting beneath a sailcloth awning on the *Cambridge*'s fantail, enthusiastically cheering for a pack of rodents . . . Cushing knew that such a tableau would have been unthinkable in the prewar navy, but such was the measure of their collective boredom. Since leaving Hampton Roads on the day after the first fight between the *Monitor* and the *Merrimac,* Cushing's warship had manned the blockade line, endlessly patrolling between Cape Hatteras and Cape Lookout, too far north of Wilmington even to see a runner, much less give chase to one. There had not been even a day in port—colliers pulled alongside every ten days or so and all hands turned to for the hot, brutal, filthy job of transferring coal. So stupefying was the monotony, after the first two weeks, that the crew welcomed even that distraction. Cushing had studied the charts and tried to extrapolate from them some strategic reason why the *Cambridge* was scouring empty ocean instead of prowling off Wilmington, but orders were orders, so here they were.

Of course, the absence of a logical purpose to be served only made the boredom and heat and discomfort seem all the more onerous. Cushing had expected blockade duty to be mostly a matter of routine patrols, but he also expected—based on the accounts of men who had pulled blockade duty off Charleston, Galveston, or Wilmington—the occasional burst of excitement, the thrill of a sea chase, the contest of wits between the wily runner captains and the dogged watchdogs of the Union navy. But as day followed uneventful day, each day the same, the men of the *Cambridge* began to lose track of time. After a month, their numbness had reached a guttering state of low despair; they were in Purgatory, helpless between the anvil of the sea and the hammer of the summer sun, which turned everything into a vast coppery glare and made the decks too hot to touch. Since blockade ships were required to maintain steam pressure around the clock, the quarters nearest the boilers were all but uninhabitable. When there was pity to spare, it went out to the stokers and engineers who actually worked next to the boilers; men fainted in the heat and the mates who carried them on deck always looked as red and gleaming as lobsters in a boiling pot.

Each day began at five-thirty with the ghastly rasp of the boatswain's whistle, ripping away whatever feeble slumber the men had found amid the nearly airless reek of their sleeping quarters. Hammocks unlashed and stowed, the crew stumbled to roll call and spent the next two hours performing routine maintenance tasks that simply could not be performed in the full heat of day. They swept and scrubbed and holystoned the decks, spliced ropes, and polished the brass fittings until they glowed. After breakfast, at eight or thereabouts, the men could attend to their own toilettes, do their sewing, and wash their hair and beards. Almost everyone had a beard now, because anyone who wanted to shave had to use a bucket of tepid salt water. Even Cushing dreaded this ordeal—it reminded him of scraping barnacles from a careened hull—but he was too fair-skinned to grow a presentable beard, and after another officer made fun of his "peach fuzz," Cushing gritted his teeth and went back to shaving.

Each day, at unpredictable and therefore "realistic" intervals, a roll of drums summoned officers and men to drill. Dry gun drills were frequent—loading and aiming on command while an officer timed the motions with his watch—intermingled with musket drills, fire drills, damage control drills, and the occasional swipe at repelling boarders. Once a week, some empty flour barrels were lashed together and tossed overboard as a target for live-fire exercises conducted at various ranges. For many of the crew, including most of the officers, this was the high point of the week. After supper, the men were left alone to amuse themselves as best they could. There was music—a bosun's pipe, two fiddles, a banjo, and spoons—and songs and yarn-spinning; fishing to supplement the tedious diet of hardtack, beans, and salted pork; letters to write; books to read; endless card games to play; and the regulation quarter-ounce of rum to savor.

And, lately, rats to race. When the starting slat was yanked away, Lord Nelson dug his claws into the track, lowered his nose, and shot forward, instantly gaining half a length over the larger but slower Honest Abe. In the straightaway at midcourse, the gray surged ahead with a surprising burst of energy. Cushing's wager was not lost, however, for Lord Nelson, observing that his rival was getting closer to the coveted cheese, evened things up by leaping on the gray rat's hindquarters and biting him on the upper leg, drawing blood as well as angry squeals. Honest Abe paused to lick his wound, and the admiral shot down the track and hurled himself savagely on the prize. Cushing won $5 and change, a fishing pole, a reasonably clean deck of cards, and two full ounces of rum, a medium of exchange more valuable than coins. Everyone liked to bet a rum ration with Will Cushing, because everyone knew that he did not drink it; instead, he used the extra grog to reward the men who performed best at drill the next day.

On this day, however, the twenty-first of June, everyone was in good spirits. In two days, another gunboat would relieve the

Cambridge, which would then steam for Beaufort for revictualing, scraping, and engine overhaul. The new captain had also promised five days of shore leave, and was cheered lustily for his announcement.

The new skipper had arrived, quite unexpectedly, on the last collier, and the former captain had departed the same way. His name was Harrington Miles, a rather plump and doughy-looking man in his early thirties with a full-moon face and a short, brush-stiff ribbon of whiskers that started at the top of one ear, made a horseshoe curve around his Adam's apple, and continued to the top of the opposite ear. Otherwise, Captain Miles was utterly smooth-shaven. It was, Cushing thought, a singularly unflattering affectation, which only emphasized the jowls and the soft, moist lips. The captain evidently loved his morning shave, though, because he commanded the preparation of hot water and was well supplied with a fragrant store-bought shaving soap that produced creamy lather along with a faint scent of violets. Miles gave the impression of being somewhat the dandy, but he did and said all the things a captain was supposed to do and say and, to his credit, he tightened up the watch discipline during these last few days before relief, knowing full well that the men's thoughts were focused on the forthcoming shore leave and not on the task at hand. "It would be very unfortunate," the captain muttered one morning, "if we do spot a runner after all this time, and the rascal escapes because we are too slow to react." Cushing thought this remark demonstrated the proper spirit and so resolved to give Captain Miles his full loyalty.

At least Miles brought news that helped to put things in perspective. Rumors had reached the Navy Department, he informed the officers during their first conference, that the Rebels had begun work on two or more powerful ironclad rams, upstream on the Neuse River . . . or the Chowan . . . or the Roanoke . . . or the Tar . . . no one was sure. Since two of those three rivers lay within the *Cambridge*'s patrol zone, she might well be the first vessel to spot, or engage, one of those powerful craft—for that reason, the captain went on, she would be rearmed in Beaufort with a 9-inch Dahlgren and a 70-pounder Parrott rifle. Because this upgrade required her deck and timbers to be strengthened against the added weight, they might have to spend more than five days in dock. This was good news indeed, and the very thought of engaging a Rebel ironclad made Cushing's pulse beat faster.

That excitement proved to be short-lived; immediately after Miles took command, the dreary quotidian routine resumed. In Cushing's most recent letter to his mother, he described life in the blockade squadron as being

> *not significantly different from serving sentence in a penitentiary. You can get a fair idea of our "adventures" by climbing to the roof of our house on a blisteringly hot day, spend four hours staring at the horizon, then climb back down and drink some tepid water full of iron rust and eat some "pork" which has a very un-pork-like texture and color, then go back to the roof again and sit there in the heat until you are bone-tired, then stumble to bed in a stifling bunk whose portholes are sealed tight to prevent the showing of any light. "Adventure"? "Ordeal" is more like it. Of course, my mood will instantly change if we do encounter a Rebel runner.*

On the night of June 21, Will Cushing got his wish. He was standing watch from midnight to four o'clock, a stretch of time that most officers referred to as the dog's breakfast because it was not only tiresome in its own right, but also interfered with a man's natural cycle of sleep, leaving him cranky and off-kilter for the whole of the following day. Cushing, however, rather liked this time. It conferred at least a stretch of privacy, and in its silences a man could feel communion with the sea. He did some of his deepest, most reflective thinking during these midnight watches.

A quarter-moon lazed in the southeastern sky behind a gauzy scrim of haze, the sea was moderate, and the warm breeze carried a sharp and humid tang of salt. Cushing paced the bridge from starboard wing to port. Through the glass, he could just make out the dark streak of the barrier banks and the scribble of restless foam that marked Ocracoke Inlet. What if a Rebel ironclad came out through that channel? Would it even be seaworthy enough to venture out? What shape would it have? How puissant was its battery, how thick its armor, how determined its captain? Would it manifest itself as a great hulking monster or would it be stealthy and low in the water? Lost in such reverie, he stared at the mute and secretive shore until spots began to dance in his vision. When Captain Miles suddenly spoke from a place just behind his left shoulder, Cushing almost leaped into the air.

"Have you seen anything tonight, Mister Cushing?"

"No sir. I was just wishing that I *would* see something."

"Yes, yes, I understand. It is an unfortunate truth, but sometimes even the most vital job in the navy brings tedium with it. An officer is lucky if he experiences three hours' worth of fighting in his whole career."

"Oh, don't say so, Captain. I could not bear to think that!"

"Nevertheless, it is a fact of life in our service. We are sworn only to do our duty; nowhere is it written that such duty must be exciting or even interesting. We must simply perform the tasks set for us, whatever they may be."

Abruptly, Miles patted him on the shoulder and walked away, moving through the pilothouse and on to the starboard wing. The man seemed tense, for some reason, and he kept pulling out his watch every fifteen minutes or so. Maybe he has trouble sleeping, thought Cushing—the captain's quarters might be comfortable and relatively spacious, but they were no cooler, no better ventilated, than any other compartment belowdecks.

One o'clock came, and the seaward haze seemed to condense into something bordering on real fog. It was, Cushing reflected, a right proper night for a runner to try its luck, and almost certainly, down the coast at Wilmington, that was happening. To port, however, visibility was still good, so Cushing continued to peer at the coast, almost willing a Rebel ironclad to come forth and do battle. But after a time his eyes grew too tired from straining to make sense out of the darkness. Since Captain Miles remained steadfastly in place on the starboard bridge wing, one arm hooked languidly over the calcium signal light mounted there, Cushing decided to approach the man and ask if he had any more details about those new ironclads. He made his way across the bridge and stood at a polite distance behind the captain, figuring that a discreet cough would not startle the man so badly as a sudden tap upon the back; for, indeed, Captain Miles seemed as deep in reverie as Cushing had been earlier. Perhaps he, too, was dreaming about capturing a runner as it came silently out of the mist, low in the water, like an aquatic greyhound. And it would look, Cushing thought, very much like *that.*

"Captain! Look there!"

"I see it, Mister Cushing, I see it."

Gray as fog, lean and fast, her single smokestack playing out a black flat ribbon straight behind her, the runner sliced through the water at a good fourteen knots, making a beeline for Ocracoke Inlet.

Through the glass, Cushing could see her name—the *Columbine*—and he could also make out some kind of signal flashing quickly from the bridge. Red light, green light . . . a pause of fifteen seconds . . . red light, green light.

"Captain, shall I order full steam and battle stations?" *Red over green—what does it mean?*

Miles seemed not to hear him. Precious seconds were ticking away. If the *Cambridge* got up to speed now, she would cross the runner's bow close enough to fire at her with some hope of success. But even with standby pressure in the boilers, the gunboat could not accelerate instantaneously.

"Captain?"

"Yes, Mister Cushing. Ring on full speed and beat to quarters, if you please."

If I please? Cushing ran to the voice pipe and called the order down to the engine compartment. Then he jumped down the ladder that led to the officers' quarters and gave the alert. In a matter of seconds, it seemed, a galvanic current surged through the hull and men came boiling up to their battle stations, half-dressed and barefoot, and began clearing the guns for action. Cushing quivered with excitement—this was the moment that justified all the previous boredom and ennui; *this* was what they were here to do.

At that moment, he heard the chief engineer shouting up the voice pipe, his voice choking with anger and vexation.

"The goddamned boiler's blown a valve! I can't raise more than half-speed!"

Cushing tore the cap from his head and stamped on it. The *Cambridge* slowly gained momentum, but grudgingly and with much shuddering vibration; the paddle wheels did not turn smoothly, but jerked in spasms, flogging the water like the arms of a drowning man. Meanwhile, the runner plowed ahead, arrogantly, it seemed, as though her skipper somehow knew the gunboat was in trouble.

Once more the engineer shouted up the voice pipe: "We must reduce speed, sir, or we'll shake her to pieces! I've got live steam shooting out in half a dozen places!"

Captain Miles listened to this additional bad news with a curious expression on his affable face, nodding gravely but with surprising equanimity, as though something had been confirmed to his satisfaction.

"It looks like tonight is not our night after all . . . Mister Cushing. Reduce speed to minimum headway—we cannot risk permanent damage to our engine."

Almost choking on the words, Cushing relayed the order to the engine compartment. Then, on the wings of a sudden impulse, he ordered the helmsman to turn 15 degrees to port. Sluggishly, the ship responded.

"Mister Cushing, I gave no order to turn the ship."

"Aye, sir, but at this angle we might still get off a few shots at her with our forward gun!"

"That would be a waste of powder, sir; the range is too great and the target too swift."

"But sir, we ought to at least *make the gesture!*"

"A ship of war does not make 'gestures,' Mister Cushing—she speaks with full authority or she maintains a dignified silence. There will be other opportunities, I'm certain of it."

How could the man speak so calmly? Or watch so impassively while the prey escaped so easily? All about the ship, men were cursing and shaking their fists at the Rebel ship, which plowed on toward the inlet as undisturbed as a ferry boat. After the runner vanished into Pamlico Sound, Captain Miles heaved a great sigh and went below to his cabin. Cushing served the rest of his watch in a state of fury, and when he was relieved, he could not sleep but lay sweating in the darkness, grinding his teeth and knotting his fists. It was intolerable that they had endured so much boredom only to be thwarted at the one time their vigilance and drilling should have reaped their proper reward.

The next day, the men were surly and tight-lipped; everyone felt raw with frustration. Cushing finally drifted into sleep during the soporific heat of midday, only to be wakened an hour later by a timid knock on his door. Groggy and resentful at this intrusion, he staggered to his feet and threw open the door with a bark of distemper.

Before him, hat in hand, clutching some object wrapped in oily rags, stood the chief engineer, a small leathery man who had been tending steam engines for almost as many years as the navy had been using them.

"Permission to speak with you privately, sir?"

Observing the furtive way the man kept glancing over his shoulder, Cushing bade him enter. He unwrapped the object he was holding and passed it over for Cushing's inspection. After a moment of puzzlement, Cushing recognized the device—a small but critical part of the engine called a bleeder valve, essentially a pressure release that automatically vented steam when the engine was running too hot. Cushing walked over to the porthole and examined the object in full light. The valve was in its open position, as it was supposed to be when boiler pressure reached a dangerous level. Which was odd, come to think of it, because the *Cambridge* had not been able to come even to half-speed last night; there was no mechanical reason for the valve to be open. But when he prodded it with his forefinger, he could not make it close.

"It appears to be jammed."

"Aye, sir, and look closely at the underside."

Sure enough, the spring hinge was broken off; the valve could not close and would continue to vent steam as long as there was minimal pressure in the boiler. No wonder the *Cambridge* had not picked up speed. Such a small thing, really, but steam engines depended on a multiplicity of small things that could go bad. Sometimes these malfunctions were enough to make a seaman yearn for the days of sail.

"Can you fix it?"

"We have spare parts, sir; it should only take a couple of hours. What concerns me is how neat the break is. A part like this usually fails by stages—you can spot the worn or rusty places long before they reach this state."

Cushing knew that blockade duty was almost as hard on machinery as it was on men. The necessity of keeping steam up 'round the clock put undue stress on the boilers and on all their attendant iron-mongery. Steam leaks and bent rods became more frequent the longer the ship was on station, until they could no longer be corrected by temporary patches—at that stage, the vessel needed some time in port, so that the boilers could be cleaned and everything else either replaced or overhauled. Since they were scheduled to reach Beaufort in two days, Cushing at first saw the problem as just one more minor irritant. Then he took notice of the tight-lipped grimness of the engineer's expression and he understood: this was no ordinary breakdown.

"Are you suggesting that someone deliberately sabotaged this valve?"

"Well, sir, it *could* have happened naturally, but for one thing: I inspected the underside of the steam cylinder only three days ago—didn't want anything to go wrong on our voyage back to the mainland, you understand. And at that time, this piece of machinery was in perfect condition—not a spot of corrosion or any sign of wear."

Cushing picked up the thread: "And if someone wanted to cripple us temporarily, without doing anything drastic that might blow us up . . . "

"Aye, sir. Tampering with this part would do that, and because it's located under the cylinder, nobody would spot the problem unless they had a reason to crawl in there and look closely."

"Which is exactly what you did three days ago, when you saw no problem at all."

"Yes, sir. It could be a fluke accident, or a badly cast part, but it don't look that way to me. I just thought you ought to know, Mister Cushing."

"Thanks, Chief. I will keep this safe and I will investigate."

The engineer saluted and turned to go. Just before he opened the door, Cushing quietly asked, "Why did you bring this to me and not to the captain?"

"You were on the bridge last night, sir. That damned runner came straight at us, like her captain knew he had nothing to fear. Seems like the logical thing for him to do was to turn around and hide in the fog until the coast was clear. So either he's a very lucky fool, or he already suspected we would not be able to stop him. I've served on this ship for almost a year, Mister Cushing, and I trust every man aboard her that I know. There's only one man I *don't* know, and that's the new captain. I've heard tell from others who were there that his behavior was a bit queer."

"Belay that kind of talk, Chief! Captain Miles is to be spoken of and treated with the respect his rank entitles him to."

"Of course, sir," replied the engineer in a very flat and formal tone.

When he was alone again, Cushing reviewed in his mind's eye the events of the previous night. For a man who professed great zeal about the duties of a blockade ship, Miles had been strangely placid when he saw that Rebel ship—in utter contrast to Cushing, who had been galvanized by the same sight. The implication, even the merest hint, of malfeasance on the part of the captain led toward a number of very dark areas indeed: sedition, inciting mutiny, insubordination . . . or an act of treason by a navy officer. Cushing resolved to act cautiously and without prejudice. This matter was delicate as well as professionally dangerous.

He could not help but be distracted during his afternoon duties. At first he attributed his clumsiness to mental agitation, but by twilight he realized that something worse had beset him. Although the waning day was still hot, every vigorous puff of wind caused Cushing to cringe with chills. He developed a ghastly headache, nausea, dizziness, and a bad case of the flop-sweats. Finally he just sagged to the deck, unable to stand. Two of his men carried him below and sent for the ship's surgeon. By the time Cushing heard the doctor say, "It is typhus fever, and a very bad case of it. He must be quarantined until we reach port, assuming he lives until then," he was passing in and out of consciousness and his very bones seemed knotted to the breaking point. In his skull, some great beast roared angrily; the air he sucked in was molten and he choked upon the reeking fumes of his burning lungs.

As the leaden hours passed and the fever took possession of him utterly, Cushing could no longer sense a demarcation between reality and hallucination; everything was a continuum of dreams. He was adrift on a wild metallic sea, on a lost ship with a dead helmsman and a crew of salt-bearded phantoms, imprisoned by a forever-wandering tide, and the captain on the bridge glared down at him with eyes like polar ice and raised one clawlike hand to point at Cushing with a gesture of sharp implacable disdain—and then spoke, not to Cushing, it seemed, but to the room at large, and to himself, and to some spectral colloquy of judges, a court-martial that would be the final arbiter of his fate, the sort of dire professional nightmare that hovered perpetually on the edge of every career officer's awareness—and its low voice was that of Captain Miles, although his visage, to Cushing's roiling perceptions, kept wavering and thrumming like a tuning fork of flesh.

"Lucky I saw the chief bring that busted valve in here—lucky for me, Mister Cushing, but not so lucky for you—and it must be ordained this way, for how else can one explain such a fortuitous case of breaky-bone fever, eh?—the surgeon does not think you will live to reach Beaufort, and in a way that is a pity, for you have some excellent qualities for one so young—no doubt you would be a splendid fellow wielding a cutlass in the enemy's midst, but in this matter, Mister Cushing, you are *out of your depth*—for I serve one of the men who controls the world, who looks beyond this squalid war and plans an empire built upon the power and profit that can be wrung from it. Believe me when I say that I hope your passing will be painless and swift, one of those deaths which is nothing more than the crash of one more wave—and your innocence, your milk-sop moral purity, will ease your journey into Heaven, of that I am sure. You have not lived long enough to grapple with the demons of ambiguity, the imperatives of self-advancement—unlike you, young master's mate, most men carry a lot of ballast, and the pockets of our souls are bulging with stones. Now, if I were you, where would I have hidden that valve?—yes, of course, in the sea chest, under the protection of your dress uniform and your unbloodied sword, where else?—such a small piece of machinery, yet it carries the weight of grave possibilities—and so I shall hide it again, in a place where anything may be hidden, no matter how small or how vast . . . "

Cushing moaned and twisted on his sopping bunk, trying desperately to rise up, but he was instantly struck by a tidal wave of dizziness, pulled back down by a dark undertow he was powerless to resist. As if to torment him further, he experienced a few seconds of preternatural clarity before he passed out, and in that sliver of time he saw the captain open a porthole and throw the evidence into the sea.

Red over green . . . what does it mean?
Green over red . . . maybe I'm dead . . .

The Sand Castle of Colonel Lamb

THE FOURTH OF JULY—As the Fourth of July belongs as much to us as it does to our enemies, if not more, and as custom has consecrated that day as a holiday, and as we really desire some rest, we shall publish no paper tomorrow (July 4th); but should any important telegraphic news be received, it will promptly be laid before the public.

—The Wilmington Journal, July 3 1862

Colonel William Lamb had many things on his mind on the morning of July 5. Just after breakfast, when he was already on board the little steamer that would take him downriver for his first day as commander of the New Inlet defenses, a rider clattered on to the dock and delivered a letter for Colonel Lamb, which had just arrived on the morning train. When Lamb examined the envelope and saw his wife's handwriting, he clutched the document impulsively to his heart, then retreated to a bench on the stern where he could read it in relative privacy.

The letter was dated May 25—six weeks earlier—and Daisy had composed it in Norfolk on the day after the city fell. She was well and safe, six months into her term, and was preparing to travel on to her family in Rhode Island, along with the three children. Because of the Peninsula fighting, all railroad traffic had been suspended for many days. The precipitate Confederate withdrawal from Norfolk had engendered considerable panic and the suffocating billows of smoke from the burning navy yard had been seen by everyone as an ominous portent. Some cried "Treason!" at the fact that the South's finest shipyard had been lost without a fight, while others fumed wrathfully about "cowardice." The mayor restored some degree of calm by traveling from crowd to crowd, assuring the citizens that Federal general

Wool, who had been designated military governor of the city, was a man of civility and honor and had promised that he intended to govern "not as a conqueror, but as the representative of a humane and civilized government." And so on the morning Daisy wrote her letter, the whole city was holding its breath, and many of the more thoughtful citizens had concluded, after a day's reflection, that it was probably no bad thing that a major battle had not been waged in their streets. The mayor assured Daisy that General Wool would grant her and the children safe conduct to Providence, so her next communication would probably be from there.

At this point, Daisy Lamb abandoned her tone of objective reportage and began to write of ardent, intimate feelings. As he read those endearments, the Young Soldier of the Lord experienced a wave of longing harsh enough to bring tears to his eyes. In the months since Daisy had left, Lamb had filled his days with duty and activity and so avoided too much melancholy contemplation. Yet all his inner discipline availed him naught at the times when his heart was thus assailed by volleys of tender words and he was stricken by emotions too long held in check. The rest of the voyage to Confederate Point passed unnoticed, for as long as he was on the great brown river, he was not on duty, not in command, not even of his own feelings. He gave way to aching nostalgia, and in his passionate young mind, a magic lantern replayed scene after scene of happiness from years gone by and intimacies that now seemed cruelly remote. Perhaps the crew sensed the intensity of his reverie, for no one approached him until the steamer turned left in midriver and angled in toward a primitive dock known as Inlet Wharf—the back door, as it were, to the defensive works on Confederate Point.

Lamb sensed the change of course and, after indulging in a few more deep sighs, he carefully folded Daisy's letter and placed it protectively in his leather cartridge box. Discipline returned. Duty was the sternest of masters, after all, and who was he to indulge in regrets and yearnings, when so many other men—men just as lonely, just as bereft, just as cut off from their loved ones by the terrible chasm of war—depended upon his example? On the riverbank, a delegation of officers waited to greet their new commander, and a riderless horse, nuzzling here and there amid the sea oats, waited for its new master. As Lamb debarked and strode to within saluting range, he recognized one of the officers: a captain named Reilly, whom he had met at the Bellamy Mansion soiree. Reilly had survived the siege of Fort Macon, it was said, escaping from that place with construction plans for a new type of ironclad. Such practical experience with siege operations would come in handy.

Once the requisite courtesies had been exchanged, the party rode east to begin their formal inspection of Confederate Point—a wedge of barren land that pointed like a mason's trowel at New Inlet. Confederate Point began at an invisible line that ran from the Cape Fear along the foot of Sugar Loaf Ridge and thence eastward to the ocean itself, just nicking the bottom of the long, fingery indentation known as Masonboro Sound, upon whose upper reaches the state government maintained a large ramshackle saltworks. For more than a mile south of that line, the land was covered by thick maritime forest—yaupon pines and wind-carved scrub oaks—until the trees thinned out, about a mile and a half north of New Inlet, replaced by undulant vistas of yellow-white sand whose heights and contours were perpetually blurred and reshaped by the wind.

Lamb's overwhelming impression was one of great vaulted space, the vastness of sky mirrored by the equal vastness of the great Atlantic, with all the land between no more than a brushstroke of white laid down on a still-damp watercolor. It was a vista both grand and desolate, and so played-upon by the forces of nature that nothing built there by human hands could be more than a temporary encumbrance upon the land. All these qualities of light and distance stirred in Lamb an elemental quickening. More than any place he had ever been, this wild circumference throbbed with a sense of the ineffable and on the wind he heard the whisper of his own destiny.

He knew that the Confederate works guarding New Inlet had recently been christened Fort Fisher, in honor of a North Carolinian officer who had fallen gallantly at Manassas, and so he expected to find, at the end of Confederate Point, a fort. Instead, he found six isolated batteries scrawled along the last mile of shore before New Inlet, none of them mutually supporting, walled about with highly perishable sandbags, plates of turf, and weedy sod, their cannons either mounted carelessly *en barbette* or embrasured behind frames of palmetto log. As Lamb rode a slow circle around the largest work—a quadrilateral wall of turf-covered sand that looked more like a child's sand castle than a serious bastion—his mouth tightened and a scowl furrowed his brow. Suddenly he turned to the man closest to him—Captain Reilly, as it happened—and blurted out: "Those palmetto logs must go! Under these conditions, they will rot into rubbish after a few months. Why was good Carolina pine not used instead? It is not exactly a scarcity in these parts."

Reilly nodded in agreement, making a note on a pad pulled from his jacket, and replied, "I cannot say for sure, Colonel, for I've only been here a short time myself. I have heard, though, that one of your predecessors insisted on importing palmetto logs because he had read somewhere that they were efficacious in the defense of Fort Moultrie."

Eyebrows soaring in amazement, Lamb remarked that Fort Moultrie had been attacked in 1776 by wooden sailing ships armed with 24-pounder smoothbores, whereas Fort Fisher, if it came under attack at all, would be hammered by steam-powered cruisers capable of showering its walls with vastly more powerful rifled shells. Whoever the previous commander had been, his grasp of military technology was a century out of date.

"Tell me, Captain Reilly, how many 'predecessors' have I?"

"Since General Whiting left for Virginia, sir? Near as I can figure, five. All sent from Richmond, and recalled after a short interval."

"That would go far to explain why this 'fort' gives every appearance of having been designed by a committee of blind men! Exactly how many guns are here, all told?"

Reilly consulted another page of his notepad. "I've taken the liberty of drawing up an inventory of all the ordnance, sir, including the field guns."

Lamb scanned the list, his frown deepening. To defend the most important channel still in Confederate hands along the entire Atlantic Coast, he had at his disposal a grand total of seventeen pieces, the majority of them marginally effective 32-pounders. Only five 8-inch columbiads, and one modern 10-incher that had somehow squeezed through the constipated supply line from Richmond, qualified as respectable coast-defense guns. Disgusted, he crumpled the paper and threw it into a rain puddle.

"This will not do! As a defense against the full might of the Federal navy, which may appear on that horizon at any moment, these batteries amount to nothing! A pair of steam frigates could level this place in a single afternoon."

Riding on in wrathful silence, Lamb soon reached the last battery, where the lone 10-inch columbiad commanded the entrance to New Inlet. He kept looking about to see where the rest of the garrison was, but finally realized that the total number of men on Confederate Point amounted to little more than the bare minimum needed to crew the guns. Well, that would change soon—Chase Whiting had authorized the movement of Lamb's own regiment from Fort Anderson, across the river, as soon as practicable, intending to replace them there with newly raised recruits from the training camps near Wilmington.

Only one thing made a positive impression on Lamb during his first inspection, and that was the eagerness of the gun crews, all young and fearless and utterly naive as to the weakness of their situation. While Lamb was visiting the 10-inch battery, he happened to glance out to sea and was dumbfounded to observe a Yankee warship steaming placidly into view from behind the dunes of Zeke's Island, across the inlet.

"Does the enemy often venture so close?" he asked the gunners.

"Oh, yes," one of them replied, "they come in close and snoop around now and then, just to see what we're up to."

"And you allow this to happen?"

The gunners looked down and shuffled their feet unhappily. "Well, Colonel, our standing orders are not to waste ammunition by firing at a ship unless it is firing on us."

Lamb vaulted from his horse and climbed into the emplacement.

"That policy ends today! Never let an enemy ship get that close to us again!"

The gun crew cheered. While Lamb bent over the notch-and-pawl elevating gear and calculated the range, the gunners loaded powder bags into the gaping muzzle and used their massive loading tongs to hoist a ponderous solid shot on top of the charge. As they went through their drill, the Yankee vessel turned to starboard, as lazily as a pleasure yacht.

"Lower the barrel two notches, gentlemen, and we'll skip the shot right into him!"

Given the right angle and sufficient propelling charge, even a 128-pound cannonball could be made to skip over calm water just like a flat stone thrown at a pond. This one did: it nicked the surf four or five times, crashed into the gunboat's whaler, blowing up a cloud of splinters, then traveled on to knock a fair-sized hole in the smoke-stack, which toppled alarmingly to one side. Through his glass, Lamb could see the startled crew running around like ants. Instantly, the ship turned and headed out to sea under full steam.

"Shall we give her another, Colonel?" shouted one excited gunner.

"No need, men. They got the intended message and will surely spread the word throughout the fleet. I doubt they will spy on us so closely in the future. Well done!"

"Three cheers for the new colonel!"

For the first time that day, William Lamb felt good, felt capitol, in fact. These men wanted to fight, and everything else could be made better as long as that was true. By the time Lamb returned to the steamer, he felt almost ebullient. As he prepared to leave, in order to deliver his full report to General Whiting in Smithville, he spoke privately to Captain Reilly, in whom he already felt complete confidence.

"Captain Reilly, I am putting you in charge of Fort Fisher's artillery, accountable only to myself and General Whiting, who, I am sure, will promote you to brevet major on my recommendation. Study the task, sir, and together we will fashion a comprehensive plan to turn Fort Fisher into a work of such magnitude that it can withstand the power of the heaviest guns in the U.S. Navy. The stakes could not be higher for our cause, and I am determined to meet the challenge."

"Just find us more guns, Colonel, and we'll build Gibraltar!"

But Gibraltar was not what Lamb had in mind. Gibraltar was a gigantic rock, and the biggest cannons ever cast could bombard it from now to Doomsday without effect—there were no useful parallels to the situation obtaining at Fort Fisher. For inspiration, Lamb cast his eye farther eastward, to the recent Crimean War, and to the accomplishments of another gentleman-engineer who had risen splendidly to an even more urgent challenge. Count Franz Eduard Ivanovich Todleben, who was thirty-six when he was called upon to improvise the defenses of the great Russian port of Sevastopol against an Anglo-French army much larger than the garrison. No one in the tsarist hierarchy had expected the allies to land so close, move so quickly, or invest the city with only a few days' warning. Todleben was Prussian by origin, and like many men who are conscious of their own innate brilliance, he had endured years of frustration, praying for a chance to distinguish himself. When that chance came, it was both sudden and overwhelming. He had been ordered simply to "survey" Sevastopol's fortifications, on the leisurely assumption that no threat would appear for months, if ever. So on the October morning when the French and British armies began digging in, just a thousand yards away, on the sullen brown hills overlooking the port, the existing works were both perfunctory and detached—"Like the low decorative walls of a municipal park," Todleben later wrote. Panic seized both the military and the civilian populations. Acting decisively, Vice Admiral Korniloff called a council of war, granted Todleben carte blanche power, then published a stirring declaration for all to see: *"Let no mention be henceforth made of surrender, none of retreat. Let us consider the town as our ship, and perish rather than surrender. I hereby empower everyone to cut down on the spot any man—be he general or private soldier, myself included—who speaks of negotiation or retreat."*

Todleben rolled up his sleeves and began literally to move mountains. Sleepless and apparently tireless, he was everywhere to be seen, exhorting, cajoling, threatening, bringing order out of chaos by the sheer force of his will. He mobilized the entire population and put them to work around the clock. While Orthodox priests sang chants and flung holy water at them, the children of Sevastopol struggled with wheelbarrows and buckets, the women moved entire hills, one lapful at a time, in the scoop of their aprons. Civilians, soldiers, and sailors from the bottled-up Black Sea Fleet toiled unceasingly with hoes, spades, mattocks, rakes, washtubs, and wicker picnic baskets. No tool was too mean, no quantity of earth too small. Earth was the only commodity Todleben had in abundance, and he made brilliant use of it. Load by load, bucket by bucket, he fashioned a gigantic earthwork seven miles long and so thick that even the heaviest projectiles buried their mass impotently within its ramparts. The allies bombarded Sevastopol for eleven months with seventy-three heavy guns and mortars before attrition, disease, hunger, and cumulative damage to the Russian cannons made it possible for them to carry the city by storm. The Crimean War had proven to be the graveyard of many officers' reputations, but when it was over, the veterans on both sides praised Todleben's genius and resolution.

Fort Fisher, Lamb reflected, would not have to withstand a siege of eleven months—any attack upon Confederate Point would be a swift and massive affair whose outcome would be known in a matter of days. But military technology had made great strides in the ten years since the Crimean War; both the accuracy and the destructive power of heavy artillery had increased exponentially. Lamb had read about, but thankfully never experienced, the penetrating power of rifled 15-inch shells, the largest caliber that could be mounted on ships, so he took those projectiles to be his benchmark. As the steamer chugged slowly toward Smithville, and the boiling sun dug a pit of fire behind the iron-bottomed clouds of an impending thunderstorm, William Lamb meditated on the art and challenges of fortification.

Some time in the dim reaches of prehistory, a primitive hunter discovered that, by sheltering behind a rampart of rocks, he could gain protection from the rocks being hurled at him by two or three hostile tribesmen, while still being able to throw his own rocks effectively at them. If he survived this encounter, he remembered the efficacy of this trick and spread the word: put something impervious between you and the enemy and your rocks are worth more while his are worth much less. From this rude beginning evolved the most complex and arcane of the military arts: defensive engineering, more commonly known as the art of fortification, which generated in time its own extensive hermetic vocabulary: *lunette, glacis, cheval-de-frise, counterscarp, ravelin, traverse, redan* . . . From the crude, brawny, motte-and-bailey hill-forts of the Dark Ages to the enormous, fugal, rococo geometries of Vauban, fortresses came to symbolize the grip and power of the princes who built them, the prestige and majesty of the state whose borders they guarded. A great fortress was a testament to human ingenuity in fullest flower. But what human ingenuity can establish, it can also overcome, especially when that cleverness is reinforced with audacity, courage, and sheer determination. Put simply: there was no such thing as a truly "impregnable" fort, and William Lamb knew it. A strong work could, however, delay the enemy greatly, exhaust his forces, compel him to pay an exorbitant price in blood, and buy precious time for a counterattack to be mounted. He also knew that no large coastal fort had ever been captured by a direct over-the-beach assault; when coastal forts fell, they did so because the enemy was able to besiege them from their landward approaches after putting ashore sufficient troops at some point beyond the range of the fort's armament.

So *that* was the crucial consideration for William Lamb. He did not think that any Federal fleet would try to force the New Inlet with the same damn-the-torpedoes brute force employed by Farragut when he lunged for New Orleans—the inlet's waters were too confined, too shallow, too treacherous; by contrast, the Mississippi Delta had been a broad highway. Lamb expected the enemy, instead, to bombard Confederate Point furiously while landing a strong amphibious force to the north, intending to crush Fort Fisher in a vise. Lamb therefore reckoned that his fort would have to fulfill multiple roles: (1) it must be strong enough to withstand for several days the heaviest naval gunfire ever employed; (2) it must be strong enough on its northern, landward face to repel an attack by ten thousand infantry—the maximum number he estimated the Yankees could deploy between the fort and Sugar Loaf Ridge; (3) it must have enough long-range guns to sustain a protective umbrella for blockade-runners making the final sprint for New Inlet, and, finally, it must be configured so that the works closest to the inlet functioned as both a highly visible landmark and as a signal station for the blockade-runners seeking its protection.

As common denominators for these requirements, Fort Fisher needed to be very big, very resistant to heavy ordnance, and very imposing when viewed from the sea. It must not only *be* strong, it must also *appear* strong, both as symbol and as deterrent. Now that McClellan's offensive had petered out, and the importance of Wilmington had so greatly increased, Lamb was confident that he and Chase Whiting could cajole more artillery from Richmond, but aside from pinewood and wicker gabions, he could not count on an abundance of any construction material except *sand.* Well, if Todleben could make Sebastopol strong by hand-moving tons of earth, Lamb could do the same thing with sand. Sand would absorb, not transmit, the velocity of heavy projectiles and minimize the blast radius of explosive shells; sand would soak up cannonballs like a sponge. Any damage sustained on Monday could be repaired by Tuesday. Sand was God's gift to the Young Soldier of the Lord. It was humble, but plentiful, inexhaustible, and like the soil of Mother Russia, it could be shaped and raised, if necessary, by the bucketful just as effectively, albeit much more slowly, as it could be with steam power.

It was at this point, when the blister of setting sun finally vanished behind the towering anvils of thunder that rose hugely above the sandhills and pine barrens beyond the far shore of the Cape Fear, that the design of Fort Fisher branded itself on William Lamb's brain, grand and sprawling, yet organic to its setting and as satisfyingly harmonious in its parts as a great symphony. His pencil flew across the paper as the details fell into place.

First, he drew the tapering triangular shape of Confederate Point, then he superimposed upon it a line in the shape of a 7. The top of the numeral, the land face, measured approximately a half mile, from the riverbank to the sea; the number's stem (the sea face) followed the beach, for at least a mile, to the mouth of New Inlet. Lamb made a notation that all foliage should be cleared north from the landface for a distance of another half mile, to deprive any landing force of cover. The main line of ramparts would be anchored by two major bastions: one at the

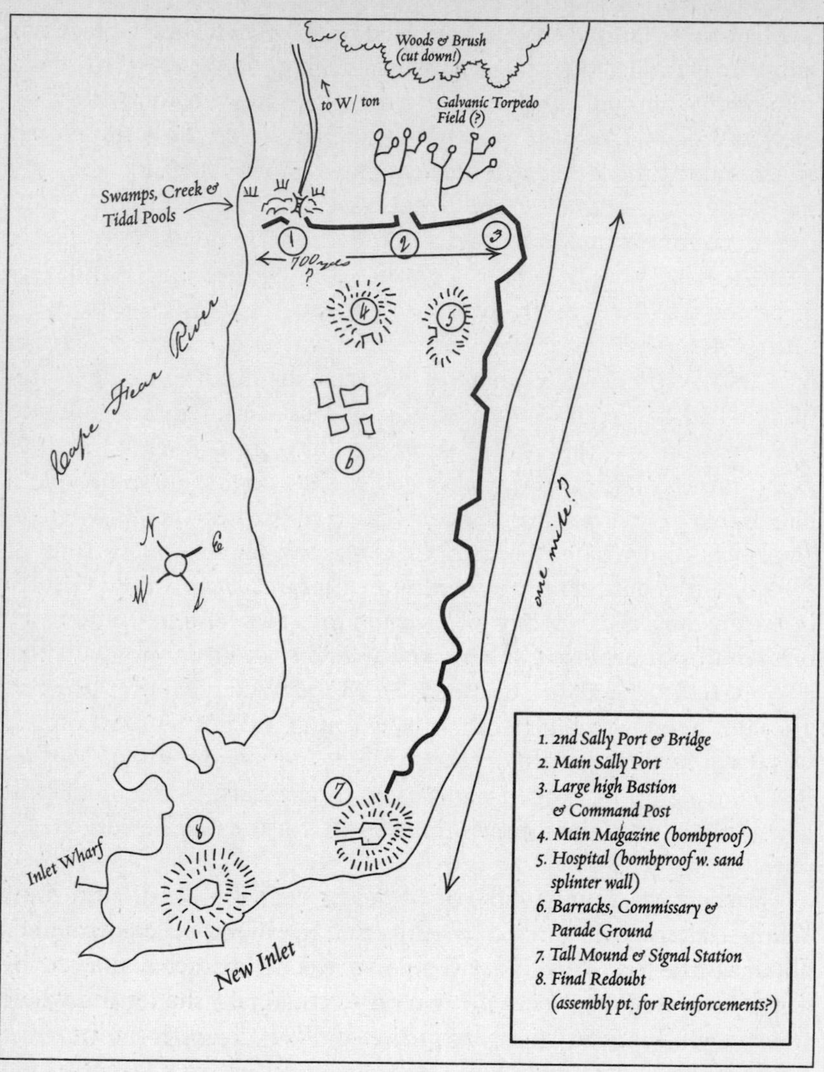

northeast corner, where the land face joined the sea face, and another massive work at the very end of the stem, dominating New Inlet and serving also as a signal platform for approaching runners.

The Northeast Bastion, as Lamb envisioned it, should be large enough to contain the fort's hospital. Another earthen wall would enclose that northeastern corner on the interior plane, so as to protect the hospital approaches from shell splinters. Might as well put the central magazine there, too, he reasoned, deep inside a mountain of sand.

So much for the overall configuration; now for the arrangement of the batteries themselves. Lamb nibbled on his pencil. The nicest thing about sand, other than its sheer availability, was that every time you removed a shovelful in order to *dig out* one place, you could immediately use that same shovelful to *raise* another place. This simple fact suggested the following arrangement:

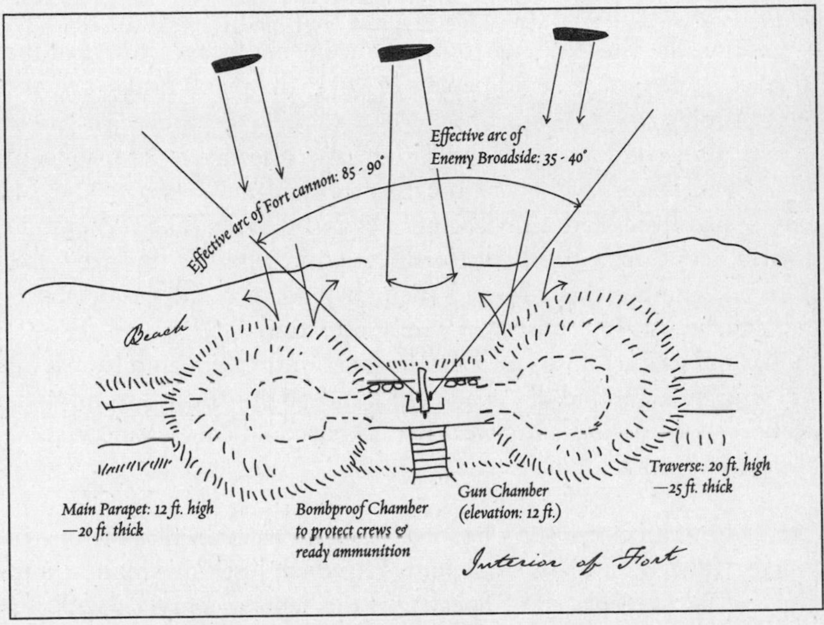

Each gun chamber—fortified with sandbags, sod, and pine beams—alternated with huge "traverses," great sod-covered mounds about thirty feet high and twenty-five feet in diameter, pierced by bombproof dugouts where the gun crews could take shelter and where "ready" ammunition could be protected; each chamber-and-traverse unit would be connected by a timbered tunnel, so that men and powder could be shifted from one threatened sector of the fort to another without ever venturing into the open. The sheer size of the traverses would make it very hard for the enemy to bring enfilade—angled fire—against any one gun chamber. In front of the whole land face, Lamb drew a palisade of nine- or ten-foot-high logs, sharpened at their tops. Near the riverbank, he sketched field artillery emplacements to cover the plank bridge where the Wilmington road finally debouched into the fort; and halfway along the length of the land face he made provision for a sally port, a fortified gate through which he could launch counterattacks if and when the opportunity presented itself. The height of the Northeast Bastion and the New Inlet Mound he estimated at forty-five and sixty feet, respectively, and he tentatively placed his own command post adjacent to the top of the Northeast Bastion, where he could observe both faces of the fort as well as the actions of the enemy fleet. And finally, he estimated the number of big guns he could mount after adopting this configuration: twenty on the land face, up to thirty on the sea face, exclusive of the smaller field guns he could deploy to cover the plank bridge and the sally port.

As for accommodations, well, there was already an old clapboard house near the inlet, where the former lighthouse keeper and his family had lived, and a small commissary building. The men would live in tents until the basic fortifications could be finished—late autumn, Lamb reckoned—and then they could build a proper barracks before the gray misery of winter settled in.

As the steamer nosed into the dock at Smithville, Lamb turned his drawings this way and that, and could find no unrealistic assumptions embodied there, no glaring weaknesses. He could hardly wait to show them to Chase Whiting.

No one in North Carolina had ever seen an election like the one in August 1862. When Governor John Ellis died, just three months into the war, he was replaced by Speaker of the Senate Henry T. Clark. By law, Clark's caretaker governance ended on the same date as his senatorial term expired, August 6. Clark had done a conscientious job, but the stress of wartime leadership had worn him down and he made it known quite early that he had no intention of running again for the office that fate had thrust upon him. A new gubernatorial election was therefore proclaimed, to be held in August.

The old-time Whigs meanwhile formed a new party, the Conservatives, led by William Holden, the feisty and intellectually astute editor of the *Raleigh Standard.* Many Conservatives had been slow to leap onto the secessionist bandwagon, a fact that made their platform suspect in the eyes of the state's other party, the Confederates. No one could accuse the Confederates of equivocating about their beliefs, which were summed up in the press by a bellicose litany: "Unremitting prosecution of the war; war to the last extremity; complete Southern independence; eternal separation from the North; no abridgement of Southern boundaries; and no compromise with enemies, Tories, or traitors."

Having proclaimed such a fire-breathing agenda, the secessionists advanced a rather undistinguished candidate: an obscure railroad executive from Charlotte named William Johnston. Perhaps Johnston was a gifted enough orator to sway the voters; no one ever found out. Newspapers representing both parties agreed that, due to the exigencies of war, no stump speeches would be allowed—the rhetorical battles would be fought entirely in print.

There was little doubt as to who the Conservatives would nominate: Zebulon Vance was well remembered for his prewar oratory, his popularity with the common folk, and his reasoned moderation during the months before the attack on Fort Sumter. Since the outbreak of hostilities, however, no prominent North Carolinian had served the Rebel cause with greater steadfastness. Many Vance supporters also looked to him as a dignified counterweight to the patronizing attitude of the Richmond papers, whose editors seemed to regard North Carolinians as poor, backward cousins. In short, Vance seemed to be the ideal candidate for the times—it would be very hard for the Confederates to discredit him.

Not that they did not try. Pro-Confederate newspapers fanned speculation that Vance would take the state out of the war; that he would oppose the controversial conscription laws Richmond had enacted in April; that his reputation for military valor was undeserved. Wildly inaccurate accounts of the fight at New Bern appeared in several prominent papers, claiming to prove that Vance had never even been close enough to smell gunpowder. When word of these stories reached the men of the Twenty-sixth North Carolina, who had gone into bivouac at Petersburg after the bloodbath at Malvern Hill, many of them sprang to defend Vance's honor by writing eyewitness accounts that could not be refuted or impugned. Deprived of that stick, the Confederate press was reduced to beating Vance with snide insults about his folksy style (*"If the State is to be governed by jokes, then Vance is certainly your man!"*).

While the newspapers traded volleys of rodomontade, Zeb Vance played a cool hand indeed. In his public letter of acceptance, he modestly called attention to the fact that he had taken the field early, at the head of a now-veteran regiment, with the intention of remaining there until Southern independence was achieved. "But a true man should be willing to serve wherever the public voice may assign him, and I should consider it the crowning glory of my life to be placed in a position where I could most advance the interests and honor of North Carolina."

When the vote was tallied, the decision was not close: Vance outpolled Johnston by a ratio of three to one. Ninety-five percent of North Carolina's soldiers, who sent in absentee ballots a week before the general polling, gave Vance their endorsement. And of the two thousand men in the Twenty-sixth, only seven voted for Johnston.

On the night of August 15, Vance made an emotional farewell to his men, at the conclusion of which a deputation drawn from all ranks came forward and presented their colonel with an engraved testimonial sword. Vance's eyes glittered in the torchlight as he accepted the gift, and the men who witnessed the event would later say that this was the first and only time anyone had seen Zebulon Vance completely at a loss for words.

Then the regimental band struck up a lusty version of "Dixie" and every man who could manage it proceeded to get drunk, officers and privates alike, and Colonel Vance in particular, with that irrepressible pour-me-a-shot-and-I'll-holler-happy gusto of a mountaineer. By one in the morning, the band was out of action, leaving only a lone fiddler out in the darkness, quietly playing "Bonaparte's Retreat," while Vance held court with forty or fifty hardy souls who had gathered around his tent.

Harry Burgwyn had not always been charmed by Zeb's manner, especially during the early months before New Bern, when Vance's rank amateurism had resulted in sloppy sanitation, lax security, and a very loose interpretation of military regulations. Terrible battles loomed ahead, Burgwyn knew, and he was confident that he could lead the men through their ordeals more effectively than his erstwhile superior. But Burgwyn knew now that, if Vance was no tactical genius, he was no coward either. They had tasted powder and smelled fear together in the chaos of New Bern, and at Malvern Hill they had borne equal witness to utter carnage. And at times such as this, Burgwyn, too, felt the impact of Vance's personality. At age thirty-two, Vance projected a commanding physical presence. He was a heavy man now, perhaps 230 pounds, but all of that weight was centered in his massive shoulders and bearlike torso. His eyes never lost their penetrating clarity, no matter how much bourbon he threw down that tree trunk of a throat. It seemed to Burgwyn that the new governor had an almost mystical aura about him—when the time and place and setting were just so, without half working at it, he compelled men to love him. And, Harry reflected, this campfire bull-session was definitely such an occasion. It was a moment Burgwyn wanted to savor, an incident to tell his grandchildren about, and so, to fully get in tune with things, even he had foregone his usual temperance. Not that he was fall-down drunk, but he was certainly full of rare comraderie—so much so that when a corporal called him Good ol' Harry, Burgwyn did not even bother to assert his rank.

There had been some singing earlier, and the telling of some bawdy jokes, but now the gathering had become more conversational, the men peppering Vance with questions and Vance responding with absolute informality. At one point, Vance took a long pull from his jug and suddenly made a fierce, angry face, causing a sudden uneasy silence among the onlookers.

"I just want to know one thing, while you jackasses are drunk enough to tell me the truth. *In vino, veritas* and all that. What I want to know is: which seven of you bastards didn't vote for me?"

Of course, no one confessed to such a sin, so Vance glowered even more sternly and growled: "Very well, you leave me no choice! I'll pick seven men at random and have them shot in the morning!"

For a brief interval, the onlookers wrinkled their brows in consternation. Then they spotted the twinkle in Vance's eyes and began whooping with laughter. When the ruckus died down, the soldiers began to throw questions at Vance once more.

"Colonel, is it true that you're going to govern the state with jokes and tall stories, like them newspapers said you was?"

"I'm afraid my fund of japery is running a bit low at the moment, son. But there's no situation so dire that it cannot be made more bearable with a sense of humor. You keep readin' the papers from home—I guarantee they'll keep you apprised of my jokes, and if perchance I don't make any during the course of a week, I'm sure they'll just make some up."

"Hey, Zeb!" called out another soldier. "First thing you ought to do when you get back home is find them sumbitches who claimed you wasn't at the New Bern fight, and throw the rascals in jail!"

"Well, now, I'm not so sure I ought to do that, Private. The whole fracas reminded me of something that happened to a lawyer friend of mine a few years back, fella name of MacDuffie. Oh, he was a speechifier if there ever was one! One time, I heard him mount a defense of his client that was so moving it drew tears from the court, the jury, the spectators, and a couple of dogs—and of course, the client was acquitted. Now on the way out of the courthouse, I overheard MacDuffie whisper to his man, 'You sonofabitch, you were guilty as sin and you know it!,' but the client looked back, all wide-eyed and innocent, and replied: 'Not a bit of it, counselor! I *thought* I was guilty too, until I heard your speech, but now I'm certain that I am not!' Now, I *thought* I was present at a couple of battles, but I'm willing to admit that I could be wrong . . . except that I do retain an indistinct recollection of the bullets that whistled around my ears."

After the chuckling subsided, a tall lanky soldier with a raw backwoods accent spoke up in a serious tone: "Your Honor, I'm from Watauga County, up in the mountains, and I hear tell that a lot of men are hightailin' it into the hills to escape conscription. I also done heard that you might be agin conscription yourself. Why should those boys be shirkin' their duty while me and these other fellers are here?"

"I admit, I am uneasy about conscription, but stern times require stern measures, and the manpower has to come from somewhere. Many people argue that it was harsh and unconstitutional. Well, by God, it *was* harsh, and it *may* be unconstitutional! But to oppose it now that it has been set in motion would only produce the greatest mischief. I am told that some people voted for me because they hoped I would oppose conscription, but I tell you now: any man in North Carolina who ought to be in the army, and who is not, I will make the state too hot to hold him!"

Cheers and applause: Vance in his element.

But even as Vance bantered on into the night, until both he and the surviving audience were too hammered by drink to keep their eyes open, there was a core of sadness in his heart. He would miss these men; even at their roughest and most profane, they were formed from the mountains' earth and tougher than a hickory knot in January. He had risen above their station in life, that was true, but he was one of them, too. If he were no longer with them in battle, he could at least use the powers of his office to make sure they had a voice and their families back home, a protector. He had a vision of their future—a cruel succession of Malvern Hills—and knew his choice had been the right one. He did not have the warrior's spirit required to lead them into such horror more than once. It was as certain as the sunrise: many of the men who laughed and drank with him tonight would die. Harry Burgwyn had the iron in his spine to lead them. They had learned to respect him now, and Zebulon Vance was sure that, in time, they would come to love him.

Colonel Lamb had been as good as his word—Frederick Reilly was promoted to brevet major, by order of General Whiting, only one week after Lamb's incisive tour of inspection. Company by company, Lamb's entire regiment was ferried over the Cape Fear from Fort Anderson and absorbed into the permanent garrison of Fort Fisher. For the first few weeks, everyone was preoccupied with the mundane details of setting up encampments, kitchens, and properly drained sanitary facilities—the latter proving predictably troublesome due to the shallow water table beneath Confederate Point. A few shipments of construction equipment had come down the river from Wilmington—buckets, mattocks, spades, and some wheelbarrows—and on the last day of August, the new telegraph line to Wilmington sparked to life, an event that cheered everyone's spirits even if it had little practical effect on the work that needed doing. One of the first messages received by the fort's telegraphist was a terse summons requesting "Captain" Reilly's appearance, at his earliest convenience, at Confederate navy headquarters in Wilmington, to discuss "important matters" with Flag Officer William Branch. Before acknowledging the message, Reilly made sure that two major's stars were sewn over the captain's bars denoting his previous status, so that Flag Officer Branch would know the rank of the man with whom he was dealing. Then he wired back that he would present himself at or about one P.M. on the afternoon of September 1.

God knows, it has taken long enough, he thought. When Reilly finally reached Wilmington in early June, after his escape from doomed Fort Macon, he had dutifully presented to Branch his drawings for a new and powerful type of ironclad ram. Then he had moped around in Wilmington, waiting for a formal assignment. Several times, he had revisited Branch and made polite inquiry as to the status of the ironclad scheme; each time, Branch had assured him that the design was "very sound" or "quite promising" and that the proposal was being studied by "the proper authorities"—whoever those might be. Reilly's last encounter with Branch, just before he was ordered to Fort Fisher, was at the Bellamy Mansion, where he had importuned the naval commander rather insistently, almost demanding some assurance that the ironclad project had not simply vanished into the slough of despond that was the Richmond bureaucracy. Branch's response was testy—he clearly did not want to be bothered about such matters during a social occasion. After this rebuff, Reilly resigned himself to his duties at Fort Fisher; at least *there* he could accomplish something.

When he showed the telegram to Colonel Lamb, the latter was quick to give him permission to go, but expressed concern about losing his chief of artillery for any extended period of time. Since Lamb had taken command of Fort Fisher, the two men developed a close working relationship. Reilly studied Lamb's designs and found them ideal. "Don't let them steal you from me," he said as he bid Reilly farewell on the dock at Inlet Wharf.

Confederate navy headquarters was located in a drab two-story brick building on Dock Street. An air of somnolence hung over the place—as well it might, considering that the Confederate navy's presence in Wilmington was more a matter of potential than actuality. Reilly knew there was an ironclad under construction at Beery's Shipyard, but the rest of Wilmington's "navy" consisted of an assortment of lightly armed tugs and ex-ferry boats not appreciably stronger, in the aggregate, than the old Mosquito Fleet.

William Branch greeted Reilly cordially enough, but Reilly sensed a certain stiffness in the flag officer's manner. It was not hard to fathom the reasons: an officer of flag rank should be commanding a full squadron of ships, but Branch had no fleet to command. He was officially responsible for the naval defense of the most important port remaining in Confederate hands, but he operated in a vacuum, unable to conjure resources from thin air, unable to strike the blockaders, unable to uphold the prestige of his service. His was almost a hollow command, very nearly a sham. What conscientious officer would not chafe under these conditions?

"Captain Reilly," he began.

"Major, sir. Brevet major, actually." Reilly tapped his new, crudely sewn stars.

"Ah. Yes. Congratulations on your promotion, the news of which had not yet reached me. But then, I am usually the last to know of these things."

Frustration Reilly could understand; every loyal Confederate felt that. But whence came this undercurrent of purest bitterness?

Branch lifted a sheaf of drawings from his desk and tapped them thoughtfully. Reilly realized, with a small frisson of pride, that these were copies of his ironclad schematics.

"I have studied your design, sir. I believe it to be sound, and feasible, and quite advanced. The long delay resulted from my having to vet the scheme past Secretary of the Navy Mallory. There are, of course, competing designs and contract bids that had to be considered. The upshot of the matter is that I have been authorized to proceed with the construction of a single ironclad of your design and another vessel of a more conventional pattern. The latter has already been laid down here in Wilmington, designated the CSS *Raleigh*. The one based on your design will be designated the CSS *Hatteras*—and may it avenge our humiliating defeat at the fort of the same name."

"Where will that one be constructed, sir?"

"Come, look at the map."

Branch walked over to a large hydrographic map of the North Carolina coast. He tapped his forefinger on a spot far up the Roanoke River identified as Holman's Ferry.

"There's a small shipyard here, I am told. The location is far from the Yankees' usual haunts, and the river is narrow, easily defended, yet deep enough for the ram to pass downstream. See, here and here and here, how the enemy's bases form a huge crescent." Branch tapped Edenton, Plymouth, Washington, New Bern, and Shelborne's Point.

"When the *Hatteras* is completed, she will sortie down the Roanoke, sweep the Yankees from Albemarle Sound—for they have no ships there that are a match for her—run past the batteries on Roanoke Island, then set course southwest and sweep Pamlico Sound. Once we have regained control of the sounds, the Yankee garrisons will be isolated and our land forces can pick them off one by one. It's a feasible strategy."

"It's a lot to ask from one ship, too, no matter how powerful. It is possible, sir, to construct two or three of my rams faster and more cheaply than one ironclad of the older type being built in Wilmington. In the same amount of time, with proper allocation of resources, we could build a small fleet and greatly improve our chances of accomplishing such a major strategic reversal. Whereas, if I may say so, the ironclad being constructed here will be too slow to pose a threat to the blockade squadron and will therefore not be useful unless the enemy tries to attack straight up the Cape Fear. I have, as you know, spent several weeks on Confederate Point, and if we have even six months in which to strengthen the defenses of that place, the enemy will not be able to pass the New Inlet. Therefore, I see no logical reason to devote our scant resources to a purely defensive end when . . . " Branch waved him silent, scowling.

"Major Reilly, I have already alluded to the fact that there are other competing ironclad designs vying for scarce resources. Contracts for such lucrative projects are not always let on the basis of military expediency. In the years before the war, we professional officers lived in a realm of hermetic idealism; the reality of today is far different. The pie, so to speak, can only be sliced into so many pieces, and it is an unfortunate fact that the largest slices always go to the firms that are politically well-connected. Everyone who has seen your drawings, from Secretary Mallory on down, agrees on the merit and economy of your design, but there are others in line ahead of you, representing vested interests whose support is deemed vital to President Davis. He ignores them at the peril of the cause in general, or so the reasoning seems to be. Be sure that circumstances are much the same on the Union side, verging in some instances on blatant corruption and influence mongering. But the enemy's wealth and industrial capacity so far exceed our own that waste, fraud, and duplication of effort, even on a rampant scale, can readily be absorbed. The arrangement I have outlined is a compromise, and it is not the one I would have wanted. It is, however, the best I can manage. As it is, I have strained my authority to secure the construction of just one ram based on your designs. If that leaves a bitter taste in your mouth, rest assured that it leaves the taste of gall in mine."

Branch's complexion had gone pale and his expression mirrored his words. Reilly felt a pang of sympathy for the man and decided that further argument with him was pointless. He bowed slightly in acknowledgment of Branch's seniority. Branch sat down heavily and ruffled through the pages of drawings for a moment before regaining his composure.

"I can promise you this much, sir: I will assign to oversee the project one of my best and most experienced officers, Captain Samuel Parker. Do you wish to be reassigned to Holman's Ferry under his command?"

"I know little about the practicalities of shipbuilding, sir. I am by training a coast defense engineer, and I feel that I will be of greater service if I remain at Fort Fisher. If Captain Parker solicits my advice, or desires me to visit the site periodically, that can be done by wire or by train. I ask only that I be allowed to meet with him and make sure he understands the principles of my design."

"Done. He's waiting for you now in a conference room on the

second floor, where he has been studying the original drawings you brought from Fort Macon. I'll take you there myself."

Samuel Parker, Reilly sensed, was an altogether different man than Branch. He radiated confidence and vigor; his handshake was warm and manly. After introductions, Branch returned to his office, and the stoic gloom that surrounded him dissipated quickly. The discussion that followed was intense and thoroughly professional.

Parker had indeed understood the essence of Reilly's design. Whereas most Confederate navy ships had been ad hoc conversions of less than ideal civilian vessels, Reilly had methodically based his design on the realities of the situation and the nature of the waters where such vessels would be required to operate. His main innovation was a new kind of pivoting mount. Reilly's system of circular rails, training trucks, and shifting tackle made it possible to shift a gun from a fore-and-aft direction to a port-or-starboard broadside position in the same amount of time ordinarily required simply to reload it. In effect, two big guns could be made to do the work of six mounted on conventional carriages. Moreover, Reilly had calculated the angles so that part of the reloading could be accomplished while the piece was being moved. The net result was a greatly reduced cost of construction, tremendous savings in weight, increased room for ammunition, and ease of maintenance. He had originally conceived of deploying two 6.4-inch Parrotts, but Parker thought the design would accommodate a pair of 8-inch Brooke rifles just as handily. The Brooke was a Confederate design, cast at the Tredegar Iron Works in Richmond and they had a good reputation. Parrott barrels were reinforced with only one iron band, Brookes by two or three—in theory, the Brookes were less likely to explode after prolonged firing.

Parker voiced admiration for the way Reilly's design elements dovetailed. Because his ship needed only two big guns, it could be powered by a smaller engine, without, theoretically, losing speed due to the weight of its armor, which Reilly had intended to be impervious to anything the Yankees might hurl at it, by alternating plates of rolled iron with thick layers of oak and pine, attached both vertically and horizontally, to further dissipate the kinetic energy of a projectile. Because of the ship's relative maneuverability, Reilly had found it feasible to cap its lethality by designing a ram, braced along the center keelson, fashioned from eighteen inches of solid oak and covered with two inches of iron plate, tapering to a cutting wedge only four inches wide. At any speed greater than five or six knots, at any angle greater than 45 degrees, such a massive spike ought to crack the hull of any Union ship it might encounter.

"I say again, Major Reilly: a very formidable craft, and one I shall be honored to steer into battle. I should like you to inspect the work at each crucial stage: the framing, the plating, the engine trials. Your Colonel Lamb won't mind you taking a few days off now and then, will he?"

"No sir, not unless the fort is under imminent threat. I must say you've given me confidence that this thing can be done, unlike . . . "

Parker sighed. "Unlike Flag Officer Branch. I understand. William and I have been friends since our midshipmen days, and we served together in the Mosquito Fleet until the end. Something changed in his character after that. We did valiant work with those little ships, you know—at the height of our commerce raiding days, the shipping insurance rates up North had trebled! We gave a brave account of ourselves at Roanoke Island, too, considering how great the odds were against us. But then, at Elizabeth City, we saw our entire command wiped out in less than thirty minutes. Mister Branch was greatly embittered by that defeat—an officer waits his entire career to lead a fleet into battle; that is his dream, his moment of fulfillment. On that day, Mister Branch's dream crumbled into dust before his eyes. I know him, sir, and I know that he would grease his boots with the tallow of the Devil's bones if he could build a real Confederate navy, a true *fleet.* If the secessionists had not been so reckless, and had spent the last year or two before the war stockpiling the resources, we would have had an armada of suitable hulls, tons of iron plate, modern engines, and warehouses full of fine English cannons—it is not as though we did not see this war looming. And now that it is here, and Mister Branch has achieved the flag rank he dreamed about as a young cadet, he feels, well, *thwarted.*"

"But you were at Elizabeth City, too, were you not? And yet you do not seem morose or embittered."

Parker smiled ruefully. "Aye, Major Reilly, I was there. I saw my ship blown up and some very brave lads killed. But the emotion I carry in my breast is that of revenge. I want, even if only for a single day, to make the American navy in these waters feel as desperate and frightened as we did. Your great ram could make that possible, which is why I swear to you here and now that I will strain every resource of mind and body to build it, and when it is built, I will smite them a great and redemptive blow. Shall we shake hands on it, sir?"

They did, each man probing the gaze of the other and finding there only clarity and understanding.

September 19, 1862
Aboard the USS Commodore Perry
Dearest Mother—

I have made a complete recovery from my illness, although I am told that my condition, when I was carried by stretcher to the hospital in Beaufort, was not such as to inspire my shipmates with any confidence. But once the crisis was passed, both my spirits and my constitution improved rapidly. Certainly my recovery was hastened by the very cheerful news that I have been promoted! According to my dear friend Charles Flusser—himself now promoted to the rank of Lieutenant Commander—Navy Secretary Welles finally received permission, in late July, to expand the list of officers beyond anything the Navy has ever known before. Many deserving young men were elevated in rank as a result of this wartime expansion, but most of them advanced only one rung up the ladder, whilst I had the distinction of being elevated to Lieutenant from the lowly status of Master's Mate, skipping altogether the intermediate ratings of Master and Ensign—something that would have been unthinkable in the peacetime Service. As far as I have been able to ascertain, I am the only man who has ever reached this rank before the age of twenty!

Furthermore, these new emergency promotions also permit us to choose which officer we wish to serve with. I had no hesitation in signing on as Charles Flusser's executive officer, aboard the gunboat Commodore Perry. *She is a vessel of humble origins, formerly a ferry boat out of Baltimore, but that is actually an advantage, given that she spends most of her time patrolling the vast but shallow waters of the North Carolina sounds and the arterial rivers that flow into them from deep in the state's interior. She is wide and stable, and can maneuver nicely in shallow water, and her broad configuration allows her to carry a relatively heavy battery: four 9-inch Dahlgren shell-guns, a 12-pounder howitzer, and a 100-pounder Parrott rifle. You may be sure that, with Flusser and Cushing in command, she will carry the fight aggressively to the enemy, wherever he may be found!*

That said, however, I must also remark upon the fact that our conditions of service are vastly different from what I hoped for when I joined the Navy. The image of a lofty frigate shortening sail and clearing for action under a blue sky far out in the open sea is now a dream from the past, relegated quickly to the realm of legend and romance. The coastal war requires the use of small, smoky vessels redolent of engine oil and coal smoke, innocent of snowy billowing canvas and gleaming spars. Instead of the blue and sunlit sea of nautical romance, we confront the shallow, muddy waters of far-reaching inland waterways, stained and discolored by the ooze of mud and the muck of vegetable decay swept down from the numberless creeks of surrounding swamps. We see no gallant flying fish or spouting leviathans, only the occasional heron and sullen alligator.

For all that, however, our patrols are much more interesting than the dreary routine of the blockade line: we cover the flanks of infantry and cavalry probes, deliver mail and ammunition to the scattered Federal outposts that dot both the Outer Banks and the riverine estuaries. Our frequent visits to the region's small ports afford us many interesting and colorful glimpses of garrison life. Most of the soldiers I have met, whatever their rank and state of origin, count themselves lucky to be stationed in such pleasant locations as Beaufort and New Bern. I spent a most agreeable 48 hours in the latter town only last week, where the men of the 24th Massachusetts, their spirits enlivened by being mustered for their pay, spent one entire afternoon indulging in the popular horse-play known in these parts as "tossing niggers in a blanket." While it was great good fun for the tossers, and probably did no permanent harm to tossed, the latter made loud and comic protestations, rolling their eyes and screeching with exaggerated fear. Of course, the louder they yelled and screamed, the more fun it was for the lusty fellows at the blanket's edge, who, when they finally tired of their sport, showered the Africans with coins and other tokens. Charles Flusser and I have combined our resources, and hired a spirited young pickaninny servant, who looks after our cleaning, mending, and any other menial chores that need doing. Charles also brought for me a copy of the book that most inspired us during our midshipman's days: Naval Enterprise: Illustrative of Heroism, Courage and Duty"*—a veritable "New Testament" of gallant parables! Of course, now that we are veterans of naval action, we can smile at the naive sentimentality of the prose, while still venerating the great heroes whose exploits are recounted therein.*

We continue to hear rumors that the Rebs are busily constructing an ironclad or two far inland, but from what I have seen of the rural areas beyond the coastal towns, I doubt they are making much progress. Nearly all the inhabitants out in the countryside seem to be what the townspeople call "white trash" or "clay-eaters." I have been told that some of them actually do eat clay, a habit they contract like any other bad habit, and while I cannot vouch for the truth of this, some of their farms are so poor in appearance that such a diet cannot be ruled out. Many of them seem not only poor, but also ignorant and shiftless. Ask one of them the distance between two points on the local river, and he will tell you "it is right smart of a journey" or something equally cryptic.

Of course, some of these same rustics might also be acting as scouts for the Rebels, in which case their seeming ignorance might well be a masquerade. Now that Burnside has departed, and the Army has settled down in its fortified coastal enclaves, the Rebs have recovered somewhat from the disorganization they displayed in the spring. Both sides seem to be watching each other warily, and occasionally provoking a small battle along one river or another. It is only a matter of time until the Commodore Perry *sails into action. I am indeed fortunate to be serving now under Charles Flusser; indeed, a greater contrast between Charles and my former skipper could hardly be imagined—but that is not a matter I should speak of in a letter.*

Pray for me, Mother. Pray that I find a battle commensurate with my new rank!

With all my love and prayers,
Your Will

"Close One, Sir!"

THE DEAR OLD MELON—We used to eat watermelon. Indeed, we loved to eat watermelon. But now we don't, because the price of that late-summer delicacy "is riz" to the point where they are beyond our reach. Well, they're no account this year anyway, or so we have heard—and we used to eat watermelons. Indeed, we loved to eat watermelons. But now we don't care for them. They are sour—they are bad—they are mean, and they are too dear. *Let them rip, if we cannot rip into them.*

We are informed by an article in the Milledgeville Georgia Recorder that dog skins, properly trimmed and tanned, make excellent shoe leather, equal to calf skin. We don't want to kill the dogs, but we welcome their skins, if they can live without them. Perhaps a further economy might be realized if the bark of the dog could be used to tan his hide.

—The Wilmington Journal, September 19 1862

By the end of September, Fort Fisher was beginning to take shape. Lamb's first priority was to link the separate sea-face batteries into one continuous rampart and then to fashion the gun chambers and traverses that would be the fort's spine. Tons of sand had to be moved; it was slow and tedious work for a few hundred men using nothing but shovels, buckets, and wheelbarrows. Lamb's other priority was to obtain more guns. Since taking command in July, Lamb had received some powder—good English stuff, purchased dockside from blockade-runners—and a few barge loads of shot and shell, but not until the last day of September did he receive his first new cannon.

Major Reilly, the fort's ordnance specialist, inspected the piece after the barrel and carriage had been laboriously winched-off at Inlet Wharf, and he pronounced it a fine specimen. It was a 10-inch columbiad—a smoothbore type of weapon designed for maximum range and elevation, cast in a single piece, the breech end rounded and bulbous and twice as thick as the muzzle, not banded with separate belts of iron; theoretically, a weapon of this design was less likely to explode from the infernal stress of prolonged firing—as Parrott guns were known to do with alarming frequency. Lying on the beach, it resembled a gigantic eleven-foot-long flower vase.

It also weighed eight tons, and the only way to move it from the riverbank to its chamber was by means of rollers, block and tackle, and sheer muscle. Once the barrel had been hauled across the width of Confederate Point and the carriage emplaced, Reilly and his crews undertook the actual mounting. This was accomplished with a device called a garrison gin—an iron-reinforced tripod made from spruce poles tapering from six and a half inches at the apex to ten inches at the base, where a massive windlass provided leverage for the men who hauled on the lines hanging down from the pulley at the top. A sling of heavy hemp line was looped around the barrel, just behind the muzzle, and again around the cascabel—the rounded, knobbed back end of the gun. A maneuvering hand-spike was rammed down the barrel, so that when the columbiad was lifted, it could be jiggered a few inches one way or another. The combined strength of ten burly men was required to turn the windlass crank and they were soaked and winded by the time the piece was raised high enough to be lowered into half-moon trunion slots on the carriage. Once the gun was snuggled into those slots, the rope sling came off and the trunions were covered by curved iron caps, fastened by square-head bolts long enough to penetrate the whole thickness of the carriage itself. In the great permanent forts that guarded Washington or Hampton Roads, hydraulic jacks and steam-powered hoists might be used, but at Fort Fisher each gun had to be mounted with the same tools and the same hard labor used in the days of Queen Elizabeth.

October was two days gone by the time the whole process was completed, and Frederick Reilly himself went out after breakfast to clean and polish the new columbiad. Only when the weapon was gleaming did he summon two other gunners to test its elevation, which measured 39 degrees plus a smidgeon; good enough, with a twenty-pound charge of good English powder, to lob a solid shot almost six thousand yards. He patted the great iron shaft with genuine affection—Fort Fisher had just become stronger and more dangerous.

"Major Reilly, you look like a proud new father."

Startled from his reverie, Reilly turned around and snapped a salute to Colonel Lamb.

"Top o' the morning to you, Colonel. And you, sir, look like a doting uncle."

"It's a fine gun. God knows where it came from, but I hope they send us twenty more just like it. Do you intend to test-fire it today?"

"I can, if that is your wish and you don't mind losing a few men from the sand-castle detail."

"I think I can spare them. It would be good to learn just how far it can reach and how fast it can be reloaded. We are expecting a rather prominent visitor tonight, and I want to extend the fort's protection as far as I can."

"Aye, sir. It's a good night for a runner to come in—the moon will be low and thin and to landward. There'll be a mist, too, unless I miss my guess. Is the ship one of our regular visitors?"

"No. I believe this will be her maiden voyage in these waters. She's called the *Florimel,* recently purchased in Glasgow, I think. Only two years old, iron hulled, with a screw propeller. She is said to be very fast and very large. Her cargo holds are immense and well shielded by iron plate, so she will be hauling approximately fifty tons of gunpowder. I don't need to tell you how badly General Lee needs that powder. Richmond has paid dearly for every grain and we are asked to be especially vigilant during her run in. I want all the guns loaded and manned by sunset and twice the usual number of lookouts."

"Any chance of us getting some of that powder, Colonel?"

"Officially, no. Unofficially, I suppose the captain might be grateful enough to skim off a few barrels. We shall see what the night brings."

Reilly did not think it likely that the *Florimel* would attempt the final dash until well after midnight, so he turned in early, leaving instructions with his orderly to waken him at one o'clock. He fairly leaped out of bed when the private nudged him and paused only long enough to gulp down some coffee before heading up to the site of the new columbiad. He was fairly steaming with anticipation, hoping that some Yankee skipper would become so distracted by the chase that he would veer into range.

Up on the windy floor of the gun chamber, Reilly and his crew were boyishly eager, leaning out over the parapet and squinting intently toward the horizon. Three A.M. came and went and still there was no sign of the *Florimel.* Had the steamer been captured far out at sea? Had she suffered engine problems and been forced to turn back? Only an hour of full darkness remained, and no sane captain would try to pierce the blockade line in daylight. Two of the gunners had given up and were hunkered down out of the wind, fighting a losing battle against sleep.

Just after four A.M., however, someone off to Reilly's left shouted, "Glory be, she's a-comin' in!"

Gray moving on gray, the ship at first seemed nothing more than a pronounced ripple in the haze. By the time Reilly spotted her, the *Florimel* was five miles north of the fort and less than twenty minutes away from the umbrella of Reilly's guns. She was indeed big, and very fast, cleaving the water like a plow blade scoring loamy earth.

"She's out too far!" cried a gunner. "They'll spot her for sure!"

Must be that screw propeller, thought Reilly. From what he understood, a screw was more efficient than paddle wheels, but it also drew twice as much water and the *Florimel*'s skipper had only been prudent to put an extra half mile between the ship and the ever-shifting sandbars closer to shore. He was gambling on speed now, and it was a horse race between the ship and the growing visibility that would reveal her to the enemy.

Too late! A signal rocket cracked the darkness, traced a vivid sparkling arc, and less than a minute later, Reilly and his men saw the flash of heavy ordnance and, by reflex, started counting the seconds until the guns' reports thumped dimly against their ears. A Yankee cruiser, not quite visible yet, had opened fire on the runner from just beyond the farthest reach of the fort's guns. It was too hazy to observe the fall of shot, but it must have been alarmingly close because the *Florimel* suddenly began to zigzag wildly. That was a mistake, thought Reilly, although it was a logical enough response from a captain whose ship was being straddled—each leg of the zigzag added a few more precious seconds to the time the runner needed to reach safety.

From several points on the compass, more signal rockets blazed skyward; the whole inner ring of blockade ships was now alerted and would be closing in with all guns cleared for action. Darkness attenuated fast now, and the first dim smudges of predawn light bled up over the horizon. Through his field glasses, Reilly could now see details of the first Yankee ship, closing fast, spewing rockets, with a great Parrott rifle mounted as a bow chaser. The enemy gunners, doubtless fired up by the prospect of significant prize money, worked the Parrott with great enthusiasm, pumping out shots at an impressive rate. Fifty yards away, from his command post in the Pulpit, a forty-foot-high revetment walled with pine and tar-covered sandbags, Colonel Lamb shouted through a megaphone, "Major Reilly, is that Yankee cruiser within range?"

"Not quite, sir! Another minute or so."

"Well, open fire anyway. Maybe we can discourage her."

Reilly's gunners, now wide awake, had already been tracking the cruiser. When the columbiad roared, firing its first shot in anger, the whole fort cheered. By now, there was enough light for Reilly to track the shot. Sure enough, it fell short by more than five hundred yards. If the Yankee crew even saw the shell spout, they paid no mind, not altering course or speed by one degree or knot. Reilly understood—weeks of tedious patrolling were forgotten in the heat of the chase. Their prey was within reach and that was all that mattered. Like phantoms suddenly looming into the light of day, two—no, *three!*—more Yankee cruisers materialized and opened fire at the hapless runner, still zigzagging at flank speed, and a veritable forest of waterspouts peppered the sea around her. From the Pulpit, Lamb's signal hoisted the flag-command for independent fire by all guns, and the very sand beneath Confederate Point quaked and groaned.

Desperate now, the *Florimel*'s captain hoisted the Union Jack, hoping to buy just enough confusion to make the final dash into New Inlet. The Yankee gunners were not fooled by such a transparant ruse and did not miss a beat. Now the runner was only a tantalizing mile or so from safety. Fort Fisher's gunners were finding the range, too, but the Federal cruisers were moving fast and each Rebel battery was tracking whatever target its gunners fancied. *Next time, we would do better to mass our fire against one ship at a time.* Reilly swung his glasses toward the Pulpit and refocused them on Colonel Lamb, who was stamping his feet and scowling furiously—obviously, the same thought had just occurred to him. Resighting on the *Florimel,* Reilly saw her Union Jack cut down, a low-lying deckhouse disintegrate in a flurry of splinters, and the vast iron hull of the great steamer lurch and shiver as multiple rounds of solid shot hammered her in quick succession. Heedless of the furious but wild fire from the shore, the pursuing cruisers kept closing in, now yawing back and forth in order to fire broadsides with every gun that could bear. A big Dahlgren shell flashed near the *Florimel*'s bridge, igniting a greasy little fire in the ship's galley. Her rigging and spars and rails were cut to pieces and her port side kept shuddering as solid shot skipped in and struck. The entire vessel seemed to be trembling with ague.

"She ain't gonna make it, Major Reilly!" cried one gunner.

"How much gunpowder did you say she was carrying?" muttered another man.

Only a mile from the New Inlet bar, the runner's captain seemed to realize his time had run out along with his options. The next hit, or the next, might cause the entire ship to vanish in one monstrous blast. He stopped zigzagging, rang on full speed, and turned sharply to starboard, running straight for the beach at fifteen knots. Every man in the fort instinctively braced for either a titanic explosion or the impact of a full-speed grounding. A hundred yards from shore, the *Florimel* rammed into a sandbar, her screw throwing up fountains of muck as it churned furiously but impotently, and Reilly distinctly heard, even above the din of cannonades, the agonizing gonglike crunch of the big ship's keel against the shaley bottom. Even before the ship stopped its forward motion, her crew began lowering their lifeboats. Lamb signaled a cease-fire and barked out a series of orders. First, he sent a company of infantry to sally out and assist the sailors into the shelter of the fort; second, he ordered Reilly's gun and two other big pieces to punch holes in the *Florimel*'s waterline with solid shot, intending thereby to flood the hold with enough seawater to dampen the gunpowder. If the powder did not blow up, there was still a chance to salvage the runner's other cargo; if the powder *did* blow up, there would be nothing but a scattering of debris to show that the steamer had even existed.

As soon as the runner's crew was safely away, Lamb's designated batteries opened fire. It did not take more than a few shots to puncture the hull, which was already dimpled and sprung from repeated hits. By the time Lamb's infantrymen reached the shaken survivors, the *Florimel* had gone down by the stern and her tormentors had drawn angrily away; no chance now of a capture or prize money and with dawn brightening behind them, they were perfect targets in their own right. Lamb chased them away by firing multigun salvos at each ship in turn and managed to tag the USS *Niphon* on the fantail just before she steamed out of range. After ordering a final cease-fire, Lamb climbed down from the Pulpit, mounted his horse, and galloped through the sally port to welcome the bedraggled and downhearted sailors, who were given blankets, coffee, and whiskey when they reached the fort.

The *Florimel*'s captain had brought the cargo manifest with him, so at full daylight, Lamb, Reilly, and several more officers rode out to inspect the vessel and determine what was salvageable. Bigger than a stranded whale, mauled by shot and shell, the *Florimel* was an immense dark vault that stank of engine oil, coal dust, and powder smoke. Until they knew the condition of the explosives packed below, none of the Rebel officers dared venture below with an open flame. For an hour they scurried about, removing tarpaulins, uncovering blacked-out portholes, and forcing open hatches until there was enough sunlight to banish the gloom belowdecks.

The civilian goods, being smaller and lighter than the military hardware, were usually packed aboard a runner last and in a somewhat helter-skelter manner—there was always room for one more box of handkerchiefs, and each item in that box brought a greater percentage of profit than a case of rifles. *Florimel*'s luxury goods were therefore crammed in every sort of nook—button cards, hosiery, linen, umbrellas, gloves, Sheffield razors, tea biscuits, Dutch chocolate, fine stationery; there was so much of it that Lamb's party gave up trying to inventory the goods. They would all be sold at auction, anyway, just as soon as Wilmington's speculators learned of the wrecking and descended upon the site like locusts. The discovery of several hundred bottles, and casks, what the manifest described as "Misc. Spiritous Liquors," occasioned a lively debate among the officers. One of Lamb's first general orders had been to impose an absolute ban on alcohol within every part of the fort except for the hospital. In this matter, he would not budge; except for two kegs of "medicinal" brandy, the whiskey and champagne remained where it was.

For maximum protection, the gunpowder had been loaded first and deepest below the deck. Most of it, indeed, proved to be spoiled by the thigh-high slurry of water that had poured in at high tide through the ragged holes torn open by Fort Fisher's cannons. Some eighteen 100-pound kegs, however, had been stored high enough to stay dry. Such a small portion of the whole was just a proverbial drop in the bucket when measured against the vast needs of Lee's army—hardly worth the trouble of extricating and shipping on, in fact. Conversely, eighteen hundred pounds of fine Woolwich powder would make a significant addition to the fort's magazine. After dithering for a moment about the impropriety, Lamb finally agreed to appropriate the barrels and smudge the numbers in his official report.

So much cargo space had been given over to the massive powder shipment that few other military goods were on the manifest, and one of them was a puzzlement: "Two Whitworth rifles, with Accessories & Ammunition for same."

"What in blazes is a Whitworth rifle?" muttered Reilly. "And what possible use can there be for only two of them?"

A search of the forward hold eventually answered those questions. The rifles turned out not to be individual shoulder-fired weapons of some exotic kind but a pair of field guns eleven feet long and weighing half a ton. They were breechloaders of a pattern that Reilly had never seen before, and despite their skinny appearance and relatively tiny bore, they gave off a decidedly businesslike aura. The Whitworths did not appear heavy enough to use against ships—or anything larger than a chicken coop, for that matter—but they must be good for something. Colonel Lamb inspected the long, thin weapons with a dubious scowl.

"Major Reilly, I want you to uncrate and mount one of these pieces, then test-fire it on the far side of the Point, where the Yankees can't see what you're doing. Find out if it is worth keeping for any reason. These things look more like toys than serious field artillery, but even popguns are better than no guns, so give them a proper workout before I decide whether or not to send them on to Virginia."

For the next two days, Frederick Reilly enjoyed one of his happiest interludes as an artillerist. Once mounted on a field carriage, the sample Whitworth proved so light and well balanced that it could be maneuvered rapidly by only four mules. You could unlimber it, aim, fire a few rounds, and be on your way to another spot in minutes. The breech was sealed by a screw plug; the propellant came in small two-pound silk bags and vaporized when fired, leaving no detritus in the barrel; and the projectile was a pointed hexagonal iron bolt weighing twelve and a half pounds, quite unlike any missile Reilly had ever seen. At first, Reilly and his gunners found the little dart risible—an example, perhaps, of the well-known British fondness for eccentricity. What damage could such a puny arrow do to a steam frigate?

And then they began to test-fire the thing. At 10 degrees of elevation, the Whitworth bolt flew forty-five hundred yards; and at its maximum elevation of thirty-five degrees, the little cannon delivered an unheard-of range slightly in excess of ten thousand yards. Evidently, that hexagonal shape of the projectile reduced air friction dramatically. Moreover, once the gunners got the hang of things, the Whitworth delivered shot after shot at any range with astonishing pinpoint accuracy. Windage and friction did not faze those sharp little bolts. If you aimed the gun properly, you nailed the target, first time and every time. It really was more like a sharpshooter's rifle than an ordinary cannon. Reilly and his men quickly changed their attitude from skepticism to adoration. Rather gleefully, they arranged a dramatic demonstration for Colonel Lamb.

On the third morning, Reilly instructed Lamb to keep his telescope fixed on a Yankee warship that was slowly prowling back and forth at a distance of two and a half miles, just beyond the reach of Lamb's conventional weapons. Then Reilly rode out to the dunes beside the Wilmington Road, where he had hidden the Whitworths, and their carriages. At a signal, the guns came charging into sight, the drivers and crewmen whooping and hollering at the tops of their lungs. When the battery reached the broad gray sand between dunes and sea, the drivers careened into position, unhitched the animals, and led them away, while the gun crews swarmed around the Whitworths, loading them in seconds. Enjoying the moment, and basking in the attention of hundreds of soldiers who had stopped shoveling, drilling, and piling sand long enough to witness the show, Reilly strode briskly from gun to gun and fine-tuned the aim. At his command, the Whitworths barked in unison—sharp little bangs that sounded like firecrackers—then commenced independent rapid fire at the targeted blockader.

William Lamb peered intently at the enemy ship and was startled to see its rigging and superstructure begin to tatter and shake under a rain of iron bolts. No serious damage resulted from the hits—although any man unlucky enough to stop one would surely be torn asunder—but the crew began running around frantically, stunned to find themselves peppered with accurate fire at so great a distance. The gunboat belched smoke as she poured on the steam, and within minutes she was in flight. Although Lamb could no longer see the little rounds' impact, Reilly's men maintained a brisk and apparently accurate fire until their target was five miles out. It took a few minutes for Lamb to realize the full significance of what he was seeing, but then it struck him like a blessing from Jehovah: thanks to the Whitworths, the blockaders would now have to patrol a line half again as far from New Inlet as their previous stations. True, the feisty little guns could not cause extensive damage, but they could sting and frighten and demoralize and kill. Reilly and his "flying battery" could have saved the *Florimel.* And in the future, they could shield any other runner whose skipper found himself in similar trouble. No, indeed, these guns would not be sent to Virginia—by their very potential to cause mischief at such unprecedented range, they materially increased the odds in favor of the runners, and that was what William Lamb had promised the Lord he would do.

Autumn descended on the Carolina coast with a slow delicacy that Will Cushing found enchanting. He was accustomed to the sudden onslaughts that characterized the seasonal shift in upstate New York, where everything from the turning of the leaves to the gathering of the harvests was dramatic, decisive, a profound demarcation that signified to everyone from schoolchildren to apple growers: "Winter is imminent. Chop the wood! Bind the sheaves! Press the cider! Time is short, so get cracking!"

On the sprawling big-skyed waters of North Carolina, the seasons changed subtly, gently, luxuriously. By mid-September, August's gross humidity had drained away, leaving the air crisp and pellucid. October brought a deepening mood; the nights turned deliciously cool and the sunlight aquired a particular tint of mellow gold. You could see farther, breathe more deeply, sleep in greater comfort, perform your duties with newfound zest. The burnished cast of light lent to every object the patina of waxen clarity, and also the strangeness, of things viewed under sunlit water. Will Cushing thought this was a lovely place to be.

He also thought Charles Flusser was the finest naval officer he had ever served under. Flusser had gotten his first taste of real naval action during the fight at Elizabeth City, and the experience had acted on his nerves like a powerful stimulating drug. Like Cushing, he was a slender, high-strung, almost elegant figure of a man, and utterly committed to the notion of relentless aggressive action. His piercing gray eyes and wide, prominent forehead always seemed to precede the rest of his body when he strode forward, as though the man's very physiognomy were the anatomical equivalent of a gunboat's bow. He constantly chivvied his squadron from one Carolina river to another. If things were too quiet for his taste around New Bern, he would lead probes up the rivers from Plymouth or Edenton or Elizabeth City, following, like a champion foxhound, every scent of Rebel activity that rumor, deserters, or runaway slaves brought to his attention. Had it been possible to attach wheels to the bottoms of his gunboats, he would doubtless already have launched them overland to attack Raleigh. Will Cushing admired him more than any other living

American sailor and loved him as a brother, and Flusser had irritated more than one superior officer by insisting that Cushing be given command of his own ship.

Cushing could not have been more delighted: the *Commodore Perry* was a stout little gunboat; the dreariness of blockade duty was behind him; and the mysterious, still-troubling incident of Captain Miles's apparent collusion in the escape of a known blockade-runner had receded like the memory of a bad dream. Perhaps the whole scene had been a hallucination caused by the typhoid fever. Cushing preferred to believe it so, rather than dwell on the possibility that a sworn officer of the United States Navy was corrupted to the point of something very much like treason.

After Burnside departed for the Peninsula, along with eight thousand of his best men, command of the Coastal Division fell upon the broad and burly shoulders of General John Gray Foster, who had commanded Burnside's First Brigade with admirable steadiness. A large, heavily bearded man with a square, honest face, Foster had fewer than nine thousand men with which to defend every Union enclave on the North Carolina coast. Such a force was scarcely large enough for defensive security and far below the number required for major offensive operations. To maximize the Federal presence, Foster set about turning New Bern, Plymouth, Beaufort, and Elizabeth City into self-contained fortresses, girded by multiple lines of entrenchments and bristling with artillery.

Foster did have one great advantage: total control of the water. This enabled him to reinforce quickly any garrison that might be threatened. He had a good working relationship with his naval counterpart, Commander Stephen C. Rowan, who had replaced the garrulous and vinegary Goldsborough when that elderly officer went into semiretirement. Rowan had plenty of small, maneuverable gunboats by the summer of 1862, and he deployed them vigorously, performing armed reconnaissance for Foster, escorting raiding parties up the rivers, bringing supplies and succor to isolated communities of Unionists. Rowan, in turn, had no finer subordinate officer than Lieutenant Commander Charles Flusser, who now commanded a three-ship flotilla. And Flusser believed there was no braver or more capable officer under his command than Will Cushing.

In late September, Flusser's gunboats had moved to Edenton, to cover the western end of Albemarle Sound while General Foster laid out a defensive plan for Plymouth, a strategically placed village at the mouth of the Roanoke River. Foster was skeptical about the rumors that a Rebel ironclad was under construction in the vicinity—local Unionists had told him there was no suitable place for such a project anywhere along the upper Roanoke—but Plymouth was a useful outpost even so, and Foster wanted it well fortified.

Flusser was elated when, on the morning of October 2, Foster took a launch over to Edenton and outlined for him the details of a mission that offered outstanding prospects for action: General John A. Dix, commander of the Federal Seventh Corps, headquartered at Fortress Monroe, had received reliable intelligence that a Rebel force said to number ten thousand was secretly gathering at Franklin, Virginia, preparing to launch a surprise attack on the Union supply depot at Suffolk, some twenty miles east of Franklin. Dix proposed a preemptive strike by a combined army-navy force, timed to catch the Rebel column as it was crossing a narrow bridge on the Blackwater River—the only practicable route for an advance on Suffolk. Twelve thousand infantry from the Seventh Corps would attack the enemy concentration as soon as their officers heard the unmistakable roar of naval ordnance near the crossing point.

After telegraphing his concurrence to Fortress Monroe, General Foster, who had personally come to Flusser's base at Edenton, asked Flusser if the operation were feasible, and after studying the maps and consulting with a couple of pro-Union pilots who claimed familiarity with the area, Flusser reported that it was. His ships could ascend the Chowan River to a point just north of the Virginia line where the Blackwater joined the Chowan as a tributary. The Blackwater was narrower and more twisty, to be sure, and there might be sandbars to worry about—for the weather had been dry as well as temperate—but the *Commodore Perry* drew only six feet of water and her sister ships, the *Hunchback* and the *Whitehead,* drew only a foot more and had bigger engines. Flusser estimated that his doughty trio should arrive at the targeted bridge between six-thirty and seven on the morning of October 3, by which time the Federal infantry should be in place, well-rested, and ready to pounce. If this hammer-and-anvil tactic worked, the Rebs should suffer a real drubbing.

If army-navy coordination went awry, Flusser was still determined to do all the damage he could from the water. Altogether, his ships mounted fourteen guns, at least six of them larger than any field artillery the enemy was presumed to have, and of the two hundred sailors he commanded, at least one hundred of them could serve as riflemen. Unless the Confederates had learned to walk on water, he thought there was every reasonable prospect of striking them hard and then extricating the gunboats before things got too hot, with or without assistance from the army.

In a state of crackling excitement, Will Cushing undertook preparations for the adventure. He ordered all the solid shot off-loaded and replaced with shells and canister, and made sure there were two rifles loaded for each of the *Perry's* thirty-six crewmen. He also requisitioned some bales of unpressed cotton, which he placed at suitable locations around the decks as extra protection. At two o'clock in the morning, Flusser's expedition cast off and steamed toward the Chowan River's broad mouth. Ninety minutes later, an urgent telegram arrived from Fortress Monroe: new information indicated that the Rebel thrust had been cancelled or postponed—there would be no Union infantry attack. Instead of delivering a surprise blow against a vulnerable column crossing a river, Flusser's gunboats were heading straight for a region where the enemy was numerous, well dug in, and screened by cavalry pickets who were certain to spot the flotilla long before it reached its objective. General Foster immediately dispatched the fastest launch available to overtake Flusser, but Flusser was steaming north at a speed just this side of reckless and there was no catching him.

Not a shot or a cry of alarm disturbed the night as the *Commodore Perry* and her charges chugged up the Chowan. Neither Flusser nor Cushing could sleep, of course, but they encouraged the nonessential crewmen to rest while they could. The Chowan marked the northern boundary of the huge peninsula that bulged out between Albermarle and Pamlico Sounds, comprising eight sparsely inhabited counties. With Rebel forces concentrated farther inland, shielding the vital Wilmington and Weldon Railroad, and Foster's units fortified in their scattered coastal enclaves, the whole region had become a no-man's-land. Troubling rumors had reached Foster concerning the growing number of outliers, deserters, and brigands who had laid claim to the pine barrens and empty cabins as the civilian population moved out, but as yet there was no hard-and-fast information about these desperadoes, whom the locals referred to by the catch-all name of Buffaloes.

These were lonesome and forlorn lands, Cushing thought. Nameless swamps brooded in the predawn gloom, cypress stumps jutting up like scarecrows or sentries carved from driftwood. When the gunboats did pass arable land, the cabins were dark and the cornfields rattled emptily in the wind. Not even a dog barked as the ships went by.

"At least the banks are low," observed Flusser, struggling to light a cigar on the lee side of the pilothouse. "No place here for an ambush, even if there were any Rebs around to plan one."

"That will change, sir," said the pilot. "Once we pass Winton, on the port side, we'll be leaving the coastal swamps and heading into the piedmont."

"Who controls this Winton?" asked Cushing.

"I don't reckon nobody 'controls' it, Lieutenant Cushing. Ain't much there worth fighting over, as I remember. Just a couple hundred farmers and fishermen. Like as not, all they want is to be left alone . . . by both sides."

"One does not blame them," said Flusser. "All the same, it would be prudent to have the guns manned when we steam past the place. Signal the other boats, Will, and make sure the howitzer is double-charged with cannister."

"Aye, sir!" Cushing was at once in motion, relaying the order to the *Hunchback* and the *Whitehead,* who were steaming in line behind the flagship, each vessel separated from the other by an interval of one hundred yards. After the order was acknowledged, Cushing strode to the fantail, where Flusser had mounted a 12-pounder howitzer on a wheeled carriage. Although useless against a warship or a fortified battery, the stubby little gun could deliver massive blasts of canister or grapeshot at close range.

Three sailors lay dozing around the cannon, resting their heads against the cotton bales Cushing had positioned there as protection against small-arms fire. He knelt and gently nudged Boatswain's Mate Babcock, a deceptively stout man who generally wore a sleepy placid expression, but who could galvanize his gun crew with volcanic energy and a barrage of fire-breathing billingsgate so colorfully profane that his very oaths could be loaded and fired.

"Mister Babcock? Dawn is not far off and we shall soon be passing a town on the port side. It is time to ready the howitzer."

Babcock's eyes flew open like two small gun-ports, and he was instantly in motion, rousing the other two gunners none too gently.

"What shall we load her with, Mister Cushing?"

"If we are ambushed, our first shot must be a daisy. If we're ever going to try out that special recipe of yours, this might be the time."

"You heard the lieutenant, you mangy sons of bitches! Time for the 'Babcock Special'!"

Cushing watched with amusement as Babcock's men rammed

home a conventional half-pound powder bag, followed by a stand of grapeshot—nine 1-inch balls nested in a banded container. Such was the regulation load. Babcock, however, had devised a fiendish addition: an empty flour tin crammed with approximately sixty-five .38-caliber pistol balls, compressed like a shotgun load by strips of tarred linen. Once that had been tamped down on top of the grapeshot stand, Babcock carefully inserted a thin wooden disc, cut to match the howitzer's bore, and on top of this he poured several handfuls of bolts, nails, and pieces of scrap iron. In effect, he was triple-charging the gun. Because the powder would be pushing so much additional metal when it fired, the effective range of this load was only about sixty yards. And since it took so long to load, Cushing figured there would only be time enough to fire the "Babcock Special" once—the idea, though, was to make that first shot so devastating that it would either sweep the bushwhackers away or so terrify them as to drive them under cover.

Dawn was gathering by the time they steamed past Winton. No one fired at them. White flags adorned many of the houses. An air of seedy decrepitude hung over the place. Only one soul came out to watch the gunboats pass—a scrawny boy who managed one timid wave before a sharp command from some invisible adult caused him to scamper off.

By the time they reached the Virginia line, sunrise was imminent and Flusser was concerned that they were falling behind schedule. He asked the pilot if it was safe to ring on another knot or two. The fellow hemmed and hawed, then admitted under sharp questioning that his knowledge of what lay north of the state line was secondhand. Flusser thought about it for a moment. Then, true to his aggressive nature, he ordered a slight increase in speed. He signaled the other two boats to stay as they were, due to their deeper draft and greater size. A gap some two hundred yards now opened between the *Perry* and the *Hunchback*.

Cushing could see into the water now, for they had passed out of the tar-colored coastal streams and in the fresh autumn dawn the river ran a clear cold olive. As the light grew, he could see mossy submerged tree limbs near the western shore, but no sandbars or dangerous rocks, for which he thanked God, for the riverbanks were solid on both sides and not as low-lying as before. Soon, he reckoned, they must reach the Blackwater's confluence and not far up that stream, the bridge . . . and the enemy. Flusser ordered every man to action stations except for the pilot, the engineer, and the stokers. Loaded rifles were passed out and the men thus armed took cover behind the cotton bales on the left side.

They came upon the Blackwater's mouth quite suddenly. Ordering a hard turn to port, Flusser scanned the banks of this new stream with wary intensity. He jumped when Cushing tapped his shoulder.

"Charles—there's a sharp bend ahead, and maybe some rocks."

"Reduce speed and keep the helm centered in midstream! You there, on the bow, take a sounding every thirty seconds and keep your eyes peeled for shoals and submerged logs!"

"I don't like the look of this," muttered Cushing, as the *Perry* turned hard to the right. At this point a sharp brush-covered wedge of land jutted out some fifty feet; what lay beyond the bend could not be seen until they rounded its knobby point. Cushing drew his revolver. Whatever lay beyond that angle, it was certain that the *Perry* would be isolated for an unpleasant length of time, uncovered by the *Hunchback*'s powerful bow chaser. Cautiously, the *Perry* nosed its way around the sharpest part of the promontory, and when the other side crawled slowly into view, the crew let out a collective sigh of relief: the river's left bank seemed deserted, a wide, shallow, gully-carved band of dry red clay, and the broad shallows at water's edge were carpeted by a profusion of smooth, water-polished pebbles. A man standing in those shallows could almost reach out and touch the side of the gunboat as it passed, but the shelf of rocks and bubbling shallows ended abruptly and the main channel still looked unobstructed and sufficiently deep.

"There's the bridge!" said the man on the bow, rather more loudly than Cushing deemed prudent.

"Any sign of that Rebel column?"

"No, sir. Everything looks peaceful."

"So far it does," said Will Cushing, and before he could say another word, the riverbank exploded with motion. Men in butternut uniforms popped up everywhere, like flocks of startled quail. "Heave, you men!" cried a Rebel officer who seemed to materialize out of thin air, frantically waving his sword. At this man's signal, a large group of soldiers rose up as one and leaned back, straining like competitors in a tug-of-war. Just aft of the gunboat's modest wake, a thick rope cable popped into view, dripping and matted with vegetation, then snapping taut across the main channel. The cable's far end was anchored deep in a grove of pines and the men hauling on the near side scurried madly to secure their end around some iron pilings that had been camouflaged by a screen of underbrush. Just before the firing started, Cushing had time to admire the cleverness of the trap. Cut off from her two larger escorts, unable to turn around because the channel was too narrow, the *Commodore Perry* was as good as bagged. Worse: the enemy was so close, and the slope of the riverbank so shallow, that her heavy guns could not depress enough to engage. Fortunately, neither could the two elderly bronze 12-pounders supporting the ambush. Both weapons fired—so close that Cushing could feel the heat from their muzzles—but their grapeshot balls passed over the ship by a matter of inches, peppering the smokestack and cutting some of the rigging, but otherwise doing no harm. Cushing yelped with relief when he felt the air over his head shiver with the missiles' passing. Then he heard a muffled *thunk* and he was knocked off his feet by the weight of Charles Flusser's body.

Crying his friend's name aloud, Cushing knelt down and examined Flusser for wounds. Flusser was breathing, albeit harshly, and his eyelids fluttered; no blood spurted, but there was a wicked bruise purpling across his temple. Cushing looked around at the bits of debris flung down by the near miss and quickly divined what had happened. A grapeshot ball had severed one of the guy wires supporting the stack and when it snapped, the wire whipped down, clouting Flusser in the head. His cap, badly torn, must have blocked the full force of the blow; otherwise Flusser would have been leaking brains instead of just knocked senseless.

You are in command now, Will Cushing! You are the executive officer and your captain is down! Act, and show no fear!

In reality, he felt none. Cushing felt his whole being—mind, body, and heart—shift into what he recognized as *battle mode:* a vivid dilation of time and vision that made everything around him unfold in slow motion and with preternatural clarity. He dragged Flusser to the starboard side of the pilothouse, where he would be sheltered from the hailstorm of minié balls now raking the gunboat from bow to fantail. As he did so, he yelled over his shoulder: "Return fire, men! Pick your targets well! Aim for the officers first!"

From behind their cotton ramparts, the *Perry's* sailors began to shoot back—twenty-five rifles against two hundred or more. All the ambushers had to do was fire in the gunboat's general direction. At this range, they could not miss hitting *something.* He heard balls crunching into wood, shattering portholes, fluffing into cotton, clanging against the ship's bell, ricochets whanging off the barrels of the impotent Parrott rifles. By act of will, he tuned out the racket and confusion, summoning a clear, abstract vision of their situation, as though he were viewing it from high above and in perfect tranquillity. The *Commodore Perry* could not move forward or it would run fast aground; it could not turn back out into deeper water, for there was not enough room. Their only hope, it seemed to Cushing, was to put her in reverse and back out into deep water near the channel bend, where all the heavy guns could at last be brought to bear, broadside, on their tormentors. But the enemy, very cleverly, had set their boom rope at an acute angle, and if the *Perry* tried to back up in its present location, the boom would either hold it fast or become entangled in the paddles. That rope would have to be cut. Cushing immediately ducked into the engineering compartment and demanded an axe. One of the black-streaked, wild-eyed stokers handed him one. Cushing climbed back on deck and prepared to run the gauntlet of fire to the fantail.

"Mister Cushing! They're going to board us!"

He looked toward the enemy shore and was stunned to see an entire Rebel company forming up, bayonets gleaming, for a charge. Only fifty yards of solid ground and ankle-deep shallows separated the *Perry* from its attackers, who dressed ranks with admirable coolness, flinching only when one of Cushing's riflemen raised up and snapped off a shot. Despite the cotton bales, such a tempest of lead beat down on the boat that several sailors were already hit and the others' fire slacked off as they huddled fearfully behind whatever cover they could find. Now Cushing saw a Rebel officer stand up fearlessly in front of the assault company—a big rangy fellow with long yellow hair and a fine curly beard whose face, like Cushing's, was bathed in the unhallowed glow of battle lust.

Without a second to spare, Cushing did not waste time moving to the more protected starboard side, but sprinted, ducking and twisting and crouching, straight for the stern. Bosun's Mate Babcock and two of his men were banging away with Springfields, but the third gunner was sprawled across a cotton bale, head down, a pool of blood spreading across the deck beneath his ruined face.

"Mister Babcock!"

"Aye, Mister Cushing?"

"Take my pistol!"—Cushing slid his Colt across the deck into Babcock's open hand—"and give me rapid-fire cover when I make this dash! On count of three! One . . . two . . . "

Babcock rested his brawny forearms on the cotton bale, gripping the revolver with both fists, and cracked off six aimed shots as Cushing dove across the last open space between himself and the howitzer. He felt something claw at his shoulder and something else drill a hole through the flapping tail of his jacket, but nothing hurt and nothing bled.

"They're working up for a charge, Mister Babcock."

"I can see that they are, yes!"

"It is very simple: if we cannot stop them with the howitzer, they will board us for sure and we will either be slain or condemned to spend the rest of the war in some hellhole of a prison camp. Can you and your men stand the fire?"

"We can if you can, Mister Cushing!"

Up rose Babcock and his two remaining gunners, each man's shoulders pinched tightly to present the smallest possible target, and began to swivel the howitzer. For a few precious seconds, the sheer audacity of their act seemed to paralyze the Rebels. Cushing added his own wiry strength and by the time the Rebel fire redoubled, he was satisfied that the howitzer was pointed straight into the path of the attackers, who were now charging pell-mell down the embankment and splashing into the pebble-strewn shallows, kicking up fans of spray, bayonets leveled, Rebel yells like Viking war cries, and the big bearded officer in front, half berserk, teeth bared and throat corded, sword in one hand and pistol in the other. Every other Confederate rifleman supported the charge by pouring a cone of fire at the howitzer crew. So many balls choked the air around him that Cushing felt like a human tuning-fork, his thin skeleton vibrating and his slender knotted muscles burning like brands.

Thok!

One of the gunners took a ball in the chest—a ragged hole spewing blue thread before the thick jellied welter of blood foamed out, like a spill of crushed wet red carnations.

"Unghk!"

The other sailor, his fist already closed around the firing lanyard, puffed blue and red feathers, like a game bird shredded in midflight, and spun away, dead before he hit the deck.

Babcock leaped for the lanyard but a ball smashed his thigh and he folded into an agonized knot, bright arterial blood spraying through his clutching fingers.

Will Cushing was now alone, his clothes already torn by several near-misses. He did not expect to live more than a few more raw distended seconds as he stepped over the fallen, took one final sight down the howitzer barrel, and yanked the lanyard.

At a range of no more than twenty yards, the blast of grapeshot and scrap iron cut down the charging infantry like Death's own reaping hook. Their Rebel yells turned to howls of agony. Limbs flew off like twigs in a hurricane, faces melted into smashed watermelons, and lengths of shattered bowel flew like snakes. When the smoke cleared, Cushing beheld a dreadful slaughter: the pebble-strewn shallows seethed with clotted red matter and pathetic strips of flayed uniform, with shattered rifle stocks and booted feet sliced from their owners' legs, with pulped and severed heads, with every imaginable ruin of human anatomy. One particular vignette burned itself indelibly in Cushing's memory: half a human skull, like a broken teacup, lined with mushy brains, the roiled waters rinsing through it as though Nature itself were trying to wash it clean. Those attackers who did not immediately die lay screaming like animals, and most of the men who miraculously escaped serious harm, fled back up the embankment as fast as their legs would function.

Yet the bearded Rebel officer and several men beside him remained upright, the discharge having swept past them by inches, and this valiant remnant came charging on. The *Perry*'s sailors, also stunned by the carnage, were slow to respond and managed only a few shots before the Confederate survivors reached the ship and began scrambling over the gunwales. Their compatriots on shore were forced to hold their fire and Cushing yelled out an order that had probably not been heard in these waters since the days of Blackbeard: "Repel boarders!"

Pistols crashed, rifle butts clubbed down, cutlasses swung. And the big Rebel officer came on, straight for Cushing, determined, at the very least, to cut down the man who had slaughtered his company. Cushing groped for his Colt, then remembered that he had given it to Babcock earlier. Desperately, he took up a ramrod and held it like a quarterstaff. But the Rebel officer disdained the implied challenge of man-to-man combat and coolly leveled his pistol at Cushing. Despite the noise and confusion all around him, Cushing distinctly heard the hammer cock, and he braced himself for the impact.

Then the Rebel officer's eyes went wide and blank and a hole appeared in his chest the size of a half-dollar, right upon his valorous heart. Slowly, like a felled oak, the big man toppled backward and crashed into the water.

Cushing turned and saw Babcock, white-faced with pain and loss of blood, but grinning wildly behind a smoking Springfield rifle. Babcock slowly lowered the weapon, with what must surely have been his last ounce of vitality, gave Cushing a big schoolboy wink, and croaked, "Close one, sir!" He was dead before Cushing could reach him.

Now the Rebels' fire became sullen and desultory, and the energized sailors on the gunboat began shooting back more vigorously and much more accurately. Dimly, Cushing saw one of the enemy artillery teams making ready to drag one of the bronze Napoleons to a new position, presumably a site from which the gun could depress far enough to rake the *Perry*. They were not out of the woods yet. Cushing retrieved his axe and waded out to the boom rope. Bullets flailed the water all around him, but to the men watching him, he seemed as cool as ice. A dozen swipes of the blade, and the boom was cut. Cushing climbed back aboard, ordered the engines reversed, and carefully steered the gunboat stern-first into deeper water. No longer obstructed by the boom, the *Hunchback* came nosing around the promontory and immediately opened fire with two Parrott rifles, blowing big red chunks out of the embankment and sending the remaining Rebels scrambling for cover.

Only when the flotilla was reunited and steaming back toward Albemarle Sound did Cushing relinquish the helm and sit down. Charles Flusser, meanwhile, had regained full consciousness, and when he heard from those who tended him about what had occurred during the ambush, he came topside to congratulate Will Cushing. But Cushing, when Flusser found him, was sitting alone near the howitzer, trembling with shock and weeping quietly as he held the cold white hand of Bosun's Mate Babcock.

The Price of Rice

MR. VANCE'S INAUGURAL SPEECH—On Monday last, the 8th instant, about 12 o'clock, the Hon. Z. B. Vance, of Buncombe was inaugurated Governor of North Carolina. The oaths of office were administered by the Chief Justice of the State, in the presence of a large number of ladies and gentlemen, the ceremonies taking place near the West Entrance of the State House, where a platform had been erected for the purpose, and from which the inaugural address was delivered. Below, we publish this document today in full.

We might express our dissent from some portions of the historical sketch which forms the opening part of Governor Vance's address, but we do not wish to mar the heartiness and cordiality of the approval which the general tone of the speech merits, by criticism of its more ephemeral parts. As a whole, the Address is bold, manly, and patriotic. It breathes a spirit and indicates a policy which, if carried out and adhered to by Governor Vance, will redound to his own credit and to the welfare of the State.

—The Wilmington Journal, September 11 1862

Pine Haven's rice crop had been planted in the usual way in the April that marked the first full year of war, and Matthew Sloane had taken some time off from blockade-running to supervise the process. This far up the Uwharrie branch of the Cape Fear River, the water's salt content was minimal, but there was still enough of a tidal cycle to permit irrigation. Matthew's father had bought this land because it reminded him of the low country around Charleston, where rice flourished with profligate abundance. He had raised stout dikes, walling off the marshlands bordering the Uwharrie, drained the acreage, and cleared away all unnecessary vegetation. The highest, thickest embankment was along the riverbank itself, perforated by wooden culverts, which were rigged with sluice gates so that water could be admitted or drained as needed during the complicated planting process. The whole expanse of reclaimed land was then subdivided into neat squares, their edges scored with "quarter-drains" in such a way as to ensure even flooding to the proper depth. Teams of oxen plowed under these fields in April and the rills of grossly turned earth were carefully hoed, almost granulated, until each plot was as level and fine-grained in texture as the flower beds of a formal garden.

Then the actual planting furrows were laid down in shallow drills, one foot apart, and the most skilled hands turned out to string the seeds, spilling them carefully through their fingers so that the seeds would be neither too skimpy to take root nor so thick as to form unproductive clumps. After the sowing, the sluice gates were opened and the fields covered with shallow water until the tender green sprouts poked up high enough to fork; after that, the water was drained or raised as needed to permit weeding, to drown certain kinds of insects, or to give physical support to the plants until they were robust enough to stand on their own. Matthew always spoke of this moment as "casting our bread upon the waters." Three months after the sowing came the final irrigation, known as the long water, then rice was left alone, for sixty or seventy days, to ripen.

If all went well—no hurricane-born floods or prolonged dry spells—the crop was ready for harvest by mid-September. This was the time of the rice fields' greatest beauty, when they shimmered like silk in response to every breeze, shoulder-high, emerald green, and crowned with golden grains. This graceful transcendence was fleeting, for the reaping, once begun, took only two or three days to accomplish. After the stalks dried, they were collected in sheaves and carried to Pine Haven's impressively up-to-date steam-powered threshing mill.

The Sloanes' plantation was rich in land, but the slave population was not large enough to bring in the harvest and simultaneously keep up with its year-round tasks, so every September Mary Harper's father, Stepney, dispatched a supplemental crew of skilled field hands from Limerick. In this way the rice could be cut down and sheaved and carried to the mill with optimum dispatch. The first wartime harvest had gone well; the extra hands showed up on time, did their work, enjoyed a big celebratory picnic afterward, and departed back for South Carolina with some extra change in their pockets.

By the autumn of 1862, however, things were starting to break down, and there were days when Mary Harper felt oppressed by the weight of responsibilities that had previously been borne wholly by her husband. As early as the April planting, she had known that it would be so, and at first she had welcomed the challenge. Rice planting was something she had known intimately all her life, and she was blithely confident that she could handle the business on her own. She wanted to present her gallant husband with a prime abundant harvest, almost as a gift, a fait accompli, proving to him that he was truly free of old, cloying domestic duties, free to pursue his new, adventurous, wildly profitable career on the high seas. Bring in such a harvest, she told herself, and Matthew would be as proud of her as she was of him.

By summer's wane, however, she was beleaguered by circumstances over which she had no control; she was frustrated and angry when harvesttime drew near and she realized that Pine Haven's rice crop would not simply fall over in gracious mannalike abundance—as it always seemed to in the past—but would have to be fought for and wrested from the earth against increasingly daunting odds.

Summer had crawled by in a great sluggish tide of enervating heat and choking humidity. Even the most reliable Negroes grew torpid and careless: one man was lamed by an accident and another died after, rather stupidly, treading on a large copperhead. There were other casualties, too, enough to reduce the labor force significantly. One woman died in childbirth, another of old age, and two of the younger men—the last new slaves Matthew had acquired before the war—ran off one night. From questioning the other blacks, Mary Harper learned that both newcomers had contracted "Abolition Fever." Apparently, they had also somehow learned that the Yankees now occupied a number of coastal towns to the north; so they lit out one moonless night with every intention of reaching enemy lines. But in their ignorance of regional geography they could not have grasped the fact that the nearest Union enclave was at least a hundred miles away and separated from Pine Haven by dangerous swamps and trackless forests. No one ever saw them alive again, but the body of one did show up a week later, drifting down the Uwharrie, so bloated and waterlogged that he could be identified only by the shirt on his back.

Mary Harper was disturbed by these events, although she gave no outward sign of it. In all her years at Pine Haven, no Negro had ever run away . . . and now—two at the same time. Matthew Sloane expected hard, competent work from his slaves, but he was a humane master in all respects. In his fields, the whip was never wielded. On the rare occasions when Fitz-John Bright discovered theft, dishonesty, or malingering, he settled the issue with his big red fists and scathing tongue, never with a branding iron or a rod. Pine Haven's Negroes lived in snug cabins, ate well from the crops they raised, and enjoyed a holiday on every Sabbath. When they were sick or injured, they were tended to, if necessary by a doctor summoned from Wilmington. A Northern observer might well conclude that the Sloanes were only protecting the large investment represented by any able-bodied slave, but Mary Harper believed that her husband's concern for the blacks' basic welfare sprang from his large fund of basic human decency.

Not once in all Mary Harper's years as plantation mistress had she detected malice or the sullen glower of incipient revolt. If her servants had even heard the word "abolition," it would have been from the random drifting conversations of guests. If their simple minds had formed any opinion from such fragmentary knowledge, it would surely be as dim and strange as the principles of Hindu theology. Such might no longer be the case. Who knew what those two runaways had said, what fantasies they had spun to the others before they made their break, what seeds of discontent they had sown?

She could not, of course, come right out and ask anyone, not even the most trusted individuals such as Agrippa and Aurelia, toward whom Mary Harper felt a genuine maternal affection. She must continue as though nothing had changed, even though something had. She was not afraid, of course, but she did experience an apprehensive *refocusing*. How well, really, did she know any of these black souls? What did they talk about in the nocturnal privacy of their cabins? What, above all, were their *dreams*? Did they now harbor some inchoate notion that this horrible war would lead to a jubilee? And if they did, were they really as trustworthy now as they had always seemed before? Did Agrippa's affable smile mask discontent, resentment, some latent malice that was now just biding its time?

As much as she hated these thoughts, Mary Harper had to confront them, if only for one primal reason: except for the brief visits Matthew made between voyages, she was alone here, with two small children and no neighbor closer than a three-hour ride on a very bad road. Her only real lifeline to the outside world was the little steam launch she used for necessary trips to Wilmington, and it could easily be stolen or disabled. So by summer's end, Mary Harper carried a new dark weight in addition to the burdens of daily management that had devolved upon her in Matthew's absence. Although she strove to maintain a business-as-usual demeanor, she had become wary.

August, as usual, brought the worst heat and the annual scourge of mosquitoes, which manifested themselves as restless grainy clouds churning above the irrigation channels. When the first case of malaria showed up among the field hands, she was not surprised. Nor was she unduly alarmed, at first, because Matthew was in all respects a progressive agriculturist; he had read that regular doses of quinine could save the lives of the fever-stricken and so he had maintained a sufficient stock of it in the house. Mary Harper simply assumed that Matthew had restocked the drug, as he routinely did every spring. But when she examined the supply, she was horrified to learn that he had neglected to do so this year. She felt a flash of irritation—even when he was off gallivanting on the *Banshee,* he should have been mindful of such a vital matter. She estimated there were enough doses on hand for five weeklong treatments. Given the way things had been going, she knew that was insufficient; if she did not obtain more quinine, the field hands would start dropping at an alarming rate.

So when two more cases were confirmed, she reached two decisions. First, she had to go to Wilmington and purchase more quinine, no matter how inflated the price had become; second, she packed up the children's trunks and told them they were going to Grandpa Stepney's plantation for a long visit. As long as she kept them indoors, away from the damp and noxious vapors that were thought to spread the disease, they were probably safe. But "probably" was not enough, not the way things were going. So many concerns pressed down on her now that she had become short-tempered with the children. She was spread too thin, and the harvest was still six weeks away. So she took them downriver to the railroad station and put them on a train for Charleston. Then she sent a telegram to her father. Stepney Harper was a third-generation low-country planter who knew full well how miasmic and unhealthy the coast could be in late summer. For that reason, he maintained a small but picturesque home in the cool green hills overlooking the French Broad River, near Asheville. Several times before, he had taken his grandchildren to that oasis, and if the train did not break down, the children would reach Charleston just in time to travel with him to the high country. Mary Harper kissed them good-bye with mingled emotions of sadness and relief.

Her other purpose for going to Wilmington was thwarted utterly.

Not a pharmacist in town had any quinine for sale, no matter what the price. Every ounce of the drug that came through the blockade was snapped up dockside by Confederate agents and routed to the battlefronts, where it was desperately needed. She reached the city just as Matthew had finished toting up the profits from the *Banshee*'s latest run. His usual pattern was to intersperse each voyage with a relaxing interlude at Pine Haven, but on this occasion he had decided to reload cargo quickly and dash out again—by God, the cotton market was on fire, and a man must strike while the iron was hot! When Mary Harper tracked him down, she found him in a state of frantic bustle and swagger, haggling and dealing, dashing like a fired-up cavalry officer from market to bank to Cotton Exchange. In fact, he seemed more irritated than pleased when his wife suddenly appeared and began reciting a litany of problems over which *he* had no control. He regained his composure when he saw how truly angry she was; he manifested appropriate guilt and chagrin for neglecting to lay in the usual quinine supply, and promised he would—if possible—purchase the drug in Nassau, but by the time the *Banshee* returned, it would almost be too late for the drug to affect the course of events at Pine Haven. Mary Harper was only partly mollified; she also reproached him for not even bothering to ask about the children's health—he merely nodded in agreement when she told of her decision to pack them off into Stepney Harper's care for an indeterminate period. For the first time in many years, Mary Harper and her husband exchanged some rather testy remarks at the moment of parting and she returned to Pine Haven without seeing him off.

In desperation, she turned to an old prequinine folk remedy: dogwood, poplar, and willow bark, macerated in whiskey, one ounce to be administered thrice a day. Mary Harper suspected that most of the supposed efficacy of this decoction derived from the whiskey, but the stuff certainly *tasted* like medicine and those who were dosed with it considered it beneficial, which was *something.*

But not enough to halt the ravages. By the end of August, three more blacks had died and more than a dozen were too sick to walk, much less work. More and more, Mary Harper assumed the additional duties of a nurse, while the rice crop matured right on schedule. Each morning, while the day was still relatively cool and the mosquitoes were dormant, she walked to the edge of the fields and contemplated that great expanse of golden translucent grain, still softly bedewed and glowing in the first slant of sunlight over the Uwharrie. In previous years, this sight had filled her with the innocent wonder of a thing that was first seen. Now, its beauty was cold comfort. With the labor force she did have on hand, assuming no more deaths, she calculated that it would take four or five days to cut down and gather all those shoulder-high emerald stalks; ideally, it should be accomplished between dawn and dusk in a single day. Inevitably, some portion of the crop would go bad on the ground or be past its prime by the time it felt the sickle's bite. One hope remained: that her father Stepney would yet dispatch a temporary labor force from Limerick.

When mid-September came and no laborers had arrived—indeed, no word of any kind from Stepney, which worried her—Mary Harper Sloane realized that she would have to make do with what she had. Some of the earlier malaria victims were back on their feet; others had more recently succumbed. It was safe, she estimated, to leave the rice alone until the twentieth. If no reinforcements arrived, that would at least give time for a few more of the sick to recover. Very well, then. She would wait a while more, then do the best she could. A partial crop was better than no crop. Meanwhile, she made sure the corn, beans, and melons were properly stored for the winter, assigned pickling and canning duties to the servants who were skilled in such chores, and oversaw the gory transformation of several hogs into hams strung up in the smokehouse.

On the morning of September 19, Mary Harper made her usual morning inspection of the rice fields. All the plants she could see were nodding over from the weight of their grains. She chose a plant at random and counted the grains, losing track after 150. It was, demonstrably and irrevocably, time to harvest. Why wait until tomorrow? Seize the day! She took a deep breath and squared her thin shoulders. She had not slept well for several nights but she knew that she had to present a picture of energy, authority, and optimism if she were to get the most efficient tasking from the workers she had. But that energy rose sluggishly and reluctant. Where was Matthew at this critical time? Off having fun on the bounding main, she presumed, or counting his profits in Jacob Landau's office, or maybe off carousing with Hobart-Hampden in some tawdry Nassau pleasure house. That last thought, and the scalding images it conjured in her imagination, finally did the trick, and her energy came surging up on a tide of resentment. As she turned back toward the house, fists knotted and mouth set in a sharp cut of marital distemper, she was practically knocked off her feet by the raucous blast of a steam whistle from the river. Like an apparition, or the answer to a prayer, there was the *Banshee,* slowly drifting toward the dock, with her husband standing on tiptoe on the foredeck, waving to her. She leaped as high as she could, then ran swiftly to find a couple of men to catch the mooring lines and make the sleek gray runner fast.

"Am I too late for the harvest?" he blurted out as soon as he ran down the gangplank and into his wife's now open and forgiving arms.

"No, my dearest! You are perfectly and wonderfully on time!"

"I've brought quinine and a band of workers, although I cannot vouch for their skills in a rice field, a just gang of stevedores and layabouts from the Wilmington docks. Had to offer them top dollar, but they are fit enough and their boss will wring the work out of them, I promise."

"Any man who can load cotton bales can swing a sickle, Matthew. Mister Bright can give them instruction this afternoon."

Matthew's expression changed. "Mister Bright will assume his traditional role as overseer of Pine Haven's slaves, but the hired men from Wilmington will work only under their boss. And here he is now."

Matthew beckoned to a massive light-skinned Negro whose weight and stride made the gangplank bend as he debarked from the ship. The octaroon was dressed like a dandy despite the encroaching heat: Hessian boots, a black satin cravat, a sparkling gold watch chain looping from his vest, a wide-brimmed Panama hat worn like a crown, as though the entire ensemble were designed to emphasize and frame his lightness of color. In one big coffee-colored fist, he beat time to his own inner music with a handsome silver-knobbed walking stick. He strode right over to the Sloanes, removed his hat, and bowed with the fluidity of a practiced courtier. He extended his hand, and Mary Harper extended hers, then flinched automatically, wondering if this black man would have the effrontery to kiss her hand under the gaze of her husband. But he did not go so far; his bow ended at a respectful distance and the extended hand was refurled over his heart—a gesture, Mary Harper thought, of considerable refinement.

"May I present Mister Bonaparte Reubens, a native of the French Antilles, freeman and labor contractor, presently a resident of Wilmington."

"Madame Sloane, I am honored to meet you," intoned the man, in a voice that blended a slight French accent with the husky mellow inflections of the Caribbean.

Mary Harper glanced questions at Matthew, whose expression plainly said: *I will explain this later.*

"I've told Mister Reubens that his men can bunk down in the barn. I trust there won't be a problem feeding them?"

Not if they like to eat unprocessed rice, she almost said. But she only shook her head: no problem. Bonaparte Reubens turned toward the *Banshee* and waved his stick at Fitz-John Bright, who was contemplating the odd dockside tableau from the portside bridge rail, corncob pipe furiously smoking.

"Mister Bright? Be so kind as to bring my crew on deck and tell them to step lively."

For a moment, Bright's countenance flashed pink with anger. *He* was the overseer on this plantation, and he was plainly unprepared to take orders from any black man, free entrepreneur or not. Matthew gave a quick nod that seemed to say: *Let it go, Mister Bright—we need the labor.*

Bright forcefully rapped out his pipe, the dusty coals spitting loudly as they hit the water, then disappeared for a moment. His muffled barks belowdecks produced a shambling parade of fourteen strangely varied men, each clutching a tatty blanket or a small knotted sack of personal belongings. Every color and breed of the Caribbean was represented in this gaunt assemblage, along with a few rawboned whites from God knew where, and one small moonfaced man who appeared to be Oriental. Reubens hurried them along with commands in several languages and authoritative waves of his stick, and they responded with eyes averted and shoulders hunched in resignation. As they passed Mary Harper, she thought they looked like nothing so much as a line of convicts weighted down by invisible chains. Here was a thing both strange and disturbing, all outside of her previous experience: a giant, black man in total command of a troupe of vagabonds representing the whole antipodean spectrum of races. By this time, several of Pine Haven's Negroes had gathered around, and they too were pop-eyed, incredulous, bemused, and a little bit disturbed by the spectacle. When the workforce had debarked and assembled in the sort of rumpled formation a gang of prisoners might adopt for the daily roll call, Reubens tipped his hat to Matthew and said, "Can you appoint a responsible field hand to show my men to their quarters and give them instruction regarding their tasks?"

Again, Mary Harper felt a lurch of violated propriety. Was she expected to treat this arrogant fellow as a guest rather than an employee? Matthew confirmed it with his next remark: "Mister Reubens will be staying in the big house, Mary. In the upstairs guest room. You will join us for lunch, Mister Reubens, after you get your men situated?"

"With great pleasure, Mister Sloane." Again, that slightly cocksure tip of the hat, a man-to-man gesture that proclaimed the unwillingness of Bonaparte Reubens to defer to any man. Matthew gestured to one of the older and more reliable hands, who shook his head at the wonder of things before obediently shouldering his hoe and leading the shambling platoon of workers off toward the barn.

"Now, my dearest, let's go inside and have some refreshment. There is much to talk about."

That remark proved to be an understatement. From what Matthew told her, Mary Harper finally grasped the feverish intensifications and upheavals great and small that had been wrought by the war's second summer. First, there was a letter from her father that had been waiting for Matthew when he checked into his usual hotel after the *Banshee*'s last voyage. The children had arrived safely at Limerick and had been conveyed thence to the Harpers' mountain retreat, where they would stay until after the peak of glorious autumn, when the whole family would return to the low country; they were well and happy and being tutored in their studies. Stepney Harper regretted that he could send no extra hands to help with the rice harvest—many of his Negroes had been impressed for work on Charleston's fortifications and the poor white farmers he would ordinarily have hired to replace them had either been rounded up by conscription officers or were hiding out in the backwoods to escape service. Besides, Stepney concluded, the rice market was stagnant, hardly worth the expense of shipping; for the first time in his life, the old planter was sorry he had not grown cotton instead, for that commodity had turned into "white gold."

Matthew also brought larger news: General Lee had mounted a full-scale invasion of Maryland. Rumors spoke of a great and terrible battle, but no reliable details had yet reached Wilmington. In that city, the blockade-runner trade had grown to staggering dimensions as more and more vessels, especially designed for the job, entered the business.

As for the formidable-seeming Bonaparte Reubens and his work gang, they were typical specimens of the human flotsam churned up by the topsy-turvy circumstances of intensified war and the consequent shortage of manpower. Two years ago, the sight of a free black man bossing a force of nonblack workers would have been bizarre, perhaps outrageous, but these days, Matthew assured her, no one gave it a second thought. The runners had to be crewed, the cotton had to be loaded efficiently, and the return cargoes had to be unloaded with dispatch—no one cared where the workers came from or what color they were. Reubens was a pompous brute who ruled his men with a hand as stern as that of any plantation overseer, and he insisted on being treated as an equal by any man who contracted for his services. Matthew had been present when some drunken wharf-rat had called Reubens an "uppity nigger" and Reubens had laid him out cold with one swipe of his cane, as offhandedly as a man swatting a fly.

"We must put up with him, my dear, just for a couple of days. He *will* drive his men until the rice is cut down, then we'll load up the *Banshee* and take the crop to Wilmington and I'll pay him off and that's the last we'll see of him. It is true, as your father stated in his letter, that the local rice market is only marginally profitable, but H-H thinks we can sell it in Nassau for a better price. The population of the place has grown so rapidly that the price of food has become dear."

"I can, as you say, 'put up with him,' Matthew, as I could put up with an itinerant snake charmer or a visitor from Samarkand, but I have worried myself to the bone about this harvest and I will not have my efforts go for naught. What I am concerned about is the example he presents to our own Negroes. We had two runaways this summer and I believe that, before they left, they spread tales about abolition and how the Yankees were coming to free every black soul along the coast. Mister Reubens will set the servants' tongues a-wagging. You must promise me one thing: he will not boss *our* workers."

"That stipulation is in the contract. Mister Bright will oversee them, as he always has done. Reubens has authority over his men only, and if he wants payment in full, he had better task them properly. We will see stranger things before this war is over."

Matthew suddenly rose and walked around the table, placing his hands on Mary Harper's shoulders. She had lost weight, and her radiant eyes were shadowed by anxiety. "I know that you are burdened," he said, bending to kiss the down on her pale neck. "And I'm not insensitive to the way things must seem to you. I am off playing cat-and-mouse with the Federal navy, or dining with English swashbucklers at Hobart-Hampden's Yellow House, or counting our profits into Jacob's strongbox, while you are here alone, striving to maintain our beautiful home. And it is true that the past year has been more of an adventure than anything I've ever done before, or even dreamed of doing."

Mary Harper sensed that he was veering off in a serious direction, so she waited for him to continue. The gentle, diffident weight of his hands felt good, and she was sorry when he removed them and walked over to cabinet, where he poured a rather large brandy, considering how early in the day it was. He was about to replace the decanter when he said, as an afterthought, "Would you care . . . I mean . . . "

"Yes, thank you, I would. If you are going to drink before lunch, I shall keep you company." Her tone was chillier than she intended. He poured a drink for her, then took his seat across the table. His hands were tight on the glass as he took a first gulp and shivered from the impact.

"What is it you wish to say, Matthew?"

"It is true—I've had a grand time. And the profits, my dear, are obscene, and getting more so all the time. Before the war, we were prosperous. Now, we are rich. But the risks are increasing with every passing month. Six months ago, the blockade line off the Cape Fear was composed of a single belt of ships, many of them indifferently suited for the task. Now there are more, and better, ships. The Yankee effort is more organized. They have signal rockets, and some of the newer vessels have calcium lights that can pierce the darkest night. There are two lines of blockaders now: one close to the inlets, and a second patrol line stretched across the distance that the average runner can cover between midnight and dawn. So far, we have been lucky, but the number of captures has increased. Some of the men I have dined with at the Yellow House are now languishing in Yankee jails—those with British passports will eventually be released, of course, but those who have no diplomatic protection will not see freedom until the war's end, and that may be a long, long time."

"Don't speak of that possibility. I cannot bear the thought."

"I must speak of it, and you must consider the possibility."

"But you said yourself that we are rich! Why can't you retire from the business?"

"Because if I did, I would be conscripted into the army, and my chances of survival would be small indeed. I don't cringe from being shot at, mind you, although it isn't a pleasant experience, it's just a matter of practicality—I am infinitely more valuable to the Confederacy as a supplier of war materials than I would be as cannon fodder."

"You could hide here! They would never come this far!"

"Yes, they would. If the losses in this Maryland campaign are as severe as I have heard, the Confederate government will comb every square inch of North Carolina and drag off every man between fifteen and fifty who is fit enough to carry a musket. Besides, I could not become an outlaw, a shirker, or one of those ghouls who hires another man to soldier in his stead—what would you think of me then?"

"I would think of you as being *alive,* Matthew."

"I would be alive if I were in prison, too. The blockade ships do not fire to *sink* us, but only to disable us or compel us to stop for seizure. Their crews want the prize money, and even the cabin boys can make more from a single capture than they could in five years of normal service. I'm not trying to alarm you, but I want you to understand that the days of carefree adventure are drawing to a close. The odds are greater now, and will grow greater still as more ships come off the ways. All that I've said is a prelude to this . . . " He extracted from his inside pocket a sheaf of formal-looking documents bound with ribbon and handed them across the table to Mary Harper.

"What?"

"Proof of deposit, along with a supply of bank drafts. I have deposited twenty-five thousand dollars in the Bank of Nassau. If anything happens to me, or if Wilmington should fall and be looted by the Yankees, you will be provided for. Both H-H and Jacob Landau know of the arrangement and can arrange transfer of funds. And one more thing: in case the blockade becomes impenetrable. I have also brought three thousand dollars in gold. It's on the ship, guarded by Mister Bright. Tonight, when no one can see us, we'll bring it up and hide it in a secure place. That way, even if the Yankees occupy Pine Haven, you will be able to buy food, or purchase your own personal safety and that of the children, should it come to that."

Mary Harper stared at the documents; how heavy they felt. Any resentment she had felt toward her husband vanished.

"You are a good man, Matthew," she whispered, reaching for his hand. She scrutinized his face, noticing for the first time the fine new lines around his eyes and the scattered gray in his hair. If she could have, she would have made a photograph of him with her gaze—this was how she would remember him, in this golden morning light, if he were parted from her for a long time. Or if he did not come back at all.

"We both have our part to play in this cataclysm," he said. "And we must play that part with honor and courage."

Then, as though embarrassed by the depth of his feelings, he drained the brandy glass, stood up, and dusted his hands.

"Now, I must go make sure that our new workers are trained to their tasks. Are all the sickles sharp?"

"Like scalpels, Matthew."

"And the threshing mill?"

"Clean and oiled and ready—I have seen to it personally."

He kissed her forehead and made a jaunty motion with his hands. "You know, my dear, our dinner tonight should be very interesting."

If Bonaparte Reubens found the dinnertime situation awkward, he gave no sign. Never before had the Sloanes sat down to dine with a Negro *guest,* but Mister Reubens was so light-skinned that, after a few glasses of wine and some mannerly conversation, it was hard to think of him as "black," especially in contrast to Agrippa, whose complexion was quite ebony. Evidently, Reubens felt the same way, for he seldom spoke directly to Agrippa. Instead, by gesture and inflection, he seemed to relish the older Negro's discomfiture—to Agrippa, Reubens might as well have been some exotic and unwelcome beast. His very presence was an ill-defined but acutely uncomfortable violation of every protocol Agrippa had grown used to. He went about his duties with an expression of tight-lipped forbearance. By the time the main course was being cleared, Mary Harper found herself enveloped with a strange brittleness of mood. Indeed, Mister Reubens made it clear, with every expansive gesture and well-spoken comment, that he was certainly the most comfortable person in the room. Questions of propriety, obviously, were something for the others to fret over.

But nothing really untoward happened until Reubens began commenting on the war—a subject that the Sloanes had tactfully avoided thus far. As the legitimized grandson of a French colonial official—and Reubens made certain to inform his hosts that he spoke three languages and had visited Paris—he claimed objectivity about the conflict. There was money to be made from it, if one were enterprising and willing to travel, but he was utterly dispassionate about the larger issues of the struggle. Until that moment, Reubens had seemed totally unaffected by the wine, but he had several times signaled Agrippa for refills during the main course, and he seemed suddenly to verge on delivering a major oration. Mary Harper had tried to make it clear that war talk was to be held in abeyance during the meal, but Reubens seemed determined to have his say, and there was no polite way to discourage him without making the situation even more strained than it was. Finally, while Agrippa was setting out coffee cups, Reubens made a rather remarkable statement.

"You realize, Mister and Mrs. Sloane, that the Confederacy is vastly outnumbered, not to say outgunned and faced with overwhelming industrial might. In many ways, I admire your culture, truly I do. After all, the French, too, maintained slavery as an economic institution, at least in the Caribbean colonies, and there is no finer civilization on earth than that of France. I fear that nothing will remain of your Confederacy in a few years except a legend of doomed heroism. Unless . . . "

"Unless what, sir?" said Matthew coldly, prepared to draw a conversational line even if it meant losing his workforce.

Now Reubens leaned forward, steepling his fingers and modulating his voice into a conspiratorial tone—a man preparing to speak some profound if disturbing truth.

"Unless you do the one thing that will give the Rebel armies the strength to withstand their foe's superior numbers."

"And that would be . . . ?"

Reubens turned suddenly and stabbed a finger at Agrippa, who was at that moment hovering near his right shoulder, preparing to serve coffee.

"Unless you give your slaves their freedom and supply them with arms! My father saw it done in Haiti, when a black army threw out Napoleon's legions. Preempt the righteousness of the abolitionists, sir! Earn the gratitude of those whom you now hold in bondage, and they will fight for you like tigers!"

Matthew Sloane's jaw dropped; Mary Harper's hand froze on her coffee cup in midair. And Agrippa, as startled as he would have been by a bolt of lightning, shuddered, lurched toward the table, and spilled a dollop of coffee down the front of Bonaparte Reubens's waistcoat. Reubens leaped up and snarled: "Be careful, boy! That is real French silk!"

Agrippa gritted his teeth and replied with all the dignity he could summon, "I ain't your *boy,* mistah, and yo' French silk don't make you any less of a nigger than I am."

Then he left the room. Reubens rubbed the stain with his napkin, then wadded the linen into a ball and dropped it on the table. He bowed stiffly to the Sloanes.

"Thank you for the meal. I'll have my crew ready to cut rice at seven o'clock."

After Reubens was gone, stalking up the stairs with heavy measured tread, Matthew and Mary Harper stared at each other in a state of paralysis. *Something* needed to be said, but neither of them could find the words. Both of them had been entertaining some thought of making love later that night, but that mood was irreparably gone now, and there seemed nothing else to do but get a good night's sleep and get tomorrow over with as soon as possible. So nonplussed was Matthew by the bizarre incident at dinner that he almost forgot about transferring the gold from the *Banshee* to a hiding place in the Big House. Mary Harper decided to walk with her husband to the ship, so they linked arms, rather self-consciously, and strode through the gardens, past the shed that housed the threshing mill, then followed the wagon track to the dock. Dense and feathery, the rice fields seemed almost luminous, threaded with starlit webs of water, and the night air was pleasantly cool. At the point where the wagon track cut through the main riverside embankment, Mary Harper pulled Matthew up to vantage point from which they could view the entire panorama: fields, dikes, crops, outbuildings on one hand, and on the other, the brooding bulk of the ship and the turbid glaze of the Uwharrie.

"I want to remember how it looks tonight," she said, "in case it all gets swept away by the war. Oh, Matthew, is it pointless to go through the trouble of harvesting? Will we make enough from the crop even to cover the expense?"

Matthew shrugged. "We may break even. But that is not really the point, is it?"

"I suppose not. What's important is the continuity of things, for as long as we can maintain them. What else are we fighting for besides the right to keep our way of life?"

"Exactly. We will harvest the rice because we have always harvested it."

After a few more moments of contemplation, they turned and walked up the gangway. Fitz-John Bright was wide awake and ready to greet them, a double-barreled shotgun snuggled in the crook of his right arm.

"Ah saw the GEN-er-RUL, ma'am!" he exclaimed, pointing with his free hand toward the open water and the far marshy shore.

"General? Which general, sir?"

"Why GEN-er-RUL BEAU-re-gard, of course! You RE-member! My all-I-GAH-tor!"

"The one you brought to Wilmington? The one you'd trained to snap at Yankee-blue uniforms? How can it possibly be the same reptile?"

Bright chuckled knowingly. "They HOME, ya know. This is his wa-TER, so this is where he came, straight UP the big ri-VER! Yessir! Ah knew him soon AS Ah saw HIM. Them big YAH-ler eyes, y'know? He keeps WATCH. Had an ol' TER-rapin sleepin' on his back, he did!"

"If you say so, Mister Bright," said Matthew. "Now let's do what we planned to do."

The gold was nested in a strongbox the size of a small steamer trunk, swaddled in cotton waste so it would not jingle. It was very heavy, so each man took one handle while Mary Harper held the lantern and walked ahead. Matthew's plan was to divide the hoarde into three equal parts, then hide each portion in the sorts of places that an intruder would not be likely to consider. One sack they stuffed inside an old porcelain commode, another they buried beneath the front porch, and the third was secreted beneath some loose boards in the smokehouse floor. Midnight had come and gone by the time they were finished, so the Sloanes went off to the master bedroom and Fitz-John Bright loped back to the *Banshee,* carrying a moldy old knuckle of ham, which he planned to feed to General Beauregard.

Breakfast was at six; the day's work began at seven. Two distinct workforces assembled on the edge of the rice fields. Reubens's crew mustered like a platoon of ragged soldiers, toting their sickles like unfamiliar side arms and wincing when their boss barked commands like a teamster cracking a whip. Reubens was dressed in the fashion of a man who had no intention of getting down in the muck with his hirelings: clean flannel trousers and a loose white cotton shirt that did nothing to hide the smooth full-moons of his broad and muscular chest. Beneath the wide brim of his hat, his eyes burned large and piercingly white. His feet were shod in well-greased store-bought brogans and he carried his walking stick like a ramrod, straight as a ruled line down the trouser crease.

By contrast, Fitz-John Bright was dressed like most of his charges: for work. A battered straw hat, a coarse woolen shirt, loose ragged rolled-up pants held up by well-worn leather-tabbed suspenders, and no shoes at all. Bright circulated among the hands and you could see at a glance that he and they were comfortable with each other. He greeted old acquaintances with a smile, patted some of the younger and older workers on the shoulder, asked after their families, commiserated with those whose relatives were still laid out with malaria. Even with the addition of Reubens's men, there were barely enough fit laborers to handle the work, so even the house servants had turned out, under Agrippa's watchful eye, to swing the unaccustomed sickle. There was a system to the procedure: each worker was given a full, a half, or a quarter task, a task being defined as the amount of work the meanest hand could perform in nine hours of industrious work. From long experience, Bright knew to a certainty what that might be and Matthew Sloane's policy was never to overtask anyone unless absolutely necessary. The very young, the old, the infirm all had their parts to play in the harvest ritual, whether it was fetching water for the hands or replacing a nicked reaper with a sharp one from storage.

Matthew decided to deploy Pine Haven's workers from the riverside, where the growth was lushest and the soil more treacherously moist; he directed Reubens's men to start on the opposite side of the fields, where the stalks were not as dense, figuring that they would become more efficient as time went on and as they worked their way toward the heavier stands.

By the time Mary Harper joined Matthew—after making sure there was plenty of food and water for the midday meal—the work was in full rhythm. Pine Haven's Negroes did their cutting with a minimum of wasted effort, knowing just how to angle their blades and how to bend into the stroke without putting excessive strain on their limbs and ligaments. Reubens's men more or less just hacked away, with no finesse, and soon they were drenched with sweat and itchy with stubble. Reubens paced restlessly along the elevations between the irrigation channels, tapping his stick against his leg and occasionally poking the ribs of someone who appeared to be slack, slow, or confused. Again, Mary Harper was struck by the topsy-turvy contrast: the *slaves* worked steadily and sang and called out encouragement to one another, while the free white wage-earners swung their reapers in sullen silence, with no word of comradeship, hardly saying anything at all except when someone's foot was trodden on or someone's sickle blade nicked someone else's clothes or flesh, and then Mary Harper could hear low curses, followed by shrill imprecations from Reubens, who called his employees "dogs" and "no-count gutter-trash," which some of them might *be,* of course, but to Mary Harper it seemed a pointlessly callous way to manage work that was already hard enough to perform. But whether she approved or not, the hirelings were making progress, the stalks were coming down, and if she blurred her perceptions, she could imagine herself back on her father's vast and far-flung fields in those now halcyon days before the war. Behind the reapers came the women and children, who gathered the fallen stalks into enormous bundles, so that their heads and shoulders vanished beneath immense green-and-gold haystacks, and all you could see of them as they drew near and climbed up the embankments was the splay of their feet and the flexing of their calves. The long flax-colored heads were laid on flat ground, and by noon the sun had dried the cuttings sufficiently for them to be bound into sheaves.

Matthew's preferred order of things was to cut and dry and sheave all in one process; when the cutting and toting had been done, all hands would carry the sheaves to the threshing mill and the day's hardest work would be over. From that point on, steam power would perform the tedious process of separating the grains from the stalks.

By midafternoon, only a few acres remained uncut and the two groups of workers had drawn close to each other. Mister Bright called a brief halt, now that the end was in sight, and water-bearers scuttled into the fields, each bucket bristling with dippers. Bright took a long drink from the closest bucket, ladled more water over his matted coppery hair, then mopped himself with a big checkered bandanna. Thus refreshed, he used this interlude to inspect the Pine Haven hands closely for signs of exhaustion, illness, or injury. His autocratic counterpart, Mister Reubens, paid scant attention to his own panting, sore-armed workers; instead, he turned away, lit a cheroot, and took a long thirsty pull from a pocket flask. Fitz-John Bright, having completed his inspection, watched Reubens with unconcealed disdain, then strode over to the elevation where Matthew and Mary Harper were making a rough tally of the crops spread out all around them.

"Cap'n Sloane?" said Bright, tossing a casual salute. "Our NEW OH-va-SEE-er smells of wisk-KEY more than HON-est SWEAT. And he has a TICK."

Matthew blinked in puzzlement, not quite able to focus on what Bright was saying. "He has a tick on him? Well, I presume he has enough sense to pluck it off."

"No, SUH. His FACE has a tick—like this!" Bright scrunched up one side of his features repeatedly, making himself look like a gangling half-wit. Before Matthew could fathom the import of this news, there was a loud groan, followed by the thud of a collapsing body, from the part of the fields where most of Pine Haven's reapers were enjoying their water break.

"My God, what's happened to Agrippa?" Heedless of his clothes and so far unsullied boots, Matthew splashed through the stubbly rows, Bright on his heels, and pushed through the knot of lathered field hands to kneel beside Agrippa. It was instantly apparent that the middle-aged major domo, who had not done outside work in many years, had been felled by a sudden wracking onslaught of malaria. Agrippa's face was contorted in a rictus of seizure, oozing bullets of sweat, and he arched his back, humping like an inchworm, as the chills shuddered through his bones. He was already delirious, moaning, clamping his teeth so hard that his grinding jawbones seemed in danger of popping out of their sockets. Matthew grabbed his arms, Bright took up his mud-slicked feet, and they began to carry him toward the house as quickly as they could. As it happened, the most direct route passed within a few feet of Mister Reubens, and Matthew could smell a strong effluvium of whiskey almost immediately. How had Reubens managed to drink so much without anyone noticing it? But the expression on his men's faces indicated that *they* had noticed, and were not in the least bit surprised. Reubens stepped close as Bright and Matthew passed his spot, already huffing from exertion. Matthew flashed an angry look at Reubens and said: "Help us get him into the house, Mister Reubens! You're a strong man and I have not seen you overexerting yourself today."

But Reubens merely stared down at the feverish Agrippa, eyes as bulgy and hard as two bird's eggs, working his cheeks and lips like a man getting ready to spit.

"It is not in my contract to rescue your house nigger, Mister Sloane. If he could not do the work, then he should not have come into the fields." Fitz-John Bright stopped suddenly, almost causing Matthew to lose his grip on Agrippa's sweating hands. He glared furiously at Reubens, who was both taller and stronger by considerable measure.

"Cap'n Sloane? Just ONE moment."

Bright lowered Agrippa's feet gently to the ground, then came up out of a coiled crouch like a snake pouncing on a rat, putting all his weight and momentum behind the blow he aimed at Reubens's hard, flat stomach. Caught off guard, Reubens doubled over with a whiskey-reeking explosion of breath. His workmen blinked in amazement but not one of them made a move to help Reubens to his feet; a few of them, Matthew noticed, even smiled at the sight of him on all fours, shaking his head and gasping like a landed fish. Bright followed the punch with a short chopping kick to the ribs. Then he bent down and grabbed Reubens's walking stick and hurled it as far as he could. Satisfied that Reubens was disarmed and incapable, for the moment, of any more violence, Bright turned back to the shuddering Agrippa and once more took up the man's feet.

What happened next probably took no more than three seconds, but to Mary Harper, who was watching the incident with her knuckles clamped to her mouth and a sick feeling growing in her stomach, the sight unspooled in slow motion. While Bright was grappling for Agrippa's legs, Bonaparte Reubens shook off his injuries, bared his teeth like a rabid dog, and snatched a reaping hook from the nearest workman. Mary Harper screamed a warning, and Matthew lunged forward with arms outstretched to deflect the swiping cut Reubens aimed at Bright's head. Matthew was not strong enough to block the stroke entirely, but he did diminish the blow's force, which otherwise would have split Bright's skull like a melon. The sickle's tip penetrated the side of Bright's head to a depth of about an inch and released a jet of cranial blood. By now, Reubens was in a fugue state, spittle bubbling on his lips, roaring defiantly, eyes bulging, swinging the sickle wildly. Angry as he was, Matthew had enough sense to realize that he was no match for this deranged and powerful man, so he flung himself to one side, reached into his coat, and drew a short-barreled .32-caliber gambler's revolver. In the quivering silence that enveloped the tableau, the hammer cock was very loud.

"Drop the hook, you black bastard, or I will shoot you down!"

Reubens responded by growling and gathering his strength for a leap. Matthew's pistol bucked and a rosette of blood bloomed on Reuben's right shoulder, causing him to drop the sickle and spin him down onto one knee. Without taking his eyes off the wounded man, Matthew called over his shoulder: "Mary Harper, get some of the hands together and have them bind this man! Use rope from the stables!" Matthew waved the pistol in a new arc, covering Reubens's workmen. "Any of you men come to his aid, and you'll get the same treatment." But none of them made any move to succor Reubens. Instead, they exchanged sly looks. One of their number, the slightly built Oriental, dropped his reaping hook, raised his hands, and said: "He very bad boss, boss. We work for you, now." The Chinaman gestured to his companions, and they swarmed forward and pinned Reubens to the ground, immobilizing him while he raged and kicked and swung blindly with his one good arm. Mary Harper picked out two of the stronger field hands and sent them off to the stables in search of rope. They returned quickly and trussed Reubens like a game bird, then carried him off and secured him to a thick timber in the barn, heedless of his yelps and curses.

Then Matthew got things organized again. He promised Reubens's men that they would be well paid for their trouble, including the substantial fee that would have been Reubens's commission, and they all went back to work in an apparent state of contentment. Agrippa was carried to his quarters and given quinine, and Fitz-John Bright, half-conscious and with small pulses of blood oozing between the fingers he pressed against the puncture, was helped into the main house. Mary Harper hurried off to fetch her box of medical supplies. After she washed Bright's scalp, she soaked a ball of absorbent cotton in brandy, coated it with powdered alum, and literally plugged the hole, keeping the dressing tight until the bleeding stopped. Then she swathed his head with strips of clean linen and poured a considerable quantity of brandy into Bright's mouth. Gradually, he regained his normal ruddy color and his pupils lost their dilation. If the wound did not turn morbid overnight, she thought, he would recover. She stayed with him until twilight, when he began showing signs of consciousness. His first word, a dry croak that she could interpret only by bending close to his lips, was another good sign: "Hungry . . . " So she fetched a bowl of warm chicken broth from the kitchen and spooned it for him. Bright lapped it up to the last drop.

"Thank you, Missuz Sloane. That hit the spot, all right."

"Don't waste energy talking, Mister Bright."

"But I must know if the harvest is proceeding."

What a loyal man, she thought. "Yes, and it may already be finished. The men from Wilmington are happy enough to be rid of their bestial boss and your assailant is tied up in the barn. I expect Matthew will turn him in to the sheriff when he takes the rice crop downriver."

"I did not like that man Reubens from the first time I laid eyes on him, ma'am. He treats his white men worse than most white men treat their niggers, yet he's a nigger, too. It seems to me that, while war may cast up heroes and cause ordinary men to find nobility in their souls that they would not otherwise discover, it also shakes things up so badly that it elevates scoundrels far beyond their peacetime station. We shall see stranger men than Reubens, and more villainous ones to boot, before the end."

Mary Harper listened with growing amazement.

"Mister Bright, I have never heard you so well-spoken before. Your speech affliction has disappeared altogether!"

He looked at her quizzically. "What speech affliction, Missuz Sloane?"

Mary Harper began to laugh so uncontrollably that she was afraid of giving offense. She pulled herself together long enough to pat Bright on the shoulder and mutter: "You just lie back and get some sleep. No more talk for now." Bright nodded, closed his eyes, and seemed instantly to drift away on a peaceful and painless tide. Mary Harper clamped her hand over her mouth and ran outside, clutching the empty soup bowl, and then she laughed until the tears came. What a day it had been! Pine Haven had experienced its first skirmish of the war! One blow, one shot, two casualties, and a seemingly magical transformation in dear old Fitz-John Bright. She would miss his bizarre habits of speech, but at least any strangers with whom Bright had to deal would no longer take him for some kind of lack-wit. When she finally stopped giggling, she returned the soup bowl to the kitchen, where Aurelia and four other servants were heaping up cornbread and peas and fried chicken to feed the exhausted harvesters. Mary Harper impulsively snatched up a warm, crispy drumstick and took lusty bites from it as she walked back to the rice fields to see how things had gone in the last part of the day.

When she rounded the smokehouse, she saw Matthew outside the shed that housed the threshing mill. He was stamping the ground angrily. *Oh Lord, what now?*

"The main flywheel belt!" he shouted when he saw her approaching. "The goddamned main belt! It snapped in two after ten minutes of work!"

"Is there not a spare?"

"Not closer than Wilmington! It was brand-new when I installed it two years ago!"

Mary Harper understood the seriousness of this breakdown. Hand-threshing with old-fashioned flails was a long, tedious, inefficient process that exhausted everyone involved. And with the price for milled rice currently hovering around $1 a bushel, the protracted effort hardly seemed worthwhile. Matthew was still overwrought from the earlier violence, and this new problem seemed to have triggered a sputtering rage unlike anything she had ever seen in him. He gestured furiously at the threshing shed and the silent hulking machine within, now just so much expensive junk.

"Damn it, Mary! I am tempted to call off the whole thing and go back to sea, where a man can make some real money! At least you will have plenty of rice pudding to eat this winter! I am finished with being a farmer!"

Mary Harper felt her own anger now, and her eyes began to fill with tears.

"Do you understand how hard I have worked to bring in this harvest? Do you? I cannot steer your ship or stoke her boilers, Matthew! Should I just close down Pine Haven for the duration of this war? I've spent all of August and half of September nursing malaria victims without any quinine, worried half to death that you would be sunk or killed or captured, constantly watching for unrest among the slaves, trying to keep things as *normal* as I can. I have sworn to bring in this harvest, even if it is the last rice crop we ever grow, because *I don't know what else to do with myself!* I am all alone out here, and when my day's work is done, I cannot relax in a Wilmington tavern like you can! Or have a grand old time wagering on cockfights with Hobart-Hampden! Or taking my pleasure in some Nassau whorehouse!"

For an instant, she thought Matthew was going to strike her; worse than that was the furtive spark in his eyes that might have signified guilt and defiance. Unwittingly, she had hit a nerve. No wonder Matthew's style of lovemaking, on those rare nights when he shared a bed with her, had become more confident and sophisticated. She felt a deep twist of inner pain. For one moment of wild speculation, she wondered what else he might have picked up from the courtesans in Nassau, or from the coarser but equally willing women in Paddy's Hollow near the Wilmington docks.

"You may not wish to be a 'farmer' anymore, Matthew, but you are still the owner of a farm, and while it may not be as glamorous and exciting as running the blockade, you cannot wish to see Pine Haven fall into decay. And that is precisely what will happen if I do not manage this plantation properly. If you cannot *be* here, you can at least make sure I have the means to do the job in your absence! Good lord, you even neglected to lay in the seasonal quinine! People died because of that, people who could have recovered. If we cannot take better care of our Negroes, Matthew, who knows what might happen the first time a Yankee cavalry patrol shows up on our land? I cannot run Pine Haven without the blacks and *they know it.*"

"They also know they will be fed and housed and kept warm in the winter!" he snapped back. "Where else would they go? What other livelihood would they pursue? You don't actually fear an uprising, do you? Just because those two bucks ran off earlier, you think Aurelia's going to poison you one night, burn down the house, and make off with the silverware? My dear lady, none of these niggers would ever raise a hand against you, and to think otherwise would be to take the council of your most absurd fears!"

"May I remind you that one of those niggers just tried to slice open your pilot's head with a reaping hook?"

"That brute is not one of ours!"

"No, Matthew, but because he is black, whether our servants like him or hate him, he is one of *them*."

They were head-to-head now, glaring defiance at each other. Matthew turned away first, making a helpless gesture with his hands.

"My God, look at us! We're practically having a civil war of our own. I'm sorry for snapping at you—but this business with the threshing machine is the last straw. Mary, I understand, I *do*, how much strain you have been under, and I know how much it meant to you, symbolically if nothing else, to bring in the rice crop. Let's please not argue any more. Tomorrow, we'll both go to Wilmington and you can do some shopping, or go to the Thalian with your friend Largo, while I track down another belt for the threshing engine and turn Reubens over to the law on charges of assault—no, charges of attempted murder! He can hang, for all I care. Mister Bright cannot go back to sea until he's healed. I'll leave him here for a few weeks, fully armed, so you won't be unprotected. As soon as your nerves are settled once more, you'll feel much better."

Mary Harper felt the tension ebb from her arched shoulders and rigid spine. She embraced Matthew—because there seemed nothing else to do at that moment—but the hug was perfunctory, a truce called rather than intimacy restored, and they both knew they would spend the night apart.

Bonaparte Reubens's wound was more painful than damaging. While Matthew stood close with pistol drawn, Aurelia bandaged Reubens's shoulder. He was fed, given water, then chained up for the night in ankle irons from the *Banshee*'s brig. He never said a word, but he glowered and growled at anyone who came near. Matthew selected two field hands whom he regarded as trustworthy, armed them with pitchforks, and assigned them to guard the man through the night, in alternating three-hour shifts.

In the morning, Reubens was gone, one of his guards was dead with a crushed skull, and the other one was found curled up in a pile of hay with a stiletto boot-knife protruding from below his rib cage, half-dead from loss of blood. He claimed no knowledge of how Reubens had managed to get free of his shackles and no knowledge of where the man had gone. His first intention probably had been to steal the little steam launch, had it been possible for him to light and stoke the furnace without attracting attention. But a flat-bottomed fishing pirogue was missing from the riverside, along with some hardtack rations from the *Banshee*'s small galley. Matthew and two armed men fired up the steam launch and went in pursuit. Five miles upriver, where the Uwharrie petered out into a trackless maze of black-water creeks, Matthew found the stolen boat, abandoned and partly sunk. Reubens must have struck out to the north, perhaps in the hope of finding a Yankee outpost. Almost certainly, that was the end of him. Wounded and unarmed, the man stood no chance of reaching safety. If the quicksand and alligators did not get him, malaria, snakes, or starvation would. Matthew was certain that no one would ever see Reubens alive again. All the same, he was relieved to learn that Fitz-John Bright was much improved after a night's rest and seemed fully prepared to guard Pine Haven while the Sloanes steamed down to Wilmington in search of a replacement belt for the threshing engine.

"Mister Bright cannot stay on guard twenty-four hours a day," Mary Harper reminded her husband at breakfast. "Can we not afford to hire another man or two?"

"You mean from that riffraff Reubens brought with him?" There was still a trace of snap in Matthew's tone. How eager he was to be rid of these domestic conundrums, these unthreshed and unprofitable crops.

"We could of course pass out arms to the slaves," she replied in an equally acidic voice. "The Chinaman seemed decent enough, and surely not all the others are bad men. Just down on their luck and compelled to work for an oppressive bully."

Matthew sighed, a bit too melodramatically, as though this additional decision were enough to turn the morning into a burden.

"Very well, my dear, I'll have a chat with the Chinaman. Aurelia?"

"Yes, Mistah Sloane?"

"There is a young Oriental fellow, out in the barn with the other hired hands. Could you please ask him to come in here?" Aurelia paused for a moment, as though not quite certain she understood. Mary Harper then realized that Aurelia might have no earthy conception of what an Oriental was, and amended her husband's instructions. "The young Chinese man, Aurelia. With eyes like this?" She lifted her eyebrows into a slant with both index fingers and Aurelia beamed with enlightenment.

He entered the room with hat in hand, bowing gracefully, head cocked alertly to one side, a slender, almost hairless man with a wiry physique and a certain appealing delicacy of features. His English was surprisingly good and his accent no harder to comprehend than the heavy patois of some Caribbean blacks. His name was Sun-Yi-Chiang, but Mister Sloane could call him Sonny.

"Would you like to stay here and work for us, Mister . . . um, Sonny?"

"Better than toting cotton bales all day, I betcha. Sure."

"What wages did Mister Reubens pay you boys?"

"Fifty cent a day and grub, sir."

"And I'll bet Mister Reubens fed you boys well."

"Ptah!" Sonny Chiang grimaced. "Bread with bugs in it! Not fit for dogs!"

"How does a dollar a day, and decent food, sound to you?"

"Very good, sah! Sonny is your man!"

"You will be asked to do heavy work sometimes, but your main job will be to guard Missus Sloane and our property while I am away on business. Can you handle a rifle?"

"Rifle? Can *learn.* It look easy enough for any fool. I also do fight with hands, legs, fists-of-harmony."

"I'm afraid I don't understand."

"You come to barn—both of you. I show you."

With sprightly step now, Sonny Chiang led them to the barn, where the rest of Reubens's men were wolfing down cornbread and coffee and squabbling over a few chunks of boiled bacon. Liberated from the tyranny of their previous employer, the men looked considerably more alert and energetic than they had when they were hacking clumsily at the rice plants. Several of them waved and greeted the Chinaman. Matthew sidled up to Mary Harper's ear and muttered, "Good choice," for it was obvious that the other men deferred to the Oriental. Considering what a polyglot bunch they were, this spoke volumes about Chiang's character, especially since almost all of them were bigger, stronger, and rougher-looking. Chaing pointed out two burly fellows and called them by name.

"Fernando! Stepan! Come on! We give show now."

The other two—a Portuguese and perhaps a Pole, Matthew guessed—made a display of fear and reluctance. "No, no! Too early to get hurt!"

"Not hurt! Just for show! I promise, no hurt!"

"Okay." The two men scowled ferociously, shouted war cries, and charged full tilt at the small brown man. Mary Harper cringed. "Stop them, Matthew! They'll murder him!" But like a phantom from an opium dream, the Chinese somehow slipped into a tiny sliver of space between his two attackers, made a couple of swift, economical movements with his hands and feet, bending like a small brown eel into their charge, and threw one of them over in a half-somersault while simultaneously striking the other across the chest with what appeared to be a very slight blow, but had the effect of a large tree suddenly crashing into his path. Both men went sprawling in the dust and when the whirlwind stopped, Chiang's foot was braced against the Pole's neck and the man's beefy right hand was vised between Chiang's palms, bent back at an angle that was perhaps a millimeter short of snapping the wrist bone.

"You see, boss? Rifle, no rifle, does not matter."

The Portuguese named Fernando nodded and dusted himself off. "You think he's good with bare hands, Mister Sloane? You should see him with a sword! Aiieee!"

Mary Harper inclined her head and whispered: "Let's hire those three, Matthew. Why break up a team?"

"You are sure? You would trust them?"

"They need a *job,* Matthew, and I think they will be grateful, and loyal, for a chance to work here instead of breaking their backs on the docks."

So it was decided. Chiang, Fernando, and Stepan were hired as guards and general laborers. The rest of the hirelings shuffled back on board the *Banshee,* while Matthew introduced the strange trio to Fitz-John Bright, who would fit them into the scheme of things, as soon as he was more fully recovered, and train them in the use of Pine Haven's bird-shot blunderbusses. As he took his leave following the introductions, Matthew impulsively stuck his head back into Bright's room, pointed at Sonny Chiang, and said: "One more thing, Mister Bright. See if you can find a sword for Mister Chiang."

"A *sword,* Cap'n? Whatever for?"

"I believe that's his weapon of choice—I'm sure he knows how to use it."

This impromptu arrangement seemed to please Mary Harper and lighten her mood considerably. Her reasoning was sound: "If by some chance that monster Reubens is still alive out there in the swamps, he is not likely to come sneaking around here again if he sees Pine Haven guarded by three men who have every reason to hate him."

"You are acquiring a certain useful deviousness of mind, my dear."

"There is a war on, Matthew. In order to keep Pine Haven intact through the storm, I shall exercise whatever degree of deviousness—*and* strength of will—as seems necessary. Do not underestimate me."

Matthew was not aware that he ever *had,* but he chose not to pursue the conversation down a path so potentially strewn with thorns. The weather was balmy, with a distinct hint of autumn now, and the river bore them along with silken ease. It should not take long to locate a flywheel belt, and while he was doing that, Mary Harper could enjoy a day of shopping or socializing, as she chose. Tonight, they would have *fun.* An evening of theater at the Thalian, dancing, a party at the Yellow House, and—why not?—a night of intimacy on neutral ground. Tomorrow, they would sail back to Pine Haven, repair the threshing mill, and finish the harvest.

Matthew's first act, after docking the *Banshee* in one of the few empty slips, at the foot of Ann Street, was to pay off the remainder of Reubens's work gang. He made sure the men had enough cash to live on until they could find other employment, and he wrote a to-whom-it-may-concern letter of recommendation, stating the "the bearer and his companions" had proven themselves to be satisfactory employees in a wide variety of tasks. He gave this to a short, stocky Irishman upon whom de facto leadership seemed to have devolved after the departure of Chiang, and the last he saw of them was a shuffling file of dispirited men making their way, presumably, to the nearest tavern. Having thus discharged his responsibilities to them, Matthew felt lighter and less encumbered. He arranged to meet Mary Harper at Landau's store at four o'clock, embraced her in a perfunctory manner, then went off to find a new steam-engine belt.

By midafternoon, he was wrung out with frustration. In Wilmington, there was no problem obtaining luxury items, thanks to the blockade-runners; you could purchase Belgian chocolates, silk hosiery, mother-of-pearl buttons, watermarked linen stationery, and tea from Ceylon. But you could not, for love or money, buy a pound of nails, a new plow-blade, a saddle, or a flywheel belt. Well known as he was, Matthew Sloane's inquiries were greeted with rueful smiles and apologetic shrugs. Everything having to do with propulsion or light industry, from boiler plates to pressure valves, had vanished from the open market. Whatever items had not been snapped up by the runner companies had been commandeered by the Confederate navy. During the course of his fruitless searches, Matthew also picked up the latest numbers pertaining to the rice market: 90 cents per bushel for prime grain, 75 cents for lesser stuff. When Matthew added to this dismal equation the man-hours needed to thresh the crop by hand, it became clear to him that, like it or not, Pine Haven was out of the rice business for the duration of the war. He did not look forward to telling Mary Harper this news, not when she had invested so much of her own pride and concern in the symbolic achievement of bringing in a successful harvest.

He was therefore pleasantly surprised, when he returned to Jacob's emporium at four o'clock, to find her in good spirits, sipping tea, nibbling biscuits, and engaging in animated conversation with her younger friend, Largo. *Like two sisters,* he thought. Jacob Landau was his usual preoccupied self, taking refuge in his ledger books and inventory lists. He put out a vacant chair for Matthew and offered coffee, but Matthew declined that beverage in favor of some port, excellent Bristol stuff, brought in on the *Banshee*'s last run.

"So tell me, Jacob, how is your project going? Do you have enough in the bank now to build your Hebrew church?"

Jacob smiled his usual distant, Diaspora-tempered smile. " 'Temple,' we call it. By the turn of the year, Matthew, by the turn of the year. Of course, one could not even begin such a project until after the war—unless you can find me a good rabbi in Nassau. And of course, some of my profits must be reinvested, to protect our interests. I have subscribed a considerable sum to the ironclad project. A demonstration of my Confederate patriotism. As a prominent Jew in an ocean of gentiles, I must be seen to fly the flag of Dixie even higher than my neighbors. Which reminds me: have you seen Hobart-Hampden yet?"

"No, but I suspect he will turn up at any minute."

"Oh, yes, I'm sure he will. The recital tonight was largely his idea, after all."

"Recital? A musical program?"

"Yes. At the Yellow House, after dinner. Largo will play the piano, H-H will play the cello, I believe, and one of his English colleagues is an accomplished violinist. They've been rehearsing for several nights.

I look forward to it keenly, and who knows, I may even pull out my own fiddle at some point."

"I did not know H-H was a musician," mused Matthew.

"He surprises one at every turn, does he not? I think that is why Largo is so infatuated with him."

Matthew hid his amusement behind another gulp of port. From what Mary Harper had told him, Largo's relationship with Hobart-Hampden had long ago ripened beyond mere infatuation. Could Jacob really be so innocent, or was he simply rationalizing a situation over which he had no control?

"By the way," Jacob continued, "I understand that H-H proposes to enlarge the Anglo-Confederate Trading Company by at least one more vessel, a sleek new runner designed especially for the task, now a-building in Liverpool. The heyday of individual runners seems to be fading; the trend now is for several ships to work as a corporation. It makes sense, you see, because that way, if one ship gets caught, the loss can be absorbed more readily. We will have to vote on it, of course, but I trust you will go along with the scheme. Naturally, we will have to put up some additional money, but with two ships running instead of one, our profits should double, too. Augustus intends to skipper the new vessel, I believe. He can tell you the details himself over dinner."

Jacob locked the store at five, and they agreed to meet for dinner at six, at the Yellow House. The Sloanes walked there from a hotel on Church Street where Hobart-Hampden had leased a suite on a yearly basis, to ensure the availability of quarters no matter how crowded the city's lodgings became—even the spacious Yellow House could not always accommodate the influx of well-to-do visitors, runner captains, and the fluctuating number of transient gentlemen whose business fell somewhere in the wide gray area between diplomacy and spying. September was waning now, and Wilmington was drenched in warm late-summer light; the month had so far been fairly dry, so the low-lying streets were neither as mucked over nor as noisome, from the dearth of proper drainage, as they sometimes were. Many passersby nodded to the Sloanes, recognizing them by face if not by name, and everyone who passed had a bustling, prosperous look. Fierce battles might be raging in Maryland, and the citizens of other Southern cities might be pinched and constrained by shortages of every quotidian necessity, but Wilmington remained the eye of the storm. So pleasant was the mood of their stroll that Matthew chose that moment to tell his wife about the failure of his quest.

"There simply is no machinery of any kind to be had. I have importuned everyone I can think of, but even H-H is at a loss to conjure up something as basic as a flywheel belt. I know how much it meant to you, to bring in the harvest, and you have done everything humanly possible. The failure is mine."

To his surprise, she squeezed his hand warmly and nodded. "I expected as much, Matthew, but you were so determined, I could not discourage you. Besides, I made inquiries this afternoon about the price of rice. As you probably did, too. Even if we could repair the threshing mill, it would hardly be worth the effort. We will process enough rice for our own needs and let it go at that. Why tie up the *Banshee* for so long, if we stand to make only pennies on the dollar?"

Clouds lifted from Matthew's spirit. The great Rice Upheaval was behind them, and before them stretched an evening of civilized entertainment, good conversation, and plentiful wine.

Mary Harper had never before heard Largo play in a formal setting, although the Jewess had played some parlor ditties when Mary Harper visited Jacob's house. And no one could remember even seeing Hobart-Hampden with a cello, much less hearing him play Beethoven, Haydn, and Mendelssohn. Nor was the visiting violinist, a wistful young Royal Navy lieutenant named Pendelton, without considerable talent. What the trio lacked in polish and refinement, they made up for in passion, digging into the music with wonderful abandon. There was ample room in the Yellow House's parlor for an audience, and numerous visitors dropped in, seduced by the music; at the back of the room were buffet tables and a goodly stock of wine, so everyone was able to satisfy several senses at once. Even Jacob Landau shed his usual reticence; after the formal program was over, he produced his own fiddle, along with a small button-box accordion—quickly taken up by another Englishman—and began playing medleys of Yiddish folk tunes. These klezmer tunes struck a perfect balance between wistfulness and rhythmic vitality—Hobart-Hampden and his accordion-playing countryman approvingly pronounced them "almost Irish"—and soon joined in, improvising. After a while, everyone was clapping, dancing, or just beating time with the silverware.

By the time the party broke up, well past one A.M., everyone was tired but happy. Hobart-Hampden ushered out the last of the guests, rewarded the accordion player with an unopened bottle of port, and asked the ladies' pardon for a few minutes, as he needed urgently to have a few words with Matthew and Jacob.

"Oh, Augustus, must you spoil the evening with *business*?" chided Largo. From the heated glances she had seen pass between the two, Mary Harper had no doubt that they wanted desperately to be alone for an hour or two; but with Jacob hovering about, awash with alcohol and teary-eyed from the bittersweet nostalgia evoked by the klezmer music, that did not seem feasible.

"It will only take a few moments, my dear. It is obviously well past your father's bedtime."

"Well, there go the Boys again!" huffed Largo as she sank into a chair next to Mary Harper, pausing long enough to refill her glass.

"Sometimes, that is what they seem to be—lads out for a lark, conquistadors in search of gold and excitement."

"While their faithful women keep the home fires glowing. Their next voyage, I think, will be a long one. H-H said 'something big' was in the works, whatever that might mean. I don't know what to do with myself, Mary Harper, while they're gone."

"Nor do I. But I have a suggestion."

"Let me hear it, please."

"Why don't you come visit me at Pine Haven? God knows I could use the company, and it is really very pretty there during the autumn. You can stay through the First Fire."

"What is that? It sounds deliciously *pagan*."

"Every autumn, on the first really cool night, we celebrate with the first hearth-fire of the season. This year, of course, there won't be the usual guests, but you and I can eat like queens, and take long walks, and go hunting. Have you ever hunted?"

"No, but it sounds exciting. Can you teach me to shoot?"

"Honestly, men make such a big thing out of being marksmen, but anyone can learn to aim a musket. There are deer in the pinewoods and if we are really lucky, we might bag a wild turkey. They are elusive, but there is no more tasty meat in all the world. Oh, dear Largo, do come! We'll live a life of leisure, just us girls, and we can talk about . . . well, *anything*. Your father can look after himself for a few weeks. And won't it be splendid when the Boys return from . . . from whatever this 'something big' turns out to be, and we are not there to greet them like concubines—only a cold and imperious message telling them where they can find *us*. It will serve them right."

"Very well, I accept. But can we time our departure so that I get to spend one more night with Augustus?"

Mary Harper inadvertently blushed. "Well, of course. I planned something along those lines with Matthew, assuming he comes out of this conference with enough sobriety left to . . . um . . . "

Largo giggled. "To *perform*?"

"Well, yes, although I had more delicate verbs in mind."

"Between us, we can be as vulgar as we like. And relish the thought of what the Boys would think if they overheard us!"

Hobart-Hampden was as good as his word, for the men returned after only a short interval. He arranged for a driver to take the Landaus home and the Sloanes back to their hotel, exchanged one final lustful glance with Largo, then bid them farewell.

When Mary Harper and Matthew were alone once more, he cleared his throat and said, "Something big has come up."

"I know, dear. Largo told me. What, exactly, is 'something big'?"

"It would not be prudent to tell you, or anyone else. But we will be gone for a long time, perhaps a month. I'm sorry, dearest, but the matter is important and the financial rewards will be large indeed. Worth two or three ordinary runs, I expect."

The coach pulled up at their hotel and the sleepy-eyed driver tipped his hat. As she climbed down, Mary Harper gave her husband a smile that verged on smugness.

"Take your time, Matthew. I have invited Largo to Pine Haven for an extended visit. We will be good company for each other . . . now that I no longer have to worry about that damned rice crop!"

"Tch, tch, my love! No need to be vulgar."

Impulsively, she leaned over and nipped his ear, murmuring, "I shall be as vulgar as I like, provided you are up for it."

"Is that a challenge?" he teased, welcoming a sudden blossom of desire. In reply, she mashed her mouth against his, startling him with the greed of her lips. He rolled his eyes, saw no one else in the corridor, and returned her passion with rampant eagerness, fumbling for the room key as he did so. When they both came up for air, she was staring at him wantonly, with an almost cruel twist to her smile.

"Show me something new tonight, Matthew. Show me something you learned from the whores in Nassau. Take me as you would take one of them."

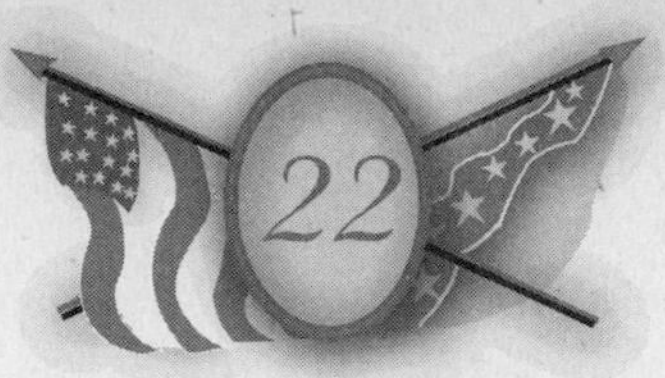

Armstrong and His Giant Gun

WOUNDED AND KILLED—It takes but a little space in the columns of the daily paper; but O! what long household stories and biographies of every one of these names, that we read over once and forget!

"Wounded and Killed"—some eye reads the name to whom it is dear as life, and some heart is struck or broken with the blow made by that name among the list.

It is our Henry, or our John, or our James, or our Thomas that lies with his poor broken limbs at the hospital, or his white, still, and ghastly face on the battlefield. Alas for the eyes that read the list; alas for the hearts that feel!

"He was my pretty boy, that I've sung to sleep so many times in my arms!" says the poor mother, bowing her head in anguish that cannot be uttered. "He was my brave noble husband, the father of my little orphaned children!" sobs his stricken wife. "He was my darling brother, that I loved so, that I was so proud of," murmurs the sister, amid her tears. And so the terrible stroke falls on homes throughout the land.

"Wounded and Killed"—Every name on that list is a lightning stroke to some heart, and breaks like thunder over some home, and falls a long black shadow upon some hearthstone.

—The Wilmington Journal, August 9 1862

According to Hobart-Hampden, it was the Battle of Antietam that really tilted British public opinion toward the Confederacy. On balance, the outcome of that singular bloodbath, waged on September 17, was a draw; both sides fought to a state of mutual prostration, and each side lost about thirteen thousand men—the greatest tally of carnage for any single day in the war so far. What impressed British observers was not the fact that Lee's invasion of Maryland had been turned back so much as the fact that Lee could launch such a major strategic offensive in the first place. Suddenly, the Confederates' military potential seemed close to Napoleonic, and anyone who understood the rudiments of strategy could see that the Rebel commanders had matured greatly since the fumbling blindman's buff operations during the Peninsula campaign, whereas McClellan seemed to have learned nothing. Despite outnumbering Lee by more than two to one, McClellan had fed his brigades into the meat grinder one at a time, much as Lee had done at Malvern Hill, and had suffered the same consequences. Perhaps neither side had prevailed at the end of that gruesome day, but there was no doubt as to which army had turned in the better performance.

One pro-Confederate Englishman, the powerful arms merchant Sir George Armstrong, had been so gratified (or, Hobart-Hampden suggested, so *royally entertained*) by the Rebels' accomplishment that he had written a flowery letter of congratulations to Jefferson Davis, offering him the gift of a brand-new 150-pounder Armstrong seacoast rifle—all Davis had to do was send a ship capable of carrying the giant weapon from Liverpool, along with an authorized representative who would formally sign for the gun at the big Armstrong Foundry in Elswick. How had Hobart-Hampden learned of this business? One of the other Royal Navy runner captains had spotted the letter in a regular mail pouch put on board in Bermuda and discreetly passed it on to Hobart-Hampden, figuring no doubt that the latter would be interested in any correspondence between Armstrong and Jeff Davis.

"So I steamed it open," he confessed to Matthew on the morning of September 25, after the *Banshee* had cleared the blockade lines and set course for Cork, Ireland, where she would take on more coal for the final leg of her ten-day trip to Liverpool.

"Even for you, that is a rash and presumptive act!" Matthew gasped. "Gentlemen do not read one another's mail!"

"George Armstrong is no gentleman, my friend. He is a ruthless, greedy, bloody-handed merchant of death, with all the manners of a cockney stablehand . . . who also happens to be a brilliant engineer. Call it a hunch, if you will. Had the contents been nothing more than flattery, I would have resealed the letter and sent it on. But once I *had* read it, I naturally thought that such a formidable gun ought to be incorporated into the defenses of the Cape Fear rather than shipped to Richmond, where it would be of no earthly use. Matthew, the damned cannon weighs nine tons! Wherever you put it, that's where it will stay forever. Besides, it's a coast defense weapon—it belongs in Fort Fisher, where the industrious Colonel Lamb will make proper use of it."

"So you are masquerading as Jefferson Davis's emissary?"

"No, old chap; *you* are. I am merely your faithful English guide. It says so in President Davis's thank-you letter to Sir George."

"Which you forged."

"Well, of course. Neither man will ever know."

"I suppose not, and I am sure Colonel Lamb will be delighted with his new acquisition, but I fail to see how we stand to make an extra profit, or any profit at all, really."

"Ahem, yes, Matthew, but there is more to this voyage than merely hauling that cannon. A lot more, actually."

Matthew sighed. *I should have known.* While Hobart-Hampden described the rest of his scheme, Matthew reveled in the crisp clarity of the morning. Abruptly, the *Banshee* drove into the Gulf Stream and the sea's cobalt blue gave way to a lush tropical green. Earlier, they had been followed by gleaming, mischievous dolphins, and now they could see a huge mysterious manta ray gliding through the sun-pocked depths. Could there be a more beautiful morning? A calm sea, a bracing wind, strange aquatic creatures that seemed to be living omens of good fortune, a stout ship throbbing with life beneath your feet, a manly friend at your side, and the prospect of genuine adventure looming over every horizon. Matthew Sloane would not have missed this for the world, and to hell with being a rice planter!

Hobart-Hampden had worked out every detail of the voyage, always with an eye toward the maximum profit. By appropriating the Armstrong gun and donating it to Fort Fisher, they would be adding significantly to Wilmington's defensive strength and therefore to the good health of blockade-running in general. Beyond that, however, Hobart-Hampden had nicely calculated how much pressed cotton they could carry in addition to the weight of extra coal they needed to reach Liverpool, where they could sell that smaller quantity of cotton for an even higher price than in Nassau. So that was one layer of profit, enough to cover their expenses. While they went to Elswick to take possession of the Armstrong gun, the *Banshee* would be loaded with lightweight luxury goods that were cheaper to obtain in Liverpool than in Nassau. In this case, Hobart-Hampden had chosen three modest commodities that could be carried in great numbers even though the ship's cargo capacity would be greatly reduced by the weight of the Armstrong and extra coal required for the trip from Liverpool to Nassau.

"Corset stays," Hobart-Hampden chuckled. "I've researched the matter. Nobody has brought any into the South and of course there are none to be had from Northern manufacturers. The ladies of the Confederacy are starved for corset stays. We can haul thousands of them, and sell them for a profit of one thousand percent! The second commodity is somewhat more ghoulish, I fear, but equally in demand: coffin screws. There is not an undertaker in Richmond who has any and they are swamped with work after the recent slaughter in Maryland. And the third commodity: *toothbrushes!* Jacob has been swamped by customers requesting them."

"*Toothbrushes*?"

"Think about it: the skill and technique of the average Confederate dentist is not far removed from that of a blacksmith. Couple that with the fact that all available anesthetics except whiskey are monopolized by the army, and most people would rather let their bad teeth rot and drop out than suffer the ham-fisted yanking and drilling of the itinerant practitioner. Clean teeth are healthy teeth, happy teeth! Which in turn yields the added benefit of sweet breath and more kissable mouths. Amazing, is it not, Matthew? On such small conveniences, such ordinarily trivial artifacts, does our civilization leverage itself."

But if the *Banshee* were to be fully loaded in Liverpool, why did they have to steam to Nassau? Why not head straight for home?

"Ah, yes, well, that's where the third level of profit comes in. You have heard of Miss Belle O'Neal, the famous Rebel spy?"

"Who has not? I thought she had fled the country."

"Yes, to escape the implacable reach of Mr. Allen Pinkerton, Chief of Lincoln's new Secret Service branch, who is obsessed with Miss O'Neal and sworn to capture her by any means, including 'foul' if my information about his character is correct. He seems blind to her charms and wishes only to stretch her pretty young neck in a hangman's noose, should she ever fall under his hand. Not a proper gentleman at all."

"So where do we fit into the picture?"

"Belle O'Neal is here. I mean, *there,* in England. Quite openly, which says a lot for her courage. She has even been interviewed about her adventures by the *London Times,* and feted royally by pro-Confederate socialites. She is using her celebrity, and her beauty, to influence anyone she can. And of course, the American consul and *his* minions are furious at her effrontery. An abduction, or even an assassination, is not out of the question, particularly if Pinkerton can find the right sort of thugs to do the job. To make a long story short, Matthew, we are rescuing Miss O'Neal and spiriting her out of England before she can be harmed. She is carrying sensitive, secret reports about the political situation in France as well as England, and the Yankees would give anything to get their hands on such information."

"Then why not head for Wilmington at full speed? We won't be loading any new cargo in Nassau."

"We won't, but she will. Something very sensitive, apparently, that is being transported under the French flag by a ship that cannot legally be searched by any American cruisers. We will stay in Nassau harbor just long enough for me to pick up this packet, or whatever it is, from the British consul. I shall turn over the documents to Miss O'Neal, and then we shall run like hell for Wilmington."

"What could be so important as to require such a degree of subterfuge?"

"That information has not been vouchsafed to me, and I know better than to ask questions, although I have heard rumors about a deal between Richmond and Paris for the secret construction of a fast, powerful commerce raider at Le Havre. One reason why we have been engaged to perform this service is my record of past experience in the Great Game."

"The what?"

Hobart-Hampden chuckled, as though one of life's fundamental pleasures was periodically astonishing Matthew Sloane.

"That's what we call it, anyhow: the constant rivalry, dating back half a century now, between Great Britain and Russia over each country's degree of influence in northern India, Persia, Afghanistan, the Punjab, all of those sultry swarthy primitive regions where there are no rules except those of expediency and no prize more valuable than strategic location. It is a world of spies and counterspies and medieval potentates, a world of plots and palace intrigues, bribery, debauchery, multiple treacheries, murders, poisonings, and the occasional truly memorable massacre. The two empires never openly clash, of course, but their surrogates, puppets, and agents are perpetually in motion, knives drawn and garrotes poised over someone's head. It's a culture unto itself, an exquisite blend of subtlety and shadowy violence, and one can become addicted to it. I was, for several years, but

I had used up all of my good luck by eighteen sixty, and there was a price on my head from several sultans and tribal chieftains, all of whom wanted me taken *alive* if possible, which indicated that they had elaborate plans for me. Torture is an art form in that part of the world—they can keep you alive for weeks while still inflicting hideous agony. Why, I remember one poor chap, a Russian operative from the Caucasus region, who was captured by the wily Pathans . . . "

"If it's all the same to you, I would just as soon not hear the details. So someone in authority in London thinks you are the man to help Miss O'Neal complete her mission. You must be gratified."

"Well, yes, of course, but the main reason I signed on for the job was to collect an extra ten thousand dollars, over and beyond the already ridiculous profits we're going to make from corset stays and coffin screws. All things considered, this will be the *Banshee*'s most profitable voyage ever. She's a lucky ship, Matthew; you can feel it in her vibrations and see it in the way she cleaves the waves. Once we have delivered Miss O'Neal safely back in the bosom of the Confederacy, I will be able to make the final payment on my own blockade-runner, the *Cossack*. I'll show her to you when we reach Liverpool."

After taking on coal at Cork, they reached Liverpool on October 6. Thus far in Matthew Sloane's life, the largest city he had visited was Charleston, and all comparisons broke down when he got his first look at Liverpool. The harbor dominated the entire horizon, thick with masts and smokestacks and speckled with the flags of many nations, the docks and warehouses and shipyards sprawled in dingy magnificence, great derricks hovering like birds of prey, and a trio of hulking black-hulled Royal Navy cruisers watching over the whole scene like heavily armed nannies. Matthew had many times imagined what a great English port would look like, but the reality of it made him as speechless as the most awestruck tourist. Ships of all sizes, functions, and description choked the winding Mersey until it vanished in the haze of English autumn. Here was the commerce of the world. Here, men spoke earnestly of *tonnage* in numbers inconceivable in any Southern port; here were kept the cargo manifests that were the ultimate record of all the goods shipped to and from all the far-flung lands of empire; tides of paperwork no less powerful in their cumulative force than the rise and fall of the seas themselves, palimpsests on which the monks of the steam age—industrious clerks scribbling their way up the ladders of career—tallied the pulse and temperature of trade, their weather-stained offices jammed together over cobbled wagon-jostled lanes on the east bank, several of them openly flying the Stars and Bars right next to the Union Jack; and on the western expanse of Merseyside, the shipyards swarmed with hull-wrights and ironmongers, riggers and fitters and victualers, brawny men jiggling red-hot rivets atop scaffolding that loomed like mastodon ribs, to the unceasing keyless music of trip-hammers, anvils, forges, lathes, saws, and a hundred chugging donkey engines—miniature railroads winding up canted ziggurats. Huge chain-cranked ramps clattery with wagon loads of plate and railings and ventilator horns and mooring cleats; ships on the cradling ways, skeletal bulwarks of rough gray steel and hull plates of iron, beaten startlingly thin, their hulls impossibly slender compared to the huge stress-curved timbers of the sail-powered ships he would have seen only fifteen years ago. With one sweeping glance, Matthew counted seven or eight turtle-backed hulls that could only be the foundations of new blockade-runners, and he was proud to realize that one of them would be joining the *Banshee* when they came off the ways—that he, Matthew Sloane, rice-farming plantation gentleman, would be a captain in a veritable *fleet;* he also spotted two very different-looking hulls, bows raked forward aggressively at the waterline, beefier in the ribs, partially scaled already with armor: commerce raiders or long-range cruisers, surely, now flagless of course, anonymous, but surely destined, after much bogus paperwork and payoffs, to fly the Rebel flag upon the high seas.

At the fringe of congestion, a sturdy little picketboat pulled alongside and dropped off their pilot, a dapper young man in the uniform of Her Majesty's Customs Service. He scampered up to the flying bridge and shook hands all around, addressing Hobart-Hampden as Captain Roberts.

"Your reputation precedes you once again," muttered Matthew from the corner of his mouth as the pilot began deftly conning the *Banshee* toward one of the few visible empty slots in the docks.

"I should bloody well hope so," grinned the Englishman, sotto voce.

When at length the runner lay snug against its wharf, secure with umbilicals of two-inch hemp, a change came over Hobart-Hampden. He was in England again, and the nonchalance he affected in Wilmington sloughed from him. His head came up, sniffing the rough wet harbor smells as though they were the most elegant fragrance ever to grace Great Britain's sky. His step became livelier, coiled, and he seemed to grow taller. God truly loves the English, thought Matthew. *I hope some of it rubs off on the South.*

After the pilot checked the manifest, the requisite forms were signed, salutations once more exchanged, and the officers of the *Banshee* were free to conduct their business ashore. Matthew had drawn up a rotating list of shore leave for the crew, placing authority in the hands of the chief engineer to enforce the roster and make sure the full crew was back on board in five days' time, sober or not.

Hobart-Hampden in the lead, walking stick all a-swagger, the two men fairly bounded down the gangplank and were instantly immersed in the cacophony and turmoil of dockside traffic. Augustus hailed a cab and gave the driver an address on Mumford Street. "Aye, Gov'ner, you'll be headed for the Confederate embassy, I reckon," replied the driver cheerfully.

"Is there a real Confederate embassy in Liverpool?" asked Matthew, as the cab swerved to avoid a lumbering dray overloaded with barrels.

"No, that's just the local name for one section of town, where the blockade-running firms have their headquarters. I say, Matthew, this will be your first visit to *our* headquarters, won't it?"

Matthew was startled to realize that, of course, the Anglo-Confederate Trading Company *did* have a Liverpool office, one that Hobart-Hampden, through his web of trans-Atlantic connections, had managed to establish via long-distance telegraph, mental telepathy, or carrier pigeons.

When the cab stopped in front of the Anglo-Confederate Trading Company, Matthew beheld a sturdy two-story brick office building topped with a slate roof and two flags: the Union Jack and the Rebel Stars and Bars They introduced themselves at the reception desk and were promptly shown to the building's inner sanctum, where they were heartily greeted by a florid man of early middle age who spoke with a pronounced low-country brogue and who introduced himself as Mister Charles Prioleau.

"Do I detect a Charleston accent, Mister Prioleau?" asked Matthew, while the man poured brandy and proffered cigars.

"Born and raised, sir! But I am now an English citizen, having lived in Liverpool for the past nine years. It is an honor to meet one of the most successful runner captains in the trade, and of course, it is always a pleasure to meet Captain Roberts again." He pronounced the nom de guerre with just enough ironic inflection to indicate full awareness of who Roberts really was. More game-playing, thought Matthew, but the masquerade did add a certain playfulness to what was otherwise a deadly serious business; perhaps that was one secret of the British character, one inimitable reason why they bore the burdens of empire so jauntily yet so efficiently. He did not think there was such a streak of self-deprecation in the French or the Russians—certainly not the Prussians!—which might be one reason why other nations made the mistake of underestimating the latent ferocity of the British Lion.

They drank several toasts, then got down to business.

"Well, Charles, here is our cargo manifest for the return voyage," said Hobart-Hampden with a twinkle in his eye.

Prioleau squinted through the cigar smoke to read the short document.

"I say, Roberts! 'Toothbrushes, coffin screws, and *corset stays*'? No Enfields, no sabers, no gunpowder?"

"Not this trip. We will make five times the profit on these goods that we would make with the usual military hardware. The Confederacy cries out for clean teeth, tight coffins, and fashionable undergarments! We can obtain all these things much more cheaply in England than in Nassau."

"Well, yes, but I'll have to wire to London for such large quantities. It will take a few days."

"We have budgeted the time. We have to travel up to The Midlands and sign off on some great bloody gun that Lord Armstrong is, um, donating to the Rebel cause."

"I know. We received a telegram from him yesterday. Here it is."

Hobart-Hampden read the message quickly. "We are in luck, Matthew. Lord Armstrong wants to show us his factory. You're a man keenly interested in modern technology, so you should find it quite fascinating."

"But what about our . . . our *special passenger?*" stammered Matthew.

"Oh, yes, the beauteous Miss O'Neal!" said Prioleau. "She won't arrive from London until Friday, according to my latest information. Just enough time for your corset stays to be delivered. The cannon, I presume, is already loaded on a train. It all comes together neatly, don't you see?"

"Indeed! And will our passenger be sailing under her own name?"

"Oh, no. She is listed on the manifest as Mrs. Roberts."

Hobart-Hampden laughed in appreciation. "That's rich! I like it!"

"Rather thought you would, old boy."

"Do I get marital privileges, too?"

"That is entirely up to her. She must have something special to offer, considering the number of important Yankee beds she has been in and out of. You must tell me all about it on your next visit."

From Liverpool to Newcastle-on-Tyne, the closest stop to the Armstrong works, was but a single day's journey by rail. Hobart-Hampden bought round-trip tickets—first class, of course—for the early-morning train, then took Matthew in tow for a visit to the construction yards of Miller and Sons, one of the city's oldest and most reputable shipbuilding firms, in order to check on the progress of the *Cossack,* their new ship. Matthew was impressed; in slightly more than a year's time, the blockade-runner trade had engendered a whole new style of marine architecture. She was nearly done, the foreman told them, and Hobart-Hampden could take delivery of the finished ship in Nassau right after Christmas. Indeed, the ship itself seemed eager, impatient, her decks and fittings all polished and spanking. She was 180 feet long and 22 feet wide, with a nominal freeboard of 8 feet and a fully loaded draft of only 10. Powered by two direct-action, inverted steam engines, each one generating at least 250 horsepower, she was the first ship Matthew had seen that was equipped with two screw propellers; she could turn on a dime, go into reverse with scarcely a pause, and cruise for days at sixteen knots with power in reserve for emergencies. Her boats were mounted flush with the decks, her stack could be telescoped down to four feet, and she discharged steam underwater. She was ribbed with steel and hulled with iron, and the hull was divided into four separate watertight compartments, so that a waterline hit in one segment would not endanger the whole vessel. She represented the acme of the shipbuilder's art; compared to her, the *Banshee* seemed almost dowdy. Throughout the inspection Hobart-Hampden glowed with pride. Here was a ship worthy of his affections, commensurate in every way with his *style.* When the two men finally left and headed off to find lodgings, he announced himself to be well pleased.

Matthew enjoyed the train ride more than he expected to. For one thing, the passenger cars were more comfortable than any he had ridden in before, and the railbeds gave such a smooth, stable ride that they seemed made of silk instead of iron. More pointedly, he was enchanted by the English countryside. On this clear sun-washed autumn day, the rolling hills glowed with a deep wet green, the kind of color, he thought, that could only be the product of undisturbed centuries. He had always been fond of Wordsworth, but not until now did he fully understand the depth of tenderness a poet could feel for such a landscape, where everything was softly focused and seemed to glow from within. They passed ivy-covered villages that, but for the telegraph wires and gas lamps, must surely have changed little since the days of Shakespeare.

Their train stopped first at Leeds, then at York, then angled northeast toward Newcastle, and suddenly the scenery changed. They were now chugging through the industrialized Midlands, and the pastoral vistas were few and cramped, walled in by factories and mills, gigantic boxes and oblongs of bolted iron, great serpents of pipe, some of which vomited thick dung-colored waste into the streams and rivers; the buildings were streaked with soot and mean-looking, perpetually damp and smoky lanes gleamed like oil slicks, as though the frequent rains could no longer wash them, but simply deposited another layer of ashen glaze. No more could he see timbered vine-clad cottages; the workers' flats were drab and characterless, no bigger than a large closet, festooned with washing that was already smeared with filth before it could dry in the pale fitful sunlight.

On the streets and stoops he saw only women with children under the age of ten, and concluded that the life span here was probably short, old men rare, and everyone else off at their jobs. No greater contrast could he imagine to the softer-edged, slower-paced life of the rural South; the pinched, bloodless wives and scrawny listless children seemed trapped in a form of bondage more cruel than slavery itself. Slaves, at least, *sang* when they worked, and smiled at the kindness of a friend or any sign of compassion from a master, and it was inconceivable that these beaten-down people might ever dance or sing or laugh. And yet, when he raised his eyes from the wretchedness of these dwellings and beheld the stupendous monuments of industry to which they were indentured, he was stirred by the awesome power symbolized by those smokestacks, cranes, conveyor belts, and conduits. Here was the wellspring of England's wealth, and the scale of it quite overwhelmed him. Rivers of artillery, railroad stock, nails and boilers, gears and levers, harvesters and lampposts, propellers and coffee grinders, stereopticons, trivets, and bone saws, rivets and steel beams, all of the hard, dark, obdurate, *forceful* things that would drive mankind into the next century, were made here in such abundance that nothing short of an edict from God could halt the forges and silence the mills. He had always believed in the power of science and invention, but his most progressive ideas were mere rustic fancies compared to this reality. Finally, as the train slowed on the outskirts of Elswick-on-Tyne, Matthew Sloane made the fearful connection and spoke of it to his companion.

"Augustus, is this what the industries of the North look like? We have come all this way to procure a single cannon, when places like this can turn them out by the dozen in a single day? I knew the South could not boast of such mighty works, but until today I did not comprehend the reality of what we are up against! What chance have we against . . . against all *this*?"

Hobart-Hampden gazed at his friend thoughtfully for a moment. When he replied, his voice was almost gentle. "You have courage, and resourcefulness, and some of the finest damned infantry in the world, Matthew, which are things impossible to measure against mass production. You saw how our workers live, in service to the barons of industry—the men who work in those factories rarely live past forty, and their lives are circumscribed by unremitting brute toil around machines that maim them in great numbers, breathing air that makes their spit turn black, knowing that their children's lives are set immutably in the same short, hopeless arc. Would you want to see your beloved South turned into such a blighted, poisoned landscape, for that is what the industrial centers of Yankeedom become? Is it not worth any hardship to preserve your land from this kind of soulless exploitation? Do not answer right away. For it could well be that all this ugliness is the very shield which protects those tranquil villages and sylvan glades you doted on this morning. England is small and her status is envied by larger powers; therefore England must be strong in order to survive. We are girded not only by the legacy of Shakespeare and the spirit of King Arthur, but also by the breech-loading field guns of Sir George Armstrong, whom you will find, I think, to be a fairly extraordinary man."

A breechloader, he continued, after they boarded the hackney sent to pick them up at the station—chatty now, a friendly lecture replacing his earlier seriousness—had inherent advantages for a colonial army such as Great Britain's. It had twice the rate of fire of a muzzle loader and all the steps in reloading could be performed at the rear, behind an iron shield that protected the crew from musketry and shell fragments. Armstrong had designed, patented, and manufactured the first really practical breechloaders, six or seven years earlier, and they had proven their worth on several far-flung battlefields at the empire's periphery. "If you have ever seen a charge by a horde of hashish-addled spear-clanging fuzzy-wuzzies—and I have, though fortunately from a distance—you can appreciate the curtain of fire laid down by a battery of such weapons." Was *their* gun a breechloader? Matthew inquired. Oh, no; it was far too big in caliber. No one had yet perfected a breech plug that could withstand the pressures generated by a hundred-and-fifty-pounder, which were something on the order of eighteen tons per square inch. Their cannon had to be loaded by winch and chain and human brawn, from the front.

All conversation ceased when they came up to the main gate of the Armstrong factory, a walled compound comprising several square miles of hard-edged facilities, the whole place looming like a smoke-colored castle atop mountains of coke and slag. Fortresslike, the main gate was flanked by two grim stone towers occupied by armed guards. Just inside the gate was a cobbled courtyard filled with horses and carriages, surrounded on three sides by squat, heavy office buildings and residences, around whose sides stunted gardens struggled to maintain a semblance of elegance amid the particulate grime that soaked down incessantly from the air above. As Matthew and Hobart-Hampden dismounted, they saw a heavyset man in a duster coat striding from the most ostentatious office building, welcoming them with pink, porky, gesturesome hands. Sir George Armstrong was a man of hale middle age—early fifties, Matthew guessed—with a hearty, florid gin-and-water complexion, thornbush brows, and a remarkable number of broad polished teeth. He gave off an aura of undisguised self-satisfaction, a sure sign of a man so wealthy and powerful that not only his deeds but his very thoughts were beyond mortal criticism, answerable only to the queen and to God. He escorted his guests into a large office filled with the sort of dark paneling and overstuffed red-leather furniture that Matthew assumed could be found in London's most exclusive gentlemen's clubs.

"How was your journey?"

"Expeditious and comfortable, Sir George, and something of a revelation to Captain Sloane—this is his first trip to England."

"Is it indeed? Tell me, sir, does our 'sceptered isle' live up to your expectations?"

"Very much so, sir. Both its pastoral beauty and its tremendous bastions of industry."

Armstrong nodded incisively. "Wait until you see the main foundry building! Nothing like it since the days of Rome! I invited you gentlemen here to show you the full might and majesty of British manufacture, so you can report back to your President Davis as to the nature of his country's support in England. I am personally convinced that it is only a matter of time until we enter the fray on the Confederate side. All it will take is one more rash Yankee naval officer stopping a British ship on the high seas, and public sentiment will demand an active role. The Royal Navy can sweep away the blockade like a hurricane, and should do it, so that any nation which contemplates using such tactics against England will be shown an example!"

"Hear, hear!" chirped Hobart-Hampden.

"Of course, I am a businessman as well as a Southern sympathizer, so I hope that my token gift will so impress the authorities in Richmond that they will order more guns of the same pattern. Ideal, positively ideal, for coastal defense! Your ports should be bristling with one-fifties—ton for ton, there's not another weapon that can shoot farther, hit harder, and boast of comparable accuracy. Anyway, the barrel and carriage and loading machinery are already on their way to Liverpool, along with one hundred rounds of self-encased ammunition. Now, if you will excuse me for a moment, I should like to take you on the grand tour!"

Armstrong darted out of the office and Hobart-Hampden leaned over to mutter: "That old bugger! He is nothing more than a salesman giving out a free sample! If he realized that the Confederacy cannot even pay for enough common howitzers to go 'round, he would probably take back his precious hundred and fifty and rudely show us to the door!"

Armstrong returned with an actuary who witnessed the signing of transfer documents and handed each of the guests a long gray dustcoat similar to Armstrong's own. These, he explained, were necessary to protect his guests' ordinary clothing while they toured the foundry. As he struggled into his garment, Matthew wondered what, if any, protective clothing might be worn by the workers who tended Armstrong's infernal machines.

Armstrong called it the Big Gun Room. It was the size of a Gothic cathedral: narthex, nave, and chancel, with transepts for mysterious subassemblies branching off into immeasurable gloom on both sides of the foundry itself. In the lofty vaulted ceilings there were windows, but the grimy light that penetrated them struggled earthward for a few yards and then expired, sucked up in the general murk. Controls, gauges, and foremen's desks were lit by gas lamps, but these provided no more illumination than candles in a coal mine. Most of the light was molten, throbbing, satanic in color. Far above, Matthew saw networks of massive girders, great loops of chain, block-and-tackle hooks that looked capable of hoisting an ironclad. The sheer volume of enclosed space was at once vast and suffocating, an unnatural darkness, a purposeful blocking out of daylight, girded like a fortress, as though the activities within could not be allowed to be seen. Matthew was overwhelmed, almost dazed, by the immensity and mephitic gloom, his sight confused by the constant flicker and pulse of forges and castings and rivers of liquid metal. An elemental vibration roared in his ears, complex as a Bach fugue, but composed of raw particulate matter. Sparks flew in great cascades, flakes of solid fire, globules of splashed-off metal hung quivering in the smoke like translucent gobbets of red flesh, the bowel-blood of earth itself. Great beasts breathed harshly, titanic hammers rang, ingots of puddled iron hissed and shrieked as carefully measured stresses shaped and directed them into preordained channels. And all through this huge and incomprehensible cavern, dwarfed by the immensity of their surroundings, moved hundreds of men, tending the fires, pulling the levers, rotating great helm-wheels that opened and closed strange sluice gates, keeping the process going, alchemists transmuting raw ore into the harsh and heavy tools of war. A few workmen, scurrying past, paused briefly to observe the visitors and to nod their respect to Sir George Armstrong, who appeared not to notice them, so entranced was he by the spectacle of his own private Hades. As if to confirm Matthew's impression, Armstrong gestured expansively and cried out in a voice commanding enough to penetrate the general clangor, "It is better to rule in Hell, than to serve in Heaven!"

Obviously, Armstrong had taken many other visitors on his "Grand Tour," for he moved them along now like a well-rehearsed guide shepherding a tourist group through the Tower of London. First, he said, he wanted to show them "King Henry," the newest and most puissant engine he had designed. King Henry turned out to be a drop-forge hammer as big as a five-story building, towering up like a guillotine designed for the beheading of titans. Standing at the dimly lit controls was a shop foreman whom Armstrong introduced as Mister Stokes, who stood dutifully at his levers and dials like a spear carrier in an opera waiting for his only scene in the production.

"Thirty thousand tons of force per square inch!" sang Armstrong, as though his guests had any standard against which such a statistic might be measured. "Nothing like it in the world, although that Prussian bastard Krupp may have something on the drawing boards. Gentlemen, this hammer can shape the largest ordnance components with the precision of a master sculptor. It combines the ultimate in brute force with the finest scientific precision. Mister Stokes, proceed with the demonstration if you please."

"Aye, Sir George." Stokes saluted the observers and removed from his overall pocket an ordinary hulled walnut. "Observe, gents! The world's largest nutcracker!" He placed the object dead center on the huge anvil, dusted his hands with a flourish, then began to manipulate levers and wheels. King Henry came alive, seemed to inhale and puff up as the steam lifted pistons as big as railroad cars and oil ran out like blood along the trembling, fire-lit cylinders and the pressure gauges' needles crept up into the red zone and trembled there. When Stokes was satisfied, he stepped back and put his finger on a large green button. Instinctively, Matthew flinched back from the impending stroke, sure that the walnut was about to be atomized.

"Voilà!"

Unthinkable tons of pressure vented in a bull elephant's roar and Vulcan's hammer came down in a blur, then simply stopped, all kinetic energy spent, with a precise, almost finicky grace. Stokes pulled another lever, the hammer slid up once more, and there was the walnut, perfectly cracked in two, the shell not even splintered and the meat within not even bruised. He retrieved the halves and offered one to each of the stunned witnesses. "Very tasty. I can put a bit of salt on them if you like."

"I don't know whether to eat it or have it stuffed and mounted as a trophy," muttered Hobart-Hampden, After staring incredulously at the thing for a few seconds, he finally shrugged and popped it into his mouth. "Very tasty indeed, sir."

"I think I shall keep mine," said Matthew, "so I can show it to my wife when I get home."

Now that his visitors had been doubly awed, Armstrong became more businesslike, leading them along narrow aisles into the depths of the foundry, from one process to the next, proudly demonstrating the steps involved in producing a seacoast defense cannon. Matthew had assumed that one merely made a mold of the proper size, then poured molten iron into it, but that technique, Sir George quickly pointed out, had become obsolete many years ago. Each hundred-fifty-pounder was cast in three parts: barrel, breech, supporting trunnions. Molding for each segment was achieved by pressing hardwood models into sand-filled boxes called flasks. Each model was then coated with a slip of cokewash—pulverized charcoal moistened with a solution of water and fine-grained clay—after which the three flasks were bolted together, dried in an oven, and placed upright, breech end down, into a big casting pit. Nearby was a reservoir of molten steel. Brawny sweat-filmed men, wielding sledgehammers, knocked out the gates. With a great mournful sigh, the liquid metal flowed. Cooling the steel too rapidly could create imperfections, even cracks, so the cooling was done gradually, over a period of five days.

The next step was "Armstrong Process" itself—the technique that had made his weapons famous for their reliability. This involved reinforcing the steel inner tube at the points of greatest firing stress with ribbons of wrought iron welded together at white heat. Once the reinforcing was complete, the whole rough casting was hoisted onto a gigantic lathe, the cascabel affixed to a turning clamp. Excess flares of metal sprue were filed off by hand. Then the boring rods were applied, a small one first then successively larger ones until the desired caliber was excavated, each rod driven by massive weights attached to cogwheels. Specialized bits then screwed out the rifling grooves. Once the whole nine-ton implement had been cast, cooled, trimmed, bored, rifled, and trunnioned, it was hung from an enormous tackle and pumped full of water so that even the most minute cracks could be spotted. When the finished weapon had passed all inspections, the cascabel was branded to mark the year and place of manufacture.

By the end of the tour, Matthew's head was ringing and his eyes were fatigued from squinting against the raw flare of so much molten metal. If Armstrong had sought to impress them, he had certainly succeeded. "I do hope President Davis enjoys my gift," he said as he bade them farewell. "And I do hope you will tell him what you have seen here. He needs more of my guns, and the price is fair."

Hobart-Hampden assured him that President Davis would receive a full description, but as they were being driven back to their hotel in Elswick, he elbowed Matthew conspiratorially and said, "Well, old boy, how does it feel to have stolen one of the world's finest artillery pieces?"

"It would feel better if there was one single factory in the South that could manufacture copies. It is, after all, only one cannon."

"True, but it buggers any other piece in Colonel Lamb's arsenal. It will be worth the trouble just to see his face light up when we show it to him."

By the time they returned to Liverpool, the 150-pounder had been loaded into the *Banshee*'s main cargo hold. Another day was needed to stow the hundreds of cartons filled with corset stays, toothbrushes, and coffin screws. At midnight on their last day in port, a shrouded hackney parked at the foot of the gangplank. Its driver requested help to bring aboard several pieces of heavy luggage, and then a tall woman, wrapped against the fog's chill in a dark cloak, strode resolutely onto the ship, where she was courteously greeted by Matthew and Hobart-Hampden. Not until they ushered her into her cabin did she unwrap herself.

From the first moment Matthew Sloane saw the face and figure of Belle O'Neal, he knew that his heart was in peril, if not his very soul.

The First Fire of Autumn

NO NEED FOR PANIC—We feel no apprehensions personally on the subject of Yellow Fever, as we do not think that there is any likelihood of its becoming an epidemic. It is not to be denied, however, that this is emphatically the sickly season here, and that there is an unusual amount of sickness in town, so that, while there is no cause for panic, there is an urgent necessity for the adoption of every proper precaution. With the public mind so directed to a particular subject, everything is referred to that subject, so that now, every form of fever is supposed to be Yellow Jack and every death is attributed to that disease.

The great amount of moisture and the continued heat, together with the suspension of the steam mills and turpentine distilleries are all unfavorable to the general health, so not on account of Yellow Fever, but on account of the general sickliness of the season, we would advise families who are out of town and can afford to remain so, ought to stay away for a few weeks.

—The Wilmington Journal, September 16 1862

Largo arrived at Pine Haven on the cusp of autumn, three days after the Boys had sailed off on their mysterious and lengthy mission. Just as Largo had once rhapsodized to Hobart-Hampden about the stern commanding wildness of Cape Fear, so did Mary Harper speak to her about the romance and lore of the low country. From the time Largo was old enough to be a fit companion instead of a childish burden, she had accompanied her father on business trips up and down the seaboard. She had seen enough of some southern cities—Charleston, Charlotte, Atlanta, Raleigh, and Richmond—to know their character and the names of their leading merchants, but as Pine Haven's gaily painted launch chugged up the Cape Fear River on that October morning, she realized that the South was the seat of other, older, prouder realms of which she knew almost nothing. Not long after Wilmington vanished astern, she felt herself entering the embrace of such a realm.

As they passed from the coastal zone into the low country, the riverbanks lost their look of cultivation and became denser, wilder, more tangled. Whole trees lay canted into the current, like fallen buttresses, trailing mops of river grass and beards of Spanish moss. A startled beaver slid from its burrow and dived into the water like a truant schoolboy sneaking out for a swim. Terrapins warmed their shells in patches of sunlight. Twice, Mary Harper pointed out the emotionless obsidian knobs of alligators' eyes, and once, like a sudden exaltation of song, a great blue heron flapped over their heads. Largo could feel the tension of the war and the jagged commercial pulse of the city fade, replaced by a growing enchantment. When the launch turned north into the Uwharrie branch, the water changed color from chill olive to a clear cognac brown, and the hundreds of tributary creeks draining from the marshes were black with the seepage of fecund autumnal decay; no smell of the sea, now, but an earthier tang that was almost bitter-sweet, a perfume pressed from all the summer's flowers as they browned and shriveled with the season.

Night had fallen by the time they reached Pine Haven's dock, so Largo saw little of the place on her first walk across its grounds, save for those small patches revealed by the moving circle of Mister Bright's lantern, while a thin, smiling Chinaman and two Negroes followed with the women's luggage. Mary Harper did pause to point out the rice fields, which were broader and more scraggly in their postharvest dormancy than Largo had imagined them to be. She got the impression of numerous outbuildings, smelled horses and mules in a barn, and saw a row of glowing doorways, stenciled with the silhouettes of curious observers which she guessed were the slave cabins. Inside the main house, Mary Harper introduced her to a moonfaced black woman of indeterminate age named Aurelia, who was tasked to look after all Largo's needs while she was there. Both mistress and guest then tucked into a meal whose plentitude and weight left them ready for bed. The tour, Mary Harper said as she embraced the younger woman, could wait until morning.

"Morning" came after nine, and when Largo woke she found her clothes laid out neatly, dusted and pressed, next to a basin of hot water and some fresh towels. There was a pleasant chill in the air, but as sunlight climbed over the forest and brightened her room, it brought both warmth and comfort. As Largo finished arranging her hair, there was a knock on the door, and Aurelia entered, bearing a tray of hot coffee and corn muffins, a big disarming smile on her mahogany face.

"Good mornin', Mizz Landau! You takes yo' time now, comin' down to breakfast. Got ham and berries and eggs and grits if you like 'em."

"I don't know, Aurelia—I've never had grits before. What do they taste like?"

The maid wrinkled her face in thought. "Well, by theyselves, they don't *have* much taste. But they come alive if'n you put butter or sugar or red-eye juice on 'em. We got all three, so you can 'speriment."

"I shall do that. Tell Mary Harper I'll be down in five minutes."

Aurelia nodded and turned to go, then turned back to search Largo up and down with a diffident but open curiosity.

"Yes, Aurelia? What is it?"

"Ah don't mean to be rude, ma'am. It's just that you the very first actual Hebrew Ah ever laid eyes on, so Missuz Sloane tell me. Preacher-man tell Bible stories 'bout de Hebrews and Moses and ol' Fay-row. Ah figure any folks stand that tall in de Bible mus' be giants or somethin'. But you don't look no diff'rent from any other white lady!"

Returning the Negro woman's disarming smile with a sly grin of her own, and a pull-your-leg tilt of her eyebrows, Largo said, "That's true *on the outside.* But some people say we have two hearts and twenty ribs on each side!"

Aurelia digested that answer with wide-eyed amazement, then realized she was being had and broke into a long rumble of laughter that followed her all the way downstairs.

From the first morning of her visit, Largo reveled in the visual poetry of Pine Haven's environs. A lavish, poised harmony existed here: the river, the fields, the gardens, the variegated woodlands, each comprised one melodic strand of the total enchantment. In the fullness of autumn, the Carolina low country proved to be a land of veils; its beauty was not brightly lyrical so much as somber; its vistas and intimacies evoked a sense of *fate,* but not unpleasantly so. Every color seemed, at some eventual distance, to verge on purple, a layered kind of lavender shading into lilac, the whole landscape suffused with an immanent and sourceless translucence: damson, amethyst, lavender-rose, shades too subtle to have names. Time thickened in this realm, its increments slow and dusty, in no hurry at all, and the slow frictionless pulse of the place got into Largo's blood. Sometimes as she wandered, she turned a wooded corner and the trees dropped back like receding curtains to reveal a sudden dramatic sweep of marsh, the water black as tar but paradoxically clear as glass, stippled with the slick, rounded stumps of cypresses, sunlight on water lilies, lazy formations of ducks, the sudden dazzling flight of a snow-white egret, rolling on the wind like a dollop of living cream; strange moody savannas, their swards of broom grass gone saffron with the change of season. Strangest and most captivating of all, to Largo's sensibilities, were the pine barrens where the tall shafted trunks seemed as precisely ordered and spaced as thin stone pillars upholding a cathedral's vaulted canopy of frothy green, twenty feet or more above a flat, spongy floor of intricately woven ferns quite soft enough to sleep on, no thorns or creepers to catch or scratch. Largo felt the air's very texture change when she first walked through such a place, as though not only time but all other mundane considerations were forbidden entry into these natural cathedrals. And always, high above in the undulating clouds of pine needles, she heard a mysterious crooning murmur that never ceased, as though each passing migratory wind paused in those boughs to be refreshed before continuing its journey. And three days' running, as she stood at the edge of one particular pine barren, listening to the wind song overhead and trying to unravel secrets for which she had no definitions, Largo saw a ghostly flock of deer come to graze near a particular canebreak on the southern edge of the region. When she mentioned it to Mary Harper, Mary Harper suggested a hunt, to provide a proper First Fire feast.

Mister Bright, now recovered to full gangling vigor, discovered that Stepan, the taciturn Pole, had once been a gamekeeper on an estate near Cracow, and in a single day of exceptional hunting, they bagged two deer and one of the region's elusive but delicious wild turkeys. A proper feast was thus assured.

Every October, as soon as the nights grew cool enough to warrant it, Pine Haven held a party to mark the First Fire of the autumn. The tradition was decades old. Friends and relatives came from as far away as Charleston, and since the occasion was more pagan in tone than Christian, the festivities were usually livelier and louder than those of Thanksgiving. Spirits flowed freely, and there was a lot of sparking among the young unmarried guests. Last year, the celebration had been cancelled because of the war, and Mary Harper had missed it very much.

So the First Fire party of 1862 was solely by and for the denizens of Pine Haven, and Largo was the only guest. The day after the hunt was given over to preparations, including the laying of five huge bonfires in a rough circle between the big house and the slave quarters, and the fashioning of several sturdy banquet tables. It was one of the busiest "holidays" Largo had ever seen. The kitchen seethed with activity, and the Negroes moved with light, happy steps, instinctively knowing that this year's First Fire party was largely for *them,* the mistress's gesture of thanks for their loyalty, a ceremony whose unspoken purpose was to underscore the fact that, whatever the future might bring, everyone at Pine Haven would face it together.

When the feasting began, promptly at six o'clock, there was no segregated band of whites standing around on one side of the yard watching the darkies dance and caper on the other. Everyone shared the same ground, even as they shared the same food and lemonade, although Largo did notice that spirits were not passed out to the blacks. When she or Mary Harper or Mister Bright wanted a drink, they went discreetly inside to fill their glasses. By the time she had eaten her fill, Largo had also consumed enough wine to feel its effects. To judge from the flush on her cheeks, so had Mary Harper. Fitz-John Bright, apparently, could absorb his weight in whiskey without showing any ill effects. By nine o'clock, the air was cold enough to draw everyone closer to the towering fires.

Largo did not want this idyll to end, although she understood that for Mary Harper Sloane, her visit was only a distraction from daily responsibilities that would descend once more in all their rigor. At least now she understood more fully why her Confederate friends were so passionate about preserving their way of life. Until now, Largo had envisioned a "plantation" as though it were a modern variation on a medieval fiefdom: the big house like a white fortress (in more ways than one), surrounded as by a moat with an aesthetic cordon sanitaire of manicured gardens, and both in turn islanded by huge dreary fields whose appearance spoke of unremitting toil, and somewhere at the edge of the property, like a dingy and half-shameful afterthought, were the wretched hovels of the serfs. Pine Haven was not such a place and she had by now learned to take it at face value. The Sloanes' Negroes dwelt in neat whitewashed cabins, adequately floored and windowed and ventilated, each with its own fireplace and a snug loft above the main rooms where the children slept. Behind the slaves' quarters were sizable family plots of melons and vegetables. The field hands were not harried from dawn to dusk in backbreaking labor. When the day's inventory of tasks was complete, Mister Bright waved them home even if much daylight remained, and once he had done so, their lives were their own. Still, Largo could not resolve one basic question: were these people better off here than they had been in Africa, where they knew famine, pestilence, and tribal slaughter? *But in Africa they were free,* whispered the Judaic conscience that was always within her, even when she chose to override it. *There is no Pharaoh to scourge them, and if they must make bricks, at least they are well provided with straw.* Perhaps the arguments of some black Moses, were such an icon suddenly to appear, could bring the matter into focus and cleanse it of ambiguity. Largo had seen the slave market at work in town; had heard the tales of cruelty and separation, and she understood why those aspects of the system had seized the imagination of the abolitionists. But what she saw at Pine Haven was not a form of bondage so much as a complex interdependence marked by reasonable civility, and sometimes more than that—sometimes she felt an undercurrent, which she sensed in glances, gestures, inflections, and stanzas of overheard dialogue, of what could only be described as affection.

"The thing about Irish music," Hobart-Hampden had said to her during one soiree at the Yellow House, "is that the drunker you get, the better it sounds." And if Largo was not yet really tipsy . . . well, maybe just a bit . . . she learned that his adage was equally true of Negro music. At first, the singing and capering and clapping were scattered and snatchy, but as the black folk settled in around the fires, bellies full, their music-making became more purposeful and choir-like. Their voices blended in a dark stately timbre and the more she listened, the more her musical training enabled her to hear and the deeper became her appreciation, for some of these a cappella renditions proved anything but primitive. Many times, the singers maintained unusual, difficult, multiple rhythms with flawless ease, throwing in syncopations and grace notes that seemed wholly improvised and spontaneous, but always apt, always emotionally effective. Unlike the formally trained European musicians she had heard or studied with, the Negroes did not seem to "follow" a song, but rather gave each song such energy and breathing room that the lyrics led *them* instead, and generated moments of accidental beauty that touched—yes—one's very soul. And as much as they sang about Jesus, there was an Old Testament gravity to their music; some of the verses she heard would not have been out of place in Ecclesiastes.

Tremblin' woman an' a tremblin' man,
God gwine to hol' you in His tremblin' hand!

By ten o'clock, everyone was singing, including the Pole, the

Portuguese, and the Chinaman, after their own peculiar fashion, and such was the spirit of the night that even the songs about death resounded with a paradoxical joy that gladdened every heart.

Ev'rybody who is livin' gots ta die, gots ta die.
Ev'rybody who is livin' gots ta die, gots ta die,
De rich an' de po', de great an' de small,
All gots to meet in dat judgment hall,
'Cause ev'rybody who is livin' gots ta die!

Just before the party broke up, not far from midnight, the Negroes—their ranks now thinned as tired, full, sleepy individuals and couples drifted back to their cabins—sang a verse that reminded Largo and Mary Harper of their men, far gone upon the vast Atlantic:

Ah look in de grave an' de grave so wat'ry,
Lawd, Ah gots to lay down in dat wat'ry grave.
Ain't nobody can swim dat water but me, Jesus,
So take mah hand upon the other side . . .

Falling gently into each other's arms, the women wept, but they were just drunk enough by that time to feel somehow ennobled by emotion's flood, as though their embrace was a prayer so strong that it could reach across the sea and touch the hearts of the men they loved.

Largo went to bed, finally, with every fuzzy intention of sleeping as late as her body desired. She was far gone in dreams when Mary Harper shook her awake in the thin light of early morning, and her head began to ache the instant she opened her eyes. Mary Harper did not look very chipper either, with her bloodshot eyes and stale wine-fumed breath, but the seriousness of her expression caused an apprehensive flutter in Largo's already queasy stomach, so she raised up on one elbow and tried to ignore her throbbing temples.

"A messenger arrived by boat fifteen minutes ago, dearest friend. As soon as you can pull yourself together, you must accompany him back to Wilmington. Aurelia has already packed most of your things."

"Has something happened to the ship?"

"No, dear. It is your father. He has fallen ill quite suddenly and he is asking for you. He sent one of the store clerks upriver to fetch you. I think the matter is serious."

On September 21, 1862, the steamer *Konstanz* ran New Inlet safely with a mixed cargo of gunpowder and luxury goods from Havana. At that time, General Lee was desperate to replenish the supplies his army had burned up in the Antietam campaign, so orders went out from Richmond that any runner whose manifest included significant military stores was to be passed through the customs station at Smithville without delay, foregoing the usual sanitary inspection and quarantine interval. General Chase Whiting once again found himself at loggerheads with his own government, for August and September were the worst months for imported contagions, even as they were the worst for domestic lowland malaria. Whiting had only recently promulgated a general order to tighten the customs' procedures at Smithville, and thus found himself in the disagreeable position of having to countermand his own orders less than a month after he had issued them.

Jacob Landau, waiting for the *Konstanz* when it docked at the foot of Nun Street, was chatting amiably with two Confederate purchasing agents eager to put the ship's powder on the next train for Richmond. He was there to take delivery of large quantities of Cuban cigars, processed sugar, and Spanish lace, all of which he had ordered and paid half down for three weeks earlier. Such commodities were plentiful in Havana, but only a few runners trafficked in them due to the extra time and coal required for the longer-than-Nassau voyage. The *Konstanz,* however, was a new ship to the trade, a large wallowing craft owned by a consortium of German investors who were eager to cash in on the situation but were not yet well informed concerning the ins and outs. Jacob had calculated that the ship stood a better than fair chance of making one or two successful runs to Cuba, if only because the Yankees were not paying much attention in that direction; as soon as the ship drew notice from the Federal consulate in Havana, of course, that would no longer obtain, and the good burghers of Bremen would lose their investment to a high-seas cruiser. But in the meantime, Jacob was quite prepared to leverage risk against profit by taking advantage of their naïveté. A good merchant, he averred, must always rotate, freshen, and enliven his stock—in wartime as in peace, perhaps even more so, there was always a keen market for the novel and the ostentatious. Confectioners' grade sugar, not to mention bolts of fine Spanish lace, had not been available in Wilmington for at least a year, at any price.

It was his God-given talent to work the margins of an enterprise with more flair and imagination than other merchants, and thus far into the war, God had favored him and his partners. He had promised God a new synagogue, in memory of Rachel and as a gesture of forgiveness to God for taking her in the first place, and Jehovah had apparently found that bargain acceptable. By subscribing very generously—much more generously than most of Wilmington's wealthy gentiles—to Editor Fulton's ironclad fund, Jacob had deftly preempted any accusations that he was a grasping Shylock, a calculating Hebrew profiteer intent only on taking commercial advantage of the South's besieged condition. He had also imported significant amounts of medical supplies, which he had donated to the city's hospitals and to the garrisons of Forts Fisher, Caswell, and Anderson. He had, in several overlapping spheres, created a vast clear space for himself and his daughter in the midst of conflict and confusion. His hands grasped the reins of these enterprises with strength and no small amount of pride, and for the first time since Rachel's death, he felt that he was doing more on earth than just marking time and toting up receipts.

And he had to admit, with regard to his manipulation of the *Konstanz* and her greedy, eager, but inexperienced skipper, that there was a sly private glee to be had from putting one over on the unseen German owners. He had enjoyed thinking about them the previous night, when he had taken advantage of Largo's absence to indulge in a lot more bedtime liquor than she would have approved of: visualizing their florid, blue-eyed, arrogant faces, stuffed with beer and bratwurst, the embodied countenance of Bavarian prejudice. How smugly they had dispatched their big, bovine freighter into the fray, blinded by the newspaper accounts of easy fortunes, ignorant as pigs of the increasingly deadly cat-and-mouse nature of the business. Jacob had toasted them, in fact, as he sat within his private shrine, the shofar in his lap and the menorah candles bathing Rachel's portrait with holy light, for who had these Germans come to first in Wilmington, for advice on how to make a quick killing in the feverish arena of the blockade-running trade, but Jacob the Jew from Munich, whose shadow they would not have deigned to spit upon twenty-five years earlier?

"That's one that won't last long in the business," observed one of the Confederate agents, pointing at the *Konstanz,* with her high freeboard, tall auxiliary masts, and Gulf Stream–blue hull.

"Lasted one trip, though," said the other. They were both dapper, rather fussy men in shiny morning coats, no longer young, self-conscious about the fact that they were not in uniform, and Jacob thought it likely that they held brief serious conversations with themselves in the mirror every morning, reminding their reflections of how important their work was to the Confederate cause, and how their talents would, really, be wasted in frontline service because, after all, who could fill out triplicate forms with greater dispatch and clarity?

The younger of the two agents doffed his hat to Jacob and wished him a good morning. They were not likely to have much disposable income to spend in Jacob's store, but just in case they needed to overextend their means from time to time—a bit of finery to impress the ladies, perhaps—they wanted the Jew to think well of them.

"Do you have a consignment of goods aboard that tub, Mister Landau?"

"I do indeed, sir. Refined sugar, from the mills of Cuba, that will sweeten your tea like angels' breath, some cigars of excellent quality, and a shipment of Spanish lace."

"Why is it, I wonder, that people will still pay a premium price for Cuban cigars, when tobacco is one of the two things the South has in abundance?" asked one of the agents.

"Some will pay the premium *because* of that, sir. Some men, indeed, will treasure those cigars all the more because they are so utterly superfluous. They will hand them out to those whom they wish to impress as a way of saying, 'I am perfectly content to pay three dollars for a cigar that is not appreciably better than the one you paid two bits for down the street.' "

The agents chuckled appreciatively at Jacob's wit. And in truth, Jacob did feel witty and keen on this unseasonably hot September morning, like a man completely at home in the world that surrounded him. On impulse, Jacob handed a *carte de visit* to each man. "Come by my store any time after tomorrow, gentlemen, and show these to one of my clerks. There is always a discount at Landau's for those who help keep strong the sinews of war. I'll throw in a few cigars on the side."

Not sure whether they were being flattered, induced, or in some subtle way even bribed, the two agents thanked him vigorously, then made a great display of checking over their papers, while the *Konstanz* made a clumsy approach to the wharf. He could hear the captain screeching *"Nein! Nein!"* as the bow made contact and several of his crew—adobe-skinned rabble who obviously had trouble with German—tripped over themselves trying to cast lines to someone, anyone, on shore who appeared to know what he was doing.

Once the ship was made fast and a gangway extended, Jacob stood back and gestured for the two Confederate agents to precede him on board, saying, "Marse Robert needs his powder more urgently than my customers need their sugar, gentlemen. Please proceed."

Much haggling commenced among the purchasing agents, the pilot from Smithville, the first mate, who spoke *some* English, and the skipper, a truculent, high-strung man who spoke none. Jacob hung back for a few moments, enjoying the Babel-like confusion, before stepping forward and offering his services as a translator. No doubt some report of the Antietam campaign had reached the German consulate in Havana, because the captain demanded a higher price for the powder than the one stipulated in the agents' contract, and did so with considerable arrogance.

"He must have been ordered to hold out for a higher price," said Jacob. "No doubt the ship's owners have learned how urgently Lee needs resupply."

"Well, we are not authorized to offer him more," scowled the younger of the two agents. "The price is fair, and would be so even if Lee had gone on to capture Baltimore."

The skipper, who reeked unmistakably of aquavit, began gesticulating angrily, threatening to steam the *Konstanz* into midstream and dump the gunpowder into the river if more gold were not forthcoming. Jacob ducked away from the shouting match for a moment, scribbled a note on the back of another *carte de visite,* then caught the attention of a bemused Confederate sentry loitering on the docks.

"Take this at once to Flag Officer Branch, with Jacob Landau's compliments, and be quick about it. Here's a gold piece for your trouble."

Fifteen minutes later, by which time the Confederate agents and the German skipper had been reduced to glowering at each other, a Rebel picketboat mounting a 24-pounder hove into view and took station directly astern of the *Konstanz.* While the German skipper flapped his arms in rage, the gun crew methodically performed their drill, charging the cannon with grapeshot and pointing it straight at the German ship's pilothouse. Simultaneously, a forty-man company of Confederate Marines, with bayonets fixed, took position at the foot of the gangway.

"Now," said Jacob in his best Bavarian German, *"either you sign over the gunpowder at the price contracted for, or those fellows will skewer you with their bayonets, while the sailors out there put a cannonball up your arse."*

"Then it is out of my hands," said the captain, suddenly deflated, *"thank God."*

As if the whole puffed-up episode had been nothing more than a quick summer cloudburst, the German meekly signed every document thrust before him. While the Confederate agents rousted up a work gang, the skipper invited Jacob to his cabin for some aquavit, and once they were alone, he collapsed into a red-faced sweating heap.

"I was under orders, you see, from the consulate in Havana—it was all a bluff. They told me the Rebels were so desperate for powder that we could jack up the price."

Jacob felt his earlier contempt start to fade.

"I do not think you are cut out for this blockade-running business, Captain. It is largely a matter of bluff, on both sides. The Yankees pretend their blockade is stronger than it is, and the runners pretend they have the power to become invisible. It is not like normal commerce."

His name was Richter, a past-his-prime alcoholic merchant skipper from Hamburg, and he was not such a bad fellow, Jacob thought, now that he was off the hook.

"Let me give you some advice, Herr Richter. Your ship is entirely unsuited for this business—it's fat and frumpy and probably much too slow on the high seas. You got away with it this time, because the Federals don't bother too much about Havana, but you've created enough of a stir on this voyage to wake them up. My advice to you is to load up with cotton and head straight back to Germany—avoid the shipping lanes between here and Nassau and you might make it. You'll turn a decent profit. Tell the owners what you saw here. It is almost too late for newcomers to get into the blockade-running trade. The rules are changing, and the odds are getting longer."

"That would suit me fine. The tropics do not agree with me." Richter fanned himself with the bills of lading he had just signed. Belowdecks, cut off from the lazy breeze over the river, he sweated profusely, and his complexion had a mottled liverish cast that seemed to derive more from illness than alcohol. "I had thought that by heading this far north, we would encounter milder weather, but by God it's as sweltering here as it was in Havana. And the insects in that town—mosquitoes the size of parakeets!"

"These are the most uncomfortable weeks of our season, Herr Richter. The natives call them dog days"—the idiom sounded funny in German, *hunden Tagen*—"and count the hours until the first cool days of autumn. The rest of the year is quite pleasant, actually. I say, are you ill? Shall I fetch a doctor?"

Between one swallow and the next, the German's florid bulk shuddered as though from a sudden chill, and it took a moment for his eyes to refocus.

"A touch of jaundice, I fear. Two of the crew are also suffering from it. The sooner we are back at sea, the better."

"You *did* pass the medical inspection, down at Smithville, did you not?"

"Customs formalities were waived so the powder could be unloaded quickly."

"In that case, I must ask that you to keep your crew on board tonight, until I can bring a doctor tomorrow to check everyone out."

"That will be hard—they're an unruly lot, and most of them aren't German, so they pretend not to understand my commands, when it pleases them. The mate and I will do our best, but after a day of unloading heavy cargo in this heat, they will have a powerful thirst."

"Order some rum brought aboard from one of the chandlers nearby. I can arrange it, if you like."

"Not a good idea. If they get drunk on board, then they will start going down the ratlines in search of whores. What's the fuss? It is only jaundice."

Jacob pocketed his copy of the shipping documents and looked closely at the glass tumbler he had drunk from, hoping it was as clean as it looked.

"That is what it looks like, to my untrained eye. But there are other illnessess that mimic the same symptoms. Be a good fellow, captain, and try to keep everyone aboard until tomorrow. I shall bring the doctor as early as he will come. Until then, I suggest you sling a hammock on deck, where you can catch the breeze, and get some rest yourself. Auf wiedersehen."

No one could have kept the crew of the *Konstanz* bottled up on board that night, especially not a sick captain who had drunk so much aquavit by midafternoon that he passed out in his bunk, a feverish sweat-slopped mass, leaving the harassed first mate to oversee the unloading of the gunpowder, wagon after wagon full of hundred-pound kegs, winched up two or three at a time from the stiffling holds, by surly crewmen who intermingled with dockside workers while Flag Officer Branch's Marines scurried about self-importantly, trying to prevent anyone from smoking within a block of the ship. By the time the last kegs were on their way to the railroad yard, several of the crew had already slipped away, having quickly ascertained, through universally accepted sign language, the location of the whorehouses in Paddy's Hollow. Others followed.

Jacob arrived at nine the next morning, with his own regular gang of stevedores, accompanied by Dr. Baccus Satchwell. The first mate was nowhere to be seen, and the handful of crewmen who had either stayed with the ship or sneaked back on during the night lay about in the morning sun, half-stupefied with hangovers. Jacob put his own men to work, and soon the cargo nets were coming up again, bulging with sugar and cigar boxes and elegant cloth. Then he led Dr. Satchwell below, into the steamy funk of Richter's cabin.

Richter was awake, but clearly disoriented. His eyes had a preternatural brightness, his thinning hair hung in lank clumps, and Jacob could feel the heat coming from his skin even at a distance. The room stank of sweat and liquor. Satchwell took the man's pulse, pried up his eye lids, and rolled his head into the sunlight in order to inspect his throat and tongue, a needful intimacy perhaps, but not a savory one, to judge from the physician's expression of disgust.

"Is it jaundice?" asked Jacob.

"It could be, and we may hope that it is. It could also be tertiary malaria." Satchwell closed his bag and motioned for Jacob to come with him. They went back on deck and sought the river breeze near the stern.

"Shouldn't you transfer him to the hospital?" asked Jacob, suddenly alarmed by the doctor's tight-lipped expression.

"Was there no medical inspection down at Smithville?"

"The captain said there was not—apparently, there were orders from Richmond to expedite the powder without delay."

"Damn those fools! Is there anyone in the Davis government with a lick of common sense?"

"It may not be jaundice or malaria, then." Jacob tried to keep his voice steady.

"No, sir. It may be Yellow Jack. And this may be a plague ship. As for the captain, if it is Yellow Jack, he will either live or die and there is nothing I, or the hospital, can do for him. The best thing for all of us—for the whole city of Wilmington—is for this ship to leave port immediately. And for the love of God, Jacob, breathe no word about this to anyone! If the crew hears even a rumor, they will run away and infect half the town—we will never track them down. If the public gets wind of it, there will be panic, maybe even a riot, because the safest thing we could do, and everyone will know this, is to tow that ship into the Cape Fear River and burn it, and everyone aboard along with it! As a doctor and a Christian, of course, I cannot countenance such a drastic measure, but an out-of-control mob might easily come to a different conclusion.

"No, the best thing for everyone is for this ship to take on whatever cargo it means to take, and head back to sea as quickly as possible. I shall confer with Flag Officer Branch, and he can concoct some bogus military necessity, send them packing at cannon point if that's what it takes, tell them there are Yankee raiders lurking about."

"They plan to take on cotton. That will take some time, given how sick the captain is and the fact that the first mate speaks very poor English. He will have to conduct the ship's business, since the cptain is indisposed. This might take a lot of time."

Satchwell placed his hand on Jacob's shoulder.

"But you, my friend, speak German. You can arrange things much more quickly with the factors at the Cotton Exchange—surely, the Germans got enough gold for their gunpowder to pay hard cash for the stuff. You can expedite this greatly. Take whomever you must into your confidence, but make it happen! *Get this damned ship out of here!*"

"If it is Yellow Jack, and the mate has certainly been exposed, then my own risk increases."

"You already drank with that skipper, breathed the same foul air in his cabin. *As did I,* sir. We will either catch it or we will not, and if we catch it we will either survive it or not; it is as much a matter of luck and general good health as anything else. In any case, it can take as long as two weeks after exposure before any symptoms appear. If they do, we shall know beyond a doubt what we are dealing with and can impose public health measures immediately. Right now, as responsible citizens, our duty is to save the town, and if we are struck down, sir, then we can at least take pride in having faced the danger bravely and resolutely, and sacrificing ourselves just as surely as any soldier on the battlefield. You have demonstrated your patriotism with money, Jacob, and Wilmington is grateful, but now it is time for men like us to face the fire of an invisible enemy who can ravage our city as savagely as any human foe. Will you swear an oath with me now, Jacob Landau, before the God of both our faiths?"

Jacob was flooded with mingled emotions. He swept his eyes over the spires and gables of Wilmington, his city, where he had made a clear and vibrant place for himself and his loved ones, and knew that God would give him strength if not mercy.

"I do swear," he whispered, clasping the doctor's hand. Then, his head dizzy with light and his limbs touched with grace, he went off to find the first mate and get things started.

Dr. Satchwell administered a strong dose of morphine to Richter, with the object of keeping the man quiescent until his ship was ready for departure. Jacob located the first mate, brought him down to see the skipper's condition, then explained that it was Richter's desire to take on a full load of cotton as quickly as possible, then sail the *Konstanz* back to Germany. On the spur of the moment, Jacob invented a tale that a Union fleet had been spotted heading for the Cape Fear, with the obvious intent on launching a large-scale raid up the river. It was imperative, he explained to the mate, that the German ship return to the high seas before this happened, or risk capture and confiscation. Flag Officer Branch would confirm this if the mate had any doubts.

No, the mate did not. Plainly, he was fed up with this whole blockade-running episode, and homesick as well, to judge from his maudlin and sentimental allusions to Hamburg.

As soon as he was satisfied that the first mate had bought the cover story without any suspicions, Jacob asked the man to round up the necessary documents and accompany him to the Cotton Exchange. His timing was fortuitous—there was sufficient cotton on hand to fill the *Konstanz*'s hold, although the agent responsible for its disposition was at first dubious, since the owners of another runner, due in port by the end of the week, had already reserved the cotton for themselves. An informal exchange of gold, drawn from a bulging leather pouch slung over the mate's shoulder, convinced the cotton factor to alter his priorities. Twenty-four hours later, the *Konstanz* was loaded and ready to sail. No additional cases of sickness had appeared among the crewmen during this interval, and Captain Richter remained quietly in his bunk, becalmed in a narcotic stupor. Meanwhile, Dr. Satchwell had informed Flag Officer Branch of the true situation, and on the night before the ship was due to sail, with the help of a muster role drawn up by the mate, a detachment of Confederate Marines swept through Paddy's Hollow and rounded up the last stragglers from the crew. Jacob dutifully waved good-bye to the mate as the *Konstanz* cast off on the afternoon of September 25. As soon as the ship reached the main channel and turned south, Jacob felt a great wave of relief. God willing, an end to the whole unsavory business. Then he rode over to the offices of the *Wilmington Journal* and placed an advertisement in the next day's edition, listing the new merchandise available at his store. As expected, the Spanish lace proved very attractive to his female customers, the Cuban cigars sold out quickly to their well-heeled husbands and brothers, and the refined sugar flew out of storage as though on wings, for it was a delicacy that appealed to everyone, regardless of age or sex.

Even for the dog days, the next couple of weeks were particularly oppressive. Wilmington steamed under a blanket of tropical humidity, day and night. Its citizens went about their business glowing with a perpetual glaze of perspiration, beset by languor, enervated, praying for a breeze, or some merciful drop in the temperature. Almost every afternoon, violent thunderstorms boiled up from the south and west, pounding the city with monsoonlike deluges. Poorly drained to begin with, Wilmington's streets became a quagmire; every low-lying plot of land turned into a stagnant pond, buzzing with hordes of mosquitoes. Everyone who came into Jacob's store was decorated with bite marks and vexed by their itching. Jacob empathized—because of the oppressive humidity, he kept his bedroom windows open at night, trying to take advantage of even the slightest breeze off the river. One night, thrashing about in the throes of a dream, he dislodged the insect netting from the bedposts and for the rest of the night, his dream was disturbed by the tormenting drone of mosquitoes performing reconnaissance around his ears. If he had been wakened by this aggravation, of course he would have replaced the netting, but on that night, he had been overcome with melancholy. He had consumed more brandy than usual while ritualistically contemplating the photographic image of his dead wife and fondling the precious icons of her personal effects. Although he had readily acceded to Largo's request to visit Pine Haven, he had never before spent so many consecutive days without her comforting presence in the house, and he was increasingly lonely as the days went by.

As a consequence of these convergent factors, he rose the next morning to find himself liberally skeeter-bit and scratching like an unwashed hound. Before going to open the store, he dabbed the bite marks with turpentine—as some of his customers had done already—and the astringency of that substance helped at least to mask the torment of his worst itches.

Four days later, the bite marks were fading and the itching had subsided from a torment to a nuisance. He ate supper with good appetite, but when he stood up from the table, he was instantly attacked by such a wave of dizziness that he staggered and fell against a wall, gasping as hard and shallow as a sprinter, until the sensation passed. Responding to his call, Wellington hurried into the dining room and fetched a large brandy, which seemed to restore Jacob's balance and clarity. He slept fitfully, and was assaulted many times by surrealistic dreams in which large swarms of ravenous mosquitoes seemed to be churning inside his skull, causing him to paw and bat at his ears.

The next morning, he was feverish. When Wellington finally came in to check on him, Jacob was semiconscious, glassy-eyed, and soaked with sweat. He kept repeating his daughter's name over and over, as though trying to summon her. Thinking he was acting on his master's wish, the butler sent a note to the store, and the senior clerk responded within the hour. He thought it was malaria and he, too, assumed that Jacob Landau was calling out for his beloved daughter. Filled with a commendable sense of mission, the clerk obtained directions to Pine Haven, hired a small steam launch, and set off to find Largo.

What neither he nor the servant understood was that Jacob's incantatory recital of Largo's name was meant as a warning, not a summons.

La Belle Rebelle

PROVEN MEASURES—Dr. Baccus Satchwell offers the following medical advice, culled from a variety of texts and articles in his library:

The first precaution against yellow fever is to move the bowels every day. Nothing is more important. If you find yourself at all costive, take some gentle aperient. But also be careful not to weaken yourself by violent purgatives, nor by excessive hard work. Try to keep your system regular, and in its normal state. You may, notwithstanding this, succumb to the fever, but the probability is that the attack will be a light one.

Second, as soon as the chill and the heightened pulse, together with the commencement of severe headaches, show the access of the fever, take an emetic. A tumbler or two of tepid water, with salt in it, will do very well. After this has acted well, take a warm foot bath to relieve the headache, and three or four hours after the emetic, take a dose of castor oil or a similar purgative. Let the patient rest in bed and be kept as quiet as possible. Dr. Finley, of Havana, says that the best treatment for yellow fever is to be seven days on your back, without so much as crooking your finger. Perfect stillness of body is of great importance.

Patients sometimes suffer very greatly from thirst. If this be excessive, it is a bad sign—though a few exceptional cases are said to occur. I have seen none where water relieved the thirst, and many more where it has hastened the death of the patient. Rather give him, from time to time, but as seldom as possible, a table spoonfull of catnip tea or hoarhound tea. I have known a few cases where the patient would hold the mouth full of water for several minutes, until it became warm, then without swallowing a drop, eject it and fill the mouth again, and again. Doing this four or five times assuages the thirst wonderfully for an hour, after which the operation may be repeated. It requires nerve on the part of the patient to control himself and refrain from swallowing the water. In every instance under my observation in which a patient so controlled himself, this means not only relieved the thirst, but also seemed to allay the fever, and in due time he recovered.

—The Wilmington Journal, September 27 1862

Three years ago, you would not have recognized Nassau! The Bahamas are coral islands, y'know, with very thin topsoil. We could not grow sugar, only flowers. Lots and lots of flowers, but you cannot build an export trade on orchids. Or on sponge fishing—a marginally profitable enterprise at best. In short: an obscure, dead-end colonial outpost. I thought, when I was appointed governor in eighteen sixty, that I was being punished for my sins. All I could look forward to was a life of useless boredom followed by retirement and a modest pension.

"Now look at us, ladies and gentlemen! Our population has trebled, our docks are piled with goods, our warehouses are bulging, and our banks are stuffed with gold."

"Not to mention our pockets!" cried a florid, tipsy gentleman who ran the Nassau branch of Bourne and Adderly, a Liverpool company whose managers had been prescient enough to invest early and heavily in the blockade-running business.

Governor Charles John Blayley hoisted his glass in acknowledgment of this bon mot. Having been miraculously elevated from colonial obscurity to international renown, Blayley manifested an almost childlike delight in playing his new role. Before the war, he had been a dour, colorless bureaucrat; now he was a man transformed: expansive, effusive, tirelessly hospitable. Hardly a night went by without a formal dinner in the Government House, with a rotating guest list that included runner captains, bankers, mercantile operators of all sorts, officers from the West India Regiment, journalists seeking colorful stories, the Anglican Bishop of the Bahamas—a cleric of large appetites, much given to bawdy jokes—and a sprinkling of gamblers, speculators, and freebooters in search of adventure and a quick profit. The only prominent Nassau resident who spurned the governor's fetes was the North American consul, who was perhaps the least popular man in town, for it was his duty to interrupt, thwart, and spy upon the very activities that had transformed Nassau into the most prosperous port in the South Atlantic. While no one had actually harmed the consul, he had been insulted on the streets, spat upon by drunks, and occasionally pelted with garbage. Consequently, he conducted his business, as best he was able, from within the walls of the consulate, almost in a state of siege.

Tonight's party was in honor of the famous lady spy, Miss Belle O'Neal, *La Belle Rebelle,* as she had been named by the cream of London society, during her recent sojourn there. Every male guest seemed smitten with her, much to the ill-concealed discomfort of the wives who were present. And many of these men cast envious glances at Matthew Sloane, who had been seated on the guest of honor's left. Governor Blayley had placed himself on her right, which was understood by all to be the prerogative of rank, but even those who knew Matthew Sloane as a bold and successful runner were puzzled as to why he rated the left hand of Miss O'Neal.

The reason, had they known it, would have set their tongues to wagging. Matthew Sloane was seated at Belle O'Neal's left hand because she had requested it. And the governor, of course, had acceded to that request, as he would have tried to do if Miss O'Neal had requested the Prince of Wales.

Only once in all his voyages to Nassau had Matthew succumbed to the town's rich and varied erotic enticements, unlike Hobart-Hampden, who was a regular and free-spending customer at the town's most elegant brothels. It might have soothed Matthew's conscience to pretend that Hobart-Hampden had "put him up to it," but H-H had merely recounted, as he often did when he came into Matthew's room for a final drink, anything exotic or unusually inventive that had transpired. On that occasion, he had waxed rhapsodic about something called a Mexican basket-fuck. So outlandishly elaborate was this experience that it seemed more fitted for a circus than a bordello, but Matthew had to agree with the Englishman's verdict that it was "absolutely unique," a once-in-a-lifetime sexual adventure. Viewed in that light, Matthew reasoned, an experimental test could hardly be considered a commonplace infidelity. Fortified by a few more drinks and thoughtfully equipped with one of the expensive lambskin condoms Hobart-Hampden always carried in his valise, Matthew went forth to explore a new erotic landscape and found the experience so amazing that he went back again the next night—merely to verify the empirical evidence of the first time. On the return voyage to Wilmington, he spent an inordinate amount of time wondering if there was any possible way to persuade Mary Harper to . . . well, at that point his imagination spiraled in kaleidoscopic confusion. He finally asked Hobart-Hampden how *he* would handle the matter. The Englishman, working hard to suppress a smirk, managed a dignified, man-to-man response.

"Matthew, a sexually active woman is more open to novelty than most men think. The problem, I fear, lies in persuading your wife that this is something you read about in a book, not something you paid for in a Nassau brothel. I don't think she will buy it. On the other hand, there are some wives who would find the idea more wickedly appealing just because of that. I would not presume to judge what Mary Harper's reaction might be."

"In other words, I'm on my own."

"In these matters, dear fellow, we always are."

Matthew was definitely on his own tonight, at the governor's soiree. And he was having a royally fine time, as would any red-blooded male who had been shown favor by a beautiful international celebrity. He felt and savored the envy of the other men at the table, perfectly content to let them speculate on just how intimate his relationship with Belle O'Neal might be. In truth, it was not *that* intimate, although he nurtured intensely guilty hopes that it might become so. He had been infatuated from the moment he first shook her hand and looked into her wide blue eyes, which shaded delicately toward violet and seemed to sparkle with enticing gleams. Her moth-pale skin, dusted lightly with freckles, was radiant, and her voice had a trace of huskiness that he found utterly beguiling, especially in concert with her full and generous mouth. She was full-figured and preferred dresses that emphasized the ripeness of her curves.

Hobart-Hampden saw at once the effect she had on Matthew, and found the situation rather jolly, although he did not tease his friend to the point of cruelty. He made it clear that he was quite immune to her charms, although he certainly understood why so many other men were not. "She's a bit puffed up for my tastes," he said, "but she has been the toast of London society, and that would turn any woman's head."

Indeed, simpering modesty was not a part of Belle O'Neal's character. She relished her fame and had even published a short melodramatic account of her adventures, which Hobart-Hampden, who knew rather a lot about the realities of the espionage trade, dismissed as "fifty percent fabrication and fifty percent exaggeration." But he never went so far as to label her a charlatan, for her contributions to the Southern cause were a matter of record and she had needed reckless courage to accomplish them.

It was that aura of gallantry, as much or more than her physical beauty, that turned Matthew Sloane into a love-stunned schoolboy in her presence: Armies had marched because of the words men had whispered in her bed. A native of Virginia, Belle O'Neal had foreseen a civil war even sooner than most secessionist politicians. Confident in her ability to seduce anyone she targeted, she had moved to Washington three years before Fort Sumter, and had industriously created a network of pro-Confederate informants and couriers. She attracted many suitors, but refused to become attached to anyone in particular, playing such an elaborate game with so many men that she managed to cultivate contacts in Congress, in the War Department, in the newspapers, and eventually in the White House, where she reportedly had warmed the heart, and perhaps the bed, of bachelor president Buchanan. She inflicted flesh wounds on dozens of hearts, but she took care never to reject anyone with such cruelty as to make of him an enemy. Those men who enjoyed her favors, and then found themselves unaccountably supplanted by someone else, tended to be more philosophical than angry—an interlude with Belle, whether it was a single night or a period of weeks, was a memory to be treasured; it signified membership in one of Washington's most exclusive men's clubs.

By the time war broke out, she had been a vivid fixture in Washington society for such a long time that scarcely anyone thought of her as being "Southern." She professed ignorance of political and military affairs, but she was always keen to listen when gentlemen tried to impress her with their own expertise. The information she gathered was supplemented by that passed on to her by her ring of operatives, and she acquired the knack of discerning significant patterns in seemingly random fragments of information; even Hobart-Hampden professed admiration for that aspect of her work.

Her moment of glory came in July 1861, when her now-legendary dispatch to General Beauregard had informed him so accurately of McDowell's intentions that Beauregard was able to counter them and win the stunning victory at Bull Run. A torrid affair with one of McClellan's corps commanders, in the early months of 1862, had produced sufficient intelligence to enable Joe Johnston to stage his strategic withdrawal from the Potomac without having to worry about Union interference. That particular coup had also aroused the suspicion of Allan Pinkerton, the zealous detective appointed to head the new Secret Service. Tipped off by one of her informants, she had slipped out of Washington in early March, only hours before a planned raid on her residence, and had taken the first available ship from Baltimore to England. Ironically enough, it was Pinkerton's obsession with her that brought her accomplishments into the spotlight—the Secret Service chief did succeed in sweeping up dozens of lesser Confederate agents and he was not shy when the newspaper reporters flocked to his office. He fulminated about the Rebels' "Master Spy," calling her a notorious harlot and vowing to put a noose around her neck if he had to pursue her to the "ends of the Earth." By the time Belle O'Neal arrived in London, she was already, thanks to the transatlantic telegraph cable, an international celebrity.

So, naturally, all of Governor Blayley's guests were eager to ask questions, and Belle O'Neal answered them with patience and grace and enthusiasm, even if she had answered the same questions a hundred times before.

"It was exciting," she replied, signaling for someone to refill her wineglass and apparently charmed when a half-dozen men responded, "but the excitement was often private, quiet. That may sound like a contradiction . . . "

"But there you were," chirped the governor's wife, who was obviously both fascinated by their guest's achievements and deliciously scandalized by the means of their accomplishment, "in the very heart of the enemy's capital! How could you not be in a constant state of agitation?"

"As I was saying, it may sound contradictory, but much of the excitement is inward. I might be walking down Pennsylvania Avenue, perhaps in the company of a Union officer or a diplomat or a senator's aide, just strolling along and making gay conversation. And then someone would pass us—a washerwoman with a basket of clothes, or a young dandy twirling a cane—and with the merest flicker of an eye, I saw that a green cloth was on top of the laundry or noted a flower in the young fop's lapel and I knew instantly that news had been received or that news was wanted, and the location I should proceed to when I was alone. These commonplace gestures were like a whole subterranean telegraph network, and I always experienced a subtle thrill when that network went into operation, for I was *in on the secrets.* A whole dialogue had taken place, and my companion never suspected, nor did the policeman on the next corner, nor any of the uniformed officers passing by. Some weeks, I knew almost as much about the movements of the Yankee forces as Abe Lincoln himself."

From the far end of the dining table, an officer of the West India Regiment waved his glass and asked: "But surely, Miss O'Neal, you are too well known, now, to return to Washington. If this detective, Mister Pinkerton, is so obsessed with capturing you, you may not be safe even within the Confederacy—surely he has his own network of agents, and they must all be on the lookout for you."

Belle O'Neal acknowledged the question's aptness with a smile that brought a blush to the young soldier's cheeks.

"Indeed, sir, that is surely the case. This voyage to Wilmington is perhaps my last important mission. But consider the matter in this light: every Yankee agent who is busy stalking Belle O'Neal is one *less* Yankee agent assigned to uncovering the other active Rebel spies, those brave men and women who work in the shadows, as far from the limelight as possible. It was not vanity alone that drove me to become a celebrity. By exploiting my fame as shamelessly as I have done, I have become, as it were, a magnet that draws the attention of Lincoln's agents. The detective who captures Belle O'Neal will grab the headlines and be lauded as a hero equal in his virtues to the alleged moral depravity of myself. In short, I am now to act primarily as a decoy, a diversion, too famous to be ignored, but too notorious ever again to be of much value as a real spy. While Pinkerton wastes time and manpower trying to track me down, the real Confederate spies can do their work more freely."

As she defined her new role in such cold, calculated terms, Belle's voice lost all flirtatiousness. For a moment, as the guests contemplated the risks and possible self-sacrifice this young beauty had taken upon her glamorous shoulders, a somber cloud passed through the room. Matthew felt a fresh pulse of admiration for her. Even Hobart-Hampden now looked at her with a newfound expression of gravity and respect.

The governor of Nassau broke the silence by proposing a toast to the gallant Miss O'Neal, a suggestion that elicited a rousing response.

Dinner was followed by dancing, to music supplied by the regimental band. Matthew Sloane was delighted when Belle took his hand and favored him with the first dance, a waltz, so there was, to Matthew's delight, a semblance of an embrace. In her arms he felt taller, more gallant, more dashing, than he had ever felt before. Every place their bodies made contact seemed radiant. His recent sexual peccadillo had been more in the nature of an experiment, an irresistible bit of scientific inquiry, than any betrayal of the heart, although he doubted that Mary Harper would view the matter quite so objectively. He had expected to feel guilt, had anticipated it in fact, as a surcharge attached to the transaction, but he had not. The thing had been done on impulse, out of near-adolescent curiosity. His attraction to Belle O'Neal, by contrast, opened Calvinistic funds of guilt, for his infatuation was volcanic, tidal, and all the more acute because there was no possibility at all of any long-term relationship with her. They would sail together for Wilmington, and three days later she would vanish from his life, as suddenly as she had entered it. If by some miracle she chose to give herself to him during that short span of time, he would regard it as Destiny and revel in every moment. Was it always the case, he wondered, that this kind of passion came too early, or too late, or in the wrong place? Hobart-Hampden would keep his mouth shut, as a gentleman was supposed to do in such a situation; indeed, he seemed to regard Matthew's emotional state with bemused detachment, as though it were a temporary derangement brought on by fever. Matthew understood the burden of guilt he would have to bear, for the rest of his life, and, however much he agonized in private, when he was in Belle O'Neal's presence he simply did not care. How intoxicating it was to dance with her, how sweet and natural it was when the music drew them closer. Was her smile meant for him, or for the room at large? Did it matter? Surely the pressure of her hand, and perhaps unavoidable brushing of her breasts, was for him and none other.

Just as the waltz was ending, when he knew he would have to relinquish her to the other gentlemen standing in line, she bent close to his ear and whispered: "Captain Sloane, you will get me safely into Wilmington, won't you?"

"I will, Miss O'Neal, though every ship in the Yankee navy tries to stop us!"

"I knew I could count on you. You will have my undying gratitude . . . and, of course, the thanks of the Confederacy."

"I do not care a rap for the gratitude of the Confederacy, madam. Your smile is my reward."

"How very gallant of you to say so."

Then the music stopped, they bowed to each other, and the governor, pulling rank on the other men waiting for their turn to dance with the famous spy, sidled forward and claimed Belle O'Neal as his partner. Matthew, still dazed from the warmth and scent of her, wandered to the nearest punch bowl and filled a cup with something whose most identifiable ingredient was a healthy portion of Royal Navy rum. Hobart-Hampden joined him, smiling wryly.

"By God, Matthew, you are smitten."

"Don't mock me, Augustus. I've been taken in ambush and cannot help myself."

"She is quite a piece of work, I'll grant you. But now it's time to weigh anchor and get out of here. Too many Yankee eyes have been watching us. If we delay any longer, I fear they may make some attempt to seize your beloved."

"Not here, not on British soil! We are under Her Majesty's protection."

"Yes, until we pass over the horizon. Have you succeeded in locating smokeless coal?"

"Not in the harbor, no. All they have here now is some second-rate Welsh stuff, crumbly and poor-burning. However, I have made arrangements to rendezvous with a collier at a point just south of Sandy Cay Island. A French ship named *La Pallice,* carrying fine-grade anthracite. Virtually smokeless. Her captain was briefly in port this afternoon, seeking to auction the stuff to the highest bidder. I offered him more than he was likely to get from anyone else. We sail at midday and rendezvous with the Frenchie between three and four in the afternoon."

"Then why didn't we transfer the coal today? It will be much more laborious doing it at sea."

"Because the *Banshee* is too well known and the Frenchman does not want to be seen doing business with us. There could be diplomatic repercussions. He left his ship at anchor on the other side of the island and took a steam launch into the harbor."

"This whole arrangement strikes me as unnecessarily complicated, Matthew. I recommend we load up with the Welsh coal and take our chances."

"If we are to get Miss O'Neal, and the Armstrong gun, safely back to Wilmington, we need smokeless coal. That French ship appears to be the only source of it for the moment. We'll sail with just enough Welsh coal to make our rendezvous and dash back into Nassau if the French ship does not show up for any reason. Then, if we must, we can load up with what's available and take our chances, as you say. As captain, it is my decision to make."

"As co-owner of the ship, I respectfully disagree. Nevertheless, we cannot tarry here any longer without losing the optimum moons and tides. Miss O'Neal has taken receipt of her dispatches, so there is nothing to detain us. We have already stirred up far too much excitement."

"I agree. But it has been fun, Augustus, hasn't it? Being the center of attention, I mean."

"Matthew, my dear love-besotted fellow, *we* are not the center of attention. We merely bask in the reflected glow of our notorious passenger."

"When I think of the sacrifices she has made . . . "

"Sacrifices? May I remind you that she has fucked at least half the Lincoln administration during the course of her career? She could not have done such a convincing job if she had not rather enjoyed it. Don't make her out to be an angel."

"And don't you make her out to be a whore!" snapped Matthew.

Hobart-Hampden scowled briefly, as though debating whether or not to slap some sense into his younger colleague's head. Then he sighed, put down his glass, clapped Matthew on the shoulder, and said: "I am going to turn in. I'll see you aboard the ship in the morning."

Gray skies and a brisk southerly wind greeted the *Banshee* as she steamed out of harbor the next morning. As Matthew had predicted, the Welsh coal generated a long greasy trail of smoke as soon as the vessel's speed rose above eight knots. Matthew doubled the lookouts—some of the Yankee cruisers who regularly sniffed about in these latitudes were skippered by men who were not too punctilious about violating British territorial waters, and the *Banshee*'s long plume advertised her course quite plainly. Miss O'Neal, who had stayed at the party until quite late, did not appear on deck until Nassau was long vanished over the horizon. Except for the needful commands, Matthew maintained a truculent silence during the first two hours, retiring to the pilothouse frequently to check and recheck the charts. At Hobart-Hampden's urging, he ordered soundings to be taken every quarter hour, for they were steering somewhat northwest of the main shipping channel and the recorded depths might well be unreliable. Finally, after Matthew had heaved one too many Byronic sighs, Hobart-Hampden grew impatient and broached the silence.

"You sound like a man rejected. Did anything untoward happen at the party after I left?"

"No. I kept hoping for another dance, but the line was too long. I consoled myself by dancing with the governor's wife, and the governor's niece, and discussing the finer points of cockfighting with a couple of very inebriated British officers. When the affair finally broke up, I escorted Miss O'Neal back to her cabin."

"To her cabin . . . but not *into* her cabin, I take it from your forlorn countenance and soulful sighs."

"Yes, damn it. Although she did give me a kiss when we parted."

"Mouth or cheek?"

"Cheek. A very sisterly kiss."

"But a kiss nonetheless, which is more than all her other suitors at the party received. Perhaps she was tired, or drunk, or both. Good Lord, Matthew, you can't expect the woman to throw herself upon you just because you are available and follow her around with your tongue hanging out. Buck up, lad, the voyage has only just begun."

"Yes, and if we don't get some decent coal, it may be a short one. Every Yankee cruiser in the Bahamas can probably see us already."

But they steamed undisturbed, and the lookouts spotted nothing until they reached the vicinity of Sandy Cay, when the man in the forward crow's nest shouted: "Sail ho! Ten points off the starboard bow!"

"Is it a Yankee cruiser?" shouted Matthew through cupped hands.

"No, Captain. She's a sloop . . . one stack . . . full sails . . . French colors."

"There's our collier, Augustus. Right on time." Turning to the voice tube, he ordered speed reduced to five knots and told the helmsman to come about and make for the other ship.

At this moment, Belle O'Neal appeared, hoisting herself up the ladder to the bridge, looking rested and vivacious, twirling a small lavender parasol in her hands, despite the overcast sky and lack of rain.

"You had best go back to your cabin, madam, when the coaling begins. It's a filthy process and the crew's language could become a bit rough."

"I have spent enough time around soldiers to be quite immune to colorful language, Captain Sloane. I don't want to miss anything exciting."

"Taking on coal is hardly that, Miss O'Neal. I merely suggest that your presence on the bridge might be a distraction to the collier's crew. They *are* French, after all."

She laughed delightedly at this remark. "On the other hand, perhaps my presence will inspire them to a prodigious expenditure of energy." She then walked aft and stationed herself on the platform atop the wheel box, an even better vantage point than the bridge.

"'Prodigious spending' is something she probably knows all about," muttered Hobart-Hampden. Matthew refused to be baited and kept his gaze on the approaching collier. The *Pallice* was not an impressive ship—her oscillating engine was obsolete and she seemed to derive more propulsion from her fully rigged sails than from its boilers. Matthew ordered a further reduction in speed, maintaining headway to facilitate minimal steerage. He waved at the French officers, who would soon be within hailing distance.

All this time, Hobart-Hampden never lowered his binoculars, but kept sweeping his gaze from bow to stern and back. He moved closer to Matthew and nudged his arm gently.

"Something is amiss here. No, no, don't act startled. Be as casual as you can. How much coal is that ship supposedly carrying?"

"I have no idea. I contracted with her captain for two hundred tons, so I suppose he must have at least twice that much on board."

"Don't you think she's riding a bit high in the water for a ship full of coal? She is light upon the waves, when she ought to be wallowing."

"She has a wide beam, Augustus. The weight could be distributed thinly across her bottom."

"Not if he plans to transfer coal at sea. It would already be piled up near a hoist, under a hatch. But that's not the only thing. If you look closely—*not so conspicuously, man!*—all the uniforms are spanking clean. So is the hull and the deckhouses. In my experience, colliers are always dingy and streaked with coal dust. I see not a trace of it.

In short, I do not think that ship is what she purports to be."

"Well, she can't be a Yankee cruiser in disguise—where are her guns?"

"I think I'll have a word with the captain, in French."

Hobart-Hampden took up the bridge megaphone and spoke a few sentences of greeting. The *Pallice*'s captain replied in kind.

"His French is no better than mine, and he has an American accent. I smell a trap here, Matthew, although I'm not sure what kind."

"I am," said Belle O'Neal, who had quietly climbed back down to the bridge and was keeping herself out of sight by crouching behind the paddle box. "It is me they are after. They learned I was on this ship and they've come to take me. The telegraph certainly makes spying more difficult."

"All right," said Matthew, lowering his glasses. "Suppose it is a trap. How can we defend ourselves . . . and our passenger?"

Their options were few. A blockade-runner could not, by international law, carry armament or offer resistance to a boarding party—to do so would automatically categorize the ship's crew as "pirates" rather than purveyors of contraband goods, which in turn meant that if captured, they could face the hangman's noose instead of imprisonment. On the other hand, the *Pallice* was not a ship of the U.S. Navy, so its crewmen, if they opened fire or committed violence to anyone aboard the *Banshee,* would also be violating international law. The situation at hand would no doubt provide the subject for a spirited debate among maritime lawyers, but as far as Hobart-Hampden could reason it out, both vessels were operating in a gray, ambiguous area. Especially since both were sailing in British waters and flying bogus flags. He and Matthew had loaded revolvers within easy reach, as did the chief engineer. The other eight members of the crew could avail themselves of belaying pins and various tools, but it was a safe assumption that the other crew, if they were indeed on a secret mission, were fully armed.

While the *Banshee's* officers discussed these things in anxious whispers, the captain of the *Pallice* readied a boat and announced that he was coming aboard, along with sufficient men to rig up the lines required to transfer coal from one vessel to the other. The gap between the starboard hull of the *Banshee* and the port railing of the *Pallice* was now down to thirty feet, about as close as was prudent, given the choppy condition of the sea.

Belle O'Neal kept peeking around the curve of the paddle box, and finally whispered, "Matthew, may I have a look through your glasses, please?"

She called me by my name—not "Captain Sloane"! Despite the incongruity of the situation, his heart thumped with pleasure. Belle focused the glasses on the "French" captain, while his attention was focused on lowering his boat. Then she made a hissing sound, as full of fear as fury. "I know that man!" she said.

Then, in the span of a quarter minute, the situation clarified rather dramatically. A nondescript deckhouse between the bow and the forward mast suddenly collapsed, like a tent whose guy ropes had been cut, revealing it to be a sham made out of painted canvas and also unmasking a 12-pounder howitzer on a field carriage, pointed straight at the *Banshee's* bridge, fully crewed by men wearing what appeared to be police uniforms. A leering gunner waved at the Rebel ship, clearly showing that his fist was on the lanyard and he was eager to shoot. At the same time, ten more men in uniform ran smartly to the port railing and took aim with rifles. Another half-dozen took seats in the lowering boat, armed with pistols and cutlasses. The "French" captain now identified himself and flourished his own pistol.

"I am Lafayette Baker, executive officer of the United States Secret Service, and I am here to arrest the notorious Rebel whore, Belle

O'Neal, for acts of treason! We shall come aboard to arrest her, gentlemen, and at the first sign of resistance, my men will open fire. That howitzer is double-charged with grapeshot, so I advise you to comply."

"We are in British waters, sir!" shouted Hobart-Hampden. "This could be construed as an act of war! Do you want to take that risk?"

"I see no risk here, sir. We are both under neutral flags. Once we have the prisoner in irons, we shall both go our separate ways and you may protest to Her Majesty until you are blue in the face. Officially, this incident is not happening, and my government can and will deny any complicity. I am under the orders of Mister Allan Pinkerton, head of the Secret Service, and no other man. President Lincoln is not involved, nor is the United States Navy. I do not intend to capture your ship, and I do not give a damn what cargo you are carrying, but if you do not turn over the spy, I shall rake you with grapeshot."

Baker gave a mocking salute with his revolver, then took his place in the longboat. It would take him only a few minutes to reach the *Banshee.*

Belle O'Neal stepped proudly forth onto the bridge, in full sight, and made an obscene hand gesture toward the riflemen. This elicited much bawdy laughter and some rough, taunting remarks.

"Don't worry, Matthew. I shall not let them take me. I have a lot of gold coin sewn into the lining of my dress—it should carry me down quickly."

Matthew gawked at her in amazement. "Go on, see for yourself," she chided him, inviting him to lift the hem of her voluminous dress. He knelt and hefted the garment, receiving for his trouble a glimpse of her full, voluptuous legs. She was in truth so weighted down with gold that it was a wonder she could move at all. If she jumped into the sea, she would sink like a cannonball.

"I will go down fighting rather than see you taken in irons," he vowed.

"Speak for yourself," muttered Hobart-Hampden.

"They mean to hang her, Augustus! Perhaps you can live with that on your conscience, but I will not!"

"If you have a plan, Matthew, I am eager to hear it."

And upon the instant's desperation, he did contrive a scheme. He explained it to Belle and Hobart-Hampden, who seized upon it with considerable relish. Working quickly and quietly, trying not to alarm the Secret Service men, he ordered the engineer to get up full pressure and stand by. Then he strode over to where the coxswain and several crewmen had gathered, in preparation for rigging up the coal transfer. They were duly apprehensive, but all of them were outraged as well—this was a dirty, a truly "piratical" business, and it did not sit well with them that the *Banshee,* which had given the slip to the navy so cunningly on so many voyages, should now be held at bay by a handful of Yankee *policemen.*

There was a lot to be done in the space of a few minutes, and it all had to be accomplished without alerting the enemy. Fortunately, Baker's boarding party were not experienced sailors and they had to struggle hard to move their longboat through the chop, against the prevailing wind. Belle O'Neal slipped off the bridge, as though intending to get her belongings, located the two officers' pistols, and secreted them inside her capacious handbag. Belowdecks, there was a lot of frantic scurrying, but the noises were too muted to reach the ears of the boarders. Just as Lafayette Baker's boat crunched into the *Banshee*'s hull, Matthew heard the chief engineer speak into the other end of the voice tube: "We are ready, Captain," and Matthew replied, "Wait five minutes, until the bastards have all come aboard, then proceed."

With a reasonable show of reluctance, the crewmen on the starboard side lowered a boarding ladder. Baker had trouble mounting it, so Matthew called out: "You there, give those men a hand! Let's conclude this business as quickly as possible."

Lafayette Baker finally reached the deck and the six men with him formed a semicircle around him, alert for any sign of trouble. Baker himself was clearly relishing the drama of the moment, for he had holstered his revolver in order to climb the ladder and had not bothered to redraw it; instead, he brandished an enormous cutlass and made a half-mocking salute toward the bridge.

"In the name of the United States Secret Service, and with the complements of Mister Allan Pinkerton, we are here to arrest the Rebel spy named Belle O'Neal. The sooner you turn her over to us, Captain, the sooner you can be on your way."

Matthew feigned an affable expression and made an exaggerated shrug. "Frankly, Mister Baker, you are welcomed to her. She's been nothing but a nuisance to us ever since she came aboard in Liverpool." Belle O'Neal rapped him smartly in the ribs with an elbow, but she too was playing her part, wearing a very convincing maiden-in-distress face and scrunching up her eyes as though she were about to start wailing.

"Give me a moment to locate the secret dispatches she was transporting, and then we shall turn her over to you. Miss O'Neal, you had better hand over those papers and make peace with God."

"Dispatches?" said Baker. "Well, well, this is indeed a bonus. I thank you, sir, for your cooperation."

"Captain Sloane, you are a traitor to the South!" She came at him with claws out and pretended to struggle, raking his cheek hard enough to draw blood, while simultaneously whispering: "Just to make it realistic. So you can lead me back out at gunpoint."

"The dispatches, madam! I know they are in your cabin. Do not make me use force."

Distraught and wailing, she allowed Matthew to force her down the bridge ladder. As soon as they were out of sight, she handed him both pistols, which he tucked into his trousers and covered with the hem of his coat. Then, she opened her handbag and showed him the four-shot Sharps pocket pistol nestled within. She also handed over a small packet of papers.

"Are these the real dispatches?"

"No. Just a bundle of letters from Liverpool. The real documents are sewn into my dress, like the gold."

"You are clever as well as brave, Miss O'Neal."

"Not half so brave as you are about to be, dear Matthew."

And then she kissed him, in the most unsisterly manner possible. She also vouchsafed one sample of her erotic arsenal by somehow contriving to wrap her long satiny tongue into a corkscrew shape and then unrolling it lasciviously in the depths of his mouth. If nothing else happened between them, even if he did manage to survive the next ten minutes, he would carry to his grave the memory of that single electrifying kiss.

"Let's do it," she said, withdrawing her lips and squeezing his hands. Matthew hoped those words were charged with double meaning. He scampered down another ladder and stuck his head into the engine room, now sweltering with the heat of pent-up steam pressure, and gave a signal to the chief engineer and his men. They hurried forward.

Matthew prodded Belle back to the bridge, openly displaying his weapon. By now, the scratches she had inflicted were convincingly enflamed and bloody.

"Here are the dispatches, Mister Baker. I'll bring her to you and gladly be rid of the vixen. She tried to tear my eyes out!"

Baker and his men were, apparently, buying the whole charade, for the sight of Matthew's wounds made them smile and their postures were now more relaxed.

Suddenly, a vivid burst of flames shot up from beneath the forward cargo hatch, and the air was tainted by the smell of furiously burning turpentine. Nothing else on board could burn so hot, so fast. Both crewmen and boarding party froze in alarm at the sight. Feigning outrage, Matthew turned on Belle and made as if to pistol-whip her. Then he yelled to Baker: "The bitch has set off an incendiary device! We must get that fire out!"

"Well, bring her down to me and we'll leave you to fight the fire. It does not appear to be very dangerous."

"You misunderstand me, sir! This ship is filled with gunpowder! We'll tie the woman up, but for now you and your men must help us put out that fire. Either lend a hand, or get out of the way!" Then he shouted down the voice tube, loudly enough to Baker to hear: "Chief, man the pumps and get a hose on deck! We have a fire in the forward hold!"

Those of the *Banshee's* crew who had been loitering on deck now sprang into action, forming a bucket-line and dipping pails into the sea. Aboard the Yankee ship, there was great consternation—the situation was stark and obvious. Both riflemen and howitzer crew had heard Matthew's comment about gunpowder and their attention was fully diverted by the prospect of both ships being vaporized in a cataclysmic explosion. Some of Baker's men, acting on the priorities of self-preservation, now joined the bucket line, while their commander, who had been rudely yanked back from visions of the glory that awaited him in Washington when he returned with not only the spy but a cache of secret documents, simply dithered in place, brandishing his cutlass as though it might at least frighten the flames a little.

"Get that hose up here!" yelled Matthew. With a commendable display of frightened energy, the chief engineer and a couple of stokers lumbered into view, dragging a canvas hose behind them.

"Now, Captain Sloane?"

"Now!"

Instead of pointing the hose at the fire, they swung it around so that it bore on the Yankee vessel, and when they opened the valve, what came out was not water but a jet of high-pressure steam. Much of the scalding vapor dissipated as it traveled the distance between the two ships, but enough of it reached the howitzer crew to drive them off, shrieking and pawing at their exposed skin. Then the engineer redirected the jet at the riflemen, who were several feet closer and hence received an even more blistering dose than the gunners. All was now chaos, and Matthew's men made the most of it. Dropping their buckets, they grappled with the boarders, thumping them with belaying pins that had been concealed until that moment and wrestling their weapons from them.

To his credit, Lafayette Baker reacted quickly. He took a swipe at the nearest crewman and laid open the man's thigh with such force that his blade got stuck in the bone and he was forced to boot the screaming man in order to free it. Matthew and Hobart-Hampden were already on the deck, pistols out. Two of Baker's men were down with cracked skulls and two of the *Banshee*'s men, incensed by the wounding of their mate, were struggling to toss a third overboard. Hobart-Hampden paused long enough to shoot a fourth man, and by the time Matthew reached Lafayette Baker and thrust his cocked pistol into the agent's stomach, the fight was effectively over.

Meanwhile, the engineer had rung on full steam and the *Banshee* was turning hard to port, putting her stern toward the other ship and gathering speed quickly. Unmarked by anyone, the hot little turpentine fire, having consumed all the rags and trash within reach, burned itself out.

"My men will fire on you, you scoundrel," gasped Baker. "They have their orders."

True to his prediction, the howitzer roared, but it was double-charged with grapeshot and the *Banshee* was already moving out of effective range. The balls rang and clattered over the superstructure, dimpling the smokestack, cutting some rigging, but doing no real damage.

"You are a fine one to call me a scoundrel, Baker. You were practically salivating at the thought of putting that woman in irons. God knows what foul plans you had for her, once she was in your power. You and your men had better return to your boat, unless you want to spend the rest of the war in a Confederate prison. And tell your master in Washington that *this* is how we defend our women in the South. Take your casualties and go, before I shoot you down as you deserve."

Baker had no choice—the distance between the two ships was increasing rapidly. Of the six men he had brought aboard, one was dead, two were unconscious, and one was floundering about in the water, desperately trying to swim to the longboat while the men who had thrown him overboard jeered roughly. Matthew's injured crewman, his femoral artery severed and blood pulsing in great jets from his wound, was beyond help.

Even as Baker and the surviving members of his party were struggling to get their injured men into the longboat, the howitzer boomed again—this time firing solid shot. The gunners were aiming at the paddle wheel, but by now the *Banshee* was almost stern-on and the round sizzled past the starboard rail and smacked harmlessly into the water. Two more shots were better aimed: one tore a hole in the aft sails and the other crashed into the galley, doing harm only to an assortment of crockery and a coffee pot. Then the firing stopped for a while, as the Yankee ship slowed down to pick up Baker and his men, and by the time it resumed the *Banshee* was out of range.

"They should have brought a bigger gun," mused Hobart-Hampden, as he watched the small 12-pounder balls plop futilely in the *Banshee*'s wake. Then he turned to Matthew and threw his arms around him in an unprecedented display of affection.

"Well done, Captain Sloane! Oh, well done!"

And Belle O'Neal, still flushed with excitement, hugged him, too. Matthew felt, for the first time in his life, like a true hero. His plan had been desperate, conceived on the spur of a terrified instant, but he had saved her from a ghastly fate.

Their ebullience did not last long. There was no chance that Baker's ship could catch them now, but they still had to return to Nassau and take whatever coal was available. If Baker encountered any Union ships, he would doubtless spread the alarm and give them a full description of the *Banshee* and her officers. If they ran afoul of a blockader now, their freedom might be short-lived.

Near sunset, a few miles from Dry Dolphin Cay and three hours out of Nassau harbor, the *Banshee* ran aground, not hard enough to sustain any damage, but hard enough to immobilize the ship. It was already high tide, so there was nothing else to do but lighten ship. Because the civilian cargo itself was so light, the only option was to jettison some of the ammunition for the Armstrong gun. They did so very carefully, one shell at a time, but by the time the *Banshee* floated free, only thirty-one shells remained.

In Nassau, they took on a full load of coal, arranged for the burial of the dead sailor, and headed back out again as soon as possible, this time following a well-charted course. Once they were headed for Wilmington, Matthew went to his bunk for a few hours' sleep.

He did not get much rest, however, because Belle O'Neal knocked on his door just as he put his head down. And for the next several hours, much to the amusement of Hobart-Hampden, who was a connoisseur of the myriad sounds human beings made in the throes of passion, she rewarded Matthew Sloane for his bravery and cleverness.

Matthew Sloane's fund of sexual experience was neither large nor—with the exception of his recent experiment in Nassau—particularly exotic. He had always assumed that history's great courtesans, the Bathshebas and Cleopatras and Marie Antoinettes, had cast their spells by means of sheer physical beauty. Now, to his amazed enlightenment, he learned that such feminine power—enough to cloud the minds of kings and sway the course of empires—might be more a function of *virtuosity* than anything else; that certain women could play upon their lovers' bodies the way Paganini played his violin.

For Belle O'Neale, when she stood proudly naked before him, her torso decorated with filigrees of reflected light dancing through the portholes from the restless sea, was not a classic beauty per se. Her proportions were Reubenesque, close to overripe, but the very ampleness of her flesh was stunning—empires would rise and fall before those breasts began to wither. He wanted to drown in her, devour her and be devoured in return. For a long time, he simply felt her with his hands, while she turned and bent and shaped herself to accommodate his explorations—patient and generous, giving him all the time he needed to pass from the stage of eager groping to slower, more methodical stroking, cupping, and probing, her smile so full of welcome, and her eyes so bright with an almost predatory intensity, that he felt himself to be the most special man on earth.

Her textures were a banquet of satin and solidified cream, and between the hot alabaster columns of her thighs, the coarse gold thatch at the erotic core of her seemed to smolder, and when she rubbed it against him, his skin trembled and his erection became heroic, achieving a crimson, near-to-bursting fullness that astonished him and certainly seemed to gratify her appraisal. Then she began to kiss him, starting off with sharp, teasing nips, then flowering her mouth into long, slow rhapsodies of tongue and lips, which in turn exploded suddenly into something more animal-like and ravenous, flesh grinding into flesh.

She seemed resolved to impress him as well as reward him, for when they finally entwined on the bunk, she hurled her flood-tide opulence greedily against his lean and charmingly awkward arrangement of limbs. It was her intent to burst him apart with delights he had never dreamed of, saturate him with sensations he could not name, dazzle him with caresses like elegant arpeggios, leave him gasping from sudden inspired improvisations of movement and muscle-flexings, sensational cadenzas of manipulation. She was an artist and fully in her element now. She was air and water, oil and fire, cinnamon and milk; she was candy, she was lava; she was an eel, a leopardess, an Olympian goddess, and a growling slut, and when she achieved her climaxes, she gripped the straining length of him like a vise. She dashed herself over him like a storm wave, leaving tidal pools of gleaming moisture, marking him with nettle-red furrows and whole astrological tables of teeth marks; she was pulp and silk and pearls and the steaming juice of nectarines. Men had volunteered state secrets for less than she gave him now, and the variety and luxuriance of her offerings coaxed from him three climaxes, the last of which was drawn out of him with her mouth and throat, and it was so long a-building that its looming intensity was almost frightening, bearing a hint of extinction, a tremendous dark convulsion that carried with its wrenching eruption of fluid some irretrievable portion of his very soul.

Matthew timed the three-day voyage back to Wilmington so that the *Banshee* would reach a point twenty miles north of New Inlet at approximately one o'clock in the morning, roughly coincident with high tide. This route would put them in danger for a longer time than a straight run for New Inlet and the protection of Fort Fisher's big guns, but they hoped, by making such a wide detour, to avoid the thickest concentration of blockade patrols. As soon as they sighted the surf, they would turn sharply south and steam parallel to the coast at full speed, trusting that their light gray paint-scheme would blend in with the spray and the breakers' roar would mask the sound of their straining engines. This was a classic runner tactic, and the Yankees certainly were aware of it, but most of the runners who tried it still succeeded.

They would, however, greatly miss Fitz-John Bright's skills as a pilot, for he knew the shifting shoals better than most and had displayed on other runs an uncanny sense for extrapolating, from wind and weather and the state of the sea, the changes that might have occurred in the vicinity of known hazards. Their course would take them uncomfortably close to the ever-shifting formation known as North Breaker Shoals. Matthew would pilot the ship himself, since he had closely observed Mister Bright's maneuvers in these waters more often than Hobart-Hampden. He would order soundings every five minutes, unless they were actually being pursued, and he ordered the engineer not to exceed half-speed unless they were being fired upon; the inferior coal they were burning produced, at night, an aggravating cascade of sparks from the stack, especially at higher speeds.

By the end of the second day, Matthew began to suspect that Lafayette Baker had indeed given the alarm—four times they spotted smoke below the horizon, indicating vigorous activity by the ships of the third, long-range blockade line. Why they were not intercepted on the high seas he could only guess, but Hobart-Hampden theorized that the Yankee cruisers probably assumed, from the *Banshee*'s own amount of smoke, that she was one of their own—no blockade-runner in his right mind would have belched such a telltale cloud.

Whether by luck or mistaken identification, the *Banshee* reached Rebel waters safely on the third night of her voyage. Matthew's revels with Miss O'Neal had continued with unabated gusto on two of those nights, but for the final run, he had resisted temptation and made sure he was well-rested. The crew went through the now-routine drill: everyone donned light gray clothing and drew woolen sleeves over their shoes or boots to deaden the sound of footsteps. All fires were extinguished except those for the boilers. Not a light burned except for the heavily shielded binnacle lamp near the compass. Any metal objects that might have to be manipulated during the night were also wrapped in cloth or rope. If the night were calm and the wind from the land, the sound of a dropped tool or of metal striking metal could carry a great distance.

But the night was not calm. Intermittent rainsqualls swept the decks and the waves grew in size as they closed on the North Carolina shore. Some of the swells broke over the *Banshee*'s turtle-backed bow, slapping the faces of the men on watch and the two officers on the open bridge. Belle O'Neal had donned an India-rubber rain cape and stationed herself next to Matthew, looping her arm through his. She had not experienced a blockade-run before and was determined "not to miss any of the excitement."

For his part, Hobart-Hampden seemed unusually energized—he was a Royal Navy man, after all, no matter what other roles he was concurrently playing, and he was in his element, raising his face into the cold spray, breathing deeply of the salt air, fully engaged by the drama and mounting tension.

"I rather hope they make a chase of it, Miss O'Neal—and of

course, that they botch the job as well. I tell you, I have hunted tigers in India, stuck wild boar in Bavaria, ridden in the steeplechase, played polo, climbed mountains, and witnessed more than a few hard-fought battles, but nothing in my experience—*nothing*—quite compares to the exhilaration of running the blockade. Certainly not the life of a rice planter, eh, Matthew?"

"Indeed. I would not have missed these adventures for all the world, and I fear that everything else will seem pale and ordinary by comparison."

"Everything?" teased Belle O'Neal.

Matthew did not answer, but went back to studying the heaving seas with his glasses.

"Any minute now," said Hobart-Hampden, "and we will spot the surf. This is where it gets tricky. We are fortunate in the weather tonight. It gives us an advantage."

Lifelined to the railing, the coxswain began dropping his lead, ducking down as the waves pounded him. When he had a depth sounding, he communicated it to the bridge with hand signals.

There! Solidifying out of the dark: restless breakers and explosions of spray heralding the sullen featureless coast, dangerously near. The coxswain raised his line and made a forceful gesture—they were running out of bottom. Matthew turned the wheel hard to port, and the ship responded. He knew instantly, from the sudden buttery play in the rudder, that they were not going to have an easy time of it. Lightened of the Armstrong shells and most of her coal, the *Banshee* was riding high and broadside to the heavy swells, bobbing like a cork instead of putting her bow solidly into the water and cleaving to her new course. So choppy had the waves become that there was no rhythm to them; they buffeted the hull at random, and for a moment Matthew feared they would literally push the keel into the shallows.

"Turn her back out to sea, man!" whispered Hobart-Hampden. "Put her bow at right angles to the current, or we may founder."

But the *Banshee* did not respond with her usual grace; the ship seemed tired and ornery and mulish, and several times Matthew had to fight hard to keep the wheel spokes from spinning out of his hands. They needed more power, even if that meant blowing sparks for a while. He spoke a command into the voice pipe and felt the paddle wheels bite deeper and the vessel gain a knot or two. No longer broadside to the waves, the runner regained some steerage and felt more stable under their feet. Matthew felt relieved—however falteringly, they had at least covered a mile or two of the distance between the shoals and the sheltering iron embrace of Colonel Lamb's columbiads. Perhaps they could zigzag up to the edge of the surf and then back out again, and still be at least partly hidden by the weather. Just as he devised this scheme, however, an oily gout of flame belched from the smokestack and for thirty agonizing seconds he could see the whole ship and the faces of those around him, as though a great red flare had burst above the bridge.

"Oh, Christ," growled Hobart-Hampden. "We're in for it now."

From a mile to the southeast came the shriek of a steam whistle, answered by another, and another. Signal rockets scratched fiery arcs in the grainy rain-pocked sky and a dazzling white light burst above the nearest Union vessel.

"What the hell was that?" cried Matthew—no need for silence now, for they had been spotted for sure and from all the pyrotechnics blazing away, it was safe to assume that every naval vessel north of New Inlet was probably converging on them at flank speed.

"A calcium flare, I presume," said Hobart-Hampden with professional detachment. "I had heard rumors that they were starting to experiment with those. Awfully bright, isn't it?"

Matthew shot him an exasperated glare and called for full speed, already turning the helm back toward the shore, searching with dazzled retinas for some patch of mist that might hide them again. As though sensing the danger, the *Banshee* trembled with acceleration. More steam whistles blew, more rockets popped, and a few more of those blinding calcium flares ignited, forcing Matthew to avert his eyes from their searing whiteness. Muffled by the surf, he heard the thump of distant gunfire but saw no splashes nearby, which meant that they had a fair chance still of reaching New Inlet.

"I do believe they were waiting for us, Matthew. I count four warships either in pursuit or steaming on a course to intercept us. This is a bit livelier than I had wished for."

"That bastard Baker must have gotten word to the inner squadron. They're swarming like hornets."

Neither man needed to mention one consequence that might arise from the knowledge that the notorious Belle O'Neal was on board this particular runner. Normally, when a blockader did intercept a runner, its gunners fired to disable rather than to kill or sink—there was substantial prize money to be had from capturing a runner, even for the lowliest sailor involved, but nothing to be gained from destroying one except the thanks of the Navy Department. Solid shot might be used to intimidate a fleeing runner's crew, or to damage a mast or a smokestack, but normal procedure was for a blast or two of grapeshot, followed by a boarding action. If the inner blockade squadron did know whom they were chasing, they might also be under orders to sink the *Banshee* if they could not capture her. Considering how brutally Matthew had humiliated Lafayette Baker, the Secret Service agent might well have issued a "dead or alive" decree with regard to Miss O'Neal. A glance at her face, sporadically lit by rockets and flares, told Matthew that she was thinking the same thing. He wanted, very badly, to take her hand or embrace her and say soothing words, but he dared not take his hands off the wheel or his eyes from the sea.

"There are now *five* gunboats converging on us," said Hobart-Hampden, as though some kind of sporting record were about to be set.

"Thank you for the information, H-H," said Matthew through tight lips.

Cannon fire whumped and flamed in a semicircle around the *Banshee*. The way things had become configured, the blockaders did not even need to worry about hitting their own ships—the runner was at the center of a cone of fire, and the shelling grew heavier and more accurate by the minute. The Yankee gunners did not quite have the range yet—most of their balls were peppering the water a hundred yards off to port, and their aim was thwarted by the mist, the spray, the *Banshee*'s color, and the distraction of their own flares. Matthew guessed they were still ten miles north of Fort Fisher. But given the intensity of this pursuit, some of those pursuing captains might not turn back, as they usually did, when Colonel Lamb's shells began to fly; instead, they might choose to brave the fort's fire if by doing so they could finish off the *Banshee*.

Solid shot now ranged over the runner's flame-belching stack: big-caliber guns, judging by the air-sucking, freight-train *whoosh* they made. And now the first shells began to crack overhead, great yellow bursts like fiery sunflowers, and he could hear the *whap* and rattle of fragments raining down on the superstructure and the viper's hiss the hot iron made when it flailed the water. Then a 9- or 10-inch shell landed at the foot of the forward mast and exploded with a deafening bang. They all ducked, and fragments spat around their heads and hummed past their ears like giant mosquitoes. When Matthew looked again, the foremast was shattered and collapsing, dragging spars and rigging with it, as well as the wet inert weight of collapsed sails. When the whole sodden mass fell into the sea off the port bow, its weight and drag carved five knots off the *Banshee*'s speed. Two terrified but loyal crewmen ran out with axes and began hacking the entanglements to free the ship.

"Miss O'Neal—Belle! You must take cover! We may still make it, but we're going to take more hits."

She stared back at him with that same startling bone-deep resolution she had shown in the face of imminent capture and calmly replied, "Matthew, I would rather die free, on this ship, than be taken alive. Given a choice between the gibbet and a cannonball, I'll choose the latter."

"I will not let either thing happen," he said, suddenly resolved that he could actually work such a miracle. He put the ship into another sharp zigzag turn just as a round of solid shot spanked the *Banshee*'s fantail, throwing up a blizzard of splinters and slicing a steaming furrow along the deck.

"Augustus, as captain of this ship, I am giving you an order."

Hobart-Hampden looked at him as though suddenly confronted with a gibbering maniac.

"I intend to take Miss O'Neal ashore in the longboat and make our way to Wilmington on foot. You can take the ship from here to New Inlet—either they will pound her to bits or she'll get through. My being aboard won't make any difference, now."

"Are you deranged, Sloane? You'll capsize in that surf!"

"Nonsense—the current is strong enough to drive us ashore in a matter of minutes. All you need do is slow the *Banshee* down for a moment, just to get the longboat away, then head for New Inlet at full speed."

"This is madness."

"No, Augustus, it is good sense. If they cripple the ship too badly for you to make it, just surrender. *You're a British subject,* for God's sake! All they can do is throw you out of the country, and then you can come right back with a new runner. And the Confederacy will not stand or fall on the strength of corset stays and toothbrushes!"

Before Hobart-Hampden could say anything more, Matthew grabbed Belle O'Neal by the waist and hustled her down to the main deck. He ordered four white-faced crewmen to lower the longboat and was gratified when the *Banshee* slowed down just enough to make that possible.

Belle climbed in and huddled in a crouch, vainly trying to shield herself from the spray. Once they had cast off, Matthew pushed the longboat clear with an oar and clutched the tiller fiercely. Waterspouts rose around them for a moment, until the runner moved off, and then they were alone, borne landward on the foaming breast of the sea. As soon as Matthew realized that they would indeed make it safely to shore, he felt a sense of peace descend upon their lonely boat, as though they rested in the cupped and merciful hands of God. Where they drifted, it suddenly grew calm. The blockaders' broadsides were no louder than muted summer thunder, their rockets nothing more than fireworks. Above them, a window of clear sky opened like a benediction and he beheld the stars breathtakingly close and it seemed to him that their mystic configurations spelled out a great promise.

Abruptly, the shoreline to the south spurted fire and much louder thunder than the Union guns. Matthew threw back his head and laughed wildly. His navigation had been off by a good ten miles; they were much closer to Fort Fisher than he had believed.

"The *Banshee* will make it after all! Bravo for Colonel Lamb and his men!"

"Sit down, Matthew! We are not out of trouble yet!"

As if in mocking reply, they were suddenly illuminated by a wobbling white light, another one of those calcium devices, he presumed. Against the clanging, clouded breakers, their boat stood out in stark relief. Shielding his eyes, Matthew turned back from the milky demarcation of the beach and saw, drifting just beyond the breakers, the unmistakable shape of Lafayette Baker's sloop, whose crew was already in the process of lowering their own longboat. The ship's howitzer boomed and the surf writhed under the lash of grapeshot. Matthew felt a numbing blow on his right shoulder, followed immediately by the shocking heat of blood, and the slippery tiller spun from his grasp. The longboat swung sideways and broached into oncoming waves, the keel instantly full of angry swirl and foam.

"We're close enough to swim for it!" he cried, reaching for her with his one good arm. But she only looked at him from a great resigned depth of sadness, shook her head slowly, with an expression he would always remember as one of genuine love, then crawled to the gunwale, grasping the oarlock for stability, and dropped into the sea. He lunged for her, ignoring the tearing pain in his back, and succeeded in clamping his fists upon the hem of her dress. But she had been soaked to begin with and her voluminous skirts were sopping and heavy. They tore apart in his hands and when he opened his fists he saw only a few sodden strands of bombazine cloth and some gold coins. Then another wave crashed over the longboat and he tumbled into blackness and felt cold sand scraping at his flesh. He willed himself to open his mouth and drink oblivion, to join her, to make amends for his sins, to escape the anguish screaming in his heart, but the boat, now spinning helplessly and heavy with water, cracked him smartly on the head.

He regained consciousness with a stout Yankee policeman pumping seawater from his lungs and the blazing pain of salt in his wound. When he finished vomiting and coughing and could sit up, he found himself staring into the muzzle of Lafayette Baker's Colt.

"Is she gone, then?" Baker yelled.

In reply, Matthew unclenched his fist and displayed the black rag and the four gold dollars that were Belle O'Neal's legacy. Baker grabbed the coins and tossed two of them to the fat policeman, pocketing the other two.

"She is gone. She preferred death to your company, Baker. Would that I had been able to join her."

"Oh, in good time you may get your wish, sir, depending on how the trial goes."

Matthew was rowed back to Baker's ship, where the grapeshot ball was roughly dug from his shoulder. Then he was placed in shackles for the dismal voyage back to the North.

In the morning, a patrol from Fort Fisher located Belle O'Neal's body. Seaweed was woven into her hair and the outflung whiteness of her arm could have been mistaken for the body of a dead, storm-battered seabird.

Bringing Out the Dead

PUBLICATION SUSPENDED—We have tried to maintain a regular newspaper, even in much diminished size, throughout the crisis of this plague. But so greatly has our readership declined, so thinned out are the ranks of our staff, and so few are the remaining advertisers, that we must suspend publication of the Journal for an unknown but hopefully brief period.

May God be with you all.

—The Wilmington Journal, September 30 1862

Largo smelled the city before she saw it—an acrid tarry stench that tainted the gentle autumn breeze coming from the sea. She saw the first refugee boats when the steam launch neared Smith's Creek, near the city's northernmost ferry crossing over the Cape Fear. Rowboats, pleasure craft wallowing under laggard sails in the afternoon humidity, a tugboat so loaded with passengers it was barely making headway, Wilmington's citizens were in exodus—whole families, with pinched and nervous faces, clutching bags and valises, their eyes filled with fear. She scanned the city's breadth and saw that its spires and rooftops were overhung with a heavy dark haze, a mysterious pestilential cloud that she assumed was the source of the growing stink. Most of the refugees paid no heed to her small launch, although a few people did point at her and the store clerk with expressions of surprise. Finally, as they neared the waterfront, they were hailed by a banker who recognized Largo and who was laboring with red-faced desperation to row his wife, children, and three female slaves in the general direction of Smithville.

"Miss Landau! You must turn back, madam!"

"Have the Yankees landed? Are we invaded?"

"No, ma'am. It is worse. It's Yellow Jack! The city is ravaged by it. Everyone who has the means to flee is doing so."

"Then who will tend the sick?"

The banker ducked his head and, having no ready answer, resumed puffing at his oars.

"We must turn back," said the clerk. "I thought your father only had a fever."

"Whatever my father has, I must be with him. If you are afraid, sir, then just land me at the nearest convenient spot and I will make my way home as best I can. I doubt very much that my father's store will be open for business until the epidemic has run its course, so you are free to go."

She thought the man was going to collapse with relief. He put her ashore just south of the railroad station and turned the launch around as soon as her feet touched dry ground. Largo looked about for someone to carry her luggage, but the streets were deserted. She spotted a wheelbarrow leaning against a nearby warehouse and decided to appropriate it. Then she headed south on Front Street.

Now she could see the source of the rank odors and the haze. On every other corner, pots full of tar bubbled and flamed, emitting choking clouds of smoke, and every four-way intersection was blocked by big hillocks of "plague soil"—earth that had been chemically impregnated at the city's gas works. No one really knew what caused an outbreak of Yellow Jack. "Noxious nocturnal vapors" and "swamp miasma" were the most common explanations—burning tar and gas-impregnated soil were supposed to "absorb" these invisible contagions, but all they really did, she suspected, was mask the stench of the dead. She could not tell which of these prophylactic measures smelled worse, but together they blanketed the city with an evil char and made it hard to breathe. After six blocks, she was wheezing and coughing. She also discovered that the city was not as deserted as it appeared, for as she drew closer to home, she saw faces peering furtively from behind closed windows. What percentage of the population had already fled?

What percentage was already dead?

As if to underscore this morbid thought, she heard a slow cobblestone rumble and saw an old threadbare hearse, drawn by mules whose ribs you could count at fifty paces, come lumbering around the corner of Walnut Street. The driver was a skinny old Negro whose hands trembled on the reigns and whose forehead was beaded with sweat. He did not acknowledge her with even a glance—his eyes were focused on something far away and dire, upon the specter, perhaps, of his own encroaching death. There were no curtains on the hearse and no coffins within, just a tangled pile of bodies, black and white, still clad in the clothes they were wearing when they died. As the wagon passed, Largo was enveloped by a vile new smell—most of these people had puked all over themselves before dying, heaving up a thick black mixture of blood and rotted tissue, and no one had bothered to clean them. Overcome by the stench, Largo gagged and struggled to control her own urge to vomit.

How strange it was, she thought, that in this age of scientific progress and innovation, her city was no better able to cope with this scourge than some medieval village.

To her relief and surprise, their butler, Wellington, had remained loyal and appeared to be healthy, although he was much dispirited by Jacob's condition. There was little he could do, he explained, other than change the bed linen and provide refreshment during those moments of lucidity when his master complained of thirst. He finished his report by admonishing her: "Miss Largo, you had best gird yourse'f for what you 'bout to see. Jus' remembah, there ain't nothin' we can do but pray for him. It all in de hands of God, now."

When she entered Jacob Landau's bedroom, she found him conscious but not lucid, his thin arms crossed tightly against his heaving chest, his feet kicking feebly beneath tangled, sweat-soaked sheets. He was burning with fever, so she fetched a basin of water and bathed his forehead. Never a large man, he now seemed withered and desiccated. He moaned as she washed him, and when his mouth opened she saw that the tip of his tongue was cherry red and the back of it coated with a thick white slurry. When he did open his eyes, the orbs were taut, swollen, congested with fluid.

When she had done all she could, and Jacob had lapsed again into unconsciousness, she went out once more and walked to the residence of Dr. Baccus Satchwell. She knocked a long time and was about to turn away—certain that the doctor was out tending the plague victims—when she heard him say, "Who is it?" in a voice much thinner and more reedy than his usual hearty tone.

"It's Largo Landau, Doctor. I have just come from seeing my father. I realize you must be flooded with responsibilities just now, but could you find the time to check on him, perhaps give him some medicine?"

"I have checked on him, girl. And unfortunately, there is no medicine I could dispense that would be the slightest help. About one-half of those who contract the Yellow Jack die; the other half survive. I could predict your father's chances as accurately by throwing a pair of dice as I could by consulting a medical text. And . . . in any case, I cannot leave the house now, for I have contracted it myself."

"Oh, God. Can you at least tell me what to expect? Are there any signs that point to recovery? Is there a definite crisis?"

"Oh, yes, my dear. If he begins to puke black liquid, that indicates the disease is entering its final stages. After that will come hemorrhages from the eyes and nose, swelling of the abdomen, and purple patches on the stomach. The final stages also involve delirium and agitation, verging on insanity. Some few people have still recovered, even then, but not many. He may try to harm himself, and as long as there is hope, however slight, you must prevent him from taking his own life or from self-mutilation."

"How can I do that?"

"Tie him down, if you must. Be brave. And pray."

"I shall pray as well for you. I'll get back to him now, and thank you."

"Wait, Largo. There is something else you must know. Your father and I did everything humanly possible to avert this disaster. Indeed, it is probable that we were the first two citizens to be exposed. Your father acted with great courage. If I should survive and he does not, I will make sure the people of Wilmington learn of his self-sacrifice."

The next morning, James Fulton and the handful of employees still with him posted a terse bulletin announcing the temporary suspension of *The Wilmington Journal*. According to Fulton's best information, between fifteen and twenty people were dying every day, the plague was still spreading, and one-third of the population had fled to the mainland. Of the city's ten registered physicians, two were dead, three infected, and three more had absconded. The corpses were now being thrown into a huge ditch on the edge of Oakdale Cemetery, black at one end and white at the other. Citizens wishing to have their dead picked up for burial should place a black emblem on their doors.

By late on his fifth day of infection, Jacob Landau was racked with the first of many black pukes. Largo did what she could to mop up after these episodes, but she ran out of clean linen and the stench inside the bedroom eventually became so ghastly that she had to wrap a perfume-soaked kerchief around her face. Ruthlessly, she submerged any fears of contamination—if the prevailing theory of "noxious vapors" were at all valid, she was probably safer nursing her father than she would be roaming the streets. Jacob's spasms eased near midnight and he lapsed into a deep sleep, so she staggered down the hall to her own bedroom and collapsed, too exhausted even to undress.

She had a dream in the morning: she was a child again, and her mother Rachel was still alive and holding her hand, and Jacob stood beside his wife, turned out in his finest suit, handsome and dignified, and in the golden mist surrounding them where they stood, an invisible choir of Jews was chanting in Hebrew. Of course, Largo had never been to a Sabbath service in a real synagogue, but her father had taught her some Hebrew and in her dream, she understood the words perfectly.

"Yis-gad-dal v'yis-kad-dash sh'meh rab-bo, b'ol-mo div-ro kir-u-sey v'yam-lich mal-chu-sey, b'cha-ye-chon . . . "

And she whispered in response: "Extolled and hallowed be the name of God throughout all the world which He has created according to His will . . . "

. . . and then, waking, she realized that the chanting was not from an invisible choir, but was coming from her father's room, bellowed in a cracked stentorian voice. As the dream collapsed in brittle shards, she ran down the hall and found him on his knees, blood streaming from his nose and his eyes bleeding scarlet tears, in front of Rachel's picture and the menorah, trying with all his waning strength to stab himself in the heart with the pointed end of the shofar. Largo screamed and ran to hold him close, but his eyes were wild and black foam boiled on his lips; his naked abdomen was swollen like a hot-air balloon and he had a maniac's wiry strength. He lashed out at her—not the slightest flicker of recognition in his hemorrhaging eyes—and struck her down. He resumed his chanting—which now she understood to be the kaddish, but she would never know for whom the memorial prayer was spoken, her mother, or Jacob for himself—and as he howled the final lines, "May the Father of peace send peace to all who mourn!" he drove the ram's horn into his stomach, screamed in too-late amazement, and rolled over on his back, dead.

Largo was not spared one final horror, for as Jacob expired, the hellish gases that filled his rotting insides spewed up through the shofar's submerged mouthpiece and the instrument gave voice to one final macabre blat of sound.

For a day and a night, she howled and tore her hair and raged against Jehovah. Why was Jacob Landau struck down so hideously, stripped not only of his dignity but his very sanity? He had been a good Jew, a devoted husband, an honest and hardworking merchant, and a loving, lenient father! Was this God's wrath for her own transgressions? Did He now regard her as little better than a harlot? Was it God's intention to force upon Largo a life of guilt and remorse? If Jacob himself, although he must have sensed the nature of his daughter's relationship with Hobart-Hampden, had never berated her, never spoken to her or treated her with any less degree of love and respect than he had always shown, what right did God have to punish both father and daughter? *It was none of Your business!*

In her grief and fury, she raised her hand to the mantelpiece where the portrait of her mother had been enshrined for so long, and took a vicious swipe at the menorah, sending it crashing to the floor. For a dazed moment, she contemplated the four candle flames that had survived the impact, and which were already beginning to singe the carpet. Let them burn, she thought. Let the rug catch fire, and the varnished floorboards, and then the curtains and walls and ceiling, until the whole room becomes engulfed. And I will sit beside my dead, disfigured father and hold his hand and stare at my mother's beautiful face until the place becomes a pyre, and God will have his purging of each and every sin. She shook her fist, Joblike, at the always mute but supposedly always watching deity. *There goes your synagogue, you cruel old bastard! I am the heir to this house and I am taking your temple with me—the harlot's heritage, going up in smoke! Will that, finally, please Your Worshipfulness?*

But the motion of her blow against the candlesticks had also dislodged an envelope, which spiraled slowly down and landed near one of the guttering flames. As it passed before her gaze, she saw her own name, scrawled in a bold but unsteady hand that she recognized as her father's. One corner of the envelope had already begun to char by the time she retrieved it; almost as an afterthought, she blew out the flames and returned the menorah to its rightful place. Then, with trembling hands, she sat down in the nearest chair, opened the envelope, and read her father's last words to her:

> *Beloved daughter—I know, from dear old Satchwell, what the progress of the yellow fever is likely to be. While I have this moment of clarity and strength, I want to tell you some things, fragments from the past which may help guide you when I am no longer able to gaze on your lovely face.*

My marriage to Rachel was arranged between our families when we were both very young—I was sixteen and she but twelve. But already, I loved her with all my heart, and loved her more with each glimpse of her as she matured. Music, of course, was the great passion of her life—but not the only passion, as I later learned. Her precocious brilliance as a pianist was noted early and encouraged by her family. When she was sixteen, she began advanced studies with a young tutor named Frederich, a handsome but perfectly honorable man in his midtwenties, and a pianist whose artistry had already drawn praise from the great Franz Liszt.

She fell in love with him, of course—in her mind, the foreordained marriage to me must have seemed remote, far away in the future, an abstraction. Unfortunately, Frederich also fell in love with her. Before the situation could develop into a scandal, he accepted a promising job in Vienna and everyone in both Jewish families felt great relief. That, they thought, was that. But somehow, they managed to correspond, and if anything, their love grew deeper with their physical separation. When Rachel was seventeen, she ran away and tried to meet him in Vienna. She never got farther than the train station, of course, and her father reacted to this act of defiance by confining her to the house for an entire year, importing another tutor who was far too old and much too ugly to pose any threat to Rachel's reputation.

But all during that year, somehow, she and Frederich managed to pass messages. Her passion for him only deepened. But she managed to convince her father that this silly infatuation was all forgotten, and eventually he returned to her some measure of freedom. She bided her time until any lingering suspicions were lulled . . . then she promptly tried to run away to Vienna again. When she saw her father, accompanied by a policeman, closing in on her at the train station, she ran to a nearby river and tried to drown herself. For this, she was sent away to a boarding school in Switzerland—a place with high walls—and forbidden to continue her piano studies.

Frederich's career, meanwhile, blossomed. He was in great demand as a chamber-music performer, he coached the lead singers at the State Opera, and he was a popular figure among the city's musical elite. He played with the Schumanns, and was a good friend of Mendelssohn. Eventually, of course, he forgot about the young Jewess who had been so infatuated with him.

And eventually, as our families had always intended, she married a prosperous but decidedly UN-musical merchant named Jacob

Landau. I had always worshiped her, and I believed that, in time, she would come to love me for my own qualities. It was partly for that reason—to remove her for good from the temptations of Vienna—that we came to America.

In time, Rachel did come to love me, but never with the passion she had felt for her handsome pianist. We never spoke of this, of course, but I always knew that the deepest, most private place in her soul was inaccessible to me. For all the time we lived together, she must always have wondered: what would her life have been like if she had gone to Vienna?

I believe I know. Her artistry was such that, even if she had not married Frederich, she would have flowered in that golden city. If she had not been compelled to marry Jacob Landau, the merchant, she would have played chamber music with the likes of Schumann and Mendelssohn and Brahms.

I am sure—smart young woman that you are—that you see where this confession is leading. This war, which is such a curse to so many, will change a great many old patterns, shatter many conventions. You, instinctively, have sensed this.

Honor my memory, and that of your beloved mother, by using some part of your inheritance to build that synagogue. But beyond that—I implore you to go and find your own Vienna! Whether or not you choose to follow your dashing Englishman to strange lands and grand adventures (if *he can put up with your occasional wilfulness!) is a choice that only you can make. But go! Find your destiny! Do not let anyone define it for you! In that way, you will be honoring the free-spirited, passionate, and deeply gifted woman your mother* was *before her horizons were circumscribed by others. By me.*

Be brave, be kind, nourish the intelligence and humanity your mother bequeathed to you, and know that you will always have your father's blessing.

Largo wept until, finally, she fell asleep. And while she slept, she had another dream and heard fragments of another verse from the Services of Atonement:

The Almighty takes no delight in the proud and arrogant . . . His help goes forth to the weak . . . He champions the cause of the oppressed . . . Affliction of the body and fasting alone cannot cleanse the soul of sin or relieve the conscience of its weight of guilt. Help us to ful-

> *fill our obligation to the needy and distressed. Incline our hearts to compassion that we may aid the homeless and the poor. On this day of* repentance, *we return to Thee with chastened heart. Receive us with favor, O God . . .*

When the words faded from her sleeping mind, she briefly dreamed once more of her parents, and saw them whole and radiant, hand in hand, smiling down at her, and then Largo awoke. She put a black swatch on her door and instructed Wellington to help load Jacob's body when the tumbrel of death came for his remains. There would be time for a proper memorial later, but she did not think he would mind being buried with the other Wilmingtonians who had perished. In the grave, at least, there was no prejudice. She bathed, dressed her hair, and changed into a simple calico dress and matching bonnet. Then she went forth into the streets of Wilmington to answer her own rhetorical question to the refugee banker: "Who will tend the sick?"

26

Nothing Less Than a Gallon

GETTING BACK TO NORMAL—Our citizens have been returning home for several days, and our streets begin to present a more lively appearance than they have for a number of weeks past. After passing through the terrible scourge our town has recently experienced, it is really gratifying to meet once more the many familiar faces that have just returned.

It is also a matter of pleasure that we are enabled to state that Market Street presented a lively appearance this morning, a number of provision carts and wagons having made their appearance, bringing in pork, beef, turkeys, eggs, potatoes, & c., all very appropriate, except we cannot see the propriety of giving 30 cents per lb for fresh pork, $2.25 for a dead turkey, 75 cents per dozen for eggs, and for every other article in proportion. How a certain class of our people are to get along under such extortion, time and circumstance can only tell. Wood, for instance, is extremely scarce, and we heard of one philanthropic dealer who sold his supply at $12 a cord. Patriotism and Philanthropy! Where art thou gone? Into such men's pockets, perhaps, for there is little evidence of them elsewhere to be found.

—The Wilmington Journal, November 25 1862

Dawn was a cold blear smudge, as though the sun was weary of its own responsibility and wanted to sleep late under cloudy blankets. Augustus Hobart-Hampden wanted to do the same. He had camped out in far more desolate and dangerous places, but it had been two years since he had spent a full day in the saddle and he was both stiff-legged and sore-bottomed when he struggled up from his blanket and rekindled a breakfast fire from last night's ashes. When the blaze was sufficient, he wedged a small coffeepot into the hottest flames and laid out some of the provisions he had brought from Wilmington: cornbread, a tin of good

London ham brought in from Nassau, and a packet of real sugar from Jacob Landau's store. Or, more accurately, from the store that now belonged to the recently deceased Jew's daughter. While waiting for the coffee to boil, he lit a cigar and stared moodily at the landscape around the rough, near-derelict road that would lead him eventually, to Pine Haven Plantation.

He had brought the battered *Banshee* into port on the afternoon of November 17, after passing the now tightly enforced quarantine inspection at Smithville. He was appalled by what he saw and heard. Instead of the gaiety and bustle of the Wilmington he had left, he found a stunned, half-empty place populated by fearful, nervous people who were just beginning to venture once more into the streets, men and women who avoided eye contact kept their distance from strangers, and were furtive and guarded even with acquaintances, a city where no cough on a dark street did not sound sinister, and where the dead were still being carted away for quick, rough, communal burial. No one could accurately tally the plague victims, but estimates ran as high as eight hundred dead, almost one-quarter of the city's population. On the night of November 13, he learned, an early frost came down on the region, glazing all of Wilmington's stagnant ponds with rime ice. No new cases of Yellow Jack had been reported after that, and refugees had started to trickle back across the river. He had gone immediately to Jacob's house, where he learned of Jacob's death, but Largo was not there, and the housekeepers had not seen her for days; indeed, they did not know if she was well or sick, alive or dead. The store was closed and had a forlorn, shuttered look.

Finally, guided by information gleaned from citizens who spoke her name almost with a tone of reverence, he located Largo in Paddy's Hollow, the concentrated nest of whorehouses and cutthroat saloons crouched against the waterfront between Mulberry and Chestnut Streets, where she had set up a free kitchen for the hungry, a makeshift infirmary for the stricken poor who had no place else to go, and where she had organized a band of roving nurses from the "fallen" female inhabitants. At the height of the plague, she and her recruits had gone forth fearlessly, bringing comfort and companionship to those so far in extremis that they had no compunction about being tended to by women of ill repute. Some of the more proper citizens, clinging to their shields of moral rectitude even in the midst of a public holocaust, professed to be scandalized, but others spoke of "the Jewess of Mercy" as though she were Joan of Arc.

He found a young woman transformed by charity's zeal: thin, pale, her exquisite eyes ringed with shadows of fatigue. When he embraced her, he could feel a deep and tightly controlled inner trembling, her heart beating small and wild as a sparrow's, her hands roughly begrimed and her clothes redolent of death, sweat, and decay. She was of course distressed to learn that Matthew Sloane was missing and presumed to be either dead or captured, but she was too preoccupied by the ocean of suffering she had waded through to spare much grief for him. And much too preoccupied, he readily understood, to fall quickly into bed with him. Without hesitation, Hobart-Hampden fell into ranks and did all he could to aid her and her fallen angels, recruiting men, wagons, and whatever supplies his connections gave him access to. There was much to be done, and the next two weeks passed in a blur of confusion and toil.

Although more refugees returned each day, as word spread down the coast that the epidemic had run its deadly course, there remained a serious if temporary shortage of waterfront labor and Hobart-Hampden could not get the *Banshee* unloaded right away, despite the light weight of its main cargo. This proved to be a more urgent matter than anticipated, for Largo had unstintingly routed a great deal of the family's liquid cash into her recent charitable ventures, assuming there was plenty more in the city's banks or in her father's safe. There wasn't. Two days after reuniting with Hobart-Hampden, she had been alarmed to discover, when she located someone competent enough to study Jacob's accounting ledgers, that her father had invested an incredible quarter-million dollars in Fulton's "Ironclad Fund," with nothing to show for it except a half-finished keel on the ways at Beery's Shipyard on Eagles Island. If the store did not reopen soon, she would run out of funds. Hobart-Hampden's share of the Anglo-Confederate Trading Company's revenues was intact and virtually untouched, but when he tried to give Largo enough cash to "tide things over," she coolly rejected the offer.

A pair of telegrams to General Whiting and Colonel Lamb finally resolved the matter. Hobart-Hampden informed both officers about the Armstrong gun and requested the loan of some troops to unload the commercial goods after the great cannon had been hoisted out and secured on a barge for its trip to Fort Fisher. Lamb was ecstatic about the weapon and readily agreed to send an entire company. By the time the goods were transferred to the store, the *Wilmington Journal* was again being published, and the advertisement Largo placed there attracted the largest crowd anyone had seen in Wilmington's streets since the start of the plague. With touching loyalty, the senior clerk had returned to his job; even Hobart-Hampden donned an apron and waited on customers, while Largo minded the till. All three had their hands full. Since the *Banshee*'s cargo was the first to go on sale since the crisis had subsided, the event had a wildly celebratory atmosphere—patrons loaded down their wagons with more corset stays and toothbrushes than they could possibly use for the rest of the century and cheered as they handed over their cash. Everything was sold out—down to the last box of coffin screws—during the course of a single afternoon, and true to the Englishman's prediction, the profits were outrageous.

Disposing of the cargo and returning Largo to a state of financial security made life simpler for Hobart-Hampden, but not by much. He made sure the *Banshee* was the first vessel in line for repairs when the shipyards reopened, figuring that a few days' carpentry and remasting would take care of the structural damage inflicted by Yankee gunfire, but it turned out that an equal amount of damage had been done by the combination of prolonged high-speed maneuvers and the trashy coal they had been forced to burn. All the ship's boilers had to be drawn down and thoroughly cleaned before she could return to the high seas. This in turn meant two weeks' enforced idleness for the Englishman who was now, by default, her new skipper.

That prospect weighed heavily on Hobart-Hampden. Largo was not exactly cold toward him, but she was perpetually occupied, usually exhausted, and still in mourning. While he had seen only the tail end of the plague's effects, and those had been depressing enough, she had fed for weeks upon its ghastly black marrow and her mood was not unlike the drawn-out state of shock that many soldiers experience after a long, brutal, dehumanizing campaign. Hobart-Hampden understood that such a mental state was not conducive to erotic enthusiasm, so he made no effort to coerce her into bed. Now that he had helped get her financially solvent again, the best thing he could give her was time and patience. Nor did he linger much at the Yellow House, where the preplague level of boisterousness had resumed, albeit with a slightly desperate edge that made the parties and cockfights seem unpleasantly shrill.

Moreover, Hobart-Hampden realized that the *Banshee*'s latest and longest voyage would not really be over until he informed Mary Harper Sloane of her husband's fate. The day after he docked the ship, he started sending forth inquiries, using channels of communication not available to the average citizen or soldier, but the epidemic had disrupted even those conduits and three weeks went by before he had definite news: Sloane was alive and imprisoned in Fortress Monroe.

His original plan had been to sail up the Uwharrie branch as soon as the *Banshee* was repaired, but that timetable was set back by the need to overhaul the engines. When Largo learned of his scheme, she pronounced it callous and insensitive. Her reasoning was part woman's intuition and part wisdom: Mary Harper, upon seeing the ship, would be overcome with joy, believing that Matthew was aboard. Her disappointment, upon seeing Hobart-Hampden descend the gangway alone and assuming the worst, would be shattering. There had to be a less devastating way of carrying the news.

So Hobart-Hampden rented a horse, packed some camping gear and provisions, and resolved that he would ride to Pine Haven. The sight of him alone, on horseback, and somber-faced, coming from the land and not the river, would signal bad news, of course, but the sheer strangeness of the sight would mute Mary Haper's darkest fears and he could swiftly soften the blow by telling her right away that Matthew was in fact alive. Besides, the prospect of a slow, solitary ride absolutely suited his current mood. He crossed the Cape Fear on the Hilton ferry and picked up the road a mile or so west of the landing. By English standards, it had never been much of a road, and since the opening of the Wilmington and Weldon Railroad, it had fallen into decline. It wound northward, meandering parallel to the tracks but never crossing them, in the general direction of Goldsboro; much of it had once been planked or corduroyed up to the New Hanover County line, but years of neglect and flooding had taken their toll. Long stretches of the route were little more than glutinous muck and his horse moved through them as though its hooves were shod in glue pots. Hobart-Hampden did not mind, for he was in no hurry to reach his destination.

The countryside through which he rode was every bit as somber as his mood, a land both shrouded and secretive. A chill muzzy drizzle beaded the pine needles with cold shimmering tears, and a dirgelike wind mourned through the tallest boughs. Evergreen trunks gleamed as though rubbed with oil, and the fallen autumn leaves, leeched now of all their glory, formed a spongy mat that soaked up every sound of his passing. On the first day, he passed scattered yeoman farms and exchanged wary nods with the very old and very young men who struggled to keep them going—no one he saw was older than adolescence or younger than bearded patriarchal maturity, no need to speculate where the young men had gone; but as he went farther and farther from the ferry landing, the number of cabins dwindled and by the time he stopped to make camp, he had seen no inhabited dwellings for two or three hours. His weariness was such that he expected sleep to come easily, but it did not, despite the canteen full of brandy he emptied after supper. Like the reverberations of a distant requiem, a chorus of images made a persistent and brooding threnody in his mind: Wilmington ravaged and haunted by the plague . . . Largo's face and eyes transformed by sorrow . . . the moment when he clasped Matthew Sloane's hand for the final time, in the shell-blasted surf that marked the end of their final voyage together . . . Matthew, his friend and comrade-in-arms, who had renounced his comfortable life as a complacent and cultured gentleman-farmer and who had pounced like a virile young hawk upon the new and stirring destiny the war had opened for him . . . Matthew, who had leaped eagerly into the pyre set blazing by his intoxicated passion for the lady spy . . . Matthew, whose lover had fallen from the heights of dawn and dragged the golden stars down with her into the abyss she had chosen. Even with the brandy smoldering inside his belly, Hobart-Hampden huddled as close to the fire as he dared, for the night had become as cold as the lilies on a grave.

But this morning he felt better—like a man rising with a hangover earned the night before at a good friend's wake—and shriven of guilt. By the time he finished his second cup of coffee, there was a faint breath of warmth from the pale lemony sun and the pine boughs that had yesterday seemed sprinkled with tears now sparkled. Winter's tang felt invigorating, no longer oppressive and menacing. He was not sure how many miles remained between his campsite and Pine Haven, but he was reasonably sure he could cover them by midafternoon and quite certain, thanks to his sources of information, that the nearest Yankee patrols were a hundred miles northeast, near New Bern. Barring an unlikely encounter with a bear or a bobcat, the rest of his journey should be pleasant enough. Of course, there were rumors, now, about roaming bands of outliers—deserters or bushwhackers or renegade slaves—who moved like ghosts through the wild no-man's-land between the contending armies, but most of them were said to inhabit the state's northeastern counties, in the bogs and neglected tobacco fields between the Great Dismal Swamp and Pamlico Sound.

It was conceivable that some of them had ventured this far south, in their quest for seclusion or loot, but he had armed himself with a revolver and a stubby double-barreled shotgun before leaving Wilmington, and the skirmish with Lafayette Baker's men had refreshed his memory about how easy it was to kill a man in a fight.

"Dey's a gen-ul-mun's coming to see you, Missuz Sloane!" chirped Aurelia.

Mary Harper's hands slowed upon their knitting, the needles clacking like twigs of bone. She put the yarn aside and rose slowly, smoothing straight lines into her skirt as best she could. Brushing at her hair and striving to maintain a dignified pace, she started toward the back door.

"No, ma'am!" called Aurelia. "He not comin' on de rivah. He on a horse, up at de *front gate!*"

Mary Harper understood Aurelia's excitement. No one had approached Pine Haven from the road in many months. She wondered briefly if she should notify Mister Bright—could this wayfarer be the herald of some far-roaming Yankee cavalry?—but decided against raising an alarm. If the visitor were truly alone, she had nothing to fear; if he were a cavalry scout . . . it would be best to display no defiance. *Well, sooner or later, a Yankee probably* will *ride down that carriage path . . . as long as this person is a gentleman, we must assume his good intentions.*

When, instead of a cavalryman, she beheld Hobart-Hampden, her emotions whipsawed: delight at seeing a friend quickly replaced by fear and apprehension. Where was the ship? Where was Matthew? The Englishman did not look so grand and swaggering as usual—his features were rather drawn, his shoulders slumped, and he handed the reins to a groom with an air of deep weariness. She ran to him as soon as he turned and wrapped him in a trembling hug. He answered her first question instantly, whispering into her ear: "He is alive and well, but there is much to tell you."

"Come into the parlor, where it's warm. I'll have some food brought in from the kitchen, and I do believe there is enough whiskey lurking about to offer you a drink or two."

"You may wish to pour one for yourself, my dear."

She ordered the fire built up and food prepared, then she closed the parlor doors and poured, as he had suggested, two drinks. Since the malaria and near-failure of the harvest, Mary Harper had learned the therapeutic value of a good stiff bourbon and Hobart-Hampden did not raise an eyebrow when she slugged back a dollop with the vigor and smoothness of a practiced gentleman.

"Matthew has been taken prisoner," he said without preamble. "As you know, our last voyage was somewhat unusual. We could not tell you beforehand, of course, for reasons of security, but we were charged with smuggling in the famous Rebel spy, Belle O'Neal. The blockaders were alerted and waiting for us. We came under heavy fire during the run into New Inlet, and Matthew volunteered to carry Miss O'Neal to safety in the longboat. He feared, and with good reason, that she would be hanged if taken alive. I am told that he almost pulled it off, but a shell struck the boat just a few yards from shore, and Miss O'Neal chose to throw herself into the sea rather than be captured. She was carrying a considerable amount of gold coin sewn into the lining of her dress, and she sank like a stone. Matthew was wounded by a piece of grapeshot and knocked unconscious. A Yankee landing party took him prisoner. My sources tell me that he is imprisoned at Fortress Monroe, and that his case will be heard sometime early in the new year. His wound, I gather, was not serious."

"I see." She also saw, or inferred from Hobart-Hampden's inflections, a disturbing hint that there was something more to the event than these bare facts. Matthew's act had either been gallant or foolish, she supposed, depending on your point of view. Or maybe *both*. Maybe there had been something between Matthew and the lady spy, whom she knew by legend and repute to be a great seductive beauty. This train of thought led exactly nowhere—she would probably never know for sure, and what difference did it make, now that the woman was dead?

"What are his chances, Augustus?"

Hobart-Hampden shrugged. "If this were an ordinary case of blockade-running, he would probably be paroled, in exchange for some captured Yankee of comparable stature, and eventually allowed to go free in one of those routine prisoner exchanges. But because we were carrying the spy, there is a double-layer of treason involved, or at least the Lincolnites may assert as much. I do not think there are sufficient grounds for, well, for a capital punishment. But it is very possible he will be incarcerated for the duration of the war. You must prepare yourself emotionally for that. At least be thankful that he was away during the plague."

Mary Harper looked up sharply.

"Is it truly over, then? We only learned about it when a wagon full of travelers stopped here, asking for shelter for the night. They were fleeing to stay with kin up near Goldsboro. They said the city was almost deserted, that people were dropping dead in the streets—all sorts of horrible things!"

He told her what he had seen and learned, and when she heard about Jacob's death, her composure finally cracked and she began to weep, partly from relief that Matthew had been spared. As soon as the tale was finished, however, she dried her tears and summoned Agrippa to put fresh wood on the fire. For a time, they sat in silence and watched the flames take hold of the pine knots. Sap boiled and spat from the wood, a sound so emptily cheerful that it mocked the parlor's gloom and summoned memories of the many parties that had enlivened these rooms in winters past, evoking for Mary Harper the sad and ghostly pomp of old events.

Seemingly anxious to broach a less somber topic, Hobart-Hampden reached into his coat pocket and drew out an envelope.

"Here is a letter from your father. I found it waiting at Landau's store and took the liberty of becoming a temporary postman—God knows when it would have reached you otherwise."

There was a knock. "Ah, that will be the food. Please help yourself, while I read this."

Stepney Harper had heard about the plague—the Asheville paper had been full of grim reports—and he had therefore decided to remain in the safety of his mountain retreat until the danger was past. The Sloane children were well and happy, and being tutored in their studies. They were excited about spending Christmas in the hills, especially the chance to see real snow. He planned to return to South Carolina right after the new year, and he would send the children to Pine Haven as soon as he could arrange safe transportation. The siege and bombardment of Charleston were not yet severe, but that was true primarily because the enemy had not yet mounted a major amphibious operation against the city itself, only against some outlying islands. If the Yankees did mount an all-out attack on the city, he wanted the children back at Pine Haven, where they would be much more removed from the threat of violence.

"Oh, that is not true!" gasped Mary Harper, when she had finished reading the gist of the letter aloud. "We are too isolated here. I am not worried about a Yankee attack on Wilmington—we are much too far away to be in the line of fire—but I am worried about Yankee raids from the upper coast, and about the slaves' attitudes, and about the bushwhackers I have heard about, up above New Bern. If you can use the road to get here from Wilmington, they can use it to get here from the other direction. No, indeed, Augustus—as much as I miss my children, I would prefer them to stay with my father at Limerick. I shall write to him about it, and you can post the letter when you get back to Wilmington."

"If I may suggest it, why don't you come back to Wilmington for the duration? It will be much easier to get information about Matthew, and your letters to him can be deposited with the American consul in Nassau—he is obliged by the rules of war to forward them to your husband, and his to you. Matthew told me you have something of a 'foreign legion' company here now, to guard Pine Haven, along with Mister Bright, who knows all there is to know about running the place."

She laughed, a short little bark tinged with bitterness.

"Oh, yes, indeed, we have quite a powerful little garrison: Mister Bright, who now speaks perfect English after having his skull punctured by a maniac, a Polish fellow and a sullen Portuguese who mostly grunt in monosyllables, and a rather antic little Chinaman who is a trained master in some ancient art of sword-fighting. I'll have him put on a demonstration for you, Augustus—you will find it amusing. But I cannot leave Pine Haven, except for the most necessary trips to town for provisions."

"Why on earth not? Bright can keep the slaves on task, surely."

"It is hard to explain, Augustus. But for the past six months, and especially now, with Matthew gone for God knows how long, the entire burden of managing Pine Haven has fallen on me—I have become both master and mistress. I have vowed to see this thing through. We will not always have a share of income from the Anglo-Confederate Trading Company, whether the South wins or loses. What we *will* have is what we've always had: this plantation and the bounty of God's earth.

"Until now, the 'duties' I performed, the ordinary daily chores required to keep this place running smoothly and profitably, were not *duties* at all. They were *delegations* of duties. I made a list, told the responsible slaves what was on it, gave a copy to Mister Bright, and those things simply *got done.* Making soap, batting the clothes, cording and carding the yarn, dyeing the cloth, drying the fruit, salting the bacon and stuffing the sausages, raking manure for the gardens, repairing the fences, filling in the potholes in the paths, repairing the shoes, putting up preserves. I knew all these things got done, and got done reliably, but I never really *saw* the labor and skill of it. The reality of toil and process might as well have been invisible, or carried out under cover of night by a band of patient, uncomplaining elves. I knew, intellectually, that there was much more to it than that, but I never really felt a compulsion to contemplate the particulars. Nor did I want to, for I was raised from childhood to accept things as they were, and to assume they were immutable. And I have learned that they are not, that deep slow currents are already undermining that castle of sand in which my class of people have dwelt for generations."

She paused for breath, her still-handsome but now lined face wrinkling in concentration, marshaling an argument, or the beginnings of a heretofore inchoate philosophy. For an instant, she looked ready to reach for another drink, but her hand settled instead on a teapot and a cup of fine bone china.

"I have never heard you speak like this, Mary Harper. Nor anyone else of the plantation class, for that matter." Hobart-Hampden smiled sympathetically, encouraging her to say more. "Please do go on—I have a taste for well-argued heresy."

"Let me tell you what a plantation mistress's 'work' consists of, Augustus, what my daily labors were, up until recently. I rose at whatever hour I chose, usually around nine o'clock, to find my clothes already laid out, brushed and folded, cleaned and ironed, hot water and clean towels on my nightstand. When I went downstairs, there was my breakfast, just as I had ordered it the night before. I ate at leisure, and read the post and the newspapers from town, if any had arrived that day. Then I drew up the menu for dinner and gave it to Aurelia, who made sure it was prepared to order, out in the kitchen—a building I seldom ventured into and never worked in at all, unless it was to mix punch for a party or to check on the quantities of staples we had on hand. Then I spent the rest of the morning walking through the gardens and inspecting the grounds, taking note of places that needed raking, or pruning, or weeding, or fence slats that needed straightening. On rainy days, I strolled through the house, taking note of sundry little things that needed dusting, sweeping, or a whack with the carpet beater—curtains, linens, utensils, plates and cups, so many *vital* things to scrutinize with the stern demanding gaze of the Lady of the Manor. And then I delegated the needful chores. My 'work,' Augustus, was to inspect and to delegate. I had not a second thought about those chores being done, completely to my satisfaction, or how, or by whose labor. I told Aurelia and she either did them herself or set other slaves to the tasks. Exhausted from all this delegating, I ate my midday meal and retired to my chambers, where I read, or answered letters, then lay down for a good long nap before dressing for the evening meal. My only *real* 'task' was to spend an hour or two supervising the children's' studies.

"If there were problems with the slaves—illness, injury, sullen behavior—I might hear a summary of them from Matthew, but all such problems were actually addressed by him or by Mister Bright—my comments and suggestions were seldom solicited and rarely voiced. After the children were in bed, my husband and I sat quietly in this parlor. He read his agricultural and scientific journals while I grazed in bovine comfort on the pages of Dickens or Brontë or Hawthorne, or some month-old issues of *Harper's,* the *Home Journal, Godey's Lady's Book,* or *Blackwood's.* Occasionally, we discussed the things we read, but never to the point of contention, always in tones of bland gentility. At ten or eleven, we bid each other good night and retired, usually to separate rooms. *That* aspect of our marriage, at least, has lately acquired a fitful new vitality. Observe that I can say this without the silly, hypocritical blushing that women of my class are supposed to affect. You are a man of the world, Augustus, and you do not pretend to being shocked by the fact that wives—the fortunate ones, anyhow—have the right to take pleasure in a subject we were once obliged to treat with feigned disgust and embarrassment. Yes: my husband has become a good and ardent lover again, and it is a cruel irony of fate that I am now to be deprived of that comfort, just as I was learning to rely upon it.

"Such was my life, and now that I look back on it from the vantage point of my present circumstances, it seems both idle and trivial. I am learning, however slowly, to understand what actually happened when I *delegated the necessary tasks.* Real people toiled and sweated and put my veriest whims above their own needs, above even the needs of their own families, to ensure that it all got done, on time, correctly, and invisibly. But the war has ripped away that complacent veil. I am studying them now, those myriad chores and how they are accomplished, and in time, I too shall learn how to card yarn and can food and boil the ingredients to make soap.

"I want my slaves to see that I am not afraid to get the dirt and dye and fertilizer under my fingernails, or the mud and manure on my shoes. I want them bound to Pine Haven by loyalty as well as law. I want them to know that *all of us*—black and white and even yellow, now—can work together to keep Pine Haven alive.

"So I rise early, now, and work harder, and show myself where the work is being done. I watch, I listen, I ask questions, and I show my respect by actually paying attention to the answers. I am even thinking about setting up schooling hours on Sunday afternoon, so that those Negroes who wish to, can learn how to read and write. I am aware that many planters would regard that as a mistake, but I fail to see any connection between ignorance and docility.

"So now I have told you how it used to be, and how it is changing. I hope this gives you some insight into why I cannot just pack up and leave this place."

Hobart-Hampden refilled his glass and lit a cheroot. In all the time he had known the Sloanes, he had never heard Mary Harper speak at such length, or with such force.

"Your feelings do you credit, my dear, and you speak of these matters with great eloquence. But, aside from moral self-improvement, am I right in surmising that one of your main reasons for adopting this new role is to forestall trouble among the blacks?"

She thought hard for a moment, then slowly nodded. "We had two runaways last summer—the first in my memory. I believe they headed north, perhaps toward New Bern, for they knew the Yankees had bases in that direction, and they knew that if they reached Yankee lines, they would be free men. One of them apparently died in the swamps—perhaps the other one made it. But I am sure that, before they left, they preached the Abolition gospel to the other slaves before they fled, and perhaps they planted seeds of discontent. I want the other Negroes to stay because they feel a vested interest in staying. I do not want them to hate me, or to harm me. And if slavery is overthrown, I want them to stay on at Pine Haven, and to regard me as an honest employer, not as their former owner."

He leaned forward and quietly said, "You don't believe the South can win, do you?"

At these words, she wrung her hands and turned her face away.

"There was a man here during the rice harvest, a free black man, very arrogant and full of himself—also a drunkard and possibly mad, for it was he who laid open poor Mister Bright's scalp with a reaping hook. He said something at our table that shocked and revolted me at the time, but it has stuck in my mind like a burr ever since. He said that the manpower advantage of the North was so overwhelming, that the only way the Confederacy could possibly prevail would be to emancipate the slaves in return for their military service. He may well have been right. But you know as well as I do, that will never happen. In the end, we may be undone by a paradox of our own making."

She stood up abruptly and gestured for him to take her arm.

"Come, now, it's time to meet the new men. And Mister Bright will be delighted to see you again. Which reminds me, Augustus, please don't take him back."

"Take him back? Oh, you mean on board the ship, as my pilot. Well, I shall miss him, of course, but with the wages I can pay, it won't be difficult to find a good replacement."

"Yes, I do need him here, but there's another reason, too. You see, even though his wound has healed, and his bizarre manner of speech has vanished, I fear the damage from that blow might have been worse than I thought. Occasionally he has dizzy spells and becomes disoriented. These episodes pass in an hour or two, and then he's right as rain, but they do rather compromise his usefulness aboard ship, especially if he has one while he's trying to navigate to New Inlet on a stormy night."

Arm in arm, they stepped into the gardens and into frail bemisted sunlight.

"Will you be at sea during Christmas?"

"I doubt it. The shipyards in Wilmington are so clogged that even simple repairs take twice as long as they should. I am told the *Banshee* won't be ready to sail until late December, at the soonest."

"Then I shall throw a gala Christmas party! Just like the old days. Bring Largo and at least two dozen other folks. Find some nice lonesome soldiers recovering from wounds, or that lovely young Colonel Lamb who commands Fort Fisher. Chase Whiting, too, if he promises not to drink too much. I shall draw up a list of what we need."

"Very well, I accept! And I promise to bring only true ladies and gentlemen who will not make off with the silverware or sing bawdy songs."

"Actually, I wouldn't mind a bawdy song or two. All part of my new and broader horizons, as it were."

Then her tone changed and she turned to look straight into his eyes.

"And when you come, Augustus, please bring us some arms. Good ones. All we have now are two ancient hunting pieces and Mister Bright's revolver. And the Chinaman's sword, of course, but it's an antique dress sword from the Revolution and probably not even intended for serious fighting. See if you can find him a nice new cutlass. Bring plenty of ammunition, too. And a good medical kit, including chloroform."

"You sound as though you're expecting a siege!" he laughed.

"I'm not expecting anything in particular. I just want to be prepared for the worst, whatever form it may take. If any man, be he a regular or a bushwhacker, wants to burn down Pine Haven, he will have to pay a bloody price for the chance to do it."

On New Year's Eve, 1862, the governor's mansion blazed with light and rang with music and laughter. The music was supplied in lusty fashion by the Johnny Reb Band, comprised of the players who had once been attached to Zeb Vance's Twenty-sixth North Carolina, and who were now the governor's official statewide ambassadors of good cheer and pomp. Gas lamps and candelabra mixed hard and steady flames with soft and flickering fires, all multiplied and embroidered by the reflections of rank and martial accoutrements worn by North Carolina's officers, most of whom sported the double stars of a lieutenant colonel or the triple stars of a full colonel, and pricked with the starry brilliance of their ladies' jewels. Governor Vance had decreed a sumptuous feast, elegant floral decorations, and the most thorough, lustrous dust-and-polish job the mansion had seen since the ball that celebrated the end of the Mexican War.

And Vance himself, of course, was the magnet around whom the lesser luminaries flocked like moths to the flame. He worked the crowd like the master politician he was, and as eleven o'clock drew near, he could be found holding court near a vast bowl of fortified punch flanked by a small mountain of ham biscuits. At his side, demure and pleasantly smiling as always, was his wife, Hattie, a petite woman with shining auburn hair, melodious voice, and manners so gracious that they compensated for her husband's occasional ursine roughness. Ranked in semicircle around the governor were the mayors of Charlotte, Fayetteville, Greensboro, and far-off Salisbury; William Holden, editor of the *Raleigh Standard* and sometimes harsh critic of Vance's war policies; Dr. Edward Warren, head of the state's new Medical Department; the president of the university; some members of the state legislature; and a smattering of Raleigh's most eligible belles, who were all too clearly scouting the ballroom for husbandly prospects, preferably in uniform and decorated with at least the single star of a major.

Vance had stationed himself beside the largest bowl of fortified punch, surrounded by a variety of guests, all of whom wanted to hear a memorable "Zeb-ism" from the master of ceremonies. But the governor's usual fund of japery was guttering low at the moment—months of unremitting toil had dulled his rhetorical edge. At the moment, he was trying to coax a jollier mood from Dr. Warren, a man who was ususally far too sober-minded to waste time with humorous banter.

"Come on, Doc," urged Vance, wagging his finger at the prim face of North Carolina's chief surgeon, "tell 'em the story about the nurse and the wounded soldier."

Warren demurred. "I'll not rise to that bait, Zebulon, for I've already told it a dozen times and I'm sure these good people would prefer to hear your version—even for the third or fourth time!"

"Very well, then: Doctor Warren and I were inspecting the North Carolina wounded in Richmond, after the battle at Sharpsburg. We were deeply moved not only by the stoicism with which our boys bore their pain, but also by the kindness of the many ladies who had turned out to act as nurses. We were approaching one young man who had lost a foot and looked as though he was barely conscious. Before we could speak to him, a nurse came fluttering up and knelt at his bedside.

" 'Hello, young fellow. Is there anything you want?'

" 'No, ma'm,' said the soldier, 'I believe not.'

" 'But isn't there *something* I can do for you?'

" 'No, I think not.'

" 'Oh, but I must help you, I must do *something*. Can't I wash your face and hands?'

" 'Well, ma'am, I reckon you can, if you want to right bad; but if'n you do, you will be the fourteenth lady who has done so this morning.' "

Even those who had heard the story before could not help but chuckle at the zest of the governor's retelling. Vance had only a few seconds to bask in their appreciation, however, because he saw his secretary, young Richard Battle—son of one of the state's most renowned judges—waving a pocket watch and pointing to the eleventh hour.

Vance gave Hattie a peck of a kiss, then announced to his audience that he had to absent himself for a while, to clear up some important business left over from the day. He would rejoin them, he promised, in time to see in the New Year. Then he and Battle walked from the ballroom together.

"Damn it, Richard, I had them in the palm of my hand!"

"Governor, you explicitly told me to fetch you a little before eleven. You wanted to finish dictating that letter to . . . "

"Yes, yes, for all the good it will do. It can't wait until tomorrow."

They passed through the chambers and climbed the stairs that separated the mansion's public spaces from the governor's suite of offices.

It always seems as though *nothing* can wait until tomorrow, thought Zeb Vance. The crises rattled through his office like runaway trains. Not six months into his term, the political hounds were already baying at his heels, and some of the newspapers that had supported him most vociferously—especially Holden's *Raleigh Standard*—were now peppering him with criticism. Fortunately, Vance had a thick skin and a seemingly unlimited fund of energy; he worked fifteen hours a day or more, and his door was always open to petitioners and delegations. It was his unshakable belief that the poorest man in North Carolina should have the same access to his governor as the wealthiest.

From the hour of his inauguration, on September 8, he had grappled with problems that always seemed intractable and sometimes really were. At that time, a majority of the legislature and most of the state's wealthiest planters and railroad executives, and a lot of newspaper editors who ought to have known better, still held fast to the notion that the war would be over soon, probably by Christmas and certainly no later than the spring of '63. But none of those gentlemen had actually *been there* on the crimson slopes of of Malvern Hill; Zeb Vance had and he knew, sure as God made pigeons and pork chops, that the war had just been warming up. His immediate and overriding objective, then, was to gird the state for a long and grinding conflict, one that might last years and years. North Carolina had contributed her share and more of soldiers—20 percent of Lee's army comprised North Carolina regiments—but within its own borders, the state was woefully unprepared for the coming ordeal. He had to start, as he sometimes put the matter, "from the scratchiest part of scratch."

Zeb spent his first few weeks in office pouring over the census figures, tax revenues, and whatever limited production figures were available. "Busier," he remarked to Dick Battle, "than a one-legged hillbilly at an ass-kicking contest." Agriculture was of course the state's main occupation, and for a quarter-century at least, cotton and tobacco planting had expanded, while the acreage devoted to food products had dwindled accordingly. Well, you could sell cotton and smoke tobacco, Zeb reckoned, but you couldn't *eat* them and North Carolina's regiments were desperately, chronically, short of rations. Nor had the state really nurtured its nascent and potentially valuable textile industry—all that cotton had been exported to the mills of New England, and had come back in the form of shirts and trousers. *That* arrangement no longer obtained, so Vance had striven mightily to encourage, subsidize, and stimulate the production of finished textile goods, both cotton and woolen. There had also been a dire and chronic shortage of leather, a commodity for which the state's regiments had an insatiable need. Until Vance promulgated new regulations, the hides of all the beef slaughtered for army rations had simply been thrown away. By December, however, the state's tanneries and cobblers had at least begun to supply some of the soldiers' needs for shoes, saddles, and artillery harnesses. Motivated by the spur of state-subsidized profit, more than a dozen new textile mills had sprung up since October. By midspring, Vance estimated, every North Carolina soldier would be able to exchange his rags and worn-out shoes for a proper uniform and a pair of good, solid brogans.

One of the more surprising bits of information Vance uncovered during his studies was the fact that between 10 and 15 percent of his state's already inadequate food production went into the distillation of liquor. After much internal debate, Zeb Vance finally came out with the most controversial and most personally distressful policy of all: in November, he caused to be enacted a drastic law prohibiting the distillation of "spiritous liquors from any kind of grain, including rice, potatoes, sugar cane, syrup, molasses, peas, peanuts, and dried fruit of every description." From the mountain counties especially, arose a great cry of protest, while the state's leading newspapers solemnly, and in many cases very hypocritically, opined that "honest men of every class will surely agree that bread is more vital to the war effort than whiskey." Vance thought that was so, but not by much. North Carolinians could still *buy* liquor, but it had to be produced by another state. Vance was a mountaineer, so he knew the law was quite unenforceable with regard to small-scale family moonshine stills, but the larger, more visible operations did start growing corn for food instead of whiskey and by the next harvesttime, there would be more bread on the tables.

One of the loudest howls of protest, oddly enough, came from Jefferson Davis, who rather testily urged Zeb to renounce at least some of the restrictions, so that good Carolina whiskey could fulfill the "medicinal" needs of Lee's army. Zeb did a bit of research before replying to the president's letter, and he discovered that the combined output of all the licensed distilleries in Virginia was conservatively estimated to be *ten million* gallons per year. Such a tide of liquor, he averred in his answering letter, should certainly be sufficient to satisfy both the medical needs of Lee's army and the seemingly unquenchable thirst of his officers.

Vance had reopened old iron and niter mines, previously regarded as played out, and in the process, the state's geologists had discovered several big new veins of high-grade ore. He had found the money to construct a new salt plant on the shores of Masonboro Sound, north of Fort Fisher, which could turn one thousand pounds of seawater into twenty-seven pounds of meat-preserving salt. He had nurtured and helped to equip more than two dozen small arms workshops, so the state would become less dependent on overpriced European rifles carried by the blockade runners.

On the whole, Zeb was reasonably satisfied with the accomplishments of his first six months as governor. There was, however, one persistent and nagging source of vexation: the Davis government's ill-disguised prejudice against North Carolina, presumably because she had been the last state to go out; and Richmond's seemingly absurd indifference to the ripe strategic possibilities along the coastline. The Federal commander there, General John G. Foster, had never regained the regiments siphoned off for McClellan's failed Peninsula campaign. Foster's fortified enclaves were isolated and his only reserves were his gunboats, which could be hurried from a peaceful location to a threatened one, but not instantaneously. The Virginia front was quiet now—after the hideous bloodletting at Sharpsburg, both sides were licking their wounds in winter quarters. If Lee could detach but one full-strength division, with adequate cavalry to protect its flanks and enough batteries to fend off Foster's gunboats, the entire coast of North Carolina might easily be retaken, one place at a time. Both the strategic and the psychological effect of such a victory would be stunning. And by giving the blockade-runners several new havens, more military goods would stream in and the Federal blockade would be stretched almost as thin as it was in the first summer of the war. One did not need a West Point education to comprehend this strategy—a monkey could look at the map and see how vulnerable the enemy's bridgeheads really were. There was a window open, here and now, for a magnificent counterstroke, but Zeb Vance suspected that the eyes of Secretary of War Seddon glazed over, and his mind sank into a torpor of indifference, whenever the very words "North Carolina" appeared on a document.

Well, thought Zeb Vance, as he took a seat behind his cluttered desk, that window will be open, probably, throughout the spring. *If I can just argue the proposition to Bobby Lee in person, maybe something will happen.*

Vance tried to conduct most correspondence in his own hand, but lately that task had become overwhelming, cutting too deeply into the time he needed to stay on top of more important things. So young Mister Battle, whose youthful stamina matched Vance's own and who was able to take rapid, accurate dictation by means of arcane symbols he called shorthand, frequently took down the governor's rapid but well-organized trains of thought, then recopied them in proper formal style.

"Here, Dick, have a drink first. Don't frown, it's legally imported from Virginia and I paid the goddamned tax on it out of my own pocket. By the way, did you pick up any useful bits of gossip whilst circulating among the aristocrats downstairs?"

"Nothing startling, Governor. I did learn that the going price for a conscription substitute has risen to about fifteen hundred dollars."

"Lord, back in April, you could hire a substitute for three hundred. As I have said before, Dick, this is a rich man's war but a poor man's fight. All right then, let's finish this onerous letter to the honorable secretary of war, so we can join our guests in welcoming the new year."

Half-mockingly, Dick Battle made a chiding motion with his pencil. "Remember now, Governor, to use moderate, temperate language. You don't want to tax Secretary Seddon's sensitive nerves and delicate constitution."

"Bah! If he's that frail, he has no business trying to run a damned *war!* I wonder if he is really as cadaverous as they say."

"Seddon? Oh, yes. I have a cousin who works in the War Department. He described Seddon as looking like an exhumed corpse after two weeks in the pine box."

"My Lord, where *does* Jeff Davis get these people from? Well, corpse or not, we must finish this letter and get it off to Richmond on the first train tomorrow. Where was I when we broke off?"

Battle consulted his notebook and replied: " . . . um, here it is, '*the actions of some conscription agents*' . . . "

Without missing a beat, Vance picked up the thread: " . . . have so far traduced the principles of both law and common decency as to warrant both outrage and prosecution by courts-martial. As an especially egregious example, let me cite one recent incident—fully and accurately reported to me by Judge Hezekiah Randolph, a man of impeccable reputation—during which a conscription squad from Georgia came into Cherokee County, North Carolina, and seized at gunpoint a number of our citizens who were clearly either too old or too young to be subject to the conscription laws, including one gentlemen upwards of sixty years old. These unfortunates were chained together like galley slaves and driven like cattle one hundred and twenty miles to Atlanta, where they were informed that they could either volunteer for the Army or remain in prison for the remainder of hostilities, however long that might be.

"New paragraph:

"Only my personal and forceful remonstrance to the governor of Georgia procured their liberation, and even then, they had to make their own way back to North Carolina, on foot, in the middle of winter, and were forced to beg for bread and shelter along the way.

"New paragraph:

"Was any conceivable military purpose served by this heinous act? Was this wrong redressed? Was compensation, not to mention a simple apology, offered to the victims? Was anyone in the conscription squad punished for this outrage? The answer to all these questions, sadly, is NO—underscore that, Dick. If the Confederate government desires the love and loyalty of common folk such as these, it must—underscore 'must'—compel its agents to treat the citizens of this state with respect and not trample cruelly on their rights. One outcome is certain, as a consequence of this evil deed: If there were no Unionist sympathizers in Cherokee County before it happened, you may be sure that there are some now.

"New paragraph:

"I have appended to this letter the names of all the mountain people who were so barbarously treated in this business, along with a copy of Judge Randolph's sworn affidavit. I know the temper of our mountain people. If prompt redress and compensation are rendered by the War Department, you may count on their gratitude and loyalty. If this request—like so many others I have sent to yourself and to

President Davis—elicits no action, then I can promise that you will receive no more volunteers from Cherokee County. I would also venture to predict that the next squadron of conscription-enforcers which sets foot in that region will be met with gunfire instead of garlands.

"Sign it with the usual flourishy nonsense and make sure somebody stays sober enough tonight to put it on the earliest train. Is there anything else, before we adjourn to greet the new and tender year?"

"Just one more petition, sir, that might give you a smile. It's from a Mister Perkinson in Wilkes County. He declares that there is much sickness in his family, and that his cousin, Ezekial, who is widely famous for his ability to prognosticate the weather and crops, has predicted with the utmost certainty that this spring will be a terrible season for snakes. Mister Perkinson requests a dispensation from the whiskey laws in order that he might make a small run of ten gallons, strictly for use in combating snake bites. If Governor Vance could give permission for this run, he will gladly send the governor a quart."

Zeb threw back his head and guffawed.

"Tell him . . . oh, Lord! . . . tell him that I could not possibly violate my official oath for anything less than a gallon."

1863

Where the Buffaloes Reign

THALIAN THEATRE
Second Night
Friday, January 20th, 1863

BENEFIT
To the
Sick and Distressed Soldiers of Wilmington
The Manager takes pleasure in announcing to the public that
The proceeds of this evening's entertainment will be appropriated
To the above cause. GO TONIGHT AND WITNESS:

MAGO DEL MAGE
The Celebrated Southern Wizard & Magician

FUN, FARCE, FROLIC, AND FOIBLES

MAGIC, MIRTH, AND MYSTERY

Presenting a grand Display of Skill and Dexterity together
With MESMERISM!

Doors open at 6:30 o'clock, Performance to commence
At 7:30 o'clock precisely

—The Wilmington Journal, January 16 1863

This time it was personal. Jack Fairless had shot two men—along with numerous dogs, a mule, and a couple of snakes—during his time with Captain Bone's Buffaloes, but neither one died, which was all right with Jack, because his Bible-whompin' father had smacked the Ten Commandments into his hide. "Ain't but two kinds of manslaughter that God will allow," Pappy had told him. "You can kill a man if he's threatening your house and family, and you can kill a man for vengeance, *if you know for certain he done whatever it was that needs revengin'*. Them kinds of killin' come under the heading of 'an eye for an eye,' boy, and God don't punish a body for doin' them!"

Jack knew to a certainty that this ambush he was part of constituted legitimate and forgiven-in-advance revenge, so he set his mind to it without any reservations. He stroked the sleek, compact shape of his new Spencer carbine. The Spencer was as good as a rifle could be: only thirty-two inches long, it was at least three pounds lighter than a Springfield musket, and it was as reliable as the sunrise—you could drop it into a creek, then bury it in sand, and it would still come up firing. Best of all—indeed it was close to miraculous—the Spencer carbine was a *repeater*. You loaded it by thumbing seven .52-caliber cartridges into the spring-fed magazine tube inside the stock and plunking another round in the chamber: eight shots! To reload, all you had to do was flip open the lever underneath the trigger, then slap it closed again. Jack had practiced until he could fire twenty-one shots a minute, including the reload time, about ten times the rate of a single-shot percussion cap rifle. Yes, by the Lord, a Spencer carbine was a wonder and a marvel.

It was also very rare and quite expensive, but somehow, through his mysterious connections, General Hawkins had managed to acquire three of them, along with a mountain of ammunition. He had, of course, kept one of the Spencers for himself, but he had given the other two to Cyrus Bone, who gave one to Jack. It was a mark of trust and favor that made Jack's heart swell with pride.

This day would mark the first time Jack Fairless had fired his carbine at enemy troops, and he intended to empty as many saddles as he could. The Buffaloes had skirmished with Rebel cavalry on several occasions, but those fights had been desultory—Confederate resources were spread very thin in the eastern counties, and mostly tied down in static defense of the railroads. What cavalry the Rebs did have was second-rate and not given to aggressive actions—they patrolled a way into the woods, sniffing around, but they had neither the strength nor the inclination to mix it up with Captain Bone's irregulars.

Six counties, comprising hundreds of square miles between the Roanoke and Pamlico Rivers, were under complete control of neither side. There were Federal garrisons at "Little" Washington, near the confluence of the Tar and Pamlico Rivers, and at Plymouth and Edenton on Albemarle Sound. Foster's main strength was centered on New Bern, which he had fortified elaborately. Everything else between New Bern and Albemarle Sound was a no-man's-land of pines and scrub oaks and black-water ponds. Even before the war, this region was sparsely populated, but the soil was good and the crops abundant: North Carolina's breadbasket. Robert E. Lee's army needed those Carolina crops badly. Farmers who had stuck it out could sell their wagon loads at any location still in Rebel hands and get top dollar for every commodity. The main task of the Confederate cavalry—even taking precedence over reconnaissance—was to escort and protect those farmers. The main task of Cyrus Bone's Buffaloes was to interrupt that flow of supplies into Virginia, while simultaneously providing Rush Hawkins with information about any threatening Rebel activity within a day's-march of Shelborne's Point.

Those were the Buffaloes' "official" objectives; they were stated in writing, signed by General Hawkins, and initialed by General Foster. Those orders legitimized the irregulars and qualified them for the Federal payroll, uniforms, arms, and mounts. But Hawkins did not much care *how* Bone disrupted the flow of supplies, or what sort of methods his men might employ to gather information from the local citizens. He and Cyrus Bone seemed to understand each other perfectly. Hawkins knew very well that about half of the Buffaloes' horses had been stolen, but he charged them all to Foster anyway, along with a monthly stipend for their upkeep, and soon he received a sack full of money, equivalent to the price of 160 horses together with the cost of feeding them for one year. In the sort of gesture calculated to make brothers out of thieves, he split the money with Bone, who in turn doled out a $10 bonus to each of his men—most of whom promptly spent it on whiskey and whores.

By early 1863, Bone commanded about two hundred men, and more were coming in every week—deserters like Fairless and Bone, who had formed the original cadre when they fled the New Bern battlefield in March of '62—refugees from the Conscription Act, longtime secret Unionists, and runaway slaves. Bone welcomed them all, even the Negroes—which did not sit well with some of the boys, until Bone drummed it into their heads that ex-slaves had a lot of scores to settle and were dependably fierce settling them.

Nobody could strip a secesh farm of anything valuable faster than Cyrus Bone's runaways, and aside from Bone himself, no one in his command was harder or more fearless than the mysterious octaroon Bonaparte Reubens, who had just appeared one day in early December, warmly clad in the skin of a large black bear he claimed to have killed with a knife. When one of Bone's most hot-tempered rednecks called Reubens a "lying black ass-sucker," Reubens struck out, fast as a snake, and broke the man's right arm so bad you could see the splintered bone gleaming white amid the torn and ruined flesh. Nobody ever called Reubens anything but "mister" after that, and he gravitated quite naturally to leadership of all the black men in the unit. They obeyed him without hesitation, admired him hugely for his obvious intelligence and sophistication, and would follow him into Hell if he asked them to.

By the middle of January 1863, the land around Shelborne's Point was pretty well picked clean. Most of the local Unionist men had come into Hawkins's lines, seeking protection or, in the case of the younger fellows, a chance to don the blue uniform. From their information, and from his own extensive reconnaissance, Bone had also identified the smattering of pro-Union farmers who remained on their land, either because they were too old to fear the Rebel conscription agents, or too proud to abandon their homes just because they were close to Rebel-held areas. To these individuals, Bone offered protection—they were valuable sources of information and they were touchingly eager to share their best produce with the Buffaloes. They were also scared to death of what this band of desperadoes might do to them if they fell from favor.

As for the Confederate sympathizers, they were fair game. Their horses and mules were stolen, their crops burned, and their houses looted of everything valuable. You could usually tell when a man was hiding something; frightened and helpless men cast furtive glances toward the places where they'd hidden their valuables. If rough talk and threats did not loosen their tongues, Bone turned over interrogations to Reubens and his fierce-looking ex-slaves. Bone usually went outside while Reubens's ingenious techniques were applied; the screams and pleas never lasted longer than the time it took him to smoke one cigar. Sometimes, though rarely, they encountered armed resistance by someone crazy enough or patriotic enough to go down fighting. These skirmishes always ended quickly. The dead Rebs were left strung up near the smoldering ruins of their homes; the badly wounded ones were marched to a nearby quicksand bog, tied up, and thrown in. One of the Buffaloes' favorite amusements was wagering on how long it took for the victim to vanish completely beneath the viscid gray muck.

Of course, the Buffaloes went after the well-to-do Rebels first; by Christmas, the only Reb farmers who remained were poor as Job's turkey, and Bone's patrols had to go farther and farther west and north to find new places to loot. Fortunately, they had acquired a remarkable if unlikely ally in the person of Dr. Claudius Edgecomb, whose plantation, Edgefield, was undoubtedly the grandest home in all these impoverished counties. Edgefield was situated almost midway between "Little" Washington and Plymouth, so the good doctor was sometimes able to supply the Buffaloes with timely information about Rebel cavalry patrols and about the occasional conscription sweeps made by their infantry. He fed the visiting Buffalo detachments until the men were stuffed, all the time proclaiming his lifelong commitment to the Union, which he had been forced to hide until now. His sympathies did not, however, extend to the realm of abolition, for he owned more slaves than any other planter in Beaufort County and worked them hard. As if to demonstrate his Unionist zeal, Edgecomb loaned Cyrus Bone a dozen field hands and some wagons full of lumber and nails, so the Buffaloes might construct cabins to live in during winter, instead of the threadbare tents they had made do with until now.

Only a few days into the new year, things began subtly to change. Bridges that Bone's men had used freely suddenly sprouted Rebel breastworks, blockhouses, and cannons; the Buffaloes could probably take these positions, one by one, but the casualties would be unacceptably high—so they found new trails and new fords. Still, their freedom of movement was newly restricted, and to Cyrus Bone this indicated that, finally, someone on the Confederate side of no-man's-land was organizing things with a firm hand.

He was right. In the second week of January, two Buffalo patrols were bushwhacked by dismounted Rebel cavalry hiding in the brush—Bone lost three men killed and eight wounded, the heaviest casualties he had ever taken. Other Buffalo detachments ran into whole companies of well-disciplined, well-mounted Rebel cavalry, and in the words of Jack Fairless, whose squad had been chased a good five miles before reaching safety behind Hawkins's breastworks, "Them men don't scare worth a damn! I ain't nary seen the like of 'em in these parts before!"

Cyrus Bone sent out scouts, paid some sniveling informants who would spy for either side in exchange for a dollar, and asked Dr. Edgecomb to poke around and see what he could learn. It turned out that Richmond had sent in a crack regiment of cavalry to reinforce the area's pathetic defenses—mostly to silence the constant nagging and incessant demands of Governor Vance, some said. These riders were all veterans of the big Virginia and Maryland campaigns, men who knew their trade and were not likely to be intimidated by Cyrus Bone's ragtag guerrillas. In overall command, Lee sent Brigadier Obed Gladdings, an impetuous ex-brigade commander who had lost a foot at Sharpsburg. Gladdings had shaken up the whole Confederate defense, sacking some incompetent or drunken officers and promoting better men to fill their places. His strategy was to divide the region into checkerboard squares, anchored by the fortifications he was building near bridges, at road junctions, and athwart the narrow paths that led through otherwise impassable swamps. Each cavalry or infantry probe went into the wilderness knowing that, if they ran into more trouble than they could handle, they could fall back quickly to one of the blockhouses.

By mid-February, Rebel confidence was visibly growing—a number of farmers who had fled the region earlier had come back, believing that Gladdings's horsemen would be their shield. Conversely, morale among the Buffaloes began to fray around the edges. Bone implored Rush Hawkins to launch raids with the well-rested regulars who garrisoned Shelborne's Point, but Hawkins had no intention of doing so. His defenses were too strong for Gladdings to attack, and he did not want to stir up trouble—or attract undue attention—by marching into the wilderness and seeking battle on ground entirely favorable to the enemy.

Despite improved living conditions, most of Bone's men grew surly, and nearly all of them stayed more or less drunk, a condition guaranteed to generate fights and the occasional act of manslaughter. Bone could hold a prodigious amount of liquor without growing a thick tongue or losing his balance, but when he passed a certain level of consumption ("Stage two!" was how Bonaparte Reubens characterized it), became maudlin and, for a man of such hardness and coarse upbringing, bizarrely sentimental. At those times, Bone sought out the company of his only close friend, Jack Fairless. Jack, too, had developed a fondness for the bottle—and when he was drunk, he thanked Cyrus Bone over and over for having given him his first real taste of whiskey—but Jack tended to become more quiet, his broad freckled face and sky-blue eyes tilted in concentration. Cyrus talked, and sometimes sang, and sometimes recited Bible verses; Jack hummed along quietly, and listened with seemingly infinite patience to whatever boastful saga Cyrus wanted to tell, and sometimes, after the whiskey silenced them and the campfire died down and the icy glaze of winter settled over their tent, they slept with their arms around each other and woke to face their respective hangovers with sheepish bad-boy grins. Jack had learned that if he could distract Bone into Stage Two drunkenness, and keep him at that level until he passed out, the night would pass in tranquillity. "Stage Three" was to be avoided whenever possible, for when Bone passed over that line, anything could happen; he might disappear into the woods and howl all night, or he might pick a fight with the first man he came across and try with all his deranged might to kill him, unless the intended target of his savagery out-ran his pursuer or a half-dozen other Buffaloes overpowered Bone and locked him in a storeroom until the fit was over. On the days immediately following a Stage Three drunk, Cyrus was invariably sweet, contrite, and transformed once more into an effective commander of irregular troops.

On one such bitter night—while the Buffaloes' camp sprawled, amid a susurrus of drunken snores, beneath a diamond-white sickle moon, Jack Fairless floated weightless on his heap of sleeping straw, vibrating like a softly struck gong between a pleasant drunken stupor and the heavy black borderline of sleep—Cyrus Bone went into a bardic fugue state, crooning softly, for his tent-mate's enlightenment, a long, elaborate interpretation of the *Iliad*, as filtered through the alcoholic prism of Bone's comprehension, gradually narrowing his narrative focus from duels and challenges down to the code of honor that obtained among the likes of Ajax, Menelaos, Hector, and Achilles—more specifically to that bond of love between great warrior brothers on the field of battle. Jack Fairless listened with half-hearted comprehension, more soothed by the husky cello tones of Cyrus's voice than entertained by the events described.

Jack Fairless could barely scrawl his name and aside from certain drilled-in Bible passages, had never read a book in his life. Pappy would not allow any other book inside the house, and would have wailed the living tar out of any child who tried to sneak in a novel or a magazine. But Jack's granddaddy had read books to his brood, and in spite of himself, Pappy had soaked up countless bedtime stories tinctured with classical references. When the old tyrant had soaked enough moonshine into the granite-veined meat of his Calvinist brain, he sometimes spun out bedtime yarns where Jericho's walls folded into the citadels of Priam's golden Troy, and the shades of Hector, Patroklus, and Agamemnon bubbled around in the same slurry-voiced stew pot with Joshua, Saul, and King David. On this particularly iron-hard night, when Cyrus Bone ruminated about the manly affection that bound such heroes, heart-to-heart, Jack Fairless drifted right along with the music of Cyrus's voice. It was as though the two were on watch in the towers of Jericho, so that even in this cramped and drafty tent beneath the crackling sheaths of ice coating the straight tall pillars of a North Carolina pine-barren, Jack Fairless dreamed himself to be a warrior poet, voyaging deep into wine-consecrated communion with a golden-skinned comrade in a silk-bedizened tent crowned with crested banners. So when Cyrus slowly reached over and began to stroke Jack's long and somnolent manly shaft, Jack's whiskey-chloroformed brain registered the sensation as merely one more element of a dream, and Cyrus Bone's now-huskier voice as the arpeggios of David's harp.

Through these damascene veils of poetic inebriation, Jack Fairless registered neither surprise, anger, nor any sense of violation. Families were large in Spillcorn Creek, and cabins were small. When an overflow of cousins stayed overnight, it was common for two or three adolescent boys to squeeze into the same bed. Nobody's house was so large that even the adults enjoyed much privacy, so by the time Jack Fairless felt the first prickly stirrings of adolescent chemistry, he had heard lots of interesting noises on the far side of paper-thin partitions, and some of those noises clearly signified pleasure-being-had. And while he could not, of course, *ask* any adults about what the sources of such pleasures might be, there were plenty of older boys who were willing to impart this whispered wisdom, sometimes followed by physical demonstrations of cause-and-effect. . . . *Now you lie there nice and quiet, Jack, while I put a little spit or tallow grease on my hand, and I'll show you something really special!* And Jack protested not at all, and soon learned that these hushed, nocturnal gropings, rubbings, strokings, and—eventually, as night follows day—some furtive etudes of mouth-music, triggered a wet spurting sensation that could spin a body off into an exalted all-too-brief spasm of transcendence.

So when Cyrus's comradely snuggles evolved into something more than just a mutual quest for warmth on a freezing night, the incident neither shocked nor angered him—it was just like those three-boys-in-one-bed experiments he had known back in Spillcorn Creek, but with one very crucial difference. Cyrus wasn't just diddling around; he *made love* to his tall, blue-eyed, naive, and very big-dicked mountaineer friend. No question about it: compared to those giggling half-guilty adolescent fumblings, Cyrus's skilled manipulations introduced Jack Fairless to more prolonged sensations of pleasure and far more volcanic culminations.

But when the two officers moved from a tent into a drafty but more spacious log hut, these cold-night communions became more frequent and ritualized, and Jack began to feel that it was wrong of him not to reciprocate at the same level of attention Cyrus displayed for him. By now, Jack had been a soldier for almost a year, and during that time had absorbed a vast amount of at least *theoretical* sexual knowledge, culled from the exploits—real, imagined, or dreamed about—recounted by the other Buffaloes.

Back in Spillcorn Creek, when lads reached courting age—usually around fourteen or fifteen—custom dictated that the tittering, innocent pleasures that came from three or four cousins cavorting in one bed should be relegated to more private venues and conducted with marrying-age females (still cousins, likely as not, but not *close* cousins). These regional mating customs were bounded by unspoken but fierce lines of demarcation, and boys who had previously pleasured each other without a single guilty thought come morning, now blushed at the very memories of all that adolescent groping and slurping.

As Jack Fairless had come to understand things during his months of battlefield service on *both* sides, the same basic repertoire of touches, tonguings, and hand-full-grabbings, were a lot more enjoyable when they involved organs named "pussies" and "titties," instead of the overly familiar inventory of organs shared between himself and Cyrus Bone. Moreover, it had been made abundantly clear to Jack that most of his comrades had a large inventory of derogatory terms reserved for men like Cyrus, who showed no particular interest in such things as "pussies."

Jack Fairless now entered a state of terrible confusion. On the one hand, he did "love" his friend, Cyrus Bone, but he thought it only reasonable to check out what a woman had to offer. His inner confusion would surely have been less if he had amassed some "pussy experience" before joining the Rebel Army, but even among the limited population of available young men in Spillcorn Creek, Jack Fairless was not a stand-out prospect. Not only was he still a virgin when he enlisted, he didn't even know what a "titty" felt like. Even his homeliest cousin, Fanny (to whom he had made a mawkish I'm-going-off-to-war-and-may-never-have-another-chance appeal the night before he left for Asheville), had refused to further his sexual education.

Of course, Cyrus Bone sensed Jack's changing moods, understood the reason for them, and responded to the increased tension by finding numerous little chores to keep Jack busy. Once each week, a courier rode up to the Buffaloes' camp and handed out some passes, courtesy of General Hawkins, to the brothels in Shelborne's Point. Somehow, Jack never got one. Finally, after a few hours of companionable drinking and yarn-swapping, Jack worked up the nerve to ask Cyrus Bone: when do I get my turn with one of them whores?

"I just want to see if pussies-and-titties combined is all they're cracked up to be, Cyrus. If you really are my friend, the way you claim, you owe me the freedom to go to town, so I can spend at least one night with some gal who's well equipped with both and presumably has some expertise in their use."

Cyrus Bone was moving from Stage One to Stage Two, so he put a brotherly hand on Jack's knee and explained that it was not his intent to deny his closest friend the pleasures of venery, but rather to protect Jack from the ravages of syphilis, a hideous disease that, Cyrus assured him, was rampant among the tarts in Shelborne's Point. Bone went on to describe, in stomach-turning terms, both the symptoms and highly unpleasant treatments of various sexual ailments.

Jack Fairless had lost most of his backwoods naïveté by now. He did not even bother to ask Cyrus why, if the whores in Hawkins's fiefdom were so riddled with disease, none of the other Buffaloes had it yet. Cyrus was lecturing him this way, Jack suddenly understood, so he could keep Jack for himself, and maintain that Patroclus-and-Achilles bond, that had originally been the scenario of their intimacy.

Jack was now a very tense and confused young man, and as the Buffaloes' second-in-command, he was expected to keep the troops usefully employed and reasonably disciplined, especially on the days when Cyrus Bone slept late, woke up in a foul temper, and tried to reassert his crumbling authority by ordering men on errands that made no military sense whatever.

Two days after Cyrus had lectured Jack about the horrors of venereal disease and the superior "cleanliness" of man-to-man intimacy, Jack waited until Cyrus Bone had ridden off to Shelborne's Point, then saddled his horse, stuffed three loaded revolvers in his saddle bag, propped a double-ought shotgun over his knees, and rode in the direction of Edgefield Plantation.

He had ridden perhaps a quarter-mile before he was suddenly surrounded by about thirty smiling and well-armed Negro horsemen—Sergeant Reubens's Colored Company. Reubens himself now appeared, dapper as a riverboat gambler in a brocaded vest, glossy knee-high boots, and a big flat-rimmed Panama hat decorated with peacock feathers. He is the strangest nigger I ever witnessed, thought Fairless, but that black cavalry company of his is the smartest-looking bunch of men in the whole outfit. Reubens too, thought Jack, exuded the same gang-leader aura of power that had once made Cyrus Bone so compelling—but whereas Bone's spiritual hold over the men was losing some of its grip, Reubens's aura had grown brighter, to the extent that even some of the white troopers turned to the black sergeant *first*, in a hot fight, rather than to Bone.

"A very good day to you, Lieutenant Fairless," smiled Reubens. "What brings you out in this direction?"

"To be honest, Sergeant Reubens, boredom. Cyrus hasn't sent any patrols in the direction of Edgefield in more than a week."

"My thinking was much along the same lines, Mister Fairless. But my men and I have another destination in mind as well, and you are more than welcome to tag along with us." Jack was puzzled when some of the Negro troopers giggled or made growling noises. Sergeant Reubens silenced them by standing tall in his stirrups and fixing each man with a glance that, Jack Fairless thought admiringly, would knock a squirrel out of a tree.

Jack brought up the rear of the small column, and Reubens soon joined him. Reubens startled Jack by saying: "You do understand, don't you, why he won't give you a pass to the whores?"

Fairless's mouth dropped open and he regarded the dignified, smooth-skinned octaroon with amazement.

"Oh, please, Lieutenant Jack, nobody in this outfit gives a rat's ass what you and Cyrus Bone get up to in the privacy of your hut. But

Bone is going into a funk more and more, and whatever's going on between you, it needs to be settled, because it's starting to get on everybody's nerves. Cyrus Bone doesn't want you to get a taste of really high-quality poontang because he suspects you will definitely prefer it to him. Keeping a fine young fellow like yourself from savoring the pleasures of a good woman's love is tantamount to keeping you under house arrest—cruel and unusual punishment, as it were. I am a man of the world, Jack—I have lived in *Paris!* Cyrus Bone does not 'love' you so much as want to possess you, to mold your body and soul to his twisted will. He senses that he is 'losing' you, and that makes him more desperate, more dangerous, and more of a drunken devil. Now, it is true that you outrank me, so all I can do is make a suggestion, but I think it is long overdue for you to broaden your knowledge of the world of the flesh. How else can you decide whether to continue living with Captain Bone, or move out and find a private hut of your own?"

Abruptly, the column halted, and Jack saw, in a clearing just beyond the path, a tumble-down cluster of buildings that had once been a turpentine factory. Gathered on the porches were at least a half-dozen very comely Negro women, now waving and shouting to Reubens's troopers.

"Just to keep things simple," Reubens explained, leaping from his own horse and helping Jack to dismount from his, "I've set up a separate brothel out here for the black soldiers. The women are all runaways from neighboring counties, all of them here of their own free will and all of them guaranteed to be just as clean and healthy as the tarts General Hawkins imported from the north. And every bit as skilled."

At that moment, a voluptuous, big-eyed girl with café-au-lait skin and a smile so lascivious that Jack Fairless felt his woodpecker grow restless at the mere sight of her, ran up and embraced Bonaparte Reubens.

"Miss Hattie Smalls, may I introduce Lieutenant Jack Fairless, executive officer of the Buffaloes, and a decent young man who has come in search of broader horizons." To Jack, he whispered: "Hattie is my special friend, and a woman whose skills in the arts of love are extraordinary. I can think of no one better suited to initiate you. I shall take a few other troopers and continue our reconnaissance toward Edgefield, leaving about half the men here—the ratio of girls to troopers leaves us no choice but to work these visits in shifts. Well, Jack Fairless, here is your chance: I make you a present of Miss Hattie and four hours of privacy during which the two of you may indulge yourselves as you like."

Jauntily waving his hat, Reubens rode on with one final admonition. "Hattie, this is Jack's first time, so do me a favor and make it special?"

Hattie Smalls, hands on hips, looked Jack Fairless up and down, licked her full lips, and said, "Big, skinny white boy like you, probably got a Johnson as long as a rattlesnake."

Jack was, for a moment, too surprised to reply or even dismount.

"Jack, honey, you gonna get down off that horse and follow me? If Mister Reubens wants you to get 'educated,' we better get to it, cause they's a lot we need to cover in four hours. Or are you some kind of queer?"

"By God," Jack Fairless almost shouted, "I think it's time to find out!"

On the afternoon of February 21, one of Doctor Edgecomb's slaves rode up to a Buffalo outpost and delivered interesting news: General Gladdings was expected for dinner at Edgefield the following evening, accompanied by "a small escort." Here was the perfect chance for Bone to get the drop on his pesky adversary. Tactics were not the Buffaloes' strongest asset; until recently, brute force had been quite sufficient. Nevertheless, Bone did not seek General Hawkins's advice; he wanted to present his commanding officer with a fait accompli that would prove once and for all the military value of his legion. The plan was simple: they would surround the house at twilight, wait until the dinner party was well underway, then storm through all the entrances in a rush, take the guests by surprise, and shoot down every man they found in a gray uniform.

There were three doors into the house, so Bone counted off three parties of about fifty men each, putting Jack Fairless in charge of one and Reubens in charge of another; he would lead the attack on the main entrance and the unmistakable crack of his Spencer would be the signal for a general rush. Their informant was correct—they counted just eleven horses tethered near the house, each with a military saddle. The night was cold and an icy half-moon cast skeletal light across the open ground and winter-barren gardens. Each detachment of Buffaloes crept to within a hundred feet of the columned wraparound porch and settled down to wait, blowing on their hands and priming themselves with gulps of whiskey. Inside, all was revelry and laughter. Finally, about nine o'clock, the visitors migrated to the dining room. Bone gave them another half hour to gorge and drink, then roused his shivering men and led them in a crouched run toward the front door. Fairless and Reubens, observing this move, got their own men in motion.

Cyrus Bone heard his boots clomp loudly up the front steps, leveled his Spencer to shoot out the lock, and fired one shot. After that, everything happened very fast and very badly. No sooner had his first bullet smashed into the door than an unseen hand flung it open in his face and he beheld not an empty hallway, but a rough barricade of furniture and flour barrels and the steady muzzles of at least twenty carbines and revolvers. A hailstorm of bullets swept through the doorway, wounding Bone in the shoulder and sweeping at least four of his men right off the porch, their crumpled forms knocking down a dozen others jammed tightly behind them. At that flame-lit instant, more gun barrels broke through the windows on either side of the door and opened a cross fire. Similar eruptions from the other sides of the house indicated that Fairless's and Reubens's detachments had also received a hot reception. Hysterical with fury and pain, there was nothing Cyrus Bone could do but shout the obvious: "It's a trap! Run for the horses!"

Bullets snapped around his head and kicked up dirt as he ran, zigzagging, toward the nearest cover. He saw a few more men go down, but nobody stopped to help them. It was a panicked rout; he had been outfoxed in an ambush so deadly he actually felt an angry flush of admiration for the Rebel general who had planned it. Stragglers wandered in all night and into the morning, some wounded, most just terrified. When Bone finally tallied up the cost of this misadventure, he discovered that almost one-third of his men were dead, wounded, or missing. He reacted to this dire setback in his usual way, by drinking heavily and raging mighty oaths of vengeance against old Dr. Edgecomb, who had apparently sold them out. But Edgecomb sent an exculpatory message that afternoon, swearing that he, too, had been deceived: General Gladdings and his "small escort" had showed up just as promised, but once inside the house, they had held him prisoner at gunpoint and filled his home with a company of dismounted troopers. Furthermore, Edgecomb protested, his house was severely damaged and two of his slaves had been cut down in the melee.

"Maybe he's lyin' and maybe he ain't. But we'll sure as Jesus find out which, and pay him back in full if he had a hand in this."

When Bone sobered up, he devised a simple plan. The Buffaloes' morale was too shaky now to mount another big operation—and they were not very good at that kind of thing anyhow. But some of them knew this country inside-out, men who had farmed and hunted and fished it all their lives, and could be as stealthy as foxes. So he sent them out to learn the truth. If Dr. Edgecomb were secretly in league with the Rebels, he would have to maintain regular contact with them somehow. Bone's scouts were set up to watch every path leading from Edgefield, around the clock, and anytime anyone left the plantation, or approached it, they were to follow that person and learn where he went and whom he met and talked to. When and if a pattern emerged Bone would decide what to do.

It did not take long for the plan to bear fruit. Twice during the first week Edgecomb rode out alone just after dawn and returned at twilight. The third time, he was followed—all the way to a Rebel strong point on the road from Tarboro to Plymouth. Five miles from his property, he picked up an escort of ten Rebel cavalry, then rode with them to the nearest blockhouse. He was welcomed like a man who was expected, then rode back, again under escort, to a point three miles from home. The doctor, it seemed, was a man of regular habits, for he made these trips, unvaryingly, on Monday and Thursday.

"Now we'll get that old bastard and a bevy of sesesh riders in the bargain!" growled Cyrus Bone, and a look came into his eyes that no man would want to cross.

The night before the planned ambush, while Cyrus Bone and Jack Fairless cleaned and oiled their Spencers, the mood in their hut was akin to the earlier manly comradeship that had been the prelude to their deepening intimacy. Cyrus had passed through Stage One alcoholism before twilight and was trying very hard to slow the progress of Stage Two, for he wanted to be clear-headed and sensitive to Jack's mood tonight.

On the day when the two of them deserted in '62, leaving John Cantwell writhing on the shaft of a shit-encrusted bayonet, Jack Fairless's worshipful admiration had touched Cyrus Bone's dark and knotted soul like a shaft of absolving silver angel-light. When the two friends' "bundling" against the icy cold had gravitated toward physical intimacy, there had been an *innocence* about the process that gave Bone the first glimpse of possible redemption he had felt in many years. And the recent intimations that he might be losing Jack's affection, or at least his unquestioning acceptance of the gift of manly love's uncomplicated pleasures, had placed in Bone's heart a sliver of fear—an emotion that his hard and violent life had purged from his consciousness many years ago.

"Fear" was a thing to be banished, and Stage Two drunkenness helped Cyrus greatly to benumb, or at least redirect, such sensations. Unfortunately for many others who knew him, that banishment was often achieved by transferring fear to someone else in Bone's immediate vicinity. But on this night, while the warrior princes, metaphorically speaking, polished their armor and refined their plans, Cyrus wanted desperately not to conjure fear in Jack's sturdy breast. So he tried to keep the conversation light and witty (there was, he knew, a subsection to Stage Two drinking during which he could in fact be very droll, and each time he made Jack smile or chuckle, Cyrus's spirit felt a budding warmth, as though the meat of his heart had been touched by a dab of camphor).

Near midnight, long after Jack had stopped drinking and Cyrus was struggling mightily to avoid crossing that dark demarcation to Stage Three, their conversation had begun to wind down and Jack was stifling the occasional yawn.

"We really ought to turn in soon, Cyrus," Jack mumbled as he finished wrapping his Spencer in oil cloth, to protect it against tomorrow's expected rain.

"We" ought to turn in, thought Cyrus, grasping at the possible implications of that pronoun. He was encouraged enough to contemplate that a night-before-battle ritual of manly bonding suddenly seemed possible. He turned away briefly from the camp table to refill his glass, the one that might mark the borderland between Stage Two and Stage Three, and when he turned back, he saw Jack Fairless reach into his pack, bring forth a piece of cloth that looked like a woman's handkerchief, and hold it up his nose, inhaling deeply. The stale fragrance of cheap cologne touched the smoky lamplight atmosphere inside the hut with a passing suggestion of feminine grace. After sniffing his lady's token once more, Jack slid it beneath his pillow, then sat up and began tugging off his boots.

"Let that be your last drink, Cyrus. It would really be best if we both got a good night's sleep, so we can give that old Rebel bastard a hot bushwhack in the morning."

Cyrus Bone's jaw clenched when he saw how easily and sweetly Jack Fairless began to drift off. Cyrus mumbled a "good night," lit a cigar, and began methodically to explore the nearest realms of Stage Three, throwing down three full tumblers of rye almost as fast as he could pour them and shuddering as the liquor's warmth fought with the pain and loneliness welling up inside his stomach.

When he came up for air, he sensed that Jack was verging on deep, contented sleep and he probed that slumber by asking, in a rusty-nail growl of a voice: "Was she *that* good, Jack, my lovely boy? Your first *woman!* Wore you out, I'll bet! What's that little token she gave you, Jack? Judging from the smile on your face, I'll bet she soaked it in cunt juice! You know, one of my cousins used to say 'All the soap twixt here and hell, can't wash away that fishy smell!'"

Jack Fairless opened his eyes and rose up on one elbow, squinting at Cyrus with a look of mingled bewilderment and irritation.

"Cyrus, what the hell are you talking about? You're drunk. Stage Three drunk. I don't want you too hungover to spoil your aim tomorrow."

"Never mind *my* aim, Jack-the-mighty-mountain-man. Did you hit *your* target? Hit the right hole? She teach you everything you wanted to learn about fucking?"

Jack wasn't sure which way this was going, but he decided to pretend he was a lot drunker than he was.

"Well, she taught me enough to make me want to learn more," he tittered.

Cyrus's voice took on a harder edge. "Did she give you a better suck than I do, and did she put as much love in it as I do?"

"It was different, Cyrus, that's all. Just different. It was all different, and I liked the differences."

"In that case, maybe I'd best pack my things and leave now."

"Go to sleep, Cyrus! You're too drunk to talk straight, and whether you believe it or not, you are still my close and beloved friend. So: climb in this here bed with me and we'll snuggle up against the cold, just like we used to do. And we'll sleep . . . just sleep."

So now they waited: Bone, Fairless, Reubens, and six of their best marksmen and, with a pair of Spencers to boot, they had enough firepower to fend off fifty men. Their orders were to kill the soldiers first and take the doctor alive; Bone had special plans for him.

That was just fine with Jack Fairless. The ambush at Edgefield had scared him so much he came close to shitting his pants, and when he finally collapsed in his hut behind the safety of Hawkins's artillery, he'd counted no less than four bullet holes in his hat, coat, and trousers. But now, after a wait at the planned site of the ambush, he was cold and wet and his nose was running like a busted pump. The doctor and his escort were late. Wouldn't it be a pisser, he thought, if the old scoundrel had gotten his wind up and decided to stay away permanently. Of course, they could steal his silver and burn down his house, but that wouldn't be enough to satisfy Cyrus Bone.

No, wait! There they came, riding slowly through the misty drizzle, talking quietly, not a suspicion in the world. There were five cavalrymen riding in a row on the doctor's right side, and Jack figured he could drop the first one easy, then work the lever on his Spencer fast enough to pop another two before they knew what hit them. One two three. But he waited, as instructed, until the little column got between two pine trees where the path straightened out and the mud got so deep they had to pick their way carefully, looking down for the sake of their horses' safety.

Cyrus Bone fired first, then the whole party blazed away. It did not take long to empty every saddle but one. Not a shot was fired in return—it was as though a biblical wind had swept the soldiers away. Edgecomb tried to turn his horse around and flee, but the beast was hit in its rump, pinning the mud-spattered doctor beneath its convulsing body. When they dug him out and bound his hands, he said not a word; he knew he was a dead man and he trembled with the fearful knowledge that his death would not be quick or merciful.

Bonaparte Reubens had learned a lot from the Creole culture of the French Antilles, where slavery had been practiced with a degree of cruelty not often found even in the Deep South. One of the things he learned was an interesting method of almost hanging a man as a means of interrogation. In his saddlebag he carried a wooden wedge, six inches at one end tapering to one inch at the other. When you put the noose around the victim's neck, you lifted him on tiptoes and balanced him on the wide end of the wedge. That was certainly uncomfortable and frightening, but unless the fellow got toe cramps, or panicked so badly he fell off the little platform entirely, he could stand that way indefinitely. Every now and then, however, you just took the hammer and rapped it against the narrow end of the wedge, instantly throwing him off balance and making his toehold more precarious. By the fourth or fifth tap, the man's boots were just barely scraping the wood and he began slowly, inexorably, to strangle. You could tell when a twitching man was about to pass into death by carefully monitoring the color of his skin—there was a certain waxy shade of blue that crept into his cheeks and lips just before he lost consciousness for good. In this fashion, the sensation of dying could be repeated again and again, as often as it took to get the desired information, or as long as Cyrus Bone's whim dictated. Or until his heart simply gave out, which is what appeared to happen to Dr. Edgecomb after about an hour of this treatment. At first, Cyrus Bone thought it best just to leave the old bastard dangling as crow food and as a symbol of the Buffaloes' wrath to any other passing Confederates. But on closer examination, Reubens detected a faint fluttering pulse still astir in the old man's corded, rope-sawed hands.

"I'm bored with this," groused Cyrus Bone, "and cold as a well digger's balls, too. Let's just shoot the fucker and leave."

Reubens counseled caution. "May I remind you, Captain Bone, that we've already dallied here for an hour. If the good doctor's escort is overdue, there might already be a bigger cavalry patrol heading this way, and another shot will tell them right where we are. We might not be lucky twice in a row."

"All right, then, sling him over a horse and we'll dump him in China Mash bog on the way back."

Even on the brightest of days, the quicksand bog was a dismal and forlorn place. On a bleak, rainy winter afternoon, it looked positively evil, as though some hideous and squamous creature dwelt just below the mushy, barren surface, ever ready to raise up its tentacles and pull down any man foolish enough to linger on its godforsaken shores.

Before they chucked Edgecomb in, Bone slapped him back to semiconsciousness and forced a big slug of whiskey down his throat, so he would at least be aware of what was happening. But in their haste, they neglected to weight him down with a big rock or a tree stump, so it took a few minutes until his mouth and nose finally went under, leaving only his wide imploring eyes bulging above the jellied surface. Say this for him, thought Jack Fairless, he didn't beg or struggle—he was from these parts and he knew that the more he thrashed about, the faster he'd be sucked under. At the last, Jack even felt a bit of admiration for the old coot: he had played a dangerous game and played it coolly. When found out, he faced his inevitable death without begging, whimpering, or be-shitting himself—the first man Jack had helped to hang who had not done one or all of those things.

But by the time the Buffalo detachment returned to friendly lines, that brief flicker of respect had vanished and all he could think about was how good that first drink was going to feel and how much fun it was going to be to brag about their victory.

Rush Hawkins was building up the fire in what had once been Judge Murdock's library, just at twilight, when an orderly came in and reported the Buffaloes' return.

"Hell, General, you could hear 'em whoopin' and hollerin' a mile away, like Injuns. Apparently, they got the drop on some Rebs and shot 'em to pieces."

"About time they did something of *military* value. Give Captain Bone my compliments and ask him to come here and give me a full report."

Hawkins went back to updating his private reports to Ben Butler and toting up the latest figures in his books. On the whole, things were going very well at Shelborne's Point. The operation had been jeopardized briefly after the trial run involving the *Columbine/Chameleon.* The corrupt and incompetent Captain Miles had become very nervous after a zealous master's mate named Cushing had caught him sabotaging the propulsion plant aboard the USS *Cambridge.* Too flustered and cowardly simply to cut the young man's throat and heave him overboard, Miles had thought Cushing was fatally ill with typhus. When he learned the Cushing had actually made a full recovery—and had later been decorated for bravery *and* promoted—Miles had come to Hawkins, almost blubbering with fear, begging for protection from all manner of imagined Navy Department wrath. Hawkins had sent a discreetly worded telegram to Butler, which resulted in Miles being promptly and permanently transferred to a mortar barge on the Mississippi, where, at last report, he had taken to drink and was in danger of being cashiered out of the service.

Pondering the lessons of that trial run, Hawkins had quickly isolated the flaw in Butler's initial scheme. Sailors on blockade duty were trained to look out for anything "different," and a ghostly ship displaying red lights over green was certainly that. Going on the theory that "least-hidden is best-hidden," Hawkins proposed to Butler that the notion should be propagated throughout the whole navy establishment that *all* mysteriously behaving ships showing that pattern were to be regarded as sailing under unspecified "special orders" and were *not* to be stopped, boarded, or fired upon. With his usual finesse,

Butler had planted the right seeds in the right places and now, apparently, everyone in the Navy Department—probably even Gideon Welles himself—assumed that this was standard procedure governing some top secret operation and paid no more attention to the phenomenon.

Now the whole system was working like a Swiss watch. Four or five times each month, ships bulging with Butler's cotton steamed out of Wilmington, sailed without incident through the inner line of blockade ships, then turned north and entered the North Carolina sounds through Ocracoke, Hatteras, or Oregon Inlet. Once docked at Shelborne's Point, their configurations and color schemes were altered to make them look like ordinary Yankee trading vessels, then they went back out to sea quite openly, flying the Stars and Stripes, and made for the bustling docks of Baltimore, Philadelphia, or New York. There, the cotton was unloaded for overland transportation to the mills and factories that were its ultimate destination. The empty ships were reloaded with ordinary-looking military supplies and sailed back to Hawkins's little shipyard, where they were reconfigured to look the same as they had when departing Wilmington. A certain percentage of those supplies comprised the tainted tinned beef, worthless gunpowder, lice-infested blankets, and dangerously unreliable muskets that were the final part of the plan; once these dubious goods had been paid for by Rebel purchasing agents in Wilmington, they became indistinguishable from all the other material gulped down and disseminated by Richmond's legendarily inefficient quartermaster service. Everyone who was in on the scheme made money; and no one who was not privy to it was the wiser.

Life was good for the garrison of Shelborne's Point too, from Rush Hawkins down to the lowliest private. Ben Butler treated his cohorts to the best. The same vessels that sailed from northern ports with holds full of slop and defective muskets also brought back to Shelborne's Point fresh meat, timely newspapers, mail, troupes of entertainers, and—most recently—a prefabricated bakery that served Hawkins's men with morning loaves hot from the oven. The civilian population—though initially surly due to the violence that attended Hawkins's seizure of the town—had gradually thawed toward the Yankee occupiers. If Hawkins had not yet made Unionists of them, he had been quite strict in regulating his men's behavior. There had been a few cases of theft and molestation, but the guilty soldiers were punished and, more importantly, *were seen* to have been punished.

Shelborne's Point reminded more than a few of Hawkins' young New England lads of their own small-town origins, and the townspeople eventually stopped thinking of these particular Yankees as horned beasts and treated them as what they were—lonesome fellows far from home and generally inclined to decent behavior. Bone's irregulars might raise unholy Hell out in the countryside, but when they came into town they were expected to follow the same orders as the Massachusetts regulars. With so many goods flowing in and out of the little port, and plenty of disposable wages in the soldiers' and sailors' pockets, the local merchants had not suffered the same pinch and penury that afflicted their colleagues on the Rebel side. Only last week, Hawkins learned that a corporal from Boston had become engaged to the eldest daughter of the former postmaster. By God, the Union was starting to repair itself before his very eyes.

In addition to the Sixth Massachusetts Infantry, he commanded first-rate detachments of engineers, artillerists, shipwrights and carpenters, surgeons and veterinarians, and a small private navy consisting of the gunboat *Trenton,* two tugboats mounting 30-pounder Dahlgrens, and a half-dozen floating batteries tethered in places where they could command the Pamlico River branch that was Hawkins's major lifeline to General Foster's headquarters in New Bern. These resources, along with Cyrus Bone's mounted irregulars—still carried on the muster rolls under the formidable name of the First North Carolina Unionist Volunteer Cavalry—made up "Hawkins's Brigade." That *did* have a fine martial ring to it, and would stand him in good stead when he embarked on his intended postwar career in New York politics. Or, with Butler as his patron, maybe *national* politics. The future was bright, either way—almost as bright as the fortune in cash and silverware locked up in the vault beneath what used to be Judge Murdock's parlor.

Most of the men in the garrison had no idea of the dimensions and depth of the plan in which they participated, and most of them would not have cared anyway. All but the most bellicose patriots had been sobered by reports of the ghastly slaughter at Antietam, and any man who requested transfer to a combat zone was sped on his way with Hawkins's warmest blessing. The rest were quite content to serve out their enlistments right where they were.

Hawkins put his feet up on an overstuffed cushion, poured a brandy, and gathered into his lap a stack of letters, newspapers, and reports dropped off by the latest ship from New York. He already knew that Benjamin Butler had been relieved of his New Orleans governorship in mid-December—partly to assuage the Lincolnites who found his high-handed antics an embarrassment, but more to soothe the ruffled fur of the British lion, for Butler had become a raging Anglophobe, publicly accusing the British of siding with the Rebellion and darkly hinting that a secret Royal Navy expedition was preparing to attack New Orleans. It was poppycock, of course—if the English were going to intervene, they would have done so a long time ago—but by being forced to deny the story, the British had given it a kind of credence. Now Hawkins got his first chance to read Uncle Ben's farewell address to the people of New Orleans, and he was vastly amused to see how Butler had used the occasion, one last time, to tweak the lion's tale (while throwing in a shot at the French for good measure):

> *I have not been too harsh! I might have smoked you to death in caverns as were the Covenanters of Scotland by a royal British general, or roasted you like the people of Algiers were roasted by the French; your wives and daughters might have been given over to the ravisher as were the women of Spain in the Peninsular War, and your property turned over for indiscriminate plunder like that of the Chinese when the English captured their capital; you might have been blown from the mouths of cannon, as were the sepoys of Dehli—and yet kept within the rules of 'civilized warfare' as practiced by the most hypcritical capitals of Europe. But I have not done so!*

One segment of the New Orleans population, at least, had been sorry to see him go: the newly freed Negroes. Butler had shown remarkable sensitivity to *their* needs, partly out of conviction, Hawkins suspected, but also because Butler smelled the scent of emancipation on the political winds and wanted to solidify his power among the abolitionists. It was reported that, as Butler prepared to board the ship that was taking him home, a big black woman ran out of the crowd and hugged him to her capacious bosom, saying: "Good-bye, honey! You ain't never stole nothin' from *me!*"

Cold-shouldered in Washington, Butler had gone home to Lowell, Massachusetts, to sulk a while and plan for his professional comeback. But his "retreat" still generated news: ordinary citizens ran up to him on the streets, begging to shake his hand and commend him for showing the Rebels what was what; patriotic groups of every stripe competed for his services as a guest speaker; the Radical Republicans were already beating loud drums to obtain him a field command in the West. In his latest letter to Hawkins, Butler made it clear that absolutely nothing had changed with regard to their private operation. If anything, his liberation from military responsibility had given Butler more time to fine-tune the whole business and a chance to personally shore up the commitment of any of his shadowy backers who might be having second thoughts, now that the war had proven to be both longer and bloodier than anyone had expected. "Do not worry about a thing," Butler had written. "A year ago, there was still a chance that someone in authority would see the necessity of shutting down Wilmington, and at that time, the thing could have been done rather easily. Now, however, the place is much better fortified and its conquest would require the diversion of many more resources than Lincoln's generals are willing to part with. The Rebels themselves have aided us!"

A sentry knocked on the door and Hawkins put his papers aside and bade him enter.

"Captain Bone reporting as ordered, sir."

"Show him in, by all means."

For the first time since his desperadoes had started to encounter serious resistance, Cyrus Bone looked happy. His oddly, almost disturbingly, pretty features showed the accumulated puffiness of too much drink on too many consecutive days, but he had recovered some of his forceful, dark vitality.

"I understand you have good news, Captain?"

"Indeed yes, General. We ambushed a Reb cavalry patrol and wiped it out with no loss to ourselves. And we uncovered positive proof that Doctor Edgecomb was playing a double game, pretending to be a Union man but actually spying for the enemy. He will not trouble us again."

"I thought as much. Well, those are good tidings, sir! I suppose, now, that you and your men will move into his plantation and set up headquarters there."

Bone twisted his fists in frustration.

"Like to, General—it's a mighty comfortable place. But too near the enemy's main encampments. That man Gladdings still has enough troops to give us trouble."

Hawkins smiled and held up a document.

"Not for long, he doesn't. He has been recalled to Virginia, with all his men. It's amazing, but every time the Rebel government gets something serious going down here in North Carolina, they pull back just as it is bearing fruit. I have heard rumors that Mister Davis does not trust our Tarheel neighbors because they were the last to secede. He is happy to soak up all the corn and bacon and supplies he can get from this region, yet he does nothing decisive to make it secure. If Gladdings had been given a good regiment of infantry and a few batteries, he could have laid real siege to us, but as usual, Richmond did a half-assed job of it. By the end of next week, Gladdings and his cavalry will be gone and all their new blockhouses either abandoned or manned by second-rate militia and raw recruits.

"Give your men a few days' rest, Captain Bone, then go out and take over Edgefield as your new headquarters. That will nicely extend the radius of your effectiveness, dampen the recent resurgence in Confederate loyalty among the locals, and still leave you close enough to me for easy communication and supply. I will even loan you a pair of twelve-pounders and two wagons full of ammunition, along with an experienced gunner to train your men in their use. I expect you to be active, and continue, as you have so effectively in the past, to put the fear of God and Abe Lincoln into every secessionist within fifty miles of this place. How does that sound?"

"That sounds mighty good, sir."

"Well, then, it's settled. As long as you're in town tonight, here's a pass for the officers' cathouse. Have some fun on Uncle Sam's tab."

Bone stared at the proffered paper with hesitation and a passing look of unease.

"Well, go on, man, take it! You have earned a little fun."

"Oh, General, whores just ain't for me. Never have been, I guess. But I thank you kindly, all the same."

"Very well, then. Give it to someone. Your man Fairless, perhaps—he's a lusty mountaineer boy."

"All right, sir. I'll take it along." Bone saluted and left the room.

What a strange man, thought Rush Hawkins. Handsome enough to have gotten plenty of women on his own, surely, but for all his temper and actions, there was also something curiously *witheld* about him.

After Cyrus Bone mounted his horse and rode part of the way back to the Buffaloes' camp, he took Hawkins's pass from his pocket, wadded it into a ball, and dropped it into a creek.

Then he rode back into town and hitched his horse in front of the tavern that Hawkins had set aside for the officers of his various commands. Tonight, the place was boisterous indeed, for word of the Buffaloes' victory had spread quickly and a delegation of officers from the Sixth Massachusetts had ridden out to the Buffs' encampment and invited everyone who had planned the ambush to ride into town and celebrate, as guests of the great state of Massachusetts. By the time Bone strode through the doors, the party was in full swing, complete with musicians, whores, a roasted pig sizzling on a spit, and enough liquor to float an ironclad. Lieutenant Stonecipher and the crew of the *Trenton* had upheld the Navy's honor by contributing a keg of rum. So many toasts had already been drunk to commemorate the Buffaloes' exploit that fully half the men involved in the ambush were already *hors de combat* and would have to be transported back to camp in the back of a supply wagon.

As soon as Bone was spotted entering the room, he was given three rousing cheers, and handed a gigantic cup of rum by the *Trenton*'s chief engineer. Rum was not Bone's drink of choice, but today's work had given him a powerful thirst and he dispatched it with such gusto that the naval contingent rewarded him with another "Huzzah!" and a refill. Eyes smarting from the cigar smoke, Bone went around the room several times, shaking hands and clinking glasses with dozens of well-wishers, until he located Jack Fairless in the center of an appreciative crowd, where Jack and Bonaparte Reubens were demonstrating the rope-and-wedge technique the Buffaloes had perfected for interrogating stubborn prisoners.

"The beauty of it," explained Reubens with bloodthirsty relish, "is that you can repeat the process over and over until the poor bugger eventually decides he's had enough and tells you what you want to know. And it has the added advantage of being quite sanitary—no need to get your clothes spattered with someone else's blood, sweat, or bodily excretions."

"Mr. Reubens has a point, gentlemen," interjected Jack, whose big-toothed, shit-eating grin indicated Stage Two inebriation at least. "Nothing worse than having to clean some terrified Rebel's shit off your boots once the day's work has been accomplished!"

By two A.M., the party began to break up, although from the look of things, one or two of the poker games might last until dawn. Cyrus Bone, like Jack and Reubens, stayed in the thick of it until all three men were reeling. General Hawkins sent word that the saloon would be locked down at three—tomorrow was a workday, after all—and dispatched a teamster and a supply wagon to cart off the Buffaloes who were either passed out or obviously incapable of riding a horse back to camp. Cyrus slung his arm around Jack's shoulder and asked if he would prefer to ride in the wagon or accompany Captain Bone on horseback, implying that Cyrus was fully capable of riding back alone, but if Jack didn't *feel up to it* . . .?

Drawing himself fully upright, so that he could actually stare *down* into Cyrus Bone's eyes, Jack responded to the implied challenge by announcing to the room at large that he was not only fully capable of riding a horse all the way back to the encampment, "but I am by God ready to race you there, Cyrus Bone, *and* give you a five-minute head start to boot!"

"Spoken like a trooper!" shouted Lieutenant Stonecipher, who promptly staggered outside and up-chucked into the watering trough.

"All right, then, Jack Fairless, your wager is accepted!" shouted Cyrus Bone, already striding out the door to unhitch his horse. "But no head starts, you redneck braggart! Just a man-to-man race. Mister Stonecipher, if you can gather your wits sufficiently, just count to three, then fire your pistol."

"What's the prize, Cyrus?" shouted Jack, already working up momentum by spurring his horse in circles.

"Ah, well, now, my lovely young Jack, we shall think of something when the time comes!"

Lieutenant Stonecipher pulled himself upright from the watering trough, cocked his revolver, yelled, "Are you ready, gentlemen?" and then contrived somehow to graze himself on the left foot.

Had there been anyone awake or sober enough to witness the end of the race, when Cyrus and Jack collided with one another near the front door of their cabin, that witness would surely have called the contest "a draw." Both men were winded and none too steady on their feet—they got so entangled trying to race up the steps that they both fell to the ground, laughing and flailing at each other. After a few minutes of this tussling, Jack raised up to attention, saluted, and bowed in the direction of the cabin's door.

"Captain Bone, sir, I concede the race. I concede your right to lead this here outfit. I concede that today's victory was accomplished through your cunning tactics. I also concede my affection and loyalty —so, if you please, you may precede me across the threshold."

Cyrus looked deep into Jack's sky-blue eyes and saw no trace of guile or hypocrisy. So what if Jack went off sometimes to get himself a little poontang on the side? Just as long as Cyrus Bone was still first in line for Jack's affections, then all was as God intended.

To prevent unseemly gossip among the rank and file, Cyrus had ordered that every hut occupied by officers and sergeants should have its sleeping space divided by a rope and a sheet, to create at least an illusion of private rooms. Jack Fairless went into his half of the hut and drew the sheet behind him, then wearily divested himself of his sword (*clang!*), his pistol belt (*ka-whup!*) and his mud encrusted boots (*bomp! thunk!*). On the other side of the partition, Cyrus made similar sounds, still chattering at Jack in an easy, bantering, reassuring tone.

"That ambush today served more than one purpose, Jack. Besides making the Buffaloes into temporary heroes, I mean. For one damn thing, it reminded the whole unit about who is in command!"

"Why, you are, Cyrus."

"Goddamned right I am, you hillbilly beanpole! I'm the one who helped you get out of the Rebel army!"

"For which I am eternally grateful, Cyrus."

"And I'm the one who figured out how to make us indispensable to General Hawkins!"

"That's what we are, Cyrus, 'indispensable,' sure as hell."

"And I'm the one who took you under his wing and taught you how to speak like a proper gentleman instead of a dirt farmer."

"That's true, Cyrus, nobody hardly ever laughs at the way I talk."

Jack was still facing his bed, his back to the partition, carefully folding his trousers over a chair back. But when he realized that Cyrus Bone's voice had gotten louder, that Bone was now on Jack's side of the hut, Jack's skin began to prickle. He turned around and gasped, for there was Cyrus Bone standing naked, his coppery flesh glowing in the lamplight, the muscles of his broad shoulders and massive thighs all bunched and rounded and his blunt, massive, blood-sausage of a penis so fully engorged that Jack thought the organ might burst asunder. How beautiful a man he is, thought Jack Fairless, who was as mesmerized as he had ever been by the ferocious commanding blackness of Cyrus Bone's eyes and the irresistible fallen-angel sweetness of his smile.

"What is your intention, Cyrus?"

"My intention, Jack, is to consumate my victory celebration by fucking you until your eyes cross."

"I done told you a hundred times, Cyrus, that you may hold me and kiss me, touch me and even take me into your beautiful mouth, but *I will not bend over for you or any man, for that is a line I will not cross.*"

"As your commanding officer, I am ordering you to cross it. What's the harm, Jack? What scares you so much? Are you afraid that you might actually *like it?* Don't worry none about the pain—you see? I have a fistful of good clean wagon grease."

Jack lunged for his pistol, but Bone threw himself across the room and struck Jack like a tidal wave of flesh, carrying him down to the bed, jabbing the point of a knife against the corded throb of Jack's femoral artery, and slathering axle grease over every anatomical part he could reach. Bending close to Jack's ear, he growled a drunken litany.

"My pretty, unspoiled Jack! What a childish boy you are to think you can allow me certain kinds of intimacy and forbid another. If not for me, Jack Fairless, you'd still be a miserable, hungry, unpaid Rebel private. Or shot dead by a Home Guard patrol because you were too fucking dumb to last five minutes as a deserter. You owe me everything, boy, and that includes your tight little cherry arsehole as well. So take a deep breath, Jack, 'cause I'm gonna bury this up to the hilt."

Jack could feel the trembling hugeness of Cyrus Bone's organ and vowed that he would not give Bone the satisfaction of crying out at the moment of violation.

"Let me say just one thing, Cyrus, before you nail me, something I've been meaning to tell you for a long time now."

"Go ahead, boy, but make it quick."

"You really ought to invest in a good toothbrush, Cyrus, because your breath would knock a buzzard off a shit wagon!"

With a vast shuddering grunt, Cyrus Bone plunged and Jack Fairless, contrary to his vow, buried his face into the pillow and screamed his head off.

"Get in there and inspect the rifling one more time, Corporal."

Corporal Ezekial Jeremiah Prosper-For-Me de Vonell Conver was the shortest, skinniest soldier in the whole Fort Fisher garrison, maybe in the whole Confederate army. Barely as big as a starving ten-year-old waif, Conver was so usefully tiny that he could actually stuff his head and one arm all the way inside the Armstrong's barrel. Using a small lantern, he could see all the way down the rifled tube, and his keen eyes could spot a single sand grain lodged in the rifling. Private Trickey boosted the little man up and supported him as he squirmed into the muzzle.

"Found something, sir!"

"What is it? Rust? Sand?"

"No, Major. I better just show you."

Trickey pulled on Conver's waving, toothpick legs and the tiny corporal squirted back out. He raised his left hand and displayed a small rumpled bird's nest containing a small gray egg. Everyone, including Major Reilly, broke into raucous laughter.

"Better put that in one of the bombproofs, Corporal," said Reilly. "I would hate for the concussion to shatter that egg next time Battery Roland opens fire!" Conver started to leap down from the Armstrong emplacement but was checked by Reilly's next command: "Do it *after* one more loading drill!"

Reilly's crew groaned, as they had already practiced loading for a full hour. Nevertheless, they popped smartly to attention and went through the motions again. It took four men to slide the semicircular, iron-handled loading tray under one of the huge shells and lug the projectile up to the muzzle. The Armstrong had come with a chain-and-tackle rig designed for this purpose, but there was not enough room in the gun pit to deploy it, so Reilly made the crew drill with this secondary apparatus. Things had gone better since he had floored the gun chamber with slabs of local pine, which gave the men much surer footing than the close-packed sand it replaced. The quartet of loaders smoothly conveyed the shell to the muzzle and braced one end of the loading tray on the two L-shaped iron hooks on the sides of the opening. Then, while Reilly counted "One, two, three, *heave!*" they tipped up the seaward end of the tray and the shell began its ponderous slide into the muzzle. They did not let it drop all the way in, for there was no easy or convenient way of getting it back out, without firing it off, as they had learned, with much cursing and hard labor, the first time they had done so.

"Halt. Return the round to storage. Well done—that was two seconds faster than the last time. Gun crew, dismissed."

Reilly watched them go. He had left a free hour for them before the midday mess call, so they could nap or play cards or write letters. Their afternoon duty would consist—as it always did—of moving sand. Colonel Lamb had staggered the garrison's schedule: one half of the gun crews drilled in the morning, while the other half worked on the defenses, and the roles were reversed in the afternoon. Sometimes, just to keep things from settling into numbing routine, Lamb scheduled infantry drills and tactics, for every man in Fort Fisher had to be prepared either to trade cannon fire with Union ships, or pick up a musket and repel a landing. Despite his, and General Whiting's, regular requests to Richmond, the garrison was still woefully understrength; on an average day, there were about five hundred men fit for duty. Vague promises had been made that reinforcements would be dispatched "if the fort is actively threatened," but promises could not fire rifles. If the fort were actively threatened, Reilly doubted there would be time to scrape up anything more than a company or two of recruits from the training camps around Wilmington—hardly a reassuring prospect.

At least now, at the end of February, Fort Fisher had enough guns to match Lamb's heroic concept of what the fort should be. Since July, by ones and twos, pieces of ordnance had trickled in, including some excellent British guns that had been purchased abroad with subscription funds provided by the nouveau riche businessmen of Wilmington. The arrival and mounting of the Armstrong gun had marked a climax of sorts. Frederick Reilly was in overall command of all the sea-face batteries, but the great 150-pounder was his special pride—there was no gun carried by the U.S. Navy that could match it for range and hitting power. Reilly thought it was also the most beautiful artillery piece he had ever seen. It was a colossus and a monument to modern technology. Five thick bands of wrought steel comprised the barrel assembly, starting with a cascabel so massive that he could barely embrace it even with both his arms stretched fully. It rested on a huge carriage of iron-reinforced mahogany, and despite weighing more than eight tons, it could be traversed smoothly by means of two long trailing levers, one on either side of the mount, thick as a schooner's spars. He had selected its crew from the best gunners on the sea face and, like Reilly, each of those men had developed a paternal fondness for the Armstrong. They might grouse about his constant drills, but many a time he had seen them wander up to the gun chamber on their off-duty hours, just to commune with the weapon, to pat it affectionately, or to scrutinize it for the slightest speck of sand or spot of potential rust. The barrel gleamed like bronze, and the mahogany pedestal shone with a patina that would have been more appropriate to a nobleman's dining table than an instrument of war.

And all of them, like Reilly, longed passionately to fire the Armstrong at one of the brightly painted barrels Lamb sometimes ordered to be released a mile or two north of the fort, when the wind and current were right. Every other sea-face battery had practice-fired at these targets, but not the Armstrong. There were only thirty-one shells for the great behemoth, so not a single one could be wasted.

Still, the arrival of the Armstrong gun, the vast amount of labor required to move it from Inlet Wharf to the parapets, and the bright, proud, defiant landmark that resulted when it was finally mounted, provided a welcome diversion for the whole garrison during the bleakest days of winter. In another six or eight weeks, the weather would modulate toward spring, and spirits would rise. But those weeks would be dreary and miserable, and Colonel Lamb—wise beyond his years—had told his officers to be on the lookout for drunkenness, desertion, increased incidents of personal violence, and all other signs, of declining morale.

Perhaps conditions were worse in Lee's Virginia camps—at least the men on Confederate Point never had to deal with snow and seldom with ice—but that consideration was remote, academic, and no comfort at all to the men of Fort Fisher. They were, for better or worse, here, and "here" was bad enough.

Reilly had lost count, sometime in mid-August '62, of the number of days when the temperature boiled close to 100 degrees. Lamb drastically curtailed heavy labor whenever the mercury rose above 90, otherwise the men would have been felled by heatstroke and dehydration. One meager cistern and two wells provided the only drinking water—brackish from the cistern and little better than mud soup from the wells. Despite all sorts of traps and the vigilance of sentries armed with clubs, rats frequented those places and the water rations sometimes bore an unmistakable redolence of wet rodent. Nightfall did not always bring relief, for the same ramparts that made the fort so strong were also high enough to cut off the sweet balm of sea breezes, rendering the interior muggy, breathless, and dense with mosquitoes. Only in the open gun chambers and on the parapets atop the big humpy traverses that separated them could a man feel the sea wind washing over him. There was never a shortage of volunteers for sentry duty on these walls.

All that changed in late November, when winter came upon them, baring its sharp gray teeth. By mid-December, conditions grew so unremittingly harsh as to make some men speak with longing about the suffering they had so royally cursed back in August. Wretched sentries huddled in the lee of the ramparts, shivering like newborn puppies. When the equinox passed, wind and weather patterns changed and there were days when icy blasts seemed always to blow straight into the men's faces, no matter which direction they turned. Nor'easters lashed the Cape Fear with freezing rain for days at a time, soaking the driftwood that was the garrison's main fuel.

But Lamb's men ate better than Lee's—at least those who liked seafood. The gentle art of surf-casting was brought to new heights and unless the weather was truly vile, there were always dozens of off-duty anglers gathered along the beach; on a Sunday, when everyone but the pickets was free to do as they liked, the cooks might have twenty barrels of fresh-caught fish to work with. Oysters abounded in the channel—good ones, too, according to those who savored shellfish. In season, the fort's gardens—located a quarter mile above the land face, on both sides of the Wilmington Road—provided modest but welcome produce. Even better were the occasional delicacies Lamb and Whiting procured from runner captains who appreciated the protection of Fort Fisher's big guns and wished to show their gratitude to the lonely soldiers who manned them. Occasionally, the men were treated to real coffee sweetened with real sugar, bananas and oranges from Bermuda and Nassau, hard candies, bits of cheese, an English tea biscuit or two—small treats, indeed, when spread among the whole garrison, but when the men received them, they became as happy as children on Christmas morning. No doubt about it, thought Reilly, the defenders of Confederate Point enjoyed a livelier and more varied diet than did their comrades in the vaunted Army of Northern Virginia.

Reilly turned his gaze away from the cluster of drafty whitewashed barracks and back toward the beach, throwing one arm over the narrow end of the Armstrong's barrel as though the gun were an old friend. Reilly had spent many long, isolated months as the solitary keeper of Fort Caswell—he minded neither the swelter nor the mosquitoes nearly as much as did men who were not accustomed to the exigencies of coastal conditions. Nor did he mind winter all that much. Perhaps it was his Celtic blood, but there were times when he reveled in the vastness and rigor of these elemental vistas. A rough nor'easter had battered the cape for the past two days, rolling up waves fifteen feet high that boomed like broadsides, unleashing thunderclaps that seemed to herald a devastating event just beyond the lightning-riven horizon. The floor of the Armstrong emplacement, like all the other gun chambers, was well drained, however, and this morning's thin silver sunlight made the pine planks gleam as though freshly varnished. Reilly smelled rain and salt and the scent of metal. Dawn had been a blinding slash of ivory across the moderating swells. As far as he could see up the beach, storm tides had left ruffling fields of brownish foam and a great strew of shells and flotsam—and perhaps, he fancied, the shards of broken pottery from deep Atlantis. Gulls settled like snowdrifts and sandpipers wrote hieroglyphic poems on the band of wet silk where spent waves retreated with the tide. It was a morning fit for solitude and reflection. Reilly ducked under the lee of the ramparts and filled his pipe, then took a notebook from his jacket and began sketching a schematic for a new artillery tactic he had worked out in his head the night before: if six to eight guns fired simultaneously at slightly different angles, but all on the same plane, it ought to be possible to create a "box" of fire around a single enemy ship, increasing the chances of multiple hits, the object being to smite a vessel so decisively, as to force it out of line and thereby reduce . . . whatever the odds might be when the Big Attack, as he now thought of it, actually came. As it surely would, one of these mornings. Colonel Lamb, he thought, would be receptive to the idea. The Young Soldier of the Lord was in fact very young, and his combat experience was scant, but Reilly had never served under a better officer or worked with a more gifted natural engineer; even Chase Whiting, whose expertise in that field was regarded as being on par with that of Lee himself, had so far found no flaw in Lamb's grand design to turn Fort Fisher into the Gibraltar of the South.

A shadow fell over Reilly's notes. He glanced up and saw Private Jonas Pickering, cap in hand, waiting respectfully for his attention. Behind him, also twisting his cap nervously, was Pickering's older brother, a tall, solemn corporal who worked as a loader far off at Shepherd's Battery, the farthest bastion on the land face, covering the plank bridge that carried the Wilmington Road right up to the fort's main entrance. Reilly did not remember the brother's name, although Pickering had introduced him once, back in September. Both men came to attention, now that Reilly had spotted them, and saluted. Reilly tucked away his notebook and returned their salute as he stood.

"Major Reilly, sir, I wonder if we could have a word, sir, about a, well, a private sort of matter. This here's my older brother, Daniel Boone Pickering, from up at Shepherd's Bat'try—you may remember meeting him a time ago."

"I do indeed." Reilly shook hands with the elder Pickering and saw on his face a look of gnawing consternation. Was the fellow ill?

And why was he here, instead of speaking to Captain Sutton, who commanded Shepherd's Battery? "What is it you wished to speak to me about, Pickering?"

Jonas fumbled in his pocket and pulled out a much-folded letter, covered with the insecure handwriting of someone not used to correspondence.

"It's this letter, Major, from D.B.'s wife. He's not much good at readin', so he'd been carryin' it around for a while, till we could get together—which we just did, over to the commissary. D.B. is much agitated by the contents. I should explain, sir, that we are from Randolph County, south of Greensboro, where there is now a large number of deserters, conscription-dodgers, and Unionist outliers, sometimes all three in the same band. There's plenty of forests and hills in the county, sir, and to some of them fellers, it don't matter if you're a Reb or a Unionist—if they gits hungry and you got chickens or hogs or a shed full of corn, they'll just come and take it, and not think twice about gunnin' you down if you oppose them. See, Major, all the fit young men are off in the army now, and there just ain't no law nor justice anywhere."

"I had heard that bushwhackers were a growing problem, but I thought the worst of it was confined to the mountains and to the swamps along the coast above New Bern. I am sorry to learn the Piedmont, too, is now affected. But I still don't understand what you boys want from me."

"Major Reilly, just please read the letter, and try to imagine yourself in D.B.'s shoes when I finally read it to him. His wife, Katy, she writes a good hand and she is a levelheaded woman, not given to 'zagerrations. If she says somethin', you can take those words to church."

Somewhat reluctantly, Reilly took the letter and spread it out on top of the Armstrong's cascabel, the pages crackling in the breeze.

Gov Vance sent two Companys of Regulars down in Jan to restore order and beat the Bushes but they got whipped out pretty quick and return'd to Rawleigh dragging there Tails. Since Conscription Agents started taking off the men 40 years to Fifty there's nobody left to stop these Brigands be they Dodgers or Union Men or just plane Bandits, it don't matter to them just so People here-abouts provide them with Food and Shelter on demand and God help you if you stand up to Them!

Oh if you knew our Condition here you would say may the good Lord deliver us, men have been shot and some Beat so badly that Life Was Despaired of, Barns and Fences Burned and some families taken as Hostages and Prisoners and compeled by threats to help the Outlaws, you know Mister Pressley of Asheboro who is now a Lt. in the Militia, he was Beat so badly his skull was Concussed and last week his house was attacked the Windows Broken and his Wife maimed by rocks thrown and his Barn and Grain burned and his house Plundered of all Valuables.

Daniel you know how Proud I was when you joined up in the Army and I would not have you do anything wrong for the World, but before God Daniel, unless you come home and help us find a Safe place to Move, we may die it is that Simple, for we have little food now and what we do have is like as not to be Stolen. And last night our Son, precious little Eddie, cried out in the Night, "What's the matter?" I asked and he replied "O Mother, I am so hungry!" and our Daughter Lucie, who never complains as you know, but she is getting thinner every Week and some Times she cannot sleep because of her Terror that "the Outlaws" might come. Before God, Daniel, if you do not come Succor us, we may die.

Your loving Katy

Frederick Reilly sighed and put down the letter, fussing with his teary eyes as though sand had blown into them. What right had Richmond to demand so much of its soldiers, if Richmond could not even protect their families from thieves and partisans and ordinary men made desperate because they could not afford to hire substitutes to serve in their place? Sure as sunrise, the *wealthy* Rebel sympathizers in Randolph County did not face such bitter choices as the humble yeomen whose "rights" were supposedly being protected by this war. Reilly knew what was coming next, and he forced his heart to be stern and his voice firm.

"I take it, Daniel, that you wish to have a furlough in order to go home and help your family?"

"Yes sir, me and Jonas here, we just want to go home for a few weeks and see to moving Katy and the children to Greensboro. We have good kin there, who can take them in and see them safely through the war. But without us to help, they cannot close down the farm or find transport, or be protected while they make the trip."

"Why did you come to me, son, instead of your battery commander, Captain Sutton?"

Jonas stepped up and spoke earnestly, man-to-man: "Major Reilly, Captain Sutton is a fiery-minded Confederate and has no family of his own. He would call us cowards and accuse us of dereliction of duty and no argument would sway him. This, you must know already. Besides, sir, you are much closer to Colonel Lamb's ear and, if I may say so, a much kinder-hearted man than Captain Sutton. If you broach the matter to Colonel Lamb, he may react more favorably. All we ask is safe-conduct passes for four or five weeks. You know sir, both D.B. and I will return as soon as we can and serve the fort loyally, yes, and fight here to the death if need be. We have been stationed here almost a year, since before Colonel Lamb took over, and in all that time we have not been absent for a single day."

There was not one thing unreasonable about the brothers' request and if Reilly had possessed the authority, he would have written passes for them on the spot and sent them off with his heartiest wishes. But he did not have such authority and neither did William Lamb; all they had, all that *any* officer had, including General Whiting, was an inflexible chain of command. Reilly could petition Lamb, and Lamb could petition Whiting, and Whiting could act on it or forward the request to the War Department, and weeks would go by before a response, if indeed there ever was one.

"Men, I understand your anguish—this letter is enough to break my heart. But I do not have the authority to grant your furlough. What I can do, I will: I shall show this to Colonel Lamb and he will try to arrange the thing. But I warn you to have patience—in the great scheme of things, the problems of one family may not weigh very heavily on any general's conscience. Above all, and I say this in all frankness, do not even think about deserting, even if you intend to come back. Once you do that, you have crossed a line that cannot be recrossed. Not even General Whiting can help you then. The army's regulations in this matter are neither merciful nor flexible. Do you both understand that?"

They nodded and mumbled their thanks, shaking Reilly's hand. He wanted to give them some assurance, so as they turned to leave he said: "Colonel Lamb will be sympathetic, and General Whiting is a compassionate man. Give it two weeks, boys, because paper moves more slowly in this army than a crippled snail."

Reilly's mood of reverie was now irrevocably gone. He folded Pickering's letter and slipped it inside his notebook, then strode off to find William Lamb.

Tomorrow Is Not a Good Day

ANYTHING TO EAT?—Not much, and we fear there will soon be nothing at all. No carts come in with produce. Nothing is brought to market. Nobody comes in to buy or sell. We are getting to be as bad off as we were during the time of the Yellow Fever.

We are disinclined to grumble at any time, and especially at this time, but really unless something be done we must soon be a starved community, since nobody from the surrounding country, in the direction from which our supplies come, will venture into town with their horses, carts, or wagons, when they have no assurance that they can get out again, nor that they can get any feed for their animals while kept here.

We bow to General Whiting's military knowledge, and have implicit confidence in his zeal and determination to defend the district committed to his charge. We are willing to make every sacrifice and submit to every deprivation that the public defense may render necessary, but we respectfully submit that some modification might be made in the present stringency of granting passports, so as to permit the intercourse between the town and the country to become sufficient to permit the people of the former to get provisions and of the latter to supply themselves with such articles as they usually obtain here.

We are not making complaints. We are merely calling attention to a state of things which does exist, and to which we have been requested to call attention by nearly every person with whom we meet. We trust a remedy can be found for this great public inconvenience, without interrupting the military arrangements made for the public defense.

—The Wilmington Journal, January 23 1863

William Lamb's endorsement of the Pickering brothers' request landed on Chase Whiting's desk exactly one week later, on the last Friday in January 1863, along with the usual morning stack of messages and telegrams. Whiting knew there was nothing inherently unreasonable about the soldiers' desire to look after their loved ones, but he also knew—much better than William Lamb—how little reasonableness had to do with it. When the Davis government passed the first conscription act in American history, in April 1862, it not only sought to provide increased manpower to prosecute a war that was clearly going to be longer and bloodier than anyone had expected, it also forced two years' additional service on the veteran soldiers who had originally enlisted for one year or the duration of the war, back in those ardent, naively romantic days after Fort Sumter. New regulations stipulated that men with two years' active service could apply for a four-week furlough and would eventually get permission to take it. The Pickering brothers were still two months shy of that qualification. Exceptions to this two-year rule were of course made in every command, on the basis of friendship, kinship, favoritism, and sometimes outright bribery, but according to the War Department's rules, those exceptions had to be vetted past the appropriate bureaucrats in Richmond—a process that added a whole new layer of kinships, connections, and favoritism to the already cumbersome procedure.

There were larger issues at stake, too. In the months following his banishment from Virginia, Chase Whiting had laid low and played things very much by the rules. His memoranda to superiors had become models of tact and respect—no more intemperate rants, no more boat rocking. Now that Wilmington was the only significant Rebel port still open on the entire Atlantic Seabord, Richmond was paying it more attention. Whiting's methodical, patient approach had gradually borne fruit. Piece by piece, over the last six months, the big guns had arrived—not yet the full complement, and to be sure, he could always use more, but at least he had obtained enough good ordnance to enable the brilliant Colonel Lamb to flesh out his concept for Fort Fisher. Now, he had to shift his priorities somewhat and begin the same slow chain-of-command process of lobbying for more infantry, more iron for Flag Officer Branch's armored rams, more funds for leasing slave labor from the local nabobs. He was also cultivating a new ally—the brash young governor in Raleigh—and he had to be careful about doing that because rumors and newspaper accounts indicated there was scant goodwill between Zeb Vance and the Davis regime.

Whiting simply could not make exceptions now for the sake of two enlisted men; if he petitioned the War Department on their behalf, that might draw unwelcome attention to him again—*Here's old Whiting, making a fuss over nothing, just like the old times; must be making too many trips to the jug again.* He would play this one by the rules; the Pickering brothers would just have to wait until the second anniversary of that glorious day when they enlisted. Fort Fisher, and all that it protected, was more important than they were.

Then he worked his way through the other documents, initialing some, setting others aside for more thoughtful consideration, losing himself in the boring rhythm of paperwork. He was nearing the bottom of the pile when an adjutant came into the office and held out a new telegram. Whiting read the message slowly, making sure he understood everything it contained, digesting its equal portions of joyful and sorrowful news.

"Shall I forward it on the wire to Fort Fisher, General?"

"No. I think it would be better if I delivered it in person. A telegram can be a very cold instrument, and Colonel Lamb has become my friend as well as a trusted subordinate. Have the boilers lit in the ferry, if you will. Just wire Colonel Lamb to the effect that I've had to move up the date of my visit, and could he please have a horse waiting for me at the Inlet Wharf. And tell him not to interrupt whatever he's doing—I shall find him, and in the meantime, I'll make a leisurely inspection of the works as a whole."

When Chase Whiting arrived at Inlet Wharf, he was met by Captain Oliver Powell, commander of Company E, Thirty-sixth North Carolina, and one of Lamb's most energetic subordinates. Powell saluted and handed Whiting the reigns of one of the fort's few horses.

"Colonel Lamb's compliments, sir. Would you like me to escort you, or would you prefer to ride alone on such a fine morning?"

"I'll ride alone, Captain; don't want to attract too much attention and divert the men from their tasks. Where might I find Colonel Lamb just now?"

Powell grinned. "Hard to say, General. He's been as busy as a duck after a June bug. Last I saw, he was up on the Pulpit with some engineers, discussing the layout for his torpedo field. The galvanic batteries and cables arrived by steamer just yesterday, and the torpedoes themselves are supposed to follow soon. Of course, everything Flag Officer Branch promises has a tendency to arrive late or incomplete, but we shall see. If you do not find Lamb there, he's most likely up at the cottage, fretting about the shingles or the shutters or some other thing. Say, General, is it true that Mrs. Lamb and the children are en route from Yankee Land?"

Whiting mulled over his answer for just a moment. "Yes, according to my information, they have passed through the lines under flag of truce and should be boarding a train in Richmond today or tomorrow. There were some complications, I gather, with Yankee customs—childish harassment of some sort. And one more thing, Captain Powell: in the future, please admonish your comrades not to be so harsh on Flag Officer Branch. He, too, has his problems—trying to forge ironclads without iron, trying to conjure a fleet when there are no suitable ships to be had, and trying to figure out some way to reassert our naval presence on the sounds in the northern part of the state. He does the best he can with a bad situation, and you would do well to remember that he has always assigned the highest priority to finding suitable artillery for this fort, even though he needs it desperately for his own ships."

Powell looked abashed. "No disrespect intended, sir. It's just that, from where we see things, the Confederate navy in Wilmington seems to be nothing but a bunch of self-important drones."

"That will do, sir. Kindly ride up to the Pulpit and tell Colonel Lamb I will be there directly."

Three-quarters of a mile separated Inlet Wharf from the existing terminus of the sea face—low undulating ground dotted with rainwater ponds and scraggles of wiry sea oats, a dismal plain combed this morning by a stiff sea breeze that was chilly but invigorating. Whiting rode slowly toward the ramparts, following a northeast bearing. As he neared the wall, he picked out more and more details and when he passed into the lee of the southernmost work, a pair of 10-inch columbiads known as Battery Hedrick, the whole mood of the landscape suddenly altered. Until then, the plain over which he rode was, like most of the Cape Fear Delta, naked and open. Had a Yankee frigate been riding off New Inlet, Whiting would have appeared as a small dark dot against a bleak gray-white field. A broadside from that hypothetical warship could have raked the entire point and carried easily into the river, shutting down all daylight movement. And while he rode over the ground, Whiting felt exposed and vulnerable. But as soon as he passed into the lee of Battery Hedrick, the chill wind chopped off as though a great blade had swept down; the air became more comfortable; distant sounds of drill and labor became audible, like the reassuring domestic bustle of a great household. Behind those walls, men felt secure. A lookout on the big domed traverse adjacent to Battery Hedrick spotted Whiting and snapped to attention. On impulse, Whiting reined in, dismounted, and climbed the broad wooden steps into the battery's gun chamber, then turned left and climbed a smaller staircase leading to the sentry's position.

"What's your name, son?"

"Private Christopher Bland, from Calabash. What can I do for you, General?"

"I just wanted to enjoy the view a moment. I find that this is the best place to contemplate the whole magnificent sweep of these works."

"Won't be for long, General." Bland pointed south, beyond the columbiads, toward the mile-square wilderness Whiting had just ridden across. "Colonel Lamb is fixin' to build a *mountain* down that-a-way, almost next to the sea and connected to this position by a new parapet. He says that when it's finished, it'll be so high we can lean out and spit on the Yankee gunners' heads. Wants to put a signal post there, too, sir, so the runners can see where their salvation lies, from much farther out than is now the case. Oh, General, it will be a wonder! Like the pyramids of Egypt. From the top of that mound, you would have as good a view as God Himself."

Whiting nodded; Lamb's proposed Mound Battery was one of the items he had come to discuss. That was one of the brightest facets of Lamb's genius: he would never become satisfied that Fort Fisher was *finished*. The works could always be made stronger, more elaborate, more resilient, more ingenious in their detail. Like some dynamic, organic, living thing, Fort Fisher *grew*. With every sandbag, every log, every new crate of ammunition, the fort became incrementally stronger. Whiting turned away from the still-barren site of the proposed mound and let his gaze take in the majestic whole of what Lamb and his highly motivated men had already accomplished. As always when he paused here, the sight stopped his breath.

In the beginning, back in July when Lamb had first shown his sketches to Whiting, the process of transformation had been not unlike a child's connect-the-dots puzzle: the isolated, freestanding batteries had had to be tied together, then reshaped to meet Lamb's requirements, then extended, and extended again, until now Fort Fisher had become the greatest earthen fortress ever reared on the shores of North America. The land face alone stretched north and slightly east for one mile, culminating in the colossal rectangular jut of the Northeast Bastion, thirty-two feet high, crowned with a huge turfed hump that contained shellproof dugouts for its garrison as well as the magazines for its armament—an 8-inch columbiad and an 8-inch Blakely rifle. Between Whiting's position and the Northeast Bastion lay chambers for eighteen more big guns, including the Armstrong, as well as the stoutly fortified telegraph station, Lamb's command-and-observation post in the crescent-shaped Pulpit, and the fort's hospital, which was shielded from shell splinters by high sand walls in front of its entrance. The outer slope of the sea face, from the berm atop the parapet to the beach, was an average of twenty feet high, angled at 45 degrees, and the parapets were at least twenty-five feet thick. Interlocking mats of heavy sod, strengthened by dense tangles of sea-oat roots, stabilized the sand and protected it from wind erosion. Each gun chamber was designed to hold no more than two weapons, and the traverses between them were massive, each one at least thirty feet in diameter, extending out twelve feet from the sea face and twelve feet higher than the unmanned connecting parapets. Besides offering ventilated, relatively comfortable shelter from bombardment and protection for the guns' ammunition stores, the traverses were also, in theory at least, an effective shield against enfilade fire from the sea—a projectile hurled at one gun chamber could not pass on to hit another, no matter what angle it was fired from. If the Yankees wanted to silence Fort Fisher's guns, they would have to overwhelm each battery in turn, and Whiting doubted that the science of naval gun-laying had reached quite that level of sophistication. The navy would simply have to *smother* the whole place with iron, wasting enormous amounts of ammunition in the process, and under those conditions, one well-aimed Rebel shot from the land could do more damage than a dozen massed broadsides from a Yankee flotilla.

From the Northeast Bastion, angling off in hazy distance, sunlight winking here and there from cannon metal, stretched the land face, seven hundred yards in length, terminating at Shepherd's Battery, one hundred feet from the river. It was constructed in the same pattern as the sea face, with the added protection of an eight-foot-high palisade of sharpened logs screening the parapet's base. Midway down its length was a sally port protected by 12-pounder Napoleons, through which the garrison's infantry might pour forth upon a presumably demoralized attacking force. Another sally port, also girded with field artillery, guarded the hundred-foot gap between Shepherd's Battery and the river; it was here that the Wilmington Road debouched into the fort proper. If the fort had a weak spot, it was there, but to *get* there, the enemy's infantry would have to march at right angles to the concentrated fire of the land-face guns, the field artillery, and several hundred muskets firing down on them from twenty feet above, then somehow negotiate their way through a marshy quagmire, over a creek, and around a large stagnant pond. The Wilmington Road crossed these obstacles over a stout wooden bridge that was already mined with combustibles and could be burned to ashes in very short order.

Oh, it was a grand achievement! Chase Whiting had spent his entire career studying the challenges of military engineering, and he had never seen anything to match Fort Fisher. Over the months he had worked with William Lamb, he had made suggestions, from time to time, on how this or that detail might be improved, but he had never found cause to countermand any of Lamb's concepts. Lamb had grasped the problem whole, on the day of his first inspection, and seen, with instincts both pristine and sublime, exactly what had to be done.

But Whiting had dallied long enough; as always, the evolving spectacle had revitalized him, and now it was time to find Lamb and deliver to him, in person, the news he had thought too personal to forward by telegram.

"Thank you, Private Bland, for allowing me to share this splendid view."

"Any time, General, sir. Come back and visit me and the boys when we're doing target practice—I swear, you'll never see finer shootin'!"

What we need most, thought Whiting as he rode north below the dour shadow of the sea face, is another regiment of soldiers as keen as that boy. *If we get them, we can hold this place against the legions of Hell.*

By the time Whiting reached the Pulpit, Lamb had moved on to a corner of the parade ground, where a large canvas tarpaulin had been erected near the flagpole. Beneath it were stacked the storage batteries and control mechanisms for the torpedoes. Lamb was in earnest conclave with his engineers, who had never before seen such apparatuses, much less been trained in their use. There were, of course, no instructions packed in the crates—the devices had been sent straight from the naval ordnance depot in Charlotte, while the warheads they were intended to detonate were still laboriously being hammered together in one of Branch's Wilmington facilities. Whiting thought the batteries, heavy and cumbersome things full of coils and reservoirs intended to hold the chemicals that would generate galvanic current, looked awfully fragile in comparison to the drubbing they would likely sustain under bombardment, not to mention the corrosive effects of salt air, moisture, and drifting sand. But Lamb radiated confidence as he scrutinized the mechanisms and debated with his technicians regarding what went where in order to make the things work. He never raised his voice or spoke harshly, and was as courteous to the lowliest private as he was to visiting generals, but the steady unwavering determination behind his calm blue eyes radiated the kind of authority that made things happen. When he spotted Whiting, he smiled and trotted over, grasping the reins of Whiting's horse and inviting the general to dismount and inspect these curious machines. Whiting declined and instead waved toward the sally port.

"Let's ride out and look at the ground, Colonel; I'm an old soldier and not used to these newfangled inventions. Perhaps you can explain your ideas better without the distraction of my trying to solve scientific riddles."

Lamb seemed a bit confused. He already had explained the torpedo field to Whiting, and was sure the general grasped the idea fully. Then he realized that what Whiting really wanted was a private conversation, so he nodded and sent an orderly to fetch another mount. Ten minutes later, the two men rode out through the sally port and into the desert of low, wind-carved dunes north of the fort. They rode carefully, for the dunes were pocked with sand-crab tunnels that were large enough to trap a horse's hoof.

"There has not been a fairer day since Christmas," said Whiting. "Let's take the advantage of it and ride over to the beach."

They halted on the crest of high dunes where the wind hummed like a bard's harp and they could see the widely spaced burned-out hulks of two beached runners, including the *Florimel.* Lamb waited patiently for Whiting to come to the point, for it was clear that there was one and that Whiting was strangely hesitant about reaching it.

"William, my boy, I came over here this morning to bring you news. Some of it is good, and some . . . dire. I cannot separate the two portions of it, and did not think it appropriate to inform you by means of an impersonal telegram."

"Daisy! My wife . . . " Lamb stammered, losing his composure.

"Is fine. And she will be joining you soon. I am informed that she has crossed the lines safely and will arrive in Wilmington on the Monday morning train. Two of the children, Little Dick and Maria, will be coming with her. I am deeply saddened to tell you, however, that Sallie—of whom I was so inordinately fond—has been taken from you."

Lamb sat rigid in his saddle, his lips drawn tight and the muscles of his jaw working silently, grinding the news like a mouthful of parched corn.

"How and when, General?"

"Scarlet fever. A month or so ago, I gather. In Providence. The infant—what is his name?"

"William, Junior," said Lamb, in a dead gray tone.

"William will stay with Daisy's family in Rhode Island. The doctors thought it best, not knowing what rigors he might have to endure while passing through the lines. Here's the telegram I received this morning, although it gives no more detail than what I have already told you."

Lamb took the message and folded it into his pocket, not even glancing at the words.

"William, I grieve for Sallie, too. She was bright as a sunbeam and filled with the Lord's own goodness of spirit."

Lamb sighed against the wind, shook his head, then turned to Whiting, his eyes full.

"I am grateful, General, for your kindness in bringing this news to me in person. And for your commiseration. I must thank God for his mercy in sending Daisy, and Ria, and Little Dick back to me safely. As for my loss, well . . . Too many fathers have lost too many children already in this terrible fight, and many more yet will lose them before it is finished. If God asks a man to bear harsh burdens, then God gives him the strength to do so. I will not weep for Sallie, because I cannot weep for all the other children who have died, or who have lost their fathers, or brothers. There are not enough tears in that ocean to measure such grief. Now, General, if you will excuse me, I must ride over to the cottage and make sure everything is in readiness for Daisy's arrival. Oh, but we have not discussed the Mound Battery or the torpedo field yet!"

"Those things can wait. For now, you must see to your loved ones and comfort them. I can find my way back on my own."

But Chase Whiting remained, for a time, on the dunes, until

Lamb's receeding figure vanished into the scrub and pine, listening for some kind of message in the steady growl of the surf and the mournful keening of the sand, but hearing none.

Daisy Lamb, with Maria and Richard Lamb in tow, reentered the Confederacy, under flag of truce, south of Fredericksburg. The Yankee customs agents in that town had been rough and ungentlemanly and none of the officers escorting the Lambs had interfered with their behavior or reprimanded them. In itself, this incident alerted Daisy to the altered mood and temper of the conflict. When Norfolk fell, William Lamb's father, and by extension, his daughter-in-law, had been treated with impeccable courtesy by General Wool, the newly appointed military governor of the port; their journey to Rhode Island was smoothly facilitated; good manners were displayed by everyone involved. But now, as Daisy traveled south again to rejoin her husband, she encountered enmity and pettiness all around. Her baggage had been opened and its contents rifled through on a big plank table for all to see. "Whoo-eee, boys, look at these Rebel bloomers!" was one of the lesser insults thrown at her.

So Daisy finally crossed into Rebel territory in a state of white-faced rage, and by the time she and the children entrained for Wilmington, she was worn out from trying to sooth the children's distress. With every mile of track, she felt more and more as though she were entering a land under siege. She had followed the war's progress in the newspapers, but only now did she realize to what extent the vast effusion of blood at Antietam had hardened the hearts of both sides. Somehow, her identity became known and on several occasions during the trip, Confederate officers had approached her, with touching earnestness, to express their admiration for the work the Young Soldier of the Lord had accomplished in strengthening the defenses of Wilmington, and so by the time the train clanked slowly across the Smith's Creek bridge and into the city, she had gained a truer understanding of just how important were her husband's responsibilities. His name was known, and seemingly revered, by many—not because he had won, or even fought, a battle, but because of some hypothetical battle he might one day have to fight.

He was waiting on the platform, standing diffidently beside a large but rickety wagon, attended by three privates and his personal orderly, Captain John Mayo, whose name was familiar to her through the irregular letters she had received. While the children jumped and waved and hollered for their poppa, Daisy studied him closely, expecting to see him profoundly altered by the weight of his duties. But to her immense relief, William Lamb looked no different than he had a year ago: the same slim, erect, reassuring figure she had preserved in memory. He radiated calmness and inner strength, and she longed once more to feel his arms around her and to hear his soft Virginia accent. Most of all, she longed for the intimacy of night, when she could finally share with him the grief she had borne alone since Sallie's frightful, fever-racked, cruelly prolonged death.

Ria and Dick were all over him, bounding from the train and hugging him, vying for his attention, almost pulling him down in their puppy-dog joy. He knelt and embraced them both, kissing each child in turn, his eyes bright. When the children finally turned loose and clambered into the wagon, he rose and held out his hand for Daisy as she negotiated the steps from the passenger car to the platform. Only when they were at last face-to-face, could she see the new and deepening lines on his brow and around his eyes.

And William could see the changes in her as well: the new strands of gray in her raven's-wing hair, the elongation of her oval face, the almost shocking newfound thinness of her bow-shaped mouth—something brittle now in her flesh when she held him, as though her skin had become infused with porcelain, her cheeks not just paper-white but paper-thin as well. Inside her body, he felt coiled springs and ribbons of tension, and knew that, if they were not standing in a public place, she would have burrowed into his shoulder and deluged him with tears. But they were not yet alone; he was a soldier and she a soldier's wife and neither husband nor wife would show their full emotions in this public setting.

On the ride from Wilmington to Confederate Point, they spoke of ordinary things: How was her father in Providence? How was the baby, William Junior? How was the weather? How stood the stars? And Dick was ablaze with martial curiosity: When could he see the big cannons? Would he be allowed to shoot one at a steam frigate? When would the Yankees come? How many soldiers did Poppa command? How brave were they? And most of all: Would they be living in a castle, inside the great walls?

"No, Dick, and believe me, you wouldn't care to live inside the fort. You would not like the food, for one thing, and the big guns would make you deaf."

"So, William, where *will* we live?" chided Daisy. "Not in tents, I hope, because I could never keep the sand out."

He folded his hands around hers. "There are few amenities hereabouts, my dear, but I have made arrangements somewhat better than a tent. We should be there soon—keep watching on the right-hand side of the road."

Ten minutes later, when they reached a point eighteen miles south of Wilmington and about one mile north of the fort, they reached the cottage, and Daisy's face brightened with the best and warmest smile he had seen all morning.

"Oh, William, it's charming! However did you manage to build such a home out here?"

He had managed it through Chase Whiting's generous allocation of carpenters, transport, and funds, and through the willing industry of his soldiers, who had made it their cause to provide a decent place for the "Colonel's Lady" to live, and through the gratitude of runner captains who had much to thank the colonel for. Before escorting her over the threshold, Lamb introduced Daisy to the servants, comprising a trio of trusted and experienced blacks on loan to the Lambs for the duration from the regal Orton Plantation, ten miles northwest of the cottage, on the far shore of the river. They were a family-connected group, lined up by seniority and status to welcome their new mistress with garlands of local flowers, platters of cookies, and a big beaded pitcher of lemonade: Aunt Charity (a stout, tea-colored woman of indeterminate middle age whose credentials, as she proudly recited them, included midwife, laundress, housekeeping dynamo, horticultural expert, and culinary sorceress); Fanny, her seventeen-year-old niece (thin, plain, soft-spoken, a minder of children, seamstress, and all-round helper to Aunt Charity, whose wishes she seemed able to fathom by mental telepathy and whose instructions she carried out with perpetually jumpy, snap-bean energy); and Cassius, Aunt Charity's twelve-year-old nephew (groomsman, blacksmith, woodworker, and self-appointed majordomo who had trained himself, or been trained, to greet every sort of guest with ramrod-straight dignity). Little Dick, with the color-blind enthusiasm of most high-spirited ten-year-olds, immediately spotted Cassius as a potential playmate, and when the Negro boy favored Dick with a disarming bright-toothed smile and said that he could teach "Little Master Dick" how to catch crabs and gig flounder, the bond between the two boys was an accomplished fact, right there on the Cottage porch.

While Captain Mayo and the privates unloaded the baggage, William Lamb escorted Daisy through their new home. Like Fort Fisher, the Cottage had been created from the things God made plentiful along the Cape Fear: doors, walls, paneling, wardrobes, bureaus, washstands, and bedsteads from varnished yellow pine, which gave the interior a sunshine glow even on the bleakest days and seemingly caressed the light of lamps and candles. It was snug, but did not feel particularly "small"—in addition to the storeroom and kitchen, attached to the back porch, there was a fair-sized parlor and the adults' bedroom downstairs, and the children's room upstairs, where they could sleep undisturbed by guests, who would—Lamb told her—be both frequent and numerous, especially if more than one blockade-runner was in port. Each fireplace mantel had been handsomely carved into graceful whorls by a master woodworker who hailed from Goldsboro. Chairs, too, were of pine, backed with cane. Plump hair mattresses, down-filled pillows, and patchwork quilts gave promise of easeful sleep. Inside the storeroom, the runners' largesse had filled the shelves with coffee, sugar, preserves, tinned fruit, sauces, wines, and liqueurs. From the wide veranda on the western side, shaded and protected by a twelve-foot awning, the Lambs could sit in rocking chairs, or read to the children, or simply sprawl in a luxuriously comfortable rope-hammock, while enjoying a sweeping view of the broad eternal river and all the ships that rode upon it. Green umbrellas of pines shaded the sandy yard and a fence of weathered driftwood planks gave privacy from the traffic passing to and from Wilmington.

The children instantly claimed their beds and began placing their toys and dolls experimentally in this corner or that. When they had settled their territorial disputes, they begged to play outdoors, their eyes flickering constantly toward the beckoning river. Lamb gave permission for Cassius to accompany them and show them how to catch crabs in the shallows, a prospect that elicited shrieks of glee. Meanwhile, Daisy was taking the measure of the servants, even as they were taking measure of her, and supervising the unpacking of the few items of silverware she had managed to save from the customhouse rogues in Fredericksburg. She did not want to tell William about that incident, so when he expressed surprise at the small inventory, she quickly replied, "I did not want to encumber myself with too many things, in case we should be forced to leave in a hurry."

Lamb nodded his approval. "That is probably wise, although I do not think the enemy will move against us any time soon."

They planned a quiet dinner, the imposition of domestic routine within the walls of their new refuge, and later, when the children were a-bed, a renewal of marital intimacy. But they both knew that the fact of Sallie's death lay between them and the joy of reunion—a demarcation they must cross together before they could look to the future. But at five o'clock, a delegation of men from the fort, including the chief surgeon, Major Reilly, and a fiddle player, came riding up to pay their respects, and there was nothing for it but to invite them to stay. There was ample food on hand, so the "quiet evening" they had planned turned into a dinner party. Maria and Dick whirled through the rooms, grabbing the attention of one guest after another and dragging them to the back porch to see the scuttling, clacking bucket full of crabs they had netted along the riverbank. Finally, at about nine o'clock, the children ran out of steam and were half-led, half-carried upstairs to their beds. The guests took their leave shortly afterward, and at last William and Daisy Lamb had the Cottage to themselves.

They sat on the parlor sofa, all lamps and candles extinguished, and let their mood be guided by the firelight's flicker and the sigh of wind against the windows. More than a year had passed since they had parted, and enormous changes had been wrought in both their lives; things had happened that must be spoken of, but neither of them could as yet bear the weight such a conversation and their awkward attempts to breach the silence sputtered out. Finally, Daisy just rested her head on his shoulder and when he glanced down, he saw a single tear gleaming on one pale cheek.

"She called for you—a lot—especially near the end, when the fever was consuming her. She thought you were in the room with us . . . "

"Would to God I could have been."

"No, William. You don't need that memory. Remember her as she was on the day you said good-bye, for that must be how she looks in Heaven."

"I haven't spared much thought for Heaven. In the fort, we are preparing, every day, for the appearance of Hell."

"Yes, the fort . . . " She touched his face with fingertips as gentle as a reverie. "You have risen in the world since the last time we spoke. You are famous, you know—I've heard men speak in awe of your achievements here. If the weather is clear tomorrow, you must give me a thorough tour of this 'Rebel Gibraltar.' "

She felt him grow tense, and the tone of his voice changed, with just a hint of command: "Tomorrow is not a good day. Better you should rest here, get better acquainted with the servants, explore the woods with Dick and Ria. No, tomorrow is *not* a good day."

Puzzled by his sudden change of mood, Daisy drew back and searched his face, surprised to see the unexpected hardness in his gaze.

"I thought you told me that one day was pretty much like another."

"Normally, yes, that is true. But tomorrow . . . I have duties to perform that require my full attention."

"Oh, I see—perhaps you're keeping a mistress inside your headquarters." She was teasing, and he seemed relieved and somehow grateful.

"Yes, you have caught me out! Actually, I have about forty mistresses, all made of iron and weighing several tons apiece, and satisfying them keeps me ragged."

So they had touched upon Sallie's death and moved on, and by unspoken agreement they had chosen not to spend these hours as grieving parents but as reunited lovers.

"Well, Young Soldier of the Lord, I am both lighter and warmer than a columbiad, and much more affectionate."

They shared their first serious kiss, and that initial contact was tentative, inhibited, exploratory, a reconnaissance of sorts. Her lips gradually softened as their bodies began to remember old pleasures, and soon they were entwined like ardent young honeymooners. Time dilated around them, and their breathing became urgent. At length, when the fire had almost burned itself out, Daisy untangled herself, brushing fussily at her hair.

"Give me twenty minutes, love, then come and join me. We will properly christen our new bed."

William watched her cross the tiny hallway and vanish into the bedroom, all slender grace, unlimbering her hair as she went so that it flowed in an inky river down to the flair of her waist. He poured a small brandy and settled back to watch the embers sift into ashes. He had not yet spent a night in the Cottage, even though he could have moved in weeks ago, because he wanted them to turn this new page together, to start afresh. Her life here would not be easy, and indeed he had vigorously suggested, in his letters, that she find more commodious quarters in the city, but Daisy had insisted on sharing his post, and for that he was thankful—how sweet it would be to return here after meeting the daily demands of duty. Especially the kind of duty that awaited him in the morning. He drowsed for a time, and was wakened by the tender rustle of her nightdress. She waited for him there at the bedroom door, candle in hand, sensual in her maturity, her still-youthful breasts dimpling the white muslin of her nightdress, dark hair spilling across her shoulders, framing her high and graceful cheeks.

"Come to bed, William," she whispered.

"I will, my dearest, and how I have longed for the moment."

He rose, replaced the brandy decanter, and was following her scent through the hall when someone began pounding on the front door.

"Oh, damn!" he muttered. "Not now, not tonight, please God, not tonight!"

But he straightened his shoulders and marched dutifully to the door. Cold wind smote him as he opened it and he shivered involuntarily. And on the wind came the distant muffled *crump* of cannon fire.

"I'm dreadfully sorry, Colonel, but there's a runner coming in. Your orders are to . . . "

"Yes, yes, my orders are to be notified and now I am. Have Major Reilly deploy the Flying Battery and muster a platoon of infantry—I'll be there directly."

Lamb pulled his overcoat from the clothes rack in the foyer, buckled on his revolver and sword. Then he ducked into the bedroom, hoping to find the right words for Daisy; but she had heard, and understood, and was smiling at him like a benediction, blowing a kiss of farewell.

"I . . . I must go. I can't disobey my own orders, Daisy. You must get used to these interruptions."

"I know. I'll keep the bed warm for you."

When Lamb returned, after tonight's runner had passed safely into New Inlet, he found the bed warm indeed. Daisy waked easily when she felt the mattress yield to his weight, and when she embraced him she smelled salt air and gunpowder and wondered at the fact that she found it rather arousing.

In the morning, she slept late, while the servants thoughtfully fed and entertained the children. The day was scoured and bright, almost springlike, and wonderfully inviting after the gloomy trip from Virginia. After breakfast, she decided to ride across the peninsula to view the fort from the beach. Remembering William's admonition, she resolved not to actually enter the fort, but surely he would not object to a little sight-seeing. She liked the emptiness of the dunes, and was intrigued by the complex shapes of the stunted, wind-sculpted trees; she made note of blackberry bushes and tried to remember her mother's recipe for boiled berry pudding with wine sauce—that would be something her husband hadn't tasted in a long while. As she rode southeast, she noticed areas where the brush had been cut down, and it was at the apex of one such barren wedge that she first beheld Fort Fisher. She had expected battlements, turrets, crenallated walls—instead she saw a sullen, frowning mass of gray sand, curiously undulant where gun chambers alternated with the elephant humps of their traverses; the half-finished palisade looked from her distance like toothpicks stood in a row. Peering more closely, she spotted the hard black reflections of cannons' mouths, like marks of punctuation. She almost laughed; the edifice was so homely and so bereft of any touch of elegance—no Arthurian castle, this, but a monument to pure, brute utility. Yet the Rebel flag added a brave splash of color, and she knew William had contrived his grand design with but one purpose in mind: to stop the enemy's shot and shell, and to keep his warships away from the river.

She wondered if it was dangerous to ride closer. After all, he had instructed her to keep away of the place this morning, but he had not forbidden her to *look* at it. Then she heard the faint rustle of military drums, fading in and out on the breeze, and she saw a small column of armed men marching out of a fortified gate, then executing a right turn and heading toward the beach. Curious, she ducked back into the spotty tree cover and rode parallel to their route, wondering what sort of drill they were about to perform. Perhaps they were practicing to repel a Yankee landing. That would be exciting—although she could not imagine why William would not want her to see such a maneuver. For a few minutes, she lost sight of the marchers, but when she rode carefully up a ridge of sand, a hundred yards from the shore, she saw them again, deploying in what looked like skirmish formation, overlooking the surf. There! There was William, in full dress uniform, standing apart from the double line of riflemen and slightly in front, apparently giving commands. If he looked this way, he would surely see her, but he was not paying attention to anything in her direction, and neither were his soldiers.

Then, a smaller detachment of men, four in all, led forward two unarmed soldiers, one man on either side, like guards. The unarmed men were left standing alone, about fifty paces in front of their comrades, and their arms, strangely, were clasped behind their backs. Not until she saw William, accompanied by a man carrying a Bible, step up to each man in turn and offer them a blindfold—which they refused—did she understand what was happening. She wanted to cry out, but horror kept her frozen in the saddle. It was over quickly, after William read something aloud from a document that kept rattling in the wind. He raised his sword; the men raised their muskets, one rank standing and the other kneeling, and the volley when it came sounded faint and puny and the two bound men jerked briefly on their feet before falling over. The crack of William Lamb's pistol, after he apparently ascertained that a coup de grace was needed, struck Daisy like a slap. Just before he rejoined the column, William looked up and saw her on the dune—she could feel the connection between their eyes, and thought she saw his shoulders slump just for an instant. Then she turned and rode back to the cottage in a state of numb despair.

He intercepted her not far from the Cottage, riding hard and grabbing the reins of her mount, forcing her to a stop. His face was twisted with anguish and some small trace of anger.

"I told you that today was not a good day to visit the fort. Now you understand why. You were not meant to see that, Daisy. There was no need for you to see it."

"Those two men—those poor men! What crime did they commit, to be shot in cold blood by their own comrades? *By their own commander!*"

"They were deserters. Good men who did the wrong thing."

"Couldn't you have thrown them in jail for a while, William? Did you have to kill them?"

A spasm of pain lurched through his eyes.

"As a matter of fact, I did. My orders are explicit and there is reason behind them. Understand, Daisy: I am desperately short of men. And there are dozens of soldiers in my command who also have compelling reasons to go back home and tend to their families. But they do not. They stay here and do their duty. If those two men had been treated leniently, I might lose five more men tomorrow, a dozen by the end of the week. An example had to be made, a line clearly drawn. Those two men understood that when they took their chances, and they died bravely, and will be remembered as brave men, not as cowards."

Her voice was still cold and shaking. "I did not know this part of you, William. I'm not sure I care to know it."

"If I am to command these men, then I must *command!* I would rather face the whole Yankee navy bare-handed than go through another execution, but because I did carry out one today, I probably will not have to order another. It was the hardest thing I have ever done, and I am sick to my soul from doing it.

"Understand me, Daisy: we are not playing soldier, here. Too much is at stake. I did not have the luxury of extending pity to those men. *They* understood that, even if you do not."

He opened his arms, a gesture, almost, of pleading, and suddenly she understood that he carried on his shoulders the weight of every cubic foot of sand in the walls, every ton of iron in the guns, every case of powder that came in with the runners he must protect. A lesser man would have been crushed. A man less honest would have sought refuge behind the stern facades of rank.

"I am the same man I was last night," he finally said. She rode over and held him awkwardly, feeling the tension knotted in his muscles and in the working of his jaw.

"Tell me, did you know their names? Those two men?"

"Daniel and Jason Pickering. I can tell you the names of their wives and children, and where they lived, and how long they have served, to the day. And tonight I will be home late, because I must stay in the fort long enough to draft letters to their kin."

"What will you tell them, William?"

"I will write that they died bravely, in the line of duty, and that they will be missed by their comrades, and by their commanding officer, which is the truth."

"I will keep supper warm. And the next time you tell me to stay away from the fort, I shall follow your orders . . . as faithfully as any of your soldiers."

Shipyard in a Cornfield

SHAD—Well, we have seen shad. We have ate shad, and now we have the pleasure of looking at shad. We have bought shad, and we like to eat shad, but shad is shad now-a-days. That is, they must be shad, if the price is any indication of their being shad. Five dollars for two ordinary-looking female shad, looks a little too much like a disposition to extortion on a person's pockets. That is according to our notion. We really wish the finny tribe would take it into their heads to come up the river a little faster and glut the market and bring down prices to a living rate, then how we would smack our lips, about half-past six o'clock some morning, after a good night's rest. Wouldn't we grow fat—for one day at least!! We think we might afford to be in a good humor all one day. We think we could guarantee that much, if only we could get a pair of shad at a more reasonable price, particularly as it is the season of Lent.

—The Wilmington Journal, February 24 1863

Four months had passed since Branch authorized Sam Parker to begin construction of the CSS *Hatteras* on the upper reaches of the Roanoke River, and during that time their friendship had grown strained. Parker had done little more than mark time in Wilmington, while Branch turned his fitful attention and diminished energies to one hopeless priority after another, focusing one week on trying to find more armor for the ironclad being hammered together in Beery's Shipyard, then trying to cooperate with Chase Whiting to locate more big guns for the Cape Fear district—Branch's paper-war with Richmond was incessant and nerve corroding. Every time Parker confronted Branch and reminded him of his commitment to the Roanoke ram, Branch testily responded that he was doing the best he could and that Parker's impatience was just one more irritant.

But finally, just after Christmas, Parker received formal instructions to proceed to the railroad yard in Weldon, North Carolina, and take command of a "special detachment" that had been assembled for the *Hatteras* project. Once the men and equipment had been gathered, he was to lead them some twenty miles downriver to the "shipyard at Holman's Ferry" and begin construction. "Adequate forces," Branch assured him, had been allocated for the defense of that site against the wide-ranging flotillas of Federal gunboats that were perfectly capable of striking so far inland and seemed likely to try, given the demonstrated belligerence and energy of their commander, Charles Flusser.

When Parker arrived at Weldon, however, on December 28, 1862, a rare snowstorm had blanketed the area to such depth that the crude wagon road to Holman's Ferry was impassable. Parker therefore spent the final days of 1862 getting to know his new command and taking inventory of what was on hand. When he had done so, his reaction was an incredulous silent howl of frustration. *Is this all?* In addition to his second-in-command, the reassuringly named Lieutenant Benjamin P. Loyall, he could count on the services of *one* carpenter (Midshipman James Snell, who hailed from Elizabeth City and whom Parker knew slightly from the days of the Mosquito Fleet), a blacksmith named Mercer Cosgrove (recruited from the railroad shops in Goldsboro), one ordnance technician (Lieutenant Torrence Tredwell, on leave from the navy workshops in Charlotte), and a sixty-man half-company of raw conscripted infantry, along with an elderly battery of 12-pounder Napoleons, which would have been about as effective against Flusser's gunboats as peashooters. Anticipating an outraged telegram from Parker, Branch sent a soothing message to the effect that "additional resources, including suitable artillery and machinery," would arrive "soon," and that Parker should commence work with confidence. As if to underscore his good intentions, Branch also forwarded a document, signed by himself and General Whiting, which conferred upon Parker the authority to purchase goods and services within a hundred-mile radius of Holman's Ferry, and to draw up contracts with any reliable workmen, merchants, or privately owned businesses who might usefully contribute to the project; more important than the document was the strongbox full of cash that accompanied it.

"Things could be worse, sir," observed the cheerful Lieutenant Loyall. "Cash will always generate more enthusiasm than promissory notes from Richmond. And Raleigh's only a day's train ride away—I suspect our best ally in this matter could be Governor Vance. He's a man who likes to get things done, and from what I hear, this armored ram is just the kind of project that would light a fire under him. I would look to Raleigh, sir, much sooner than to Wilmington, never mind Richmond."

"That sounds like good advice, Mister Loyall. As soon as we get things going down at the shipyard, I shall arrange an audience with Vance and take his measure."

"It's more likely that he will take *yours,* Commander. Win him over to our cause, and the ram is halfway built already."

Snowfalls did not last long in eastern North Carolina. By New Year's Day, the landscape was back to its normal red-clay drabness and a quick hard freeze on the night of January 2 rendered the road to Holman's Ferry passable, even for Parker's artillery. His little force clanked and jingled out of Weldon at daybreak, riding parallel to the Roanoke River under an achingly blue sky, past wide fields of withered cornstalks, winter-crumpled tobacco plants, and occasional small farms, whose curious inhabitants came out on their porches and waved—rather halfheartedly, Parker thought—at the unusual sight of wagons and field guns.

Although the straight-line distance to Holman's Ferry, as scaled on Parker's map, was about twenty miles, the river made several deep elbow-bends that added another ten miles to the traveling distance, so they camped for the night in a large tobacco shed. There was lively talk around the campfires, especially from the mostly beardless infantrymen, none of whom had seen action, but all of whom were unalterably convinced that they and their popgun artillery could close the Roanoke River against anything the Yankees sent their way. Sam Parker and the handful of other veterans knew better, of course, but they said nothing to dampen the lads' spirits. If nothing else, his sixty-odd boys could cut and haul a lot of timber, and even a moderately well-equipped inland shipyard would provide enough tools and machinery to build the ironclad's keel—he would worry about finding the necessary iron, engine, and ordnance later on.

As he dozed off, Sam Parker entertained a pleasing vision of hammers rising and falling on mighty timbers, and sparks flying in orange swarms from chiming forges. His months of frustrating inaction were over; he was in command of a vital undertaking, and with the help of God and William Branch, he would construct the very instrument of vengeance he had dreamed about since the day he had watched, in impotent fury, as the Mosquito Fleet was torn to pieces.

There was a crackling frost in the ditches and ponds and bright glaring grins of sunlight on the river when they set out the next morning, and high good spirits among the men. Sam Parker saw a propitious day ahead and he was eager to reach the shipyard and take stock of what he had to work with. An hour's ride brought him to a hand-painted signpost: HOLMAN'S FERRY: 2 MILES. PETER RUFFIN SMITH, PROP. PASSENGERS: 10 CENTS & HORSES A QUARTER. GOODS NEGOTIABLE. Everybody cheered as they marched past. Low hills sloped up from the riverbank, spotted with woods, and after two more miles, Parker rounded a bend and drew his reins so he could pause and survey his new fiefdom. The river here widened to a hundred yards and its current was slow, almost gentle; a good place for a ferry, he reckoned. Some distance ahead, he saw a small dock and a stout wooden trestle festooned with sagging pulley ropes, another matching apparatus on the far side, but no sign of the ferry itself. To the right of the road lay vast empty stretches of cornfield. He saw nothing else except a tiny shed scarcely big enough to shelter the ferry operator. Lieutenant Loyall rode up beside him and gestured toward the barren landscape.

"Well, here is Holman's Ferry, all right. But where did they hide the 'shipyard' part?"

"Damned if I know," muttered Parker. "Maybe there's somebody we can ask."

He waved the men forward and halted them near the shed. Inside he found a plank bench and a rough wooden desk and a mildewed accounting ledger that provided him with the knowledge that the last recorded ferry trip took place on August 8, 1862. Attached to the shed was a toolbox fastened shut with a rusty padlock. Loyall tugged on the device and the whole assembly came off in his hand. Inside was a modest assortment of hammers, saws, crowbars, and a few tins worth of corroded nails, screws, and fasteners. The truth now dawned on Samuel Parker: *This was it!*

"Gentlemen, I do believe that we are looking at the Holman's Ferry shipyard in its entirety."

One could either laugh at the colossal absurdity of it, he thought, or one could howl imprecations at Heaven. Parker chose to laugh. Not only was he expected to create a formidable armored ram out of thin air, but, before he could even begin that Herculean task, he would also have to conjure a working shipyard in the middle of an empty cornfield!

"We must suppose," mused Lieutenant Loyall, "that the term 'shipyard' is some sort of local joke, although the humor of it eludes me at the moment."

Just then, one of the privates lounging by the roadside called out: "Rider coming, Cap'n Parker. Looks like a local boy."

Clearly impressed by this display of Confederate military power, the boy reined in his horse and gawked. Parker dusted some cobwebs from his uniform, smiled broadly, and waved a friendly greeting to the lad. He grinned back at Parker—a wide, sunny, farm-boy face under a haystack of uncombed yellow hair—and saluted with gusto. His name, it turned out, was Charles Smith, and his daddy, Peter Smith, owned the ferry landing and all the woods and fields you could see.

"So, Charles Smith, can you tell me where the so-called shipyard is?"

"Why, sir, that would be the toolshed over yonder, where my daddy used to make repairs on the ferry. Some folks called it a shipyard, speaking in jest, back when the ferry was running regular-like."

"Why doesn't the ferry run anymore?"

The boy shrugged as though any fool could plainly see the reason. "Ain't nobody had call to use it. Farm traffic dried up after the last conscription law got passed—most folks don't have enough goods left over from feedin' theyselves to justify a trip to the market up at Weldon, or downriver at Scotland Neck. Ferry itself got carried away by a flood back near Thanksgiving, and Daddy's so shorthanded now, what with so many of his hands sucked up by the army, he figured it weren't worth the trouble to build and maintain another one."

Charlie Smith seemed impatient relating these old, stale facts, and finally worked up the grit to ask the question that had been roiling his fifteen-year-old brain ever since he saw Parker's little force.

"What is it that brings you here, Captain, sir? With Napoleons, too! Are the Yankees planning to raid Weldon from the river, or what?"

"I don't think they are, Charlie Smith, and I surely do hope they don't. Now, I need to know something about you, honest injun and man to man: Can you keep a military secret?"

His face lit up and he jittered in the saddle, barely able to contain his excitement. "Captain Parker, I am your man for secrets! Yankee bayonets could not prod a word from me—whatever you tell me."

"Spoken like a soldier, lad. Well, as strange as it may sound in view of the landscape which surrounds us, we are here to commence the building of a great and powerful ironclad ram, and when it is built, we intend to sail down that river and sweep the Federal gunboats out of Albemarle Sound. How does that sound to you, Charlie Smith?"

Evidently, it sounded exciting enough to cause the young man to ride around in circles hollering "*Yippee!*" at the top of his cracked adolescent voice. When the lad settled down again Parker asked: "Will your father be as excited as you are? Can he help us?"

"You have come to the right place, sir! My daddy, he's a wizard with machinery and mechanical contrivances. If it's broke, he knows how to fix it, and if it ain't been built yet, he can figure out how to get it started. Ride on up to the house with me, and see for yourself."

"And your mother, Charlie?"

"Oh, she passed back in fifty-nine. Had a tumor the size of a mush-melon. You should have seen it."

Smith's plantation was quite the largest, handsomest building Parker had seen in this part of North Carolina, built of honest red brick, encircled by stout, brightly whitewashed outbuildings and gardens that were productive rather than decorative, including a large patch of scuppernong grapes that suggested, even in their gray winter tangles, the possibility of sweet wine and summer shade. A Negro met them near the hitching posts and bade them welcome with a heartiness that did not seem feigned. This seems a happy place, thought Parker. *I must try to protect this farm as well as my ironclad, for the Yankees will surely pillage it if they come upriver.*

"One thing, Captain Parker," said the boy as he led them up the broad flagstone steps. "My daddy, well, you'll see. He'll be sitting behind his desk, where he conducts his daily business, but he won't be able to rise up to shake your hand, although he certainly would if he could."

"Is he ill, Charlie?"

"No sir; he's in the pink of health—hasn't been sick a day in his life that I can remember. It's just that he lost both his legs, up to the knee, when he charged up Malvern Hill with Governor Vance. But he gits around just fine, even outdoors. See that device over by the well?" Parker followed the boy's pointing finger and saw a strange contraption indeed: a bucket-shaped wicker seat and a steering wheel attached to the front of what appeared to be a threshing-mill steam engine. A pair of servants was shoving pine knots into the small boiler, which hissed and trembled with seeming eagerness.

"You mean to tell me," said Lieutenant Loyall, " that your daddy rides around in that?"

"Yessir!" replied the boy. "He calls it a 'self-propelled prosthetic carriage' and when the war's over, he intends to patent the design and make it available to all veterans, on both sides, who have suffered similar wounds. When he needs to inspect the plantation, we just plunk him down in that seat, strap him in, and off he goes. Hit can reach five or six miles an hour, on level ground, and he says it's 'a damn sight cleaner than a horse.' "

"Well, Mister Loyall, we are in need of a mechanical wizard and it seems we have come to the right place. Let's go meet him and see if we can enlist him in our venture."

Peter Smith was a stout, smiling man of early middle-age, with the shoulders and arms of a blacksmith. Charlie ran into Smith's study to prepare him for his military guests, and Smith chose to greet them by means of a striking demonstration of his vigor and mobility: instead of rolling around the desk in his wicker wheelchair, he leaped down and propelled himself forward with the strength of his forearms and hands alone, even balancing on one arm while he shook hands with a bone-crushing grip. Then, having proven his point, he hopped back into the wheelchair, panting just a bit from the exertion. During the impassioned hour of conversation that ensued, Sam Parker became convinced that they had, indeed, come to the right place. It would take more than the loss of two legs to dampen Peter Smith's secessionist zeal. He might not be able to shoulder a musket anymore, but by God he could help create an ironclad that would smite the invader like an extension of his own brawny fist.

There was no shipyard? Very well, they could build one! His uncle, Ruffin, owned a portable sawmill down in Tarboro—he would send a slave to Weldon this very day, with a telegram requisitioning the apparatus, and Ruffin would probably have it on the morning train. There were not enough infantry or cannon to fortify the river? Very well, they could be procured! His younger brother, Benjamin Smith, commanded a militia company at Scotland Neck, five miles downstream; they weren't doing much except running scout patrols in the direction of Plymouth, and the Yankee garrison there was quiescent, so Benjamin could get by with a couple dozen men—he could send the rest to Holman's Ferry, which would give Parker another hundred soldiers and his own cavalry detachment. As for the cannon, well, sir, Peter Smith's brother-in-law was a clerk in the office of Secretary of War Seddon and *he* could plead their case better than any amount of written memoranda—would a battery of banded, rifled 32-pounders do for a start? Maybe a couple of 6-inch Brooke rifles, too? With properly trained crews and sufficient ammunition, of course. It could be done! It *would be done!* Might as well start looking for suitable timber, too, so when the sawmill arrived, they could get to work immediately. They would not have to look far, no sir! His cousin, Elliott Smith, whose land abutted the line between Edgecomb and Halifax Counties, owned five thousand acres of prime yellow pine and good Anglo-Saxon oak and he had the wagons to haul it.

"What about iron?" asked Peter Smith, near the end of this intense and optimistic discussion.

"*That* will be our major problem, I fear," said Parker. "Even more of a problem than finding the cannon and the engine. There simply isn't enough of it, anywhere in the South. If we can get it, the Tredegar Works in Richmond will roll it into armor plate, but for the time being, all we can do is proceed with construction of the keel and hope the iron will show up. There was a boat full of three-quarter-inch spikes, three tons of them, and a like amount of pig-iron bars, anchored down in Tarboro, set aside for our use . . . but the Yankees raided up there in November and burned and sank it. So we have to start from scratch."

"From the scratchiest part of scratch, as Governor Vance likes to say. Correct me if I'm wrong, Captain Parker, but the raw iron does not have to be of any quality, does it?"

"No, Mister Smith. Any old scrap will do—once it's all mixed together and melted down, it's all the same."

Smith rubbed his grizzled chin and jotted down notes. Then he looked back up and nailed Parker with his fierce, wounded-eagle's gaze. "Well, then, man, hire some divers to go down to the bottom of the Tar and scoop up whatever they can find in the burned-out hulk. The river's not that deep and it should all be in one big moldering pile. Trouble is, you'll have to wait until this summer—river's so damn cold right now, it'll stop your heart."

"Damn my eyes, I should have thought of that! Mister Loyall, draft a message to Flag Officer Branch, requesting the loan of some experienced divers . . . with large buckets. May as well send it now, since it will probably take him months to get around to it."

He turned again toward Smith, this time with an expectant look that said: *You are the man, sir, abbreviated or not!*

"Two more things occur to me, Parker. One is *railroad iron.* The Yankees have torn up all the track between New Bern and Kinston, to prevent us from massing troops close to their base. There is no civilian use for busted-up rails, so all that bent and dismembered track is probably still lying there in Gum Swamp, in the middle of no-man's land. Chances are, we could send patrols in there and just drag it out—the Yankees don't send big units into that godforsaken wilderness any more often than we do. And don't you believe for one minute that Governor Vance doesn't have railroad iron stocked away somewheres! I've heard it said that Richmond wants desperately to extend the line from Greensboro to Richmond, to create a more secure line of supply than the one that runs from Wilmington through Goldsboro. Now the governor, he don't want that new line to be built, 'cause that would take away Richmond's incentive to protect the coastal line. And who constitutes the most powerful and influential lobby in the state legislature? Why, the railroad stockholders, that's who! I suspect that Vance, if you can persuade him of how valuable your ironclad would be for protecting the state, might be inclined to do a little political arm-twisting and choke a few tons of rail iron out of those boys. It's certainly worth a trip to Raleigh to find out where he stands on the matter.

"Additionally, we should examine the proposition that a whole lot of *little* iron can be melted down into *big* iron—it just takes more effort to gather it up, that's all. Gentlemen, this is the middle of the nineteenth century and *everybody*, from the poorest sharecropper to the richest planter, has some kind of scrap iron lying about—nails, horseshoes, worn-out tools, broken muskets, hinges, shit buckets, you name it. Why, hell, we've probably got two hundred pounds of such rubbish right here—all we got to do is scrounge around and find it. Same thing for every farm along the Roanoke and the Tar, not to mention the shops in the towns. Issue a proclamation! Send out agents with wagons! Them that won't give it to the cause outright, well, offer 'em a nickel a pound for their scrap and they'll suddenly remember where it can be found. Make up a cover story, so if the enemy hears of it, they will at least be kept guessing; say it's for the ironclads a-building in Wilmington. It would be a slow process, to be sure, but then, so is building the keel and superstructure. Do you have the authority and the funds to undertake such a program?"

"I do, and the power to requisition outright, from those who will not either give or sell their scrap."

"Excellent. Well, gentlemen, if you would kindly transport me to my steam-powered carriage, we should go down to the river and find a location suitable for laying the keel. I have a place in mind. And by the way, Mister Parker, you and your officers are welcome to make this house your headquarters; there is plenty of room. You can quarter your men in the outbuildings until my workers can throw up some temporary barracks. Let's get to it!"

Parker and Loyall had to walk behind Peter Smith's sputtering, lurching machine, for the racket it made petrified their horses. Smith took them to a grassy meadow that sloped gently to the river's edge—flat enough to provide a stable platform for the immense weight of the vessel, angled enough to facilitate its eventual launch into the water. That very afternoon, riders were dispatched downstream to Scotland Neck and upstream to Weldon. And in the evening, Peter Smith's servants prepared a dinner of ham and fried chicken. Parker's men dug into the food with rapacious gusto, and there was music and dancing and storytelling well into the night. When Sam Parker finally retired, sinking blissfully into the luxury of the four-poster bed where Peter Smith's wife had breathed her last, four years earlier, he felt genuinely content for the first time since the battle at Elizabeth City, thirteen months ago. Mister Smith and his resourceful mind, not to mention his extensive and well-connected family, were a godsend, and the men were fired up with enthusiasm for the project, which had seemed so daunting only a few hours earlier. This thing can be done, he thought as he fluffed up the down-filled pillows and closed his eyes. *This thing can be done!*

Within days of the dispatch of Smith's letters up and downstream, events began to quicken. Sixty men from the Scotland Neck Mounted Rifles, commanded by Benjamin Smith, rode into camp and put themselves under Parker's command for the duration of the project. They were among the better militia units in the region, well armed and mounted, and they had the confidence borne of several skirmishes with General Foster's cavalry based in Plymouth. They even boasted a distinction that, to the best of Parker's knowledge, was unique in military history: the first time mounted cavalry had repelled a naval force. Back in December, they had bushwhacked one of Flusser's gunboats at a place where the river narrowed and was crowned by heavy brush, and where the gunboat's cannon could not be sufficiently elevated to return fire. They had peppered the vessel with so many bullets that its skipper had been forced to throw the engine into reverse and withdraw. Parker liked their spirit.

Parker retained half of them as laborers and guards, then dispatched the rest, along with his two 12-pounders, to fortify a bluff five miles downstream.

Two weeks into February, the first of many barge-loads of pine and oak lumber arrived, cut down and transported by Peter's cousin, Elliott Smith. And during the next few days, the disassembled parts of Ruffin Smith's sawmill came rattling up in wagons, covered with canvas to keep out the late-winter drizzle. By the time the machinery had been knocked together, there was enough timber on hand to begin actual construction.

Parker and Loyall had tried to educate their landlubber craftsmen in the requisite naval terminology that decorated Reilly's set of schematic drawings, but they proved remarkably obtuse when it came to grasping the definitions of, never mind the differences among, carlings, garboard strakes, rabetts and futtocks, although the latter term amused them greatly and gave rise to some ribald figures of speech having nothing to do with marine architecture. Finally, the naval officers gave up lecturing and simply pointed to the various subassemblies and said, "This part fits into *this* part, like so."

The meadow chosen for construction and launching had first to be subjected to a painstaking survey. For a vessel intended to weigh 400 tons, the smallest variations of slope were critical. A few degrees too steep, and its growing weight might create instability; one armor plate too many and the whole thing might slide into the river or break in two from massively uneven stress on the keel; a few degrees too shallow, and gravity itself might betray the project, creating a monolith too ponderous and inert to be moved by any available combination of men and beasts. When Parker finally finished recording all his finicky measurements, he found an ideal oblong of meadow sloped at just the right angle and just barely large enough to contain the *Hatteras*'s completed bulk, which would measure 45 feet in width and 152 feet in length.

After choosing the right ground, Parker and his men had first to build the stocks to hold the keel, and next, the frame members that would form the hull. Every day, the sawmill buzzed like a giant hornet from eight o'clock in the morning until twilight, cutting the rough tree trunks into timbers, which were then measured and trimmed by the carpenters. The frame members measured eight by ten inches, morticed at the joints so they could be bolted to each other on the keel. Boring the bolt-holes proved to be both slow and exhausting, for the wood was green and winter-damp. Yet the joinings had to be done quickly, to minimize warpage when the wood began to dry. Once again, Peter Smith came up with a practical solution: he ordered the removal of the engine from his steam-driven wheelchair and rigged it up to drive a mechanical drill-bit, thus cutting, by about 60 percent, the time required to bore those holes. This act of ingenuity was also, of course, a personal sacrifice, for it greatly reduced Smith's mobility at the same time it destroyed the only prototype of the "steam-propelled amputee chair" that could have brought him wealth and fame after the war. Even so, he managed to get around quite handily, propelled in his conventional wicker wheelchair by relay teams of out-of-breath Negroes.

Where the father could not go, the son was there in his stead. Charlie Smith, whom Parker's men had quickly adopted as a kind of mascot, was a study in perpetual motion, riding or running here and there, carrying messages, fetching tools and nails, bringing pitchers of well water to the thirsty work crews. On the occasion of the boy's sixteenth birthday, March 11, Parker and Loyall, with the unanimous support of their troops, officially swore Charles Smith into Confederate service, bestowing upon him the semiofficial rank of chief courier. Peter Smith had secretly ordered his best seamstress to make a brand-new uniform, which was presented to Charlie along with a gallant red sash, a new pair of boots, and a .36-caliber revolver. The boy inflated with pride during this ceremony, as did his father, even though Parker detected just a hint of sadness and ambiguity when Peter Smith's eyes flicked downward to the blanket that covered his truncated legs.

Throughout March, while the ribs and spine of the *Hatteras* grew until they resembled, from a distance, the colossal skeleton of some great prehistoric beast, Sam Parker and Ben Loyall went forth with small detachments and wagons to scour the countryside for iron. They covered a fifty-mile radius from the shipyard, systematically dividing the map into pie-shaped sectors and posting handbills listing collection points at every suitable crossroads store, post office, and railroad siding. From the more patriotic citizens came buckets and hampers full of pitted, rust-flaking oddments; from the more mercenary citizens, they purchased scrap for 5 cents a pound. But by April, the aggregate amount thus collected was only a ton and a half. Their attempts to locate and drag out the torn-up rails between Tarboro and the outer defenses of New Bern yielded very disappointing results; General Foster had by now heard plenty of rumors about ironclads a-building on the interior rivers and had dispatched his own patrols to find the rails and drag them into the nearest bog, where they sank beyond any hope of reclamation. One result of all this to-ing and froing was that Samuel Parker became known, throughout that part of North Carolina, as the Iron-Monger Captain. Parker did not know whether to be pleased or chagrined.

By the time the corn in Peter Smith's fields was starting to turn feathery and verdant, it was clear to Parker that something more drastic had to be done in order to secure the amount of iron required to finish the ship. Telegrams flew between Weldon and Wilmington, and Branch's dithering, excuse-laden messages promised iron in abundance, from a puzzling array of possible sources, but so far, not one pound of it had materialized.

"Whatever he's laid hands on, he's hoarding for his own ironclad," said Parker, after reading one-too-many evasive replies.

"You can hardly blame him," mused Peter Smith. "Iron is worth more than gold these days, and the blockade-runners can only bring in a drop in the bucket. I believe it is high time you paid a visit to Zeb Vance. If there is any stockpile of railroad iron in the whole state, he will know where it is and who controls it. Explain to him just how powerful a weapon the *Hatteras* will be—how much it will deter Yankee aggression in eastern North Carolina, by virtue of its mere existence, and he may find a way to shake some of that iron loose. There is no greedier or more tightfisted kind of businessman than a railroad magnate, and I have heard Zeb Vance say as much, more than once. I shall write him a letter this very night—if a veteran of the Twenty-sixth Regiment solicits an audience with the governor, the governor will grant one. Of that, I am certain."

Throughout most of 1862, the North Atlantic Blockading Squadron was tasked with sealing off the coast from the mouth of the Piankatank River, in southeastern Virginia, down to the South Carolina border. On paper, it comprised a total of forty-eight ships, not all of them ideally suited for the job, at least six of which were off the line on any given day due to repairs, refueling, and resupply. Admiral Goldsborough, who had little stomach for the job to begin with, became ever more crotchety and hard to deal with as he neared the age of compulsory retirement. Gideon Welles yanked him off the job with unseemly haste, only days after the old sailor's birthday, and replaced him, on September 4, with Admiral Samuel Phillips Lee, a Virginian who was, in fact, distantly related to Robert E. Lee, but who had remained steadfastly loyal to the Union. This Lee had spent almost his entire life at sea, beginning with his Midshipman's cruise aboard the legendary USS *Hornet* in 1827. He had served with distinction in the New Orleans campaign and during several other, early, Federal naval actions. More to the point, Samuel Phillips Lee had spent eight years working for the Coastal Survey program—no other officer in the U.S. Navy knew the Atlantic shoreline as intimately as he. Shortly after being promoted to head the blockade squadron, he had received a personal letter from Gideon Welles that read, in part: "I am thankful that I have lived to see the day when old age, rank, and imbecility are no longer the sole qualifications for senior command. Go after the blockade-runners like a parcel of cats keeping watch on a mouse-hole . . . "

Lee took command with a mandate to make the blockade *work*. He reenergized the squadron almost immediately and began to implement fresh ideas. He demanded, and soon began to receive, more and newer ships, but he did not wait for them—he had studied the blockading system long before he rose to command it, and he regarded it as being damnably slack and haphazard. He insisted that all ships keep up steam at all times, so they would be ready to give chase the instant a runner hove into view. He shifted the picket lines closer to shore—as close as the surf and bottom conditions permitted—then implemented an intense series of drills designed to improve ship-to-ship communications and lessen the chances of collision at night.

The Cape Fear estuary posed the greatest problem for Lee, as it had for his predecessor. Old Inlet and New Inlet were only six miles apart on the map, but the big, irregular bulk of Bald Head Island and the deadly, extended elbow of Frying Pan Shoals made the actual traveling distance between the two inlets more than fifty miles—a four- or five-hour voyage for most of his ships. Wilmington, then, presented Lee with not one, but two distinct fronts, one of which was dominated by the firepower of Fort Fisher's big guns and the range of its pestiferous little Whitworths. After a detailed personal inspection, Lee requested and got an enormous amount of information from his former colleagues in the Coastal Survey bureau: charts, hydrographic data, tide tables, weather records, anything that might help the blockaders in their work.

Lee was methodical. First, he closed off the peripheral inlets at Shalotte and Topsail, neither of which had been continuously picketed before. Then, he refined his tactics with regard to the two Wilmington inlets. Closest to shore, he stationed his oldest, slowest, least seaworthy vessels; they were incapable of a high-speed chase, but they could deliver massive broadsides and their high masts enabled them to signal the course and speed of outward-bound runners to the faster, newer picket ships stationed farther out in two concentric rings. A day's steaming to the east, athwart the Bermuda and Nassau routes, he placed his biggest and fastest cruisers, ships that could remain on-station for months at a time and whose lookouts stood at least a theoretically good chance of spying a runner in broad daylight, either coming or going. Finally, to sharpen the skills of his crews, Lee doubled the number and frequency of drills: gunnery, signaling, small-boat handling, amphibious landings, boarding tactics, and damage control. The men did not complain—any sort of activity was a reprieve from the sodden boredom that was their usual lot.

Back in October 1862, at Charles Flusser's insistence, Will Cushing had been given his first independent command: a gunboat named the USS *Foxglove*. She was an iron-hulled steamer of one hundred tons' displacement whose shallow draft made her well suited for inland waters. On the foredeck, she mounted a big hulking 6.4-inch Parrott rifle, which could fire either an 80-pound solid shot or a 100-pound shell, and on the stern she carried a 24-pounder naval howitzer. Of the twenty-eight crewmen, all but six were older than Will Cushing, and his second-in-command, Lieutenant James K. Valentine, was an old salt nearly twice Cushing's age. Despite his remarkable youth, Cushing's reputation for boldness had preceded him, and his crew believed that Cushing's arrival guaranteed the prospect of action.

In February 1863, they got the chance for it. The *Foxglove* was temporarily detached from Charles Flusser's gunboat flotillas in the sounds. Admiral Lee wanted a "vigorous officer" to secure the waters around Topsail Island, as part of his new tighten-the-screws strategy, and Flusser could think of no one better suited for "vigorous" duty than his friend Cushing. Cushing, of course, jumped at the chance, hungry as always for action. The *Foxglove* arrived at Topsail Inlet in mid-February, and the very name of the place excited him: it was said that Blackbeard frequently hid *The Queen Anne's Revenge* in the channel behind the island, which was so flat that his lookouts could spot the topsails of potential victims and then dash out to capture them.

But the area was barren of targets. Day after boring day, Cushing scoured the region in vain. Periodically, just for the hell of it, he sailed down to Masonboro Sound and lobbed a few shells into the big saltworks located there. But, at best, his bombardments constituted a minor nuisance; as his executive officer, Lieutenant Valentine, observed, "There's not a lot of damage you can do to a big pile of salt, even with a hundred-pound Parrott shell."

There were few inhabitants in the Topsail area, but Cushing took pains to visit them and treat them with courtesy—sometimes sending a surgeon to tend for their sick and injured—on the theory that at least some of them might secretly be Unionists and could become valuable sources of information. This investment in diplomacy finally paid off during the second week of March, just before Cushing was scheduled to return to Flusser's command in Pamlico Sound. The *Foxglove* was anchored just west of the northern end of Topsail Island and Cushing was contemplating a quick dash up the New River to check out any Rebel activity in the little village of Jacksonville. He had been wanting to do that—Jacksonville was the only local hamlet he had not visited—but he was deterred by the fearsome reputation of a dangerous sandbar known as the Rocks. Not even Cushing was imprudent enough to risk a valuable gunboat that deep in Rebel territory without the guidance of a good pilot who knew the river well. On March 14, fate provided him with just the man.

He was an old coastal pilot named Jason Pedrick, whose skin had turned to brown leather under fifty years of summer suns and whose eyes blazed like tiny ebony beads from deep inside corrugated wrinkles. His hands were clawed from arthritis and he had more fingers than teeth. He appeared from a glaze of sunset-golden water, materializing like a specter, at the oars of a weather-beaten whaler, and as Cushing watched him approach, he remarked on how calm the man looked and how steadily his corded old muscles worked the oars. He came to a stop right beneath the gunboat's bridge, solemnly packed and lit a stubby clay pipe, then introduced himself, requesting permission to come aboard.

Pedrick had retired from piloting just before the war began, and then had started, with the help of his three sons, a modestly profitable tobacco farm in the rich loamy soil near Jacksonville. He had once been "as Southern as the next man," he recalled, but his loyalties had not been deep and circumstances had altered them. One by one, conscription had swept up his sons, making it first difficult, then impossible, for him to keep the farm going. One of his boys died at Antietam, another at Second Bull Run, and the third son, after learning how desperate his father's economic condition had become, tried to desert, got as far as Petersburg before being captured, and was now languishing in Castle Thunder prison in Richmond. He might well have been shot, had not General Lee himself commuted the sentence after learning about the family's other sacrifices. The last straw was the day in October when Confederate tax agents came on his land and confiscated half of what little curing tobacco he had, compensating him with a promissory note that was worth more as "an ass-wiper" than a financial document. Pedrick had had enough. From everything he could see, the Confederacy was oppressing him far more than the distant Federal government ever had. He wanted the damned war to be over, so he could get back his only surviving son, and he was prepared to do his little bit to hurry the process along.

Did Mister Pedrick know how to navigate a boat this size through the Rocks? Yes, by God, he did; better'n any pilot left in Jacksonville, of which, admittedly, there were few, given the lucrative employment opportunities down in Wilmington. The *Foxglove* was wider than ideal, but its flat bottom and shallow draft made the passage possible.

And what was there up in Jacksonville to justify the risk, asked Cushing? Oh, several things, adumbrated the old pilot: two schooners filled with naval stores, for one, just waiting for the next moonless night to make a quick dash down to Wilmington, not to mention the mail depot, where much interesting correspondence might be read, including a lot of letters to and from various Rebel outposts in the region. And a big new warehouse where the Confederate tax collectors stored and guarded all the crops and valuables they had squeezed out of the regional populace.

What kind of resistance might be expected? Not one hell of a lot, Pedrick avowed. Some militia companies scattered around. The gunboat could be in and out before they had time to assemble. There were some earthworks around the village, but they were not manned and mounted no artillery.

Cushing ordered food and drink for his serendipitous guest, then motioned for Valentine to follow him back to the fantail, where they could speak privately.

"Can we trust him, sir?"

"If his story is true, we can. But then, if it's false, we might not learn that until we're in serious trouble. The thing is, Mister Valentine, we have cruised these waters for weeks and seen no sign of Rebel forces, not even a scouting party. The other thing is that we have absolutely nothing to show for our time here, *nothing*. If we have the chance now to achieve even a small victory, I think we should seize it."

Valentine smiled and patted Cushing on the shoulder. "I have seen that look before, sir. You are burning for action. Well, so am I and so are the men. Somebody should pay for all our recent boredom."

Cushing ducked his head and sheepishly grinned, looking less like a naval officer at that moment than a schoolboy scheming mischief. If the Rebels in Jacksonville had pigtails, he would dunk them in an inkwell.

"All right, we'll do it by stages. If Pedrick is as good a pilot as he claims, we will know that soon enough. And if he gets us safely through the Rocks, then we can extend him a greater dose of trust. And if we reach the town and see two schooners docked there, as he claims, then he passes all the tests. But just in case, I want you stationed at his side all the way there, with your revolver clearly visible. If he is honest, he won't mind that obvious precaution. If he is deceiving us, his manner will likely betray him when he first sees that pistol. At the first sign of trouble, let him hear you cock that hammer. And if I order it, shoot him."

Next morning, they hoisted anchor at dawn and poked the gunboat's bow into the turbid brown confluence of the New River Inlet, as cautiously as a surgeon's probe venturing into unexplored flesh. Today, Cushing reflected, was the Ides of March, and one could take that as a propitious coincidence or as a warning. Both the big Parrott rifle on the bow and the howitzer aft were manned and loaded; muskets and cutlasses were propped within easy reach. Mister Pedrick quickly proved himself to be a skillful pilot indeed—smoothly conning the ship around half-submerged logs, sandbars, and occasional large rocks—and he accepted the proximity of Lieutenant Valentine's revolver with a phlegmatic nonchalance that reassured the others standing in the wheelhouse. The Rocks proved to be somewhat less fearsome than their name, comprising mostly a jumble of shallows and pebble-covered sandbars spotted with a few boulders. At high tide, in daylight, they were easily passable if one knew the twists of the deeper channels. Pedrick rang for dead slow when they approached this stretch, however, and everyone tensed while he threaded the needle, figuring that if they were going to be ambushed, this was surely the place for it. But the tangled woods on either bank remained peaceful as they passed and when Pedrick rang on "one-third revolutions," everyone began to relax. The *Foxglove* cruised into Jacksonville about midday, and there, as promised, were the two schooners, tied up at the town's modest docks.

Thunderstruck at the gunboat's sudden appearance, the townspeople assembled to witness the event with mouths agape. Cushing swept the surroundings alertly with his glasses and saw some rudimentary earthworks, just as Pedrick had described them—but no cannon, no gray uniforms in sight, nothing but the Confederate flag drooping listlessly from the courthouse. Lieutenant Valentine disembarked a well-armed landing party, accepted the town's surrender from its elderly and flustered mayor, then traded one flag for another, while the sailors on the gunboat shouted their huzzahs. A few stands of small arms were located in the courthouse basement and promptly dumped into the river. All the mail in the post office was seized and taken aboard for whatever intelligence it might contain. Both schooners were indeed loaded with tar and turpentine, to the value, Cushing estimated, of $30,000 each. They would make nice prizes when towed back to New Bern, and the gunboat's crew would get a tidy cut from their value, once the paperwork had been done. Pedrick stated that there should be no problem pulling them back down the river, as long as they crossed the Rocks while the tide was still high. There was one flare up of excitement when some of Valentine's shore party descried two previously hidden men in Confederate gray hightailing it out of town on horseback, forcing Cushing to cut short his brief but satisfying occupation. After little more than an hour, the gunboat weighed anchor and chugged away, its two prizes wallowing behind like a pair of leashed dogs.

Two hours downstream, however, they were fired on from the western bank by a small detachment of mounted men. The carbine volley caused no damage and no one was wounded, but Cushing was forced to halt and swivel the Parrott rifle in reply. A few charges of canister chewed up the foliage and drove the bushwackers off with dispatch, but Cushing now had to assume that the alarm was being raised all over Onslow County. Whatever odds and ends of Rebel troops there were in the vicinity would surely be converging on some other ambush site downstream. Time had been lost, the element of surprise squandered. Darkness fell, with near-tropical suddenness, while the gunboat and her two charges were still a mile above the Rocks.

"Well, Mister Pedrick, can we make it over?"

"I'm sorry to say it, sir, but there's not a pilot alive who would try that at night. I earnestly beseech you to believe that I had nothing to do with that skirmish—how could I? I was with you all the time."

In the fading light, the old man looked so pitiable, chewing nervously on the stem of his pipe, that Cushing could not help but believe him. He slapped Pedrick on the shoulder and tried to cheer him up.

"No one could have done a better job today than you have, sir. If we must wait for daylight and high water, then so be it. If they try to board us tonight, they will meet with a hot reception. Now, sir, consider yourself relieved of duty. Go below and get some rest. I will see to it that you receive a generous dole of rum—you've earned it."

Pedrick's relief was palpable. Before he left the wheelhouse, he drew close to Cushing's face and said, with fierce sincerity, "Commander Cushing, I swear before God that I will get us safely out of here tomorrow morning or die trying!"

"God willing, no one will have to die, but I thank you for your promise. When we get back to New Bern, you'll find all the piloting work you could desire, and be paid for it handsomely."

No one slept much that night. Both cannons were manned and muskets distributed to every man. Cushing forbade any illumination—anyone desiring a smoke had to take his pleasure belowdecks, behind blacked-out portholes. There was no moon, and a sharp frost keened the air. Every sound was magnified in significance and jumpy sentries heard Rebel infiltrators rustling in the bushes, but no shots were fired. Cushing kept watch on the bridge, a Colt on the chart table, a cutlass propped against the wheel, and a double-barreled shotgun on the floor beside his feet. Until midnight, he strained eyes and ears for any sign of the enemy, but the effort caused his eyes to swim with fuzzy lamps of fatigue and, eventually, his head drooped and he began to snore softly. Valentine shook him awake at three A.M. and pointed out some dim reddish lights in the distant woods: campfires. An hour later, they heard muffled metallic sounds that signified some kind of military accoutrements in motion and they exchanged worried glances. The sounds might be coming from horses, or men, or field artillery. If the Rebels had managed to scrounge up even a single Napoleon, they would be firing from so close, and at such a big immobilized target, that they would surely score some hits before the *Foxglove*'s gunners could even spot their location.

Well before dawn, every man aboard was alert and taking aim at the hostile shore. Mister Pedrick was at the helm, and the tide, he assured them, was favorable. As soon as daylight permitted, he would take them through the Rocks and on to safety. The pilot vowed once more, "My life is forfeit if I fail you, Commander Cushing."

The first mile of the voyage passed without incident. Whoever these Rebels were, they were as well led as they were determined: they did not fire until the *Foxglove* had actually begun to negotiate the Rocks. They had managed during the night to deploy a pair of 6-pounders behind some thrown-up earthworks. Dismounted cavalry and some infantry, amounting to at least forty men, followed the guns' first salvo with a blistering fire from rifles and carbines. Fore and aft, the gunboat's cannons returned fire steadily, momentarily suppressing the enemy's fire in one place or another. But to Cushing, the effect was not unlike throwing buckets of water on a brushfire—you might douse the flames in one spot, but as soon as you took aim at another, the fires leaped up again. A whirlwind of waterspouts surrounded the *Foxglove* as it twisted and jerked and sideslipped and spurted briefly forward in cumbersome lurches, yanking the two schooners roughly in its wake. At one point, about halfway through the shallows, one of the schooners veered so close to the hostile bank that two bold Confederates suddenly leaped from cover and began chucking tar-covered torches at the boat. Cushing's sharpshooters cut both of them down, but not before their incendiaries did their work. The turpentine cargo detonated in a stinking oily cloud of flames, whole barrels of the stuff blowing skyward like rockets. Cushing ordered the towrope cut and the gunboat gained a knot of speed as it shed the weight and drag of the now-blazing schooner.

Jason Pedrick never took his eyes off the river. He ran this gauntlet of fire with iron nerves and icy judgment, even when shattered glass blew across his head and minié balls gouged fat ragged holes in the woodwork. Gritting his teeth against his pipe stem, sweat rivering down his adobe-colored cheeks, knuckles white on the wheel spokes, he *piloted,* like no one else Cushing had ever seen. Yard by boiling, lead-lashed yard, hull plates ringing like handbells and superstructure shredding, the gunboat kept grinding forward. Distance and widening angles finally masked the fire of the enemy's cannon. Clear and blessedly calm water loomed ahead—they were almost through. The volume of rifle fire diminished, no great damage had been done to the ship, no one had been injured except by splinters—and they still had one valuable prize in tow. Cheers soared up from raw throats.

"By God, I got you through!" cried Pedrick, just before one solitary and very patient sniper fired the last shot of the engagement. Cushing turned to congratulate the faithful pilot, just in time to see a perfectly round, silver-dollar-sized hole open on the side of Pedrick's neck. The old man shook his head in disbelief, spitting out his pipe and raising his right hand as though to confirm the wound. Jugular blood jetted between his fingers and drenched Cushing like scalding tar.

"Well, Commander Cushing, it appears that I am killed. Up to you now. Watch out for them big sandbars two or three miles above the inlet. Steer to the . . . "

"*Left or right?*" shouted Cushing to a man already beyond hearing. As Pedrick toppled to the left, the loosened wheel spun to the right, so Cushing lunged for the helm before anything else, just in time to avoid running hard aground. By the time he got the gunboat back on course, Pedrick's blood had flooded the wheelhouse floor to the depth of at least one inch. It sloshed suckingly around Cushing's feet while freshly shed, but turned into a greasy, sticky pudding as it solidified. He ordered Pedrick's body to be wrapped in canvas and placed under cover on the port side, vowing to God and crewmen that he would arrange a sailor's burial, with full honors, as soon as they rejoined the fleet. Buckets of river water sluiced most of the blood into the scuppers, where it drained away into the river in a long, sad, rusty cloud.

It had taken two hours to make the contested passage of the Rocks, plenty of time for additional Rebel troops to set up another ambush downstream. But numerous creeks, brisk and deep from seasonal runoff, cut through the western bank and should hinder pursuit, unless, of course, the enemy had thrown up some bridges, in which case they might well be able to redeploy more artillery. A few of those creeks, moreover, were broad and deep enough to carry small boats, so the gunboat's crew remained alert for the possibility of a boarding attack.

Despite the continued danger, Cushing maintained a slow speed. Now that *he* was piloting instead of the experienced Pedrick, he was uncharacteristically cautious. He remembered some of Pedrick's maneuvers, but had difficulty keeping in mind the fact that he was traveling downstream now and would have to reverse the order of Pedrick's decisions. Fatigue warred with adrenaline in Cushing's blood, but he forced himself to appear calm and steady. When three o'clock passed with no further sign of Rebel action, Cushing started to relax. Only three or four miles to go now, before he saw the wide safe waters of Topsail Sound.

But wait! Pedrick's last words . . . a big patch of sandbars coming up soon . . . Cushing tried to remember how they had gotten past this obstacle on the original voyage, but that now seemed as remote in time as some Elizabethan exploit. Left or right, God damn it! *Which?* Now he could see how the river was shallowing under the bow. No time left for dithering. The winter sun was already low, gilding the waters with dazzling slices of deceptive light; overhanging trees speckled the surface with shadows. He tried to read the white water ahead and rang for "dead slow" on the engine. Things looked more promising on the left, but maybe if he nursed the boat forward at the slowest possible speed, he would have time to reverse engines and back up before he was committed to the wrong channel. According to the wheelhouse chronometer, the tide had only just turned, so he had both depth and current on his side.

It was the current, in fact, that thwarted his plan. By the time he saw the wide gravelly hump of bottom coming up, the current was moving too fast for "reverse engines!" to have much effect. With a long, surprisingly gentle sigh, the *Foxglove* struck the bar and drove herself firmly aground.

Lieutenant Valentine had never heard Will Cushing scream "*Shit!*" before, but that was only the first shot of a barrage of oaths that erupted from him on this occasion. Professional decorum quickly asserted itself, however, and the crew began to do what sailors have always done when their ship runs aground. They deployed a kedge anchor, the men got out into the lowering water and hauled with ropes, and the engines roared in reverse until the water boiled—all to no avail. Time and tide opposed their every effort. They would have to lighten the ship considerably, which would take hours, and wait for the next high tide. As soon as Cushing realized the futility of all the straining and groaning and cursing, he ordered a halt and had the cooking fire lit in the tiny galley. After a glum meal of beans, biscuits, coffee, and rum, he gathered the men about.

This was, he knew, his moment. All of his career up to this hour had verged on this scene, and he knew that the time had come to make a speech that good old Charlie Flusser would have included in his favorite collection of stirring oratory and naval valor: *Naval Enterprise, Illustrative of Heroism, Courage, and Duty.* The setting sun bathed the fantail in ruddy, operatic light—he felt God setting the stage for him—and he knew that what he was about to say might later be accounted sheer melodrama. He also knew that he was in danger of losing his first command, and that he was still basically a skinny twenty-year-old boy whose uniform hung loose about his bony shoulders. This was the moment for him to display what Annapolis called "command presence," and he would do it with all the style and flair and bravado he could summon. A few deep breaths—he felt his stature expand and his face become transfigured in the day's last offering of warmth. The officers and men formed a semicircle around him.

"Men," he began, then paused and tried again when he heard his voice come out pinched and a little squeaky. "*Men!* We must bring the remaining schooner alongside and put every spare thing aboard her. Dismantle the howitzer, too, and dump it overboard. Keep only the pivot gun, the shells, and the canister. Also a sufficiency of coal and some small arms. I see no chance of getting this vessel off until the next high tide. We will probably be attacked in the morning, and by an overwhelming force. It therefore becomes my duty to provide for the safety of you all."

It was working. Grim-faced and silent, their eyes were riveted on him.

"If we are attacked in the morning, and overpowered, either by artillery or boarding or both, the only alternatives left are to blow up the ship or submit to unconditional surrender. I will not do the former except as an absolute last resort; to do the latter, well, that is unthinkable.

"I want all the men except five or six—and these must be volunteers—to go on board the schooner. Take it downriver to a point that is beyond the range of the enemy's guns, anchor there, and wait for us. For myself, and those volunteers, I intend to work the pivot gun in the morning and fight her to the last, and set a long fuse to the remaining powder. I will not surrender while a shell remains on board. Now I will turn my back for a minute. Choose among yourselves who will go and who will stay. The volunteers should take five steps forward."

It was a very long minute, and the men were disconcertingly silent. When Cushing turned around, he was astounded to see that the men remained together, all standing as they had before. Had he overdone the rhetoric? Did they find him ridiculous, a vainglorious young pup who had lured them into this trap and was now deciding their collective fate? Then it dawned on him: the men had *all* stepped forward.

"By God, I won't forget this, men! I won't forget it as long as I live!"

Lieutenant Valentine smiled. "Guess you'll have to chose, sir. Doesn't seem like anyone trusts that schooner to get us out." So Cushing did, counting off Valentine and five of the older sailors. For the rest of the night, the crew worked to lighten the ship. The schooner's draft was shallow enough bring it within a few yards of the gunboat; water, provisions, muskets, and personal belongings were passed across to its deck, the men working waist deep in cold, black water. Then they stripped the *Foxglove* of everything except the Parrott rifle and about fifty rounds of shell and canister. There was no way to do this quietly—shoving the howitzer overboard made a stupendous splash that could probably be heard all the way back in Jacksonville—and by now, almost certainly, the enemy knew where they were and how helpless they would be in the morning.

An hour before dawn, the schooner slipped anchor and inched carefully around the sandbars. Cushing told its twenty-two-man crew to anchor at the mouth of the New River Inlet and wait there. If he had to blow up the gunboat, he would try to bring off the volunteer crew in the ship's rowboat and rendezvous with the schooner as soon as possible.

Then, there was nothing to do but wait, hunched and shivering, around the Parrott gun. In the first cheerless gray of predawn light, Cushing was relieved to see a thick mist rising from the river, along with the tide. In another hour or two, there would be enough water under the keel to get up steam. He ordered the boilers stoked, figuring he and the other six men were far enough away to escape scalding if a Rebel shot punctured the furnace.

But the Rebels did not even wait for proper daylight. And when they opened fire, they did so with three guns well sited at cross-fire angles and protected by hastily dug earthworks. Cushing and his volunteers worked the pivot gun bravely, and managed at least to keep the Rebel gunners' heads down some of them time. But when daylight burned off the fog, shells and solid shot slammed into the *Foxglove* with methodical, hammering accuracy. Roundshot pierced the hull in several places; a shell exploded on the boiler, releasing a wild banshee howl of jetting steam, as though the wounded vessel were screaming in pain. Grapeshot balls tore the flagstaff in two, and Cushing watched in despair as the flag twisted in the heated steam-wind, like a bird shot down in flight. Although the gun crew continued to return fire, it was all pointless now. The power plant was hammered into junk, the hull was a sieve, the superstructure knocked to pieces, and Cushing could count at least four fires taking hold in various places. There was still enough powder in the magazine to blow the ruined vessel to kingdom come—preferably while the enemy was trying to climb aboard and salvage her—and there was no point in prolonging the struggle. He ordered Valentine and his sailors to bring the rowboat along the port side, where it was shielded from enemy fire, but first he told them to reload the Parrott and insert a slow match. "That way, she can still fight on her own even after we leave."

They pulled on the oars like madmen. So intent were the Rebel gunners on punishing the *Foxglove,* and so dense was the smoke from her fires, that only a few wild shots were thrown at them before they passed around a protecting bluff. Cushing was close to tears—the youngest ship captain in the U.S. Navy had risked his vessel and lost it. Valentine, pausing to wipe the sweat from his furrowed brow, punched him lightly on the knee and grinned: "I'll say one damn thing for the navy, sir. They sure teach a man how to row a boat!" Cushing shook off his grief and redoubled his pull.

Fifteen minutes later, they heard a violent clap of thunder and, looking back, saw a great mushroom of smoke boiling over the trees, marking the final resting place of the *Foxglove.* After that, no one spoke. Cushing consulted the charts he had brought and figured they were close to the river's mouth. He strained to catch a glimpse of the schooner. At least they could sail home with a prize; the enemy had lost $60,000 worth of naval stores and two schooners, and he had certainly raised hell up and down the river, which had been his general intention to begin with.

"Stop!" he suddenly barked. "Back oars! And be quiet!"

There was the schooner, all right, but it was encircled by a dozen boats filled with Rebel soldiers, and the enemy flag was already flying above it. There might have been a fight—he hoped it was a good one—but they would never have heard the musketry over the din of the shelling. In any case, twenty-two of his men were now lost or captured, and he alone was responsible. For a moment, Cushing was paralyzed by a sense of loss and failure.

"Christ, sir, what do we do now?"

That question snapped Cushing out of his funk. He was still responsible for the lives of six remaining men, and he was damned if he would meekly surrender after all they had endured up to this moment.

"Beach the boat here." Cushing stared at his map, desperately seeking some way out of this trap. He had not come this far only to meekly surrender and live out the war in some shit-hole of a Rebel prison camp. Then, like a touch of God's grace, an idea came to him.

"Gather round and look at this chart. We are here, at the mouth of the New River. Due west, about three or four days' march, is a branch of the Cape Fear called the Uwharrie. We have provisions and water, we have weapons, and the enemy will not be looking for us. What I propose is simple: we go inland, navigate by dead reckoning, and sooner or later we'll reach that river. There must be farms along its banks. We can steal another boat, a steam launch if we're lucky, traveling by night and hiding by day, and in a couple of days, we'll be close to New Inlet. No one will be looking for a few men in a small boat. The moon will be low, and we might be lucky enough to time it while a runner's coming in. We run past Fort Fisher, and by morning we'll be out among the blockade lines. While we're doing it, we can take detailed notes of the enemy's defenses, maybe get a glimpse of those ironclads they're supposed to be building in Wilmington. Well, men, what do you think?"

What they thought—and it was plain on their faces—was that he had gone mad. Then Lieutenant Valentine put things in perspective by saying: "I hear the food at the Salisbury prison is pretty gruesome. We might get captured anyway, but at least this gives us a chance. I, for one, haven't yet had a surfeit of adventure. Come on, lads! If we pull this off, we'll all be heroes! Your wives and sweethearts will read about you in the papers!"

"I already thought we *were* heroes," grumbled one old salt, staring balefully at his blistered and powder-blackened hands. Then he shook his head, not quite believing he was signing on for this craziness, and laughed. "Hell, why not? We can at least steal some chickens along the way!"

"No, sir," admonished Cushing. "We shall pay for anything we consume. Unless, of course, it happens to be running around with nobody's name on it."

They tossed the oars into the underbrush, removed their scant supplies and firearms, then sank the rowboat and followed Will Cushing into the wilderness of Onslow County.

Cushing and the Lost Sailors

MR. LINCOLN'S TROUBLES—The Lincolnite Congress has passed a law declaring every man in the Northern States between eighteen and forty-five to be subject to military duty at the call of the President, to be drafted into any corps or employed on any service that the War Department may designate. The enrollment, drafting, etc., is to be done exclusively by Federal Officers.

Yankeedoodledom is stirred to its lowest depths, yet Lincoln has now got the Army and Navy. The sword is wholly in his hands, and he has been vested with the authority to make it as long as he pleases. The purse is also in his hands, or at least, the power of turning out green-backs. These things being so, it strikes us as being very doubtful whether there will be sufficient spirit left in the North to strike a blow against the despotism that is gradually absorbing all the powers and abolishing all the liberties of the states and the people. If there be anything in the talk now coming from the Northwest, now is the time to show their grit. Now must they indeed "Awake, arise, or be forever fallen," bound hand and foot in the grasp of Seward and Lincoln.

It is true that although armies may be called out, these armies may refuse to fight, or cease to be efficient. Such is, in great measure, the present position of the Army of the Potomac. But we must not calculate too largely upon that. We must be prepared to bear every energy and every resource to meet the new hordes which this wholesale conscription gives Lincoln the authority to call out and hurl against us.

—The Wilmington Journal, February 27 1863

Mister Bright found them, at first light on the morning of March 31. He and Sonny Chiang were out on the final night patrol, from three A.M. to breakfast time, Bright riding on a sorrel mare and the diminutive Oriental following—Sancho Panza–like—on a scrawny mule. True to his word, Hobart-Hampden had returned to Pine Haven in early February, at the helm of the newly repaired *Banshee,* with provisions, mail, and a formidable collection of arms: five Enfield rifles, four Colt revolvers, a huge meat-cleaver cutlass for Chiang, and two brand-new .52-caliber Sharps breech-loaders, weapons so advanced that only a few companies of Yankee skirmishers were yet equipped with them. With Pine Haven's polyglot little garrison thus fitted out with better arms than those of any band of bushwhackers they were likely to encounter, Mary Harper had established a rotating schedule of patrols each night. No one would sneak up on the place if she could help it.

But, somehow, these men had done so, and were now sprawled on beds of cold pine needles on the edge of the rice fields, apparently so exhausted, and so ignorant of their proximity to a plantation, that they had not even bothered to post a sentry. Mister Bright stayed to watch them, pistol drawn, while Sonny Chiang hurried back to the big house and told Agrippa to wake "the mist-less." Mary Harper was already up and washing her face when the summons came. Still damp and sleep-befuddled, she rushed downstairs, afraid that someone had been injured. She flung open the back door and almost laughed at the sight of the little Chinaman, face twisted with earnest alarm, his body listing to port from the weight of the enormous sword he insisted on wearing at all times.

"*Yankees,* Mistress Sloane! Yankee-men asleep near the rice paddies! Mistah Bright, he says you come double-time-quick!"

"Oh, dear God," she cried, hands rushing to her mouth. "We are invaded! Quick, go wake up Stepan and Fernando! Tell them to arm themselves and meet me here at once! How far is it? Do we need to ride?"

"Faster to walk," said Chiang, already heading off to rouse the other men. "We get there quicker if we don't wait for horses!"

Mary Harper ducked back inside and picked up her own weapon—an old bell-mouthed hunting piece, which she kept charged with buckshot. By the time she pulled on her field boots, Chiang had returned with the rest of what she thought of as the "Pine Haven Posse."

A brisk ten-minute walk brought them to the spot. Mister Bright sat alertly on his mount, covering the little encampment with his pistol. Mary Harper and the reinforcements fanned out to encircle the sleeping men.

She had often rehearsed this scene in her mind, convinced that some day the enemy would indeed appear. But she had not expected it to happen quite this soon—simple logic, combined with her general knowledge of the strategic situation on the coast, suggested that either guerrillas or a cavalry patrol would appear long before Yankee regulars. Yet there on the ground before her were a half-dozen *sailors,* at least a hundred miles inland from the nearest occupied port. Their inexplicable materialization could not be more incongruous if they had descended from another planet.

They certainly did not look very threatening. Their gaunt, bearded features spoke of hunger and exhaustion; their hands and faces were cross-stitched with cuts, abrasions, and bramble scratches, suggesting many days of hard marching through the swampy wilderness of Onslow County. One of the sleeping men groaned and shifted weight to relieve the pain of a hip wound; another, paler, fellow had sustained what looked like a bullet wound to his right hand, which was swollen and morbid-looking beneath a rough cocoon of blood-soaked bandages. That hand cannot be saved, she thought. *It must come off, but we have no doctor and he will surely be dead before we can fetch one from Wilmington.* These thoughts surprised her—her first instinctive response had not been properly hostile, but almost motherly. These poor souls did not signify "the enemy." Instead, they looked like a pack of lost boys, utterly worn out and helpless beneath the Rebel guns now pointed at them. Their sleep was so heavy that she scarcely wanted to wake them, much less take them prisoner.

Her somber gaze kept returning to the sprawled-scarecrow figure of the group's commander, or so she assumed him to be by the torn epaulets on his shoulders and the chevrons on his sleeves. *Why, he's just a boy, no more than twenty!* His sunken, high-boned cheeks seemed too frail and thin to hold a beard, just a faint dusting of down like the feathers on a baby duck. His fine, straight, light brown hair reached the base of his neck, and had his nose been less Roman, his mouth less *determined*-looking, even in slumber, he might almost be considered effeminate. *A young poet's face.* But withal, she thought, *a warrior*—for his right hand rested lightly on the exposed butt of his Colt and his left was curled firmly around the pommel of his sword. What was left of his uniform hung loosely on his frame, for whatever meat had sheathed his bones—and there could not have been much to begin with—had melted away during his trek. The more she studied his face, the more certain she was that he presented no danger to her or to Pine Haven. Even in the sleep of profound exhaustion, he had a look of *honor,* like a fiercely dedicated young squire who wanted nothing more than to gain the spurs of knighthood.

While Mary Harper studied this curious tableau of "enemies," Mister Bright and the other armed men were staring at her expectantly. *What shall we do with him—with them?* She motioned for Bright to bend close and whispered: "Let me wake them. Perhaps the sound of a woman's voice will ward off any reaction of panic. Wherever these sailors come from, they are a long way from where they ought to be, and we don't want them coming up with their guns drawn."

"Yes-um, they sure look rode-hard-and-put-up-wet."

As quietly as she could, Mary Harper knelt beside the young officer and gently covered his pistol hand with her own.

"Young sir? Please don't be alarmed when you wake up—we mean you no harm."

Will Cushing's eyes—sky-blue and clear—flashed open and he jerked his right hand from beneath hers as though her flesh were scalding. For just an instant, as the young man came up to a sitting position and saw a half-dozen muzzles held straight by grim-faced men, some kind of inner lightning slashed across his gaze and his mouth curled in a snarl. Yes, thought Mary Harper, he is a warrior. She held him with all her strength until he saw her frank disarming smile and realized he was not, in fact, surrounded by Rebel soldiers, which caused him to relax somewhat.

"My name is Mary Harper Sloane, and I am the owner of Pine Haven Plantation, upon whose grounds you have wandered, although I cannot imagine how or from where."

"Lieutenant Commander William Barker Cushing, madam, United States Navy. It appears that we are your prisoners."

"For the moment, you are my guests and will be treated as such if you behave as such."

Lieutenant Valentine, who appeared both relieved and slightly amused by this turn of events, dusted off clumps of wet pine needles, drew himself erect, and bowed. Then, since neither party quite knew how to proceed, Valentine introduced each sailor by name and rank.

Mary Harper reciprocated this ritual, and was amused to see the Yankees' reaction to the motley mix of her own little army. The sailor with the hip wound elbowed his nearest comrade and said, "My Lord, Henry, that there's a *Chinaman with a cutlass!* " in the same tones he might use to indicate the sudden appearance of a pachyderm or a two-headed cow.

Cushing sullenly got his band together and they all marched back toward the grounds, considerately setting a pace that matched the gait of the limping sailor with the hip wound, who jacked himself along with the help of a makeshift crutch. Mary Harper fell in alongside Cushing, while Bright and the other men followed, weapons still at the ready. By the time they all reached the big house, their route was lined with astonished Negroes, some of whom reached out shyly to touch the tattered blue uniforms, as though verifying that these specters were really human.

"Two of my men need medical attention, ma'am. The sailor with the limp will probably recover—the ball merely passed through the flesh—but the other fellow's hand is in a bad way."

"We have no doctor, Mister Cushing, but we will do what we can. I think the first order of business, however, is a good meal." She turned and spoke over her shoulder. "Mister Bright, please run ahead to the kitchen and make sure that, whatever has been prepared for breakfast, the quantity of everything should be doubled. These men look as though they haven't eaten a good meal in weeks."

Bright scampered off. Cushing, obviously in the grip of conflicting emotions, thanked Mary Harper and assured her that such was indeed the case—they had consumed nothing during the past four days but some varmints and a handful of crawfish.

"I suppose you'll turn us over to the local Confederate garrison . . . "

"Well, Mister Cushing, that would be a half day's trip downriver to Wilmington, and I . . . oops!" She covered her mouth and laughed. "I suppose that information is a military secret—dear me, I could be hung for treason!" Then, more soberly: "Frankly, I don't know what I will, or can, or should do with you-all. Things might become clearer if you tell me exactly how in the world you ended up here . . . after you've eaten, of course."

Once she was back in her own house, Mary Harper became a flurry of authority. She ordered the two wounded men to be made as comfortable as possible and saw to it that their filthy dressings were changed. Valentine and the sailors were seated, under rather casual guard, around a couple of plank tables near the smokehouse, for the morning had turned pleasantly warm and they were too grubby and smelly to go indoors. At the sight of coffee, biscuits, bacon, and molasses-dripping pancakes, the famished captives moaned with pleasure, and soon they were swapping yarns and personal information with the men who guarded them. All in all, except for the obvious pain of the more seriously wounded sailor, the mood soon veered in the general direction of a picnic. Mary Harper invited Cushing into the house and asked Agrippa to set a place for him at the dining table. Now that a tone of civility had been established, she really was anxious to hear his story. In between great bites of food, he told it.

Within minutes of plunging into the woods near the mouth of the New River, the rowboat's crew had been set upon by a mounted Rebel patrol that had, apparently, been expecting them to try just such an escape. Tracking dogs came first, setting up a racket that must have alerted every Confederate within a mile or two. Reluctantly, Cushing had ordered his men to shoot the animals. In a chase that lasted all day, Cushing had no recourse but to abandon his straight-line-to-the-Uwharrie plan and strike deeper into terrain so roughly wooded and creek-veined that the horsemen could not ride through it for any long stretch. Cushing's command decisions often came down to sniffing the air, scanning the terrain quickly, and pointing, "This way, men!" as though he had absolute confidence in each change of course. Periodically the hunters and hunted caught sight of each other and exchanged fire; Cushing's men emptied several saddles, but one of his own men was killed and two others were wounded in the skirmishing. By nightfall, they had managed to give the cavalry the slip, but they spent a miserable night on a hummock of saw grass surrounded by black-water bogs and funereal tree stumps that reminded them of tombstones. Able Seaman Conners, whose hand had been shattered like dropped china by a minié ball, clamped his teeth on a scrap of leather belt and shivered in agony, while his uninjured comrades took turns holding him for warmth.

Dawn of the second day brought rain and black clouds so low and dense they could not even see the sun and so could only guess their direction. They decided to wait out the storm before proceeding. Cushing doled out about half of their rum supply and everyone used their cutlasses to hack down pine branches and construct a lean-to. Beneath its meager shelter, Cushing spread out his soggy map and fidgeted over it with compass in hand. Its depiction of the land between the coast and the vague meanderings of the upper Uwharrie was mostly a patchwork of guesses, no more reliable than the charts of Elizabethan explorers—"*Here be Monsters.*" Most of the afternoon was taken up with desperate efforts to collect enough dry kindling to coax a fire. Near twilight, the clouds thinned just enough to permit an educated guess as to where the sun was. Throughout the night, men coughed and sniffled in their damp, torn uniforms. Before allowing himself sleep, Cushing made meticulous notations on his chart and in his pocket notebook—distances, azimuths, uncharted waters, quicksand pits—a regular reconnaissance of this dismal region, hoping that his notes and observations, if he ever managed to get them into naval hands, might be used to update the maps and improve the chances of any other stranded sailors who might find themselves castaways in Onslow County.

Day three dawned fair and mild, raising their spirits. Sunrise over the swamps brought forth a thin, pale, lemony disc of sun. Squaring their backs to it, the men broke camp and headed west. They made several miles before coming upon a vast tract of wilderness more water than land; the ponds and streams were too deep and too wide to cross, so they made long slow detours to find fords and embankments, walking two miles north or south, Cushing estimated, for every mile west.

From the fourth day on, things became a blur. Scourged by brambles and slowed even further by their injured, they were often forced to hack rough trails with their cutlasses, which were now, like their firearms, speckled with rust. After consuming the last of their rations, they were forced to spend their time and dwindling energy trying to find game. As rich with wildlife as these acres were during the summer, they were all but barren in March. Perpetually damp, they could find no dry place to store their small supply of powder. Once, to their amazement, they broke through a dense screen of brush and saw a deer grazing peacefully not fifty feet in front of them. Galvanized by the sight, every man raised his firearm and pulled the trigger, but the guns just went "thunk!" when their hammers smashed on wet percussion caps. Pausing long enough to give them a disdainful glare, the deer bounded off and was never seen again.

After carefully drying their remaining powder, they managed to do better, knocking off the occasional varmint, including one fat opossum whose flesh, when roasted on sticks, proved to be so greasy and gray-tasting that half the men could not keep it down and the ones who did had to struggle on the following day with pernicious cramps and gruesome diarrhea.

Each day they grew weaker and slower. One night—it might have been the eighth or ninth—Will Cushing asked wearily for their attention and in a silence made deeper by the crackle of damp firewood, he asked for their forgiveness. He had meant to lead them to freedom but instead he had led them into Hell. If and when they found a Rebel outpost or a farm, any man who wanted to surrender should consider himself free to do so, and no one would—no one possibly *could,* after the magnificent effort they had made—think that man a quitter. As for himself, Cushing went on, he had learned something valuable about human limitations, and if he somehow did make it back to the bosom of the navy, he would be a better officer because of it. The pursuit of glory, he now understood, might sometimes cost too much. When his tired, small, almost little-boy voice trailed off, Able Seaman Conners struggled upright on his one good hand and glared back with fever-racked eyes. "Mister Cushing," he grated, "you did not order us to follow you. We *chose.* That choice has cost me a hand—don't try to tell me otherwise, because I can smell the putrefaction better'n any of you swabbies—but I've still got two good legs and as long as I can make them move, I'm following you. All the way through Hell and out the other side, if need be." Every man grunted in agreement.

At dusk the following day, they clawed through a bramble patch toward a dimly seen elevated bank that gave promise of dry sleep, and finally saw a body of water so broad and deep that it could only be the Uwharrie. In the morning, the men's faces were lit once more with hope. Surely, in one direction or the other, they would find a farm, a plantation, a fishing camp, *something.* Cushing sent out scouts at first light but when they returned at midday, their reports were uniformly glum. A mile to the north the river forked, and the easterly branch apparently flowed right back into the watery maze from which they had just escaped. Conditions were no better for a mile in the opposite direction, where numberless creeks carved the land into a flooded morass that they could not hope to cross in their weakened condition. But *across* the river, the scouts had glimpsed a few abandoned fishing huts and a stove-in dock, indicative, perhaps, of a nearby plantation.

So the choice was made for them: they would have to cross to the opposite shore. They made a dispirited search for logs that might be used to construct a raft, but the few limbs they found were sodden and impossibly heavy and they found no vines suitable for lashing them together. Cushing digested these tidings solemnly, then announced that he would attempt to swim the river in the morning, then head south until he found someone to surrender to. He would then appeal to that person's sense of humanity and, God willing, the men stranded on the eastern bank would be rescued in a day or two. But when he suggested this plan, the men looked at him with downcast expressions. He was skin and bones now, and for several days he had been wracked by the sort of cough that usually heralded pneumonia. Lieutenant Valentine immediately volunteered to go instead of Cushing, for he was much stronger. Cushing thanked him, but insisted that the first attempt was his responsibility. "If I don't make it across, Mister Valentine, command devolves to you in any case, and you may then do as you see fit. I can make that an order, if you like."

At sunset, Will Cushing climbed to the highest point on the shoreline embankment and sat alone. Like Moses, he had led his people through the wilderness, and yonder lay their Promised Land, their only hope of salvation. In truth, that far shore did look inviting, compared to what lay behind them. Over there, and not too far away, he sensed the presence of settlement, cultivation, and ordinary human beings who would surely give succor to the helpless, even if only to turn them over to the nearest Rebel outpost. He turned his scratched and parchment-thin face into the sun's last benediction and he prayed. "Dear God, I ask forgiveness for my vanity and recklessness. I have chased after glory and dragged other men in my wake. Now, if it is your wish, I am ready to make atonement for all the suffering I have caused. Grant me only the strength to save my brave sailors, just that, then do with me as you will. Take my life for theirs."

Just before he got to the "Amen," he was startled by a loud splash almost beneath his feet. Leaning carefully over the embankment, he saw a large swamp-turtle that leaped into the river from what appeared to be a moss-covered hummock. Then, like a blessing, one last slant of ruddy light redefined the shape and he felt his throat catch with gratitude and relief. Thanking God repeatedly, and not forgetting to ask His blessing on the poor tortoise, he slid down the bank, and confirmed his discovery. There at his feet, securely wedged into a thicket of roots and jammed-up driftwood, was an old, half-flooded flat-bottomed pirogue. There was just enough light coming from the burnt-orange glaze of the river to reveal the words PINE HAVEN painted on the boat's stern. He called out to the men and by nightfall they had baled out the bottom and ascertained that the pirogue's leaks could be caulked with moss.

That night they built a huge fire and sang every hymn they could recall. Daybreak came, a blessing of bright sun and generous warmth. With eagerness and newfound reserves of strength, they dragged the pirogue to a suitably flat patch of shoreline, upended it, and rendered it river-worthy. There was no way to fashion proper oars, but Valentine waded out almost to midstream and verified that a couple of seven-foot poles ought to suffice to get them far enough across for the current to take them the rest of the way. Fitting everybody into the little craft proved impossible until Cushing suggested that he might float along behind without impeding the crossing. "Hell, boys, I'm the skinniest runt of the litter. Just hang on to me good and I'll kick you across!"

"Obviously, you made it," said Mary Harper. "That pirogue you found—it was stolen from us last autumn by a scoundrel we mistakenly hired to help bring in the rice crop. I am glad the boat survived, but I rather hope the man who stole it did not."

Cushing, stimulated almost to garrulousness by sheer relief and five cups of coffee, shook his head and grinned wryly.

"Oh, getting across the river was not difficult. We would have drifted down here yesterday, but for one final, very strange thing that happened. About a mile upstream, we were suddenly attacked once more."

"Attacked? By whom? We heard no gunfire."

"Not by 'whom,' " Cushing replied. "By *what.* Out of nowhere, coming up out of the depths almost beneath our keel and right beside me, rose the gaping, dripping jaws of an enormous bull alligator. I've never heard of one just attacking human beings like that, without provocation, and I declare to you that I'd just as soon never see one again."

"How horrible! Usually, they mind their own business, unless they're crippled or provoked. What did you do?"

"After we all screamed, you mean? Well, there wasn't much else we could do but head for the shore as fast as possible, while trying to fend off the reptile with our poles. He submerged after Mister Valentine poked him in the eye, then came back up right beneath us. With enough force to flip over a boat containing six men! I, of course, being the only one actually in the water with it, scrambled ashore as fast as possible, then turned around just in time to see the boat and all its occupants go flying. Thank God the water there was shallow enough to stand in—we all managed to haul ourselves out while the great brute was busy demolishing the boat, actually ripping it to shreds with teeth the size of belaying pins!"

"Surely he left you alone after that?"

"No, ma'am, he did not. He chased us all the rest of the day, stalking, then spurting along like half a ton of scaly lightning! What made it even more strange is that he could not possibly have gotten our scent, for there was a westerly breeze all day and we mostly kept downwind from him."

"They have a poor sense of smell. Mostly they just sit around half-submerged until they catch sight of a bird or a turtle or some other flash of colors. Stealth and keen eyesight, those are their assets."

"Well, madam, I can verify that for a fact! I know this sounds crazy, but it was almost as if the sight of our blue uniforms actually drove him to a frenzy! In fact, that's how we finally got rid of him. One of the boys took off his clothes, stuffed them with pine needles, and hung them off a branch, six feet up. Sure enough, ten minutes later, here came that crazy 'gator, and as soon as he saw the dummy, he reared up like a snake and opened his jaws wide enough to swallow a locomotive. That's when myself and Lieutenant Valentine jumped out and hacked off one of his paws with our cutlasses. That sent him packing! We could hear him growling and thrashing as he fled back to the river. And not long afterward, we all collapsed at more or less the same moment . . . on the spot where your men found us."

Mary Harper, who had been hanging wide-eyed on every word of this saga, now coughed and sputtered and shook her head.

"Poor old Beauregard!"

"Ma'am?"

"That is the alligator's name, Mister Cushing. At least, I assume it was he. Forgive me if I laugh at what must have been a terrifying ordeal for you and your men . . . it's just that . . . . we used to have a big bull 'gator who hung around these parts, whose behavior was sometimes eccentric. We named him Beauregard. Until now, I thought he was long gone—the last time I saw him was far downriver, near Wilmington."

Cushing mulled over these remarks while he savored the last swallow in his cup. Then he replaced it in its saucer and favored Mary Harper with a knowing and altogether disarming smile.

"Perhaps . . . they *home.* Under conditions of wartime stress, at least."

Their eyes held for a moment, probing for each other's sense of humor, and they began to laugh in unison. Mary Harper dropped her hand over the young man's, fleetingly, while they enjoyed the outlandishness of the story. Before she withdrew her hand, their eyes met, blue delving into hazel like a handshake but tinged with something else, which Mary Harper chose to identify as mutual admiration.

"You are very young, sir, to bear so much responsibility. Yet your men look up to you, and I sense that mere rank is the least of their reasons."

"Once they get some rest and put some flesh on their bones, they will surely not thank me for leading them into such hardship. I did not lose a man during the fight along the river . . . but twenty-two men were killed or captured when I ordered them downriver in a schooner we'd taken at Jacksonville, and when I led the six survivors into the swamps, I got one of them killed and two hurt, one seriously. I do not call that great leadership."

"Speaking of that, we must decide what to do about . . . Mister Collins, is it?"

"Conners, ma'am, Able Seaman Conners."

"Yes, of course. And please, Lieutenant Commander Cushing, you must call me 'Mary Harper' instead of 'ma'am,' for I am not your mother."

He blushed—this fierce-eyed slayer-of-men and daredevil raider—and cleared his throat. "Well, Mary Harper, I see no alternative but to take off that hand. I am no surgeon, but I have certainly seen it done enough times to know that no great skill is required, just quickness. I shall have to do it. Have you any medicines, any surgical instruments?"

"A fair stock of common remedies, for malaria and such. But we do have saws and plenty of whiskey. However, I have another idea. You saw our Chinaman, Mister Chiang?"

"How could I miss him?"

"My overseer, Mister Fitz-John Bright, sustained a bad head wound last year and has been suffering from periodic seizures ever since. Mister Chiang is very learned in certain exotic Oriental practices. He uses needles, inserts them at the junction of certain nerves, blocking the sensations those nerves convey to the brain. When Mister Bright feels a spell coming on, Chiang puts him in a bed, cleans the needles in boiling water, then inserts them carefully, just into the skin. Mister Bright assures me that the technique works like magic. Since these treatments began, Bright has not experienced a single attack. It may be that Chiang can use his magic needles to block the transmission of pain. He also has another skill which might be useful. I would rather show you than describe it."

She rang for Agrippa and sent him to fetch Chiang. After she introduced the Oriental to Cushing, she suggested that the demonstration be conducted out of sight of the other sailors. She selected a log the same approximate width as a human forearm and placed it in the notches of a sawhorse. She took a piece of sewing chalk and marked a line on the log.

"Mister Chiang, please demonstrate how you can cut that log with a single blow."

"Understand, Mist-less Sloane. Sunny pretend that is an arm, yes?"

"You are way ahead of me, Mister Chiang. That is the general idea."

Chiang drew his cutlass, a hefty blade that was almost as long as he was tall, fixed the log with a look of burning concentration, and puffed like a toad, gulping in oxygen and limbering his arms and shoulders, grunting and barking strange Chinese syllables. Then, in a great arc, he raised the blade in both hands, shouted something that sounded like *"Heee-YAH!"* and struck. So precise was the stroke that it bifurcated the chalk line and stopped a quarter inch below the log, which fell asunder in two smooth-ended halves, the cuts so smooth that the severed ends appeared to have been sanded and varnished. A steam-powered band saw could not have made a cleaner, faster cut.

Cushing was impressed—the best surgeon in the navy could not have bettered this mock amputation, and a pine log was considerably tougher material that a human tibula.

Mary Harper patted Chiang approvingly on the shoulder, and he bowed graciously.

"And your nerve-needles, they can be used to block pain? Serious pain?"

Understanding glowed in the small man's eyes.

"Yes, Mist-less. Sunny has never done this, but the master I studied with, he show me how. Need plenty hot water! Sword must be very clean! Lots of bubbles!"

"Boiling, he means," muttered Cushing, still goggle-eyed from the demonstration. "I've heard of that theory, though most surgeons dismiss it. That would lessen the chance of secondary morbidity."

"All right then," said Mary Harper. "We should proceed as soon as possible. I'll have the water prepared, and the needles. Mister Cushing, perhaps you should go to your men and explain. Take a jug of whiskey for Seaman Conners."

"No, no, no!" cried Chiang. "Must not be drunk! Needles not work so good!"

"That'll be a hard sell on Conners," said Cushing, "but if Mister Bright can verify the needles' efficacy, he may go along with it."

"It's settled then. We'll do it on one of the picnic tables, where the light is good."

" 'We?' Madam, I mean Mary, I cannot allow you to witness this. It is men's work, and horrible to see."

"Mister Cushing, you must understand—I am in command of this plantation every bit as much as you are in command on your ship. I need to see how it is done, in case . . . in case I ever have to do it myself. I promise you I will not faint or throw up or do anything *feminine.* I will see you in thirty minutes."

With that, she gathered her skirts, somewhat defiantly, and strode briskly away, barking orders to the servants. Cushing watched her with new admiration, thinking that she certainly did not conform to his preconceived image of a typical Southern plantation mistress—some flighty, arrogant "belle" flouncing along in hoopskirts.

Able Seaman Conners, his belly full for the first time in many days, was in an affable mood, though his freshly bandaged hand was swollen to twice the size of the other one. When Cushing explained the needles, however, his eye grew wide with apprehension. He would not let some dirty Chinaman stick pins in him, then lop off his hand with a sword, no sir! Patiently, Cushing explained what he had seen: how quickly the amputation would be over, and added pointedly that the "dirty Chinaman" was in fact much cleaner and certainly less fragrant than his patient. Fitz-John Bright weighed in with assurances that the needles were relatively painless and that he had come to rely on them to assuage the effects of his own grave head wound. Conners was wavering—between Cushing's untrained hand on a saw and a single flash of the Chinaman's cutlass there was a clear choice to be made—until Cushing mentioned that, for the needles to work properly, there would be no preoperative whiskey. Conners almost bolted at that news, but Cushing assured him that as soon as the deed was done, he could have all the whiskey he wanted.

Bright and his men cleared the table and spread a clean linen sheet. Cushing suddenly wondered what to do about tying off the severed blood vessels. Overhearing him, the big stolid Pole, Stepan, spoke up for the first time that morning. Polish army technique, he explained:

immediately after the amputation, push the stump into a bucket of gunpowder and light it off. Instant cauterization, with much less tissue damage than searing it with a red-hot implement or trying to tie off the veins with ligatures. Everything would be over, literally, in a flash.

When both the cutlass and the needles had been well boiled, Mary Harper accompanied Chiang to the site of the operation, her stomach fluttering and her resolve wavering, now that the moment was at hand. She introduced herself to Conners, who was lying on the table, trembling. She bathed his forehead with a compress and said: "I will hold your hand, sir. Be brave."

Lieutenant Valentine unwrapped the bandages and Mary Harper got her first look at what a minié ball could do: the hand was a puffy mass of morbid flesh, the gaping hole swarmed with maggots, slivers of shattered bone gleamed, and when the arm was placed flat against a second picnic table, so Chiang would have a clear swing, a thick black ichor welled up from it. Gangrene was already creeping up Conners's wrist—the cut would have to be made in midforearm if he were to stand a chance.

"Aw, Jesus and Mary, it hurts," the man finally admitted, fixing his eyes on Mary Harper's. "Go on, Chink, take the fucking thing off! Beggin' your pardon, ma'am."

"You may curse all you want to, Mister Conners. My ears are not delicate."

That brought a wan smile to Conners's lips.

"When do those needles go in?"

"Going in now," said Chiang in a calmly professional voice. "Hand not hurt so much now, does it?"

"By God, he's right! It doesn't! Put some more in, Chinaman! You can be my doctor any day of the week!"

Mary Harper looked at the arm, at the bright yellow curls of hair and the brawny muscles, at the gleaming festoons of needles quivering in certain nerves and conduits, shutting down the connection between wound and brain. Chiang stepped back and nodded that he was ready. Several men stepped forward to hold Conners down, but Cushing shook his head. Better if it happened without that signal, for the laying on of rough hands would cause the man to tense, needles or no.

"*Hee-YAH!*"

Sunlight on steel, blinding, a decisive crack. The bloated hand fell away and Mary Harper was amazed to see, for one instant before the blood welled, the cross-sectional anatomy of a man's forearm, as clear as a drawing in a medical text. Stepan and Cushing lunged forward, while Conners was still processing the implications of that sudden sound, jammed the stump into a heap of gunpowder, and touched it off. Now Conners roared, more from amazement than pain, reared up—Mary Harper still holding him to her bosom—took one look at the stinking cloud of smoke curling up from his truncated arm, and fainted.

"Best goddamn amputation I ever saw," whispered one of the sailors, before he, too, keeled over.

I will not faint! I will not! Mary Harper sponged the sweat from Conners's face and took deep breaths.

"Thank you, Mister Chiang," she said. "That was skillfully done. I told you he was good, gentlemen. Now, if someone would get rid of . . . that thing on the ground . . . we'll move this man into a bed. Mister Bright, make sure he has a full jug of whiskey on the table for when he wakes up. Any of the rest of you gentlemen care for a drink, I think you've earned it."

As she passed by, Cushing heard her mutter: "And so, by God, have I!"

By midafternoon, most of Cushing's men were passed out on whatever pile of straw happened to be convenient. Mary Harper slugged down two shots of bourbon as soon as she got back to the big house and washed her hands, then switched to sherry, not wishing to appear *too* unlady-like. She invited Cushing to join her, after he made sure Conners was laid out comfortably on one of the upstairs beds.

She asked him about his home, his family, the brother who was serving with General Meade's artillery. He spoke of his mother with such childlike affection that she, once again, could only wonder at what a strange composite he was: face of a poet, eyes of a killer, body of a gawky adolescent. When Cushing finally ran out of praises for his mother, he politely inquired about the Sloanes.

"Before we go further along those lines, Will Cushing, I need to know one thing: are you stationed on the blockade line, and if so, where?"

"I pulled a tour of duty on the line, yes, until God mercifully sent me a case of typhoid fever. When I recovered, I was saved by an old friend, Charles Flusser, who helped me get command of a gunboat. The boredom of blockade duty was driving me crazy—we were reduced to holding races with pet rats just to pass the time! I would resign my commission rather than go back to it."

"When did you become ill?"

"I don't remember the exact date, but it was early in the summer of sixty-two. Why do you ask?"

"My husband, Matthew, was captured by a blockader last autumn. He presently languishes in the prison at Fortress Monroe. I merely wanted to be certain it was not you who took him from me. He was captain of the *Banshee*—perhaps you've heard of it?"

"Everyone knows that ship, Mary. It's a saucy runner, and a lucky one. Your husband must have become very wealthy."

"He already was wealthy, before the war. He thirsted for adventure, though, on the high seas. You of all men can understand that. And now I pay the price for his bravado."

"I don't understand why he is still incarcerated. Captured runner skippers are usually paroled within a month or two— Oh! Now I remember! He was taken when he tried to help the famous spy, Belle O'Neal, escape. She drowned, of course, and the *Banshee* got away scot-free. All of which means that he ran afoul of the Secret Service—a bunch of ruffians, I'm told. It was in all the Northern papers."

"He was captured *with* this woman, you say?"

"Well, with her corpse, at any rate. He apparently behaved with great gallantry, trying to save the woman from being hanged. A dirty business, all around. That, surely, is the reason why he's still in jail."

Her voice grew wooden, her eyes distant.

"Thank you for the information. Some things are clear now that were mysterious before."

"Madam . . . Mary, I am not without connections in the Navy Department. If I get back safely, I promise I will see what can be done to expedite his release. At the very least, I can surely get a letter to him, if you want me to carry one."

"A letter? No. I would not know how to begin, much less when to stop. But I would be grateful if you could pass along word that I am well, and Pine Haven is managing nicely. Oh, and tell him that our children are safe with my father, down near Charleston. I miss them terribly, of course, but they are safer there than they would be here. If you and your ragged warriors could sneak up on the place, so could other men, with worse intentions. The countryside northeast of here is swarming with deserters and bushwhackers, I'm told, all the way up to Virginia. And there is always the possibility of a big attack on Wilmington, in which case the river may one day be swarming with bluecoats. They might not be as well behaved as you, and they certainly will not find the same reception."

"If it were up to me, Wilmington would already be captured. Beg pardon, ma'am, but closing down that port would do more to shorten this war than a dozen victories in the field."

She laughed teasingly. "Come now, sir, the last thing you want is for this war to end before you have done a few more imperishable deeds of valor."

"You know me too well, and in only the space of a single day. It is true—I am happiest when I can go in harm's way with a stout ship beneath my feet and men like those you've met manning the guns. It might be different, if I had a family of my own, but . . . "

"But your mother, surely . . . "

"Oh, Mother understands me. I write her regularly, and I know she enjoys hearing about my exploits in battle."

"She knows how much *you* enjoy telling her about them, William, but that is not the same thing. Believe me in this matter, for I am a mother, and if you were my son, I would not cease to worry. But enough of this—I must decide now what to do about you and your men."

"My original intention was to reach the Uwharrie, find a boat, and sail by night down to New Inlet, then run past Fort Fisher and simply rejoin the fleet. I cannot of course ask you to facilitate that plan, for it might be construed as treason."

"Oh, I feel the noose tightening 'round my neck already! See here, I cannot simply turn you over to the nearest Confederate authorities. Let me propose this: you and your men remain here until you are fully recovered from your recent ordeal. We have a steam launch that we use for supply trips to Wilmington. I think I can prevail upon Mister Bright to take you all downriver to some place where you can find a boat. Between Sugar Loaf and Confederate Point, probably. After that, you are on your own. If you steal a boat, please leave an appropriate sum for the owner—I have cash, if you need it. I draw the line at allowing you to keep your weapons, however. Well, perhaps you and Lieutenant Valentine can keep your side arms, but the muskets stay here. If you run into trouble, I do not want anyone's death on my conscience, on either side. Mister Conners can stay here and we will nurse him back to health. I can always use another good man, even an abbreviated one."

"He will want to come with us. Twelve years in the navy—he would be miserably unhappy if he were left behind. He can at least look forward to honorable retirement and a pension."

"Well, then, it is settled. And Godspeed to you, sir. I don't suppose it would do any good to ask that you not take notes on the defenses or vessels you might see along the Cape Fear . . . "

"Not the slightest. The temptation would be irresistible."

"I thought as much, you rascal."

Impulsively, light-headed from the sherry she poured him, he reached for her hand. She did not withdraw it.

"I am grateful beyond any words, Mary Harper Sloane. I swear to you that I will do everything in my power to affect your husband's release. And I want you to know that if, for any reason, Pine Haven is threatened by outliers—by anyone other than regular troops, who will treat you decently when and if they arrive—I will be your defender. It will not be hard to get word to me, for I am well known in the fleet and Charles Flusser commands a whole flotilla of gunboats. If there is trouble, send word to me, and I will move heaven and earth to help you."

"How very gallant. But how will your gunboats get here?"

"I took notes, made sketches, during our trek through Onslow County. I could lead a force overland in half the time it took us to make the journey, for I know the lay of the land now, and would know how to properly equip the men. If you have another pirogue or two, I could hide them safely on the eastern bank, just in case."

He really would, she thought. *He would come with drawn sword and fire in his belly.* She placed her other hand on his.

"The prospect seems remote, thank God, but we have a few such boats lying about, and no one uses them much for fishing these days. Let it be as you suggest."

Fitz-John Bright calculated that it would take about eight hours to steam from Pine Haven to the vicinity of Sugar Loaf Ridge, after Cushing and his men climbed into Pine Haven's steam launch at eight o'clock on the morning of April 8, 1863. During their recuperative week at the plantation, Mary Harper had ordered the house servants to clean and stitch the sailors' uniforms, but she also donated a motley assortment of civilian shirts and pants for them to wear over the uniforms—theorizing that, if the wandering crew were captured, they could strip off their disguises quickly and surrender as regular troops and not as spies. She also provided them with a lightweight tarpaulin they could hide beneath as soon as the launch reached the heavily traveled waters near Wilmington.

"No peeking, now!" urged Bright as they drew abreast of the ferry crossing that marked the northern boundary of Wilmington proper.

Having said that, Bright then proceeded to give a tourist guide's lecture on every landmark feature they passed. Crouched uncomfortably under the tarp, Cushing peered through an inch-wide slit and took copious notes about everything he saw on the port side, while Valentine did the same on the starboard. He counted three blockade-runners in port and the timbered keel of a large ironclad on the ways in a shipyard—at least six months away from completion, he noted with satisfaction, knowing how valuable that information would be to the blockade squadron. Starting at the tip of Eagles Island, he saw several small earthwork batteries between the city and the prominent snowy hump that could only be Sugar Loaf. The one thing he did not see was any boat suitable for his purpose.

"Mister Cushing?" called Valentine. "Come over here and take a look at this." "This" proved to be Fort Anderson, a strong and well-sited bastion that was, Bright cheerily informed him, the largest Confederate installation between Wilmington and New Inlet. And there, at a small dock a hundred yards south of the fort, was a single-masted pinnace large enough to hold them on the last, most dangerous stage of the journey. At the foot of the dock was a small tin-roofed shed and a stack of oars.

"That's the very ticket," Cushing said. South of the dock was a shoulder-high bluff indented with ravines and covered with scruffy underbrush, angled sharply to the southwest. A Rebel sentry in the fort would have to lean over the walls and peer at just the right angle in order to see them disembark. "We can hide out there until dark, then backtrack and steal that pinnace."

"What if it's guarded?"

"We will deal with that eventuality if we must."

He poked his head above the tarp, blinking against the sudden light, and asked Mister Bright to put them ashore.

"You're the doctor, Cap'n C.," replied Bright as he obediently turned the rudder and reduced speed, casting an apprehensive glance at the big black ovals of Fort Anderson's river-face cannon. Like nearly everyone else at Pine Haven, Bright had become rather fond of these unlikely visitors—had in fact struck up something like a real friendship with Able Seaman Conners, whose grit he admired and whose inexhaustible fund of bawdy jokes had generated many a belly laugh—but he was ambivalent about this particular assignment. Not that he wanted to see these lads marched off to prison at bayonet point, but he did not relish the idea of aiding and abetting the enemy, even if these enemies were admittedly pretty decent fellows. He wished them well, but the sooner he was rid of them and on his way back to Pine Haven, the better. Once he had fulfilled Mrs. Sloane's instructions, he planned to stop over in Wilmington for the night, find a nice cozy tavern, and maybe pay a visit to one of the whorehouses in Paddy's Hollow.

He cut back the throttle as the launch neared the embankment. Valentine threw a small anchor into the brush. Then Cushing and his six surviving mates quietly dropped over the side, waded ashore, and hid themselves as best they could. Cushing turned back and waved.

"Thank you, Mister Bright, and tell Missuz Sloane to remember what I said. I am her obedient servant, should she need . . . um . . . ?

"A knight in blue armor?" Bright suggested.

"Something like that, yes."

"Well then, I am gone, boys. Y'all come back after the damned war is over and we will show you a real old-fashioned plantation party."

He pulled in the anchor, backed up the launch, and chugged off.

For the rest of the afternoon, Cushing's men crouched or knelt or stretched out in their chosen thicket, still camouflaged with civilian clothing. Twice they heard Rebel voices nearby—men from Fort Anderson, out for an evening stroll perhaps, but the voices came and went. By eight o'clock, darkness cloaked the river and Cushing whispered it was time to make their move. Cautiously, he climbed to the rim of the embankment and found a rough path that seemed to lead toward the dock. Pistols drawn, he and Valentine led the way. From behind the fort's earthworks came the familiar sounds of a military camp settling in for the night, including the music of a not-bad fiddler and voices raised in song. Cushing nodded in time with the music: perfect cover, he thought. Five minutes later, they were standing on the edge of the dock. No light shown in the hut, but there was a solitary sentry sitting in a cane-backed chair, musket across his knees. Cushing crept forward, pistol extended, ready to knock the man on the head, but lowered it with a smile when he heard how deeply the man was snoring. *This fellow is going to be in big trouble in the morning.* Valentine was thinking the same thing: he gestured at the sleeping sentry, then made a throat-cutting gesture with his index finger. Cushing nodded and whispered into Valentine's ear: "They'll shoot him for dereliction if we don't help him out. Don't want that on my conscience."

So while Cushing positioned his pistol where it would be the first thing the sentry saw when he opened his eyes, Valentine and another burly sailor grabbed the man, pinioned his arms, and clamped a hand over his mouth. Eyes popping like fried eggs, the private came instantly awake and, when he realized what was happening, began to shake with fear.

"Listen carefully, soldier. We are going to steal this boat. The reason why we can steal it so easily is that you were asleep at your post. You understand what the penalty is for that offense?"

Oh, yes, he did, to judge from the panicky way he bobbed his head.

"But if we make it look like you put up a fight and got overpowered, you'll get a commendation instead of a court-martial. Understood?"

Yes sir, replied the bobbing head.

"We're going to have to rough you up some to make it look good. Then we'll tie you up and gag you inside that shed. That's your best choice. Your only other choice is to be taken prisoner and sail with us out to the blockade line. Which will it be?"

"Ain't much of a choice, Admiral. Just please don't bust my nose."

"Fair enough." Cushing nodded to the big sailor holding the sentry's arms. With theatrical exaggeration, the man rolled up his sleeves, spat on his hands, then clouted the sentry across the jaw with a right hook and followed with a left to the temple. His face conflicted between pain and relief, he slumped over, unconscious.

"He'll look mighty convincing when they find him," muttered the pugilistic sailor, admiring the contusions and swellings already taking shape.

"Take him into the shed. Grab his rifle and cartridge pouch. Then, boys, off we go!"

The "Old Cushing" was back, eyes afire and voice like steel. They could smell the distant sea now, and so far luck had been with them. Ten minutes later they were in midstream, moving toward Smithville at a brisk clip. Cushing ordered the mast taken down and stowed, for stealth.

When the lights of Smithville hove into view, Cushing checked his watch. If all went well, they could reach the blockade line by dawn, with time to spare. Huddled under the furled little sail, he consulted his map of the Cape Fear Delta. They could turn east now and run New Inlet under the guns of Fort Fisher, which presented the added risk of placing them amid the blockade ships in pitch dark—one jumpy lookout and a single roundshot would ruin them, if they were mistaken for a runner. Or . . .

"I propose a change of plan, men."

"Uh-oh," grumbled someone at the oars.

"We have plenty of time, thanks to our good fortune so far. What do you say we sneak ashore at Smithville and kidnap General Whiting from his headquarters? We can get in, do the deed, and get back out before anyone catches on—then we can hoist the sail and make straight for the Old Inlet, past Fort Caswell and those new batteries on Bald Head Island—they won't be as alert there as they will be at Fisher, and the channel is much wider."

Valentine stared at Cushing. "Sir, with respect, don't you think we have pushed our luck about as far as it can be pushed?"

"Yes, yes, of course, but think of it! What a feat! The very impudence of it is magnificent!"

"May I remind you, sir, that we only have one musket and two pistols? And we are not likely to encounter another sleeping sentry. Not at a general's headquarters, we won't. Please, sir, enough is enough!"

Cushing merely stared back at him in silence. Where they saw recklessness, he saw a grand opportunity to tweak the Rebels' noses one final time before making his getaway. Valentine's shoulders slumped in acceptance.

"Very well, sir. What's your plan?"

"We will improvise that when we get to Smithville. Well, men, get cracking on those oars."

When they drifted past New Inlet and the shadowy bulwarks of Fort Fisher, the crew cast longing eyes at the beckoning expanse of the channel. But there was no more grumbling, and in the minds of even the most reluctant, there was a vision of some future occasion when they could say to other old sailors, or to their grandchildren: "Yes indeed, I sailed with Cushing on the Smithville raid! Would you like to hear the tale?"

They beached the boat a hundred yards north of town. It was ten-thirty and all was silence except for the lazy lap of water and a dog's bark. Leaving one man with the boat, Cushing led the others boldly into town, weapons hidden, keeping a ten-foot interval between each man, sliding from shadow to shadow and detouring away from lighted windows. Cushing halted them when he turned into a side street and saw a campfire in the backyard of a residence. Two Negroes were sitting beside it, conversing in slow, sleepy drawls. They gaped in pop-eyed amazement when Cushing suddenly appeared in the firelight, pointing a pistol at them and gesturing for silence. Then he opened his civilian coat to reveal the Yankee uniform beneath and the two exchanged grins. Would these two Negro gentlemen like to be liberated on this very night? If so, freedom was theirs, provided they would cooperate and lead the raiders to General Whiting's residence. The two blacks exchanged looks of astonishment, then nodded vigorously, as though they were being invited to participate in a frolic.

Following the Negroes, Cushing's party resumed their stealthy progress. Smithville was not a big town and when they reached the center of its small commercial district, the Negroes signaled a halt, pointed to a large whitewashed building fifty feet away, and announced that they were now passing the Confederate barracks, where three hundred men lay sleeping. Here, there *would* be sentries, so Cushing detoured down an alley and gave the place a wide berth. When they looped back to the main street, they came upon a large residence whose broad veranda overlooked the river. The windows were dark, but one on the bottom story was partly open, signaling an invitation with a curtain that ruffled out to dance with the breeze. Cushing knelt at the windowsill and peered into the room, impatient for his eyesight to adjust to the darkness. He was again in luck, for this was obviously the general's dining room. Seeing no immediate danger, he climbed through, turned left in the main hallway, and unlocked the front door. As each man entered, Cushing whispered an order and pointed in various directions. While the others fanned out to investigate the lower rooms, Cushing cautiously went up the stairs, pistol extended. The second-story landing was pitch-dark, so he struck a match, cringing as each sulfur grain detonated with what seemed like a thunderous blast. Three closed doors faced the hallway. Trusting to luck, he chose the middle one. There was no outcry when he stepped in, but he knew, from the prickling of the hair on his arms, that *someone* was in the room. Gripping the pistol in his right hand, he struck another match with his left.

By its flare, he beheld an alarmed man in a nightshirt, flinging aside his covers and struggling to rise. As Cushing stepped forward, the man grabbed a chair and waved it around his head in wild defiance.

"I have you covered," said Cushing, making sure the match light glinted on his revolver. "A shot will bring the garrison running, sir, but it will also be your death sentence. You are my prisoner, General Whiting."

Incredulously, the sleep-fuddled man lowered his chair.

"You, sir, have the wrong man. General Whiting is spending the night in Wilmington."

"Ah. Too bad. In that case, who are you?"

"Major Francis Hardman, General Whiting's adjutant."

"You'll have to do. Please get dressed, Major, as we have a long voyage ahead of us."

"You are insolent, sir!"

"I am the one holding the pistol. Get dressed and be quick about it." Cushing lit a candle and scooped up some papers he saw lying on a writing desk, hoping they might contain useful information. Sputtering with indignation, Harding pulled on his trousers and jacket, but his hands were shaking so badly he could not manage the boots.

"Leave them!" Cushing hissed. "Those slippers will do fine—we can send for proper clothes tomorrow."

From downstairs now came Valentine's alarm: "Captain! Time to go! I spotted some jackass running out the back door and heading for the barracks!"

At the front door, Cushing paused long enough to stick his *carte de visite* under a small flowerpot, where it would easily be discovered in the morning. On the back, he wrote: *"My dear General Whiting: I deeply regret that you were not at home when I called. Another evening, perhaps? Very respectfully yours, W. B. Cushing, U.S. Navy."*

Keeping his Colt pressed against Hardman's spine, Cushing ordered the men just to meander back toward the boat as though nothing in the world were amiss. But as soon as they started filing down the street, they heard a long drum roll from the Rebel barracks, followed by excited clamor and shouting voices. Gunners ran pell-mell toward the waterfront battery, half-naked, nightshirts flapping, most of them obviously convinced that a Yankee fleet was steaming through Old Inlet. In minutes, the streets were jammed with confused soldiers searching for their company commanders. The two Negro guides led them through the crowd at a cool, measured pace, and because of their civilian clothes, not one soul paid them the slightest mind. By the time they reached the pinnace and shoved off, the wind had freshened enough to warrant raising the sail. By the time they entered Old Inlet the alarm had spread to Fort Caswell and to the newly commissioned Fort Holmes across the channel on Bald Head Island. So many rockets blazed over the inlet that it almost seemed as though the enemy was saluting them. But not a shot was fired at the harmless-looking little sailboat. When they reached the open sea, Cushing ordered the men to jettison their civilian rags, so that they might approach the nearest blockade ship in proper uniform.

Attracted by the curious fireworks display, several frigates sniffed closer in shore. At 3:45 A.M., April 9, 1863, Lieutenant Commander William Barker Cushing and the survivors of the USS *Foxglove,* missing in action since March 15 and long ago given up for lost, were sighted and picked up by the astonished crew of the USS *Monticello.*

Cushing saw to it that his chagrined prisoner was given dry socks, a generous portion of rum, and a decent bed in which to sleep. The next morning, under a flag of truce, the *Monticello* signaled Fort Caswell, requesting that Major Hardman's clothes be brought out from Smithville, along with enough cash to enable the major to have as comfortable a sojourn in prison as possible. A picket steamer would dock at the fort at twilight to convey the prisoner's belongings back to the *Monticello.*

Will Cushing, of course, chose himself for this errand. While Hardman's luggage was being transferred, a Confederate officer saluted Cushing and told him that there was someone who wanted to meet him. Cushing followed the man into the fort and was ushered into a small office. A dapper middle-aged man rose to greet him, struggling hard to maintain a stern expression and wearing a general's stars on his epaulets. Wordlessly, the officer handed Cushing a *carte de visite,* identifying himself as General Chase Whiting.

"I thought it only proper, Mister Cushing, to reciprocate your courtesy. Be assured that the next time you call on me, you will find a more appropriate reception."

Whiting stuck out his hand and Cushing shook it, inhaling as he did so a faint waft of bourbon.

"May I offer you a drink, sir?"

"Not while I'm on duty, General, but thank you."

"Ah, yes. I have almost forgotten what it's like to be *off*-duty. In that case, don't let me detain you. I'm sure poor Major Hardman is anxious to have his clothes."

Cushing studied Whiting's face for a moment: refined, intelligent, penetrating gray eyes, but some great hidden fund of weariness, too, beneath the demeanor of command. Suddenly, Whiting began to quake with laughter. He threw a fatherly arm around Cushing's shoulder and said: "That was a damned splendid business last night, son! The very essence of impudence! Some day, when our two navies are no longer shooting at each other, you must tell me exactly how you pulled it off. Now get back to your ship, before I change my mind and clap you in irons!"

May 2, 1863
Washington, D.C.
Dearest Mother—
Much has happened since my last, rather hurried letter from aboard the Monticello. *As I told you then, I requested, and was granted, a court of inquiry with regard to the loss of the Foxglove, to determine for the official record if the honor of the flag suffered at my hands because of the decisions I made during that affair. Admiral Lee declined to convene the court of inquiry, stating in a letter to me that "the Navy does not prosecute an officer for the loss of a ship, when that ship was fought so gallantly." In fact, I have been promoted—at the unheard-of age of twenty-one!—to the rank of Captain, and am presently enjoying ten days' leave in our Capital, whilst the Navy Department decides what to do with me next. I have just returned from the office of Secretary Gideon Welles himself, who shook my hand and congratulated me on my exploits—very colorful accounts of which have appeared in the newspapers. He offered me a choice of commands, between a new fast steamer named the Violet and an older but more powerfully armed vessel named the Commodore Barney. I inquired as to where each of those ships might be stationed. The Violet, being much the sleeker and faster, would be assigned to harry the blockade-runners off Wilmington; the* Barney, *however, would most likely patrol Hampton Roads, where her heavy guns could be used against any Rebel mischief by either land or water. I asked Welles if the rumors were true that General Longstreet had recently been given command of Lee's forces in Eastern Virginia. If so, I surmised, then there would almost certainly be action along the waterways south of Norfolk, for "Old Pete" was not likely to be supine. Mister Welles arched his eyebrows in surprise, saying that Longstreet's appointment was not yet public knowledge and that I was probably not supposed to have that information. Then he admitted that the War Department also expected trouble from that source. In that case, I told him, I would much prefer command of the* Barney*—not adding that in order to escape the numbing dullness of blockade duty, I would as readily accept command of a rowboat.*

I invested two days of my leave so that I could have a look at my new ship, which was in Hampton Roads for routine maintenance. The

<u>Commodore Barney</u> may indeed be a bit slow for blockade work, but she is big (512 tons) and a veritable floating fortress. Her crew consists of 13 officers and 125 men! Command of her more properly belongs to an officer of higher grade than myself, but the Powers That Be are pleased to think that I have earned the distinction, and of course I am proud as a peacock.

Alas, I am punished for my pride—fate has deprived me a chance to visit with my dear brother Alonzo, whose artillery regiment was until yesterday encamped across the Potomac in Falmouth. I learned of this at the same time I learned that General Hooker has set the Army in motion for a grand and crushing offensive against Lee, and I knew that Hancock's Division, to which Ally's battery is attached, would surely be decamping for that campaign. I obtained a pass from the Provost Marshal, along with the name of the boat that was to make the run this morning. After being robbed blind by a hackman, and being forced to slog through that special kind of mud for which our Capital is widely famed, I took my seat aboard the ferry, only to learn from the man who inspected my pass that the <u>correct</u> boat was two wharves down! I hurriedly disembarked and tramped off through the mud once more, weighed down by the carpet bag full of food and liquid refreshment, which I intended to set before my brother with a great flourish.

Remember that sentimental lithograph Aunt Mildred used to keep in her parlor—the one that depicts a forlorn gentleman gazing sorrowfully at a departing train, from whose coach window an equally despairing young woman is waving good-bye? Under that picture, if I remember correctly, were the words: "Just One Minute Too Late . . . "

Sometimes, it is the small things that break our hearts, dear Mother. IF I had not wasted time arguing over the fare with that hack driver . . . IF I had not been forced to wade through ankle-deep mud . . . IF that other boat had pulled out just a few moments later . . . THEN I would now be writing you an account of the jolly reunion enjoyed by Ally and myself on his last night in camp. But the chance was missed, and I fear it will be a long time before our paths cross again. We both know that Alonzo will conduct himself valiantly in the coming battle—that is not even a question. But for all Joe Hooker's boasting that he "will show no mercy to Bobby Lee," this engagement will most certainly be hard fought and costly, for "Bobby Lee" does <u>his</u> boasting with fire and sword, not empty bombast. I shall not dwell on it further, not wishing to cause you more worry about your heroic sons than you must already feel . . .

The Whores of Paddy's Hollow

VIGILANTES NOT REQUIRED: Word has reached us that yet another rhetorical crusade has been launched from the city's pulpits against the sinful waterfront blocks known collectively as "Paddy's Hollow." Certain citizens, alarmed by the increased patronage of said district by the transient sailors who throng our port, and by the enlarged population of females and unsavory "businessmen" who have adopted the Hollow as their wartime home, have gone so far as to suggest that a Committee of Vigilance be formed to purge these hovels with torch and sword.

It is true that many of the inhabitants of Paddy's Hollow are people of the lowest and most vicious character imaginable, dwelling in circumstances so vile that it would tax the pen of Mister Dickens to describe them. But we urge caution, for, if this blighted district were purged from our city, where else would the sailors go? At least now, the vice and crime are contained, and the good citizens of Wilmington know which blocks to avoid in their daily rounds.

Moreover, we applaud the efforts of Miss Largo Landau, the "Little Jewess of Mercy," who has, since the ebbing of the Yellow Jack epidemic, striven heroically to bring order, sanitation, and some measure of controlled decorum to activities which would otherwise be chaotic and more dangerous to the city as a whole. It is ironic that so selfless an example of "Christian charity" has come from one of our Hebrews. We take this opportunity to remind our readers that donations of clothing, medicine, and food are welcomed at the Landau Store, during regular business hours.

—The Wilmington Journal, April 25 1863

"I see you made the paper again," mused Hobart-Hampden, reaching languidly for the coffeepot on the dining table of his Yellow House suite, pausing long enough to hand Largo a plate of fresh Nassau-bought orange slices.

"At least, this time, Mister Fulton did not hide quite so coyly behind the usual veils of hypocrisy and euphemism."

It was Sunday morning, and a clear lemon light blessed the city with spring's eternal promise. The *Banshee*'s repairs had taken until mid-January; she had just returned, Friday night, from her second voyage since the encounter with Lafayette Baker. Hobart-Hampden had recounted the whole story to Largo during one of their many low-key conversations in the weeks after his trip to Pine Haven. He had shown an honorable diffidence to her somber mood, now that he had learned more about how deeply the plague had marked her soul. She accepted his solemnity as a mark of hard-earned respect. She thought, perhaps, that she was now a more *interesting* lover, even though the delicious naughtiness and romance of their early months had been flensed-away. But last night she had sought release, something beyond mere recreation, something wild and far removed from the daily responsibilities she had taken upon herself; she had learned a few new love-tricks from the ladies of Paddy's Hollow, which she had presented to him like courses in a banquet. She understood that a man so widely traveled and so worldly had dined on every conceivable sexual novelty, but not *with her*. They had cavorted and experimented and thrashed around all night, until the cork-lined walls of his bedroom nearly melted, then passed out in a tangle of soaked and trembling limbs. To judge from the well-fed smile on his lips this morning, and from the sultry purr she heard in her own hoarse voice, the encounter had been both remarkable and therapeutic. Largo bit into an orange slice and licked the juices with relish, while Hobart-Hampden smoked and read the rest of that day's edition of the *Journal*.

"Do you think Mister Fulton's editorial will soothe the distempered mob, my dear?"

She gave a tart laugh and sucked her fingertips.

"For the moment, there is no danger. They are *all* in it, H-H. The sheriff and his men take a cut every week from all the licensed establishments—in cash or 'services rendered,' depending on their mood, and the property owners charge inflated rents for tumbledown hovels that are partly submerged whenever it rains. As long as the war rages, the city will be flooded with lecherous, well-paid sailors who would otherwise be roaming the streets and making a nuisance of themselves to the proper citizens. The preachers can fulminate all they want, but the fact remains that at the moment there are more whores in Wilmington than Methodists—and to be honest about it, there are times when I prefer the company of the whores. If the Yankees ever occupy this town, you will see a lot more proper young ladies bargaining their virtue for a good meal and the luxury of protection."

A warm breeze stirred the curtains. From the rooms around and above, she could hear the Yellow House revelers stirring to life, seeking coffee or some other stimulant to ward off last night's hangovers. Far-off church bells signaled the end of morning services; the prosperous burghers of Wilmington, wives and children in tow, would now be dispersing from their various houses of worship to enjoy their Sunday dinners.

Replete with oranges, buns, and coffee, Largo indulged in a luxurious stretch. A hot bath steamed invitingly in the bedroom, but she was not quite ready for it. Once she had bathed and changed, she would have to leave and go about her Sunday rounds.

Hobart-Hampden heard the church bells, too, and gestured toward the waiting tub.

"Our revels are at an end, I fear."

"Not quite yet. Pass me the pipe, dear Augustus, so that I may fortify my spirits for the day to come."

His eyebrows went up in mock disapproval. "Don't become too dependent on the hashish, sweetheart. It is not always easy to get, you know."

"Hypocrite! You're the one who told me it is not addictive, remember?"

He refilled the pipe and handed it to her, along with a box of matches.

"Not 'addictive,' perhaps, in the medical sense. But people can grow too fond of it, and it blurs the edges of reality for those who do."

"I *want* the edges of my reality to be a bit blurred, thank you." She sucked down two deep lungfuls of the sweetish smoke, shivering with pleasure at the way the sunlight on her face suddenly became more tactile, the very outlines of the furniture somehow more *significant.* "And, anyway, it is better than alcohol. Must be. Every day, I see men and women whose lives have been laid waste by drink, but I have yet to see anyone ruined by a little smoke."

"Oh, really? The next time you meet Flag Officer Branch, our illustrious naval commander, observe the faint yellow stains on his fingertips. I have seen it before, in the Orient—the man smokes opium. I'd wager my royal commission on it. The only reason no one knows about it is that no one in these parts recognizes the scent that clings to him on some mornings."

"Oh, surely not! Our Admiral of the Confederate Drones? Where on earth does he get it?"

"Not from me, I assure you. Other runner captains, with fewer scruples, probably keep him supplied. You cannot blame the man—his entire 'navy' consists of corncracker schooners and converted tugboats. And that great hulking ironclad, the *Raleigh,* for which he is unable to obtain either iron or a big enough engine. By the time that vessel actually slides off the ways, the war will probably be long over."

"Well, I have learned that every upright citizen has his secrets . . . or *her* secrets, for that matter. And every city has its Paddy's Hollow, at least in spirit." Abruptly, riding the current of hashish-energy, she tossed aside the bedclothes and scampered for the tub.

Hobart-Hampden put down the newspaper, snuffed out his cigar, and followed. He alternately scrubbed her back and shoulders, and cupped her breasts with palms full of suds. She sighed at the luxury of sensations; she would miss them when he left again, and that would be fairly soon.

"You did tell me the next run will be a long one, back to England?"

"Mmm, yes. Our second ship, the *Cossack,* is ready. But first I have to make a trip to Raleigh to meet with your Governor Vance. He has a scheme to put North Carolina into the trade in a big way. If he offers terms that are sufficiently attractive, we might consider a partnership between the state and the Anglo-Confederate Trading Company. I meant to discuss it with you last night, but somehow became distracted. . . . Of course, at the moment, you and I *are* the Anglo-Confederate Trading Company. I think we have room on our truncated board of directors for the redoubtable governor of North Carolina. I've been in correspondence with him and studied his proclamations to some extent—I like his sharpness. And unlike the usual run of Confederate politicians, he has a certain armor-plated transparency to his character. Speaks his heart, but thinks with his head. I look forward to taking his measure, man to man."

"And no doubt writing a full report on him to . . . whoever it is you send those secret dispatches to. You know, Augustus, when this war is over, I swear I will withhold my favors from you until you tell me the full story of your clandestine activities."

"In that case, my dear, we would go a long, long time without intimate relations."

And that, Largo knew, was all she could pry from him. No matter; this aura of mysterious doings was one of the things that most attracted her to him. "Has it ever occurred to you that I might actually be able to help you in that regard?"

"Has it ever occurred to you that you already are?" He leaned forward and favored her with a slightly wicked leer. She splashed him playfully, then changed the subject.

"When will you leave for Raleigh?" She turned, foam dangling attractively from her nose, her voice anxious.

"Monday morning, if the train is on time. Only for a few days. We shall have time for another private party before I take the *Banshee* out again."

He kissed her and slid his hands over her warm, slippery body. She had grown thinner, since the days of the plague, and had lost the coltish, youthful glow that had first attracted him, but hardship had only accentuated the exotic cast of her eyes and the fullness of her mouth. Whatever changes the war had wrought, they remained well suited to one another's tastes.

Bathed, relaxed, and primly dressed, Largo slipped out of the Yellow House at two P.M. through her usual backyard route, and emerged on the bright, crowded streets looking exactly like any other Wilmingtonian lady on a fine Sunday afternoon. Largo drove first to the store and collected the weekend's charitable donations for the downtrodden (not much, as it happened, for people had learned to hang on to anything that was not actually disintegrating): some clothing, an assortment of books, a few boxes of buttons, needles, ribbons, and gee-gaws. The steadfast clerk, the same one who had ferried her over the Cape Fear after bringing her news of Jacob's illness, had given up his Sunday to help load the wagon with sacks of flour and rice and a few bags of coffee and tea. Once the supplies were loaded, she dismissed the boy with thanks and a silver dollar.

She drove slowly north on Front Street, delayed briefly by a company of raw, whey-faced recruits marching back to Camp Whiting after drilling all morning in the sandy fields south of the waterfront. Gone now were the eager, bloodthirsty expressions of those who answered the trumpet in the spring of '61—these youngsters were the latest sweepings of the reviled but necessary Conscription Laws and they knew what was waiting for them in Virginia, and knew that it was not glory by any stretch of the imagination. Some of them doffed their caps and waved at her, and she waved back, trying to keep pity from showing on her face.

When the road was clear again, she flicked the reigns and steered the cart, as best she could, around the fresh heaps of dung and the deeper mud puddles. As she drew abreast of Walnut Street, the unofficial southern boundary of the Hollow, she thought: At least you cannot smell the place the way you could last summer. No one knew exactly why the city's red-light district bore the name "Paddy's Hollow." She was reasonably sure there never had been anyone named Paddy associated with it—but the place was low and vile, and so, by repute, were the Irish, which was probably explanation enough.

During her mostly carefree adolescence, Largo had often heard the grown-ups speak of the place, in guarded and scandalized whispers, and Jacob had made it forcefully clear to her that Paddy's Hollow was one of those places where Young Girls Did Not Go. Nevertheless, she had gone there, in November 1861, when she had first made up her mind to become Hobart-Hampden's lover. Who better to give advice on contraception than one of the Hollow's madams, for whom the subject was not a matter of evil speculation, but a simple business necessity? She had wandered those blocks, thinking herself well disguised in a cloak and floppy bonnet, trying to decide which of its establishments was the least evil looking. Finally, she chose a two-story house that looked almost respectable, even rather cheerful, built on brick pillars above the floodplain, festooned with clotheslines from which bloomers and stockings stirred in the soupy breeze like illicit flags. MADAM MURPHY'S RESIDENCE FOR LADIES proclaimed the nicely painted sign over the front entrance, ESTABLISHED IN 1850, MADAM LEOTA MURPHY, PROP.

Mrs. Murphy herself answered Largo's timid knock—a broad, floury woman with merry green eyes and copious gray hair swept back in a chignon, watermelon-sized breasts swinging proudly under a cotton shift, Juno-esque hips, and big muscular legs that looked capable of snapping a bullock's back. Aside from the fact that semi-naked women kept peeking out from various bedroom doors, Largo saw little that was unusual, and nothing that was threatening, about Mrs. Murphy's establishment. Leota invited her into a clean but cheaply furnished parlor, served tea, and listened sympathetically while Largo stammered her request for arcane knowledge. Two hours later, armed with new terminology ("*le sponge pessaire,*" "French Letters," "abortifacients"), and a well-thumbed copy of *The Married Lady's Companion,* Largo sneaked back home, her horizons and options considerably widened. Several of the resident girls came in and out during this tête-à-tête, to replenish the tea service or to bring certain items in for Largo's inspection, and Leota Murphy addressed them all with affection and courtesy. Largo had been prepared to hear moans of Dickensian despair, perhaps even the sounds of domestic violence, but the girls' laughter had been gay and unforced, and none of them seemed to be held there against her will.

"You see, my dear, we are like a family here. My girls are healthy and clean, and I do not demand an unreasonable percentage of their, um, wages, in return for their room and board. Our gentlemen callers are encouraged to use one or another of the contraceptive devices I have explained to you—never let it be said that any man's wife was made to suffer from the consequences of her husband's occasional recreational visits to my house. That is why we have 'Mrs. Murphy's Motto' displayed in all the rooms. Here is my *carte de visite,* with the motto printed on the back."

To guard yourself from shame or fear,
O Votaries of Venus, hasten here;
None of my wares e're found a flaw,
Self-preservation is Nature's Law.

Now, as Largo drove into Paddy's Hollow proper, she experienced the familiar prickly awareness of crossing a profound but invisible line of demarcation. Since the blockade-running boom began, the district had spilled over its prewar boundaries, and Mrs. Murphy's house was now surrounded by newer, lesser, and altogether more unsavory establishments. But when Largo had chosen to go forth and "tend the sick," it was back to Mrs. Murphy's she had gone.

The Yellow Jack plague had been a great leveler, cutting across all the strata of Wilmington society, creating in a matter of days two new classes of citizens: the dead, of course, who were all thrown into communal pits during the worst of it, regardless of their class, status, or occupations; and the seriously ill, who verged for one terrible week on the border between life or death. Largo had been determined to go where the need was greatest and by the time of Jacob's death, that place was Paddy's Hollow, whose destitute and desperate inhabitants had been left to fend for themselves. The Dead Carts did no go there, but only stopped on the outskirts to pick up corpses that were dumped at collection points. The handful of doctors who had neither fled the plague and had not succumbed to it were overwhelmed; the hospitals were packed to overflowing; and no medicine was to be had save for the rich and well connected.

When Largo ventured into the Hollow for a second time, on the day after Jacob's grisly demise, the first thing she saw was the body of a newborn child, floating facedown in a pool of sewage, the umbilical cord twined around its wrinkled husk like a jungle creeper. During that second visit, she heard moans and shrieks galore, and saw young women cowering indoors, half-mad with terror, and furtive bands of depraved criminals who scurried from victim to victim, stealing every ring and broach and coin purse they could find and savagely beating anyone who raised a hand in protest. In these narrow, cloacal alleys, the dark stench of burning tar generated a dense, greasy fog that clung to the skin and burned the nostrils, and on every intersection leading to or from the district, big stinking heaps of gas-impregnated "plague soil" rose like fortifications. Two armed deputies tried to stop her from entering the place, saying that they had standing orders to arrest or even shoot anyone who tried to flee from this mephetic Hell into the city's "better" districts. There *were* no "better districts," she told them angrily; the Yellow Jack made everyone equal, and how could they call themselves "Christians" if they turned their backs on the poor devils on the other side of these reeking barricades. And, besides, if they did not let her pass, she would return later with documents signed, if necessary, by the mayor, the chief of police, or General Whiting himself, for she was a rich and well-connected woman. The deputies clearly regarded her as a *deranged* woman, and finally stood aside, shrugging their shoulders as though she were already dead.

But Largo did not die, or even take sick. During the epidemic's final weeks, she had emptied her purse to provide food, comfort, and even a bit of ragtag medical care for the people of Paddy's Hollow. When she learned that Baccus Satchwell had recovered from the fever, she reminded him of his debt to Jacob, cajoling and finally shaming him into setting up a clinic and some recuperation sites adjacent to the Hollow. Thanks in part to the cleanliness that was her tradition, Mrs. Murphy's "Residence for Ladies" proved to be an island of wellness—only one of her girls died—and it was there that Largo set up her headquarters. She recruited a small band of nurses, either from the residence itself or from the handful of other establishments that met with Leota Murphy's exacting criteria, and Dr. Satchwell trained them in the rudiments of care or palliation. To combat rampant thievery, Largo even organized, from a list of names provided by Mrs. Murphy, a small detachment of watchmen, armed mostly with clubs, knives, and brass knuckles. Composed of discharged, one-armed soldiers, sailors stranded between runner contracts, bartenders, bouncers, some middle-aged men who had either married or entered into long-term relationships with their favorite whores, and one or two shifty-eyed but basically reliable part-time pimps, her "Provost Guard" reclaimed the streets and alleyways from the low-life ghouls who had emerged to prey on the helpless.

When the epidemic abated and the renewed runner trade brought back the old business-as-usual bustle, Largo did not consider her business in Paddy's Hollow to be done. She had come to know these people well, and she had seen them rally 'round one another during the plague's worst days with commendable spirit and selflessness. Many of them she knew by name, and many a heartbreaking story had been poured out to her by young women who had never, in their worst nightmares, expected to find themselves in a place like Paddy's Hollow. Young wives whose husbands had died in the war, cast-off mistresses abandoned by rich blockade-runners, widows forced out of their paltry homes by wartime inflation, waifs who had been seduced by some opportunistic monster and then indentured to some madam or pimp when their seducers had grown tired of them—none of these women ended up in the Hollow because of inborn moral depravity, although eventually they all became tainted by depravity's smothering embrace, hardened to it, forced to abandon one line of moral defense after another just to survive.

There was, Largo discovered, a surprisingly elaborate hierarchy of vice inside the Hollow. At the top, socially and aesthetically, were Mrs. Murphy's "Residence" and two other establishments that had been landmarks for more than a decade. In Leota's saloon, the tangle-foot whiskey was more potable, the atmosphere more genteel, and the entertainment—the public entertainment, at least—aspired to a touch of class. There was always a crowd on Friday and Saturday nights, when Leota's three handsome daughters—Winona, Maggie, and Kate—performed their "Cyprian Interpretation of the Dance of the Seven Veils," accompanied by some fairly accomplished musicians.

Largo found the show more cleverly titillating than lascivious, with its cheap plaster urns and painted palm trees, its teasing use of diaphanous curtains and silhouettes, of incense, and interludes of recited sort-of-biblical poetry.

On the next-lowest rung of Paddy's Hollow society were the newer, rougher, cruder establishments that had sprung up with the coming of war, places with names like the Ironclad, the Haystack, and the Riding Academy. Their inmates tended to be women of transience—in town for a season or two, then gone, and God knew where to—and their owners, ruffians and opportunists. On weekend nights, or nights when there were multiple runners in port, these places seemed to explode with noise and raucous activity. Drunken women displayed themselves at open windows, shouting lewd enticements to the men staggering past. Pimps from these places fanned out across the waterfront, accosting sailors, or loitering near the train station, the training camps, or the hospital, where they touted their women's attractions to recuperating wounded, furloughed men on their way to or from the battlefronts, and hayseed draftees with a few dollars in their pockets, gangling youngsters who wanted, in however base a fashion, to lose their virginity before risking their lives.

Lowest, and newest, of the Hollow's substrata were the fly-by-night entrepreneurs who worked out of tents, lean-tos, abandoned shacks, and moving wagons. These, in Largo's opinion, were the lowest of the low, equal in their callous depravity to the skulking rats who stole the rings from dying girls' fingers during the plague. Drifters and draft dodgers, career felons and jailbirds, they dispensed raw vice in the form of shit-or-go-blind moonshine, rigged card games, crooked cockfights, bare-knuckled boxing matches, and quick tumbles with whores too poxed-out, too ugly, too old, too young, too malformed, or too black to find a berth in any respectable establishment. These operations floated through the district like garbage heaps on a noxious tide, setting up in one alley on Monday, another on Tuesday. In these roving enclaves of sin, murder was not unheard-of, theft was common as grass, and disease flourished.

Just after Christmas, Largo had presented to Dr. Satchwell a prospectus for containing the excesses of the Hollow's worst denizens. She had the figures: one diseased whore, she estimated, could infect between twenty and thirty sailors or soldiers every week—and those men, in turn, would carry their illness abroad or into camp, infecting an ever-widening circle of partners before the first signs of gonorrhea, syphilis, or tuberculosis were manifest. In the interests of the *war effort* alone, she argued, never mind simple human decency, would it not be better to organize medical inspections on a regular basis? Some of the transient whores would fall through the net, of course, but the ones who proved to be healthy could then obtain a proper license, and display that document to their clientele. It stood to reason that any man looking for a quick "night with Venus" would prefer to take his business to a certifiably healthy woman, a companion who would not condemn him to a subsequent "lifetime with Mercury." Every licensed woman would then be required to contribute $1 a week from her income to underwrite the cost of maintaining a clinic and a small salary for the men of the Provost Guard, who helped Largo keep a lid on the simmering violence and crime. If the city would implement such a rational system, she would use all of her now considerable influence to keep the Hollow as free from open sewage, foul language, and unsightly public outrages as humanly possible.

She presented these ideas to a secret meeting of the city's leading businessmen, who agreed to hear them only after considerable arm-twisting by Dr. Satchwell. Largo spoke with passion and a lack of embarrassment that reddened their faces, and there was much grumbling about this "meddling Jewess" and her "Tart's Crusade," but some of these same men had been known to frequent Mrs. Murphy's establishment from time to time, and Largo made sure to deliver a very *informed* glare at each of them in turn. She clinched her argument by reminding them that she was "inclined," for the moment, to continue donating "a tithe" of the Anglo-Confederate Trading Company's runner profits to Editor Fulton's Ironclad Fund, but she was under no legal obligation to do so; if the city fathers did not agree to support her charitable and sanitary program, that money could easily be diverted elsewhere. Ultimately, and of course motivated solely by a desire to keep the town's brave soldiers and sailors in a state of robust good health, suitable arrangements were made. And for the moment things were, for the most part, as orderly as might reasonably be expected inside eight square blocks of back-to-back whorehouses, cockpits, saloons, gambling dens, and flea-ridden flophouses.

Or were they? One block from Mrs. Murphy's, Largo saw a couple of windows spiderwebbed by pistol balls, a heap of scorched bedding, a chaotic strew of playing cards and poker chips, a forlorn Confederate soldier's cap that looked as though a pack of wolverines had been chewing on it, a Bowie knife broken off near the hilt, and some splotches of what appeared to be dried blood on the planks in front of a saloon named the Old Kentucky Home. In this particular establishment, evidently, Saturday night's revelries had gotten of hand.

Letoa Murphy greeted Largo with her usual generous stuffed-bear hug, then snapped a few orders to make sure her cargo was unloaded and properly stored for later distribution. Then she invited Largo into her parlor and closed the door. She poured tea for Largo and another cup for herself, which she spiked with a liberal dollop of Scotch whiskey.

"It appears that things were lively last night, down at the Old Kentucky Home," said Largo.

"You could say that, love. A wee incident."

"No one killed, I hope."

"Not so far as I've heard, although the tally of the wounded must have run into the dozens. Flag Officer Branch finally had to dispatch a company of armed Marines to clear the streets and cart off the injured. What I fear the most is that the circumstances which triggered this outburst will soon be commonplace, and next time it might be more than our watchmen *and* the Confederate navy can handle."

"What was so special about the circumstances? I thought I had seen just about all the circumstances Paddy's Hollow has to offer."

"Well, it's like this," Leota Murphy said, "and the Yellow Jack only speeded up the process: Wilmington's changing, girl, and the Hollow is changing with it. All those well-to-do families who used to run the city's affairs—not all of those who fled the fever bothered to come back. Them that has families on the mainland, they left their women and kids in relatives' care. That's taken down the *tone* of the place somewhat, made the ol' town rougher around the edges. Oh, sure, on a Sunday morning like this, things look pretty much the same as before, but what you saw when you drove here today was just *clumps* of normality, the stage props of illusion.

"You saw how many soldiers there are in the streets now. Some of them are this season's sweepings from the draft, of course, the babies of the cause. But whole companies, even regiments, are rotating through Wilmington now, to and from the front lines, because this is the main railroad terminal between Charlotte and Richmond. And this much I know from an old gentleman friend o' mine who's a stockholder in the railroad—the tracks are always breaking down now, just being pounded into the ground from all the traffic, and there's no more iron to replace the worn-out rails. So now, more often than not, a trainload of soldiers heading to Virginia, or a trainload of soldiers heading south on furlough, why, they don't just camp around the railroad station and hop on the next train, no indeed. Sometimes they have to wait days until they make their connection, and they get bored and resentful at the whole cocked-up mess that dumps them here, stranded and idle. Do those boys care a two-penny damn for our fair city? It isn't *their* hometown. They see Wilmington as a place grown fat and prosperous as a result of the same situation that's rendered their poor bodies dirty and half-starved; they see fine uniforms in our shop windows while they are clad in rags. They see the purchasing agents from Richmond sipping good coffee in their hotel cafés, while all they have to drink is some foul horse-piss made from stable-sweepings and chickory.

"These are not the same men who passed through town a year ago, Largo. Well, some of them may bear the same names, but they're not the same men even so. They've grown hard and bitter—they've supped on brutality and blood and their eyes have been burned by sights of horror such as you and I never saw, even in the worst days of the plague. So there they are, often in their hundreds, sleeping out-of-doors in shit-caked fields on the outskirts of town, watching the days of their furloughs being chipped away because some stretch of track is broken between here and Charlotte. They're bored as well as angry, and heartily sick of playing poker with the same tent-mates every night, with the same frayed and greasy cards.

"And then, along comes some slicker from the Hollow, some panderin' pimp with Satan's own promise in his smile, and he tells 'em, 'Boys, there's cheap likker and high-class poontang just a short march away from here, down in Paddy's Holler! Y'all come with me, and I'll show where a good time's at!' and off they go, sometimes in whole companies, and any sergeant who tries to stop 'em knows he might make an enemy who'll put a minié ball twixt his shoulders the next time they go into battle.

"This weekend, it was worse'n usual. A whole dang company from the Fifteenth South Carolina, stranded in town for three days and ready to rip up the train tracks with their teeth, came flooding into the district on Friday night, thirsty as devils and horny as jackrabbits. Mind you, there were also two big runners freshly docked, so the place was already hosting fifty–sixty sailors who were also randy enough to fuck a monkey, plus another hundred or so local recruits, out larkin' on a weekend pass, plus the usual fluctuating number of recuperating wounded, discharged veterans, and dockside laborers, and, Largo honey, *the place damn near blowed up!* That fracas down at the Old Kentucky Home? That was just the most visible outbreak—bunch o' sailors went to it with a couple-dozen South Carolina boys for no better reason than the fact that there *weren't enough whores to go around.* Once a fight like that gets started, it can spread from bar to bar like wildfire. I saw the hunger riots in Ireland, when I was a kid, and I can smell the brimstone startin' to accumulate in the air just before the first punch gets thrown or the first knife comes flashin' out. 'Tis a wonder that the whole district did not go up in flames."

"But everything looks peaceful in here, Leota." During Mrs. Murphy's monologue, Largo had been scrutinizing the room for signs of mischief; the zest and optimism of the early morning was draining from her and her stomach had grown knotted.

"Everything is, now, but heroic measures were required. I called in the Provost Guard and had them draw up a cordon around the house. Once I saw how things were going to hell in the neighborhood, I gave orders not to admit anyone who was obviously drunk, foul-tempered, or brandishing any weapon more dangerous than a stiff cock. We were an island of calm in a sea o' madness."

"I take it that there was no sign of the sheriff and his deputies."

"No more than there was a visit from the Pope!" Leota cackled. "Leastways, not until this mornin', when they swept through flashin' their badges and wagging their billy clubs under people's noses. Lots of talk about revoking 'business licenses' from the most violent establishments."

"Which translates into a higher weekly payoff to the coppers if those places want to stay in business." How easily, now, such rough vernacular came to Largo's lips. Six months ago, she had never used words like "copper." And a year before that, she had never even heard someone speak of "stiff cocks," much less developed a personal appreciation for one.

It was early afternoon now, and the westering sun struck the river and transformed it into molten pewter. Odd, snaky rays of that refracted light slithered through the Hollow's mazey lanes and finally came to rest inside Leota Murphy's plain but respectable parlor. By this furtive light, Largo could see the tiredness in the madam's eyes, the pouchiness of age on her cheeks, and a new, disturbing droop of discouragement in the downturn of her normally cheerful mouth. She put down her teacup and reached out for the older woman, who responded by hugging her close, pillowing her against her mighty bosom, and giving vent to a sigh that seemed to have no bottom.

"What can I do, Leota?"

"Why, darrlin' girrl, you have already done all that you can. You helped us when no one else would—and that at a time when your own poor heart was grievin' something fierce. Back then, this house and the others that had been here for years, we were like a family. But now, we're outnumbered by the newcomers. And the worse the war becomes, the longer it lasts, the more we will be outnumbered. If there was a company of wild soldiers here yesterday, there'll be a regiment soon. 'Tis a maelstrom that sucks everyone down its gullet, sooner or later. There are men amongst us now who would cut your lovely throat and never give it a second thought, if you crossed 'em the wrong way or showed up in the wrong dark alley when the madness is at flood tide. And there's worse things that could happen to you, love—no need for me to elaborate."

Leota Murphy drew back and made a tired, heavy effort to rearrange herself in a pose of dignity, gazing at Largo with a motherly sternness.

"Largo, I do not want you venturing into the Hollow anymore by yourself. If you have donations and food to deliver, send me a note and I'll have some of the Provost Guard lads meet you at the boundary and escort you in. But never again at night, do you hear? And never, ever, between sunset on Friday and noon on Sunday. Things are on a downward slide, now. Last night's brawl was the first pebble in a long slow avalanche. We might be swept away by it, but you *must not* be swept away along with us."

She rose and walked over to the open window, gazing into the light as though hoping to glimpse some sign of peace upon the great river's patient shoulders.

"I hear there is opium coming in now on some of the runners—and *that's* a scourge we've never had before in the Hollow. Some folks say the Yankees are behind it, hoping to weaken us by making addicts and dreamers of our officers—as if whiskey and frustration were not already sapping the will from some of them! Now, mind you, every man's entitled to his own vice, but even a confirmed tippler like Chase Whiting, God bless his gentle soul, can put down the bottle when duty requires him to. But once opium gets its hooks into a man, he *must* have it. So the scoundrels who deal in that heathen poison will make more money than those who still have some scruples—more money means more bribes to the coppers, to the customs inspectors, to the human apes who unload the cargoes. The most ruthless 'entrepreneurs' will form gangs and rule by naked fear. Oh, I saw it in the Irish quarter of New York, when I was a girl. Brute force will become the rule. Anarchy will be the norm. And when the blockade really starts to pinch, and the speculators suck the blood from what's left of honest commerce . . . Ah, Jaysus, I see it coming, girrl. Black and wild as a hurricane."

She spun back and glared hard at Largo, who sat as though benumbed, the tea in her belly roiling.

"When it comes to that, I will take my daughters and pull out. I'll know when the time is right. And then this whole place can go to Hell, as it surely will. God knows, I have more sins on my back than a month of confessions could even begin to list. But one sin I will not carry is the knowledge that some *avoidable* evil has brought you harm. One day, I'll send a message to you: do not come here again, not even in daylight. When I send that message, I will also send enough money to arrange passage out of Wilmington for me and my daughters and anyone else who's been welcomed under my roof. If you and your handsome Augustus can help us out, that will be the last service I ask of you. Now, promise you will do as I said!"

Largo felt the leaden weight of some vast but ill-defined failure sinking into her shoulders.

"All right, Leota. Between sunset on Friday and noon on Sunday, I will not venture into the Hollow. But I will come on other days, to make sure the clinic is running, the licensed girls are being cared for, and the Provost Guard boys receive their stipend. I am not afraid."

"I know you're not, dear girrrl. What I'm tryin' to tell you is that you *should be.* From now on."

Largo stayed long enough to make her usual inspection of the clinic and the general state of sanitation in the blocks immediately surrounding Mrs. Murphy's. Then she drove back to the Landau house, and changed clothes, to get rid of the clinging redolence of the Hollow. She told Wellington and the other house servants to take the rest of the day off, then drove off again to the Yellow House—no longer caring very much who saw her come and go from that rowdy establishment. She told Hobart-Hampden what she had seen and heard.

"I am decidedly unamazed. Now that we are the only significant Confederate port still open, all the riffraff in this hemisphere are being drawn to Wilmington like iron filings to a magnet. I warned you to be more cautious in your dealings with the Hollow. Mrs. Murphy and her longtime neighbors may be something of a 'family' to you, but I assure you they are not typical of the people who inhabit such places. Now that old Leota herself has felt the change of climate, maybe you'll take my advice more seriously. Largo, you've done noble work on behalf of those people, but the kind of scum that's settled there since the epidemic, well, by God, 'noble work' is wasted on them."

She was already feeling scratchy enough; his offhanded, almost lecturing tone made her snappish in reply. "Augustus, I will not abandon the friends I have made there just because the population of rats has increased. Will you stand by me in this, or not?"

His expression softened. "You know I will. I just don't want to lose you to some rotten-livered gutter trash. I'm bound for Raleigh on the morning train, and I had rather hoped to spend the night with you before embarking. Give me the rest of the afternoon to see what I can put in motion. Will you be at the store, or at home?"

"The store is closed on Sunday, and I doubt there have been any new 'charitable donations' in the last three hours."

Hobart-Hampden arrived at precisely four-thirty. In the carriage with him was another one of the Yellow House's Royal Navy waifs, the same slender straw-haired lad who had played along with Hobart-Hampden and Jacob Landau during that long ago and innocently happy musical soiree that preceded Matthew Sloane's final voyage—the night Mary Harper had invited her to Pine Haven—the night Jacob had played his fiddle—the last night she had seen her father happy. The young Royal Navy man now sported a rakish little goatee and his eyes were no longer quite so innocent.

"You remember Lieutenant Standish Pendelton, my dear? Just returned from diplomatic business in Brazil, and impatiently waiting his turn to be a runner captain, so he can make his own fortune before he turns twenty-five. If he sucks up to me properly, I may even make him my first mate aboard the *Cossack*. But for the nonce, he is to be your escort—your fully armed escort—whenever you venture into the Hollow. He looks like a winsome fellow, I know, but his hands reek of heathen blood and he's a crack shot."

"At your service, Miss Landau. Just call for me at the Yellow House, whenever you need me."

"Thank you, Mister Pendelton. I shall try not to interrupt the customary round-the-clock entertainments any more than necessary."

"I believe he plans to seek some 'entertainment' this very afternoon," chided Hobart-Hampden. "All right, Lieutenant, you may go.

And when you get to Mrs. Murphy's, take my advice and ask for Kate. I am told she has remarkable dexterity."

"Augustus!" Largo feigned a swipe at him as the young officer strolled away, heading in the general direction of Paddy's Hollow.

"Now, my dear, jump up here beside me. We're going to take a lovely, romantic ride out to the seashore."

They rode all the way through town, out to the high dunes below Young's Pond, where the beach spread out before them, empty and tranquil, hushed under the saffron drapery of imminent sunset. Hobart-Hampden had done some quick horse-trading with the current crop of Yellow House boarders and had procured for Largo a compact, elegantly engraved LeFaucheux revolver. They were all the rage in Europe, he said, and there was not another one in all of Wilmington. They fired one-piece metallic cartridges, ignited by a small vertical steel pin instead of a copper cap. Hence, they could be loaded, fired, and reloaded in a matter of seconds. The LeFaucheux was also ingeniously designed to fit in pockets, purses, saddlebags, even boot tops; the pistol's hammer fitted smoothly into a groove above the firing pin, so there was no sharp protruding tang to catch on cloth or leather. One squeeze sufficed to fire a round, rotate the cylinder, and recock for the next shot. Hobart-Hampden had also purchased two boxes of ammunition, fifty rounds in all, and they invested twenty rounds in target practice. The piece was well balanced and did not kick hard in Largo's hand. There had been a time, before the plague, when she would have felt uncomfortable toting around a loaded pistol, but now she accepted both the necessity of going armed and the possibility that she might have to draw down some thuggish assailant. Her first two shots were wild, but she took the gun's measure quickly and thereafter smashed two empty wine bottles and a row of large seashells at a range of fifteen feet.

Night came upon the beach slowly. They build a driftwood fire, ate a wicker-basket supper of bread and cheese and potted ham, then spread a blanket on the dunes and made love while the stars came out and the moon dredged up from behind a bank of enormous cumulus cloud-towers, its color as red as a lunatic's eye, and then held each other until the air grew cold and the wind began to moan over the sands like a whispering dream.

Zebulon Vance arrived at the governor's mansion in Raleigh at precisely six A.M. He was routinely putting in fifteen-hour days, so the only clear and peaceful time he had for his personal reflections was this two-hour slot before his office opened for business at eight—by which time there was usually a whole waiting room full of petitioners haggling with his secretary for appointment times.

For the past month or so, part of this personal time had been devoted to a slow, methodical reading of John Lothrop Motley's *The Rise of the Dutch Republic.* One of his old professors at the Chapel Hill university had urged this monumental tome on Vance, saying that there were uncanny parallels between the South's struggle for independence and the protracted heroic resistance of the Dutch to the distant tyranny of Philip II of Spain. That proved to be the case, and the steadfastness of Orange was an inspiration—aside from Motley's illuminating accounts of strategy and high politics, the element that fascinated Zeb was the author's passionate advocacy of civil liberty as a sine qua non of a noble society. Hanging now on the wall closest to his desk was an enlarged, framed quotation from Motley's introduction:

"If ten people hate despotism a little more and love civil and religious liberty a little better in consequence of what I have written, I shall be satisfied."

Since Motley had labored ten hours a day for the better part of a decade to compose his epic history ("like a brute beast," he avowed), it was reasonable to suppose that he damn well *meant it.*

Most mornings, Zeb devoted one hour to the book, a rapt and stimulating ritual he followed as faithfully as a mountaineer Baptist reading his Bible. But on this bright, soft morning in early May, the governor's attention kept wandering from the printed page. Through the open window behind his chair, nature's bounty seduced his senses. Dogwoods were exploding in their brief, feathery glory, and every breeze carried the sweet heavy perfume of riotous honeysuckle. Yielding to the mood, Zeb swiveled around, propped his long legs on the windowsill, and let reverie caress his mind. Lord, how he longed to be back in the mountains on such a morning as this, when the rhododendron blossoms were thick and profligate on the hillsides, and the black-crystal cascades in dark ravines made the air taste almost like mint. Hell, he wouldn't even mind the occasional homey stink of a passing skunk, or the sweet dumb rolling hump of a fat groundhog undulating toward its burrow. Or the proud, posed silhouette of a buck against the azure vault of a mountain sky.

But he was chained to this desk like a galley slave to his splintery oars; he could not excuse himself even for a weekend trip to Asheville.

The only legitimate reason for the governor to travel back to his beloved mountains would be the eruption of some sudden crisis *in* the region. Sadly, the ingredients for such a crisis were already present. Conscription had hit the western counties very hard, the new and flint-hearted tax laws even harder. Patriotic zeal for the Confederate cause had always been brittle in the mountains, and confined mostly to the wealthy landowners and merchants; the hardscrabble mountaineers out in the countryside had mostly wanted to be left alone, as they always had and always would. And if the reports reaching Zeb's desk were correct—he had no reason to think they were exaggerated—things had gotten much, much worse in the past six months. Deserters and draft dodgers, hundreds of them if not thousands, roamed the wilderness, most of them ready to kill or die rather than be shipped back to the army, and, since many of them had carried their rifles back home with them, they were at least as well armed as the Home Guard units that were supposed to comb them out of the woods and send them back to their regiments. Things had not yet come to a boil, but by God they were simmering. Vance's springtime reverie evaporated. He turned back to his desk and picked up the latest issue of the Asheville newspaper. On the front page was a petition signed by a group of citizens calling themselves the Loyal Confederates of Watauga County which read, in part:

> *We have very little slave labor in this mountain country, and if all the white labor is pressed into the Army, how are the women and children to be fed? Unless wiser policies prevail, our people will have to choose between starvation and immigration. We respectfully and earnestly call Your Excellency's attention to this matter.*
>
> *And will you be so kind, Mr. Editor, as to inform Jeff Davis and his Destructives, that after they take the next draw of men from this region, will they please, as an act of great and special mercy, also be so gracious as to call out a few, just a few, of their exempted plantation-owning pets from Mississippi, Georgia, and South Carolina, to come to the mountain counties and simply shoot our women and children in the head, to put them out of their misery . . .*

I could not have said it better, Zeb thought, though Lord knows I have *tried*, in letter after letter.

There was a knock on the door, which then swung open to reveal the head and shoulders of Richard Battle, Vance's tireless amanuensis. Zeb glanced at the clock. Time to go to work.

"Good morning, Governor. Time for your first appointment."

"Refresh my memory, Dick. Is it military, political, or civil?"

"A bit of each, I'm afraid. Mister Whitford, chairman of the North Carolina and Atlantic Railroad."

"Quite so. This will probably be brief. I'll try to twist his arm, and he will remind me of how many votes he can swing against me in the next election. But simply as a matter of protocol, I must confer with him *on the record,* so to speak. Show him in."

Sleek, well-fed-looking, the walking embodiment of political influence, Jonathan D. Whitford strode into the governor's office like a man doing a favor merely by showing up on time. Immaculate in his swallowtail coat and glossy stovepipe hat, a diamond stickpin sparkling on his cravat, he did not bother to take off the hat until after he had pumped the governor's hand. Vance inquired after Mister Whitford's large and socially prominent family, skipping lightly over the names of his two strapping young sons—both of whom had obtained draft exemptions because of their "essential" work in the railroad corporation; from his own inquiries, Vance had learned that this "essential" work consisted mainly of lobbying the state legislature in favor of policies that favored the railroad's financial interests. Raleigh boasted no more ardent Confederate patriot that Jonathan Whitford who, along with his associates, had prospered greatly from war-related contracts.

"So, Your Excellency, what service can I render on this fine spring morning?"

"I have read, sir, your latest report on the state's inventory of surplus track. If the numbers are correct, and I assume they are, down to the pound, we have enough iron on hand to maintain the existing network until sometime in the year eighteen sixty-five. That is good news indeed, considering how much wear and tear the rails must endure from the constant flow of men and vital supplies to General Lee's brave army."

Whitford waved a deprecating hand. "Governor, that is a very, very *provisional* estimate, as I'm sure Your Excellency can understand. If General Lee mounts his grand offensive this summer, the demands on North Carolina's rail network could multiply greatly. And, I need not remind you, the enemy enclaves on our coast could become more active—we have already lost quite a few miles of track on the lines around Kinston, from cavalry incursions and raids up the rivers by their cursed gunboats."

"Yes, I know. I have repeatedly urged President Davis to assign more troops to those vulnerable counties. They are our prime agricultural districts, and General Lee himself has referred to them as the 'Breadbasket' of his army. As loyal Confederates and patriotic North Carolinians, we must defend them tooth and nail. Unfortunately, at the moment, our 'teeth' are rather blunt and our 'nails' trimmed to the quick."

Whitford shifted uncomfortably, crossed his legs, and flicked an imaginary speck of dust from his highly polished boots.

Vance rose, came around the desk, and sat informally on the edge, so close to the railroad magnate that his burly frame seemed, from Whitford's point of view, intimidatingly large, even looming—exactly the effect Vance wanted.

"Mister Whitford, what if I were to tell you that we now have, or quite soon will have, a weapon so powerful that it can, by itself, do more to protect the eastern counties than a full division of troops."

"I assume Your Excellency is referring to the ironclad now under construction on the upper Roanoke."

Vance glowered sternly. "That, sir, is a military secret."

"Well, yes, of course, but one hears rumors. It's rather too large to go unnoticed, after all."

"Quite so, and you may be certain that our worthy opponent, General Foster, has heard those rumors, too, down at his headquarters in New Bern. Every additional week of delay in completing that vessel raises the chance that Foster will mount a major attack up the Roanoke. On the other hand, if the ironclad were finished, armed, and fully girded with armor, he would not dare—I can assure you, sir, without violating any secrets, that this one ship, when completed, will be able to sweep Foster's gunboats from our waters. The only naval vessels strong enough to take it on are the great steam frigates off the Outer Banks, and they are too big and too heavy to pass through the existing channels."

Vance picked up some papers and riffled through them. They were, in fact, nothing more than routine enlistment statistics and summaries of corn production, but Whitford did not know that.

"Despite the greatest difficulties and shortages, work on the ironclad is progressing steadily. Her keel is laid and most of her timbers. The main problem now is finding sufficient iron to roll the plates that will form her armor. I have discussed the problem with you before, sir, and the only solution would seem to be a greater allotment of railroad iron. For every eight to ten miles of track, the Tredegar Works can manufacture thirty tons of rolled armor plate. And the vessel requires three hundred tons of plate in order to fulfill its design."

"Governor Vance, my companies have already donated twenty-eight tons of worn-out rails, and we have agreed to sacrifice any damaged rails that can be salvaged from the spur lines around Kinston, which were so badly broken up by Yankee raids. We can spare no more, sir, not a single span—not if we are to maintain reliable service on the tracks that have not been damaged. It is all but impossible now to meet the wartime demands on track and bridges and rolling stock."

"Yes, yes, I understand that. But I could not help noticing, in your most recent inventory, that some thirty-five miles of track, in depots at Greensboro, Durham, and Hillsborough, are listed as being, how did you say it?" Vance picked up another set of documents, this one embossed with the corporate seal of the North Carolina and Atlantic Railroad. "Yes, here it is: 'held in reserve against future construction contingencies.' Now, sir, a reasonable man might interpret that as a reference to the new line the Confederate government wants to build between Greensboro and Danville. Mathematics was never my best subject, but it seems to me that all the rails held in reserve in those depots are just about the amount needed to construct that forty-mile connection, assuming two miles of double track for every statute mile of finished roadbed. You *do* still use two sets of rails, I assume."

Whitford acknowledged Vance's little jape with a pinch-lipped smile. "We are businessmen, Your Excellency, and sooner or later, that contract *will* be let. The obvious strategic value of such a connection makes it a high priority for the Richmond government."

"Oh, come now, sir! Even Richmond's *highest* priorities seem to require almost geological periods of time to set in motion. The immediate threat to this state, and by extension to the whole Confederate cause, is the enemy presence on our coasts. If Lincoln came to his senses and sent John Foster a full corps, he could be in Raleigh in three weeks. The one thing that deters him from pressing such a strategy on his superiors is the potential threat represented by our ironclad. If that vessel could be finished, armed, and sheathed in good iron plate, the enemy would never mount such an offensive. Indeed, if the ironclad were in full commission *at this moment,* we could turn the tables on Foster and force him to hunker down in New Bern until Hell froze over."

Whitford was fidgeting now, but his mouth was set and his eyes stubbornly fixed.

"I am the governor, sir, not a dictator. I have neither the legal authority nor the means to order the release of some of that reserve iron. I can only appeal to you, man to man, as two loyal sons of the Old North State—*give me that iron* and we can purge the enemy from our shores! If the eastern railroads are made secure, there will be no need for any hypothetical link between Greensboro and Danville. And let me assure you that if you do release that iron, I will do everything in my power to guarantee even greater profits for your companies than you now enjoy."

Whitford regained his composure; he had taken Vance's heaviest rhetorical broadside and weathered it.

"Your Excellency, I will pass along your request to my boards of directors, as a measure of my respect for you, but the only way that iron could be released would be the passage of a law by the state legislature. Candor compels me to remind you, sir, that many of the railroads' directors are members of that body, as are most of the major stockholders. You are of course entitled to introduce such legislation, sir, but I must tell you frankly that you have about as much chance of getting it passed as you do of catching a weasel asleep. I will, however, go back over our records and see if perhaps there are a few more tons of rusted scrap lying about in out-of-the-way facilities."

"Please do, sir. Every pound, every bolt, every nail will help. And now, I won't detain you any longer from enjoying 'this fine spring morning.' Good day."

Somewhat taken aback by this abrupt dismissal, Whitford bowed and retreated, closing the office door with just enough of a bang to communicate both his pique and his unassailable rectitude.

Zeb Vance watched him go with an angry stare that followed the man like a hornet. "You lying, greedy, puffed-up son of a bitch," he growled. He waited five minutes, enough time for Whitford to be gone from the capital building and driving off in his elegant carriage. Then he rang for Dick Battle.

"Well, Dick, that went just about as I expected it would. Had to give the man one more chance to do the right thing, just for appearances' sake. Send in the other gentlemen, please, and make very, very certain that we are not interrupted for the next half hour. I don't care if Jefferson Davis shows up—especially if Jefferson Davis shows up!"

Into the governor's office now filed an unusual and varied group of men: Captain Samuel Parker, head of the *Hatteras* project; Colonel Wentworth C. Graves, commander of the infantry and artillery defenses of Weldon, the rail junction and river port closest to Holman's Ferry; a tall dashing Englishman in Royal Navy dress uniform; and a sharp-featured civilian named Porter, who worked as a journalist for William Holden's *Raleigh Standard,* but who was also on Zeb Vance's payroll as an informant, political spy, and, when necessary, an agent provacateur. During their half-hour wait in Dick Battle's reception room, the four men had introduced themselves to one another, but as yet they had not the slightest idea why the governor of North Carolina had summoned them to his office.

Once they were all seated, and Battle had brought in coffee and biscuits, Vance wasted no time.

"Commander Parker, will you please give us the very latest figures about the iron available for the *Hatteras*?"

"As of yesterday, the situation was this: three hundred tons of iron are needed to roll the armor plate, along with between five and eight tons of nails, bolts, and miscellaneous fittings. My 'ironmonger' sweeps through the countryside have collected approximately eleven tons, from the lines damaged by enemy action around Kinston, and from dredging operations in the Tar River, we have retrieved twenty-two tons; Flag Officer Branch has managed to ship about fourteen tons from the vicinity of Wilmington; the North Carolina Railroad commissioners have *generously* sent us about twenty-eight tons. And finally, there are thirty tons of rolled and finished armor plate at the Tredegar Works in Richmond, awaiting clearance to be sent down by rail.

"In toto, therefore, we have one hundred five tons. As you can see, gentlemen, we are a long way from having enough to finish the ironclad."

"Captain Hobart-Hampden, whom I assume you have all now met, is an experienced and highly successful blockade-runner. The state of North Carolina has just entered into a contract with him to go into the runner business as a state-sponsored venture, in order that North Carolina herself may clothe and arm its regiments, and procure weaponry to defend its shores, since the government of President Davis has not done a satisfactory job in any of these areas, despite the remarkable contributions we have made to the Cause. Captain Hobart-Hampden has contracted for a load of first-quality iron bars, directly from English factories. The stuff is damned expensive, and my treasury is not bottomless, but . . . well, Captain, you tell us what's coming."

"On the maiden voyage of our new ship, the *Cossack,* four hundred twenty bars, approximately fifty-two tons. Already in transshipment to Nassau, on various subcontracted vessels, another five hundred fifty bars. The *Cossack* will bring another fifty-two tons on its second run, and one of our other ships, the *Banshee* will bring in another one hundred thirty bars, comprising sixteen tons—bar iron is an unstable, tricky sort of cargo. The weight has to be distributed with a careful hand and it all has to be tied down firmly so the bars do not come loose and slither about in rough seas. All of this will take some time, gentlemen. I first have to take the next available runner to Nassau, then book passage on another ship to Liverpool, then take delivery of the *Cossack* and bring her safely into Wilmington. Quite frankly, we could make a great deal more profit by filling our holds with goods other than raw iron, but as a gesture of solidarity with Governor Vance, I've given top priority to that commodity. I agree with the governor's strategy with regard to the coastal waters, and as a career naval officer, I have a keen professional interest in seeing just what the *Hatteras* can do."

Sam Parker, who had brightened up considerably at Hobart-Hampden's news, scribbled figures and added sums.

"That is very heartening news indeed, Captain. Counting what we already have on hand or in route, that makes two hundred twenty-five tons, give or take. I will consult with Major Reilly at Fort Fisher—he's the ordnance expert who actually designed the *Hatteras.* Perhaps by shifting some of the armor thickness around to less critical areas of the ship, we can find a compromise."

"We are not yet done, Commander Parker," said Vance, raising his hand, with a twinkle in his eye that suggested he was enjoying this unfolding chamber-drama. "Just before Lincoln's election, the trustees of the university at Chapel Hill approved a plan to construct a new facility, one dedicated to modern technology. A showcase of all the latest . . . *stuff.* Logically enough, the building's architecture would incorporate the latest in construction techniques—including riveted iron girders. The project is, of course, suspended for the duration, but some of the materials arrived before North Carolina seceded, including a warehouse full of big iron girders. Since the university is a state-funded institution, and since I happen to be an alumnus as well as the governor, I think a simple decree is all it would take to donate to the cause. Might even be a gesture worthy of some good newspaper ink."

"Er, Your Excellency," interjected Parker, "just how much iron are we talking about?"

"At a rough guess, eight or nine tons."

Parker's face fell again. "Every bit helps, of course, but that still leaves us far short of what we need to sheath the *Hatteras,* without weakening some parts of the ship in compensation . . . "

Vance was clearly enjoying himself, but none of the others could guess what gave the governor his cunning, expectant smile.

"Patience, gentlemen. We have yet to hear from my confidential aide, Mister Porter. At my urging, he has been doing some diligent research into the railroad company's prewar archives. Please share your information with the room at large."

Porter cleared his throat and brought forth a notepad.

"Back in Eighteen Fifty-seven, when the state's railroad network was expanding vigorously, orders were placed with Northern factories for more than one hundred fifty miles of track. All of it was laid down and duly accounted for except for a temporary surplus of approximately twenty-two miles' worth. The records make no further mention of that track. If it was not laid down, then it must still be somewhere. Two weeks ago, I discovered the location. It is stored in a large, unmarked, warehouse near Weldon on the end of a small spur line, now quite overgrown with weeds, but conveniently close to docks on the northern shore of the Roanoke River. Twenty-two miles of track equates to roughly sixty tons of iron. One might think the whole consignment had been forgotten entirely."

"One *might,*" chuckled Zeb Vance, "seeing as how it was not listed on the company's most recent inventory of available resources. But I rather think that omission was intentional. Mister Whitford and his associates are practically drooling at the prospect of getting a fat contract to extend the Piedmont line from Greensboro to Danville. While I can see the strategic value of such a direct line, I am in no particular hurry to see it built. Its existence would give Richmond one more excuse to neglect our eastern counties—which must now be defended, however poorly, because the line from Wilmington through Goldsboro and thence into Virginia, carries so many vital imported supplies and so much Carolina-grown food. For all their hand-wringing about shortages, those railroad rascals already have half the track they need hidden away. I have, to put it bluntly, been lied to, and I *do not like that!* We need that iron now, not later. We need the *Hatteras* more than we need another, superfluous, stretch of track."

Vance swung a penetrating gaze toward Sam Parker. "Captain Parker, if you could get your hands on sixty tons of brand-new railroad iron, could you somehow contrive to scrounge up the rest of what you need to make that vessel as powerful as it was intended to be?"

"Governor, I will send patrols as far as the Tennessee border if necessary, and rake every barnyard and cornfield along the way."

"By God, sir, I like your spirit! That won't be necessary, however. When the time comes, I shall issue a proclamation to the mountain people, urging them to comb every inch of their land for every nail and broken horseshoe they can find. I know their temper—they will respond. Hell, I'll even go to Asheville and make some stump speeches about it—give me a good excuse to get out of these stifling chambers of government, breathe some cool mountain air for a change."

"But sir," Parker stammered, not quite sure where all this might be leading, "the fact remains that the warehouse at Weldon belongs to the railroad companies. If they don't even acknowledge its existence, how will you persuade them to part with it?"

"I don't intend to persuade them, the lying skunks. I intend to seize it. Or, more accurately, I intend for you and your men at Holman's Ferry to steal it."

Now that Vance had arrived at the core of his outrageously bold plot, his enthusiasm boiled over. To cover the operation, a phony Yankee "raid" would be staged along the Roanoke. Parker's men, dressed in blue uniforms, would tow their barges up to Weldon, strip the old warehouse bare, then burn it to the ground. Colonel Graves's two militia companies, whose main encampment was two miles away, guarding the railroad bridge, would, conveniently, be marched off for an extended training exercise on the chosen date, except for a handful of picked men who would provide the wagons and extra muscle needed to haul the rails down to the barges.

"No problem there, Governor," said Graves. "Most of my boys are local farmers and more than a few of them got royally screwed, if you'll pardon my language, when the railroad men bought up parcels of their family land back in the fifties. They will not only keep their mouths shut, they will relish the chance to stick it to the plutocrats."

Of course, Vance continued smoothly, revealing another layer of his plan, there would be a great public uproar about the "enemy's" deep penetration up the river. But that would only serve to underscore his case for reinforcements to be sent to the region, and, indeed, for the ironclad to be finished so that no more such incursions would be possible.

Parker saw one serious flaw in the scheme, however. How could this "enemy" force make its way past Holman's Ferry undetected, and unopposed by the batteries he had erected down at Scotland Neck? Vance had that covered, too. The *main* enemy force, the gunboats, would in fact be stopped by those batteries, indeed, they would be valiantly repulsed, or so the story would be told in the newspapers. Parker need only schedule a loud and vigorous hour of target practice at the appropriate time. The actual raid on Weldon would be attributed to a cavalry force that had been disembarked below the batteries and had ridden ahead to burn the warehouse, then scampered back and reboarded their transports just out of the batteries' range.

"But a cavalry force could not possibly carry off sixty tons of railroad track," protested Parker. "Dump it in the river, maybe, but not actually move it. The railroad moguls will raise a howl all the way to Richmond. Once they figure out what's really happened, they might cost you the next election!"

"Ah, but that is the beauty of the thing, Parker. If they make that assertion, they also admit to committing fraud against their state—by deliberately falsifying official documents, out of greed and self-interest. *These* documents, right here on my desk, copies of which can speedily be released to the press. If they did not admit the existence of this secret cache of track, they cannot publicly complain about its disappearance. Especially if the public already believes the warehouse was pillaged by Yankees. Oh, they will suspect that I pulled a fast one, and it will probably cost me some votes, but by that time, I hope, the *Hatteras* will be finished, and victorious in action, and if the electorate suspects that the railroad men were deliberately holding back the iron that made it possible, it will not be myself who is burned in effigy."

Vance sat back, beaming, and spread his hands as if to say, "Any questions?"

Parker and Graves agreed to coordinate the plan in detail, inform the necessary accomplices, and report back to Vance when everything was ready and a suitable date selected. Parker asked where the blue uniforms would come from, but Vance was ready for that one, too. Before the war, he said, the Raleigh militia had drilled in blue, but those outfits had, of course, been put in storage as soon as blue became the enemy's color. He would arrange for the clothes to be moved to Holman's Ferry, suitably labeled as Confederate uniforms from one of the state's textile mills.

Sam Parker was almost light-headed by now; with this one, brilliantly devious, plot, the governor had cut the Gordian knot and would deliver the iron to bring the *Hatteras* alive. When there were no more questions, and the assembled ringleaders had agreed that this entire discussion had never taken place, the conclave adjourned, and the wheels of Vance's plot began to turn.

When Parker, Graves, and the mysterious Mister Porter had left, Vance motioned for Hobart-Hampden to remain. When they were alone, the Englishman shook his head in appreciation and said: "Governor, when the war is over, I seriously suggest you consider moving to London and becoming a British citizen. You could have, sir, an absolutely brilliant career in Parliament! Or the Foreign Service, come to think of it."

"You flatter me, Augustus, and I thoroughly appreciate it. You will find me a staunch Anglophile, which is one of the reasons I want you to take command of my state's first blockade-runner . . . what was the name of it again? The *Maharajah*?"

"I had named it the *Cossack,* Your Excellency. After the hard-riding, fearless horsemen of the Russian steppes. I have seen that elite cavalry in action during my service in Central Asia. However, now that the vessel has a new and distinguished investor—the great state of North Carolina—it occurs to me that another name might be more appropriate, one that pays tribute where it is due. I propose to rename her the *Ad-Vance.*" He lifted his hand as though proposing a toast.

" 'To Vance!'—from the Latin, of course."

"I remember my declensions in that honorable but now quite useless tongue; they were drummed into my brain by a professor who was old enough to have served in the Roman senate. I like the name, sir—how could I not? The *Ad-Vance* it shall be, then. Captain, I do believe we shall do a prosperous business together."

The Mound Battery

CONSCRIPTION AGAIN—North Carolina has been distinguished for the faithfulness with which she has enforced the Conscription Law, as well as for the large numbers of troops she has placed in the field, and for the unparalleled gallantry of her sons. Still, there are many—too many!—remaining at home, whose sphere of usefulness, and therefore of duty, in this crisis is in the field. We feel it is our duty to impress upon these and upon all, the nature of the events now happening. To assure them that upon the strength or the feebleness of the effort now made, much of good or evil for the future may, and in all human probability, must depend. To ensure decisive success, a greater effort must be put forth than has ever yet been made. All apathy must be cast aside, and enthusiasm in recruiting for the ranks of the Army must take its place. We will go farther, and say plainly, and in so many words:—The ranks of our armies, thinned by sickness, battle, and desertion, must be recruited more rapidly than is now the case. If we are successfully to cope with the hordes of the enemy, swelled by the immense accessions which they are now receiving—if we would close the Spring campaign without disaster to our arms and with disaster to theirs. This can only be done by every man who can go, going. Conscription or no conscription, and by every straggler, absentee or other person not at his post, repairing thereto promptly—at once! Now is the time!

—The Wilmington Journal, April 6 1863

Looking south from his command post in the Pulpit, Colonel William Lamb contemplated once again the strangely biblical appearance of the construction project that, when finished, would form the most visible and dramatic symbol of Fort Fisher and the men sworn to defend it. Stark against the prevailing flatness of its backdrop, the Mound Battery rose higher every day, inch by painstaking inch. He had conceived the idea months ago, while he was refining his design for the complete system of works, but he did not order the actual construction to begin until after the sea and land faces, together with their integral array of huge humped traverses and gun chambers, their bombproof-ready magazines and dugouts, had all been built, and the heavy guns procured, mounted, and tested.

When he was satisfied that the fort's primary defenses were operational, he ordered work begun on the Mound. Starting on New Year's Day, he assigned one full company, on a daily rotating basis, to pile up sand for the foundation. But so enormous was the base circumference relative to the projected height, that by the end of January, all you could see was a lumpy plateau, scarcely a foot high. Lamb appealed to Chase Whiting, and Whiting released more troops, drawn from the mostly idle garrisons of Forts Anderson, Caswell, and Holmes—another four hundred men, whose field tents had sprawled over every empty acre of Confederate Point, as though a clan of Bedouins had camped out in a patch of desert. Whiting also sent an urgent request to Richmond, seeking authorization and funding to lease as many Negroes as possible from the owners of surrounding plantations. To Whiting's amazement, the request was granted and the money transferred. By mid-March, therefore, Lamb commanded a racially mixed workforce of almost one thousand men, and the Mound's prodigious foundation grew perceptibly.

Once Whiting and his chief engineers had inspected the foundation and pronounced it strong enough to hold the weight of the remaining elevation, plus the pair of heavy guns that would ultimately be emplaced there, Lamb moved on to the next stage of his plan. The old wooden lighthouse was dismantled and from its timbers Lamb's carpenters cobbled together a sixty-foot-tall scaffold, its platform centered directly over the Mound's intended apex. A long wooden ramp, wide enough for two columns of men and wheelbarrows to pass abreast, connected that platform to a mountain of sand. Every day, from dawn to nightfall, endless files of men sweated and strained up the incline, pushing wheelbarrows or towing carts, blacks and whites intermingled.

Observing their progress from the Pulpit, Lamb colored his impressions with biblical metaphors: This, surely, was a sight not dissimilar to that of the pyramids' construction, or perhaps, considering the mixture of black slaves and white soldiers, of the Tower of Babel.

And in his moments of fancy, Lamb thought of himself as the Pharaoh who ruled this motley tribe—and was happily amused by the fact that he needed only his righteous authority as commanding officer to set these minions in motion, not the scourge of overseers' whips. As soon as the weather turned warm, in late March, many of the workers shed their shirts, and the bright sheen of sweat on their shoulders and backs made it look as though two shimmering strands of multicolored pearls were undulating back and forth.

Even with the scaffold, the ramp, and the larger workforce, progress on the Mound went slowly. By April 6, its average height was only twenty feet, and the slaves' labor contracts were about to expire. But a few days later, a miracle happened: a convoy of barges tied up at Inlet Wharf, carrying a small but powerful locomotive and enough narrow-gauge track to build an inclined railroad from the sand dumps to the summit. It was a gift from Hobart-Hampden and a consortium of wealthy blockade-runners, who had leased both the donkey engine and the track from a now-idle granite quarry in Georgia and then dispatched the machinery down to Fort Fisher as a gesture of thanks to Lamb and his overworked garrison. Once the scaffolding had been knocked together and the doughty little engine fired up, the railroad moved more sand in one day than Lamb's men could move in a week. The Mound grew prodigiously.

And now, on the afternoon of May 14, it was complete. Lamb watched the last column of workers wind down the scaffold; heard a raucous celebratory toot from the little locomotive. He was too far away to hear the clink of discarded equipment, and the sea wind rushed forward to fill the sudden quiet. The Mound's western slope glowed golden-white in the lowering sun, and to the east, across the surf, it cast a huge conical purple shadow, as though a volcano had magically risen on the tip of Confederate Point. Halfway down the slope, the colors changed to a tough, weedy green, for the base of the cone had been massively shingled by plates of thick coastal sod, bearded with sea oats and dune grass, to prevent erosion by wind or storm-driven waves.

The Mound Battery was forty-three feet tall and visible from a great distance out at sea; no single thing on the whole Cape Fear coast reached such a height, or made such a defiant statement to the beholders' perceptions. On the stout circular revetment that formed its crown rose the fort's main flagstaff. Heliograph signals from Lamb's command post in the Pulpit flew in a straight line down the sea face to the Mound's summit, and signals from the Mound's summit were visible from every point along the walls—thus Lamb could relay tactical orders to every battery in Fort Fisher in a matter of seconds. There was another signal apparatus on the Mound as well: a pair of range lights that were turned on whenever a blockade-runner made its dash for New Inlet. When the runner's pilot saw those two lights line up straight, he knew it was safe to begin his starboard turn into the channel. There was still room on top for two big guns—a 10-inch columbiad and a double-banded 6.4-inch Brooke rifle, fresh from the gun foundry in Selma, Alabama. If the Union navy were rash enough to emulate Farragut's damn-the-torpedoes tactics at New Orleans and try to storm straight through the inlet with light-draft gunboats, those two potent weapons could sink them easily with plunging fire.

William Lamb smiled into the tangy wind and savored a moment of rare fulfillment. With the Mound now operational, all of Fort Fisher's basic elements were in place. Whatever time remained to him, before the inevitable Yankee onslaught, he would devote to small refinements and to the unending task of making the walls, traverses, and gun chambers ever stronger. *Be not too proud, Young Soldier of the Lord,* he reminded himself. You must still find more ammunition—there could never be too much—and above all, more men. The enemy could still make an amphibious landing on the broad sandy plains to the north, and if all the fort's artillery was fully manned, he had only a few companies of raw infantry to oppose such a maneuver. There was still much to be done.

Very quietly, someone coughed behind his right shoulder, someone who understood the colonel's mood and did not wish to invade it. Lamb recognized that diffident cough.

"Good afternoon, Major Reilly. The Mound really looks impressive from here, does it not?"

"It does indeed, Colonel, and all the gun-crew lads are fixing to celebrate its completion. A rare allotment of whiskey would go well with their suppers, sir."

"Have we enough?"

"I think so, under lock and key in the commissary storage house. I may have forgotten to mention that a delegation of grateful runner-captains shipped us a few extra barrels, last week, to celebrate their grand victory at Chancellorsville.

"By all means, then! Share the bounty with the men. It's their vigilance that keeps our runner friends in business. By the way, Major

Reilly, we're having an unusually lively group of guests to dinner at the Cottage tonight, and I distinctly recall issuing you an invitation several days ago . . . Daisy and I look forward to your company."

Reilly ducked his head uneasily and performed a little shuffle with his feet. "Well, Colonel, thank you, sir, but I'm not a man of easy social graces. Bump on a log, you might say. I promised the gunners I'd spend the evening with them, make sure that whiskey allotment gets distributed fairly, maybe play some cards." Suddenly Reilly snapped his fingers. "Oh, I almost forgot the reason I came up here. Those new torpedo-exploding devices, the ones Hobart-Hampden promised to have sent to us from Bermuda? Runner brought 'em in last week and they came down from town on this afternoon's supply steamer. You should take a look at 'em, sir, before you leave for the day. They look like just what the doctor ordered."

Lamb was excited by this news and he rubbed his hands together with something approximating a little boy's gesture of glee. The torpedo field north of the land face was his pet project, his ace in the hole against massed infantry attacks.

"Where are they, Reilly?"

"Down with all the other torpedo batteries and stuff. I couldn't resist opening one of the crates."

"Lead on, man! I'm anxious to see the latest advances in British technology."

All the torpedo-activating equipment had been stored in a canvas-covered pit, dug into the sand at a safe remove from the big whale-hump of the central magazine. Not even the engineers who had studied this new and controversial brand of weaponry felt entirely comfortable around the actuating equipment: hulking galvanic batteries that generated—or theoretically generated, since the apparatus was temperamental at best—jolts of current sufficient to ignite a waterproof charge of fulminate powder packed inside a goose-quill tube, which would, in turn, detonate a rhomboidal iron cylinder packed with one hundred pounds of explosives. Lamb had sowed the northern approach with twenty-four such bombs, connected by India-rubber coated wires into groups of three; until today, his skeptical ordnance specialists had striven to maintain eight separate galvanic "cells" composed of zinc plates submerged in sulfuric acid, thirty-five gallons of it for each battery. On several occasions, he had tested the system, using smaller torpedoes with token charges, and had learned to anticipate a success rate of approximately 50 percent. Not good enough. So he had asked Hobart-Hampden to find out if Britain's scientists had come up with something new, less cumbersome, and more reliable. Apparently they had, and the faithful Augustus had managed to acquire some specimens.

Reilly led him over to the newly arrived crates and proudly displayed what appeared to be a large telegraph generator attached to a burly, walnut-handled crank. The manufacturer's seal proclaimed these machines to be "Wheatstone's Magnetic Exploders," built in Manchester.

"If these do the trick, Colonel, we can dump all that stinking sulfuric stuff into the sea. No one will be sorry to see it go—I've been half-expecting some damned fool to stick his finger in it, just to see what happens."

"Don't throw it into the ocean, Major Reilly," Lamb chuckled. "It will probably kill all the fish for miles around. Well, these newfangled devices certainly should be an improvement, if they work. We'll unpack the rest and set up an experimental trial. Have some of your gunners rig up a twenty-pound charge in a tin box or something. Maybe give it a whirl next Sunday, if the weather's fair. Meantime, make sure all the existing torpedoes are in good shape, and send some men out tomorrow to make sure none of them have become exposed, due to the recent rains. I don't want any accidental explosions."

Lamb clapped Reilly on the shoulder, thanked him for the good news, then strode off to his tactical quarters. There were no new telegrams on his desk, and no more duties to perform, so he rode out through the riverside gate, beneath the hulking embankments of Shepherd's Battery, content in the day's events and already looking forward to an evening of good food and stimulating company.

We shall all drink a toast to the Mound Battery. May it be the salvation of many a doughty runner and the bane of the enemy!

At least once a week, there was a dinner party at the Cottage. The runner captains customarily brought a wagon or two full of food and luxury goods after each successful run into New Inlet, as a grateful tribute to Colonel Lamb's vigilance and the protection offered by Fort Fisher's big guns. Daisy's larder was always full, and she made sure the excess food and coffee were shared with the garrison.

Tonight, the party celebrated the successful runs of two famous skippers: "Plucky Tom" Taylor, captain of the *Night Hawk,* just returned to Wilmington from his tenth consecutive round-trip to

Bermuda, and "Jolly Jack" Cubbins, skipper of the *Comet,* which had been so hotly pursued two nights earlier that only some fancy shooting by Reilly's Flying Battery had saved her from running aground. Other guests included Editor James Fulton; the fort's chief surgeon, Dr. Reece; Chase Whiting and his wife, Katie; Captain Henry Savage, Collector of Customs and Smithville; Hobart-Hampden; and another Englishman, a Mister Frank Vizitelli, artist-correspondent for the *London Illustrated Times.* Reverend Dane, the pastor of St. James Episcopal Church, had tagged along, possibly to represent Wilmington's clergy, but more likely to chaperon his eldest and only unmarried daughter, Clara, who was being escorted, apparently as a matter of political and military protocol, by none other than Flag Officer William Branch. Even more taciturn than usual, Branch gave the distinct impression that this arrangement was more of a duty than a social pleasure—Clara Dane was a bony and relatively charmless woman who tried to compensate for her equine features by sprinkling her conversation with frequent girlish giggles that seemed to dribble from her prim little mouth at the rate of three per minute, whether they were remotely appropriate or not. Branch attended to her with impeccable stoic courtesy, but not even the lavish spread of good food—constantly replenished by Aunt Charity and her niece, both sparkling in starchy white aprons—seemed to afford any real pleasure to Branch. As week followed uneventful week, Branch had come more and more to embody the local Confederate navy's status as "uniformed drones." Between Branch and Whiting, there was a pronounced coolness that neither officer made any great effort to disguise.

After tucking into a lavish buffet supper, the guests dispersed, some to stroll the grounds, some to sample the excellent wines brought in by the runner captains who were the guests of honor. Hobart-Hampden had decided to leave the party fairly early. He and Vizitelli would ride back to the Yellow House, the correspondent to wager on a cockfight or a whist game, and Hobart-Hampden to embrace his dark-eyed, lush-lipped Jewess. Or so he hoped. He had returned on the train from Raleigh with just enough spare time to change for the party and to scrawl a note for Largo that he had thrust into Lieutenant Pendelton's hand on his way out the door. He needed one more serious drink before concluding the evening's business, preferably consumed during a slow meditative smoke on the riverbank. Lamb's "butler," the efficient young Cassius, struck Hobart-

Hampden as a black youth of considerable intelligence, and he paused a few minutes to chat with the lad before seeking solitude beside the darkening river.

"You and young Dick Lamb seem to have struck up a lively friendship, Cassius."

"Yes, sir, Captain. Little Dick, he and I be reg'lar playmates. I teach him how to ketch crabs, show him how to care for the horses, where to find the seabirds' eggs, and right now, we makin' a raft, with a sail and a rudder, too. When it's done, me and Dick and young Rufus Pender, we gone form a pirate crew, out on the river. My sister Fanny, she's stichtin' up a pirate flag, too. With, what you call it, a skull and sawbones."

Hobart-Hampden laughed. "Skull and *crossbones* is how the real pirates would say it. Did you know, Cassius, that the bloodiest, most feared pirate of them all, the ferocious Blackbeard, used to use the Cape Fear as one of his hideouts? Why, he might very well have anchored right there, and he might have buried a treasure chest or two nearby. Right here on Confederate Point! So, when you and little Dick and . . . what was the other boy's name?"

"Rufus Pender, Cap'n. He's thirteen and his mammy runs that little store 'bout two mile up the road, on Sugarloaf Hill. He's the onliest boy to help out now, 'cause his daddy and two brothers, they off fighting with Marse Robert in Virginny. The Penders be mighty poor these days—all they gots to sell is fishin' line and crab buckets and oyster rakes and some poor-grade cloth and crackers. But they good people, Cap'n, even so. Us three boys, we get together whenever we can, go explorin'."

"Not too close to the fort, I trust . . ."

"Oh, no, sir! Miss Daisy and the colonel, they very strict 'bout that. We can't go no closer than the line where the trees been cut down." Aunt Charity's voice summoned, so Cassius straightened his jacket and bowed politely.

"Very nice talkin' with you, Cap'n. You enjoy that drink, now—outside by the river, this time on a spring night, it be mighty peaceable."

"Nice talking to you, too, young man. Remember—you boys keep your eyes open for one of those pirate treasure chests."

Surprisingly, the lad winked and made a sly grin.

"Oh, Cap'n, I think we already done found one!"

William Lamb climbed the narrow stairs very quietly. He and Daisy were fortunate, he reflected, in having the services of a well-trained "big-house slave"; Aunt Charity had served many years at Orton, before crossing the river to help out at the Cottage. Maria and Dick followed her around like happy ducklings, and the Negro woman wooed them into slumber every night with her extensive fund of bedtime stories, some African, some European, some apparently of her own devising, a colorful mixture of both cultures. She made sure they visited the chamber pots, brushed their teeth, and said their prayers—all this without seeming to miss a moment of her downstairs duties as well. Every night, when the children were tucked in, she notified Daisy with a quiet word and a reassuring nod. Later on, when the Negroes were dismissed for the night and had retired to their small but cozy cabin—conveniently close but screened from the Cottage by a grove of wind-bent yaupon trees—the Lambs went upstairs, hand in hand, and peeked in on their darlings.

Lamb wondered, sometimes, if he had made the right choice by bringing Daisy and the children here, instead of putting them up in one of the fine Wilmington houses whose owners had generously volunteered to host the famous colonel's family. Even though it was not visible from the sea, the Cottage *was* within range of the biggest Yankee guns—that alarming fact had been confirmed a month ago, when a couple of solid-shot fired by a frigate in hot pursuit had zoomed over the chimney and thrown up water-plumes in the river.

Lamb had felt duty-bound to raise the matter with Daisy, but she would not hear of moving. Small and plain as it was, the Cottage had become *her home* the moment she stepped across the threshold. As for those two errant cannonballs, they had merely added a frisson of excitement to the routine of her days. There was plenty of room for the children to play and work off their energies, and relatively little danger. Cassius watched over them with sharp diligence, and the children understood that, even though he was a slave and they were technically his "little master, little mistress," he was their mother's appointed deputee and they were to obey him in all things when Daisy was not around. It was Cassius who had taken Dick and Ria up to the "borderland," the edge of that barren killing ground a half mile from the land face, where the garrison had stripped away all vegetation, and Cassius who had explained to them that this raw demarcation was the absolute limit of their world; they were not to venture into that man-made desert unless accompanied by their parents.

At the top of the stairs, William Lamb lit a candle stub and quietly opened the door to the children's bedroom. They slept like angels, their hair tousled and their sweet mouths softly open. Their presence made the very air in the room smell pure, and this image of innocence always acted on Lamb as a powerful tonic, causing him to feel, just for an instant, that all the great hulking power of his fort existed, in some part, to offer them protection. From the moment he kissed Daisy good-bye in the morning and rode into the fort over the plank bridge, past the gleaming muzzles of the bronze Napoleons emplaced there, his days were rigorous, his obligations stern, his responsibilities enormous and sometimes—as on that forlorn and awful day when he had ordered the execution of the two deserters—bitter as gall. But he bore the weight of each day more calmly, more resolutely, because he knew that when the garrison stood down for supper and the Stars and Bars was lowered from its staff atop the Mound, he would ride back to a place that was home.

Satisfied that the children were deep within their dreams, he tiptoed to their bedsides and kissed their foreheads in turn. Sometimes, he fancied that as he did this, he caught some faint emanation of those dreams, a feather-soft vibration of sweet, inviolate peace.

Refreshed as always by this nightly ritual, Lamb closed the bedroom door, pinched out the candle, and drew himself erect, remolding his features to fit the role of host and commander. The party downstairs was winding down, and he would not be sorry to wave farewell to the last guests, but that would not be for another two or three hours.

Dick Lamb thought that yellow pine was just about the most cheerful kind of wood there was. For most of his ten years, he had lived amid the dark, heavy furniture that was popular with the adults of his time, but the cottage and its yellow pine walls and simple, welcoming furniture seemed, even on the gloomiest gray days of the previous winter, to be made of sunlight itself. And because the wood was not yet seasoned, it often made interesting sounds at night, when the house was quiet: sighs, quirky little questions addressed from one plank to its neighbors, tiny bursts of wood-song. And the fourth step down from the upstairs landing always made a distinctive little squeak when his father trod upon it on his way back down from his ritual candlelight inspection. And so, when the pine slab made that little squeal, which to Dick's vivid young imagination sounded exactly like a mouse whose tail had just been pinched, Dick knew that his father was gone for the night and would soon retire to the adults' bedroom below.

He slid down the covers and bent close to Ria's head, making absolutely certain she was deep inside her six-year-old dreams. He quietly pulled on his shoes and covered his pajamas with a dark, knee-length winter coat. Then he silently padded over to the window and peered out, searching the brushy undulating dunes on the ocean side of the Wilmington Road. Sure enough: there was the signal—two quick winks of a lantern shutter, followed by two more. Earlier, there had been adults standing around the front porch, near the hitching posts, and while their horses and carriages were still there, the owners had apparently taken their business indoors, or had gathered on the backyard terrace, to savor the fade of twilight across the broad slow river. Dick had already tested his escape route on previous nights—lowering himself from the bedroom window to the roof of the porch that encircled three sides of the Cottage, then shinnying down a stout beam until his feet touched the rim of a rain barrel. He could make this getaway in less than two minutes, bedroom-to-ground, and unless some adult happened to wander around to the south side of the house, no one would see him. He knew his parents would disapprove of his nocturnal rambles, but they had apparently never considered this possibility, so they had not *expressly* forbidden it. If he got caught, he could always fall back on that excuse, flimsy though he knew it to be.

Pirates took risks, he reminded himself as he dropped the last two feet and crouched quietly, straining to hear any approaching adults. *Especially pirates who were hot on the trail of real buried treasure.* When Rufus Pender found the treasure chest, and showed it excitedly to Dick, they had both dutifully reported it to Cassius—but they hadn't told him exactly where it was; they just described it as being "near the beach," which it was, in a way. And tomorrow, all three of the Fort Fisher Pirates were supposed to check it out, appropriately equipped with shovels and a pick, of course, which Rufus could supply from his mother's store.

But Dick knew that when Cassius realized that the treasure chest was buried just inside the Forbidden Zone of cleared land, he would not allow the younger boys to dig it up until he had cleared the project with the Lambs. And neither Dick nor Rufus could wait that long. They planned, instead, to uncover the tantalizing object tonight, and if it did not weigh too much, they would drag it back to the tree line and rebury it. That was a *real* pirate scheme—Dick and Rufus could just imagine old Blackbeard smiling down on them, twisting the ends of his fierce moustache and commending them for their cunning.

Dick scampered like a rabbit, crossing the pale expanse of the road so quickly that any adult who happened to see him might think him a deer. Rufus was waiting, crouched beneath some scraggly trees, fully equipped for the expedition with shovel and pick and lantern. Barely able to contain their excitement, the boys quickly located the scraps of cloth they had tied to branches during the day, marking the trail to the tree line's edge nearest the treasure chest, a half mile from the cottage and slightly closer to the fort itself.

Rufus was barely a year older than Dick Lamb and a year younger than Cassius, which made the pirate gang a very symmetrical and complementary trio of boys. Rufus has spent a lonely year before the Lambs arrived; his brothers and father were off in Marse Robert's army, as were most of the draft-age men who made up the sparse prewar population of Confederate Point. Between Wilmington and the fort, there were perhaps a hundred scattered cottages; poor but honest families who loved the solitude and privacy, and lived on seafood, small patches of garden produce, and whatever rabbit, squirrel, or venison they could bag. During the hurricane season, they were also "wreckers," for by ancient custom, whatever goods the sea cast up after the great Cape Fear storms were fair game for the first beachcombers who stumbled on them.

Dick and Cassius had been as delighted to make a new friend as Rufus had been to discover that he had new neighbors, and over time the three boys bonded strongly. Rufus was their guide, leading them through the tangled maritime forest and pointing out the saline creeks where crawfish thrived. To the imaginations of three boys, Confederate Point was a vast canvas that invited every sort of pretending. Its enormous windy sands could be the exotic Sahara. Its beaches were strewn with an ever-changing variety of exotic and wonderful flotsam: shells of every color and form, driftwood statues, seaweed in great storm-knotted clumps that looked like green, tentacled monsters. Sometimes, there were fabulously *gross* specimens of decomposition, an occasional glassy-eyed shark, or one of the magnificent Portuguese men-o-war that sometimes drifted in from the Gulf Stream. Rufus avowed these jellyfish could stun a full-grown man with their venom even when they were dead—and you could never tell *if* they were dead, but you could derive great squealing joy from puncturing their weird translucent air sacs. There were also cannonballs lobbed from the Yankee ships offshore and the black, sinister mass of two sunken runners, just tantalizingly visible at low tide. Two or three times, they had tried to get close to the burned-out hulk of the *Florimel,* but a mounted patrol from the fort chased them off and that same night, Colonel Lamb delivered a stern lecture to the boys—a burned-out runner was off-limits, a place of danger, every bit as forbidden as the cleared zone north of the fort. On two occasions, though, the colonel had arranged for the three boys to actually visit inside the walls of the fort, and he had used one of those excursions to show them what various calibers of unexploded shells looked like, eliciting from them a solemn promise that they were *never* to approach such objects, but were to report their location to him so that ordnance experts from the fort might either retrieve them and shoot them back at their original Yankee owners, or, if they were too rusted to use, or did not fit any of the fort's guns, destroy them where they lay.

But the treasure chest did not resemble any of those shells. From what they could see of it, it looked exactly like a storybook image of an iron strongbox. Who knew what might be inside? Doubloons! Cutlasses! Silver looted from the Indies, perhaps by Blackbeard himself! Dick was a bit troubled by the fact that the black iron object lay inside the Forbidden Zone, but only by hundred feet or so. It was far enough from the fort so that no one would see them dig it up, not at night, and even if its contents were too heavy for them to drag back to the tree line, it did not appear to be secured by a very strong lock, just some ordinary iron hinges and bolts: a few lusty swings of the pick, and its contents would be revealed.

Augustus Hobart-Hampden enjoyed three of North Carolina's four seasons—like most of the natives, he merely endured the humid, broiling summers and spent as many days as possible either on or near the water. The storm that had battered the *Comet* two nights before was almost certainly the last tempest of spring—both his sailor's instinct and the almanac suggested as much. And a May night such as this, with the river still holding a suggestion of soft twilight, could be as sublime as any riverbank vista in England. He was also stirred by the moody ferocity of the whole Cape Fear region. He often thought back to the maiden voyage of the *Banshee,* when Largo spoke of the river and the cape in phrases of near-Wordsworthian eloquence, paying homage to its untamed wildness, its magnificent indifference to the ships and men who plied its shoal-littered and riptide-carved channels. Her casual poetry on that occasion had stirred in his breast an interest somewhat deeper than carnal curiosity; had confirmed his early suspicion that she might be worth a considerable investment of time and emotion.

As he sipped his drink and expelled a few neat ovals of cigar smoke, he considered once more the curious situation of Matthew Sloane. Hobart-Hampden had pulled every string in his grasp to expedite Sloane's parole—not only out of loyalty to a friend but also for a very practical reason: he wanted Matthew to take command of the *Banshee* again, while he took the helm of the new *Ad-Vance.* But because of the Secret Service's vendetta against Belle O'Neale, and Matthew's spirited repulse of Lafayette Baker, none of the usual protocols had worked.

Finally, with the help of the governor of Nassau and the British embassy in Washington, he had managed to get a letter through to Matthew, informing him that Mary Harper was well, the children were safe, Pine Haven was thriving, and that Jacob Landau had died in the plague. He did not directly mention the *Banshee,* on the assumption that Matthew's jailers would read any mail addressed to him, but he did hint broadly that great opportunities and new adventures were waiting for Matthew, should he be paroled.

Sloane's return letter was flabbergasting: a grim, terse, breast-beating wail of self-loathing. The gist of it was: *I do not want to be paroled; my sin was so great that I belong in this prison cell; I can never look my wife in the eyes again.*

What utter sentimental Calvinistic rot!

Hobart-Hampden would have none of it. He had prepared an official report (on Royal Navy stationery) about Lafayette Baker's high-seas ambush, emphasizing that this act of near brigandage—*unworthy of a gentleman and certainly unworthy of a president as highly principled as Abraham Lincoln*—had taken place on British territorial waters. To this initial report, the governor of Nassau had appended an official letter of protest. The queen herself—by means of a tight-lipped statement from the prime minister—had expressed her displeasure at Mister Baker's dishonorable behavior. All of these documents were formally portfolioed by the Royal Navy attaché at the British embassy in Washington, and the resulting diplomatic furor was so severe that President Lincoln himself reportedly had ordered a thorough review of Sloane's case. If things continued to move in this direction, Matthew Sloane, whether he wanted to or not, might soon be back on the bridge of the *Banshee,* where the sea wind would soon cleanse him of his confounded guilt.

Altogether, Hobart-Hampden reflected, it had been a good piece of work, one of his best.

His reverie was interrupted by the appearance of Flag Officer Branch, who asked politely if he might join the Englishman for a drink and a cigar. Hobart-Hampden of course agreed. He felt sorry for the fellow. He knew the saga of the brave but hopelessly outgunned Mosquito Fleet, and understood the frustration Branch lived with daily, as the massive ironclad *Raleigh* sat on the ways at Beery's Shipyard on Eagle Island week after week, not yet armed, fitted with a clapped-out ferryboat engine that might, at full speed and in calm water, propel the behemoth at the dazzling speed of five or six knots. And having just returned from Zeb Vance's Machiavellian conference on the subject of iron, he knew that Branch had faithfully sent Sam Parker all the iron he could spare. Every month, a few rolled plates of armor did arrive from Richmond, but at the current rate, the *Raleigh* might not be finished for another year, and Branch understood as well as Hobart-Hampden that the war might be as good as lost by that time, especially if Lee's great summer offensive did not restore momentum to the Rebel cause. No wonder poor Branch had taken to the opium pipe; especially if his social life had narrowed to such an extent that the Reverend Dane's horse-faced daughter was the best female companion Branch could find.

For a while, the two men discussed naval affairs, one officer to another. Branch had visited Fort Fisher and practically drooled with envy at the sight of the giant Armstrong gun. If he had the resources to start another ironclad, Branch averred, it would be patterned on the Union navy's monitors and it would have a rotating turret large enough to mount a pair of Armstrongs—with such a dreadnought as that, in combination with the *Raleigh,* Branch could sally from New Inlet and break the back of the blockade in one stunning attack. But this was a fantasy, and he surely knew it.

Hobart-Hampden saw the value of the *Raleigh*—even if it proved too underpowered to venture far from shore, its existence as a floating battery on the Cape Fear River would be a powerful backup to Fort Fisher. He confirmed to Branch that the state itself was going into the runner business and offered to bring him 120 bars of good English iron on the *Banshee*'s second voyage. He did not, however, tell Branch that the *Banshee*'s first voyage for Governor Vance would bring in iron for the *Hatteras;* there was already enough ill feeling between Branch and Sam Parker. When he heard the offer, Branch seemed stunned with gratitude; his eyes actually glistened when he pumped Hobart-Hampden's hand.

Just then, with his usual punctuality, Cassius stuck his head through the back door and asked if the two gentlemen would care for another drink. Yes, they would.

Hobart-Hampden then brought up a technical question, one he had been meaning to ask Colonel Lamb, but one that Branch could probably answer just as well. How, he inquired, did Fort Fisher's land torpedoes differ from the tethered submerged torpedoes that Whiting had sewn around Fort Anderson and the other river batteries? Did the land torpedoes resemble the nautical ones—like giant iron fishing corks studded with friction detonators?

"Well, the principle is the same, except that Lamb intends to detonate his bombs on command, by sending electrical current through buried wires when the enemy infantry is marching over them. Nor do they resemble the river devices. Actually, Lamb's torpedoes look like ordinary iron chests, though tapered at the bottom, so the blast will radiate more effectively—at least that is the theory. Personally, I doubt the detonating cables would survive a heavy shelling, and every time they have a big storm out here, they have to rebury some of the iron casings."

Young Cassius, who had been standing quietly behind them carrying a tray full of glasses, suddenly cried out in alarm and dropped the tray. Then, without a word of apology or explanation, he fled into the Cottage.

"I wonder what that was all about?" mused Branch.

"Perhaps he was spooked by our discussion of those 'infernal devices,' as the Yankee papers like to call them."

Cassius was much more than spooked. When he heard Branch say the words "actually, Lamb's torpedoes look like ordinary iron chests," a terrifying intuition flashed through his mind. Heedless of Aunt Charity's angry glare, or Daisy Lamb's look of astonishment, he ran up the stairs and crashed open the door to the children's bedroom. Ria stirred awake and saw him. Cassius forced himself to look calm, placing a hushing finger to his lips and winking at the little girl. Reassured that all was well, she put her head back down and fell instantly back to sleep.

By this time, the adults were gathered anxiously at the foot of the stairs and General Whiting had gone so far as to put hand on sword, wondering if this young black man had suddenly turned into a homicidal maniac. But by the time Cassius reached them, he blurted out enough to galvanize the men into action.

"Cuh-nul Lamb! It's Little Dick, suh! He's gone out the window! Ah think I know where! Get all the lights you can grab and follow me! He may be in danger! No time to lose!"

As soon as Cassius spotted the boys' cloth trail markers, he knew which direction they had taken, for the Fort Fisher Pirates had often used that technique to mark their favorite routes through the woods. As he crashed through the scrub pines, he explained about the "buried treasure" the other boys claimed to have found . . . a partly buried iron chest. And William Lamb's blood ran cold as he stumbled behind, crying his son's name as loudly as he could above the eternal sea wind.

"There it be!" whispered Rufus Pender, unshuttering the lantern and raising it high: a dull black wedge of iron, six inches of it uncovered by the recent storm. Using hands and Rufus's small shovel, the boys scraped away more sand, until they could see the hinges and the strange little cylinder that seemed to serve as the treasure chest's only lock. Dick was now seized with foreboding—surely the sentries on the land face could see their lantern—might even construe them as Yankee spies—might, oh Lord, even fire upon them. If a mounted patrol rode up now and caught them in the Forbidden Zone, his daddy would give them both such a whipping they wouldn't be able to sit down for a week.

"Come on, Dick, help me pull it loose."

But the combined strength of both boys could not budge the heavy cask and the hundred pounds of gunpowder it contained.

"Oh, Rufus, I hear my daddy callin'. We better hightail it back into the trees right now."

"Not before I bust open this sum-bitch and see what's in it!"

Rufus stood back and raised the pick.

Just as he started to swing it, a black shape flew out, swift as a panther. There was no way Cassius could tackle both boys, so he acted from the loyalty Aunt Charity had drummed into him all his life. He grabbed Dick Lamb by the waist and spun him around, throwing him down into a slight depression in the sand and covering him with his own body just as Rufus Pender brought down the pickax with all his might.

On the front porch of the cottage, Daisy Lamb held on to Aunt Charity and Katie Whiting held on to Clara Dane, who was only now figuring out that something fearful was taking place and was attempting, without much success, to suppress one of her nervous little giggles.

Then a sudden yellow light flared in the direction of the fort, and a few seconds later they heard a dull and distant crump of thunder.

Daisy Lamb screamed.

At noon on Saturday, June 12, 1863, the Pirates of Fort Fisher launched their flagship—appropriately christened, in a nod toward both Blackbeard and a more contemporary legend, *Stonewall's Revenge.* Thanks to God's grace, the quick thinking of Cassius, and the fortunate fact that two-thirds of the powder in the "treasure chest" torpedo had been too soaked from the latest storm to blow up the way it was supposed to, all three of the boys had survived. But none had escaped injury, and William Lamb did not think he could ever forgive himself for the incident. He *thought* he had made it absolutely clear to Dick and his friends that the treeless half-mile Forbidden Zone between the scraggly edge of the maritime forest and the land face of the fort was "forbidden" for good reasons. In the conscience-tearing days after the explosion, he wondered if some other choice of words, some sterner threat of punishment, might better have enforced that boundary. He had not told the boys about the torpedo field because he was afraid that such knowledge would increase their curiosity, their desire to actually see some of the "infernal devices" they had heard about. He had, however, made it daylight-plain to them that the maritime forest had been cut down there, at his command, for one grim reason: to make it impossible for a Yankee landing force to approach the walls unseen, and to make it easier for his artillery to kill them if they tried. He might have used other words, a different approach, but there was no guarantee they would have averted the tragedy, either. He would never know. Just as he would never know if Daisy could forgive him.

A patrol had come galloping up from the fort right after the blast, with pistols drawn, and somewhere inside the ramparts, the garrison's drums were sounding the long roll, turning the gun crews out and summoning the infantry to fall in. In the one corner of his mind not spinning from the blood and confusion of the moment, William Lamb was pleased at how quickly the garrison was responding; but the rest of him was mired in sand and blood, screams and the stink of exploded powder.

Cassius had hurled Dick down and partly shielded him with his own tall body, but a piece of iron had sliced across Dick's forehead and in the sudden jittering light of many lanterns, the boy's face was a sheen of blood, a scarlet jack-o'-lantern defined by the wide stunned glaze of his protruding eyes. Cassius has broken an ankle and the starched white back of his butler's jacket was like a dartboard, studded with small daggers of shrapnel. As he raised himself up again, uncovering the rest of Dick Lamb, each protruding sliver generated its own spreading stain until his back was sopping with red. With courage befitting a veteran soldier, however, Cassius struggled until he found one leg that could support him and somehow he managed to help Dick to stand as well, and was exploring his young master's body, with gentle methodical hands, searching for additional wounds.

But Rufus Pender had taken the full force of the blast at the instant his pick cracked open the fulimate-and-powder quill detonator and he lay screaming on his back, his clothes shredded, his face a mass of raw and rearranged meat, the left arm just *gone,* terminated at the elbow in a ragged spurting stump and the right hand so badly mangled, and flailing so wildly at his facial wounds, that Lamb could not make an accurate count of how many fingers the boy still had. Without waiting for orders, two of the mounted scouts turned around and galloped back to the fort, promising to return with a wagon, and to alert the fort's surgery to be ready to receive casualties.

At that point, Dr. Reece and Daisy showed up, riding as passenger in Flag Officer Branch's buggy. Even before his feet touched the sand, Branch had removed his belt and handed it over for use as a tourniquet. Daisy Lamb, quickly recovering from her shock and stifling her sobs, inspected her son's wounds first, then those of Cassius, understanding at once that poor Rufus Pender's injuries were by far the worst. While Dr. Reece, Lamb, and one of the soldiers from the fort shifted the mutilated boy onto a blanket and began ministering to him, Daisy walked over to Branch and calmly asked him for the loan of his sword. Then she began cutting off long strips of her petticoats to make bandages. By the time a second wagon arrived from the fort, she had swathed Little Dick's head with mummy-wrappings and had managed to stop the worst of his bleeding. There was no more screaming now, for the blessed morphia of shock had closed down Rufus Pender's nerve endings, and except for the urgent whispered consultations of the surgeon and those assisting him, the only sound was Dick Lamb's quaking voice, over and over again, saying: "Oh, Mother, I am so sorry . . . I am so sorry . . . you and Poppa *told* us not to go here . . . "

One thing Lamb had insisted upon, from the day he assumed command of Fort Fisher, was that the fort's hospital should be as modern and as well stocked as any in the Confederate army. Dr. Reece had recruited two more reputable surgeons to assist him and had trained a dozen good men as nurses and aides. Grateful runner captains had brought in the most complete and up-to-date surgical kits available in England, cases of the finest linen bandages, and copious amounts of both chloroform and morphine—the anesthetic now preferred by Europe's surgeons, but still comparatively rare in both American armies. By the time the wounded boys and their rescuers reached the hospital, the operating theater was brightly lit with gas lanterns, the assistant surgeons aproned and ready, and all the necessary instruments, bandages, and suturing threads neatly laid out. All three boys were quickly anesthetized with chloroform, and the work of repairing them commenced with the rasp of saw, the bobbin-thrust of probes, the sponging of blood, the prompt disposal of cut-off flesh.

Word of the accident flashed through the garrison, and in the days that followed, Lamb's regiment adopted the Fort Fisher Pirates as mascots. While the boys were recovering in the hospital, humble privates came in to ask after their progress, to cheer them up with tales and songs, bringing them flowers and the most exotic seashells from the garrison's many collections. It was Dr. Reece's opinion that these displays of comradeship and kindness had a great restorative effect, when added to the youth and general good health of the wounded boys. Five days after the explosion, he judged it safe to discharge them from the fort and send them home.

Everyone who had been at the Cottage party that night felt in some way responsible for the boys' recovery and made a concerted effort to help them return to normal life. Cassius would probably have a limp for the rest of his days, but none of the shrapnel wounds in his back proved to be very deep and none of them grew infected; he thumped around on his crutch, pretending it was a pirate's wooden leg. Dick Lamb's scalp wound was expertly sutured and most of it followed the natural line of his hair, so the scar would not blemish him in manhood. In the meantime, he proudly sported a black-leather eye patch presented to him on the day of his discharge by one of Reilly's gunners.

Rufus Pender's injuries, however, were both extensive and permanent. Dr. Reece saved all he could of the boy's left arm and managed to save enough of the elbow's structure to support, at some future date, a prosthetic arm—*that* branch of medical science, the surgeon grimly observed, was progressing by leaps and bounds as the war went on. But nothing could be done for his left eye; a chunk of torpedo iron had scooped it out and left only a red swollen hole; so, naturally, he too wore a "pirate's eye patch." Of the boy's right hand, only half the original complement of digits remained: half a thumb and the two middle fingers.

On the day of Rufus's discharge, Flag Officer Branch and a delegation of Confederate sailors from Wilmington presented to "Pirates' Mate" Rufus Pender a masterfully fashioned "hook"—attached to a metal cup containing a hand-carved grip designed to fit the boy's remaining fingers. The sailors also gave the boy an outlandish horsehair beard, fitted with small leather straps, which he could put on or take off like a mask. When the whole outlandish costume was strapped on, the boy did in fact look like an actor portraying Blackbeard in a gaudy melodrama. As their pain receded, and with it their guilt about sneaking out to dig up the "treasure chest," they took much delight in being the now-famous Pirates of Fort Fisher.

The only person intimately involved with these events who did *not* find solace in the Pirates' amazing recuperation was Rufus Pender's mother. On the morning after the accident, Lamb and Dr. Reece rode north in the Lambs' carriage to the ramshackle Pender store, located on the Wilmington Road at the base of Sugar Loaf Ridge, and broke the news to her, in phrases that touched briefly on the seriousness of his injuries, but lingered emphatically on the fact that Rufus was alive, that none of his wounds appeared mortal, and that he was receiving the best possible care. She insisted on returning with them to the fort; they could hardly forbid it, but she chattered nervously all the way, repeatedly emphasizing that she had already sent a husband and two sons to serve the cause, and that it was manifestly ungrateful of the Confederacy that her only remaining boy should be wounded *here,* for God's sake, and not on some distant battlefield. She extolled Rufus's manly virtues, praised him for his help at the store, made certain the two officers knew how difficult their lives were and how impossible things would be if Rufus could no longer help her as he had always done.

When they finally ushered her into the hospital, everything was utterly quiet. The ventilation shafts had sucked out the smell of blood, leaving only a faint lingering stink of chloroform, and the three boys were peacefully asleep. Dr. Reece firmly suggested that it might be better for all concerned if Mrs. Pender contented herself with a moment of prayer—in time, they would prepare her for the shock of seeing her son as he had become.

For a moment, she was docile and mild, wrapped in vague confusion, smiling at her sleeping boy. Then, without warning, uttering something like a growl, she broke free of their restraining hands, lunged across the room, and threw back the sheet covering her son's truncated body. Her breath came in harsh gasps—she could not grasp the enormity of what had happened to him, despite their attempts to prepare her. Then she whirled around and ran from the hospital out onto the parade ground, screaming like a mad woman and tearing at her hair and arms. A hundred soldiers turned to gaze at her. And it was to them that she cried: *"Haven't you had enough? You men with your flags and uniforms and causes! Haven't you filled your bellies with sufficient blood? Do you not all have mothers, too? Don't the Yankee soldiers have mothers? How long will you butcher each other before it all ends? Will you fill the sea itself with mutilated boys? Don't you understand? Your mothers do not* care *who wins this cursed war! Neither do the Yankees' mothers! All we want is for our sons and husbands to come back to us—with the same number of arms and legs they had when they left! Why is that so hard to understand?"*

The stillness that followed her outcry was the most profound William Lamb had ever known inside those walls. Not he, not Surgeon Reece, not any of the men on the walls, not Lincoln or Jeff Davis or maybe God Himself, had a ready answer. And the sky and sea, as always, were as mute and inscrutable as they were vast.

In the days that followed, Mrs. Pender rallied, helped greatly by her son's courage and determination. At first she had refused to go along with the other adults' "Pirate" therapy, but when she realized how much that charade was helping to speed the boys' recovery, she began to play her part. She was also cheered by the Lambs' promise that they would share some of the runners' bounty with her, so that her store would be stocked with more and better goods than ever before.

Therefore, she too was on hand for the launching of the *Stonewall's Revenge.* Branch had continued to help, sending a few sailors down to help the boys finish their raft, to make sure it was safe enough for its intended voyages on the river; they had even brought with them a small wooden cannon, which was mounted on the raft with great ceremony, and a pirate flag, and wooden cutlasses for all three boys.

Once the young cutthroats were afloat, the Lambs served refreshments and gave Mrs. Pender a large basket full of fruit, tinned meat, tea, and genuine sugar—luxuries she had not seen in more than a year. The picnic went on until dark, when the boys poled their raft back to shore. The Wilmington sailors put mother and son and provisions into their wagon, and dropped them off at the store.

Exhausted from playing pirate, Rufus fell asleep early. Mrs. Pender discovered a bottle of wine in the depths of the basket and decided to celebrate the day by consuming most of it while she decided which items she would keep and which she would place on her shelves. Not until nine o'clock did she bother to check the mail that had been dropped off at the store by the morning postal rider from Wilmington. Since Pender's Store was the closest thing to a post office on Confederate Point, she sorted out the letters addressed to the region's handful of literate denizens, then sat down near the lantern to finish the rest of her wine and read the latest issue of the *Wilmington Journal.* When she unfolded the paper, she gasped and clutched at her heart, for the front page was bordered in black, and that could only mean one thing: the local casualty lists from Chancellorsville had finally arrived and were now duly published. Silently praying, she ran her finger down the alphabetized list until she read:

Sergeant Avery Pender—killed in action
Corporal Anson Pender—mortally wounded
Private Josiah Pender—missing in action

No one closer to the Pender Store than half a mile even saw the fire, and by the time those neighbors arrived, there was nothing they could do. When the ashes cooled the next morning, Mrs. Pender's charred body was found beside an upturned can of kerosene. Rufus Pender had tried to pull her from the inferno, so desperately indeed that he had driven his pirate's hook through one of her shoulders, but with only one arm, he could not have moved her more than a foot or two before being overcome by the smoke and so had collapsed upon her breast and died there.

33

The Colonel and Cleopatra

GALLANT VICKSBURG—We have nothing direct from Vicksburg, but we have reason to know that the report of its fall is untrue. As late as yesterday, it was certainly in our possession. It is very hard to know what news from the West is true and what is not true, or no longer true.

How the story of Vicksburg's fall got afloat is more than we can presently ascertain, but we take it to be one of those flighty optimisms so often reported as fact by the New York Herald. If wishes were horses, beggars would ride. It is certainly a relief to know that the gallant little city "still lives," for, apart from the prestige the place has already gained, the importance of the position can scarcely be exaggerated. Its bearing upon the fate of the whole State of Mississippi would be vital. The State Capital would be endangered, not to say the whole State itself, for it is doubtful whether a defensive line could be taken up west of the Tombigbee River, the western branch of the Alabama.

We have a telegraphic report from the Jackson Mississippian, only three days ago, which confirms the fact: Gallant Vicksburg still stands defiant!

Long may she remain so!

—The Wilmington Journal, June 20 1863

Brigadier General Rush Hawkins planned to sleep late on the morning of June 14, 1863. He had played a marathon game of high-stakes poker until 3 A.M., with Lieutenant Stonecipher and two officers from the Sixth Massachusetts, then rode back to his headquarters and collapsed.

Hawkins rolled out of bed at eight-thirty to empty his throbbing bladder into a chamber pot, fully intending to flop back down for another four or five hours of blissful oblivion. The morning was dry and temperate, and a mild pine-scented breeze caressed his naked body as he stood before the open window and delivered himself of an Olympian piss.

Unfortunately, as he was shaking off the last drops, he heard businesslike boot-clomps on the stairs, followed by an almost apologetic knock.

"Christ on a pair of stilts, what *is* it?" he groaned.

"My apologies, General! Urgent message from the docks, sir!"

"From the docks? There's no ship scheduled to come in until Tuesday. Oh my God, is it a Rebel ironclad?"

"No sir. It's General Foster's flagship, and General Foster's on it. He sends his compliments and requests your presence at a strategy conference, at your earliest convenience."

"Saddle my horse, and have Calliope bring up a clean dress uniform. And a pot of fucking coffee!"

Hawkins reeled away from the open window, the chamber pot, and the promise of renewed slumber. He could feel the morning-after headache beginning to eat like acid at the meat of his brain. His hands were shaking too badly to risk a shave, but he did manage a cold-water scrub under his arms and around his crotch.

This was unprecedented—unthinkable! In all the months John G. Foster had commanded the Union enclaves on the North Carolina coast, not once had he personally visited Shelborne's Point. If something was up, why hadn't Butler warned Hawkins? What was the purpose of this visit? A surprise inspection? An official notification that the whole scheme had been uncovered and Hawkins was relieved of his command? It sure as hell wasn't a friendly visit from one officer to another, Hawkins knew that much.

He had just managed to worm into fresh underwear when there was another knock on the door. Calliope Keen entered, bearing in her massive ebony arms a freshly washed, ironed, and neatly folded uniform. There were times when the old Negro woman showed an almost maternal affection for Hawkins, and this was such a moment.

"Sweet Jesus, Gen'ral Hawkins, you gots to look yo' best this mornin', and that ain't gonna be easy!"

"Yes, Missuz Keen, I'm well aware of that. Thank you for the clothes."

"They's a pot of hot coffee, just the kinda strong you like, on the table in the front hall, and a couple of chicken biscuits, too, so's you can get somethin' on yo' stomach while you ride. *If* you can keep it down, that is!" Cooing and cackling, she retreated down the stairs, while Hawkins wrestled with his boots, sword belt, and side arm. By the time he reached the foot of the stairs, Calliope had thoughtfully poured some cream into the coffee so that it would not be dangerously hot. Balancing the coffee mug in one hand and a napkin-wrapped biscuit in the other, Hawkins let the horse find its own way back to town. By the time Hawkins reached the outskirts, he was beginning to feel slightly human again.

Thank God it *was* Sunday, so Foster would not be expecting to see smartly turned-out companies executing drills or marching hither and yon on various assignments. Instead, the general was standing nonchalantly on the dock beside his flagship, one leg propped up on a mooring cleat, enjoying a cigar and apparently savoring the pastoral panorama of the river, the village, and the workshops and warehouses arrayed near the docks.

Hawkins dismounted, walked forward as briskly as he could, and snapped off a reasonably crisp salute. Foster returned it, then shook his hand. He was a large, burly, heavily bearded man with close-set intelligent eyes and blunt, honest, but rather homely features. His performance as a brigade commander during the Roanoke Island–New Bern campaign had been rock-solid, so when Burnside left to join McClellan, on June 25, 1862, he promoted Foster to commander in chief of all Union forces in North Carolina. Unfortunately for Foster, Burnside also took many of his best regiments with him, leaving Foster with barely nine thousand men—scarcely enough to defend the towns Burnside had captured and far below the number required for serious offensive operations. Foster was an engineer, and a good one, so he concentrated foremost on fortifying the Union enclaves. But whenever the opportunity presented itself, he mounted bold little raids up the rivers, aggressively supported by Charles Flusser's flotilla of gunboats.

"To what do I owe the pleasure of this unexpected visit, General?" asked Hawkins.

If Foster was bothered by the fact that Hawkins was unshaven, irritable, and clearly hungover, he did not show it.

"Well, sir, we have scarcely laid eyes on each other since the end of Burnside's campaign, and since I was on my way up to Little Washington anyway, I thought I would stop by and chat for a while—take a look around—that sort of thing."

That sort of thing was a phrase loaded with implications Hawkins did not want to speculate about, not while striving to cope with a headache of apocalyptic dimensions.

"Well, General, it's Sunday morning, so there's not much activity. I have an office over by the shipyard—we can talk there in private, and then I'll show you around."

Hawkins fervently hoped that one or two of the orderlies on duty had seen Foster's arrival and taken appropriate actions, such as firing up a pot of coffee in the office. He led the way, Foster falling in on his right side. As they passed the enclosed shed where Butler's ships were reconfigured, Foster halted for a moment and narrowed his eyes, scanning the building and surrounding facilities.

"I admit, General Hawkins, to an abiding curiosity as to what, exactly, your people *do* here. . . . I gather it's some kind of top-secret operation under control of the Navy Department, or *somebody* in Washington. Technically, your regiment and its ancillary units are part of my coastal command, but I am not supposed to call on you for field operations except in case of 'operational necessity.' I may have to do that sometime in the near future, but I don't want to call down the wrath of the War Department by interfering with some larger scheme."

They reached Hawkins's dockside office and the scent of brewing coffee told him that somebody had indeed been minding the store. A well-turned-out sentry had also materialized, although from his bloodshot eyes and faintly liquorish breath, the man had clearly been just as involved in Saturday night's revels as Hawkins had been. Foster, again, did not seem to notice, or care—he returned the sentry's salute and passed quickly into the office. As Hawkins passed the sentry, he leaned in the man's direction and whispered, *"Well done, Corporal. I'll remember you!"*

The coffee was still half-brewed and strong as naval tar. Foster helped himself to a mug, lit another cigar, and strode over to the big map of coastal North Carolina covering the wall behind Hawkins's desk. He studied it for a moment, seemingly lost in strategic contemplation, while Hawkins fidgeted nervously with his own cup of coffee, not knowing whether to stand at attention, offer the general his own chair, or slouch against the wooden filing cabinet . . . what he *really* wanted to do was lie down on the nearest sofa and cover his head with a cold towel. When Foster turned around, his previous air of affability was gone, and he stared at Hawkins with such a penetrating gaze that his eyes were almost crossed.

"My gunboats control these waters, Hawkins, and Captain Flusser's crews are extremely vigilant. There is not much that goes on around here that escapes their attention. Ships come into Shelborne's Point, ships that look for all the world like ordinary blockade-runners, displaying red and green signal lights, and my standing orders are to ignore them. Ships of the same size, but significantly different configuration, leave Shelborne's Point two or three days later. At other times, the same process happens in reverse. My guess is that this is some kind of long-range plan to undermine the *genuine* blockade-running enterprise—although I am but a simple engineer and cannot fathom what the subtleties may be. You may very well be acting under orders from someone or some agency in Washington whose authority supercedes my own, and therefore under no obligation to answer my questions, but you and I will get along much better if you can at least give me some assurance that this peculiar arrangement is, in fact, contributing significantly to the Union war effort."

Hawkins stirred his coffee nervously, afraid to speak for fear of stammering and giving Foster the impression that he had something to hide.

Once more putting on a hearty smile, Foster came around the desk and clapped Hawkins on the shoulder.

"Come, come, man! I've cooperated fully with this operation, whatever it is, and the reports your Unionist cavalry have provided about the local situation have been both valuable and timely. I'm not here to shut you down or poke my nose into your business. It's just that I'm planning a rather large operation sometime during the next six or eight weeks, and I need to know if your troops can contribute to it. In fact, their cooperation may be vital to its success—but it will mean temporarily shutting down your other activities. If you can just give me a general idea of what those activities are . . . "

Hawkins sighed. Foster had never asked for anything from the Shelborne's Point garrison except intelligence reports about regional Rebel activity, and the Buffaloes had done a pretty good job of supplying that kind of information . . . at least until recently. It would not be wise to alienate Foster at this stage of the game.

"Very well, General. It is as you surmised: basically, we hijack prime Rebel cotton, divert it to the Northern mills, and send the same ships back into Wilmington loaded with defective weapons and tainted food. It's more complex than that, of course, but that is the gist of it."

"Ah! A very cunning scheme, I must admit. Now, let me ask you: can you suspend these activities for a period of two or three weeks in late July or early August? If I leave the *Trenton* here to support your fortified artillery, and a company of infantry, can you deploy the rest of your regiment and the Unionist cavalry in support of a raid on Kinston? I have information that there's a Rebel ironclad on the Neuse River, just below the town. Of course, I also have information about an ironclad up on the Roanoke, near Weldon, but I'm told it's many months away from completion. I want to take out the one on the Neuse first, and tear up the railhead at Kinston while I'm doing it. Your men will go by ship to Little Washington, join forces with the garrison there, and march south, to prevent Rebel reinforcements from coming to Kinston by rail."

"This operation will take place in late July?"

"Yes, provided I receive the cavalry reinforcements I've asked for from General Hooker's Army of the Potomac."

Hawkins tried to think quickly. He could arrange it with Butler to interrupt the red-over-green system for a few weeks; Butler would surely see the necessity of having Hawkins's troops actually make a *military* contribution. And it would give the Buffaloes something to do besides terrorize the countryside, pick fights with the Massachusetts regulars, and loll around Edgefield Plantation all day in a drunken stupor. It would serve them right, too, thought Hawkins, because Cyrus Bone was one of the agents who had spread reports of an ironclad on the Neuse, even though Bone himself had probably never even sent a patrol to that river. Foster's remarks confirmed Hawkins's growing suspicion that Bone sometimes fabricated colorful "intelligence reports," just to make the Buffaloes' importance as a military unit seem much greater than it really was.

"You can count on us, General Foster. Just give me a couple of weeks' notice, and we'll be ready to march."

Foster shook hands and beamed affably.

"I'm glad to hear it, General Hawkins. And now, before I resume my trip to Little Washington, I think I'd like to inspect this mounted unit of yours . . . what's it called now? Oh yes, the First North Carolina Unionist Volunteers or something like that."

Oh, God, not that—not today! Hawkins blanched and stammered, "Well, er, sir, it is rather a long ride out to their camp . . . and I doubt that they'll be at their best on a Sunday morning . . . "

"All the better for me to get a candid opinion of them, Hawkins! Besides, it's a lovely day for a ride."

At first, General Foster looked approvingly at the Buffaloes' encampment at Edgefield Plantation: the position was protected by well-dug rifle pits and a thick abatis of sharpened, interlocked pine branches. The two 12-pounder Napoleons were well-sited to command the wagon road leading west and the open cornfield through which any attacking Rebel force would have to deploy. Unfortunately, both cannons were draped with wet laundry, and the two sentinels on duty at the main gate were asleep.

Things deteriorated quickly from that point on. Just beyond the sleeping pickets, Foster saw a bloody-mouthed, half-naked man hanging by his thumbs, toes barely scraping the ground, obviously being punished for some infraction against Cyrus Bone's wishes. Next came a half-dozen mud-spattered, roaring-drunk soldiers chasing a scrawny chicken—none of whom paid any attention to Hawkins and Foster, much less saluted. Lolling on the steps and front porch of the main house were several slutty-looking Negro girls, bare-breasted beneath loose cotton shifts—local runaways who had attached themselves as camp-followers to Bonaparte Reubens's colored company. The rest of Bone's two hundred-odd men lay snoring inside the farm buildings and former slave quarters they had turned into barracks after taking possession of Edgefield. Hawkins could count at least ten men who appeared to be passed out on the bare ground, several of them still clutching jugs and bottles.

His jaw clenched, casting furious sidelong glances at Hawkins, General Foster stamped up the front steps. One of the colored girls reached out languidly and grabbed the general's leg, inquiring, in a throaty voice, if he would like "to get his Johnson pulled?" Foster jerked his leg back in disgust. Just at that moment, the front door flew open, and a burly sergeant named "Big Red" Elliott came flying backward, blood squirting from his nose, followed by a red-eyed Cyrus Bone, who had just pistol-whipped Elliott with a bloody-barreled Colt.

"You lyin' ass-suckin' son of a bitch!" shouted Bone. "I wouldn't piss down your throat if your gut was on fire! You cheat me at cards again, and I'll tear your arms off!"

Not knowing what else do to, Rush Hawkins stepped forward and tried to place a restraining hand on Bone. "Captain Bone! Get a hold of yourself! This here is General John Foster, commander in chief of all Union forces on the North Carolina coast!"

Bone slumped against the door frame. There were whiskey and bloodstains on his shirt, black crescents under his armpits, and he stank like a goat.

"I don't give a rat's ass if he's Abe Lincoln."

"General Hawkins?" shouted Foster. "Arrest this man at once! Is there *any* sober officer in this goddamned outfit who can take command?"

From the shadowy, trash-strewn interior of the house came the tall, thin figure of Jack Fairless. Hawkins almost did not recognize him. Darkened by the sun, his hair pulled back in a ponytail, his eyes now colder and harder, Fairless was no longer the gangling hillbilly he had been when Hawkins first saw him, standing worshipfully in Cyrus Bone's shadow. Fairless at least wore his uniform, although the jacket was open to his waist, and his boots were clean and polished. He might have been every bit as drunk as Bone, but he held it much better. He came to attention and saluted Foster, then introduced himself as "Lieutenant Jackson P. Fairless, executive officer."

"I apologize for this sorry spectacle, General Foster. Captain Bone has not been himself lately and I'm afraid his fondness for the bottle has gotten the better of his good judgment."

"Well, Fairless, why did you not report this state of affairs to General Hawkins?"

"Frankly, sir, because the last man who threatened to lodge a complaint against Captain Bone was tied to the muzzle of one of those Napoleons and blown in half with grapeshot."

By now, several apparently sober Buffaloes had gathered around this confrontation. Some of them covered Bone with their weapons while two others bound his hands behind his back. Bone looked dazed, uncomprehending. His eyes sought Jack Fairless.

"Jack? Jack, you ain't gonna let 'em truss me up and throw me in jail, are you? You know I can't stand that, Jack! Don't turn on me, Jack! Jack, you mother-fucker, if you turn on me, I swear I'll come back and cut your goddamned throat, and *you know I will do it, too!*"

"Jesus Christ, shut up!" said one of the men holding Bone, who then stepped back two paces and drove the butt of his Springfield into the pit of Bone's stomach.

Foster looked around in disgust. "Lieutenant Fairless, you are now promoted to brevet captain and placed in command of this unit. I'll do the paperwork to confirm your rank as soon as I get back to New Bern. You have six weeks to turn this rabble into a military unit again. And as for you, Hawkins, I would advise you to keep a closer eye on *all* of your men, from now on. When we get back to town, I want you to send a platoon of *disciplined* regulars out here to help Captain Fairless clean up this shit-hole."

Then they tied Cyrus Bone to Hawkins's saddle horn with a long piece of rope and half-dragged, half-pulled him back to Shelborne's Point.

Jack Fairless sneaked up to the brig late that night, knocked the sentry unconscious with his pistol butt, and broke Cyrus Bone out of jail. He did this because he knew perfectly well that if he did not, Cyrus Bone would escape on his own and come back to Edgefield and cut Jack's throat, just as he promised to do.

The two men rode in silence back to the plantation, but once inside, Cyrus embraced Jack and began to weep with gratitude.

"I knew you couldn't turn on me, Jack! Not my fair, sweet Jack!"

The big house was dark and silent. The two officers climbed the stairs to the master bedroom. Cyrus was fumbling all over Jack, like a grateful dog, going through his usual transformation from drunken bestiality to maudlin emotionalism.

"Jack!" he whispered. "Jack, my fair boy! In the morning, you can help me get away, but for tonight, let's you and I share the bed one more time, like we used to do on cold nights. For you know I love you, Jack, with all my heart."

Jack allowed himself to be borne back onto the mattress. Cyrus Bone flung off his shirt and trousers and bent over Jack's prone body, his thick strong fingers fumbling with the buttons on Jack's fly.

Suddenly, the hall door flew open and there stood Bonaparte Reubens, grinning evilly and holding aloft a very bright lantern.

Cyrus Bone blinked in confusion, and as he turned around to stare at the light, Jack Fairless drew a pistol from under the pillow and shot him in the heart.

"You are a witness, Lieutenant Reubens."

"Yes sir, Captain Fairless. Mister Bone, after escaping from the brig in Shelborne's Point, made his way here and attempted to sodomize you by force."

"A plain case of self-defense."

"Yes sir, indeed it was."

Zeb Vance had been warned that the train trip from Raleigh to Wilmington would be "slow" and probably "interrupted" from time to time, so he budgeted—or so he thought—plenty of time. The *Ad-Vance* was due to arrive from her maiden voyage on Sunday, June 26, and the governor was so excited about the event, he told Dick Battle that he was "happy as a dog with two dicks." The two men boarded the train on

Saturday at three in the afternoon; it was supposed to depart Raleigh at four; it finally creaked out of the station at a quarter-past five. Vance had been able to requisition a semiprivate compartment, no sleeping arrangements, but at least there was room enough for him to stretch his long legs out on the opposite bench. He and Battle shared a basket supper, played a few hands of cards, then broke the seal on a "properly taxed and paid for" quart of bourbon and made serious inroads in the contents while the direly overloaded train creaked southeast, toward Goldsboro, at an average speed of seven miles per hour. While they drank, Vance insisted that Battle take out his shorthand notebook and take down yet another fulminating letter to Secretary of War Seddon, who would no doubt welcome its appearance on his desk with the sort of enthusiasm usually extended to an importuning leper.

"I have checked the records, sir, and learned that, at latest count, the Confederate government has promoted to the rank of brigadier general a total of three hundred and sixty-five men. Out of that number, however, only sixteen have been North Carolinians. Considering the great efforts this state has made on behalf of our cause, and the sterling record of her regiments in battle, I find this disproportion not only alarming, but also bordering on a calculated insult.

"And now comes news of the most egregious and callous act so far perpetrated on our honor. I have just learned that a Virginian, Colonel T. P. August, has been placed in command of all North Carolina conscripts. Whatever this man's other qualities, he cannot possibly know anything about the localities from which those conscripts have come. I find it ludicrous to believe that we have no North Carolina colonels suitable to this task."

Vance refilled his glass and gathered steam; Battle struggled to pay attention.

"Merely alluding to the obvious impropriety and bad policy of wounding our people's sensibilities by the appointment of a citizen from another state to execute a law both harsh and odious, I wish to say, sir, in all candor, that is smacks of discourtesy to our people, to say the least of it. Having furnished as many, if not more, troops for the service of the Confederacy as any other state, and being, as I was assured by President Davis, far ahead of all others in the numbers raised under the conscript law, the people of this state have justly felt mortified in seeing those troops commanded by citizens of other states, to the exclusion of claims of their own. There is now a feeling of heightened indignation due to the appointment of this Virginian colonel. Our people regard this as tantamount to a declaration that North Carolina has no man in her borders fit to command her own conscripts, even though hundreds of her noblest sons and best officers are now back home with mutilated limbs and ruined constitutions, though still able and willing to serve in any noncombatant role they are given.

"Having submitted in silence to the many, the very many, acts of administration heretofore, so calculated to wound that pride, which North Carolina is so pardonable for entertaining, it is my duty to inform you that if persisted in, the continued appointment of strangers over her native troops will result in . . . *Dick?* Still with me, man?"

Though Battle strove mightily to keep up with the governor, he had not the mountaineer's bred-in-the-bone capacity to handle whiskey, and he abruptly dropped off to sleep in mid-dictation, at nine-thirty, an hour after full darkness had descended on the rolling, mostly empty spaces of the eastern Piedmont.

Vance, however, was in a very mellow mood indeed, and continued to sip his sour mash and contemplate the great starry void that covered this part of his beloved state. The letter to Seddon could wait; Vance had more pleasant things on his mind. Not only was *his* ship coming in, but his scheme to appropriate iron from the grasping, dishonest rogues of the railroad company had worked to perfection. Parker and his men mounted their "cavalry raid" on Weldon during the weekend of June 12 and 13. The press had raised the expected outcry about the vulnerability of the state to such impudent Yankee incursions—which would bring additional weight on Richmond to do something about the situation—but there was also great praise for the defending batteries at Scotland Neck, which had apparently fended off a sizable armada of Yankee gunboats, thus averting an even greater humiliation. Details of the engagement—as Vance had anticipated—were quite vague; folks read into them what they wanted to read. Whitford and the other railroad magnates suspected that some kind of flim-flam had been perpetrated, and were suitably furious about it, but they could not make public accusations without also revealing their own greedy deceitfulness. Meanwhile, all that iron was now safely under guard at Holman's Ferry and the railroad agents who had come snooping around had found themselves firmly blocked by vigilant sentries. Parker had jiggled the paperwork, mixing the stolen iron with other stocks legitimately obtained, and by now, the first twenty tons of it were already on their way to the Tregedar Works, where—eventually—they would be rolled into armor plate and transported back to Parker's little shipyard. Once the tonnage now strapped in the *Ad-Vance*'s hold was added to the stockpile, the *Hatteras* would become an actual threat instead of a potential one, and Vance could hardly wait until Parker could unleash her on Albemarle Sound. He saw that fiery retribution in his mind, and finally fell asleep, lulled by dreams of martial vindication.

A conductor shook him awake just before dawn, at the Goldsboro junction. Passengers continuing to Wilmington would have to change trains now, he said. This one was being turn-tabled around and loaded with troops and supplies for Virginia. The new train was not as crowded, and it left Goldsboro more or less on time, but it was shorter, composed of much older and shoddier carriages, and pulled by an engine that lurched and wheezed with age and decrepitude. Vance and Battle rated window seats, which proved a blessing, for the summer heat rose in quivering waves over the sandhills and cornfields and pine woods, and the open windows admitted some kind of breeze, even if it was frequently laced with engine smoke. Somewhere in the middle of Duplin County, about halfway between Goldsboro and Wilmington, the ancient locomotive encountered a long stretch of soggy, worn-out track, and its average speed, Vance estimated, dropped to about five miles an hour. It also came to frequent and unexplained stops, which caused the governor to fidget anxiously and glare furiously at his watch as though willing Time itself to run backward.

"If this keeps up, it will be dark by the time we reach the ship," he growled.

"Yes, sir. I reckon it will." Battle glanced out the window at the barren sand road that paralleled the tracks. "Why look there, Governor! I believe we passed that same darkie about three miles back."

Vance leaned out and beheld a solitary grizzled Negro plodding along stoically, pulling a small hand cart loaded with farm tools, probably on his way from one temporary job to another. He waved. The Negro flashed a good-natured smile and waved back, then resumed his lonely trek. "I believe you're right, Dick. Hell, at this rate, he might get to Wilmington before we do."

Five minutes later, the train lurched forward again, over roadbed so rough and ill-repaired that its long-suffering passengers could have counted each piece of track—*thumpa-thumpa-thump*—if boredom so inclined them. After a torturous progress of perhaps two miles, it screeched to a halt again, while crewmen jumped out to shore up another section of track. By now, the cars were like ovens, and Vance was beside himself with impatience. He reached for the whiskey jug again, and washed down the stale remnants of the sandwiches his staff had packed. The minutes ticked by. Vance looked again at his watch, then leaned out the window, muttering: "Just about time now. Yes, by God, here he comes."

The old Negro, still maintaining his steady, league-covering stride, his ragged shoes kicking up dust, once more drew abreast of the train. This time, Vance waved vigorously and signaled for the man to halt.

"Good day, sir," he boomed. "I am the governor of North Carolina!"

Pausing to scratch his gray-wool hair, the old man made a small bow and replied: "Is that so? Well, Ah'm mighty pleased to make your acquaintance, in that case."

"You seem to have a long, hard journey. Might I invite you to climb aboard and ride with us, as my guest of course, and we'll put you off at your destination . . . whatever that might be hereabouts."

The old man thought for a moment, then replied: "Ah thanks you very much, Boss Man, but Ah really ain't gots the time."

Vance was still laughing when the train rumbled forward. Evidently, the rest of the line into Wilmington was in better shape, for the train rattled on slowly without further stops, and pulled into the Wilmington depot at four-thirty. Plenty of daylight left for the governor to make his grand entrance. The *Ad-Vance* was already tied up at the Dock Street Wharf—because the ship had come straight from Liverpool, General Whiting had waived the usual two-week quarantine stop at Smithville. Vance and Battle hopped into a waiting carriage and sped to the river.

And there she was: sleek and spanking clean, not yet begrimed by bad coal, 268 feet long, with two huge side wheels and a pair of engines that could drive her at seventeen knots with reserve power for twenty if she was pursued. She could show a clean pair of heels to virtually any Yankee ship afloat. There was a goodly crowd assembled to welcome the governor, and at the top of the gangway, resplendent in his finest uniform, was Hobart-Hampden. Vance immediately noticed that the runner-captain was "making eyes" at a dark-haired, rather exotic-looking young beauty at the forefront of the crowd. Pausing long enough to glad-hand editor Fulton and several other dignitaries, Vance led a gay parade up to the decks of his proud, swift, audacious new ship.

A mass of cheering people followed their governor aboard, including, he noticed, that ravishingly attractive young woman with the gypsy mouth and deep black almond-shaped eyes. In the crush, she managed briefly to squeeze the English captain's hand, then moved back to a discreet distance. *A girl in every port,* thought Vance, as he followed Hobart-Hampden on a guided tour. *Perhaps I should have chosen the sea, instead of the jungles of politics.*

The *Ad-Vance* had performed splendidly, and her engines were so reliable that you could set your watch by her scheduled arrival time. She had zipped through the blockade so slick and fast that not a shot was fired at her. Her holds were crammed with iron, as promised, but also with eight thousand pairs of infantry shoes, three tons of uniform cloth, and hundreds of cotton-cards, which were in desperately short supply in the state's burgeoning textile miles, since the fine-gauge wire they mounted, badly needed for combing cotton and woolen fibers into yarn-strands, was nowhere manufactured in the South. And of course, in whatever odds and ends of cargo space were left over, there were luxury goods that Hobart-Hampden was free to sell on the local market—after Governor Vance got his pick of them, as was only fitting and proper. It was an altogether propitious voyage: the state had gotten iron for its armored ram, enough shoes to shod two full regiments, and enough good English cloth to double the output of her mills, at least for a month or two. And the Englishman and his unknown business partners, who owned 50 percent of the ship, had made a tidy profit without having to haggle with tight-fisted Confederate purchasing agents.

In the jolliest of moods, Vance returned to the main deck and was struck at once by the unexpected quiet and somberness of the people who had been milling around in his wake. Striding back to the head of the gangway, he quickly discovered the reason.

Blocking his passage at the foot of the way stood a puffed up young cock of an officer in the full dress uniform of the Confederate navy. He glared defiantly at Vance, backed up by a platoon of Marines with fixed bayonets.

"Who are you, sir?" demanded Vance in his most stentorian voice. "And what is the meaning of this?"

"I am Lieutenant Commander Albert Thorburn, sir, adjutant to Flag Officer Branch, commander of naval forces in Wilmington."

"I know very well who he is, Thorburn. What I want to know is why you are here and he is not."

"Flag Officer Branch is . . . indisposed. I am here to carry out his standing orders. This vessel is in violation of quarantine regulations and must return immediately to the inspection station at Smithville, where it shall remain, as specified by law, for a period of not less than fourteen days."

The crowd reacted instantly and angrily; none of them had any intention of spending two weeks in quarantine and could scarcely believe the absurd drama playing out before their eyes.

"General Whiting has issued orders that this ship is not required to undergo inspection—she comes directly from Liverpool and has not stopped in any unhealthy places on the way."

"I am not aware of any such orders from General Whiting, and in their absence, I must do my duty."

"This pompous fool is not backing down," muttered Vance. He snagged Dick Battle by the coat sleeve and whispered, "Where the hell is Whiting, anyway?"

"I mentioned it to you earlier, sir—he's gone off to Richmond again, to plead for a field command. God knows when he'll be back." Vance turned scornfully toward the officer blocking his departure.

"What state are you from, Mister Thorburn?"

"I am proud to be from the great state of Virginia!"

Vance groaned. In a voice frigid enough to coat the air with ice crystals, he leaned over the railing and fairly shouted, "Do you dare to say, sir, that the governor of North Carolina shall not leave the deck of his own ship?"

Thorburn swelled like a toad, intoxicated with his own authority.

"I shall let no one off this ship, be he Governor Vance or Jesus Christ Himself! And I have instructed my men to fire on anyone who tries to disembark."

At this point, Vance had to be physically restrained from rushing down the plank and attacking this young fool with a pair of large, rawboned, gubernatorial fists. This arrogant popinjay seemed at that moment to embody everything about the Richmond government that drove him to fury. His moment, his ship, his triumph—spoiled by a goddamned *Virginian!* Here was a huge vessel, loaded to the gunwales with vital military supplies, already cleared for docking by the highest Confederate authority in the region, and this idiot wanted to quarantine it for two weeks, holding a crowd of Wilmington dignitaries and the governor of North Carolina incommunicado from the entire outside world.

While the deadlocked tension simmered, Editor Fulton had the good sense to beckon to a prominent citizen he knew on the dock and throw to him a scribbled message:

"Go find Branch, bring him here naked if need be, and have this madness resolved! I do not care if he is drunk or in the arms of some whore or dying with fever! Just GET HIM!"

For the next fifteen minutes, Vance and Thorburn glared daggers at each other while everyone else, especially the very uncomfortable-looking Marines, sweated in the heat. Then there was a ruckus on the edge of the crowd, and Flag Office Branch appeared, still fumbling to button his uniform. He looked ghastly, with dark shadows under his eyes, pale cheeks, and trembling hands. He did not move like a drunkard, and no one afterward recalled smelling liquor on him as he passed by, but he was clearly not well, and his head kept lolling from side to side as though a trip-hammer were belaboring his brain. Obviously the situation had been explained to him on the way, but when he beheld the reality of it, he gaped in disbelief. He raged up to Thorburn and spun him around, practically lifting him by his collar tabs.

"You . . . you . . . *cretin!* Have you gone mad, or are you really stupid enough to think you were carrying out my wishes?"

Thorburn quickly diminished in size. He stammered something about "taking the initiative" and "following your standing orders while you were indisposed, sir."

"You will follow these orders, sir: get *out of my sight!* I will have you 'indisposed' right out of the service, do you hear me? Go back to your quarters and consider yourself under confinement, and the rest of you men are dismissed!"

Now somewhat revived, Branch saluted the quarterdeck and said: "With my deepest apologies, Governor Vance, you and the other people are free to go. And this ship is free to unload at her captain's convenience."

Branch turned around and marched back whence he had come, but there were many on the ship who saw the heavy, defeated sag of his shoulders as soon as he thought he was out of view.

Thoroughly vindicated, Zeb Vance thundered to the crowd, "No man is more prompt to obey lawful authority than myself, but I will not be ridden over by bayonets and epaulets!"

The crowd gave him three lusty cheers, Hobart-Hampden set about arranging a lavish party on board for later that evening, and William Branch locked himself in a darkened room and reached once more for his opium pipe, understanding even as he reloaded the bowl that he was sucking on the ashes of his own professional dreams, the smoky dissipation of what remained of his dignity.

It rained so hard on the afternoon of Sunday, July 3, that William Lamb eventually gave up hoping to return to the Cottage that night; the sandy road was a quagmire and the normally placid little creek in front of the land-face terminus had turned into a raging torrent, periodically submerging the plank bridge that connected road to fort. At day's end, therefore, he retired to his tactical headquarters, a small tin-roofed shed that was the only remnant of the old Federal lighthouse station, the remainder of which had been cannibalized to build the scaffolding for the Mound Battery's construction. He shared a modest supper of beans and cornbread with Major Reilly, Surgeon Reece, and a few of his other officers, read some Bible passages by candlelight, sparingly treating himself to a few glasses of French cognac recently presented to him by a grateful runner captain, then lay down on his narrow cot and let the drumming of fat coastal raindrops lull him to sleep.

Shortly after three A.M., he was wakened—indeed, nearly hurled out of bed—by a prolonged detonation of thunder so loud and ominous that, for a sleep-blurred moment, he feared the enemy fleet had crept close under cover of the storm and opened a stupendous bombardment on his fort. As the explosions rumbled and crashed, now close, now far, as though a demonic percussion orchestra were playing antiphonal chorales from the choir lofts of a sky-high cathedral, he became convinced that he was hearing no naval bombardment, but some long-traveled and sinister reverberation of the great and possibly decisive campaign now raging far north of the Potomac. Lamb could only speculate, from sketchy and contradictory reports, but it seemed logical to him that Lee would try to capitalize on the momentum gained from his stunning victory at Chancellorsville; his power was at its zenith, while the Army of the Potomac had just lost one commander—the disgraced Joe Hooker—and had not yet grown used to its new one, George Meade. According to the latest news, Lee had marched deep into Pennsylvania, perhaps seeking to interpose his forces between Meade's army and Washington. Such a bold stroke was typical of Marse Robert's audacity. He would, Lamb reasoned, find some patch of superior ground, as he had at Fredericksburg, dig in there, and compel Meade to assault him at a disadvantage. No one knew, as yet, just where this battle was actually raging, but every Confederate officer knew in his heart that it would be the greatest engagement of the war thus far, and that it might well be the fulcrum on which the fate of the Cause was balanced.

Finding it impossible to sleep, Lamb got dressed, struggled into his rain cape, picked up his umbrella, and headed toward the Pulpit. His puddle-hopping journey was illuminated by fitful bone-white arcs of lightning, and by its savage, knife-edged glare, the ramparts of Fort Fisher loomed like a citadel carved from yellow ice, and the wet-iron masses of its giant guns seemed to soak up the lightning, retaining a brief mephitic afterglow even after the flashes were spent. The Pulpit was sheltered from the storm's worst fury by a slanted wooden roof, and its half-moon interior was protected from flooding by several drainage channels that emptied onto the beach, each of them now choked with runoff and frothing like mountain streams. The sentry posted here was huddled and miserable, but commendably alert and quick to salute at the sight of his commanding officer. Lamb recognized the man: the diminutive corporal with the improbably long name, Ezekial Jeremiah Prosper-For-Me de Vonell Conver. Swaddled against the rain and wind, the peak of his cap barely reaching as high as the stacking swivel on his musket, Conver resembled a twelve-year-old boy dressed up to play soldier. But Lamb knew that Major Reilly respected the pint-sized corporal, for he projected an innate man-sized dignity that had long since put an end to teasing. Anyone who ventured a joke about Conver's size received a withering stoic glare that clearly implied: if you make fun of my stature, you are a littler man than I.

"Good evening, Corporal. Or, rather, good morning." Lamb found himself having almost to shout above the vast frying roar of the tempest.

"And to you, Colonel, sir. What brings you out on such a foul night?"

"Even on the Cape Fear, you don't often see a storm so wickedly violent. I wanted to get a good look at it, I suppose. Catch a glimpse of God at his most fearsome."

"Well, this is the place to be, all right."

Sensing Lamb's brooding and solitary mood, Corporal Conver

nodded respectfully, then withdrew to the other side of the position, resuming his sentry's stance and dutifully scanning the violent seas, even though there was no possibility of a Yankee fleet appearing on such a night. Even the inner ring of the blockade line had drawn farther out to sea, hunkered down far beyond the horizon, riding out the tempest. After fifteen minutes, as though to herald the second act of some heroic opera, the rain suddenly slacked off, the air along the shore grew clear, and the gigantic mass of the storm drifted eastward, so that Lamb could see it whole: a great angry beast, tearing itself to shreds and creating, as it slowly moved away, a spectacle that loomed across the whole sky's vaulted arch, from north to south; a soaring, pinnacled distance, ripped apart by a wild astral light that seemed a thing apart from all ordinary water and sky, illuminations beyond the mortal spectrum, while gargoyles of cloud—some gray and smooth-skinned as dolphins, some as coarse-grained and purple as a bruise on the cheek of night—brooded on the spectacle. Such ascendancy and almightiness, such planet-scouring violence—how could its weight possibly be upborne by an element as frail as air?

He had not known, or even fancied, that lightning occurred in so many shapes, varieties, and baroque configurations. Some bolts drove straight into the sea like harpoons; others, miles long, cut jagged, horizontal slashes that leaped with seeming ecstasy from one saw-toothed citadel of cloud to another; still others, farther out and shrouded by intervening cloud mass, exploded in gauzy coronas that had enormous radiant mass but no clear edges, like stars exploding in the depths of space. What these disparate pyrotechnics revealed was a veritable continent of thunderheads, ranged in alpine vistas, some low and mysteriously veiled, others towering like ebonite crags—cliffs in motion—wedges as black and hard as cannon iron—and between these lofty monster-shapes, these Olympian horse manes and thrusting obelisks, he glimpsed stupendously deep canyons and plunging cataracts whose sinuous demarcations glowed like molten pewter, streamed and smoked like waterfalls whose span would dwarf a dozen Niagaras. Two symmetrical meteor-falls of lightning framed one colossal mass of darkness and ripped into it a crevasse narrow as a blade, then joined in a cataclysmic fusion, forming a column of blinding white, then dispersed into a luminous bell, revealing to Lamb's dazzled sight a great lofty abyss so clogged with slow-tumbling geometries of thundercloud that Lamb felt he was watching the fallen stones of some forgotten realm, one that mirrored the deep green nighted temples of Atlantis, a rare and privileged glimpse of the dark inscrutable tides of Time.

Spellbound, he watched the storm front slowly haul away to the east, until its depths were blurred, its thunder muted as distant drums, its fires remote and unrevealing. But even at this great distance, some conflagrations of lightning were so immense as to reveal the horizon-wide drapery of rain being dragged in its wake, as though the clouds were unrolling the sea like a vast sable carpet behind them. It was quiet enough now, an hour or so before the first light of dawn, to hear the turbid restlessness of the surf.

Corporal Conver spoke quietly: "Ever wonder, Colonel Lamb, what would happen if the tide just kept on going out one day? Could we walk the streets of vanished empires, or hear the tolling bells of sunken ships?"

Lamb considered this unexpectedly mystical comment for a moment before replying: "Yes, I suppose we could. And take the measure of leviathan. And solve uncountable mysteries. But would you *want* all the sea's mysteries to be solved, Corporal Conver?"

The little man grinned slyly. "No sir, I reckon not. Not if it meant puttin' up with the stink of all them dead fish."

Lamb chuckled. He felt strangely purged and calm.

"I think I will take a walk along the beach, while it's still dark and cool. Pass the word to the other sentries, if you would please."

"Yes, sir!"

Conver scurried off to notify the next sentry post, up on the Northeast Bastion. Lamb exited the fort through the sally port, telling the outposts there that he would return in an hour. He also picked up a large shuttered lantern—some of the washed-up wreckage from the beached runners contained embedded nails, and experience had taught the garrison that it was always wise to throw some light over any dark object on the shoreline before deciding whether to step over it or walk around it, or in the case of an unexploded Yankee shell, mark it for later cleanup.

He walked at the silken juncture where the last feeble slickness of the spent incoming waves vanished into the soak of coarser beach sand, in the last and purest hour of the seaside night. He replayed in his mind the wild spectacle of the storm, then remembered the brief tocsin of alarm that its thunder had wakened him with. Could Nature deal in symmetries, if they were of sufficient magnitude? If, as rumor and fragmentary reports indicated, the war's greatest battle was presently unfolding in Pennsylvania, could that titanic emotional and physical convulsion so disturb the ether as to generate a resonance in God's elements, hundreds of miles away? Had some primal receptor in Lamb's soul sensed that atavistic connection at the instant of his waking? On one hand, the notion smacked of primitive superstition—and William Lamb was certainly no heathen. But he had seen plenty of Cape Fear storms by now, and not once had he beheld anything so apocalyptic, so disturbingly insistent that someone *bear witness.*

Ah well, thought the Young Soldier of the Lord, no man who is not wholly a fool can possibly live by the sea for a year and not become a philosopher.

He was about five hundred yards north of the fort when he was stopped in midstride by the appearance of a large, oddly shaped object in his path. Whatever it was, it was no stranded fish, no chunk of hull from a derelict runner hulk. But it seemed, in a subtle vibratory way, to be *moving.* Cautiously, he drew near, knelt down, and flipped open the shutter of his lantern.

And gasped in wonder at what he saw. He had heard from local residents that the great loggerhead turtles, in the summer of every year, sometimes came to these beaches to lay their eggs. No one knew from whence they came—vast distances, it was said in nautical legends—or what drew them to these barren and storm-tossed shores. It was a primordial part of the huge, mysterious, and utterly benign creatures' cycle of life, and very rarely did humans observe it. Those who had, spoke of the sight in hushed, near-mystical tones. Now he understood why.

This female was a creature of breathtaking size: more than five feet long, from the tip of her great horned cleaver-shaped beak to the vestigial points of her tail, and with both flippers extended she had the reach of a good-sized man. The massive hump of her shell was predominately reddish-brown in color, but was so overgrown with encrustations, ornate filigrees of coral-like shells, and masses of freshly deposited seaweed, that he could barely make out the original pattern of its plates. Loggerheads with distinctive markings had been observed returning to the same nesting area for the span of whole generations; no man knew the span of their lives, but those who managed to survive their predators were thought to live for centuries, and from the heavy accretions on this one's shell, Lamb was willing to fancy that she had been coming to this beach longer than white men had dwelt in North America. On impulse, he named her Cleopatra.

She was backward to the surf, and well above the high-tide line from the recent storm. She had found a spot where the sand was soft and comparatively dry on top, but still cool and moist at the bottom of the cavity she had excavated, which appeared to be at least eighteen inches deep. Through instinct or antique cunning, she had found a place that was also well drained and covered with only thin, scattered vegetation. She exhibited no alarm when Lamb bent closer, regarding him and his lamp with a gaze of stoic indifference. *I have seen centuries pass,* her eyes intimated, *and drifted in depths you cannot imagine, evaded predators who could dispatch you with a single bite and leave nothing but red bubbles to show you had ever existed.* He circled around the nest and was startled to see the copious amounts of sand she had excavated. How many hours had she labored to fulfill this pre-Adamite ritual? Peering into the cavity, he saw dozens, perhaps hundreds, of tiny spherical eggs, each thin leathery shell coated with her birth secretions. Even as he watched, a slow rhythmic tremble passed across her shell, and a fresh clutch of glistening eggs, six or seven, rolled down into the nest.

Apparently finished with the laying, she appeared to heave a glacial sigh of relief, then began methodically to refill the cavity with sand, her flippers working with a deft economy of motion that belied her enormous bulk. He watched in rapt fascination as she finished covering the nest, then slowly, so slowly, she used flippers and beak to scatter the soil so that its location would be camouflaged from the crabs and gulls that would surely hold a ravaging feast if they discovered what lay beneath the sand. Glancing to the horizon, Lamb saw that the stars were beginning to lose their brightness and the turtle, too, seemed to understand that dawn was not far off, for her motions acquired as much urgency as her evident exhaustion permitted. When she was satisfied that she had done all within her power to protect her offspring, she raised herself up and began to move once more toward the sea. Every lurch forward seemed a labor of heroic determination, and she had to pause long moments between each movement, mustering her strength. It occurred to him that she must reach the water before daylight, and her incremental progress was so slight—each tremendous effort moving her only a matter of inches—that he wanted, if possible, to help her. Setting down his lantern, he gently placed his hands on the rough surface of her shell and pushed with all his strength. He might as well have been trying to shove the Armstrong gun—she could not have weighed less than five hundred pounds. If she minded his gesture of sympathy, she gave no sign. Finally, he worked it out so that, if he pushed just as she was reaching the apex of each forward strain, he was actually able to add an inch or two to the distance. Here was Nature's own "ironclad," and together, man and beast, they raced the sun. By the time she reached the glimmering band of moisture that marked the wavelets' farthest cast, he was sweating hard and his hands were covered with tiny, brine-stinging cuts. Then one small wavelet, stronger than most, came up far enough to lap the bottom of her beak. That first light kiss of seawater seemed instantly to revive her and she put on quite a burst of speed. When she was deep enough actually to use her flippers for propulsion, she fairly leaped ahead, seeming to rejoice at the increased vigor of the wavelets that pelted her and washed across her shell. How wonderfully cool that must have felt, Lamb thought, and how triumphant was her safe return to her natural world. When she finally gathered full speed, plunging into water deep enough to cover her, Lamb cheered for her and clapped his hands and called out toward the gathering dawn: "I will try to protect your babies, Cleopatra! You have my word as an officer and a gentleman!"

Now almost giddy, Lamb relocated the nest and marked its approximate circumference with a few oddments of driftwood. Then he brushed the wet grit from his trousers and strode back toward the fort, so happy and so amazed at the thing he had just seen, that he was actually whistling when he returned the lantern to the bemused sentries at the sally port. He reached the pulpit again just as Corporal Conver was due to be relieved. Rather breathlessly, he told the sentry what he had just witnessed, and Conver, who hailed from Onslow County and had heard tales of the great loggerheads all his life, seemed to understand his colonel's boyish excitement.

"Well, sir, you have seen a once-in-a-lifetime sure-enough wonder, all right."

"I shall send a patrol out later, mark off the nesting place, so Reilly and the Flying Battery do not roll over it and crush the eggs. How long before they hatch? I would like to witness that, having been present, so to speak, at the moment of birth."

"About six weeks, as I recall. But don't get too fond of them little wigglers, sir. Once they hatch, they're helpless. Half of 'em probably won't make it from the nest to the water, once the gulls and the crabs get wind of 'em."

"By God, they will make it if I have anything to say about it."

"That's just it, sir. Only one who has anything to 'say' about it is God. Well, Colonel, here comes my relief, so I'm off to the barracks for breakfast and some shut-eye. It was a pleasure visitin' with you tonight, sir."

"Thank you, Corporal. I am glad we shared these hours."

As the little soldier withdrew down the stairs and his replacement arrived, Lamb gave the newcomer a perfunctory nod, then turned around to watch the dawn. Daybreak came swiftly, in a glorious blinding spread of silver, and it seemed to Lamb, after the storm's stupendous violence and his encounter with the prehistoric turtle, to be a sunrise as weird as the first experimental dawn of Creation.

He scanned the dazzling horizon with a telescope and saw that, except for one blockade ship that was little more than a black speck, located more or less exactly where it was on every other morning, the sea was empty.

So: today was not the day.

Nor, probably, would tomorrow be.

But one morning, when he mounted the pulpit and looked to the sea, it would be. For on that particular morning, he would look out and behold the gathered might of the United States Navy, and he would learn on that day the true strength of what he had created upon these windswept sands and meet the destiny that would be the measure of his life.

Author's Note and Acknowledgments

The Sands of Pride is a work of fiction, based primarily on the extensive research I did for my nonfiction trilogy, *The Civil War in North Carolina* (particularly *Volume III: Ironclads and Columbiads: The War on the Coast*). While the major historical characters do, say, and act pretty much as history tells us they actually did, and the major events and battles took place when and as I describe them, I have not hesitated—in the interests of clarity and narrative flow—to conflate some of the more confusing and complex circumstances in the historical record.

I appeal to regional historians and Civil War buffs: please do not write and tell me that there were no such places as Shelborne's Point, the Uwharrie River, or the South Roanoke, or that the CSS *Hatteras* is actually the legendary *Albemarle. I know.* My intention was to capture, in all its drama and colorful variety, the essence of the Civil War experience in coastal North Carolina. Historical novelists are entitled to some poetic license; my deviations from literal truth are minor and intended to bring alive the spirit of the times and the people who lived through them.

With but two exceptions, all the quotations from *The Wilmington Journal* are verbatim, and I owe my deepest thanks to Beverly Tetterton, of the New Hanover County Library, for her generous help in making this material easily accessible. In his Wilmington newspaper, Editor James Fulton, for all his pomposity and unabashed racism, left a vivid and historically important record of daily life during the Civil War period. His irascible voice simply could not be ignored.

Special thanks are due to Mr. Rick Smith, who has written the definitive study of wartime Wilmington and the blockade-running phenomenon; Rick generously shared his encyclopedic knowledge of the period, and tirelessly answered many questions during the early stages of the project.

Many other people helped, often in strange and diverse ways: Dr. John Saunders, the late, beloved, Janelle Lavelle, Randall von Seggern, Stuart Norman, Mark and Peggy Rainey, Nancy Slayton, Prof. Chris Fonvielle, Rod Gragg, Jennie Ashlock, with the Cape Fear Museum, Warren and Toni Tucker, Matthew McMillan, Ralph Speas, and Dr. Veita Bland, who kept me healthy and (at least partially) sane throughout four exhausting years of work. I am grateful to all of you.

Special thanks are due to my agent, Betsy Nolan, whose faith in my work has exceeded all reason; to Philip Turner, my expert and patient editor at Carroll and Graf; and, as always, to my beloved wife, Elizabeth Lustig, for her unwavering support and sustaining devotion.

William R. Trotter
Greensboro, N.C.
January 14, 2002

Prospect Free Library
0001500132236